USA Today bestseller

THE CLUB

Trilogy

Lauren Rowe

Published by SoCoRo Publishing
Layout by www.formatting4U.com
Cover design © Sarah Hansen, Okay Creations LLC

Table of Contents

The Club Trilogy book one

Lauren Rowe

Published by SoCoRo Publishing
Layout by www.formatting4U.com
Cover design © Sarah Hansen, Okay Creations LLC

Chapter 1
Jonas

Name?

I inhale and exhale slowly. Am I really going to do this? Yes, I am. Of course, I am. The minute Josh ever so briefly mentioned "The Club" to me during our climb up Mount Rainier four months ago, I knew it was only a matter of time before I'd be sitting here on my laptop, filling out this application.

"Jonas Faraday," I type onto my keyboard.

With this application, you will be required to submit three separate forms of identification. The Club maintains a strict "No Aliases Policy" for admission. You may, however, use aliases during interactions with other Club members, at your discretion.

Yeah, okay, thanks. But the name's still Jonas Faraday.

Age?

I type in "30."

Provide a brief physical description of yourself.

"Extremely fit. 6'1. 195 lbs."

Wait a minute. I've been working out like a demon this past month. I walk into the bathroom and stand on the scale. I return to my laptop.

"190 lbs."

With this application, you will be required to submit three recent photographs of yourself to your intake agent. Please include the following: one headshot, one full-body shot revealing your physique, and one shot wearing something you'd typically wear out in a public location. These photographs shall be maintained under the strictest confidentiality.

Jesus. Am I really going to send my personal information and three photos of myself to who-knows-where to some unknown "intake agent" for a dating service/sex club I know nothing about?

I sigh.

Yes, I am. I sure as hell am. Even if it's against my better judgment, even if doing this flies in the face of rational and analytical thinking, even if my gut is telling me this is probably a horrifically bad idea, I've known I was going to do this since the minute I heard Josh talk about The Club four months ago.

"It's incredible, bro," Josh said to me, getting a foothold on a boulder and stretching his hand toward a nearby crag. "Best money I've spent in my life."

The best money my brother had ever spent—and this coming from a guy who drives a Lamborghini? It was an endorsement I couldn't ignore. In fact, thanks to Josh's intriguing recommendation, I've thought of little else since our climb. Even when I've been smack in the middle of what should be an epic fuck with a hot kindergarten teacher or state prosecutor or barista or flight attendant or personal banker or dog groomer or graphic designer or court reporter or waitress or hairdresser or pediatric nurse or photographer, all I can think about is what I'm probably missing out on by not belonging to The Club.

"It's like a secret society," Josh explained. "You can find members anywhere you go, anywhere in the world, on a moment's notice, and the members matched to you are always ... uncannily *compatible* with you."

It was the "uncannily compatible" part of that sentence that grabbed me and wouldn't let go, not the part about being able to find other members on a moment's notice anywhere in the world. Because God knows I can find a sexual partner virtually any time I want, anywhere I go, on my own.

I hate to be blunt about it, but women throw themselves at me, I guess based on my looks (so they tell me) and money (so I surmise) and, sometimes, thanks to the Faraday name (which, believe me, ain't such a prize). Young, old; married, single; hot, mousy; blonde, brunette; bookish, badass; full-figured, heroin-chic. It doesn't matter. It seems I can have anybody I want, as easily as ordering "fries with that" if I'm so inclined. And, yes, over the past year or so, I've become increasingly, incessantly, obsessively so inclined. And I'm beginning to hate myself for it.

Before anyone gets all up in arms and starts righteously listing off all the women I could never bed—"Well, you could never fuck Oprah or Mother Theresa or Chastity Bono before she became Chaz"—let me be crystal clear about what I'm saying here: I can bed any woman I *want* to. No, not literally every woman on planet earth. I fully acknowledge I couldn't nail a nun or Oprah or an eighty-year-old great-grandmother or a pre-op-transgender-lesbian. Nor would I want to, for Chrissakes.

What I'm saying is that if I, Jonas Faraday, *want* a particular woman to be naked and spread-eagle in my bed, if that's what I *want*, if a woman turns my head and makes me hard, or, hell, makes me laugh, or think about something in a whole new way, or maybe if she can't find her sunglasses and then chuckles because they're sitting on top of her head, or if her ass is particularly round in a snug pair of jeans—oh, yeah, especially if she has an ass I can really sink my teeth into—whoever she is, she will, eventually and most willingly, float onto my bed like the beautiful angel she is, spread open her silky thighs and, after a only a few moments of mutual bliss, beg me to fuck her.

I wish I could say "end of story" right there, but, unfortunately, I can't. Because sex is never the end of the story when it comes to me. And that's why I need The Club. I can't keep going to the same pond with the same fishing rod, dipping my rod into the same waters—no matter how warm and inviting those waters happen to be—and just keep bringing up the same goddamned tilapia, regardless of how moist and delicious. I just cannot do it anymore.

If I keep doing the same thing I've been doing, over and over, the same way I've been doing it, then I'm going to go completely insane—which is something I've already done once, albeit a lifetime ago and under completely different circumstances, and I'm not willing to do it again. What I want is something different. Something brutally honest. Something *real*. And if the only way to get what I want is to ignore my better judgment and shell out an enormous monetary sacrifice to the gods of depravity, then so be it.

Please sign the enclosed waiver describing the requisite background check, medical physical examination, and blood test, which you must complete as a condition of membership.

No problem. I'm relieved to know every member gets rigorously vetted. I sign where indicated.

Sexual orientation? Please choose from the following options: Straight, homosexual, bisexual, pansexual, other?

"Straight." That's an easy one. Just out of curiosity, though, what the fuck does "pansexual" mean? I Google it. "Pansexual: Not limited or inhibited in sexual choice with regard to gender or activity." Ah, okay—anything goes. Interesting concept, solely from a philosophical perspective, but it most definitely doesn't describe me. I know exactly what I want and what I don't.

Do any of your sexual fantasies include violence of any nature? If so, please describe in detail.

"No." Emphatically, categorically, no.

Please note that your inclination toward or fantasies about sexual violence, if any, will not, standing alone, preclude membership. Indeed, we provide highly particularized services for members with a wide variety of proclivities. In the interest of serving your needs to the fullest extent possible, please describe any and all sexual fantasies involving violence of any nature whatsoever.

Hey, assholes, I answered honestly the first time. "None."

Maybe I should move on to the next question, but I feel the need to elaborate. "There is nothing whatsoever I enjoy more than giving a woman intense pleasure—the most outrageously concentrated pleasure she's ever experienced in her life. Now, granted, if I do my job, her pleasure, and therefore mine, is so overwhelming, it blurs indistinguishably with pain. But, no, my fantasies do not tend toward violence or infliction of pain, ever. I find the entire idea repulsive, especially in relation to what should be the most sublimely pleasurable of all human experience." What kind of sick fucks do they let into this club, anyway? My gut is churning.

Are you a current practitioner of BDSM and/or does BDSM interest you? If so, describe in explicit detail.

"Never," I write, my fingers pounding the keyboard for emphasis. A distant memory threatens to rise up from its dark hiding place, but I force it back down. My heart is racing. "My extreme disinterest in bondage and sadomasochism is absolutely non-negotiable."

Payment and Membership Terms. Please choose from the following options: One Year Membership, $250,000 USD; Monthly Membership, $30,000 USD. All payments are non-refundable. No exceptions. Once you've made your selection regarding your membership plan, information for wiring the funds into an escrow account will be immediately forthcoming under separate cover. Membership fees shall be transferred automatically out of escrow to The Club upon approval of your membership.

What did my father always used to say? *"Go big or go home, son."* Oh, how he'd laugh heartily from his grave to know the son he derisively called the "soft" one is harkening back to his father's mantra to choose a sex club membership. *"I guess you're more like your Old Man than I thought,"* he'd say. I can hear his ghost laughing wickedly in my ear right now.

It's not the amount of money that gives me pause. I could buy either membership plan multiple times over and never hear so much as a peep from my accountants—but I don't throw money away, ever, in any sum. Regardless, though, if I'm going to do this, which I am, doesn't it make the most economic sense to join for a full year? My hands hover over the keyboard. My knee is jiggling.

All right, fuck it, yes, I admit it—it's crazy and irresponsible to spend this kind of money on a club, or dating service, whatever the hell this is, especially sight-unseen. I'm Jonas, after all, not Josh. I'm not the twin who buys himself Italian sports cars on every whim or who hired Jay-Z to play his thirtieth birthday party (which would have been our joint birthday party if I'd bothered to attend). And yet ... I sigh. I know damn well what I'm about to do here, no matter the cost or how loudly the voice inside my head is screaming at me to retreat.

"One year membership," I write, exhaling loudly.

Please provide a detailed explanation about what compelled you to seek membership in The Club.

I close my eyes for just a moment, collecting my thoughts.

"I love women," I type. I take a deep breath. "I love *fucking* them. And most of all, I love making them come." I smirk at the stark boldness of the words on my computer screen. There is no other context in which I'd ever make these crude statements to anyone.

"Perhaps what I'm supposed to say is, 'Oh, how I love the smell of a woman's hair, the softness of her skin, the elegant curve of her neck.' And, yeah, all of that's true; I'm not some kind of sociopath. Yes, I've been known to lose my composure over a woman's sharp mind and wit—and that's not sarcasm, by the way; when it comes to women, the smarter the better—or her husky voice or raucous laugh, or, yes, even a flash of genuine kindness in her eyes. Yeah, that's all sexy as hell to me. But in my view, a woman's hair only smells so damned good, and her skin is only so damned soft and inviting, and her laugh is only so infectious all as a delicious prelude to one thing—the most honest and primal and fucking awesome thing our bodies are designed to do. Everything else is just prelude, baby, glorious prelude."

I take a deep breath. I've never articulated these thoughts before. I want to get this exactly right—otherwise, what's the point of filling out this application?

"From as early as I can remember, I've always particularly admired women. As I grew up, that translated into a powerful sexual appetite, but nothing I couldn't control. I could take a woman to an art gallery or concert or movie or candlelit restaurant and pleasantly ask her about her work, her passions, and even her beloved Maltese Kiki over a bottle of pinot noir and not even once feel compelled to blurt out, 'I just want to fuck you in the bathroom.'"

I stare at the screen. I'm pretty sure I sound like an asshole right now. But it can't be helped. The truth is the truth.

"And then, everything changed. About a year ago, I went on a typical date with a very pretty woman, and when I fucked her after dinner—and not in the bathroom, mind you—she did something a woman had never done with me before. *She faked it.*" I grimace. "She fucking faked an orgasm. It was so obvious as to be insulting. And it pissed me the hell off. Sex isn't supposed to be about *humoring* someone or being *polite*—it's not high tea with the goddamned Queen. Sex is supposed to be the *truth*, the most real and raw and honest and primal expression of the human experience. And orgasm, by its very nature, is the height, the very culmination of that honesty."

Jesus, after all this time, I still get riled up about this. My chest is heaving. My cheeks are flushed. I can't think straight. I need music. Music is the thing that calms me when my thoughts are racing and my pulse is raging. As a kid, my therapist taught me to use music as a coping mechanism and it still works for me. I click into the music library on my laptop. I choose "White Lies" by Rx Bandits and listen for a few minutes. Quickly, the song soothes me and clears my head, opening a window for my bottled thoughts and feelings to fly through. I listen for several minutes, until I'm calm again.

"I couldn't understand why she'd lied to me," I continue. "Why would she prematurely and artificially end a damned good fuck (or what I *thought* was a damned good fuck) and thereby exclude even the *possibility* of her actually getting off? Was I that big a hack at fucking her that she preferred ending the intolerable tedium to at least *trying* to come for real? I was beside myself."

I inhale deeply and exhale slowly.

"One night, as I was tossing and turning and thinking about it, the truth grabbed me and wouldn't let go. I suddenly knew she'd lied to me precisely because, yes, indeed, I was just that terrible at fucking her—because she'd thought getting off with me was so hopeless, that *I* was so hopeless, why even bother to try?

"It might have been enough to send me to a very dark place, a place I've been before (and it ain't pretty), except for one thing: I knew down deep that I hadn't really *tried* to get her off, not like I knew I was capable of doing. I'd concentrated solely on my own pleasure, not hers, and assumed that whatever I was experiencing must have been mutual. The more I thought about it, the clearer it became—she'd given me exactly what I deserved. And I was ashamed of myself.

"It was a watershed moment. From that instant, I became a man obsessed, singularly focused on fucking that woman again—only *excellently* the second time around—and making damned sure she came for real and harder than she ever had before. I wanted to teach her a lesson about truth and honesty, yes—but even more than that, I wanted *redemption*.

"Well, of course, she agreed to see me again—she actually seemed excited to accept another invitation from me, despite my apparent hopelessness—but this time, when I fucked her again, I was a new man, a man possessed, a man *enlightened,* you might say, singularly focused on her pleasure and nothing else. And the result was mind-blowing. Her entire body convulsed and undulated against my tongue from the inside out, slamming open and shut violently like a cellar door left open in a tornado. And the noises that came out of that woman were fucking amazing, too, the most primal, desperate sounds I'd ever heard—nothing at all like the hollow bleating she'd tried to pass off the first time around. She was a fucking symphony. Of course, women had come with me before then—but never like that. No, no, no, never, ever like that. I'd held her in the palm of my hand and pushed her over the edge, at my will, and into another realm."

My heart is racing. My cock is hard.

"And the best part—the true epiphany—was that getting *her* off like that got *me* off. Holy fuck, did it ever. In fact, pushing that beautiful liar into untethered ecstasy, making her surrender to the truth, to me, to her pleasure, turned out to be the most epic fuck of my life—a high like nothing I'd experienced before. After that, I wanted that high again and again (though not with her, of course—never again with her)—and ever since, I've been chasing that high like a horse running to the barn with blinders on."

I take a deep breath.

Has any of this babbling answered the question? Shit. I don't know. But this is the best I can do.

"And that's what's brought me to The Club."

I stare at my screen. I shrug. That's all I got.

Please provide a detailed statement regarding your sexual preferences. To maximize your experience in The Club, please be as explicit, detailed, and honest as possible. Please do not self-censor, in any fashion.

My hands are trembling over the keyboard. The question I've been waiting for.

"Some guys say fucking a beautiful woman brings them closer to God. But, really, they should aim higher. Because when I make a woman come like she's never come before, when I make her surrender and leap into the dark abyss, I don't just get closer to God, I *become* God. *Her* god, anyway, for one, all-powerful, fucking awesome moment."

I stare at the screen. My dick is straining painfully inside my jeans.

"Making a woman come, at least the way I'm talking about, is an art form. Every woman's orgasm is a unique puzzle, a treasure locked away by a secret code. Almost always, the best and most reliable way to crack a particular woman's code starts with licking and kissing and sucking her sweet spot, but even that seemingly 'sure thing' only works if, as I do it, I pay close attention to her body's special cues and adjust accordingly as I go. I can't just lick her—I have to *learn* her. Usually, after only a few minutes, though, I've got her figured out.

"I always know I'm on the right track when she suddenly and involuntarily arches her back, thrusts her hips reflexively into my mouth, and spreads her legs as wide as they'll go. That's when I know her body's preparing to give in to me, that I'm breaking down her defenses—that she desperately *wants* me to unlock her secret code."

I'm rock hard. God, I love that moment. I lick my lips again.

"When she thrusts herself into me and begins to open herself, I become ravenous, myopic, relentless. I lick her and kiss her and suck her with increased fervor, and maybe even nibble and gnaw at her, too, depending on what her body's telling me to do, and she continues rapidly opening and unlocking, spreading and unfurling, untethering and breaking down. It's fucking incredible.

"She's a beautiful, blooming flower. The trick, of course, is to catch her the exact moment before her petals fall off, and not a second before or after, because what I'm aiming for—the holy grail, if you will—is to plunge myself into her at the very instant when doing so will push her over the edge. It's tricky. Too early, and she might not come at all. Too late, and she'll go off without me."

I unbutton my fly and my cock springs out. I want to jerk myself off right now, but I want to get these thoughts onto my computer screen even more.

"She's on the verge—so fucking close—and I'm out of my mind, a shark in a frenzy. Finally, she reflexively *shudders* in my mouth—a feeling so delicious, I often dream about it—and I know her body's teetering right on the very edge, hanging by a thread, aching to give in, but her mind is keeping her from what she wants, usually thanks to daddy issues or a raging good girl complex or low self esteem (take your pick, it's always something). Whatever it is, her mind is getting in the way of her body surrendering utterly and completely to the intense pleasure she yearns to experience.

"But I won't be denied. She claws at me, gulps for air, her

pleasure mounting and morphing into an agony she increasingly cannot contain. She whimpers, groans, writhes—and I'm so fucking turned on, too, I can barely contain myself. 'Fuck me now, *please, please,*' she often says, or some variation thereof, but I won't do it, even though I'm losing my fucking mind, because I know she's not maxed out just yet."

I breathe deeply.

"Finally, like a key turning in a lock, something inside her clicks. She opens. Her mind detaches from her body. She becomes untethered. She *surrenders*."

I let out a shaky breath.

"That's when I plunge into her like a knife in warm butter and fuck her with almost religious zeal—sometimes pulling her on top of me to do it, sometimes turning her around, sometimes slamming into her the good old fashioned way—by then, any which way is equally effective—and the moment I enter her, her body releases completely, reflexively shuddering and constricting and undulating all around my cock, over and over again. Sure, she's come before, of course. But never like this. No, never like this. It's pure *ecstasy* in the way the ancient Greeks defined that word: *the culmination of human possibility*. For both of us."

I let out a long, controlled exhale and shift in my seat. Holy shit, I've really gotten myself worked up. I breathe in and out deeply several times. I'm trembling. I take a moment to compose myself.

"I should be clear about something, in the interest of full disclosure. What I've described here is the ideal. The *aspiration*. Sometimes the timing works out exactly this way, and sometimes it doesn't. Sometimes, especially when I'm still learning a woman, or if she's particularly hard-to-read for some reason, she might come like a freight train before I manage to get inside her. And if that happens, it's nothing to complain about, believe me—fucking a beautiful woman immediately *after* she comes is also a delicious privilege, no doubt about it. But the pinnacle, the peak, the perfection to which I aspire—the holy grail—is and always will be bringing a woman right to the edge of ecstasy and pushing her over it from the inside out."

I shift in my seat again, but my erection is too intense to ignore. I have to stop typing. How could anyone fill out this application without having to jerk off? I grip my shaft and pump up and down until a staggering wave of pleasure wells up inside of me and finally releases in fitful spurts. I go into the bathroom and pull off my jeans. I hop into the shower and let the steaming hot water rain over me, relaxing me, cleansing me.

Getting women into my bed isn't my problem. The problem occurs right after a woman has had the best sex of her life, when her body has finally functioned at full-tilt capacity for the first time. That's when a woman invariably confuses discovering the full extent of her sexual power with the ridiculous notion that she's found her soul mate. Thanks to a lifetime of brainwashing by Disney and Lifetime and Hallmark, she naively believes glimpsing God during an epic fuck somehow translates into some kind of happily ever after with her Prince Charming. No matter what I've said beforehand, no matter how clearly I've presented myself and the limits of what I'm willing to give, she's suddenly convinced she's found The One. *"He just doesn't know it yet,"* she tells herself.

And that's when I hurt her, whoever she is—whether she's a librarian or tax accountant or personal trainer or pediatrician or makeup artist or singer or bioengineer or therapist or paralegal. Whether she's funny or sweet or shy. Whether she's serious or sexy or smart. Whether she's a tree hugger or a Sunday school teacher. I hurt her, whoever she is. Because I'm too fucked up to be The One. Not for her, not for anybody. She can't change that fact. No one can. *I* can't even change that fact—and believe me, I've tried.

Damn. How am I going to accurately convey all this information in my application? I get out of the shower, throw a towel around my waist, and get right back to my laptop. I stare at my computer screen for a brief moment, trying to find the right words to succinctly express my thoughts.

"No matter how honest I am right from the start about how little I'm willing to give outside the four walls of my bedroom, women always seem to get hurt by me, nonetheless," I type. "Either they don't believe me when I tell them what I really want, or they think they can change me. And they can't."

I sigh.

"I'm not out to hurt anyone." And it's the truth. "All I want to do is give a woman pleasure like nothing she's experienced before—which leads to my own ultimate pleasure. After I taste her and fuck her and teach her what true satisfaction feels like, I might want to lie in bed and talk and laugh with her, too—because, believe it or not, I enjoy talking and laughing quite a bit, as long as everyone understands it's not going to lead to a heart-shaped box of chocolates and a weekend shopping trip to IKEA. Maybe I'll want to get into a hot shower with her and lather her up, running my soapy hands over her entire, beautiful body. Maybe I'll want to dry her off with a soft, white towel and then fuck her again, maybe the second time so intensely, so deeply, so expertly, we'll come together, both of us gasping for air and shuddering simultaneously as our bodies discover the culmination of human possibility together.

"After all's said and done, I'll surely want to tell her how beautiful she is and how much I've enjoyed our time together. I'll want to kiss her goodbye, gently and gratefully, thanking her for our glorious time together. And then, almost certainly, I'll never want to see her again."

My hands hover over the keyboard for a brief moment.

"And I don't want to feel like an asshole for any of it." I sigh. "Because I'm sick and fucking tired of feeling like a complete asshole."

I pause again.

"You've asked me to state my *preferences*, but clearly what I've described here transcends preference. I *need* smart, sexy women who *honestly* want what I do—no lies—and who, most importantly, can clearly and rationally distinguish physical rapture from some kind of romantic fairytale."

I stare at my computer screen, a sense of hopelessness threatening to descend on me. Am I kidding myself here? Do women like this even exist?

I type again. "If I could find even one woman, just one, whose 'sexual preferences' are uncannily and genuinely compatible with mine, I'd be ... " What would I be? *Elated.* That's what I was about to write. *Elated.*

Jesus. I quickly delete that entire last sentence. It's a non sequitur, for Chrissakes. I mean, shit, I'm either a sexual sniper with a rampant God complex or I'm fucking Nicholas Sparks. I can't be both. I have no idea what bizarre place in my brain that last ridiculous sentence came from. I guess that's what happens when a guy like me tries to articulate his deepest, darkest needs without a filter—the thoughts come out in a jumbled, desperate, douche-y mess, inexplicably intertwined with all the fucked up shit I've tried unsuccessfully to fix with years of useless therapy.

What the hell is this mysterious "intake agent" going to think of all my incoherent rambling? I cock my head to the side, an epiphany slamming me upside the head. An "intake agent" is going to read my application—yes, of course—and that intake agent's going to be a woman. *Of course.* And not the eighty-year-old pre-op-transgender-lesbian variety, either. They can't let assholes like me, or, worse, crazy fucks with violent fantasies or bondage fetishes or some other latent form of psychopathy into The Club without first passing a woman's gut check. Right? *Right.*

I grin broadly and place my fingers back on my keyboard.

"And now a message directly to you, My Beautiful Intake Agent." I lick my lips again. "Have you enjoyed reading my brutally honest thoughts—my deep, dark secrets? I've enjoyed writing about them. I've never expressed these truths to anyone else—never even thought about them quite like this. It's been enlightening to arrange the bare truth so clearly on the page and confess it to you—and therefore confess it to myself, too. In fact, telling you the brutal truth turned me on so much, I had to take a break midway through writing this to jack off."

I smile again. I'm such a bastard.

"So, tell me, My Beautiful Intake Agent, are you surprised at how wet your panties are right now, considering the fact that you've been brainwashed your whole life by Lifetime and Hallmark to think you want flowers and candy and a candlelit dinner followed by silent missionary sex, a chaste kiss goodnight, and a trip to IKEA the following morning to shop for a mutually agreeable couch? And yet, despite a lifetime of conditioning about what you're supposed to want, here you are, anyway, aren't you, My Beautiful Intake Agent, imagining my warm, wet tongue swirling around and around your sweet button, wishing I were there to lick and kiss and suck you 'til you were jolting and jerking like you'd gripped an electric fence? You're a unique puzzle, My Beautiful Intake Agent, yes you are—a rare treasure locked down by a padlock. But guess what? My words have already begun to *unlock* you, as surely as if I were there to turn the key myself.

"So what are you going to do about the dark urges clanging around deep inside you right now, My Beautiful Intake Agent? Are you going to ignore them, or are you going to let them rise up and eventually untether your body from your mind? Perhaps you should use this opportunity, as I have just done, to touch yourself and think honestly about your deepest desires, to think about what *actually* turns you on, as opposed to what's *supposed* to. Touch yourself, My Beautiful Intake Agent, and go to the deepest, darkest places inside you, the places you never allow yourself to go—and embrace the brutal truth about your wants and needs. Your whole life, you've been taught to chase all the Valentine's Day bullshit, haven't you? But that's not really what you want. Tell the truth—to me and to yourself. You'd ditch all the Valentine's Day bullshit in a heartbeat to howl like a rabid monkey for the first time in your life, wouldn't you?"

I'm smiling from ear to ear, imagining some frazzled, middle-aged woman sitting in a cubicle in Dallas or Des Moines or Mumbai, reading my words with wide eyes and a throbbing clit.

"I know what you're thinking: *Cocky bastard! Asshole! A legend in his own mind!* All true exclamations, my dear. But guess what? Cocky bastard or not, if I were there to lick you, nice and slow, right on your sweet button, the way you deserve to be licked, the way you've only ever dreamed of being licked, the way no man has ever done for you before, I guarantee it'd take me less than four minutes to deliver you unto pure ecstasy that would make you surrender to me, totally and completely." I smile to myself.

"Yes, My Beautiful Intake Agent, if I were there to teach you what your body's divinely designed to do, you'd be forced to admit an immutable truth, whether you wanted to or not: In addition to me being one cocky-bastard-asshole-son-of-a-bitch motherfucker, I'm also the man of your dreams."

Chapter 2
Sarah

I'm stunned. Like, mouth hanging open, eyes bugging out of my head, I've turned into a strand of wet spaghetti stunned. I can't believe *this* is the first application I've been assigned to review and process all by myself after three months of supervised intake training.

What an asshole. What a flaming, unparalleled, self-absorbed, self-righteous, egomaniacal, self-important asshole. I don't know whether to laugh or scream or cry or throw up. Talk about emotionally stunted. Pathetic. Delusional. Narcissistic. And maybe even a little bit scary. He wants to lick my "sweet button" 'til I howl like a monkey? It'd take him less than four minutes to "deliver me unto pure ecstasy that would make me surrender to him, totally and completely?" What the hell? Who talks like that? Who *thinks* like that? Freak.

Oh, and the best part of all, he'd make me come harder than I ever have in my entire life? Ha! That one made me laugh, considering the situation. I'm sure he'd be shocked, and oh so titillated, to find out that making me come *at all* would *de facto* qualify as making me come harder than ever before. Yeah, I'm sure that little nugget would make his head explode into a million tiny pieces.

Maybe the woman who faked it with him wasn't the devil incarnate, after all—maybe she just knew she wasn't capable of having an orgasm, no matter what he did. Did he ever think of that? Maybe she pulled the chord on her parachute when it became clear things were going to end the way they always did for her—with a big, fat nothing. Sure, he *says* he made her climax the second time around, but can he be sure? Maybe she faked it again. Maybe she just wasn't wired to have an orgasm. Maybe she was wired like me.

Jerk.

But if he's such a jerk then why am I squirming in my chair right now, trying to relieve the pounding ache between my legs?

Dang it, despite my brain's firm desire to be disgusted by what he wrote, his words, and especially his message to me personally, lit my body up like a Roman candle. Wow, just sitting here, staring at my laptop in my little student apartment, I want to reach down past the waistband of my pajama bottoms and touch myself—and I *never* have that urge, ever.

I need to get a grip.

But when I close my eyes to clear my thoughts, all I can think about is his warm, wet, flickering tongue on my skin—between my legs—right where I'm pulsing mercilessly right now. I feel my face flushing crimson.

What the heck has gotten into me? I'm not some kind of sex-addicted nympho. I mean, I'm no virgin, either. I lost my virginity during my freshman year of college to a guy I thought was hot (who then promptly turned into a cling-on), and in the five and a half years since then, I've had two long-term-ish boyfriends (both of whom were cute and sweet, even though things eventually got too boring to continue), one fairly forgettable one-night-stand (thanks to my best friend, Kat, who lured my guy over by flirting with his friend), and, to top it all off, a second one-night-stand six months ago I can barely remember (thanks to a fourth cosmo that pushed me well past Fun-and-Confident-Sarah and right into Hot-Mess-What-Were-You-Thinking-Sarah—something I swore to myself I'd never let happen again).

So, yes, even if I'm not a sex fiend, *per se,* I've definitely had my share of sex, including oral, by the way—both giving and receiving—so it's not as though I'm some kind of squeaky clean fairytale princess who blushes at the sight of a penis. I'm certainly not gonna swoon and pass out just because some jerk refers to my clit as my "sweet button," for the love of Pete. And, anyway, even if I'd had any hang-ups about words that begin with the letter "c" before I started this bizarre "intake agent" job three months ago, they're long gone now.

But I digress. Big deal if my body's not wired to have an orgasm. I'm not alone in this predicament, or, situation, rather—it's not a *predicament*. I've done my research. Seventy-five percent of women never reach orgasm through intercourse alone and a full *ten to fifteen percent* of women like me never reach climax at all, ever, under any circumstance, no matter the tongue or toys or position or emotions involved.

So, okay, I'll never suffer a horrible backache after having a mind-blowing orgasm like Kat "complains" about. Big deal. It certainly doesn't mean I can't experience sexual pleasure at all, because believe me, I do. I thoroughly enjoy the physical sensation of sex, especially when there's an emotional connection with the guy (or, occasionally, when alcohol creates the *illusion* of an emotional connection with the guy).

The more I think about it, I can totally relate to what this Jonas Faraday guy is saying because, much like him, I get most turned on when I'm pushing my partner over the edge hard and fast—particularly when he's trying desperately to hang on. Getting a guy off, especially when he's like "no, wait, not yet, I wanna hang on," makes me feel powerful, like I've got a superpower. So, yeah, I totally get it.

But *understanding* the guy certainly doesn't explain why I'm so frickin' *turned on* by him. I mean, seriously, why the heck do I feel like touching myself right now? I *never* want to touch myself. What's the point? I've tried in the past, and all it does is make me feel defective in the end.

And it's the same regarding a guy going down on me. Getting licked to death by some well-intentioned guy with a frenetic tongue might be pleasant at first, sure, but it can only do so much for me when I know I'm not going to come. The whole exercise inevitably begins to feel kind of pointless—and, honestly, kind of embarrassing and anxiety-producing, too. And if he keeps going and going with no success, the whole situation becomes soul-crushing, actually—especially if it's obvious he's frustrated or, worse, disappointed.

That's why, almost every time sex heads down the whole "oh let me make you come, baby" path, I wind up faking it, usually right off the bat, so he won't wind up feeling disappointed and I won't wind up feeling like a flaming failure. It's not his fault I'm a ten-percenter—and it's not mine, either. It's just the way it is.

But I'm sidetracked. All I'm saying is I'm not the kind of girl who's going to get hot and bothered by some guy talking about licking a woman's "sweet button" or "fucking her brains out" or making her "come like a freight train." So why the heck is this guy's application turning me on like this? Wow, I mean, I'm really, really turned on. This is a first. In my three months on the job, I've had all kinds of reactions to the twenty or so applications I've processed, but never once before now have I been close to feeling like my panties are on fire—not even when the applications are a little bit sexy or kind of sweet.

Often, the applicants are just normal (rich) men searching for true love in an overwhelming world who are hoping The Club will curate their search. I have no problem with that. I mean, if you have a particular sexual quirk—whether it's a foot fetish, wearing women's lingerie, or being whipped while dressed in a bunny suit—it must be kind of difficult finding women (or, men, or both) who'll accept, and maybe even enjoy your freaky thing, whatever it is.

The way I see it, most of these guys are just diehard romantics who, yes, happen to have some kind of sexual peccadillo. Sometimes, I read their heartfelt confessions and yearnings and desires and I actually think, "Aw." But I never, ever think, "Oh, pick me, Mr. Bunny Suit Guy." Hellz no.

In addition to the diehard romantics (as I prefer to think of them), the second largest contingency of applicants consists of globetrotting tycoons and celebrities and professional athletes who apparently want to find compatible companions wherever their global travels might take them. Again, I have no problem with this. Some of the guys in this category are pretty hot, actually, and not particularly weird or anything—some are even sexy as hell—but even the hottest globetrotter/athlete guy has never once made me want to slide my fingers into my pajama bottoms. So why now?

The third category of applicants, the group I call "the wack jobs," not only *doesn't* turn me on, the whole lot of them makes me want to shower in Lysol. They're the ones who, without exception, apply for a full year's membership, apparently seeking to indulge their every depraved fantasy without the pressure of a ticking clock. These guys aren't interested in finding true love like the diehard romantics, and they're not looking for love despite a hectic travel schedule like the globetrotters and pro athletes. They're simply not looking for love, period—or else they'd never pay for a full year's membership up front.

Who in their right mind, *if* they were looking for love, would commit to paying a year's membership fee if there were even the *possibility* of finding someone special after only a few months? That's the thing I hate about the wack jobs the most—that they're motivated solely by their hedonism and demons, and not even a little bit by their hearts. They're all diehard cynics, every last one of them, led uncontrollably to their next nameless, faceless sexual encounter by their gigantic, throbbing dicks—without even an ounce of hope or romanticism coursing through their horny veins.

Reading the wack jobs' sexual preferences is like driving past a horrible car wreck. Disgusting. Horrifying. Shocking. But you can't look away. These guys are the ones who want to tie a woman up and shove steel balls up her cooch (what?) or dress a woman in a Goldie Locks costume and make her do unthinkable things with porridge (I almost quit after reading that one).

My least favorite wack job so far was a guy who wanted a secret gay life on the down low, concealed from his wife and four kids, even though he was a politician who'd recently campaigned vigorously based on his vehement opposition to gay rights. (I flagged that application as "do not approve," but my recommendation was ignored.) It wasn't the secret gay life part that got me so riled up—I figure half these guys are joining The Club to cheat on *someone*—it was his disgusting and inexcusable hypocrisy, his self-loathing disguised as moral superiority that got me seething. That guy almost made me throw my hands up and quit—but then, after I cooled down a bit, I decided not to throw the baby out with the bathwater.

True, twenty percent of the applications are revolting, but eighty percent of them are semi-titillating, or at least fascinating or amusing or even sweet; the pay is fantastic; and the work schedule is pretty easy. So, all things considered, it's an ideal part-time job for a first-year law student who needs the money but also needs time to attend classes and study. If I quit, I'd have to find something else, anyway—I'm drowning in student loans as it is, and the law job I've committed to take after graduation doesn't come with a lawyer-sized paycheck.

But, anyway, the point is that even the most appealing applications haven't made me fantasize about having monkey-sex with the applicant. And yet, here I am now, after reading a certain megalomaniac's application, doing just that. What the hell?

Jonas Faraday.

Who is this guy? I mean, really? Despite all The Club's warnings and demands for complete honesty, most applicants lie about *something*—hence the reason The Club hires law students like me to rigorously vet applications. Sometimes, the guy shaves years off his age, or says he's single when he's married, or describes himself as "extremely fit and 190 pounds" when his pictures tell another story.

So what's "Jonas Faraday" lying about? That he's some kind of woman wizard who can have any woman he wants and make them come as easily as shooting ducks in a barrel? *Puh-lease.* No man can have any woman he wants—no matter how rich or good looking he might be—and I'm living proof the second part is impossible, too. But what else is he lying about?

Let's find out.

I put my curser over the first photo attached to the application and click on it. This ought to blow an icy frost into my blazing panties pretty damned quick.

Oh. My. Gawd.

I'm looking at a picture of the most exquisite male specimen I've ever seen, dressed to perfection in a meticulously tailored suit. Holy crappola. His eyes. His lips. His jawline. Did I say "his lips" yet? Okay, let me say it again. *His lips.* Wow, I'd give anything to kiss them, even once. I just want to run my fingertip over those lips. I want to lick those lips. Holy moly.

The photo is from some sort of professional photo shoot. I can tell by the quality of the image and the lighting. Obviously, whoever this guy is, he's a male model. I sigh. Okay, that's a relief. I might have had a stroke if the guy who wrote about licking my "sweet button" until my "mind detached from my body" actually looked like this.

Damn. If this alleged "Jonas Faraday" guy looked even remotely like this male model he's pretending to be, I'd believe he was some kind of pied piper for women. I mean, a guy who looked like this could certainly bed *me* any time he pleased, thank you very much (assuming I didn't know he was a narcissistic asshole, of course). But it's a moot point because there's no way he looks like this. No effing way. This is a blatant "catfish" attempt if I've ever seen one—where the applicant tries to pass himself off as some ridiculously perfect human specimen, as if nobody's ever going to discover the discrepancy between the Greek god he's claiming to be and the elf from *The Lord of the Rings* he actually looks like.

I click on the next picture and, this time, I practically black out.

"Wow," I say out loud.

The bastard attached a bathroom-mirror-selfie, wearing nothing but tight briefs and a cocky grin. Oh man, there are muscled cuts above his hips, and his stomach is rock hard and chiseled. His nipples are small, perfect little circles. There are tattooed inscriptions running down the inside lengths of both forearms. I can't make out the phrases, but I'm drawn to them. I touch them on my screen with my fingertip.

I suddenly imagine this Adonis' naked body pressed against mine, and every drop of blood in my brain whooshes directly into my crotch. What the hell is happening to me right now? I'm like a frickin' cat in heat. This is so unlike me I want to slap myself silly right now. And, anyway, I don't know what I'm getting so worked up about. This Greek god is not the one flirting with me—the one flirting with me is some normal-looking guy who swiped these images off a European ad for condoms.

I click on the third picture. Another selfie. A headshot this time, as instructed. He's staring into the camera, unsmiling. His gaze is matter-of-fact. Unapologetic. Intense. Magnetic. Confident. I can't look away. He's stunning. Well, the *male model* is stunning. I'm transfixed. I'd really like to have sex with a man that looks like this just once before I exit this planet. I'd really like to feel someone like this touching me, kissing me, making love to me—and, wow, imagine if he did it all expertly, like this Jonas Faraday claims to do. Talk about a perfect storm.

I close my eyes.

Maybe that's the thing that's got me so hot and bothered about this guy's application—I'm realizing I desperately want to have sex, just once, with a guy who knows exactly what he's doing.

The guys I've been with have been cute and well-intentioned but just sort of ... I don't even know how to put it. Functional? Clumsy? Clueless? Or maybe it's just been so long I'm just not remembering it right. I haven't had sex in six months—and that was a drunken one-night stand I don't even remember in any detail. But reading "Jonas Faraday's" words, and now looking at the photos of this male model, I just can't help thinking—what if I were to have sex with a guy who was masterful at it *and* looked like this, too? Yeah, that'd be *my* holy grail.

I sigh.

I'm really veering off task here. I've got a job to do. I force myself to click out of Mr. Perfect's photos. Okay, no more ridiculousness. Time to work. Job, job, job. Do, do, do.

I load the three photos onto my Google images software to run them against all the existing images on the Internet. I don't normally start my research this way, but, more than anything, I'm dying to find out the true origin of these photos. After I press the "go" button, I grab myself a glass of wine in the kitchenette and put on some music. I linger for a moment against the counter, sipping my wine and listening to Sarah Bareilles sing me a happy song, trying to distract myself from the tingling inside my body that won't go away.

I shake my head and take a big swig of wine. And then another. I can't believe I'm getting turned on by a wack job who signed up for a *year's* membership in a sex club. I mean, come on, he admits explicitly he can't form any kind of emotional connection with a woman to save his life. So why is my body reacting this way? Even before I saw those three mesmerizing photos, I'd already physically reacted to his application exactly as he predicted, and quite emphatically. As I lean against the counter, thinking about those photos again—his body, his eyes—an insistent ache keeps tugging at me. A throbbing I can't ignore.

Damn, I can't resist.

I take another big swig of wine and slide my fingers inside my pajama bottoms, just for the hell of it. When my fingers reach their target, I close my eyes and let out a low moan. Wow, I've never been so wet in my life. If he were here, he could enter me like a hot knife in warm butter, just like he said, without needing to do a damned thing first.

My laptop beeps and my eyes pop open. There's a result window on my computer screen. I pull my hand out of my pants and lurch over to my kitchen table. "No matches" is the message on my screen. What? Surely, if this guy took those images off some gay porn site, or a Facebook profile, or an ad for ass-less chaps, there'd be a frickin' match. How can these photos not be posted *anywhere* on the Internet? Where'd he get them, then? My heart's thumping in my chest. He couldn't possibly look like this, could he? No way. He couldn't turn me on with his bare words and then turn out to look like a Greek god, too—could he?

All right, I'll start at the beginning, like I usually do. I Google "Jonas Faraday," even though I'm sure he's using an alias (despite The Club's strict instruction against it). Much to my surprise, the search instantly calls up countless links for a "Jonas Faraday" in Seattle. I click the link at the top—a website for Faraday & Sons, Global Investments, LLC, based in Seattle with satellite offices in Los Angeles and New York, and much to my shock, there he is, boom, right on the homepage. *Jonas Faraday.* The Adonis himself. The most beautiful creature I've ever beheld. Ever, ever, ever. Like, seriously, ever. He's standing next to another very good-looking guy with darker hair but similar looks, both of them in sleek suits. The caption under the photo says, "Brothers Joshua and Jonas Faraday carry on the legacy of their late father, company founder Joseph Faraday."

So, there you go. He really looks like this. Oh my God.

I scrutinize the photo. The other guy, his brother, seems authentically happy, smiling with what appears to be genuine glee. Jonas, on the other hand, stares at the camera with such burning intensity, it's not clear if he wants to murder or devour whoever's behind the lens. I smirk. The photographer must have been a woman—which, of course, would make the answer to my question "devour." I bet he took that photographer home after the photo shoot, whoever she was, and "delivered her unto the culmination of human possibility."

I feel a pang of envy.

His muscled torso flashes across my mind. His abs. His eyes. His sculpted arms with those elegant tattoos along his forearms. His lips. I imagine those lips whispering "Sarah" in my ear as he makes love to me—or, ha! Who am I kidding?—as he *fucks* me, as he so clearly stated was his predilection. I imagine those lips smiling up at me from between my open thighs. I shiver. Another swig of wine. I'm losing my mind here. Have I had a brain transplant recently and I just don't remember? These thoughts are not normal. At least not for me. My heart is racing.

I click onto the selfie-headshot he submitted and stare into his smoldering eyes. In this shot, unlike the one in the suit, there's a sadness behind his eyes. Is that loneliness? Exhaustion? Whatever it is, I can't resist it. He looks totally different here than in the suit and tie photos—bare, somehow. Vulnerable. The more I stare at his mournful face, the more I'm sure: This is the money shot for me, the one that makes me want to touch him and kiss him the most, even more so than his almost-nude selfie. It's just so disarming. Beautiful, really. It makes me ache all over, and not just in my panties. In my heart.

A nagging realization begins washing over me, nipping at me, threatening to consume me—a slow but steady drip, drip, drip of a deep and secret truth. I want to feel the sensation of losing myself completely to someone. I want to know what it's like for my body to detach from my mind, just once. I want to convulse and shudder and whimper and shriek the way other women do—the way he describes it. I want to experience the kind of pleasure that blurs into pain. Yes, I admit it—I want to howl like a rabid monkey. *I do.* And something tells me Mr. Jonas Faraday, the cockiest and most self-aggrandizing human being on planet earth—and yet the most physically alluring creature I've ever seen, too—with the saddest and most captivating eyes—just might be the man for the job. In fact, if I'm being honest here, I'm ardently hoping he is.

But why am I wasting time fantasizing about him? This is a man who just applied to The Club—*for a year*—and I'm his frickin' intake agent. It's a non-starter. I need this job more than I need to howl like a monkey.

Damn.

He told me to touch myself and think about what turns me on. Well, there's no harm in doing that, job or no job. I grunt with exasperation, grab the bottle of wine off the kitchen counter, and stomp into my bedroom, slamming the door emphatically behind me. If I can't have him in real life, then I'll just have to crank up the music, close my eyes, and imagine a world where I can.

Chapter 3
Jonas

My entire morning was hijacked, stranding me in a conference room with my management team, half listening to a phone call with Josh in Los Angeles and my uncle in New York and their respective teams. "That new acquisition isn't performing as projected." "Yeah, but the question is whether that's a trend or a blip?" "Can someone put that into a spreadsheet?" Blah, blah, fucking blah.

Ever since I submitted my application to The Club the night before last, I can't concentrate worth a shit. Even when the checkout girl at Whole Foods last night smiled and asked me what I was doing later, I just grabbed my bags off the conveyor belt and said, "I've got a busy night." And she had piercings, too—which means she had major daddy issues. I can't remember the last time I passed on a woman with daddy issues—they're usually my Achilles heel. But my head's just not in the game right now.

Within minutes of sending in my application, I received an automated email from a "no reply" address, informing me that my application had been received by my intake agent and would be queued up for immediate processing. "The review process takes up to two weeks and is designed to ensure maximum protection, privacy, and satisfaction," the email said. "Thank you for your patience."

I was pissed as hell to find out things would take so long. I'd hoped to get a warm and quick welcome from The Club—like how a Hawaiian hotel hands you a mai tai as you walk into the lobby. What could possibly hold things up for two weeks? I'd answered every question honestly and followed all directions to a tee; I'm not a serial killer or felon or druggie; and God knows they've got my full membership fee, in cash, sitting in the bank earning interest. So what the hell could possibly take two weeks? I can't stop checking my private email account, hoping things will somehow go faster than expected.

Now that I'm finally in my office alone, I close my door and quickly open my private email account, even though I know nothing will be there. My heart stops. There's a message in my inbox time-stamped at 2:12 a.m.—about an hour after I went to sleep last night. My breathing constricts just thinking about this message sitting here all morning while I've been trapped on a conference call about "projections" and "action items."

The email is from a sender identified as "Your Beautiful Intake Agent." Holy fuck. When I click on the sender name, the actual email address is "Your_Beautiful_Intake_Agent @gmail.com." Oh my God. My pulse is racing. My mouth is dry. I click open the email.

"My Brutally Honest Mr. Faraday:

"This email is not an official Club communication. In fact, if anyone at The Club ever found out about it, I'd lose my job faster than I could say 'my sweet button' or 'petals falling off a flower' or 'plunging into me like a hot knife in warm butter,' or, perhaps, my favorite, 'cocky-bastard-asshole-son-of-a-bitch motherfucker.' So, in the interest of me being able to make my next rent payment, I'm hoping you'll keep this message just between us—you know, our little secret. *Gracias*.

"I went back and forth and round and round, trying to get up the nerve to send you this note, and then trying to convince myself not to send it (because it's obviously a horrible idea), and then trying to stop myself from obsessively reading and re-reading what you wrote to me (I wasn't successful), and then trying to figure out exactly what to say to you if and when I actually sent you a note (which, of course, I knew was inevitable). So, here I am, after consuming a significant amount of two-buck chuck for some liquid courage (or maybe liquid stupidity?), finally writing this note to you and swearing to press 'send' when I'm done—even if doing so qualifies as felony stupid.

"I think I've finally figured out exactly what's so freaking important to say that I'm willing to risk the best-paying job I've ever had to say it. It's the thing you value the most, Mr. Faraday—the truth. You so kindly showed me yours, right? Well, then, I think it's only right I show you mine. Yes, Mr. Faraday, I'll give you my tit—in exchange for your tat, of course. (What did you think I meant?)

"But the truth is like an octopus when you start trying to pin it down—it's got lots of moving parts. So for starters, let's just start with pinning down the easiest parts—the parts I think you'll like the most.

"Yes, Mr. Faraday, I am indeed a woman. You're so damned smart. But you already knew that.

"Yes, Mr. Faraday, I thoroughly enjoyed reading your

application, just as you predicted I would, particularly your personal note to me at the end. Given the fact that I've been raised on Lifetime and Disney and Hallmark, and since I do, no doubt, have a raging good girl complex (among other self-sabotaging complexes, some of which are none of your business), I really wanted to hate your message. Actually, I just wanted to hate you, you cocky bastard asshole motherfucker. But my body had a different idea.

"As I read your note to me, despite my mind's unyielding desire to hate you, my body went rogue on me and *ached* for you. It *throbbed* for you, Mr. Faraday. Yes, my body had the exact physical reaction you predicted it would have. I won't go into too much detail, because I'm a fancy lady and all, but, yes, a change of panties was most definitely in order. Or, if we're being honest, the minute I started touching myself, just like you told me to do, I just tossed them on the bedroom floor.

"And, now, goddamn you, Mr. Faraday, I'm having that very same unmistakable physical reaction to you, yet again, just from typing this email to you. And, shoot, I'm all out of clean panties in my pretties drawer, too—and I don't have quarters for the laundry room downstairs! You really are a bastard, aren't you?

"That's a nice segue for another truth. Yes, I think you're a cocky bastard, as I've already mentioned. And worse, you're a cocky bastard with a raging God complex. Your God complex is so big, in fact, it rivals the size of your raging hard-on, if you can believe it.

"But you've also got honest eyes, Mr. Faraday. And they're sad, too—which is something I apparently cannot resist. And damn, you've got some effing kissable lips. And you make me laugh, too (though not intentionally). Oh, yeah, and you've got smokin' hot abs, by the way—but I probably don't need to tell you that. I mean, you've got a mirror, right?

"Yes, Mr. Faraday, it's true. I wanted to touch myself after reading your note to me, long before I even saw your photos, in fact. Your words alone—your crass and cocky and self-congratulating but honest and confident and insightful and spot-on words—made me want to slide my hand inside my panties. But I resisted because I don't touch myself, Mr. Faraday. Ever. There's never been any point.

"However, when I saw your photos, I must admit my self-restraint and 'not seeing the point' flew right out the window along with my brain. Suddenly, I was spread out on my bed next to an almost empty bottle of wine, music blaring—and I was touching myself and wishing your warm, wet tongue was doing the touching instead of my fingers. I imagined your gorgeous face smiling up at me from between my open thighs, your lips slick and shiny with my wetness. And then, Mr. Faraday, I touched myself some more and imagined you inside me, whispering in my ear. And for the first time in my life, I felt the promise of incredible pleasure simmering and bubbling inside me. No, it didn't erupt, of course, because it never has and probably never will—but for the first time, I believed it *could.* Or, hell, maybe I'd just had too much wine.

"Now, before you start gloating or jacking off or doing whatever it is a cocky bastard like you does to celebrate your sexual godliness, let me tell you a few more truths—the ones you might not like quite as much as the above entries. Brace yourself, Mr. Faraday.

"Despite what you think, you haven't made every single woman you've ever graced with your godliness come harder than she ever has. The unpleasant truth is that some of them didn't come at all. Perhaps every single woman you've ever been with has *appeared* to come during sex with the Magical Fuck Wizard himself, but, statistically speaking, at least ten percent of them are lying to you. Why? To enhance your pleasure. To spare you from feeling like a failure (considering how much effort you undoubtedly exert). To convince you she's worthy of an invitation to dinner or some other "Valentine's Day bullshit" you so abhor. Or, most likely, to avoid her own feelings of inadequacy and shame at not being able to perform what her body is apparently designed for, despite her desperate desire to do so. You think that first faker who inspired your current odyssey of box-lunch-munching is the only woman who's ever faked it with you or who ever will again? Maybe. But I highly doubt it—statistically speaking.

"Think back on some of those allegedly epic fucks of yours, Mr. Faraday. Really think about them. Could I be right?

"Or, hey, okay, okay, don't get all worked up about it. Maybe I'm dead wrong. Maybe you really are lighting up each and every one of your sexual conquests like Christmas trees. It's not a statistical probability, but I suppose it's *possible.* There are documented cases of people being struck by lightning on three separate occasions, after all; and I just heard about some guy in Chicago winning the lottery three different times in the same week. So I guess it's *possible* you've somehow managed to randomly avoid ten percent of the female population during your apparently many, many, many sexual exploits over the past year. It could happen. If that's the case, though, there's no way to know if you're as good as you think you are, is there? Think about it—if you've somehow been so lucky as to avoid the really tough nuts to crack, then you really haven't tested the limits of your skills, have you? I mean, I'm sure you'll agree that being able to climb *Mount Rainier* doesn't guarantee a successful climb of *Mount Everest*. (Speaking of which, that article about you and your brother in *Climbing Magazine* was excellent. I particularly liked it when they referred to you as 'enigmatic.')

"Of course, there's also a third possibility. Perhaps you have some kind of innate radar that kicks in subconsciously during your selection process? Perhaps the women you instinctively *want* in your bed happen to be those women who are innately disposed to go off like bottle rockets at the slightest flicker of your golden tongue—because you can sense it. If so, it doesn't necessarily prove your alleged sexual prowess, really, it just means you've got a handy talent for spotting and plucking low-hanging fruit (which, in and of itself is a dandy talent, indeed). It also makes a girl like me a little bit annoyed, if you want to know the truth. I mean, if you really are that good in the sack, where's your spirit of charity? Why not use your superpowers to help the less fortunate occasionally? Throw us ten-percenters a bone, will ya? Look at it this way: Is it really fair for you to pass right by a homeless shelter and waltz into the Ritz Carlton next door in order to serve some rich, fat lady a free turkey dinner smothered in gravy? And on top of that, once you've done that, should you really go back to the homeless shelter and saunter right up to the poor, starving girl in the corner and *brag* to her about how expertly you just served turkey to a fancy lady? Really, Mr. Faraday, how rude. (And just to be clear, the poor, starving, homeless girl in this elaborate metaphor is lil ol' me.)

"I'm not sure which of these three scenarios is The Truth. But it doesn't matter. Whichever one it is, the result is the same: Despite your alleged hunger for brutal honesty, you clearly haven't experienced it like you think you have. Why? Because *honesty* is just the flipside of a little thing called *humility*. (This word is pronounced 'hyoo-míl-uh-tee.' It's a noun. Look it up.) Without having one, you simply cannot have the other.

"Well, my Brutally Honest Mr. Faraday, have you enjoyed reading *my* secrets and confessions and wine-induced thoughts? Because I've enjoyed sharing them with you. In fact, I've enjoyed writing this note to you so much, I took a break midway through to touch myself (again)—all the while thinking of you and your warm, wet tongue and your beautiful, sad eyes and your luscious lips. I'll leave it to your active imagination as to exactly where in my narrative that pleasantness occurred.

"Well, Mr. Faraday. Perhaps this is goodbye. Probably so. I hope you find everything you're looking for in The Club, especially the honesty you so desperately crave. And don't worry—despite the horrific lapse in judgment I've displayed by sending this email to you, I'll diligently process your application according to all protocols and standards of professionalism going forward.

"Oh, yeah, and one last thing (in the interest of brutal honesty, of course)—yes, Mr. Faraday, I would indeed ditch all the Valentine's Day bullshit to howl like a monkey for the first time in my entire life. Hellz yeah, I would. I'm already apparently willing to risk my job to send you this email, so why not throw a little Valentine's Day bullshit under the bus, too? The only question I have is whether you, or any man for that matter, could accomplish the job for a ten-percenter like me, a Mount Everest kind of a girl. I highly doubt it. But, damn, I sure do wish someone, someday, somewhere, would prove me wrong—especially someone with exactly your sad eyes and luscious lips and chiseled abs. At any rate, even if you could do it, Mr. Faraday, on the following point I think we can both agree: It would most certainly take you a helluva lot longer than four minutes—two hundred and forty measly little seconds—as you so confidently claim, to do it. Puh-lease.

"Truthfully yours,

"Your Beautiful Intake Agent."

"Yo," Josh says, picking up my call on the first ring.

"Is it possible to trace an email to identify the sender?"

"What?"

"How the fuck do I find someone who sent me an anonymous email?"

"Whoa, no need to yell. Someone's a little high strung today."

"Josh, I don't have time for bullshit. Can it be done or not?"

"Calm down. It depends."

"On what?"

"On what server she's using."

"How do you know I'm looking for a 'she'?"

He laughs. "A wild guess."

"Fuck you."

He laughs again. "If I can get her IP address off the email header, then we're in business. If we're lucky, that'll cross-reference with her name on the server's account records. But I'll have to get a hacker involved to check the server's records on the down low—"

"Do whatever you have to do. Just keep it confidential."

"How much are you willing to spend?"

"Whatever it takes."

"Wow. What's—"

"Don't ask."

He sighs. "Okay. Don't get your hopes up on getting the name, bro. It's unlikely. We might get a physical address, but more likely it'll be a defined area—you know, like a one-mile radius. Maybe just a city. It depends."

"Can you do it right now?"

"What's going on?"

"It's personal."

"Sounds fun."

"Josh, seriously, I can't—"

"I'm just fucking with you, bro. Forward me the email. I'll take care of it."

"I'll forward you the email *header*—not the message itself."

"Damn. Sounds like it would have been some interesting reading."

"Oh man, you have no fucking idea."

I gather up my laptop and burst out of my office.

"I'll be gone the rest of the day," I murmur to my assistant as I whiz past her.

"What about your appointments this afternoon?" she calls after me.

I don't answer her. I've got to get out of here. I reach the reception area and punch the call button for the elevator. My head is spinning.

My Beautiful Intake Agent has never had a fucking orgasm! Not even once! Oh, what I would do to this woman. How I would lick this woman. How I would fuck this woman. Just the thought of her feeling so warm and wet and convulsing around my cock for the first time in her life makes me so hard I have to hold my laptop in front of my pants as I wait for the elevator. I'm going to be the first man ever to witness pure ecstasy on her face, to watch her eyes roll back into her head and her cheeks flush as she comes for the first time in her life—with me—because of me—*thanks to me.* The thought makes me moan involuntarily, just standing here waiting for the goddamned elevator.

Thankfully, the elevator arrives before I have a heart attack. I step inside and pound on the button for the parking garage over and over as the doors close.

Fuck. I don't even know what she looks like. I can't even imagine her face experiencing rapture because I don't know what her face looks like! Fuck, fuck, fuck. No woman has ever turned me on like this. Especially not a woman I've never even seen.

The elevator stops after a couple floors, before I've reached my destination, and a woman from the bank two floors down gets on. She's hot, but I don't give a shit.

"Oh, Mr. Faraday." She smiles and bites her lower lip. "Hi."

I can't even speak, I'm so distracted. So hard. So utterly disinterested right now in anyone or anything other than My Beautiful Intake Agent. All I want to do is get home so I can close my eyes and let her words wash over me and think about fucking this woman and licking her and making her come. I've never wanted to make a woman come so bad.

I nod at the woman and pretend to look at my phone. She gets off at the next floor, her nose out of joint.

I press the button for the parking garage again, even though it's already lit up.

I've got to get home. I want to read that email again and again and again and jerk myself off. Through her written words alone, My Beautiful Intake Agent's managed to turn me on like nobody ever has. That woman just kicked my ass. Hard. And I liked it. *My Beautiful Intake Agent.* My smart, sexy, hilarious, pulls-no-punches, kicks-my-ass intake agent. She called herself a "Mount Everest kind of a girl." Now that's a girl who knows how to dangle a fucking carrot. Damn.

When the elevator doors open, I sprint toward my car on the far end of the garage—not an easy thing to do with a raging hard-on, mind you. *A raging hard-on to rival the size of my raging God complex.* I can't help but smile. Holy shit, I've got to find this woman.

Who is she? *Where* is she? She could be anywhere in the world right now, working remotely from some intake center in Malaysia or India for all I know. But, wait, no—she mentioned Chicago, the Ritz Carlton, two-buck chuck. And, hey, she easily adopted my references to Lifetime and Hallmark, too. Yeah, she's definitely American.

I reach my car and jump inside, fumbling with the key.

She's here in the States. Somewhere. And I'm going to find her.

I pull out of my parking spot and peel out toward the exit.

Yes, I'm going to find her. And when I do, I'm going to lick her and then fuck her like she deserves—so well, so expertly, in fact, with such care and attentiveness and precision and unflinching devotion, she's finally going to discover the incredible power that's lain dormant inside her for so long. Yes, I'm going to make that woman come so hard, and with such velocity, she'll see God for the first time in her life. And when she does, she'll be surprised to find out he's a cocky-bastard-asshole-son-of-a-bitch motherfucker with so-called "sad eyes" and "luscious lips" who doesn't have an ounce of humility or charity in his body. Oh my God, I've got to find this woman before I have a fucking stroke.

Chapter 4

Sarah

By all outward appearances, I'm doing my job right now, exactly the way I've been trained to do it. I'm sitting in my nondescript Honda hatchback, scoping out my assigned applicant's place of business from an unobtrusive vantage point (in this instance, from across the street), for the purpose of visually confirming the man works where he says he does, looks roughly the way he claims to look in his photos, and, generally speaking, appears to be the man he claims to be.

I am emphatically *not* staking him out to get my rocks off. I am emphatically *not* feeling all gooey inside at the possibility that I'm going to lay eyes on the most gorgeous creature on the face of the earth. Nope. Hellz no. Not me. I'm all business, people. This is precisely the way I've been taught to do the surveillance portion of my application processing procedure. So, really, I'm just following protocol. So why do I feel like a stalker, then?

Because I'm a stalker. A sick, perverted, obsessed, panties-on-fire, spent-all-night-scoping-him-out-on-the-Internet stalker. Last night, I researched and researched online and read every bit of information I could find on the guy. Which wasn't much, really, unless you're super interested in acquisitions and real estate investment trusts.

Here's what I know so far: Jonas Faraday is a "well-respected" business up-and-comer with a "shrewd" mind for crunching numbers, who has "unconventional" but almost always "uncanny" investment instincts. He's a Seattle native, though it seems he travels frequently, often with his twin brother, Josh. He attended Gonzaga undergrad and went on to get an MBA from Berkeley (which makes me think he must be pretty liberal, but I couldn't find anything about his political affiliations).

Jonas Faraday runs Faraday & Sons with his twin brother, Josh (who lives in Los Angeles but apparently travels the world for business and pleasure even more than Jonas does) and also their uncle, William Faraday (who lives in New York). The company website says his father, Joseph Faraday, the founder of Faraday & Sons, died thirteen years ago (when Jonas and Josh were seventeen). Looks like the uncle stepped in to run Faraday & Sons after Joseph's death, seeing as how Jonas and Josh were still teens at the time. Countless business and investment-related articles and blogs recount the rise and rise of Faraday & Sons, detailing and analyzing the key acquisitions and investments that have put them on the map in the global investment community.

I devoured everything I could find—all the while feeling like I'd found absolutely nothing of any interest. What I really wanted to read about wasn't Jonas Faraday the businessman—I wanted to know about Jonas Faraday the man. But I kept coming up with zippo. He's not engaged in any kind of social media whatsoever—no Facebook or Instagram or Twitter or Pinterest. No pictures of his eggs benedict. No snapshots of him partying with his buddies in Vegas. No "likes" to tell me his favorite books and movies and places to eat. He doesn't write a blog or otherwise post information about himself, and he doesn't seem to attend fundraising galas or sit on any boards or date socialites or models or otherwise seek attention of any kind.

Now, if I were researching his brother, Josh, I'd have an endless supply of reading material, since Josh, unlike Jonas, has a penchant for attending parties all over the world with his high-profile-celebrity-athlete friends and girlfriends and tweeting out pictures of his adventures. Seriously, Josh was at Justin Timberlake's birthday party? What the hell? But not Jonas. Jonas is nowhere to be found on the party scene.

Unpredictably, the most detailed personal information I uncovered about Jonas Faraday, by far, came from a short transcription of an interview for a local middle school's career day. How the heck that interview came about, I cannot even begin to imagine—Jonas Faraday doesn't strike me as a charter member of the Big Brothers of America program—but Jonas seemed surprisingly forthcoming in the short interview.

When the boy asked Jonas' advice about picking a career, he was quoted as saying, "Find what you're good at, whatever it is, and become excellent at it. Excellence isn't magic—it's habit, the by-product of doing something over and over and striving to be the best at it. Simply figure out what your passion is, and resolve to make excellence your habit."

When asked about his hobbies and interests, Jonas responded, rather curtly, "Climbing," and I could almost imagine him squirming uncomfortably in his seat as he realized the interview was verging away from career advice and into personal information. But the kid pressed for more information, bless his little heart, and Jonas obliged him. "Rock climbing, mountain climbing. My goal is to climb all ten of the world's highest peaks during my lifetime."

"What else do you like to do besides climbing?" the kid asked, apparently uninformed of his subject's innate distaste for human interaction outside the walls of his bedroom.

"Well," Jonas was quoted as saying, "I also enjoy reading, particularly books about psychology, philosophy, fitness, and, especially, the mysteries of the human body." I liked that last topic the best—*"books about the mysteries of the human body."* A clever euphemism, I'm sure, for books about the puzzle of the female orgasm. Just the thought of him studying up on female sexuality turned me on more than I care to admit.

"Anything else?" the kid asked, and I laughed out loud, wishing I could have seen Jonas' body language at that point.

"I love music," Jonas answered. "And, of course, going to football and baseball games, as you know."

"As you know?" That part of his answer intrigued me. Why did the kid know Jonas likes going to football and baseball games? Is Jonas Faraday's interest in sports a well-known fact in the world at large—like, does his family own a sports team or something?—or was this information known specifically by this kid? And if so, how? Did the pair have a casual chat over juice and cookies before the interview started? Or do the two share some other relationship that led to this interview in the first place? The latter seemed more plausible to me, or else why on earth was Jonas there, but my research uncovered nothing to answer that question or any other. I couldn't figure out who the kid interviewer was, other than his first name (Trey), and I couldn't find anything in particular to explain Jonas' "as you know" comment.

The kid wrapped up his interview with a real humdinger of a question: "Do you have a favorite inspirational quote?" he asked.

"I have many," Jonas replied, and I could almost feel his intensity leaping off the page. "But one of my all-time favorites is from Plato: 'For a man to conquer himself is the first and noblest of all victories.'"

And that was the entire interview. Not much, really, and yet that little two-hundred-word interview by a middle-schooler revealed more about Jonas Faraday, and inspired more curiosity and interest in me, than every other business article about him combined. I must have read that little transcript twenty times, parsing and analyzing every word obsessively, feeling more and more attracted to him each time.

And now, here I am, sitting in my car, staring across the street at his building like a lovesick puppy, waiting to catch a glimpse of the hottest physical specimen I've ever seen—who also happens to quote Plato and read books about psychology, philosophy, and "the mysteries of the human anatomy." Be still my beating heart. And other pulsating parts, too.

If I were dealing with any applicant besides the scrumptiously delicious Jonas Faraday, I'd probably just walk into his office lobby and ask the receptionist if Mr. Faraday might answer some questions for my law school newspaper (since, hey, it seems like the guy is open to school-related interviews), and regardless of whether the receptionist were to say yes or no, I'd at least be able to minimally confirm his identity for purposes of my surveillance checklist by snooping around his office lobby and looking at the plaques and pictures on the walls.

And yet, for some reason, when it comes to conducting surveillance on Jonas Faraday, I'm instead sitting in my car, staring across the street at his building, freaking out about whether or not he's read my email from last night, worrying he's going to report me to headquarters, and just generally losing control of my mind, impulses, and body in general. For some reason I can't fully understand, I don't want to go in there and let him catch a glimpse of me.

Damn! Last night, I was so cocky and sure of myself when I sent that crazy-ass email, drunk on three glasses of cheap wine, listening to loud music, my head swimming from his sexy note to me and those intriguing answers in his career day interview. But today is a different story. Today, I can't stop worrying that maybe I made an epically huge mistake.

Why was I so damned sure I could trust him not to tattle on me? And what was so important to say to him that it was worth risking my job in order to say it? And why on earth did I tell him the embarrassing truth that I've never had an orgasm before? I've never told anyone about that. Ever. Not even Kat. Why on earth did I tell *him*? Ugh. He must have been, like, "Thanks for the over-share, dearest intake agent, now please get back to processing my application."

Gah.

What if he feels like I've compromised his privacy so egregiously, he withdraws his application and demands his money back? Oh my God, The Club sure as hell won't take kindly to an applicant demanding a quarter-million-dollar refund because their horny pony of an intake agent couldn't keep her hands in her pants and hormones in check. Oh man. I screwed up. I never should have sent him that email. I never should have had that third glass of wine. I never should have given in to temptation and touched myself like that—

Oh my God! There he is, racing like a bat out of hell from his parking garage in a sporty BMW. I cover my face with my hands as he flies past my Honda, but a split second is all I need to confirm he's even more gorgeous in person than in his pictures. Holy crappola, what a beautiful-looking man. Damn.

My heart is racing.

I start my car and try to wedge immediately into traffic, but a fast-moving stream of cars prevents me from pulling out from the curb. Damn.

I wait. And wait.

When traffic clears after half a minute, he's long gone from my sight.

Shoot! He could be headed anywhere right now. It'd be a wild goose chase to try to find him. I'm certainly not going to park my car outside his house and stare at him with binoculars like some kind of creeper. It's one thing to camp out on a busy commercial street and another thing entirely to stalk the man at his house. Wow, that probably would be actual "stalking," come to think of it, like, technical, legal "stalking" according to statutory definition. I'll have to research that. But I digress. I'm sure he lives in some fancy mansion behind a gate, anyway, even if I did want to legally stalk him. Which I don't. Of course not. Because that would be desperate and pathetic. And out of control. And bordering on obsessive behavior.

Gah.

My breathing is shallow. I groan. Good God, I'm desperate and pathetic. And out of control. And completely obsessed. Damn. I didn't expect him to fly out of his parking garage like that. I wasn't ready. I'm so bad at this.

I turn off my ignition and sit in my parked car, staring out my windshield at the leafy trees lining the street.

Holy moly, the man is gorgeous. Like, insanely, utterly, undeniably, breathtakingly gorgeous. Like, holy shit on a stick I've never seen such a good- looking man in all my life kind of gorgeous. Like please, please, please, for the love of God, please let me have sex with a man as good looking as him once in my entire life kind of gorgeous. Like, God have mercy on my soul I cannot be held accountable for my actions kind of gorgeous. Like, maybe sending him that email wasn't such a bad idea after all kind of gorgeous. Like, yes, maybe having a one-night stand with a man like that, with no tomorrow, and letting the door hit my ass on the way out, would be just fine with me kind of gorgeous.

I groan and rub my eyes in frustration. Aw, who am I kidding? It's time to stop the insanity and get real for a second here. I'm exactly the kind of girl he loathes—a hopeless romantic who naively mistakes physical chemistry for emotional connection. I'm his kryptonite.

Even after that drunken one-night stand six months ago, the following morning, I was idiotically hoping the guy would call me and say, "Hey, can we start again? How about I take you to dinner tonight?" Right then, I promised myself I'd never, ever do a "one and done" again. I'm just not cut out for it. I sigh. Or maybe promises to myself are meant to be broken when unforeseen and irresistibly compelling and good-looking circumstances present themselves.

Rain begins to dot my windshield and quickly turns to a steady downpour. Hello, Seattle.

I stare at the rain for a moment.

My first solo review and I've already hopelessly messed everything up, and then some. When I conducted surveillance during my training period with supervision, it seemed so easy: Observe the applicant in a public place, note the time and details on my intake log, and file report confirming the guy is who he says he is. Done-zo.

I recline my seat, gazing out my windshield, watching the rain batter my car.

I guess, technically, I've already fulfilled my surveillance if I think about it. Jonas Faraday, the same guy in the pictures, just came out of Faraday & Sons, looking the way he claims to look—only way better. So I should be done-zo, right? Not just with the surveillance, but with the application review process in total. I've got everything I need to mark him "recommend approve," don't I? I could go back home right now, note my successful Jonas Faraday sighting on my intake report, package my findings and research and recommendations together with the "all clear" that just came back from his psychological and medical testing (great news—he's definitely not a psychopath!), and when I get the go-ahead from headquarters, send out the automated "congratulations!" email to him and overnight his welcome package and instructions.

But goddammit! I don't want to do that. I don't want him to become a member of The Club just yet. The mere thought of him going on an epic cunnilingus spree with a long line of nameless women—all of them as depraved and devoid of humanity as he is—just makes me sick. Approving him would be like giving a toddler cotton candy for dinner, when what he needs is a big bowl of grilled fish and kale. He's a crack addict stumbling desperately into a crack house, when what he needs is a month of rehab. I could scream right now.

For such a smart man, he's so dumb. He may think he wants *less* human connection in his life, but what he needs, desperately, even if he doesn't realize it, is *more* human connection. Idiot. Sex-crazed, egotistical idiot. If only I had a little bit more time to ... To what? What the hell am I thinking? My Lifetime/Hallmark brainwashing is rearing its ugly head again. Man, he sure has me pegged.

What do I really expect to happen here? He didn't apply for membership so he could diddle the lowly intake agent. And he didn't apply for Club membership so he could find true love, either. And he certainly didn't join The Club to learn something new and beautiful about the depths of his fragile heart. Ha! The man explicitly wants unfettered access to women who are just like him, women who are as emotionally disconnected and damaged as he is, women who allegedly want pleasure and nothing else—women so motivated by this elusive pleasure he allegedly provides that they're willing to pursue it without even *hoping* for something more, without even leaving the door open the teensiest bit for the mere *possibility* of something more, of something beautiful. Something real.

Who are these hopeless, cynical, untethered women he hopes to find? What woman could possibly be happy being so hopeless and shutdown and hedonistic and out of touch with her own heart? Even if you know you're just having a booty call with a hot guy (and I've had *two* of those, mind you, including one I remember, so I'm pretty effing qualified to give my opinion on this subject), isn't part of the fun the slim *possibility* that it *could* lead to an unlikely romance? Or, at least, a fleeting but unforgettable romance in a "We'll always have Paris" kind of way? (Or, in the case of two of my booty calls, a "We'll always have the Wild Onion" kind of way?) No matter how cynical we think we are, isn't the whole point of being alive and interacting with other humans—and especially having sex with other humans—about believing love is possible for even the lowliest and loneliest of fools?

If Jonas Faraday doesn't understand that, okay. He's a man. But who the hell are these women in The Club, who don't understand it, either? And why would any man, including Jonas Faraday, ever want those kinds of women, anyway, if indeed they exist? If that's what he wants, if that's what he really wants, then why not just date other men, for Pete's sake?

And the worst part is I know for a fact that each and every woman in The Club is going to lie like a rug when they see My Brutally Honest (and extremely hot) Mr. Faraday and tell him every ridiculous thing he wants to hear, no matter how far from the truth, because they won't be able resist the fantasy of taming this unbreakable stallion any more than I can.

Wow, I'm really going off on an internal rant here. Kat would laugh her ass off at me right now. I'm so predictable.

I sigh.

I just wish I had access to female membership profiles, so I could see exactly what I'm up against here. But all I've ever seen are male applicants—and only those in the greater Seattle area, at that. Why the hell am I so goddamned upset at the thought of all these other women sleeping with My Brutally Honest Jonas Faraday, all the while telling him what he wants to hear? Just the thought hurts my heart, even as my body aches for him.

I'm being an idiot.

I'm imagining something between us that doesn't exist. He sent that note to me on a lark, sight unseen—and it wasn't even a message to *me*. It was a message to some fantasy girl who bears no resemblance to me—a nameless Intake Agent without a romantic bone in her anonymous body. He was just having a bit of pre-approval fun with the idea of me—but not with me, personally.

Certainly, once he reads my response email and realizes the kind of hopeless romantic I am (not to mention the kind of smart-ass I am, too), all the fun of it will be gone for him. Even if by some small chance he likes my reply (which, I know, is a ridiculous thought), where could it lead? Nowhere. He sleeps with swimwear models and glamazons and socialites I'm sure—women who look like Kat—and probably not women who look and talk and act and think like me.

Now don't get me wrong; my self-esteem is just fine. In any crowd, I can usually count on at least a couple guys being drawn pretty enthusiastically to my vaguely exotic Latina looks like moths to a spicy little flame. But it's never a sure thing, not like how it is with Kat. What if "vaguely exotic Latina" just isn't Jonas Faraday's thing? That'd be a cruel pill for me to swallow.

Of course, in my fantasy, I'm the woman who gives him an indefatigable hard-on like no other (which is probably saying a lot, considering how indefatigable his hard-on already seems to be), and he wants me like no man has ever wanted a woman, anywhere, anytime, ever in the history of the world. Mark Antony and Cleopatra? Pffft. They'd have nothing on Jonas and Sarah.

But even if that were the case, what would be the point? He's a one-night stand kind of guy and will never, ever change—he even says so himself—so, at best, even in this fantasy, I'm talking about having mind-blowing, orgasmic sex with the most gorgeous man in the world, just once, and that's it, nothing more. Is my job worth that? *Well, damn, when I say it like that, hellz yeah, it is! Hellz yeah!*

I feel like slapping myself. No, it's not worth it.

Maybe if the job weren't part of the equation. But, no, I can't risk it. If The Club ever found out, I'd be fired on the spot. And I need this job. I'm the one putting myself through law school, after all, and it was frickin' hard to get here in the first place. I'm not going to risk everything to have one heart-stopping orgasm that can't lead to anything else, ever. No matter how gorgeous he is. Or how cunning a linguist. Or how gorgeous. But I already said that.

And, anyway, the odds of me being this godlike man's cup of tea are slim. After all this build-up and dirty talk and masturbation and confession and "honesty," if he were to finally see me, there's a very real possibility he'd exhale and say, "oh." And I don't mean, "*Oh!*" with naughty raised eyebrows, I mean, like, "oh," with a droopy frowny-face. And that would be kind of soul crushing, I have to admit.

I look at my watch. Crap. I've got Constitutional Law in an hour. I bring my seat to an upright sitting position and start my engine.

Yeah, I've made a decision—a mature, responsible decision.

The minute I get back from class tonight, I'll delete that intake-agent Gmail account I made for him and forget this ever happened. I'll get approval to trigger the automated "congratulations!" email and overnight him his welcome package. And then I'll just try to erase the allegedly Brutally Honest Jonas Faraday from my memory. I won't even think of his mournful eyes and luscious lips and ridiculous abs and tattooed arms and round little nipples and intriguing interest in philosophy and "human anatomy" ever again.

I sigh. Yep, I'll just erase all of that from my memory. Boom.

I turn on my windshield wipers and pull my car into traffic.

But even so, there can't be any harm in keeping his photos on my laptop for occasional future viewing, right? Or, perhaps making his face the background image on my desktop? I mean, for Pete's sake, I might be mature and responsible, but I'm not freakin' dead.

Chapter 5

Jonas

I've read and re-read her email to me twenty times, jerked off and showered, and now I'm sitting at my computer, staring at a blank screen, trying to figure out how to reply to her.

I've got to be honest with her—this woman can spot bullshit a mile away—but I have to be careful not to spook her, too. She's already nervous about risking her job. Whatever I say to her better not make her wig out and delete her email account. That account is my only means of reaching her.

"My Beautiful Intake Agent," I write.

I stare at the screen, my fingers resting on my keyboard.

What do I want to say? Do I really want to say I want to fuck her, sight unseen? What if it turns out she's not at all physically attractive to me? What if she's a great-grandmother or something?

Fuck it. I can't think like that. She's hot. I know she is. I've got a sixth sense about these things. And I can't worry about scaring her off. I just have to tell her the truth. It worked the first time. I have to believe it'll work again.

I lay my fingers on my keyboard again.

"The only thing bigger than my raging God complex right now is my raging hard-on for you," I type, making myself smirk. "Your email made me hard from the minute it hit my inbox to the moment I stopped reading it for the twentieth time and jacking off to it fifteen minutes ago. Thank you for your brutal honesty. And, of course, for telling me your delicious secret, too. Yes, indeed, you're Mount Everest, my dear—and you must know what kind of allure you therefore present to a passionate climber like me.

"You're driving me fucking crazy, you know. (Of course, you do—and you like it.) I'm a man who needs to be in control, a fact that probably hasn't escaped your notice, and in this bizarre but delectable situation, you're the one holding all the cards right now. This is an upside-down distribution of power for a man saddled with a raging God complex, as I'm sure you can appreciate. But for some reason, I'm enjoying the torture.

"You know everything about me, and I know nothing about you—well, wait, that's not completely true. I know what I need to know. You're smart. And sexy as hell. And not afraid to kick my ass with some seriously brutal honesty of your own. And, of course, I know you've never experienced the most fundamental and ultimate pleasure known to human experience, a fact that pains me as much as it excites me. It's a fucking travesty, My Beautiful Intake Agent, it really is.

"I want to know everything about you. But let's start with your name. And where I can find you. At the very least, you owe me three photos, my beautiful one. One in clothes, one full bodied, and one headshot, of course. It's only fair. Take out your phone right now and send them to me. Show me your tit. (For my tat, of course. What did you think I meant? You have such a dirty mind.)

"And, by the way, of course, I won't tell a soul about your email, rest assured. I would never do anything to harm you in any way. I promise.

"Undeniably, faithfully, and truthfully yours (and also going crazy and losing my mind and thoroughly *not* enjoying the imbalance of power, though I have a hunch you *are*), Jonas."

What is it about this woman that gets me off like this?

I quickly press send, without even reading what I've written. I know if I don't just send it, as is, I'll start obsessing over whether the wording is exactly right, and whether I'm going to scare her off, and trying to make it perfect. Because I like perfect. But I've already left her hanging far too long without a reply, and I'm sure she's starting to wonder. And worry. And regret. Oh shit, what if she's already deleted her email account? That would be very, very bad for my mental health. I can't lose my only means of contacting her.

My cell phone rings and my heart instantly leaps in my throat.

"Josh," I say, my chest constricting. "Please tell me you've got good news."

"She's in Seattle."

I can barely breathe.

"Are you there?"

"Yeah, yeah. I just can't believe it. You sure?"

"Oh yeah, I'm positive. She's on U Dub's server."

"She's a student at Washington?"

"Or a professor, I guess. One or the other."

I've read her email so many times it's part of my gray matter now. *"Hellz yeah,"* she said. *"Helluva lot longer." "Puh-lease."* She said this job is the "best paying job" she's ever had.

"She's a student," I say slowly, putting the pieces together. Yeah, I'm sure of it. She said she was drinking "two-buck chuck." Yes, definitely a student. She said she's got rent to pay—and that she's got a laundry room downstairs. Okay, so she lives in an apartment. Student housing? My mind is clicking and whirring, gathering the pieces of the puzzle. Something is niggling at my brain. Something important. She used the word *allegedly,* didn't she? Yes, more than once. I smirk. Who uses that pretentious word but lawyers ... *and law students?*

"She's a law student," I whisper, smirking. And, suddenly, I'm sure of it—because, holy fuck, can that woman argue a point.

Josh laughs. "You always did like 'em smart. You're so predictable, man. Okay, let me see if my guy can get onto the university's server and take a peek around. There's probably some sort of distinction in their records between law students versus the entire student population. That would at least narrow the field. Do you know anything else about her?"

"Not yet. But I will."

"All right. When you get more information, get it to me."

"I will. Keep your phone handy. Thanks, Josh."

"No problemo. You know how much I love the chase—even if it's chasing a law student for you."

I'm about to hang up.

"Jonas."

"What?"

"Does this have something to do with The Club I was telling you about?"

I don't say anything.

"I knew it!"

"No."

"You joined."

"No."

"Bro, you're acting like a sexual deviant right now. That's exactly what The Club does to a man. Oh man, you're about to have the best month of your life." He laughs again.

Wait, what? Josh only signed up for a *month*? Wow, I really *am* a sexual deviant. "It's none of your business," I mutter.

"Really? You've got me hacking the server of the fucking University of Washington, just to get you laid by some mystery law student with a fake email address—and it's none of my business?"

I exhale. "I submitted my application a few days ago. I'm not a member yet. And now, it doesn't even matter. I've gotten myself distracted. Hopelessly distracted." I grunt. "I don't give a shit about The Club. All I care about is finding her."

Josh laughs again. "Wow. Distracted from The Club? That's pretty intense. Sounds like this girl is a real stand-out." He exhales. "Okay, bro. Sit tight. I'll see what I can find out."

"Thanks again, Josh."

"Aw, you know I'm a sucker for true love."

"Fuck you."

I've been pacing around my house for the past hour.

She hasn't replied to my email.

And Josh hasn't called back, either.

I'm going crazy.

Why hasn't she replied? What's going on in her beautiful head? And, shit, what if her head's not quite as beautiful as I imagine it to be? No, that's impossible. I've got a sixth sense for hotness. I'm never wrong.

I change into my workout clothes and head into my home gym, music from Kid Ink blaring in my ears. Maybe lifting some weights will burn off some of my manic energy. I don't like feeling out of control.

I let the hot water beat down my back. How old is she? If she's in law school, she's probably anywhere from twenty-two to maybe twenty-five? Twenty-six at most? Right? Unless law school for her is a later-in-life, change-of-direction type thing. But that's probably not the case. God, I hope it's not.

Just as I'm wrapping a towel around my waist, I hear my computer beep with an incoming message. I sprint out of my bathroom to my laptop on my bed. I click open my private email account. I'm panting.

It's from her.

"Here you go," her message says. There's a photo attachment. I inhale sharply as I click on the photo and open it. Oh my God. It's a picture of a breast. One breast, singular. The smart-ass showed me her "tit"—for my tat, of course, just like I requested. I don't know why I'm even surprised.

I sit down on the bed, my erection poking up from beneath my towel. I can't stop staring at the picture. Her skin is smooth with an olive undertone, or is that barely-there mocha? I can't tell. Is she Italian? Greek? Latina? Light-skinned black? I can't tell from this tiny swatch of skin. All I know for sure is she's definitely not a platinum blonde Swede or a redheaded Irish Catholic. No, that skin is definitely tinged with some flavor. And the breast itself is round and plump, the perfect size for my hand plus a little extra. Definitely real. Her nipple is dark and round and standing fiercely at attention for me. Oh God, this woman. I wonder what she did to herself to make her nipple stand up like that? I wish I could have been there to see her do it, whatever it was. No, I wish I could have been there to do it to her myself.

"Thank you," I type. "You're beautiful. I can't stop looking at the photo. I'm totally obsessed."

"I know the feeling," her reply comes back immediately.

I practically growl with excitement upon getting her reply. "Tell me your name," I quickly write.

"No," she replies—again, immediately.

I can barely contain myself. This woman is somewhere in this city right now, staring at me through her computer screen. My heart is racing. "Not fair. You know my name," I type.

"Life isn't fair."

I half-smile at my screen. "Ain't that the truth," I type. Truer words were never spoken. I sigh. "If not your name, tell me something else. How about your age?"

"I just turned 24."

I'm thrilled. She finally threw me a bone. And I'm relieved, too—twenty-four is good. Very good. "See? That wasn't so hard. Happy Birthday," I type, smiling.

"Thank you."

"Pisces, then?"

"Oh my God. You did not just ask me, 'What's your sign?'"

I laugh out loud. "Yeah, I guess I did. I'm dumb like that sometimes."

"With cheesy pickup lines like that, it's clearly thanks to your supernatural good looks and *not* your sparkling personality that you've managed to be worshipped as a supreme sex-god by so many. Gosh, I expected a little more panache from you, Mr. Faraday. Aren't you supposed to be some kind of woman wizard? Oh, wait, that's only inside the four walls of your bedroom—never on the outside."

I can't help but smile from ear to ear. She's kicking my ass again. I love it. "You're right. I'm not very good at this." And it's true. I mean, I can *talk* to women, of course. I can even flirt. Sort of. But I've never been great at doing it. And especially not in a situation like this—when I can't look into her eyes and get a read on her. "I'm hopeless at small talk," I type.

"There's no such thing."

"No such thing as small talk?"

"No such thing as *hopelessness*. There's always hope. 'We must accept infinite disappointment, but never lose infinite hope.'"

Oh God. My cock has been leaping and lurching throughout our entire exchange, but my brain just joined the fray, too. "Who said that?"

"Martin Luther King Jr.," she types.

She's a whole new breed of woman I've never encountered before. I exhale loudly. "Here's one," I type. "'Hope is the dream of a waking man.'"

"Oh, I like that. Who's that?"

"Aristotle."

"That'd be an awesome episode of Epic Rap Battles of History—Martin Luther King Jr. vs. Aristotle. Hard to say who'd win."

I grunt. How did we get from her erect nipple to Martin Luther King Jr. and Aristotle waging an epic rap battle? "Stop trying to distract me, My Beautiful Intake Agent. I know exactly what you're trying to do, but I demand to know more about you. Come on."

"Okay, okay. You've worn me down, especially when you 'demand' like that. You're so manly when you do that, by the way—I like it. Okay, here's everything: I am a woman. I am 24. I have a Maltese named Kiki. I buy her little outfits with rhinestones on them. She is my world. The End."

She's killing me right now, even as I'm laughing out loud. "Come on. Please. Tell me something real," I type.

"Why?"

I sigh. Jesus, she's frustrating. "Because you know everything and I know nothing. It's not fair. Where's your sense of fair play and justice?"

"Just so you know, I'm sighing right now. Oh, and rolling my eyes, too."

"Please."

"Okay, okay. You wore me down *again*. You're so persuasive, Mr. Faraday. Irresistible! Okay, here you go: Blah, blah, blah. Prelude, prelude, prelude."

I burst out laughing. That's fucked up. I never under any other circumstance would have disclosed my thoughts about "prelude" to a woman—especially a woman I'm trying to get into bed. "Come on. Anything. How about this: What was the song you listened to when you touched yourself and thought about me?"

"How do you know I listened to music when I touched myself and thought about you?"

"You told me so."

"Did I?"

I've read her email so many times I can recite it word for word. "Yes, you did. You said you were spread out on your bed next to an almost empty bottle of wine, music blaring, and that you touched yourself and wished my warm, wet tongue were doing the touching instead of your fingers. Best line ever in the history of the world. Gave me a gigantic woody."

"Gee, thanks. But I'm sure you get a gigantic woody reading a grocery list."

"Only if it's yours."

"Oh, smooth, you woman wizard, you. See? You're not as bad at this as you think."

"Stop trying to change the subject. What was the song? Did you turn on Pandora and roll the dice, or did you choose a specific song?"

"I chose the song. The perfect song. Of course."

My kind of woman. "What was it?" My heart's pounding in my ears.

"'Pony.' The cover by Far, not the original."

Okay, this girl officially just blew my mind. That cover's not a mainstream tune—I'm shocked she knows it. The original song by Ginuwine is an old R&B cheesefest from the nineties about a guy looking for a horny pony to ride his saddle. The original was unintentionally hilarious, but Far's rendition of the song rocks—heavy guitars, crashing drums, crunchy bass. And the vocals are tongue in cheek and sardonic, while still managing to be raw and gritty and dirty. If she picked *that* song for a session of self-love, that tells me I'm not dealing with the usual kind of girl—a fact I already knew.

"Excellent choice," I type. My entire body's coursing with electricity. I've got to find this woman.

"I agree," she types. "Hence, the reason I chose it."

I inhale and exhale deeply. I don't like being out of control like this. I don't like her holding all the cards. My knee is jiggling wildly.

"I want to meet you more than I want to breathe," I type. And it's the truth. "Please," I add. I've never begged a woman for anything in my entire life, but I'd get down on my hands and knees if I thought it would make her tell me where to find her.

She doesn't reply.

Up 'til now, her replies have been instantaneous. I wait.

My heart is pounding in my chest. Why isn't she replying?

As long as there's a break in the action with her, I reach for my phone to text Josh. *"She's 24."*

He texts back right away. "*Good. If we don't get a name, we can narrow the field by age. But get a name if you can, obviously."*

Why isn't she answering me? Did she get up to pour herself a glass of wine? Did she get up to turn on "Pony" again? Or is she just sitting there, staring at the screen, second-guessing herself and freaking out?

Still no reply.

I click onto the picture of her breast again and stare at her hard nipple. Oh man. You'd think I'd never seen a nipple before the way my body's reacting to the sight of hers.

Why isn't she responding?

I place my hands over my keyboard again. I've got to reel her back in. She's obviously starting to second-guess herself here.

"I interpret your silence to mean you're not ready to meet me. (As you can see, I'm super smart at interpreting a woman's nonverbal cues—just one more stunning example of my woman wizardry.) That's okay. We don't have to meet. Just send me another picture, then, to tide me over. It's only fair—you've got three of mine, after all. You owe me two, but I'll settle for one. How about a headshot?" My breathing is shallow. I want to type the word "please" fifty times, but I restrain myself.

"I'm thinking," she says immediately.

I exhale in relief. She's still there. Thank God.

"Don't think. Thinking is the enemy. Just do it. Right now. One picture. I won't breathe 'til I get it. I've officially stopped breathing. Please, please, don't let me suffocate over here. Hurry! I'm not breathing! Hurry! Aaaah!" I press send and sit and stare at the screen. Oh God, this woman is making me crazy.

After a moment, there's another email. Thank God.

"Please don't suffocate, for Pete's sake. That'd be a dumb thing to do. Here you go." It's another photo file.

I open the image. It's her thigh? Her hip? It's hard to make out. But there's that skin again. Smooth and even. And olive-toned. Definitely olive. Oh man, I want to touch that gorgeous olive skin. I want to touch every square inch of it, inside and out.

"Thank you," I reply, but that doesn't even come close to expressing what I'm feeling. "You're so beautiful. I want to touch you." I'm hard as a rock.

An immediate reply. "I want to be touched by you, My Brutally Honest Mr. Faraday."

My heart leaps. And so does my cock.

"Call me Jonas."

Again, an instant reply. "I want to be touched by you. *Jonas.*"

I am losing my fucking mind. "Tell me where to find you."

"I shouldn't."

"You should."

"Bad idea."

"How can I touch you if I can't find you?"

No reply again.

"I just want to touch you," I type again, not waiting for her reply. Thank God we're conversing over email. If I were speaking these words to her, I'm sure I'd be shouting them, I'm so amped up. "I won't tell anyone about our communications. I promise."

"I know you won't tell. I trust you. That's not why it's a bad idea."

I grunt in frustration. If she's not worried about her job, then why is it a bad idea? I don't understand. As far as I'm concerned, this is a fucking fantastic idea. Okay, new tactic. "How about you touch yourself and pretend it's me?"

"I already did that. That's what got me here in the first place."

"So do it again. Maybe second time's the charm. You never know."

There's a long pause. I'm just about to email her again, when her reply comes.

"Okay," she says.

I inhale sharply. "Good. Do it now."

"Yes, sir."

"Right now."

"Jeez, I said okay. You're so effing demanding."

I can't hold back anymore. I'm losing control. I shouldn't say what I'm about to say—it might scare her off. But I can't stop myself. "Go lie on your bed and touch yourself." My fingers are moving quickly on the keyboard. "Imagine my hands all over you, my lips on your neck, your nipples, your belly, inside your thighs and all around your pussy. Imagine my tongue caressing every inch of you 'til you're writhing and moaning and begging me to kiss your throbbing tip. Finally, imagine my warm tongue finding it, swirling it around and around, lapping at you, kissing you, licking you. Imagine yourself letting go in that moment, giving in completely to the pleasure—so completely your mind flashes into a blinding light and ceases to exist. And right then, right at the moment you imagine your mind disappearing into oblivion, I want you to say my name again, out loud. Go do that for me right now. I'll wait." I press send.

"Yes, lord-god-master," the answer comes back immediately. "Stay tuned. And keep breathing, for Pete's sake. This may take a while."

I wait. I'm shaking. I put my laptop next to me on the bed and yank my towel off. I lie there, naked on my bed, my hard-on straining up toward my stomach. I raise my hands above my head and grab at my hair for a moment, the muscles on my naked body tensing. I feel like I'm losing my mind. If only she were sitting on top of me right now. I moan, imagining her there, riding me. Oh God, how I wish she were on top of me right now, throwing her head back and coming.

I can't believe she's never had an orgasm, not even once.

I need to find this woman.

I need to fuck this woman.

I need to make this woman surrender to me.

I can almost feel her on top of me right now.

I'm going out of my fucking mind.

After what seems like forever, my computer finally beeps with a new email and I click on it.

"Jonas," the message says. "Jonas, Jonas, Jonas, Jonas, Jonas, Jonas, Jonas, Jonas, Jonas, Jonas, Jonas, Jonas."

I stare at my screen, losing my shit. Moments ago, somewhere in this very city, not too far from where I've been lying here naked on my bed and imagining her, she put her beautiful olive-skinned hand between her legs and touched herself at my command, all the while imagining my warm tongue on her sweet spot—and she said my name over and over and over again when she did it.

Fuck.

I'm trembling with the physical need to touch her, to put my hands on her body, to whisper her name in her ear—if only I knew her goddamned name, that is.

"Tell me your name." I type quickly, pounding on the keyboard. If I were saying these words out loud, she'd be shocked at the forcefulness of my tone.

"No," she replies.

I grunt. Why is she being so difficult? "Please," I type. If she understood my desperation, she'd give in and do what I tell her to do.

"Bad idea."

"Good idea. Please."

"Why?"

I grunt again. *Why?* What does she mean *why*? Why does she think? Because she's driving me out of my fucking mind, that's why, and I've never even laid eyes on her. Because she's somehow managed to hook me like a marlin on a line, that's why. I sigh. My fingers hover over my keyboard. "I want to know what name I'll be whispering into your ear as you experience pure ecstasy for the very first time." I swallow hard and press send.

I wait. No reply. Four minutes pass. Nothing.

My heart is in my ears. Oh man. She's not answering. Fuck. That wasn't the right message. She's scared to meet me, for whatever reason, and so what did I do? I told her I want to fuck her, sight unseen. Have I gone totally insane? If she's at all sane, unlike me, then I'm sure she's freaking out right now. Damn. I need to reel her back in, show her I'm not crazy, that I just sound that way.

"Just tell me your first name," I type quickly, even more frantically than before. "Have mercy on me. If you won't meet me, then I'll have no choice but to jack off again, thinking of you—and when I do, what name should I whisper into the dark, sad, lonely void of my bedroom? You're not really going to make me moan 'My Beautiful Intake Agent' over and over, are you? That doesn't exactly trip off the tongue. Come on, I'm begging you—and, believe me, I never beg."

I press send.

Almost immediately, my inbox beeps with a reply. It's a one-word message. But it's all I need.

"Sarah."

I exhale in relief and elation. I grab my phone and tap out a quick text to Josh. *"Sarah."*

"I'm on it," he immediately texts back.

Sarah.

I can only hope a first name is enough to find her. Because a first name is all I've got. That, and hope. Infinite hope. My fingers find my keyboard again. "Thank you, my beautiful Sarah. Sarah, Sarah, Sarah, Sarah, Sarah, Sarah." I grin. I feel like a little kid. I might even be blushing right now. "Please, Sarah, just let me meet you. Please, please, please, please, please. Tell me where you are."

I press send and wait. My stomach is flip-flopping. My heart is racing. She's close to giving in; I know she is. I can feel it—taste it. I stare at my screen. *Come on, Sarah. Don't think about it. Just take a leap of faith.*

Five minutes later, an email finally lands in my inbox. But it's not from her. It's an automated email from The Club. My breath catches and my heart sinks at the same time.

"Congratulations!" the automated email says. "Your application for membership to The Club has been approved. Once your membership funds have successfully transferred to us from escrow in approximately two business days, you will receive a welcome package containing detailed instructions about how to use and maximize your membership. Welcome to The Club. Where your every fantasy becomes a reality."

I'm frantic. "Sarah," I type out. "Did I scare you? I won't tell anyone about you, I promise. I just want to meet you. I just want to touch you. We could even just talk. I just want to see you. Please. Please reply right away." I'm typing like a maniac. I press send and wait.

Two minutes later, I receive a bounce back notification that makes me scream out in frustration. "Delivery failed. Server unable to locate email address. Please check your records and, if you feel this message is in error, try sending your email again."

Chapter 6

Jonas

"Hold your horses, bro. He's going as fast as he can," Josh says.

"It's been three days."

"Jonas, hacking into a major university's server is kind of a big deal. You have to be patient."

I grunt.

"I know patience isn't your strong suit. Just, please, try to relax."

"There's no way in hell I can relax."

"Well, try. I'll get back to you soon. He said he's close."

"Thanks. Sorry I'm such an asshole. I appreciate your help."

"No worries. You can't have the looks *and* the personality—you gotta leave me a little something."

"Call me the minute you hear—"

"I will. Bye."

Relax? I'm supposed to relax? There are only two things in this world that ever help me relax, and for the past three days since Sarah cut me off, I've only been doing one of them—working out like a madman. But I'm still relentlessly amped up. I can't get her off my mind. I don't understand what I did to make her run scared—other than show her what an asshole I really am. Yeah, come to think of it, maybe that was it. But she knew the truth about me when she first answered my email. So what changed? What did I do? Just the thought of her freaking out and wanting nothing to do with me is killing me right now. One minute she was touching herself and saying my name, and the next minute she was cutting off all ties. I have to find her and make her feel safe again, make her understand I'd never harm her.

I sit at my kitchen table in a pair of jeans and nothing else, my head in my hands. I should be working right now. We're planning another big acquisition and there's plenty to do. Josh has been picking up my slack, but there's only so much he can do from L.A. on this particular deal. Really, I should be in the office right now, managing my team. But I can't concentrate. I just keep staring at my phone, waiting for Josh to call me to say he's found her.

A couple times, I've tried her email address again, hoping maybe she'd calmed down and reactivated it. But no luck. Same bounce-back message both times.

I open my laptop and click into my email again, just in case.

There's a message from The Club, dated yesterday afternoon.

"Dear Mr. Faraday,

"Welcome to The Club! This is to notify you that your membership funds have successfully cleared from the escrow account. You are now a full-fledged member of The Club. Tomorrow, you will receive a welcome package at the address provided on your application, which will give you everything you need to maximize your membership. If you have any questions or concerns or suggestions, you may contact us at Member_Support@TheClub.com. Of course, all communications will be held in the strictest confidence. Please do not reply to this email, as your reply will not direct to anyone. Welcome to The Club. Where your every fantasy becomes a reality."

I feel sick. I just spent two hundred fifty thousand dollars on something I don't even want anymore. It kills me to waste money. Especially a quarter of a million dollars.

Two nights ago, I lay in bed all night, trying to figure out how I could withdraw my membership application and not cause a problem for Sarah. I went over it and over it in my head, lying in the dark, but I couldn't imagine a scenario where canceling that payment wouldn't end with Sarah losing her job—which, in turn, would mean breaking my promise to her. For a while, I considered withdrawing my membership application and agreeing to pay her a year's salary instead (which most certainly is a mere fraction of two hundred fifty thousand dollars). But it always came back to me breaking a promise to her and losing her trust forever—something I'm not willing to do. And, anyway, what if the big wigs at The Club are vindictive fuckers? They could sue her ass for intentional interference with contract and demand payment of my entire membership fee from her. The more I turned it over and over in my head, the more I knew I had to let that damned payment go through—even though joining The Club is the last thing I care about right now. I promised her I wouldn't harm her in any way. And I'd rather pay money—any amount of money—than harm her. Or break a promise to her. I'm a lot of things, but a liar I am not.

Hopefully, when she finds out I didn't stop the wire transfer she'll realize she can trust me completely. She'll understand I'm a man of my word. Maybe then she'll contact me again. I can only hope. Because right now, I'm out of my head.

The doorbell rings. After a minute, I drag myself up from the table and shuffle to the door like a dead man walking. It's a guy from FedEx with a box.

"Jonas Faraday?"

"Yeah."

"Sign here, please."

Getting this box should feel like my birthday and Christmas all rolled into one. I should be chomping at the bit to open it. So why do I feel like throwing it, unopened, against the wall? I leave it on my kitchen table and head into my gym. I need to clear my head—and that means listening to music and working out 'til I'm dripping with sweat.

Two hours later, after a long workout powered by The Sound of Animals Fighting, a hot shower, and answering some work emails, I sit at my kitchen table and stare at the box. Fuck it. I can't resist.

When I open the box, there's a handwritten note sitting along with whatever else. My heart races as I pull out the note.

"My Dearest Jonas,

"You want brutal honesty? Well, here it is. When it comes to you, there's just too much downside and not enough upside. I lost my mind momentarily, but I've regained control of myself. If I were willing to lie to you, like everyone else apparently does—like you *want* everyone to do, despite what you delude yourself into thinking you want—things might have been different. Enjoy your membership. I'm sure you'll get exactly what you want out of it. My wish for you, however, is that, someday, you'll realize what you *want* and what you *need* are two very different things.

"Truthfully yours, Sarah."

I sit and stare at the note in my hand for a good long time.

Her swirling handwriting is distinctive and smooth and beautiful, just like her skin. And it's confident. Feminine. Bold. I run my finger over the indentions made by her ballpoint pen and an unexpected tidal wave of melancholy slams into me. Shit, I feel like crying for the first time since I was a kid. I feel alone. No, that's not it. I feel *abandoned.*

The scent of her dresses hanging against my face fills my nostrils for a fleeting moment—the image of her vacant face on the pillow. I shake my head, but her eyes—her beautiful blue eyes—are still staring lifelessly at me. I push it all back down. I wipe at my eyes and shake my head.

Why do I feel like she just ripped my heart out of my chest? My heart was never involved here. My attraction to her is purely sexual—out of this world, off the charts, insane, inexplicable, unconventional, maybe even bordering on obsessive, yes—but still, purely sexual. Well, no, maybe not *purely* sexual. Because I know she's smart as hell. And funny. And witty. When she cuts me down to size, I actually enjoy it. But all of that is just prelude, right? Just the lead-in to the main event, the sexy little things that make me want to fuck her, right? And that's all. Right?

I wipe my eyes again.

I've never even *seen* her and I was willing to take a giant leap of faith—to meet her and taste her and fuck her and make her come. And on the flipside, she knows everything about me—she's seen my photos, heard my secrets—and won't even agree to sit in the same room with me. What did she mean there was no upside to me? That I'm not the IKEA-shopping-on-weekends kind of guy? That I tell the truth about what I want, and what I don't? Is she saying she's not interested in what I'm willing to offer her? No, she's interested—or else she wouldn't have emailed me in the first place. Is she saying she would have wanted *more* than what I can give her, so why even bother with me? Yes, I think that's exactly what she's saying. But she knew that up front, so why'd she even reply to my note in the first place? I guess she realized she wouldn't give up all the Valentine's Day bullshit to howl like a monkey for the first time in her life, after all. Well, good to know, then. She saved us both a lot of hassle. Good to fucking know.

She thinks everyone lies to me—and that I want it that way? What does she mean? Is she calling me a liar—or, at least, a self-deluding prick? Fine. Maybe she's right.

I sit at the table, rubbing my face.

I remember how she looked over at me from the bed, her blue eyes frantic. *Don't move,* her eyes commanded me. *Stay hidden.* And I did. I stayed hidden. I didn't move. I didn't do a damned thing. And she paid the price for my worthlessness.

No upside, huh? Is that what she thinks about me? Well, guess what? She's right. I'm all downside, baby—I'm a fucked-up pile of shit without a single redeeming quality. You want to play with Jonas Faraday? Be prepared to get hurt, then. Boom. Because that's all I've got for you. A big, steaming pile of hurt.

Fuck it.

I pull the box toward me. Let's see what "all my fantasies becoming reality" looks like when delivered to my doorstep by FedEx. Hopefully, the rest of the box will be kinder to me than Sarah's brutal note.

There's an iPhone pre-loaded with an app, a welcome booklet, and a rubber bracelet. According to my brief skim of the booklet, if I'm in the mood to meet up with a female Club member, any time of day or night, anywhere in the world, I check-in on the app and register my current or future location with an anonymous pin number. "You have been meticulously matched with other members within The Club, and only compatible members will have access to your posts and check-ins," the instructions say. When I show up at the meeting spot, I'm required to wear my color-coded bracelet—I've been assigned purple, whatever that means ("self-deluding prick," maybe?)—and then wait for all the purple-coded women in The Club to flock to my registered spot and descend upon me like purple moths to a purple flame.

The instructions go on to explain, "Male members are required to wear their assigned color-coded bracelets at all check-ins. Women may choose to wear their bracelets or not—at their sole discretion—ensuring them the opportunity to assess the situation before identifying themselves. After much experimentation, we have determined this system maximizes satisfaction and safety for all involved."

Apparently, I can also send requests and invitations to specific members, soliciting their attendance at my check-in spot, or, I can just roll the dice and see who shows up. "No matter how you decide to check in, however, rest assured that only compatible persons, pre-selected for your preferences specifically, will respond. Persons outside of your color-code cannot access your posts and check-ins."

She sees no upside to me, huh? Fine. She's sure I'll get everything I want out of my membership? Damn straight I will. I spent two hundred fifty thousand dollars on this goddamned membership, might as well fucking use it. Why not? Why fucking not? Apparently, that's what she expects me to do. Apparently, that's what she *wants* me to do.

I unlock my Club-issued iPhone and open the pre-loaded app. I look at my watch. 3:06 p.m. Using the pin number assigned to me, I check myself into one of my favorite bars, a nearby place called The Pine Box, at 5:00 p.m. Fuck it. Let's see if someone besides My Beautiful Intake Agent—*Sarah*—can see an upside to me. Maybe some woman besides Sarah—whoever the hell she is—will be able to see an upside to a guy who can give her the best fuck of her life.

Chapter 7

Jonas

The Pine Box is packed, as usual. I take a seat at the bar.

"A Heineken."

The bartender nods.

I touch the purple band on my wrist. It feels like a neon sign flashing "pervert." I look at my watch. I'm a few minutes early. How long does it usually take for the purple moths to descend, I wonder? I scan the bar. I don't see any purple bracelets out there in the crowd. But, apparently, under the rules, I might never see one. Any one of these women could be a member, I suppose—and many of them are attractive. Highly attractive, actually.

Two women tucked into a booth in the far corner catch my attention. One of them is exactly the kind of woman I'd usually make a beeline for—tall and honey blonde with an athletic frame. Vintage Christy Brinkley. She's what anyone would go for—anyone who watches Hollywood movies or football or porn. But for some reason, it's the woman sitting across from her who's peaked my interest the most. And that's weird because I can't even see her face. She's intently studying a menu, and her face is completely hidden. All I can see is the top of her forehead poking out from behind the menu, and her long dark hair cascading down her shoulders. Her hands are particularly striking—long, slender fingers, natural fingernails and a simple silver band on her right thumb. Sexy.

But the thing that pulls my attention to her the most is her skin—what little I can see of it, anyway, on her hands and forearms and that tiny sliver of forehead peeking out from the top of the menu. Her skin is the exact same olive tone I imagine Sarah's would be, and it looks smooth and soft, too, just like Sarah's looked in the two photos she sent me. I can't peel my eyes away from the woman behind the menu. I just want to see her face. If I could just see her face, just once, maybe it'd give me something—anything—to imagine when I'm in the shower, lathering myself after a workout and fantasizing about making Sarah come.

The bartender puts my beer on the counter in front of me. I nod at him and throw down a ten.

But what am I thinking? I'm not going to think about Sarah anymore. That's the whole point of me coming here tonight wearing my pervert-purple bracelet, isn't it? I'm here to rid myself of her. She doesn't want to have anything to do with me? Fine. I'm done with her, too. Tonight, I'm going to give my undivided attention to my new purple fuck buddies, whoever they may be.

I glance at my watch. Five minutes past five o'clock. Come out, come out, wherever you are.

Once things get rolling with The Club, I surely won't have time to think about Sarah ever again. I'll be too busy making all my new purple partners lose their minds and then serenely saying goodbye to them without the tiniest need to feel remorse. And they'll be content and satisfied, too—because that's exactly what they'll have signed up for. Nothing more. There'll be no thoughts of soul mates and some sort of "deeper connection." We'll both be sexually satisfied, and that will be enough for us. No hurt feelings. I'll be like a kid in a candy store. Why did she say everyone lies to me and that's what I want? That's exactly the opposite of what I want. What did she mean?

I suddenly find myself wishing the woman behind the menu would turn out to be one of my new purple playmates. It seems quite possible, because it sure feels like she's been secretly staring at me every time I look away. Or maybe it's the blonde that's making me feel that way—the blonde's not even hiding her repeated glances and smiles over at me. Hey, maybe they're both up for grabs. But, no, that can't be. I didn't write anything about wanting a threesome in my application. Been there, done that. It's not my thing. Both times I tried it, I wound up focusing on one woman to the exclusion of the other, and the "extra" woman started getting all pissy and insistent and overcompensating, until finally she became a downright hindrance to me accomplishing my mission with the woman I wanted to focus on. I realized pretty quickly that I strongly prefer to give one woman my undivided attention.

To be honest, even if the blonde were wearing a purple bracelet right now, I'm not sure I'd be all that interested, even though she's exactly what I usually go for. For some reason, I just don't want my usual tonight. Tonight, I want to witness an olive-hued beauty writhing around on my white sheets. Hell, even if the woman behind the menu isn't a member, maybe I'll take her home anyway and give her the night of her life.

But that's just stupid. If I came here to pick up a random woman in the bar, why the hell did I just pay two hundred fifty thousand dollars for The Club to set me up with "uncannily compatible" women? I need to just cool my jets and focus on the task at hand.

I take a large gulp of my beer and look around the bar. There are a lot of good-looking women here. I still don't see anyone wearing a purple bracelet, though. I feel like the hunted, rather than the hunter, and I'm not used to it. I'm not sure I like it. In fact, I'm sure I don't. I like being in control at all times.

Maybe I'm supposed to check the app to see if someone else has checked in? And then go on some sort of wild goose chase, looking for her in the bar? Yeah, I bet I'm supposed to do that. I couldn't concentrate on all the instructions and materials The Club sent me—I was so fucking out of my mind about Sarah—I figured I'd just wing it.

Sarah.

Why'd she give up on me like that—without giving me a say in the matter? I thought things were going so well between us. I've never wanted a woman so much in all my life—and I've never even *seen* her! What the hell did she expect from me? What kind of *upside* did she expect me to promise her just to meet her in person? Talk about demanding. Unreasonable. I probably dodged a bullet there.

No, even in my anger, I know that's not true. The only one who dodged a bullet here was Sarah. She ran like hell because she's so damned smart. Even though I'm pissed, I can't help smiling, thinking about our email exchange. *"You did not just ask me, 'What's your sign?'"* she said. *"Smooth, you woman wizard, you,"* she said. Even when she kicked my ass, I loved it. If only she would have let me see her, things would have been different. I know they would have. The kind of chemistry we have—via fucking *email*—doesn't happen every day. It pains me to wonder how off the charts our chemistry would have been in person. It sure would have been nice if she'd have let *me* decide what I was or wasn't willing to give her, rather than her deciding that, whatever it was, it wasn't enough. Shit, I can't even think straight just thinking about her.

I look over at that corner booth again. Menu Girl's still hidden behind that damned menu. How long does it take to decide what to order? The skin on her arm is luscious. Yeah, I don't know if I can resist going after that woman behind the menu tonight, a quarter-mill spent on membership fees or not. I've got a whole year to dabble in The Club's offerings, after all. Why rush? Tonight, maybe I'll partake in Sarah's olive-skinned double. Yeah, Menu Girl can be my Sarah stand-in. What better way to help me lose interest in Sarah? I'll imagine that woman in the corner is Sarah, take her home, taste her, make her come, fuck her brains out, and then let the usual wave of complete disinterest wash over me. If Menu Girl gets her feelings hurt, that's her problem. It'll be classic aversion therapy—*A Clockwork Sarah*—and I'll be cured of Sarah forever.

I stand up from my stool. That's exactly what I'm going to do. Whoever she is, her feelings be damned tonight. If I can't get Sarah off my mind, then I'll fuck someone else's brains out until I can.

"Hi there."

It's a fair-skinned brunette with startling blue eyes. She's stunningly attractive—a real head-turner. She grins at me and pushes a lock of dark hair behind her ear, plainly showcasing the purple bracelet on her wrist as she does it. She smiles broadly when my eyes lock onto her bracelet. Her teeth are white and straight.

"Hi," I reply, glancing over at the corner, but a lingering group of people has moved between us and I can't see Menu Girl. Shit.

"I'm Stacy," my new friend says, putting out her hand. "You're a brand new member, right?"

"Yeah." As I take Stacy's hand, I glance back to the corner again. I'm startled to see Menu Girl's big brown eyes glaring at me over the top of her menu. The minute our eyes meet, she abruptly looks away and raises the menu again. What the hell? She was *glaring* at me just now.

Every hair on my body suddenly stands on end. Oh my God.

I look back at my would-be purple companion. "Would you excuse me for just a minute?"

Her face falls. "You're not going to buy me a drink?"

"I'm sorry, yes, of course, I am. What would you like?"

She stops to think about it for a moment and I feel like I'm going to explode with nervous anxiety. Come on. Please. Make up your mind. It's not a life-changing decision. It's a drink order.

"A glass of chardonnay would be great," she finally says, flashing me her most alluring smile, and I quickly place her order.

A growing urgency is swelling inside me. I'm having a crazy thought right now.

Stacy puts her hand on my arm. "You never told me your name."

"Jonas."

"It's nice to meet you, *Jonas*." She licks her lips. Her features are ridiculously well put together. "What a pleasant surprise you are, I've got to say."

I try to smile back, but I'm too distracted to focus on her. I'm having an insane thought, a maniacal and self-deluding-prick thought. I'm thinking that Sarah came here tonight. I'm thinking Sarah, my beautiful Sarah, is sitting in this room right now, forty yards away, watching me from behind a fucking menu. I'm thinking that, despite her handwritten note, she can't stop thinking of me any more than I can stop thinking of her.

"You, too, Stacy. I'll be right back. Just enjoy your wine for a minute." I turn away from Stacy, without waiting for her reply, and instantly lurch toward the corner booth, my heart clanging in my chest all the while.

"Excuse me," I say, making my way through the lingering crowd, my pulse pounding in my ears.

No.

No, no, no.

She's not at the booth anymore.

I look around frantically, but she's nowhere to be seen. The woman behind the menu and her supermodel friend are both long gone.

Chapter 8

Sarah

"This is a bad idea," I say, looking at my watch. It's twenty minutes before five o'clock. My stomach is flip-flopping. He could walk through the door any minute.

"Why?" Kat sniffs. "You said yourself he has no idea what you look like—well, other than your boob." She laughs. "That was so badass of you, Sarah. I can't believe you did that."

I roll my eyes. "I know. It was so unlike me—I don't know what got into me."

"Oh, I know exactly what got into you."

I blush.

"Just relax, okay? He won't even know you're here. And the bar's plenty crowded, too. You'll have plenty of time to watch him and gather your courage."

"Courage to do what?"

"To say hi to him."

"There's no way I'm saying hi to him."

"Then why the heck are we here?"

"I just want to look at him." I sigh. "I can't resist. When you see him, you'll understand."

"You dragged me to The Pine Box on a moment's notice just to *spy* on him?" She looks at me dubiously.

I nod. "I've only seen him in photos—well, and for a split-second when he was speeding past me in his car. I just want to get one good, long, lingering look at him in the flesh." And, truth be told, I can't resist seeing what kind of woman The Club deems his perfect match.

"Sarah, I still don't understand—why not just sleep with the guy, even if it's just once? If he's as hot as you say he is, why not have one amazing night you'll always remember?"

"I don't know if I'm capable of enjoying 'one amazing night' with him," I say. I don't know how to explain my unexpected feelings toward this guy. He's awakened a yearning inside of me like nothing I've felt before. Somehow, I know, deep in my bones, if I play with this fire, I'll surely get burned to a blackened crisp. Or at least my heart will. I'm exactly the kind of girl he joined The Club to avoid. I know I am. And I can't change any more than he can. So what's the point? There isn't one.

Kat shrugs. "Well, then, why are we here? You just want to torture yourself? I mean, come on, you know what he's looking for, and it ain't a relationship. This is a guy who joined 'The Club,' after all."

"Shh," I say. "Please." I've told Kat a thousand times that the very existence of The Club is über confidential. But she loves the whole idea of a secret underground club for rich freaks and always wants to know every juicy detail. "I just have to see him in action. Maybe it'll help me get him out of my system." I shrug. "What time is it?"

"Quarter to five."

My stomach flip-flops. I've imagined this man licking me and smiling up at me from between my legs countless times, for goodness sakes, and even imaginary sex with him has been the best sex of my life. I can only imagine how my nerve endings will react to seeing the genuine article in person. I'm not sure I'll be able to keep myself from screaming his name like a groupie at a rock concert.

"Oh my God. Is that *him?"* Kat whispers, cricking her neck toward the front door. I follow her glance and immediately throw a menu in front of my face.

I feel my cheeks flush. "Yes," I whisper.

I peek at Kat around the side of my menu. She's openly gawking at him.

"Holy shitballs," she says. "Wow. He's ... wow. I thought you were exaggerating. But, no, not at all. He must have made a deal with the devil or something."

"Don't look at him," I hiss. "Act natural."

"I *am* acting natural—"

"No, you're not."

"Yes, I am. If I *weren't* looking at him, now *that* would be totally unnatural."

"What's he doing?" I'm shoving my nose so far into my menu I can't see a thing—not even the items on the menu.

"He's sitting at the bar." She pauses. "He's ordering a drink." A long pause. "A beer." Another pause. "He's looking around." A long pause. "Drinking his beer." Another pause. "More looking around."

My heart is in my throat. My pulse is in my ears. My stomach is in knots. "Is it safe for me to look?"

"Yeah, he's not looking over here."

I peek over the top of my menu. "Oh." It's all I can manage—and it's a "maybe I made a huge mistake by blowing him off" kind of "oh." A "maybe I shouldn't have said there's no upside to him" kind of "oh." An "oh hell maybe it's worth getting my heart smashed into a thousand pieces to get a piece of that" kind of "oh." He's gorgeous.

His head starts to swivel in our direction, and I cover my face again.

"Sarah," Kat chastises me. "He doesn't know what you look like. Why are you covering your face?"

My hands are shaking as they hold the menu. Just that one glimpse of him was enough to send me into some kind of hormone-induced seizure.

"He's looking over here," Kat announces flatly.

I peek at her on the far side of my menu again. Her face is turned toward the bar. She's smirking at him.

"Don't look over at him!" I command. "Please. At the very least, don't *smile* at him. When you smile at a man, he comes over to talk to you. Every time. Kat, please," I whisper with urgency.

"And remind me why don't we want him to come over here again?" she asks between her smiling teeth.

"Because I'd have a nervous breakdown," I say, my voice cracking with anxiety. I think it's an accurate statement. I'd surely have a nervous breakdown or some other life-altering medical crisis, if Jonas Faraday waltzed over here at all, but especially if he came to flirt with *Kat*.

"Okay, okay, I'll stop," Kat says, apparently sensing my sincere anxiety. "Oh, hey, he's looking the other away again."

I peek at him over the edge of my menu. He's looking around the bar again, obviously waiting for a parade of purples to show up. The whole situation makes my flesh crawl. But what did I expect? For him to cancel his club membership and declare, "I don't care about The Club! I just want *My Beautiful Intake Agent!*"—for a woman he's never met or even spoken to on the phone? Talk about Lifetime-Hallmark-Valentine's Day brain-washing. What was I hoping for—some kind of meaningful human connection thanks to a little email-sex? Ha! I really am exactly the kind of woman who made him want to join The Club in the first place.

"What's he doing now?" I whisper, afraid to look.

"I don't know. A group of people just stood in my line of sight."

"Damn." A minute passes. "View still obstructed?"

"No. Would you just put that down already? Anyone looking at you would think you're deranged or something. Who takes this long to decide on a simple food order?"

I sigh. I'm being ridiculous. Life is short. I'm in the same air space as the scrumptious, if arrogant, Jonas Faraday. When will I ever get this chance again? I'm acting like a scared child—something I thought I'd given up for good a long time ago. "You know what? You're right. I should just go over there and talk to him like an adult."

"There you go—put your big girl panties on." Kat's beaming at me.

I put the menu down on the table. "I mean, even if I crash and burn, at least I'll never wonder 'what if.'"

"Exactly."

I gaze over at Jonas, resolving myself to just go talk to him.

I gasp. Oh crap. He's talking to a stunning brunette—and even from here, I can see the purple bracelet around her wrist. I grab the menu again and hurriedly raise it up, just below my eyes. Miss Purple smiles at him and licks her lips. Oh wow, she's really coming on strong—and she's smokin' hot, too. Even though Jonas' head is turned away from me, there's no doubt in my mind his eyes are bugging out with unfettered lust right now. She's frickin' spectacular—and clearly ready to jump his bones.

I want to scream. Or throw up. Actually, more than anything, I just want to cry. And, honestly, I'm confused. Why on earth did this gorgeous woman join The Club? What is she hoping to gain? Is she a gold digger? Is she looking for a husband? What? Because I don't believe for a second she's here to find serial sex partners with no strings attached. A woman like that could have any man she'd ever want. So why on earth was she matched to Jonas, a guy who wants to give her nothing but an orgasm and a polite farewell?

What's going on here? And why isn't Jonas wondering the same thing?

Out of nowhere, while I'm still peeking over my menu at Jonas and that woman at the bar, Jonas turns almost completely around and looks directly at me. My eyes are hard slits. *Bastard.* His eyes go wide. So do mine. Shit.

I quickly glance away and raise my menu to cover my entire face. I feel like I've just been caught in the act—the act of what, I'm not entirely sure. I'm seized with a sudden panic. Does he know who I am? No, that's a silly thought. And yet, for a split second there, I swear I thought I saw *recognition* in his eyes. But that's impossible. He can't *recognize* me—he's never seen me before. The man couldn't pick me out of a line-up (other than a line-up of left boobs).

I quickly peek again, but he's turned back to her, buying her a drink. Of course, he is. I could puke. Sure, Sarah, there was *recognition* in his eyes—so much so, he immediately decided to buy his new purple friend a drink. I'm such an idiot. Anger and embarrassment and humiliation flood into me all at once. And jealousy, too. Let's not forget jealousy.

"Let's go," I bark at Kat, leaping up from my seat. Without waiting for Kat's reply, I bolt to the front door like the place is on fire. In a flash, I'm flying up the sidewalk, away from the bar, as fast as my legs will carry me, the sound of Kat's high heels clacking on the cement behind me.

I can't believe I almost said hello to him in there. That would have been an awkward moment at best and a mortifying catastrophe at worst. I can't believe I got so wrapped up in the ridiculous fantasy of our little forbidden whatever-it-was (I was about to call it a romance, but obviously, that's the last thing it was). I can't believe I touched myself and said his name, that I wanted to have sex with him so much it physically pained me, that I researched him online for seven hours straight, a good six hours more than necessary for my intake report—when I should have been reading the next three cases for my contracts homework. Oh good God, I can't believe I sent him a picture of my boob! I've never done anything like that in my life. What the hell is wrong with me? And most of all, I can't believe I let my heart ache for the sadness in his eyes—a sadness I stupidly thought I could fix. A sadness I *wanted* to fix.

I was a fool.

I reach my car, panting. I bend over, catching my breath. After half a minute, Kat reaches me, equally out of breath.

"Wooh!" she breathes.

"Sorry," I choke out.

"I understand." She grimaces. "Ouch." I'm pretty sure she's referring to what we just witnessed in the bar, not her sprint up the sidewalk in heels.

My chest is heaving. "Ouch," I agree.

A minute passes. "I knew he was a man-whore," I say, "but seeing him in action like that . . ." I let out a shaky breath. "If that's the kind of woman I'm up against, I never stood a chance, anyway."

Kat shoots me a commiserating frowny face.

My shoulders slump. "I don't know why he has this hold on me." Tears are threatening my eyes, but I suppress them. "I keep pushing him away from me, telling him to leave me alone—and then I'm crushed when it works." I roll my eyes at myself. "I'm a mess."

Kat wraps me into a hug, and I put my cheek on her shoulder. "If he wants to chase tail for the rest of his life rather than have the most incredible girl in the entire world, then he just doesn't deserve you, anyway," she whispers.

Chapter 9

Jonas

I'm grateful to be showering alone right now. I usually like showering with a woman right after I've fucked her. But not tonight. Sex with Stacy was ... unfulfilling. No, actually, it was bordering on repulsive, if I'm being totally honest. I can't believe I just used the word repulsive to describe sex with a woman who looks like Stacy. But there you go.

The woman has an incredible body—tight and lean with curves in all the right places—and soft skin and thick hair and the bluest eyes I've ever seen. And yet, I wasn't into it from minute one. I definitely wasn't enthused to go down on her, so I don't for the life of me know why I did it anyway. Force of habit I guess. Convincing myself I was "back," maybe. Perhaps I thought I could fool myself into enjoying it, if I just gave it the ol' college try. But it was a huge miscalculation on my part. The minute my tongue hit her cunt, my stomach jerked, if you can believe it, like I was tasting rancid milk or something.

But Stacy didn't seem to notice me practically gagging down there. Nope, the minute my tongue hit her bull's-eye, she moaned and groaned and did all the right things—writhing and pleading and howling and begging—like I'd flipped some magic switch on her. She ramped up so fast and so hard, in fact, I actually rolled my eyes and pulled away from her, staring. It was all I could do not to yell up to her face, "Really, Stacy?"

I didn't say that, of course—I am a gentleman, after all—but I did stop licking her right then and gape at her in total disbelief. And the minute I stopped, do you know what she did? She whimpered and begged me to slam her with my cock like she'd never been so turned on in her life. It was almost funny. Even I knew I hadn't done a goddamned thing yet, and there she was, following the blueprint I'd given in my application, to the letter. Un-fucking-believable. But it's hard to resist a hot woman begging you to fuck her, even if she *is* a fucking liar. So, I did. I fucked her, though I'm not proud of myself for doing it.

When I entered her, which I did kind of roughly, to be honest, my only thought was getting myself off, as opposed to bringing her any form of pleasure. And guess what? Shocker! I was no sooner inside her than she came like a Mack truck—or so it seemed. (Or, as Sarah would say, she *allegedly* came like a Mack truck). And you know what I was thinking during her *alleged* orgasm? I was thinking, "Give me a fucking break." That's not the greatest thing in the world to be thinking while a woman squirms under you in apparent rapture. In fact, it's pretty fucking gross.

And that's when I thought, rather distinctly, "I want Sarah." And the minute I started thinking "I want Sarah" while my dick was pounding into Stacy, I felt so disgusted with myself, so physically repelled, so depressed, so fucking *lonely*, I wanted to pull out and not even bother coming at all. But that's not what I did. No, being the high caliber individual that I am, I did quite the opposite. I closed my eyes and forged ahead, imagining my cock was inside Sarah—Sarah with the olive skin and perfect breast and the hard nipple I'd give anything to twirl around in my tongue. Sarah with the bullshit-o-meter like no one I've ever met before. Sarah who's never come before, and who decided to trust me with that delicate pearl of truth. Sarah who knows I'm an asshole but touched herself and said my name, anyway. Yep. I closed me eyes and let my mind construct a blurry image of Sarah—a kind of amalgam of Sarah and Menu Girl fused together, and I fucked the shit out of Stacy.

Thinking about Sarah made me pump into Stacy even harder. As I slammed into Stacy—as she groaned and writhed under me—I told myself Sarah couldn't stay away from me, even though she deleted her email account, even though she wrote me that fucking handwritten note. With each thrust, I told myself Sarah had looked me up on the check-in app, that she'd figured out I'd be at that bar, that she couldn't stop thinking about me, aching for me—that she wanted me as much as I wanted her. I imagined everything went differently at The Pine Box—that Sarah was Menu Girl, and that I went straight over to the corner instead of buying Stacy a drink, that I went right over to her and took the menu out of her hands and said, "You're coming home with me right now." As my naked skin moved against Stacy's soft, fair skin, over and over, I imagined the rapture of feeling Menu Girl's smooth, olive skin rubbing against mine. I imagined Menu Girl's sweat was mingling with mine, that her long, dark hair was unfurled on my white pillowcase, that her slender hands were clutching my back, her fingernails digging into me, the silver band on her thumb scraping against my skin.

All of that pretending worked for me, and I was right the verge of coming, right on the verge of shouting Sarah's name—but then Stacy moaned and whispered in my ear. "You're amazing," she said, and I was instantly jolted back to reality. I opened my eyes and saw Stacy's blue eyes staring back at me, not Menu Girl's big brown eyes.

That's when I remembered Sarah didn't want me.

That's when I remembered Sarah didn't think I was worthy of her.

That's when I remembered Sarah didn't see an upside to me.

And that's when I got pissed.

I started fucking Stacy without mercy. I'm not proud of it—in fact, I'm so disgusted with myself, I feel almost physically ill about it—but I fucked Stacy so hard after her "you're amazing" bullshit comment, and with such animosity, I can't imagine she experienced anything but unadulterated humiliation, maybe even pain.

Though, of course, she pretended to like it.

Because she's a fucking liar.

"That was incredible," Stacy said after I finally came and collapsed on top of her in an angry, sweaty heap. I pulled back and looked into her face, ready to apologize—to beg her forgiveness—and she smiled at me. It was a smile that didn't reach her eyes—her very, very blue eyes—and it felt like a punch in the gut. I pulled out of her and yanked off my condom. I couldn't muster a return smile or any kind of reply to her hollow compliment. I certainly didn't feel like apologizing to her for fucking her so hard anymore. I knew I'd just sold my soul to the devil—for two hundred-fifty thousand dollars, to be exact—and I hated myself for it.

"I'm gonna hop in the shower," I mumbled, hoping Stacy would get the hint.

And guess what? She did. Without batting an eyelash. Of course, she did. Good ol' Stacy. I shouldn't have been surprised, since she's an android programmed to make my every fucking fantasy a reality. Well, an android programmed to make what I *thought* was my every fucking fantasy into a reality. As it turns out, what I wanted—what I *thought* I wanted—doesn't exist.

"Yeah, you go ahead," she said cheerfully, gathering up her clothes. "I've got to get going, anyway." Wow, big surprise. Right on cue. "Thanks for everything, though. You're amazing. Maybe I'll see you around." Without another word, she threw on her clothes and waltzed out the door, just like that. No request for my phone number.

No hints about Radiohead coming to town the following week and, hey, they just happen to be her favorite band. No hopeful expression in her eyes. Not even a request for my Club identification number so we could check-in with each other again. Just in and out. Fuck and duck. Hit it and quit it. Exactly what I said I wanted in my application. But, ah, wasn't the second half of my "sexual preferences" that I didn't want to feel like an asshole afterwards? So why do I feel like the biggest asshole who ever lived right now? Actually, I feel like more of an asshole right now in this very moment than I've felt in my entire adult life.

I lather my body with shower gel, practically scrubbing my skin to get Stacy off me. I close my eyes and let the hot water pelt me in the face for a moment, and then I open my mouth and let the searing water flood my mouth, trying desperately to cleanse my tongue. Before getting into the shower, I brushed my teeth and tongue for, like, seven minutes, but I still can't get the sour taste of Stacy's cunt out of my mouth. Just the thought of my tongue touching her makes me shudder. What the fuck was I thinking?

I don't want Stacy.

Or Marissa. Or Caitlyn. Or Julie. Or Samantha or Emily or Maddie or Kristin or Lauren or Rachel or Bethanney or Natalie or Darcy or Michelle or Charlotte or Grace or Katie or Shannon or Juliana or Tiffany or Andrea or Melanie or Hannah.

My chest constricts. The truth is dawning on me as the hot water pelts me.

I want Sarah.

But Sarah doesn't want me.

I lost my mind momentarily, she said, *but I've regained control of myself.*

I'm what happened when she had an aberrant lapse in good judgment? I'm what happened when she let her guard down for once in her repressed life? I'm the bad guy who forced her to acknowledge and claim her deepest, most honest desires, instead of chasing bullshit rainbows like everyone else tells her to do? She's regained her control now, huh? Well, lucky for her. Who knows what could have happened if she'd deigned to meet me—if she had lowered herself to giving me a fucking chance rather than unilaterally deciding I wasn't worth her time.

Fuck.

I lean my hands against the marble in the shower and let the hot water slide down my naked back. My head is spinning. She thinks I'm unworthy of her.

When it comes to you, she said, *there's just too much downside, and not enough upside.*

I grab the shampoo and massage a drop into my hair.

Thanks to that application, she knows better than anyone—literally, *anyone*—just what a cocky-bastard-asshole-son-of-a-bitch motherfucker I really am.

If I were willing to lie to you, like everyone else apparently does—like you want everyone to do, despite what you delude yourself into thinking you want—things might have been different. Her words sting like razors slicing my chest. Before Sarah, I fooled everyone else. Even myself. But not her. She knows the truth. *Enjoy your membership,* she said. *I'm sure you'll get exactly what you want out of it. My wish for you, however, is that, someday, you'll realize what you want and what you need are two very different things.* Shit. I don't know what the hell I need. But I sure as hell know what I want.

My cell phone rings in my bedroom, pulling me out of my thoughts. I leap out of the shower and run to my phone on my bed, dripping water across my wood floor as I go. I missed the call—fuck!—it was Josh. I call right back, my heart in my throat.

He picks up right away. "We found her."

I'm sitting on my bed in a pair of jeans, staring at Josh's follow-up email, trying to gain control of my breathing. Of the three Sarahs currently enrolled at the University of Washington's law school—Sarah McHutchinson, Sarah Jones, and Sarah Cruz—two of them are twenty-four years old: Sarah McHutchinson and Sarah Cruz. With Sarah's olive skin, my money's on Sarah Cruz. I suddenly remember she said *gracias* in her first email to me. I smirk. Yeah, she's Sarah Cruz. It doesn't matter if I'm right or wrong about my guess, though, because Josh styled me with all three women's cell phone numbers and email addresses, plus their physical addresses, too. But I know in my gut I'm right. *Sarah Cruz.*

"We can get their social security numbers and transcripts, too, if you want 'em," Josh said during our call, about ten minutes ago.

"I don't want to run a credit report on her," I said, "or interview her for a job. I just want to find her."

Josh laughed. "Lemme know what happens. At this point, I'm probably as invested in this romance as you are, bro."

I bristle. "It's not a romance."

"Jonas, you're such an idiot."

I Google the name "Sarah Cruz," but so many cluttered results and links and images come up there's no way I can possibly make heads or tails of all the information. I try "Sarah Cruz Seattle" to narrow things down, but it barely makes a dent in the white noise of information, and nothing that comes up looks even remotely promising, anyway. I try "Sarah Cruz University Washington" and a link to a pdf document pops up on some student forum—a list of first semester standings for the University of Washington Law School, Class of 2016. I open the document and scan the names, beginning at the top of the list. I don't have to go very far down the list—Sarah Cruz is ranked fourth in her entire class right now. Yeah, my clever Sarah is Sarah Cruz, I'm sure of it. And she's kicking everyone's ass, not just mine. Of course she is.

I pick up the phone and Josh answers immediately.

"Can your guy see if there are photos in the Sarah files—like for student IDs or something? I only need a photo for whichever one's got olive-ish skin. I know my Sarah's definitely not fair-skinned."

"Wait, you don't know what she looks like?"

I don't say anything.

"You've never seen her?"

I'm silent. Shit.

Josh makes a "mind officially blown" kind of sound. "I assumed you started this quest after she sent you some anonymous, sexy photo that rocked your world. But you've never even *seen* this girl? This is all because of something she *wrote* to you in an email?"

Well, shit, the whole thing sounds fucking insane when he says it like that. I sigh, unwilling to answer the question—but my sigh tells Josh everything he needs to know. Even I can hear how ragged and desperate it sounds when I exhale.

"Wow. This really *is* a romance of epic proportions." He laughs.

I can't even muster a "fuck you." I'm a wreck.

"Don't worry, I'll see what my guy can find. Sit tight."

"Hey, Josh, one more thing."

"Yeah?"

"Get me the transcripts, too."

I don't know what's taking so long. I thought Josh would get back to me right away with those pictures. But he hasn't called or emailed and I'm on pins and needles. So close, and yet so far. I can't concentrate on anything. I certainly can't do any work. Or even work out. I don't want to do anything that pulls me away from my phone and makes me miss a call from Josh.

I pace around my kitchen, staring at my laptop on the counter. I pull my phone out of my jeans pocket. Nothing.

Sarah Cruz. I can't stop thinking about her breast. Her nipple. Her thigh. Her skin. And about how she said she wished I'd realize what I *want* and what I *need* are two very different things.

Fuck it. I don't need to see her photo to call her. Whatever she looks like, I still want to talk to her, at least. I still want to meet her. If it turns out she's not classically beautiful, so what? Or even if it turns out I'm not physically attracted to her in the slightest ... But, no, I can't even imagine not being physically attracted her. She's hot; I'm sure of it. Her skin is heavenly. Her breast is perfect. Her nipple standing at attention gave me a raging hard-on. What more do I need to know? If her face isn't what I'd normally go for, all I'd have to do is look down at that nipple of hers, and I'd be all good.

I pull up Josh's email with the contact information for all three Sarahs and squint at my computer screen for the phone number listed under Sarah Cruz's name. I suppose she could be the other twenty-four-year-old Sarah—Sarah McHutchinson?—but I doubt it.

With shaky hands, I slowly dial the digits for little miss bullshit-detector, I-lost-my-mind-momentarily-but-now-I've-regained-control-of-myself, doesn't-see-the-upside-in-me, number-four-in-her-law-school-class, never-howled-like-a-monkey-once-in-her-well-ordered-little-life, makes-me-fucking-crazy, I-want-her-but-she-doesn't-want-me, Sarah Cruz.

Chapter 10

Sarah

Watching Jonas move in on that ridiculously hot woman in the purple bracelet was a sobering slap in my face—a wake-up call that Jonas Faraday is and always will be exactly the horndog he claimed to be from day one, and nothing more, and that all the depth and gravitas and yearning and loneliness and innate goodness I thought I saw in his eyes was a figment of my imagination. A mere projection. As much as it ripped my heart out to realize all that, the silver lining has been that I've decided to vigorously focus all my time and attention on my studies and crazy-ass job, just as I should be doing. Jonas Faraday was a distraction, an unwise and time-consuming distraction, that's all, and now I'm done with him.

I pulled a marathon study session after coming home from the bar last night, and now I'm all caught up on my reading for every one of my classes (and I've even read ahead in contracts, too). This morning, I started making myself a detailed study outline for torts that covers the issue, rule, analysis and conclusion of every case we've read since week one, and next week, I'll start my outline for contracts, and right after that, I'll dig into constitutional law. If I keep up this pace, I'll be completely prepared when finals roll around with plenty of time to spare. The top ten ranked students at the end of the first year are granted a full-ride scholarship for the remaining two years of the law program, and I'm hell bent on getting one of those coveted slots.

The Club has kept me busy, too. A new application from a guy in Seattle landed in my inbox this morning, and I've just now gotten back from conducting my confirming surveillance. I've only been back home for ten minutes and I've already logged into my intake report and recommended approval (contingent on an "all clear" from pending medical and psychological testing, of course). The guy signed up for a one-month membership (always a good sign), and his sexual preferences section was the biggest vanilla-snoozefest I've seen yet. He's refreshingly normal. Sweet as can be, in fact—but, whoa boring as hell. I'm guessing he hasn't had a heck of a lot of luck with the ladies up to this point. Hopefully, membership in The Club will give him a shot at finding love—and, if not, then I hope it will bring him the most thrilling month of his life. Either way, I'm rooting for him.

When I clicked on the pictures he sent with is application, they were bursting with his normalcy and utter loneliness, and it was very obvious to me he was exactly who he said he was—I mean, who would pretend to look like that guy in a catfish attempt? All I had to do was stand in the lobby of his office building (he's a software engineer) at lunchtime and I quickly spotted him leaving his building to grab a sandwich, looking every bit the thirty-seven-year-old, five-foot-seven, introverted computer nerd he claimed to be in his application. Done-zo.

Maybe I'm just feeling emotional lately, thanks to seeing Jonas on the prowl flashing his purple bracelet, but when Mr. Normal walked past me, all alone and looking sad among his departing co-workers (all of whom were rushing off to lunch around him in animated, chatty groups), I felt like crying for him. Or maybe I just felt like crying for myself. Everyone deserves love, whether that simply means being invited to lunch with co-workers once in a while, or finding that one person with whom you can share all the sides of yourself, no matter how normal or boring, or maybe even a little bit freaky—or, as the case may be, no matter how cocky or arrogant or emotionally disconnected or, possibly, just a little bit sad. But, anyway, if a person can't find love on his own, who can blame him for plunking down his hard-earned savings for a shot at finding it through any means possible—or, at least, for a shot at experiencing a little excitement for once?

After appropriately logging the details of my surveillance onto my intake report, I pull out my phone. I've got a text from Kat asking if I feel better about the whole Jonas situation today. I was upset yesterday, but I'm fine now. It's time to move on. I text her that I'm good, followed by a string of winking emojis to emphasize the point.

Just as I'm about to put my phone down, it rings with an incoming call. I don't recognize the number. I usually let unknown calls go into my voicemail, but what the heck, I'm sitting here with a few minutes to burn before I jump back into my torts outline.

"Hello?" I answer.

There's an audible exhale of breath on the other end of the line. "Sarah?"

I'm suddenly uneasy. "Who's calling, please?" Why is my stomach doing cartwheels?

"It's Jonas."

I inhale a sharp breath, but I can't speak.

"Jonas Faraday," he clarifies.

I still can't speak. His voice is masculine. Sexy. It sends tingles up my spine and back down again.

"Are you there?"

"How did you get my number?" I'm suddenly panicked. Did he get my contact information from The Club? Did he tell them about me?

"I figured out you're a law student at U Dub." He clears his throat. "So I hacked into the university's server to find you."

I'm speechless. Did he just say he hacked into U Dub's server to find me?

"I had to find you, Sarah. I had to talk to you. I'm going crazy." His voice is low, intense.

There's a long pause. He's waiting for me to say something.

"You didn't get my number from The Club?"

"No, of course not." He sounds offended. "I would never contact The Club about you." Yeah, definitely offended. "I told you I wouldn't."

I can't believe what I'm hearing. I can't believe he called me. I can't believe he found me. And he hacked into a major university's computer system to do it? I'm silent for a minute, trying to process the fact that I'm talking to Jonas Faraday right now—that he *tracked me down*. I'm ashamed to admit it, but my body's beginning to react to his voice exactly the way it did to his application.

"Sarah, I have to see you—"

"How'd you figure out I'm a law student at U Dub? I didn't tell you anything except my first name." My mind is racing. What did I tell him? My first name and age, and that's it. How did he find me? I can't for the life of me understand how he's calling me right now.

He explains the deductions and conclusions and clues in my email that led him to this very moment. I'm impressed. Electrified, really. He loves my sense of humor, he says. He calls me "smart" like four times. And, wow, he's pretty fixated on my olive skin tone. Hearing him go bananas about my skin makes it zip and zap like a live wire. If he likes my skin, then maybe he'll like the rest of me, too. But, wait, hold on. It's suddenly occurring to me he hasn't complimented my looks, other than my skin. So, overall, he must have been disappointed by whatever photo he saw. I mean, isn't a guy saying, "You've got gorgeous skin" sort of like saying, "You've got a great personality?"

"So you find my *skin* attractive, huh?" I ask.

"Yeah," he says. "And now I can add your voice to the list, too. It's so sexy. I love that little edge in it. I was already dying to know what you look like, but now I'm losing my mind."

Hold up. He's never seen me? No, surely, he just means he hasn't seen me in person. "You mean you want to know if I look like my picture?" I wish I knew what photo he has of me.

He pauses and my stomach drops. Why is he pausing?

"Did you see the photo on my student ID?" I ask. "Because when that photo was taken, I'd just gotten back from the gym and I wasn't wearing any makeup—"

"No, no. I've never seen your photo."

My face flushes. He's never seen my photo? He hunted me down and called me—and has been going on and on about how attractive he finds me—and he has no idea at all what I look like? "Oh." I don't even know what to say. "Why did you pause before answering?"

He sighs. "Because I want to see you more than I want to breathe. And I had to get control of myself before speaking. I'm feeling pretty intense right now. I don't want to scare you off."

The floor drops out from under me. A throbbing in my panties announces itself. "Are you telling me the truth, Jonas?" I whisper.

"Say that again," he whispers back.

I know exactly what he wants. "Jonas," I say. And when I do, the pulsing between my legs becomes more insistent.

He lets out a shaky breath. There's another long pause. I can feel the electricity of his arousal on his end of the line. "Yes, I'm telling you the truth. I'll always tell you the truth, Sarah."

Well, that breaks the spell. I laugh. "Seeing as how your 'relationships' last two to seven hours max, depending on Your Holiness's mood on a particular day, your promise to 'always' tell me the truth isn't all that impressive a commitment."

He huffs. "Wow." By the tone of his voice, I know I've broken the spell for him, too.

"Yeah, well," I huff right back. What did he expect from me? I just saw him drooling over Miss Purple last night.

"You don't like me very much."

"I don't even know you."

"Yeah, you do." He pauses. His voice is surprisingly wounded. "You know you do."

My heart leaps.

Damn. I know I'm supposed to be all "righteous indignation" in response, maybe laugh at him or read him the riot act, maybe make him chase me and try to convince me, and all that other stuff I've been conditioned to think is the normal reaction of a sane, rule abiding, self-respecting woman—but suddenly, I don't feel like a sane, rule abiding, self-respecting woman. And I certainly don't feel like saying anything that's not one hundred percent honest.

"Yeah, I know you," I concede. I don't know why I understand this man, but I do. I just get him. And I want him, despite myself. "I'm sorry," I say. "I'm being a bitch."

He lets out a huge burst of air, like he'd been holding his breath.

"I'm coming to pick you up right now. I can't wait another minute to see you."

That pisses me off. "Yeah, okay, let's see, we can 'fuck' for—what?—about an hour?—does that work with your schedule?—because after that I've got to study, and you've probably got to go screw yet another hot brunette wearing a purple bracelet."

"Oh my God!" he shouts with glee. "I knew it!" He's effusive.

Did he not just hear a word I said? I just ripped him a new one—did he not hear that?

He chuckles. "That *was* you behind that menu yesterday! I knew it." He's thrilled. "Oh my God."

Oops. Oh, damn.

"You couldn't stay away." His voice is pure elation.

I can't speak. Shoot.

"You just couldn't stay away," he says again. He's utterly thrilled.

I'm silent. Pissed.

"I knew that was you. Just from the little patches of skin I saw on the photos you sent me." He sighs with delight. "I'm just that good."

"Fine, yes, it was me. Curiosity got the best of me. But then I saw you drooling over Miss Purple at the bar and I felt physically ill. No, actually, I felt like a piece of trash. Believe me, I think I'll be able to 'stay away' from now on."

His tone shifts to panic. "Oh man, we are so not on the same page here. You've got to let me explain something to you—"

"There's nothing to explain. You've paid two hundred fifty thousand dollars to have sex with a different woman wearing a purple bracelet every night of your life for the next year, and by God, that's what you're gonna do. I get it. Please, feel free—enjoy yourself—but leave me the hell off the roster—"

"Sarah, could you please let me get a word in edgewise here?"

I huff into the phone.

"Please? I know you're angry and confused right now—"

"I'm not angry or confused." The minute the words come out, I know they're not entirely accurate. "Okay, wait, yes, I'm angry. In fact, I'm really, really angry. But I'm not confused. At all. I'm pretty clear on everything—"

"No, wait, listen, you have no fucking idea what's going on—"

"I have no fucking idea?"

He sighs. "Correct. You have no fucking idea."

"I've read your application. And I saw you in action last night with Miss Purple. What more is there to understand?"

"If I gave a shit about The Club, then why the hell did I track you down? Why the hell am I calling you right now?"

"Because I'm Mount Everest, plain and simple—and you, Mr. Faraday, are an avid climber."

He lets out an exasperated noise. "I don't even know what you look like and all I've been able to think about is finding you, touching you, hearing your voice. I've been going out of my mind for you, Sarah. And then I finally find you and—"

"You sure didn't look like you were going out of your mind for me last night."

"I was going out of my mind for you *especially* last night."

"Really?" I chuckle. "Was that before, during, or after you fucked Miss Purple?"

He pauses. "Yes. All of the above. But especially during." His voice is soft but impassioned.

I laugh heartily. Spitefully. He wants me to believe he was losing his mind over me while having sex with another woman? Is that supposed to make me feel all mushy inside? Or turn me on? Even if it turns out I like things a bit naughtier than I realized (as I'm recently learning, thanks to His Supreme Holiness), I'm not effing deranged.

"Listen, it's not easy to explain." He sighs. "And not over the phone. But, goddammit, please, please, please, just let me see you. Just let me talk to you in person."

"Why? Talking is just 'prelude,' right? Right along with eating or laughing or going to a concert or doing just about anything that isn't 'fucking.' It's all one long, drawn-out 'prelude' to you becoming 'God.'"

He makes that exasperated noise again. "This is so fucked up. There is no other circumstance where you'd know all of that. This is . . ." He grunts with frustration. "This is so fucked up."

I don't say anything. He's right. There's no other circumstance where I'd know every single one of Jonas Faraday's twisted thoughts before he's had a chance to dazzle me with his smile and perfect abs. I smirk. It must be killing him that I know what I know. And thank God I do. Otherwise, I'd be in for a heart-shattering ride, I'm sure.

"Would you please just let me take you to coffee? Or dinner? I just want to talk to you."

"Why go through the motions of Valentine's Day bullshit, when I know you'd hate every minute of it?"

He grunts. I don't know what that sound means. "This is so fucked up," he mumbles again.

"And anyway, it'd be hard to have a normal conversation with you, knowing all the while you just want to 'fuck me in the bathroom,' anyway."

There's a long pause. He's not talking.

"Hello?" I say. "Are you still there?"

He lets out a shaky breath. "God, you're everything I thought you'd be." He swallows hard. "I want you so bad," he finally says.

That's not what I expected him to say. His words hit me right between the legs. "So," I huff, but there's no conviction in my tone—only sudden arousal. What just happened? "So I'm right—about the bathroom thing?" I can barely get the words out. I'm not sure if I want him to admit it or deny it.

"Halfway right. Yes, I absolutely want to fuck you. More than I've ever wanted to fuck any woman in my entire life. But not in a bathroom. In my bed. Nice and slow."

He lets that hang in the air for a second.

The throbbing between my legs is becoming insistent.

"When I finally get to fuck you, it's going to be in my bed where I can take my time, where I can see your gorgeous skin against my crisp white sheets." He lets out a ragged sigh. Oh, wow, he's really turned on. "But that's not why I called. I just want to see you," he continues. "And talk to you. I have so much to tell you, but I can't say it all in a telephone call. I mean, yes, of course, I want to do more than talk to you, much more, but if you let me see you tonight, I'll be happy to get to touch any part of your skin—any part at all—your hand, your arm, your face. Whatever you'll let me touch. Your ear. Your toe." I can hear him smiling. "Your elbow."

I'm on fire. He's ignited something inside me I didn't know existed. These are not the words I expected to come out of Jonas Faraday. Especially not directed at me.

"Sarah?"

"Did you fuck Miss Purple last night?" My tone is even.

"Yeah," he says gruffly, without hesitation.

"That was an odd thing to do if you supposedly wanted me, don't you think?"

My question is rhetorical—meant as a cynical, mocking barb. But he surprises me by answering in earnest.

"Not odd at all. You deleted your email account and wrote me that handwritten note, basically telling me to fuck off. So I decided to make myself stop wanting you the only way I knew how. I paid for that stupid membership; might as well use it, right? And then, it serves me right, the whole thing with Miss Purple turned into the biggest cluster fuck—the worst sex of my life. Totally backfired. Being with her just made me want you more." He exhales again. "So much more."

I'm breathless. I didn't expect any of that.

I know I'm supposed to be appalled and offended and skeptical, and I'm probably supposed to hurl some angry or snarky comment at him, cutting him down to size and lashing out at him for being sick and twisted. Maybe I'm supposed to say something simple and sarcastic like, "Oh, how sweet." But the truth is, I *do* think what he's said is sweet. He's never even laid eyes on me, and he spent last night screwing an incredibly hot woman and wishing she were *me*? Maybe someone else wouldn't understand—maybe someone else would judge me harshly for what I'm about to say—but I don't care what anyone else thinks. I know I just got the equivalent of a Hallmark card from Jonas Faraday—and it makes me want him. It makes me want him bad.

I unzip my jeans and let my hand wander in.

"Did you make her come?" I ask, arousal seeping into my tone.

He pauses a long time, considering. I'm sure he's wondering if this is a trap.

"Did you make her come?" I ask again. This time, there's no doubt I'm totally turned on.

He inhales sharply, obviously realizing I'm blazing hot. "No." His answer hangs in the air for a long time. "She faked it," he finally adds. "Just like you said."

After what he said in his application, I know how much her faking it must have upset him, but I'm selfishly glad she did. My fingers continue their exploration. "I'm touching myself, Jonas," I say.

I can hear him trembling across the phone line. "Sarah," he whispers.

"Did you go down on her?" I ask. I should be disgusted. Outraged. Hurt. But I'm not. Far from it. My fingers find their target.

I moan. "Touch yourself, Jonas, touch yourself and tell me if you licked her," I say.

His breathing hitches sharply. "I started to, but the second my tongue touched her, I couldn't do it." He groans. "I was repulsed."

I should express utter indignation. I should call him a man-slut and hang up on him. I should say something about him being a pig. But instead, I fondle myself with even more enthusiasm. He was *repulsed* going down on that incredibly hot woman? "Tell me, Jonas."

As if reading my mind, he instantly adds, "Because she wasn't you." His voice is hoarse. I know he's handling himself roughly.

"More," I say. I can't for the life of me understand why I'm so turned on right now, but hearing him say he went down on that ridiculously good looking woman and wished she were me is the hottest thing I've ever heard. My hand is becoming insistent inside my jeans. "Touch yourself and tell me more," I insist. Oh God, my head is spinning. "Touch yourself, Jonas."

He tries to catch his breath. "I started in on her with my tongue ... and she started moaning and groaning and thrashing around right away." His voice has taken on a tone I haven't heard from him. It's guttural. "She said I was 'amazing.'"

A deep-throated chuckle escapes my throat. I can hear him smiling on the other end of the line in reply.

"Your laugh is sexy," he whispers.

"What was her name?" I ask.

"Stacy," he spits out.

"Stacy the Faker."

"Stacy the Faker," he repeats quietly. "I wanted her name to be Sarah."

My hand is getting pretty good at this. I moan. "What happened next, Jonas?" My heart is racing.

"I was down there for twenty seconds, practically gagging the whole time, and she acted like I was the second coming of Christ."

I lick my lips. "So what'd you do?" I begin sliding my fingers in and out of my wetness with surprising skill. I'm getting better and better at this.

"Oh, Sarah," He groans. "I love your voice."

"Tell me," I say. "Tell me, Jonas."

"You're driving me crazy. Let me come see you right now. I didn't call you to—"

"Tell me," I say, and my tone leaves little room for argument. My fingers are finding ways to give myself pleasure I've never discovered before. I'm frantic.

"I fucked her."

The words send a shiver down my spine. My breathing hitches.

"I closed my eyes and imagined she was you, and I fucked her. Hard. I didn't care if she came—I didn't want her to come. All I cared about was fucking her and imagining she was you." He lets out an animalistic sound that makes me want to leap through the phone and straddle him.

"Tell me how you imagined she was me."

"I imagined she was the woman behind the menu—I imagined you were the woman behind the menu."

I'm flabbergasted. How the hell did he make that connection? I was tucked away in the corner of a crowded bar, my face hidden. Why did he even notice me in that bar, let alone make the connection? "Why?"

He doesn't answer. I can tell he's busy on the other end of the call.

"Jonas," I whisper. "Tell me."

"Your skin, Sarah." His voice halts, like his pleasure just escalated on his end. "Your hair. Your hands. That ring on your thumb." He lets out a low groan. "Oh my God, that ring."

"You like that?"

"Oh, yeah," he moans. "I like that. And your big brown eyes over the top of the menu, glaring at me. You were so pissed at me. I liked it."

My hand is frantic now. I touch my thumb ring with my index finger and imagine he's the one touching it. If he were here right now, I'd take him into me and ride him as deeply as my body could manage. "What else did you imagine?"

"Your breasts. I imagined licking your nipples and making them hard." He moans again.

"What about my face?" The hair on my neck is standing up.

"I don't know," he mumbles. "It doesn't matter. Whatever you look like, I want you."

I am so aroused I'm almost in pain. "I'm so wet," I whisper. The nerve endings between my legs are frantic for him. I throw my head back and moan into the phone.

I hear him come on the other end of the call. It's an unmistakable sound. Wow, it's a total turn-on. Oh God, he makes me feel wild, like I can say or do anything, no matter how depraved. I feel like such a bad, bad girl with him. And I like it.

My fingers continue their assault on myself. I want to join him in his climax so badly, and I've never been so hot in all my life.

Maybe this is finally the moment, right here, right now, with him. Maybe discovering this bad girl inside me is what I've needed all along to finally let go, to finally let it happen . . .

I keep trying, insistently.

But after a moment, I realize it's not going to happen, no matter how crazy-aroused I am. It's just not going to happen. As usual.

And if not now, then probably never.

I pull my hand out of my pants.

He's quiet on the other end of the line.

There's a long pause.

That was the hottest thing I've ever experienced in my entire life, and I still didn't come. I'm hopeless. If I couldn't let go and let my deepest desires overtake me when I was having dirty phone sex with an outrageously sexy man who hacked into U Dub's server to find me, when I was feeling tingles and waves of pleasure I've never felt before, when his husky voice described fucking another woman and imagining she was me, sight unseen, then I'm obviously never going to get off.

I just have to face it.

And that's not good. In fact, when it comes to Jonas Faraday, it's a frickin' disaster. Getting women off is all this man cares about. If I can't get off, then what can I offer him? Frustration and disappointment. For both of us. Plus, quite possibly, a little heartbreak, too, at least on my end.

This is a no-win situation for me, I suddenly realize. If I never come with him (most likely outcome), he'll move along quickly to someone who will. And if I *do* eventually come—glory be!—he'll move along quickly then, too, just like he said he would on his application. Either way, this story ends with him moving along quickly—whether I want him to or not.

He's been honest about his disdain for messy female emotions—but I'm not sure my heart is capable of distinguishing the feelings he invokes in me from my perhaps naïve but sincere belief in love and hope and meaningful human connection. I don't need weekend trips to IKEA, mind you—I've got a whole lot of living to do before I start picking out end tables with anyone—but I certainly don't want to knowingly enter into some kind of meaningless fuckfest with a man who tells me right from the start he's going to toss me into the trash right after he gets what he wants. (Or doesn't, as the case may be.)

My high has crashed down around my ears. My brain has elbowed its way to the front of this parade, past my heart, way past my crotch, and taken over.

Jonas Faraday is a climber. And, yes, right now, he's climbing me—which of course feels pretty damned good. Intoxicating, like a drug. But I've got to get off the drug. For my own sanity. Once he's had me and gone on to tomorrow's purple-bracelet-wearing hottie, I'll be left in a state of pathetic withdrawal, like a junkie in a back alley hankering for my next fix—and wishing to God I'd never taken that first hit of Jonas Faraday in the first place. I might think I'm ready to give free reign to the bad girl I've recently discovered inside of me, but the good girl who's been in charge a helluva lot longer knows that even one hit of this addictive man will probably lead to irreversible, regrettable, heartbreaking pain. If not brain damage. And it's just not worth it. Look at what he's already done to me! For the love of God, I just masturbated to him telling me how he licked and screwed another woman last night. What's happening to me? I'm becoming just as sick and twisted as he is. Why, oh why does he make me so crazy?

I sigh. I'm resigned. "Did you come?" I ask him. My tone is matter-of-fact, though my intention is cruel.

I hear him smile. He sighs. "Mmm. I couldn't help myself. I've wanted to hear your voice for so long. You've got that little bit of gravel in your voice—"

"Well, I didn't."

There's a long pause as he figures out what to say. "Shit," he finally says, reality dawning on him. "I'm so sorry." His distress is palpable. "Sarah—"

"No need to be sorry. That's just the way it is with me, like I've been telling you."

"I'm sorry. I didn't call you with the intention of—"

"Don't apologize. You've been clear about what you want, and I can't give it to you. The reality of me just doesn't live up to the fantasy, as it turns out."

"You're better than any fantasy." His voice breaks with sudden emotion.

"No."

"Why are you doing this? Tell me what's going on inside that beautiful head of yours right now."

"Beautiful head? You've never even seen my 'beautiful head.'"

"I'll come over right now and fix that."

"What's the point?"

"Why are you doing this?"

"I'm not doing anything."

He doesn't say anything.

"I've got a lot of studying to do," I finally say.

He remains quiet.

"So, I'm gonna go."

"Why are you withdrawing all of a sudden? You don't have to do that. Just let me come see you. If you'd just talk to me in person, I know—"

"What's the point? Don't you see? What just happened is a gigantic metaphor—a metaphor for how it would be for you and me. Neither of us satisfied in the end."

"What do you mean?"

I don't answer him. I can't figure out how to explain what I'm feeling.

His voice suddenly flashes acute anger. "Oh, I get it. Not enough upside for you, huh?" He lets out an angry blast of air.

I pause, giving the matter due consideration. Well, that's one way to put it.

"Correct," I say evenly. "Honestly, when it comes to you, I don't see any upside at all."

Chapter 11

Jonas

I blew it. I fucking blew it. I'm such an idiot. She already thinks I'm chasing her with my dick and nothing else, and I just proved her point in spades. Fuck! I didn't call her intending to have phone sex with her! I actually wanted to *talk* to her—to tell her I can't stop thinking about her, that I've been going fucking crazy over her, to tell her she kicks my ass and I love it, that I moved mountains to find her, sight unseen, because she's worth it. I even wanted to tell her she's made me start to rethink a few things, that I might even have been wrong about a thing or two, and that's a hard thing for me to admit to anyone. I wanted to tell her I want to make her come more than words can say—*and I haven't even seen her yet*. So what does that say? It says she's driven me goddamned crazy, that's what. And then, despite all my good intentions, I just went right ahead and jacked the fuck off on our phone call—exactly what she would have expected me to do—and left her hanging out to dry with her hand in her own ice-cold pants, feeling like a cheap phone operator at 1-877-SEXTALK.

Why didn't I stop and *think* before I reached down and started jerking off like a jackass? This is a girl who's never, ever had an orgasm in her entire life. Why can't I get that through my thick head? I can't assume anything. I have to handle her with kid gloves so she doesn't freak out and get all up inside her own overthinking head and start getting some kind of complex about not being able to "give me what I need." If she would just trust me, learn to let go and trust me, I know I could deliver her to Nirvana. I know I could. But she doesn't know that—and that's the point. I can't even begin to understand how it must screw with her mind to have sex, time after time, without coming even once—to not even believe there's a *possibility* of coming. I can't even fathom it. I mean, I've never had sex and *not* gotten off. Ever. Literally. Not even with fucking Stacy the Faker.

So what is sex all about for a woman like that? It's all about getting the guy off, right? Getting him off gets her off, I'm sure—but that can only take her so far for so long when there's no payoff for her at the end of it all, time after time. I mean, yes, I love making a woman come, but isn't that because, ultimately, it makes me come so hard I almost pass out? Huh. What if making a woman come was all there ever was for me, and it never led to my own satisfaction, ever? Huh. Something to think about. That puts things in a whole new perspective.

Who are these guys she's been with in the past, for Chrissakes? Do they not even *notice* she's not getting off—or do they just not care? Or does she fake it so well they don't know the difference? And didn't I used to be just like them, not too long ago? I have a pit in my stomach. Yeah, I was. I most definitely was. Hell, maybe I still am. Shit. It's suddenly hitting me like a ton of bricks. I'm no different than any of the guys she's been with. I just proved that in spades on the phone. Damn. I never should have jerked myself off—I should have kept my hand out of my pants and just *talked* to her.

But, hang on a second, she *told* me to touch myself, she *wanted* me to do it—oh God—her gravelly voice when she said, "Touch yourself and tell me how you licked her" was so hot, *so fucking hot,* how was I supposed to resist? No mortal man could have resisted. It was the most incredible thing a woman's ever said to me, hands down. Oh God, it brought me to my knees.

But I should have resisted, no matter how impossible. I should have had the presence of mind to say, "What's the rush? Let's just talk. Let me take you out for coffee." But when she ordered me to touch myself in that gravelly voice of hers—when she was *turned on* by the idea of me licking another woman's pussy and wishing it was hers—when she asked me for details about it and started moaning and saying my name as I told her—it was so hot, I almost came right then and there. I just couldn't believe what I was hearing, couldn't believe how hot she made me, couldn't believe she *understood* what I was trying to explain to her. She didn't pull the predictable "shocked and indignant" bullshit reaction on me. Nope. She understood what I was trying to tell her; it turned her on, and she admitted it.

Epic.

No one would even believe me if I told them what just happened (which, of course, I'd never do). I can barely believe it myself. When she told me to touch myself and tell her everything, that was when I knew this woman gets me like nobody ever has.

And now I've blown it. Was that one orgasm *during a fucking phone call* worth it, Jonas? Fuck! I never would have guessed I could lose control of myself so completely. I don't understand why she affects me like this. She thinks there's no upside to me, and I just proved it. Never mind I let a wire transfer for a quarter-million dollars go through just so she wouldn't lose her part-time desk job. *When it comes to you, I don't see any upside at all,* she said. None at all?

Well, what the fuck does she expect from me? I've never even laid eyes on this woman. What am I supposed to do—profess my undying love to her? Ride in on a white horse and swoop her up into my saddle and ride off into the sunset? Send her roses and candy and Hallmark cards? Hey, how about a teddy bear, too? That's such total and complete bullshit, all of it. Even if I were "normal," even if I were brainwashed into believing in happily ever afters like the rest of world, I wouldn't be able to make her any promises. Even normal people go out on a date or two or three before they run off to elope in Las Vegas, don't they? For Christ's sake, am I supposed to swear she's my soul mate—wear a vial of her blood around my neck—before she'll grab a cup of coffee with me?

I mean, yes, of course, I don't want to just grab coffee with her—I'm not saying that—yes, of course, I want to take her to my bed and lay her down on my white sheets and lick every inch of her olive skin and suck her hard nipples and kiss her everywhere and bury my face between her legs and look up and see her big brown eyes looking back at me and fuck her 'til she's screaming my name. Yes, of course, I want to do all that. But to get to do all that, I'm supposed to sign some contract that I'll never make one wrong move? That I'll never be an asshole? That I'll never hurt her feelings? Well, I can't guarantee that. Who can? Can normal people guarantee that? I don't think so.

What the fuck does she want from me? I've already hacked into a major university's server to find her, and it wasn't cheap. I called her sight unseen and poured my heart out to her. I knew full well a normal woman would bolt when I told her about fucking Stacy, and I told her anyway—because I promised to tell her the truth, no matter what. Fuck, I've already told her more than I've ever told any other woman, ever—which, by the way, she's using against me in the most fucked up way, considering how she acquired the information. And, worst of all, thanks to her, I've already gagged and quite sloppily banged my way through fucking a very hot woman, all the while thinking of her. What more does she want?

I'm done.

She doesn't want me? There's no upside when it comes to me?

Fine.

Guess what? There's no upside to *her*. That woman has been all downside from day one. I was happy before she replied to my note. I was looking forward to my membership in The Club. I was ready to have the best year of my life in that stupid club. She doesn't want me? Fine. I can have any woman I want—other than *her,* apparently—so I guess it's time for me to get out there and fuck them all. I've spent two hundred fifty thousand dollars on my Club membership, this supposedly mind-blowing, best-money-I-ever-spent-in-my-life-hands-down membership, so I'm going to start getting the most out of it. Or, hell, I could just go down to Whole Foods right now, crook my finger at that cashier with the piercings, and she'd come running to my bed like I was pulling her on a fucking string.

Fuck!

I get up and pace around my room like a leopard.

No upside.

Fuck.

I want her. Not whoever's next in the purple parade. Not the girl with the piercings at Whole Foods. I want *Sarah.*

Fuck.

I don't give two shits about The Club right now.

How am I supposed to know if I'd want to spend more than two to seven hours with her, anyway? I've never even *seen* her. Can she honestly expect me to know how much time I'm willing to give her, sight unseen? Yes, she turns me on now, of course, but *seeing* her might make a difference. A huge difference. All I've seen of her are pieces of a jigsaw puzzle—a breast, a nipple, a thigh. Some hair over the top of a menu. Smooth olive skin. Big brown eyes. Beautiful, soul-stirring, brown eyes. A ring on her thumb. That voice.

I close my eyes. Shit. I just gave myself a woody.

I'm losing control of myself. No, I've already lost it. It's long gone. Joining The Club in the first place—for a fucking year, no less!— proved it. What was I thinking? I can't act on every single urge and whim. I need to reel it back in, take control.

From now on, I'll focus on two things: climbing and work. Yeah, Josh and I will climb Mount Everest next year when they reopen it. I know we said we'd do a bunch of other mountains first, but why wait? We can use this coming year to train like madmen. I'll put my head down and train and get in the best shape of my life. And I'll refocus on work, too. There's plenty of it. Business is through the roof.

When I need the kind of relaxation only a beautiful woman can bring, I'll check in on my Club app and meet some lonely, all-too willing Purple. No feelings involved. Especially not mine. But I won't do it every day. It won't be an addiction. I'll just do it occasionally, when I need to blow off steam. And by the time the year has passed, I'll be standing on top of the world, at the pinnacle of Mount Everest, as close to God as a human can get while still standing on planet earth—and, by then, I will have forgotten all about her.

Yes. That's the plan. And it's a good one.

I sit down at my desk and open my laptop. I've got a mountain of acquisition prospect reports to analyze and emails to send out. It's time to get back to work and get over myself. And get over her. I've never even seen her, for fuck's sake, it shouldn't be hard to forget her.

I've barreled through two acquisition reports in ninety minutes and sent out at least fifteen emails to my uncle in New York and Josh in L.A. and various members of my team here in Seattle regarding some due diligence action items. Being productive is calming me down. With each passing minute, I like my plan of action for the next year more and more. Train for Mount Everest, fuck purples in The Club, as needed (no feelings involved), climb to the tippy-top of the world, forget she ever existed. Everything back to normal.

It's foolproof.

I'm about to start on a third acquisition prospect report when my cell rings with a call from Josh.

"Hey," I answer, and launch right in as if we've already been talking for ten minutes. "I'm thinking we climb Everest next year. I know we projected ten years, but I don't want to wait." It's pretty much how phone calls with Josh always go—we don't have individualized conversations so much as one continuous conversation that's sporadically interrupted by life.

"Whoa, slow down, high-speed. What happened to us climbing Kilimanjaro next year? And K2 after that?"

"Scratch all that. Everest is the highest. Why bother with anything else?"

"Um, because we both agreed we need more experience before we tackle Everest. What's going on?"

I grunt, but I don't answer him.

"Jonas, you're freaking me out. *I'm* the reckless one. You're the look-before-you-leap twin. Stop trying to steal my thing."

There's another brief silence.

"You do realize *I* called *you*, right?" Josh finally says. "You don't even want to know why?"

"The EBITDA on the Jackson deal? I just emailed you about it."

"No, dummy, why would I call you about that? I don't give a shit about the EBITDA on the Jackson deal. No, bro, I got the photos." I can hear his shit-eating grin across the phone line. "I wanted to make sure you check your email."

My breath stops short. "I've been working."

"Do you know for sure which of the Sarahs is yours yet?"

I pause. I don't want to talk about her. "Cruz," I finally mutter.

Josh hoots like I just gave the right answer on *Jeopardy*.

"But she's not *my* Sarah, as it turns out."

"What?"

"I just talked to her."

"You *talked* to her? What the fuck! When were you planning to tell me this little nugget—"

"She's not interested in me. Doesn't even want to meet me for coffee."

He pauses. "You hacked into U Dub's server to find her, without knowing what she looks like, and she's *not interested*? How the hell did you fuck that up? Is she married or something?"

"No, she's just not interested."

"I can't ... She knows you hacked into U Dub's server to find her, right?"

"Yeah."

"And she didn't go all weak in the knees over that?"

I'm silent.

"Well, has she *seen* you, at least? I mean, does she know what you look like?"

"Yeah."

"Really? Wow." He pauses, considering. "I'm shocked." He sighs. "Oh man, that sucks. Wow." He exhales loudly, totally deflated. "I was kind of excited for you—especially after seeing her picture. I was really hoping your Sarah was gonna be Cruz."

"You saw her photo?" My heart's suddenly racing, despite myself.

"Yeah, and she's—"

"No, don't tell me. Please. If she looks good, I'll just be even more bummed. And if she's the Bride of Frankenstein, I don't want to know that, either. I'd rather hold onto the fantasy I've created in my head."

"Bro."

There's a long pause. With just that word, he's chastising me—telling me I'm an idiot. I don't reply.

"Check your email," he says slowly, condescendingly.

I grunt.

"Bro."

I'm dying of curiosity, I must admit.

"Trust me."

My stomach is lurching. "Really?"

"Really."

"Really good or really bad?"

"Really, really, really good."

Holy shit, she's a knockout. I can't stop staring at her. It's just a snapshot for her school I.D. and she looks like a fucking model. Her dark hair is swept back into a ponytail and she's not wearing a stitch of makeup (the way I prefer most women, actually), and she's still an absolute head turner—distinctive, not a cookie-cutter beauty, by any means, faintly exotic—but fucking gorgeous. She'd definitely stand out in any crowd. There's something about her face—the way her features all come together—she slays me. Her eyes are the best part. They're big and brown and brimming with intelligence and humor and warmth and take-no-bullshit confidence. There's depth in those eyes. But, wow, her lips are a close second. Good God, I keep thinking of those lips moaning and saying my name and asking me about how I fucked Stacy—and all with that gravelly voice of hers, too.

Damn, what a fantastic surprise this is. It's Christmas morning right now. And to think I'd been bracing myself for disappointment—priming myself not to be overly critical when I saw her, telling myself I'd have to find one particularly attractive feature and focus on that to the exclusion of the not-so-great parts. But there's not a single not-so-great part. Especially when I look at her features all put together. If I didn't even know her, I'd beeline right to her in a bar. She's gorgeous.

Now that I know what she looks like, what just happened on the phone is even more catastrophic. If I'd only known she looked like this, I wouldn't have called. I would have gone straight over to her apartment and beaten down her door and made her talk to me. And then what might have happened? She wouldn't have been able to turn me down then.

But I couldn't wait to call her, could I? I just *had* to pick up the phone and call her, sight unseen. I thought calling her without seeing her first was some kind of proof of my good faith—some kind of romantic gesture of my unconditional attraction to her. I figured she'd get all swoony about it. Man, I calculated all wrong.

If I'd just waited 'til seeing this picture, I would have handled things differently. I wouldn't have let her take control of the situation like I did. I would have been in charge. She wouldn't have rejected me if I'd showed up on her doorstep, that's for sure. No woman has ever been able to resist me when I bring my A game. Damn, I should have brought my A game—but, instead, I brought my dick. I didn't even call her to talk dirty to her, I really didn't. And what did I do? I had phone sex with her. Why couldn't I control myself and talk to her like a lady and keep my pecker in my pants?

I blew it.

And now I'm drowning in regret.

She's stunning.

I should have known my gut is always right when it comes to women. I could sniff out a hot woman blindfolded—and, actually, that's exactly what I did, come to think about it—I sniffed her out blindfolded.

Yeah, this is a game changer.

She doesn't get to dictate what happens between us anymore. I'm taking charge now. She's not interested in rolling the dice with me? She doesn't think there's enough *upside* to me?

Fuck that shit.

I'm done being a pussy-ass, sentimental whiner. I'm done begging her to pretty-please give me the time of day. I want her and I'm going to have her and that's all there is to it. Sarah Cruz is about to learn one of the immutable laws of nature, a principle as immovable and unavoidable as the theory of relativity or Boyle's law of gases or motherfucking gravity. It's called Faraday's law of attraction and it goes a little something like this: When Jonas Faraday wants a particular woman, Jonas Faraday shall have her. And in this particular instance, Jonas Faraday wants the magnificent Sarah Cruz. End of fucking story.

Chapter 12
Sarah

"But *why*?" Kat asks. "I mean, jeez, he went to all that trouble to find you, and you won't even go out to dinner with the guy?"

We're sitting at my little kitchen table eating Pasta Roni and Caesar salad for lunch after coming back from a yoga class.

I sigh. "It's complicated," I say.

"Even if he turns out to be a douchebag, worst case scenario you could just sit there and look at him and still have a spectacularly good time. Oh, and a free meal."

"We're fundamentally incompatible," I say evenly.

"But how do you know that if you won't even meet him?"

"Because I know," I say.

"So you say. I wish you'd tell me what he said in his damned application that's got you all aflutter." She turns her head and glances at me sideways. "Is he some kind of freak?" She winks.

I roll my eyes. "You know all that stuff is confidential." I lower my voice. "But no."

"He's into S and M, isn't he?"

"I can't talk about it—but no. We're just not compatible on a basic level, personality-wise, goal-wise, so it's pointless to subject myself to disappointment and maybe even heartbreak."

"But what if you're the *one* girl in the *whole* world who can change him?" She smirks.

I know she's kidding—mocking that clichéd impulse that attracts every girl to an irredeemable bad boy at least once in her life—but she's hit the nail on the head. That's exactly what I keep hoping I am—the one girl in the whole world who can change him. It's ludicrous. "Yeah. If he could just find The One, he'd be a changed man," I say, trying to keep my voice light and bright. But I don't feel light and bright. I feel miserable.

Kat laughs. "You're obviously obsessed with him. And he

wouldn't have tracked you down like a big game hunter if he weren't at least slightly obsessed with you. So why not take him for a spin and at least *see* if you're more compatible than you think?"

"It's not as simple as test-driving a car—"

"Yes, it is. It's precisely as simple as test-driving a car. I say this with love, girl, but you make everything more complicated than it has to be. No offense."

"None taken." She's absolutely right. I hate that about myself. I sigh. "Maybe you're right. Maybe I should—"

There's a loud knock at my door.

Kat's eyes go wide. "Oh my God," she whispers. "I knew he wouldn't take no for an answer!"

My heart's in my throat. I'm wearing sweats and a T-shirt and no makeup right now. Oh my God, please, Lord, no. He wouldn't just show up at my house, unannounced, would he? Yes, he would. I know he would. That's exactly the kind of thing he'd do.

"I guess he's not letting you off the hook that easily, little Miss Over-thinker," Kat says, marching with glee to the front door.

I bolt to my bedroom like a mental patient escaping from a psych ward, trying frantically to think what clean clothes I have in my drawer that don't make me look like I'm dressed for a marathon study session. My heart's beating out of my chest and my pulse is raging in my ears. I can hear Kat opening the front door and greeting whoever's on the other side of it. I hold my breath, listening.

A male voice says, "Sarah Cruz?"

Oh God. This is disastrous. Worst case scenario. If he sees Kat first, he'll only be massively disappointed when I show my face and say, "Sorry. Sarah's me."

"No," Kat says, squealing. "But you've got the right place. I'll take those for her."

"There's more stuff in the truck, too. I'll be right back."

What the hell is going on? I march out of my bedroom back into the living area to find Kat standing before me with the most exquisite arrangement of roses I've ever seen—at least three dozen roses of every imaginable hue bursting out of an elegant crystal vase.

Kat laughs. "Looks like someone's not accustomed to being turned down."

Kat and I take stock of the various goodies littering my kitchen table. In addition to the six arrangements of outrageously beautiful flowers, there's a gigantic box of chocolates in a heart-shaped box tied up in a huge red bow (which Kat has already untied and dug into), a gigantic white teddy bear holding a red, heart-shaped pillow embroidered with the phrase "Be Mine," and, to top it all off, a sealed, pink envelope with my handwritten name across the front.

I stare at my treasure trove, unable to speak.

"Aren't you gonna open the envelope?" Kat asks, picking it up and handing it to me.

"Yeah, I'm"—I gesture toward my bedroom and begin walking quickly toward it—"just gonna read it in private."

Kat looks mildly disappointed, but she says, "Okeedoke."

In my room, I perch on the edge of my bed and stare at the sealed pink envelope in my shaking hands. I want to open it more than I want to breathe. But I'm nervous. If I know Jonas Faraday, the card will surely include words like "lick" and "come" and "fuck" and maybe even "clit," and I don't want to read those words right now, to be honest. I've got romantic visions of flowers and candy and teddy bears dancing in my head, and I don't want his unique form of "brutal honesty" to burst my bubble. Even if I know he's just making some sort of sardonic point with all this clichéd stuff, I can't help but enjoy the over-the-top romanticism of it all, even if he's only mocking traditional romance. Frankly, if all he's got to say to me at this point is "I want to make you come," I'm not in the mood to hear it.

I stare at the envelope in my hand. I feel so excited right now, so genuinely hopeful, I almost don't want to open the card and get let down. The odds are high that whatever's inside this card is going to ruin this moment—and the silly hopes that are rising up involuntarily inside me against my better judgment. I mean, no matter how cute that teddy bear is out there, we're still talking about Jonas Faraday, after all—and he's not a teddy bear kind of guy.

Well, there's only one way to find out what it says.

I take a deep breath and tear open the envelope.

It's a Hallmark card. I can't believe my eyes. It's a frickin' Hallmark card, covered in pink and red hearts. The cover of the card says, "Happy Valentine's Day" in swirling gold letters. Where did he find this card in March?

The inside of the card is imprinted with a stock message that makes me gasp: *You are everything I never knew I always wanted.* The message is followed by a handwritten letter "J."

This is the last thing I expected him to say. My mind is reeling. I don't even know what to think.

"Sarah!" Kat calls from the kitchen. "There's a note in the flowers!"

I rush out of my room into the kitchen, and she hands me a tiny envelope. I open it to find a handwritten notecard.

"My Magnificent Sarah,

"I hereby decree today to be Jonas and Sarah's Valentine's Day—and since I am God, thus it is so. A car will pick you up for our traditional Valentine's dinner at 8:00, and we will dine at a candlelit restaurant, out in public, like normal people do. At the end of our dinner, I will kiss you goodnight, if you'll let me, and nothing more—like normal people do—and then the car will take you directly home, without me in it. (Come on, Sarah, it's just dinner. You need to eat, right?)

"Truthfully yours, Jonas

"P.S. After we spoke yesterday, I saw your photo for the first time—hence the upgrade in your name from 'My Beautiful Sarah' to 'My Magnificent Sarah.' Damn, Sarah, you're absolutely gorgeous."

Holy frickin' moly. My cheeks are burning. My head is spinning. My knees are weak. What the hell is going on here? I can't make heads or tails of it. I know in my head that this entire charade is a big fat satire to him—some kind of nod to an alternate, surrealistic reality he's poking fun at somehow—and yet it's making me swoon nonetheless.

"What does it say?" Kat asks.

I wordlessly hand her the card, my mouth hanging open.

"Oh my," she says as her eyes scan the note. When she's done, she looks up at me, smiling from ear to ear. "Oh my," she says again. "My, my, my, my, my."

Chapter 13

Jonas

It took an outrageous chunk of change to rent out every table at Canlis for the entire night on such short notice. I had to agree to buy out their highest projected nightly revenue, times *five*, before they finally agreed to shut down the entire restaurant and cancel all dinner reservations (on the pretense of a possible gas leak). But what the hell—I've already thrown a quarter-million dollars down the toilet plus twenty thousand on hacking into the University of Washington's server—what's another thirty thousand for a dinner date? Tonight, I'll pay and do and say whatever I have to if it will make her understand I'm more than just a gigantic, throbbing hard-on.

I look at my watch. It's just past eight. Soon. Very soon. I'm jittery.

What if she refused to get into the limo when it pulled up in front of her apartment? What if she got my gifts and threw them into a dumpster, or smashed each and every crystal vase to the ground?

"Is everything as you wish, Mr. Faraday?" the owner of the restaurant asks me, gesturing to the twinkling white lights strung around the place at my request.

"It's perfect," I reply. "It looks very Valentine's Day-ish. Thank you." I look out the floor-to-ceiling window overlooking the city. "And the view is incredible."

"Seattle never disappoints."

I exhale. I'm way more nervous than I thought I'd be. There's no guarantee she's even heading here right now.

I sit down at the table the restaurant has prepared for us and stare out at the twinkling skyline. My knee is jiggling. I force it to stop.

My cell phone buzzes with an incoming text. I look at the display and smile. *"ETA 5 min,"* the text reads. I'd told the limo driver to text me when he was five minutes away. Looks like she got into the car. That's a start—an excellent start.

As I stand in the cold night air in front of the restaurant waiting for her limo to pull up, my senses are heightened, like I'm a jungle cat stalking my prey. It's going to take all my restraint not to pounce on her when she arrives.

The limo finally pulls up and I open her door, adrenaline flooding my entire body.

And there she is.

Damn.

Wow, her photo didn't even begin to do her justice.

Some sort of primal hunting instinct is threatening to overtake me. I want to tackle her and ravage her right here and now. But, of course, that's not an option. I've got to make her understand I'm not all about fucking her. If that were all I wanted, I could get that in The Club. Somehow, I hold it together well enough to pretend to be a civilized human being, capable of normal conversation.

"Sarah," I breathe, holding my hand out to her. "Happy Valentine's Day."

She smiles up at me. Oh, those lips. They slayed me in her photo, but in person, they make me want to get down on my knees.

"Happy Valentine's Day, Jonas," she replies. Oh, that hint of gravel in her voice. Maintaining control over myself tonight is going to be a tall order.

She takes my extended hand.

Her skin is soft and warm. I look down at her hand in mine and see that damned thumb ring of hers, and that just about does me in. For a split second, I contemplate pushing her back into the limo, crawling on top of her, and running my hands over every inch of her. Instead, I bring her hand up to my mouth and gently kiss the top of it—and then, slowly, pointedly, I lay a gentle kiss right onto her thumb ring.

Her eyes blaze—she knows I'm already a goner. She smiles and slowly pulls her hand away from my mouth—but the expression on her face tells me she likes the feel of my lips as much as I like the feel of her skin. Just that simple exchange, and the air is sexually charged. Not good. I mean, it's *fucking awesome*, don't get me wrong—but tonight is supposed to be about everything *except* my insatiable hard-on for her. In fact, tonight is emphatically *not* about that. Tonight is about showing her she's not some phone sex operator to me. Tonight is about showing her I'm quite functional in ways that don't involve my tongue or dick. I've got to make her understand that what she knows about me, she's learned only thanks to a uniquely exposing circumstance—a situation unlike any other that, by its nature, compelled me to reveal the darkest, most primal parts of myself, parts I've never shown or talked about with anyone else. In real life, I swear, I'm really quite charming.

She needs to understand that, if you only look at my sexual appetites, out of context from other stuff about me that's actually kind of normal, you'd get a pretty warped view of me—which she undoubtedly has. Wouldn't that be true of anyone? I'm sure of it. I've got to show her that, despite my insatiable and seemingly uncontrollable desire for her, I really do possess some attributes that aren't even the least bit sociopathic. So, yeah, the more I think about it, tonight is all about showing her the parts of me that aren't the least bit sociopathic.

I exhale, trying to get ahold of myself. I can't allow myself to have a raging hard-on all night long. I'd never be able to concentrate on anything she's saying—and that would blow my show-her-I'm-not-a-sociopath strategy to bits.

"So nice to finally meet you," she says, smirking.

"No, Sarah, believe me, the pleasure's all mine."

The view is spectacular, all right. And I'm not talking about the skyline. She's wearing a green dress that hugs her curves in all the right places, and the view of her backside as we follow the maître d' to our table is something else. Now *that's* an ass I could really sink my teeth into.

"We're alone?" she asks, scanning the empty restaurant.

"I didn't want there to be any distractions."

"You rented out the entire restaurant?" Here eyes are wide.

I love the look on her face right now.

We reach our table and take our seats.

"Wow. This is amazing." Her face is awash in childlike giddiness. "You rented out Canlis," she mutters, seemingly to herself. "Wow. Thank you. That's ... wow."

A man could get addicted to trying to make her face look like that.

I take my seat across from her and smile. Or, at least, I try to smile. I'm finding it hard to relax my face into any kind of normal facial expression. It feels unreasonably warm in the restaurant.

I flag the maître d' back to the table as he's leaving.

"Yes, sir?"

"Can you turn down the heat just a tad?"

"Of course, sir."

Sarah smiles at me, her eyes flickering with some sort of amusement.

Oh, that mouth. Oh God, if I let myself focus too long on those lips, this dinner date will take a sharp detour. And I'm not going to let that happen. Not tonight. I already made that mistake on the phone, and I'm not going to do it again. Tonight, I'm going to show her the upside of Jonas Faraday—yeah, tonight, I'm all upside, baby.

A waiter comes to the table with wine and an appetizer.

"You're gorgeous," I say after the waiter leaves. And she is. "That dress is incredible."

She looks down as if to remember what she's wearing. "Thank you. Unfortunately, I couldn't wear my favorite dress for you. Such a pity." She smiles mischievously and takes a sip of her wine.

"Why not?"

"It's *purple*." She laughs her gravelly laugh.

Somehow, that laugh of hers puts me at ease. I can feel my shoulders relaxing a bit. I lean forward onto my elbows. "If I could order a woman out of a catalogue to my precise specifications, I'd order you."

There's a brief silence.

Shit. I need to reign it back in. I'm coming on too strong. I can't blurt out every damned thought that flitters across my mind. I take a long swig of my wine.

She moves her mouth to speak—to make some sort of snarky comeback, I'd guess—but then she closes her mouth without speaking.

"What are you thinking right now?" I ask.

She purses her beautiful lips. "A thousand things. Mostly, I can't believe I'm here right now. At Canlis. With you." Her mouth twists for a moment. "And, well, that you're probably the most outrageously good-looking man I've ever laid eyes on, let alone been on a date with. And, yeah, that I can't believe I'm here. With you."

Damn, I want to take that dress off her. "I'm so glad you're here. You're absolutely beautiful."

She looks at me like she's trying to figure out the last piece of a jigsaw puzzle that doesn't fit. "What are *you* thinking right now?" she asks. She leans forward onto her elbows in mimicry of my position and the tops of her breasts push out of her neckline.

My cock springs to attention. "If I answer that question, my entire strategy for the night will be blown to bits."

"You have a strategy for the night?"

"Absolutely."

"What is it?"

"If I answer that question, my entire strategy for the night will be blown to bits."

"So you won't tell me what you're thinking, then?"

I exhale, thinking about her olive skin writhing around on my crisp, white sheets. "You know exactly what I'm thinking."

She licks her lips. "Oh, well, good luck with your strategy, then." The candlelight flickers across her face. She leans back and so do I. I'm not sure who just dominated and who submitted in that exchange. Maybe it was a draw.

There's a brief silence as we assess each other and sip our wine. We each sample the appetizer. It's delicious.

"Thank you for the Valentine's Day gifts," she says. "You shocked the hell out of me."

"Did you like them?"

She pauses. "If I answer that question, my entire strategy for the night will be blown to bits."

"You have a strategy for tonight?"

"Absolutely."

"So you won't tell me if you liked my gifts?"

She smiles. "No, I'll tell you. Strategies are over-rated." She leans forward again. "I felt light-headed and weak at the knees when your gifts arrived. The scent of the flowers wafting through my little apartment made me swoon. As I got ready for our date this evening, I danced around my apartment just for the heck of it—out of sheer joy. Oh, and I must have hugged that teddy bear fifty times, imagining he was you."

My heart is suddenly pounding a mile a minute. I'm smiling from ear to ear. "Yeah, okay, but did you *like* them?"

She laughs.

"How could that answer ruin your strategy for tonight? It's the best answer ever."

"Well, considering how you feel about Valentine's Day 'bullshit'—and the women who are brainwashed into wanting it—it's fifty-fifty you might run for the hills now that you know for sure I'm one of the droning, brainwashed female masses. Honestly, I wasn't sure if you *wanted* me to like everything or if you sent it as some sort of test—like, if I swooned, then I failed the test and proved I'm brainwashed."

"You thought I sent you all that so I could say, 'gotcha'?"

"I'm not sure why you sent that stuff." She shrugs. She takes a sip of her wine.

I look at her, incredulous. Wow, I've really got my work cut out for me tonight. I have to keep remembering that, thanks to that application, I'm starting out in a deep hole, trying to dig my way out. "I'm sorry you even had to wonder. That sucks."

"Come on. You're the one who insists a woman has to choose between 'Valentine's Day bullshit' and monkey-sex that makes her see God. I didn't want to be an idiot and think you were serious if you weren't."

I sigh. "Oh, Sarah, just forget that stupid application, okay? I sent you those gifts because you deserve to have *both* Valentine's Day bullshit *and* monkey-sex." I lean forward again. "And because I want to be the man who gives you both."

She blushes. There's a long beat. "I think you missed your calling as a greeting card writer," she finally says. "'My darling, you deserve Valentine's Day bullshit *and* monkey-sex. Happy Valentine's Day.'" She throws her head back and laughs a full-throated, gravelly laugh. It makes me want to kiss her neck. She beams at me. "Did you come up with the message inside the card you sent me? 'You are everything I never knew I always wanted.' I loved it." She sighs.

"Well, I selected the quote to be printed onto the card, but I didn't write it. It's from a movie."

"What movie?" she asks.

"*Fools Rush In.*" I take a bite of food.

"That one with Matthew Perry?"

"I like to think of it as that one with Salma Hayek."

"Oh, yeah, of course you do." Her eyes blaze. "I can't imagine how you wound up sitting through that movie."

"I didn't mind it at all. I've had a thing for Salma Hayek ever since. Good soundtrack, too."

"But it's a romantic comedy. Like, hopelessly, unabashedly romantic."

"I didn't say it was great cinema. I just said I didn't mind it."

"But that movie was all about two mismatched people finding true love against all reason and logic. A movie like that represents everything you abhor."

I'm quiet for a moment. She thinks I "abhor" true love? I don't abhor true love. Do I? Is that the gist of what I said in my application? Have I become that big an asshole? Maybe I'm a sociopath, after all.

She shifts in her seat and studies me. "Did a former girlfriend force you to watch that movie? I mean, I guess what I'm really asking is have you ever had a committed relationship, or have you always been like this?"

"Have I always been like what?"

"Emotionally damaged—seemingly incapable of forging any kind of intimate human connection."

I feel like she just punched me in the gut. My sociopathic, asshole-y gut.

I consider. What's the honest answer here? "Yes," I answer, "I've always been like this—or, at least since I was seven years old. And yes, despite the way I am, I've had several girlfriends—all of whom complained of my 'emotional unavailability.' And, yes, it was a former girlfriend—a live-in girlfriend, briefly—who forced me to watch *Fools Rush In.* But I didn't mind it."

"What happened to you when you were seven?"

Shit. Why did I mention that?

She waits. When I don't respond, she continues. "Okay," she says softly. "Not a casual dinner topic." She pauses. "I'm sorry."

I want to tell her, "Oh, no problem," and make the tension in my jaw go away, but I can't. The muscles in my jaw are pulsing.

She barrels right ahead. "So when was your last relationship?" She takes a long sip of her wine.

I sigh. At least it's better than talking about what happened when I was seven. "It ended a couple years ago. That was the live-in relationship."

"Why'd it end?"

"Because she said I 'wouldn't let her in'—and it was true. Because I never told her even one of the things I've already told you. Because I knew if I told her the truth about me, how I really think, how I really talk, how I really am, she wouldn't sit across the dinner table from me, looking at me the way you are right now. And at least some part of me knew I wanted a woman who'd know everything you know and still sit across the table and look at me the way you're looking at me right now."

She opens her mouth but doesn't speak. She blinks slowly at me. Her cheeks are flushed.

"But enough about that. The Internet is very clear we're not supposed to talk about past relationships on a first date."

"You read up on what's appropriate first date conversation?"

"I didn't want to fuck up dinner like I fucked up our phone call."

She looks at me sympathetically. "You didn't fuck up our phone call. That was all me. And, anyway," she says, "this isn't a first date. We're way, *way* past that, and you know it."

I can't hold off anymore. I reach out and touch her hand and then her arm. Her skin is so smooth. Our eyes lock. An electricity courses between us.

"You drive me fucking crazy," I whisper.

Her eyelids lower to half-mast. Oh, she wants me, too. "How's that strategy of yours going?" she says. She parts her lips.

"It's about to be blown to bits."

She leans forward and whispers to me. "You drive me fucking crazy, too."

And that does it. She just hurled my strategy right off a cliff. I want to swipe the dishes and cutlery to the floor and take her right here on this table.

Thank God, the waiter comes with a refill on the wine and another appetizer. His presence gives us both a chance to collect ourselves.

"You like seafood?" I ask, suddenly anxious that everything I've ordered won't be to her liking.

"I grew up in Seattle," she says.

I take that to mean she loves it.

She takes a sip of wine. "This is really good wine, by the way. I'm not really knowledgeable about wine, to be honest, but it seems like a good one."

"Well, yeah, anything's better than 'two-buck-chuck.'"

She laughs. "I like two-buck chuck."

I shake my head.

"What can I say? I'm a cheap date."

I resist the urge to roll my eyes. If she only knew everything I've shelled out to be sitting here with her right now, she wouldn't say that. "I'm no wine expert, either," I assure her, and it's true. "I just know what I like." Again, there's that heat between us. "I ordered seven courses for us. I hope that's okay. They'll just keep bringing us food all night long."

"Wow, thank you. That's amazing."

"So you grew up in Seattle?"

She nods. "With my mom. You?"

"Haven't you researched me?"

Her mouth twists. "For hours and hours."

"Well, then, you already know the basics. Which means you've got a distinct advantage over me. It's only fair we talk about you for a while." I take a bite of the new appetizer. Again, the food is delicious.

"You want to know about my 'passions and hobbies and my beloved Maltese Kiki'?" She takes a long sip of her wine.

"Exactly."

"Ah, but you see, I happen to know—unlike any other girl who'd otherwise be sitting here right now under any other circumstance—that you don't give a crap about my precious Kiki—not even about her new rhinestone jacket and tutu—because the only thing you're thinking about is getting down and dirty in the bathroom."

I sigh. "You're misquoting me. I never said I don't give a crap about your precious Kiki."

"Well, okay—you didn't say you don't give a *crap* about her, which is good, because she's the apple of my eye—what you said is that when you ask a woman about herself you're *actually* thinking the whole time that you just want to get down and dirty in the bathroom. Of course, you didn't use the words 'get down and dirty'—you used your all-time favorite word—but this is the nicest restaurant I've ever been to in my whole life and I'm trying to act like a fancy lady."

I rub my eyes. "Oh my God, this is so fucked up," I mutter.

She nods and picks up her wine goblet. "Hey, your words, not mine." She takes a dainty sip.

To my surprise, I laugh. Not too many people can make me laugh—especially not at myself. I lean back in my chair. "Actually, I *want* to know all about you—even about your Maltese Kiki, if you happen to have one. Surprising, but true."

"Let's not go overboard. No one wants to hear about anyone's Maltese named Kiki."

I laugh again. God, I want to take that green dress off her and touch every square inch of her.

"So let me see if I understand this situation correctly. You want to know about my hopes and dreams and passions (and my imaginary Maltese Kiki), and you emphatically *don't* want to get down and dirty with me in the bathroom?" Her eyes are suddenly on fire as she picks up her wine glass again.

Oh, wow, my dick is at full attention. I can't formulate a verbal response. My heart's clanging in my chest. I bite my lip. Oh shit, suddenly, that's all I want to do right now—fuck her in the bathroom. But that's exactly what I absolutely cannot do if we're going to get off on the right foot here.

When I don't speak, she grins. "Oh, yes. Your brilliant *strategy*." She leans forward. "Well guess what? I don't want *strategic* Jonas. I want *honest* Jonas." She licks her lips. "I like My Brutally Honest Mr. Faraday." She smiles slyly. "A lot."

I'm so turned on right now, I can't think straight. I lean forward, too. I whisper, "Yes, I want to fuck you—more than anything. But not tonight. And not in the fucking bathroom. Because fucking you in the bathroom would be no different than what we did on the phone yesterday—and I promised myself I'm not going to do that to you again no matter what. When I finally do fuck you, Sarah—and, believe me, fucking you is the highest priority in my entire life right now—I'm going to do it right so that we *both* experience something we've never felt before." My erection strains inside my pants. "We're going to wait and do it nice and slow and right—and it'll be worth the wait, I promise." My brain is quite certain of this entire speech, even if my hard-on begs to differ.

Her eyes are flickering, and I can't tell if that's because of the candlelight, or because of something heating up inside her. "So that's your strategy? A slow burn? Making me wait? Making it worth the wait?"

My nostrils are flaring. "In a nutshell." I can't read her expression. "What are you thinking right now?" I ask.

She takes a bite of food, and then a long sip of wine, making me wait. "Two things. First, that I really, really like it when you're honest." She grins.

I smile.

"And second, that your precious strategy is about to get blown to bits."

Chapter 14

Sarah

Oh, he's yummy, all right. Just yummalicous. Of course, he's gorgeous—but I already knew that. What I didn't know is that he'd smell so good, too. Or that he'd rent out a fancy restaurant just for me and send a limo to pick me up, too. I don't consider myself a materialistic girl, but come on—who wouldn't swoon just a little bit at all this *Pretty Woman* treatment?

But the thing that's getting to me right now above everything else is the way he's looking at me like he's going to devour me in one bite like a great white shark snacking on a sea lion. I don't think a man has ever looked at me quite like this before—and, if so, certainly not a man I find this irresistibly attractive. His eyes are mesmerizing to me—full of exactly the kind of soul and depth and even sadness I thought I glimpsed in his photos. Now that I see him in person, I know there's something behind those eyes—and I can't wait to find out what it is. When he said that thing about him being incapable of human connection ever since he was seven—oh my God—the look on his face, it was like he was seven years old right then. He looked so small in that moment, so lost, I wanted to reach over the table and take his face in my hands.

Coming here tonight, I was nervous. Nervous I wouldn't live up to all the hype. Nervous he'd regret all the effort he's taken to find me. Nervous the chemistry I'd felt in emails and on the phone somehow wouldn't translate in person. Well, damn, I was nervous for nothing. Our chemistry is through the roof. It's taking all my effort to sit in my chair like a civilized person, rather than leaping onto him like a cheetah on an impala. It's all I can do not to pull the tablecloth off the table and jump his bones right here, right now. I don't know what it is about him, but I feel like someone else around him—but in a good way. Not so inhibited. Not so worried about what anyone else might think. Like I want to take a risk—something I usually avoid at all costs.

What if I got up from my seat and sat myself down on his lap right now and helped myself to those incredible lips of his? Would he be able to stick with his strategy then? I'm dying to find out. In fact, the minute he revealed his stupid strategy, the only thing I wanted to do was force him off it. I guess he's not the only one who loves a good challenge. What if I went over to him, lifted up my dress, pushed my G-string aside and slammed his hardness into me, deep inside me, right here at the table? I can't stop imagining myself doing just that as I sit here sipping my wine and staring across the table at him.

I think it's distinctly possible I'm going insane. These thoughts are not the things a normal woman imagines while sitting in a nice restaurant, overlooking the Seattle skyline. I'm not some kind of sex addict. I'm not some kind of pervert. I'm a "good girl" kind of girl. Dependable. Responsible. A rule follower. So why does he make me want to be so, so, so, so bad? If only he knew what I was thinking. I wonder how he'd feel about his stupid strategy then?

The waiter comes to the table and places salads in front of us.

Jonas looks across the table at me mournfully, as if he knew exactly what I was thinking right before the waiter showed up.

"So, how do you like working for The Club?" Jonas asks. He takes a bite of his salad.

I shift in my seat. "I like it a lot. More than I ever thought I would."

There it is again—that look. It's like he's going to swallow me whole.

I clear my throat. "I've only been working there three months," I say. "Your application was the first one I processed all alone, without supervision."

He meets my direct gaze with a smoldering stare of his own. "I'm your first." He grins broadly. "I like that."

My mouth twists into an amused smile. I like that, too.

"How did you start working for The Club?"

Why are we going through the charade of carrying on a normal conversation? We both know what we'd rather be doing right now. And it starts with the letter "f."

"I answered an ad in a law school forum seeking a student for a work-from-home, part-time research position. It was really vague and kind of mysterious sounding, but the pay was ridiculous, so I applied. I had to undergo all this testing and psychological assessment and jump through weird hoops and sign a non-disclosure agreement before I ever found out the details on the job. But the pay was too good to pass up. After all that, when I finally found out what the job really was, I was floored, but intrigued. Kind of compulsively curious, you might say. And the work turned out to be so fascinating and the paychecks started depositing like clockwork, so . . ."

"Do the applications ever freak you out?" He takes another bite of his food.

"All the time. Including yours." I smile. "But as it turns out," I say, leaning forward, "I like getting freaked out."

The smile that unfurls across his face is wicked.

"I like knowing people's secrets," I say.

His eyes are twinkling.

"Well, mostly. Some of it's totally disgusting, I have to admit. Some of it, you can't un-see. But it's like a car crash, you know? You can't look away. Even the disgusting stuff is fascinating."

"Tell me some of the disgusting stuff."

I tell him the worst of the worst and he laughs heartily. Midway through my storytelling, he has to put down his fork and wipe his eyes, he's laughing so hard.

I love his laugh. Something tells me it's hard to elicit.

"And that's all in the first three months?" he asks, bringing his napkin to his eyes.

I nod. "I'm only planning to keep the job 'til the end of the school year. Hopefully, my grades will cooperate with my big plans—the top ten students at the end of the first year get a full-ride scholarship for the rest of the program, so I'm crossing my fingers." I bite my lip. "I've got an unpaid internship this summer, so I'm really gambling on that scholarship."

"Is your internship at a law firm? I bet you had your pick of jobs—fourth in your class." He smiles.

"You looked that up?"

"I told you, I'm obsessed with you."

My nerve endings sizzle and pop for just a moment. I shift in my seat again.

"No, my internship's with a nonprofit—it's where I'm gonna work when I graduate."

"Really? What nonprofit?" He looks genuinely interested.

I'm a bit caught off guard. Why is he interested in this? Isn't this the part where he yawns and wishes we were having monkey-sex in the bathroom right now? This isn't how I pictured this night going. I never expected Jonas Faraday to ask me about my hopes and dreams. I thought, maybe even hoped, he'd make it easy to resist him by being self-involved and going on and on about what he planned to do to me.

"It's an organization that provides aid and free legal services for battered women." I feel my cheeks involuntarily flush with the fierce emotion I feel about the topic.

He pauses, considering me. "A cause close to your heart, I take it?" he asks softly.

My heart is beating fast. I can't speak, so I simply nod.

There's a long pause. Clearly, he expects me to elaborate. But I'm not here to regale Jonas Faraday with the sob story of my childhood. I don't want to talk about what my dad did to my mom all those years ago that made her run away—to escape, really—and raise me all by herself. I'm not going to talk about how she worked two jobs my whole life, dreaming of a better life for me. No, I'm not here to talk about how brutally he used to beat her while I cowered in the corner, or about how much she's sacrificed for me, or how strong she is, or how much I admire her, or how important it is for me to make all her sacrifices worth it. I'm not here to tell him all that just so he can file me away in a folder with all the other "girls with daddy issues" he's banged. I might not know what I'm here to do, but it's certainly not to talk about any of that.

I shrug.

"So, no interest in corporate law, then? There are plenty of top law firms in Seattle offering ridiculous salaries to starting lawyers. Trust me, I know—I've probably funded a sizeable number of their salaries myself over the years."

I don't like this topic. I want to know more about *him,* not tell him about *me.* "I didn't go to law school for the money," I say simply.

His eyes flash and I feel his desire for me in no uncertain terms. The way he's looking at me, I know he's hard right now. Yet again, I imagine myself sitting on his lap and taking his hardness into me. I wonder if his "strategy" could withstand *that.* By the expression on his face right now, I'd swear this man can read my exact thoughts.

"What are you thinking right now?" I breathe.

"Why do you ask?"

"Because you're looking at me like you want to swallow me whole."

"I'm thinking I want to swallow you whole."

I can't help but smirk.

"I'm thinking you're everything I fantasized you'd be. And more. And I'm thinking I want you so bad, it's causing me physical pain. And, most of all, I'm thinking you're so fucking beautiful."

Boom. Just like that, I'm throbbing. And wet. I want him.

We stare at each other for a moment.

He leans back and sighs. "Tell me more about what you do for The Club, My Beautiful Intake Agent."

I sigh, exasperated. "Why?" I whisper. I hope my voice doesn't sound as impatient as I feel. I don't understand why he's so chatty tonight. Isn't this the man who thinks about fucking a woman in a bathroom while chatting over a nice glass of pinot noir? I check the label on our wine bottle. Yep. Pinot noir. So what gives?

"What do you mean, *why*?"

"Why do you want to know more about me? I thought you didn't care about any of that kind of thing."

He rolls his eyes. "I'm not a monster." He leans forward. "Talking to you is turning me on. And I like getting turned on."

There's that throbbing again. I lean forward onto my forearms. "I review applications assigned to my geographic territory—Seattle—and read all about people's deepest secrets and fantasies. I research to find out if they are who they say they are, and then I do surveillance on each applicant—"

"Did you do surveillance on me?"

"Of course." I tell him every detail about how I saw him fly past me in his BMW.

He exhales sharply, his mind blown. "To think I drove right past you when I was desperate to find you." He shakes his head.

I grin. "Normally, I would have just waltzed into your office to ask about you. But I didn't want you to see me. When it came to you, I didn't do anything the 'usual' way."

"Why didn't you want me to see you?"

I purse my lips. "I guess I wanted you to see me for the first time ... on a night just like this."

He arches his eyebrows and smiles. "Good call."

I grin.

"So, usually, you just walk right into a guy's office when you're doing surveillance?"

"Yeah, I just go wherever they are and waltz right in. Who cares, since they'll never see me again?" As an example, I tell him about my recent trip downtown to watch that software engineer leave his building for lunch.

"What did that guy write in his application?"

"Actually, he didn't care about the sex all that much. I think he's genuinely looking for love."

Jonas scoffs. "In The Club? Yeah, right."

I'm offended. "Anything's possible. And he only signed up for a month. So that says a lot."

"Why does that say a lot? A fucked-up deviant can't sign up for a month?"

"No, the fucked-up deviants are the ones who sign up for a full year."

His eyes flash at me. Was that anger? Humiliation? I can't tell.

"I don't understand," he mutters, his cheeks blazing.

"The ones who sign up for a year have zero faith they'll ever find love—or else they wouldn't commit to a year up front. For them, it's all about the sex. Nothing more."

His eyes are hard.

Shit. Clearly, I'm pissing him off right now. I forge ahead anyway. Screw it. He wants "brutal honesty," right? "The ones who sign up for a month are the romantics," I explain. "They're hoping to find love right off the bat and never need The Club's services again. I think they're sweet."

"Ah," he says. Yeah, he's pissed.

"Not everyone is scared of love, you know." I sniff. "Some people actually think love is the most important thing in the world. And why shouldn't that software engineer find someone to love—in The Club or however he can find it? He deserves love as much as anyone." I'm becoming angry and I don't understand why. "Even if *you* don't believe in falling in love, Jonas, that doesn't mean the rest of the world doesn't believe in it. When I saw that software engineer leaving his lobby for lunch, he looked so alone, so lonely, so *sad,* I actually cried a little bit." And, what the hell, I feel like I could cry all over again, just talking about that guy. Why am I taking up the software engineer's cause so passionately? Why am I blasting Jonas right now? I knew what he was before I agreed to dinner. So why hold it against him now?

Jonas looks at a total loss.

"I'm sorry," I say quickly, but my pulse is racing. "I don't know why I got so riled up there. I've known all about you from the start. It's not fair to hold it against you now."

He runs his hand through his hair.

I exhale. "I'm sure you're plotting your swift escape right about now," I mutter.

"Correct," he says.

My stomach drops. I've blown it. I've totally and completely blown it.

"But only to take you away from this table to a place where I can touch and kiss every inch of you."

I exhale sharply.

His eyes are on fire. He's like a caged lion.

"Why me, Jonas?" I ask. I can't help myself. This man can have any woman he wants. I wish I could let it go, go with the flow and not ask, but I don't understand why he's moved heaven and earth to find me, and rented out this restaurant for me, and is now looking at me like I'm a bottle of whiskey and he's an alcoholic, especially now that I just ripped him a new one. "Please. I don't care about your strategy, whatever it is," I whisper. "I just have to understand why you've gone to such extremes to pursue me."

His eyes darken with intensity. "You want to know?"

I nod. "Please."

His eyes are blazing. "The minute I read your email—the minute I saw the *sender name* on your email—even before I'd read the goddamned message—I knew you'd change everything."

I can't breathe. My heart's thumping in my ears.

"And, Sarah, I *wanted* you to"—his jaw muscles pulse—"change everything." He puts his fork down and stares at me.

My heart is beating like I just ran a hundred-yard dash. That throbbing between my legs has returned with a vengeance. I'm a whirl of unbridled emotion right now.

His chest is heaving.

I stand up from my chair. I'm his for the taking. *Take me.*

He leaps out of his chair and grabs me, pressing his body fervently into mine, his hardness nudging against my hip. He swoops down to my mouth for a kiss, and electricity floods my every nerve ending. Oh my God, his lips are warm and soft and delectable. When his tongue parts my lips and enters my mouth, I smash my body against his, and we're both instantly impassioned. In a flash, we're moaning and clawing and grasping at each other, both of us savage animals.

"Now," I whisper. "Right now."

"Sarah—" he begins, and it's clear he's going to protest.

I reach down and touch the bulging package between us. I want to wrap my legs around him and take him into me right here. "Jonas," I moan. I'm so turned on I'm in danger of losing my legs out from under me. If he doesn't take me into the bathroom this very second, I just might unzip his pants right here in front of the waiter.

"It's either on the table or in the bathroom," I breathe. "Take your pick."

He looks around for a brief second and back at me.

My stare is unwavering.

He grips my hand and pulls me toward the back of the

restaurant. Everything is a blur around me. I'm in sensory overload. I'm having trouble walking—my legs are rubber under me. I'm enraptured by the scent of him, the rawness of him—by the all-encompassing throbbing between my legs. Oh God, I want him.

We're in the bathroom. The women's bathroom. There's an anteroom with a feminine-looking couch. He brings me to the couch, his lips assaulting mine, and lays me down on my back. He's frantically unzipping the back of my dress and pulling it down, roughly, while at the same time pulling up the hem. He's groaning. His hands are all over me. Now there are soft, warm lips on my shoulder, my neck. Oh God, a finger slips inside my underpants, inside of me, eagerly working me, rhythmically caressing me, making me wet. I cry out. Lips on my nipples. I fumble for his zipper. I'm clawing at him. I can't breathe.

His fingers work themselves to my clit. I cry out again and reach for his hard shaft. He yanks my underwear off. My dress is pulled down from the top and hiked up from the bottom, bunched around my waist. I'm soaking wet between my legs, aching, yearning for him. My thighs are covered in my wetness.

"I'm on the pill," I whisper. "Now, Jonas."

"No," he says, bending down toward my crotch, clearly intending to lick me.

I pull at his head, forcing his face back toward mine. I glare at him, desperate. "There's no time for that," I hiss back. "Now, Jonas."

I grab feverishly at his penis and pump his shaft up and down as his fingers work their way to the exact spot that drives me wild. I groan and lean back onto the couch, pulling his hardness toward me, positioning him right at my wet entrance.

"Now," I plead. "Please, now."

"No," he says, but I feel the tip of his penis resting at my entrance. He moans.

I thrust my hips toward him, urging him to enter me, teasing him. "Do it now," I say, gritting my teeth.

"We're at cross-purposes here," he says, trembling, but a second later, he plunges into me, making me cry out.

He slams into me, in and out of me, over and over. He lets out a choked noise that tells me he's already close.

I reach my hands under his shirt to find warm, taut muscles. He pulls down my bra and pinches my nipple—and when he does, something deep inside me faintly ripples at his touch. I make a sound I don't recognize—a sound I've never heard myself make before—and he shudders visibly with his arousal.

He pulls out of me and bends down toward my crotch, yet again intending to lick me, but I get up and push him onto the couch, onto his back. In one swift motion, I straddle him and take him into me again, riding him roughly. I gyrate on top of him, moaning. His fingers quickly move to massage my clit.

I'm on fire. I'm feeling so much pleasure it's beginning to feel like pain. My nerve endings are zapping me like live wires. Glimmering waves of pleasure begin nipping at me from a distance. Again, that foreign noise escapes my throat.

He cries out and I feel his ejaculation inside me, spilling into me.

I'm shaking. Panting. Wanting more. I'm not done yet. I've never been this aroused in all my life. I want more.

I open my eyes to look at him.

He's looking right at me. He looks like a Greek god reclined beneath me. I've never even kissed a man this good looking—and now I've just had the best sex of my life with him. Holy crap, this was amazing. I'm panting like a rabid dog, aching for more. Needing more.

He's still.

He touches my clit again, but I jerk away.

Now that he's done, I don't want to be touched. The moment has passed for me. When he was fucking me and touching me at the same time, my body belonged to him. But now—now that he's climaxed—my body has closed up shop. I don't want all attention on me—I know exactly how that ends. Not well.

But, oh God, I was close. I know I was. I was closer than I've ever been before. I felt like I was about to lose myself—like I was losing control. And I liked it. I really, really, really, really, really liked where this was heading.

I want to do it again.

I feel his hands on my breasts again. And then on my stomach, my hips, my butt.

He moans underneath me. I tilt my head back and sigh, remembering how I felt a moment ago—how everything started warping inside me. I want to feel that way again—I think I could feel that way again.

His hand moves between my legs and I gently guide him away again. No. The moment has passed.

He looks defeated.

Oh, I've disappointed him. My stomach drops into my feet. Of course I have. Good sex means only one thing to him. How could I forget that? I get off him quickly and angrily and start pulling my dress back down and up, trying to put myself back together.

"What's the matter?" he says, shocked.

"Sorry to disappoint you," I hiss.

"Oh my God!" he shouts, throwing up his hands. "And here I thought I was supposed to be the fucked up one. Sarah, do you even know how fucked up you are?" Wow, he's angry.

I wheel around to look at him, incredulous. "*I'm* fucked up? Why? Because I won't pretend to have an orgasm for the sake of feeding your ego?"

"No, because you're hell bent on sabotaging yourself. Look at you. It's text book defense mechanism." He grabs my shoulders. "Well, guess what? I'm not going to let you do this. Do you understand me?"

"Do what?"

"Sabotage this."

"There's nothing to sabotage," I say.

He looks wounded. "You don't mean that."

He's right. I don't mean that. Not at all.

And he's also right that I'm so fucked up. I've been fucked up for a really long time, now that I think about it, despite how much it might appear I've got it all together. No matter how hard I try to be perfect, and rule-following, and smart, and keep it together, no matter how great my grades are and how well I convince the world I'm Sarah the Straight Arrow, Sarah the Studious One, Sarah the Snarky One, I'm always one hair away from falling apart, pushing people away, quickly rejecting before I can be rejected. Holy shit, he's right. I'm so fucked up. I've always been so fucked up, despite appearances. And he figured it out this fast? No one ever figures me out this quickly, because I don't let them.

I finish putting my dress back together, slowly, and then I sit on the edge of the couch and put my head in my hands.

"I'm sorry," I say. "You're right."

"About which part?"

"All of it." I bury my face into my hands. Tears are threatening. "I'm trying to screw this up." I turn to look at him, cringing.

"Why?"

I sigh. "Come on, Jonas. I've read your application." I search for the right words. "I know you're just going to move on. I'm damned if I do and I'm damned if I don't. Either way, you're gonna reject me. Sooner rather than later, too."

He exhales. "So you're gonna do it first, then. Is that it?"

I nod slowly. "I guess so."

He sighs. "Understandable. Given what you know about me. And who you are."

I shrug. I am what I am. So is he.

He puts his finger under my chin and guides my face to look at him. The moment my eyes meet his, my eyes moisten.

"I'm glad you're fucked up," he whispers. "If you weren't, you wouldn't want me. No one's more fucked up than me. You have no idea."

I can't help but smile through my impending tears. I trace his lips with the tip of my finger. "Why are you so fucked up?" I ask him.

His eyes are soulful, earnest. Sad. He leans his forehead against mine. "It's a long story."

I understand. I don't know why I understand, but I do.

"Why are *you* so fucked up?" he asks, his nose touching mine.

"It's a long story," I say quietly.

He leans back, exhaling. "Oh, Sarah."

I look up at him and a lone tear escapes down my cheek.

He wipes it away and kisses me. It's a gentle kiss—a kiss of sheer kindness.

He reaches into his pocket and pulls out his cell phone. "Bring the car to the front now," he says, never taking his eyes off me. "Thank you." He stands and grabs my hand. "Come on. I'm taking you home."

I bristle. He banged me, and now it's time to send me packing—is that it?

He shakes his head, obviously bewildered by my facial expression. "To *my* home, you big dummy. I'm taking you home *with me*."

The streetlights flash on his face as we sit together in the backseat of the limo, our bodies close and our hands clasped. He holds my hand with supreme confidence, like I'm his. I like it. I want to be his. Even if I wanted to freak out again (which I don't) I couldn't possibly muster the effort—not with him holding my hand like this.

I hate the way I reacted in the bathroom. I shouldn't have done that. I ruined what should have been an incredible moment. I need to just turn off my brain and go with the flow and see where this leads. No more self-sabotaging. He was right.

I don't know what's going to happen next, it's true—but I don't need to know. We're going to his house, and that's exactly where I want to go. I want to see him naked. I want to touch every inch of him. I want to find out everything there is to know about him. I want to see his family pictures. I want to see how his house is decorated. I want to see if he's neat and tidy or a slob. I want to see what's in his fridge. I want to make love to him in a bed. And I want to turn the tables on him and lick every inch of him 'til he begs me for mercy. Yes, for some reason, I want to bring him to his knees and thwart his every strategy.

I shudder at my inner monologue. Where are these thoughts coming from? I never think this way, about anyone. I don't understand what he ignites in me. It's something primal—not controlled by conscious thought. I want him. I want to know what makes him tick and deliver it to him, whatever it is. That's just not like me. Usually, if I'm being perfectly honest, when it comes to sex, I could take it or leave it. So why am I so sexed up around him?

He turns and sees me staring at him. He squeezes my hand. "That wasn't how I wanted tonight to go."

"I thought it went pretty frickin' well."

He glances up at the driver. "Put the partition up, please," he says, and immediately a dark barrier rises up. Jonas squints at me. "Of course you did. Sex for you is all about one thing—getting the guy off. And as fast and hard as possible because, without the possibility of an orgasm for yourself, that's how you get validation. Totally unacceptable." His tone is matter-of-fact.

My mouth is hanging open. "Do you always say whatever the heck you think, no matter how rude?"

"I'm not being rude. I'm being honest."

I stare at him.

"But no, I don't. Only to you—and also to my brother Josh."

"Because that was pretty damned rude."

"Maybe. But true."

I consider for a moment. "Making you want me, forcing you into me, even though you wanted to hold out, even though that wasn't your plan—yes, that turned me on, I admit it." I sigh, remembering that glimmer I felt as Jonas slammed into me. "God, that was hot. I liked feeling like you were powerless to resist me."

"Aha." He smirks. "I'm not the only one with a raging God complex."

I laugh. "Apparently not." We smile at each other.

"Well, there's only room for one god in this limo," he says. "And it's me." He pauses. "And, yes, I *am* powerless to resist you, by the way."

"Good," I say. There's a beat. "Sex for you is all about getting the girl off," I challenge. "What's the difference?"

"There's a big difference. I want to get you off, true—but only because it gets *me* off. I mean, it *physically* gets me off. I'm quite selfish—as I'm innately wired to be. But you? Your only pleasure is derivative."

I look at him, not sure I understand his meaning.

"You're sexually co-dependent," he clarifies.

I glare at him. "No I'm not. I get off, too—just not culminating in an orgasm. What we did back at the restaurant was incredible."

"You don't even know what you're talking about. You've come to expect nothing for yourself sexually, so you don't even try anymore. You get the guy off as fast and hard as possible to prove your sexual worth, end of story."

"You really are rude, you know that?"

He shrugs. "Honest."

"I really don't like how you've turned everything around and made it all about *me* being the weirdo here. Maybe you've forgotten—I've read your application, Jonas. You're the one who's fucked up, not me."

"Absolutely, I'm fucked up. No argument there. You don't even know the half of it." He looks out the window, thinking. "I know I am," he says softly. He turns back to me. "But you're totally fucked up, too, and you don't even know it."

"So you're some sort of expert in psychology, huh?"

"Yeah, you could say that."

Oh. That's not the answer I expected. "Really?"

"Well, not technically. But I went through years of forced therapy as a kid—most of it total bullshit, of course—and I picked up a thing or two." He looks out the window again and the flickering lights illuminate his perfect features.

My stomach drops. Why was he forced into therapy as a kid? What the hell happened to him when he was seven?

He doesn't give me the chance to broach the topic. "And, in recent years, I've acquired what you might call a healthy interest in female psychology." He turns back to stare right into my eyes. "And sexuality."

I'm turned on and I'm sure my face shows it.

"I've read everything I could get my hands on about the female brain, female psychology, the female sexual experience. Female sexuality is definitely my favorite topic." His eyes blaze. "Fascinating stuff."

I don't know why this revelation titillates me, but it does. "Well, then, surely you know that for a woman, sex is about so much more than the big 'O.' It's the whole fantasy of it—more mental than physical."

"Yeah, yeah, yeah. But with all due respect, My Beautiful Intake Agent, you're not qualified to give me this speech, whether it's true or not." He unclasps his hand from mine and places his hand confidently on my thigh, under the hem of my dress, as if he's been touching me for years. "It's like you're trying to tell me green beans taste better than chocolate—but you've never had a single bite of chocolate in your whole, deprived life."

I can't help but laugh. He's got a point.

He smirks. "You're one of the shackled men in Plato's cave."

I raise my eyebrows. *Please explain.*

He smiles and begins lifting the hem of my dress to reveal my bare thighs. He exhales a loud breath at the sight of me. "Oh God, your skin," he whispers. "I can't resist it." He reaches out and gently caresses the tender skin on the inside of my thigh, causing every hair on my body to stand at attention. When he sees my eyelids go heavy with desire, he smiles at me.

I bite my lip.

"Plato wrote an allegory about some men sitting in a dark cave, all of them shackled together in a line, facing the cave wall."

I nod. *Go on.* With the story. And the touching, too.

His hand travels back down my thigh and begins caressing the sensitive skin on the inside of my knee. "There's a line of men sitting shackled in a dark cave, facing a cave wall. A bonfire rages behind them, but they've never seen it, since they've been shackled and forced to sit facing the wall their whole lives." Now his hand works its way back up my leg, up my inner thigh.

I let out a shaky breath, anticipating where his hand might travel next.

"The only thing the shackled men have ever seen is the cave wall—their own shadows dancing in the reflected firelight. Of course, since they don't know any better, they think the reflected light and dancing shadows are the ultimate in beauty."

I can instantly see where this is heading. But a man explaining Plato to me while touching the inside of my thigh is by far the sexiest thing I've ever experienced, so I'm not about to interrupt him. Now his hand moves farther up my leg, toward my G-string.

He's staring at me, his eyes like laser beams.

I'm trembling.

"One of the men in the cave, a guy at the end of the line, breaks free of his shackles." His voice is low and measured. His hand caresses the crotch of my panties, making me jump.

I close my eyes and exhale, trying to control my breathing.

He brings his lips right to my ear as his hand continues caressing the fabric of my panties, right over the exact spot that's throbbing for him. "The one who's broken free of his shackles turns around for the first time and sees the bonfire behind him," he whispers. "And he cries at the sight of it. He didn't know anything could be so bright and beautiful."

He kisses my neck as his hand forcefully yanks at the waistband of my panties. I lift my hips so he can get them off. He quickly succeeds in guiding my panties all the way down and I kick them off. My heart is racing. He licks my neck and his hand returns to the inside of my thigh, slowly working its way back up again. Oh my God, I'm on fire. My hips are writhing beneath me, straining toward him, yearning for him to penetrate me.

"I've unshackled you, My Magnificent Sarah," he whispers in my ear, "but you've only seen the bonfire." His hand reaches my wetness. His finger gently enters me.

My body jerks involuntarily toward him, aching for him.

He leans into my mouth and kisses me as his fingers work in and out of me. I moan loudly. He pulls his mouth an inch away from mine, but his fingers continue their exploration.

"The man sees a distant light at the mouth of the cave and he runs toward it." His fingers expertly plunge in and out of me, owning me, making me slick and wet and hungry for him. "And when he finally bursts out of the cave, he's blinded by the light, by the beauty he beholds."

His fingers find the most sensitive spot on my entire body, and I cry out.

He moans. "He sees sunlight and blue sky outside the cave." His voice has become ragged. He presses his body against mine. His erection bulges into my leg from underneath his pants.

"Fuck me, Jonas," I say, shocking myself. I've never uttered these words to anyone in my life.

He nips at my ear as his fingers move expertly back and forth from my tip to my wetness and back again. Oh my God, I've never been so turned on in all my life.

"The man sobs at the sight of the beauty outside the cave." His fingers are making me delirious. "He didn't know such beauty even existed. Oh, Sarah." His voice is hoarse.

His fingers are massaging me like no one ever has. My entire body ignites into sudden flames.

"Fuck me," I whisper urgently. "Please." Oh God, he's so good at this. I've never been touched like this, ever. Not by anyone, not even myself. My body is writhing and gyrating in syncopation with his magical fingers. "Now, Jonas."

"You want me to fuck you?" he asks, his voice suddenly edged with aggression.

"Yes," I say hoarsely. "Right now."

"No," he says, his voice steely. "We're gonna do things my way. No more hard and fast for you."

"Please, Jonas," I moan. "Now." I lift my hips toward him, begging him to enter me.

"No." His fingers slide back into my wetness and then to my clit again with fervor, and back and forth again, back and forth. "I'm gonna take you to the mouth of the cave, baby. No more bonfire bullshit. No more fucking around."

He kisses my mouth, and I respond with voracious enthusiasm.

"Now," I beg again. I'm whimpering. "We'll do it your way next time." I feel like I'm going to scream if he doesn't give me what I want. I can't contain this rising tide of hunger inside me. "Now, Jonas."

"No," he says. "You want the bonfire, but I'm gonna give you the true light. You're gonna surrender to me whether you want to or not."

"Please," I beg. I'm desperate. Pathetic. What if my body can't come, no matter how golden his tongue? Right now, I'm not ready to find out. I just want to enjoy this delicious moment with this amazing man. Suddenly, I'm pissed. He's not in charge here. He doesn't get to tell me how we're going to do this. He doesn't get to call the shots. I grab at his crotch and his hardness makes me moan. "If you won't fuck me, then I'm gonna fuck you," I whisper.

He grunts and I feel his body shudder. I know he can't resist me, despite his big talk. I know it.

I frantically unzip his pants and his shaft springs toward me.

He tilts his head back and groans as I grip his full length. Quickly, before he can change his mind, I lean down and take him into my mouth. His entire body jerks and shudders with pleasure. He lets out a long, strangled groan. He touches the back of my head and grabs at my hair, moaning. "Sarah," he mutters. "Not fair."

My crotch is throbbing. I reach down and touch myself as I take his hardness into my mouth, all the way to the back of my throat. My nipples are so hard they hurt. He moans again, and suddenly, there's that faraway glimmer again, deep inside me, just like the last time—like a butterfly fluttering inside me far, far away. I can't stand it. I can't wait anymore. I pull away from him and swing my leg over his lap, briefly positioning his tip at my wetness, and then I slam myself down on top of him, as hard as I can, plunging him into me.

We both cry out at the same time. He shudders and immediately begins thrusting into me and grabbing my ass like it's his lifeline. I rest my palms on the limo ceiling and ride him like he's a bucking bronco, craning my neck so my head won't bang into the ceiling. My body's never felt this much pleasure, ever.

"Sarah," he mutters again, his thrusting becoming savage.

"Harder," I gasp. "Harder."

He complies, making me gasp. His hand reaches down to my clit as his shaft burrows into me and I throw my head back, yelping. I'm not myself right now. I'm a wild animal—a wild animal trapped in the back of a limo—trying to break free. Sweat is beading down my back. My head is spinning. I grab the back of his neck as I ride him and pull him to my mouth for a voracious kiss. I'm riding him as hard as my body will tolerate, gyrating, my nerve endings exploding as he so expertly touches and fucks me.

He pulls at my hips, forcing himself into my body even farther. Oh God, he's deeper inside me than anyone's ever been. I look down at him, and his eyes are closed, his face enraptured. Those butterfly wings are fluttering inside me, rising and gaining strength. I lean down and lick the entire length of his beautiful face, groaning and slamming my body down onto him as I do.

"Oh God," he moans. He gasps as his body finds its release.

My heart is racing.

I'm trembling.

Sweat is dripping down my back.

But my ache hasn't released. I'm still throbbing. Yearning. Desiring.

The faraway fluttering begins to recede.

It's gone.

After a moment, we unravel from each other. I look out the window and realize we're parked in front of my student apartment complex. What the hell? How long have we been sitting here? Thank God the windows are tinted. Thank God the driver didn't open the door to announce our arrival—or maybe he did. Who the hell knows? I wince at the thought. And why are we here, anyway? I thought Jonas was taking me to his house?

"That was the last time we do it your way," Jonas says evenly. His voice is surprisingly stern. "You keep hijacking me against my will—and against your higher interest."

I shrug. It sure seems like he's enjoying getting hijacked. And I'm sure enjoying doing the hijacking—turning the tables on him and making him abandon his strategy. Fuck his strategy. What if an orgasm just isn't something my body's designed to do? Why must he be so damned focused on that one small thing? Why can't we just keep doing things this way—my way—and not worry about it one way or another? If it's meant to be, it's meant to be. But we don't have to *try* for an orgasm, do we? Why set me up for failure—and set him up for frustration and disappointment?

"From here on out, we do things my way," he says.

I'm noncommittal. "I think my way has worked out pretty damned well."

"Of course you think that—but you're clueless, remember? You're too fucked up to know that what you *want* is different than what you *need*."

"That's my line," I mutter.

He smiles. "I know."

"Are you always this rude?" I ask.

"Only with you." He touches my face and sweeps my hair away from my eyes. His eyes have that mournful look in them again. "Sarah." He kisses my neck. "You make me crazy." His lips graze my neck. "I can't resist you."

"I don't want you to resist me."

"I know. But you *should* want me to. If you'd just let me do things my way, your body will thank me."

"I think maybe you're too focused on the whole orgasm thing."

He takes my hand and kisses it. "You don't even know what you're missing. Just wait 'til your eyes behold the sunlight outside the cave, My Magnificent Sarah."

What if I can't deliver what he wants? How long will he keep trying? Certainly not indefinitely. But how long? A night? Two? What if he does his damned best—what if I let him lick me with his allegedly masterful tongue—and absolutely nothing happens? What then? Then I'll know for sure I'm a lost cause. Men have tried before him and they've failed. Could he possibly be so much better at it than anyone else?

"We do things my way next time," he commands. "And after that, we can do it again any way you please." He kisses the ring on my thumb.

I close my eyes, enjoying the feel of his lips on my fingers. "I'm just saying women don't always need to have—"

"No," he cuts me off. "Stop. When you finally know what the fuck you're talking about, then I'll sit and listen to you talk all day long about how sex isn't about coming, and that men and women are wired differently, and that women are more about the mental and emotional blah, blah, blah. Okay? But until then, I'm in charge. No more hijacking. No more going for the jugular. No more fucking around."

I don't know whether to pout or smile. I'm nervous and excited and anxious and exhilarated at the same time. "I think I was close," I whisper.

He pulls back sharply from me, his eyebrows arched. "When?"

I'm surprised at his sudden excitement. "Both times. I felt something new. Like I was just about to tip over the edge of something." I close my eyes, trying to recall the faraway glimmering I felt, especially just now in the limo.

"Oh man, we're close," he breathes. "If I'd only stuck with my strategy." He runs his hand through his hair, thoroughly energized. "You're wired so fucking hot and you don't even know it, Sarah. When I finally light your fuse, it's going to be the Fourth of fucking July."

I guess there's only one way to find out. "Okay," I say. I want nothing more than for him to be right about that.

His smile spreads across the entire expanse of his beautiful face.

I look out the window at my building. There are students lingering out front, chatting.

"I thought we were going to your house? Why are we here?"

"We're just stopping here so you can pack a bag. You're spending all night with me." He rubs his hands together like a villain in a James Bond movie. "I'm finally gonna get to see your beautiful skin on my crisp white sheets."

Chapter 15

Jonas

I'm sitting on my couch, waiting for her to come out of my bathroom, and, if my rambling thoughts are any indication, possibly spiraling into madness, too. I think I'm addicted to her. I can't get enough. Everything she does, everything she says, everything she *is*—she's perfect. She's better than any fantasy. I can't resist her. One command from her, and my plans are shot to hell. I never, ever planned to fuck her in the bathroom at the restaurant. Or in the limo. Jesus. But I'm not complaining, believe me. Missing out on either one of those delicious fucks would have been a goddamned travesty. And, anyway, it's clear to me now she has to get the crazy out of her system before she'll be anywhere near ready to start her long, slow, sweet surrender. She's like breaking a wild horse. I've just got to let her jump and buck and jerk a little before I try to throw a saddle on her. And that's fine with me—every second with her has been sheer perfection. Except for when she cried. Damn, I never want to see her cry again as long as I live. Just that one tear and I was wrecked.

So it turns out she's got daddy issues after all. I've always been drawn to the girls with daddy issues. I'm so predictable. She didn't say that, of course, but I knew her whole story the minute she talked about helping battered women—could see it playing in my head like a movie. I guess her daddy did quite a number on her and her mom. Bastard.

I sigh. I've really screwed things up so far. I had it all worked out in my head exactly how the night was going to go—she was going to be Meg Ryan in *Sleepless in Seattle* or some other fairytale like that—but damn, I didn't count on her being so damned bossy and taking control. Orgasm or no, that woman fucked my goddamned brains out. It turns out she's got a little crazy inside of her—and, damn, I love me a little crazy. Damn. Damn. Damn. When she turned all bossy on me, when she turned into a fucking she-devil on me, it was so hot. Sure, I came into the night with my big strategy—and I'm gonna get back to it, I swear I am—but who could resist her? Who'd *want* to resist her? Her ass, oh my God—her ass. It's the best ass I've ever laid hands on. And her eyes. When she looked at me like she was going to pounce on me ... "Fuck me," she said, right in my ear, and my head just about exploded. When she said that, that's when I knew for sure: she's perfect.

But I've got to take control now, as pleasant as it's been having her boss me around. From now on, I have one purpose in life. I am on this earth to make this woman experience pure ecstasy, no matter what. And to do that, I've got to show some goddamned restraint around her for once. She needs a slow burn. She needs to feel safe. She needs to feel an emotional connection—because, of course, she was right, women are all about the emotional connection. But the weird part is, I honestly *do* feel an emotional connection with her. When I asked her about herself at dinner, I genuinely wanted to know the answers to my questions. If she'd had a fucking Maltese named Kiki, I actually would have listened to her talk about it all night long—and I would have *cared.* (Though, I was relieved as hell to find out she didn't have a Maltese named Kiki.) If I'm being honest, I already feel more emotionally connected to Sarah than I ever felt toward any of my girlfriends, even Amanda—and I lived with Amanda for almost a year. I've never felt so open, so comfortable as I do with her. It's like I can do no wrong with her. No matter how big an asshole I am, no matter how disgusting the truth is, no matter how honest I am, no matter how twisted I am, she's turned on by it. She actually likes the real me. Go figure. It's addicting.

And, holy fuck, the real Sarah turns me on like nobody ever has. When she said she didn't go to law school for the money, oh man, that was too much. I wanted to take her right there on top of the table. And when she got all pissy about me joining The Club for a full year, I *liked* feeling ashamed about it, because she was right. I *liked* feeling like I should be a better man for her. Hearing her talk about the one-month membership guys like they're all John Cusack holding up a boom box in *Say Anything* was pretty adorable, even though the whole idea is ridiculously naïve. Of course, a guy joining for a month is a diehard romantic, looking for love, *of course* he is. He couldn't possibly have signed up for a month simply because he didn't have enough cash for a longer term. But, hey, if she wants to see romance in the one-month guys, so be it. I think her optimism is cute.

And, hell, maybe she's right. What do I know? Josh certainly has all the money in the world, and he only signed up for a month—

and that guy's as big a romantic as there ever was. At any rate, when she told me about that software engineer guy, when she defended his honor like he was a knight in Camelot, she was so sweet—so idealistic. So *kind.* Damn, that woman just gets me off.

My mind is racing. I think I'm losing my mind. I exhale. I have to calm the hell down. I just have to show some restraint and slow things down and stop letting her bring me to my knees every two seconds. Because, right now, I want to make her come more than I want to breathe—and to do that, I've got to take control of this situation.

The door to the bathroom finally opens and Sarah comes out.

"Do you want to finish the tour?" she asks.

"Sure," I say. "There's not much to see."

She laughs and rolls her eyes. "Ah, rich people. So funny."

I look around. By my standards, my house is modest. I mean, don't get me wrong, it's got all the important amenities—a home theatre, a gym, a killer view, a pool, a gourmet kitchen, a wine cellar. But, seriously, it's not outrageous. It's understated. Normal. No bowling alley or basketball court. Pretty modest square footage. Clean lines. Well, yes, the artwork on the walls is spectacular—but I like art. Always have. And, yes, all the floors and finishings are premium, some of the marble is even imported from Italy, but that's only because a person should surround himself with beauty whenever he can. Beauty feeds the soul. I look around, seeing my place through her eyes.

"You know what? Fuck the tour. Are you hungry?"

"I am," she says. "I've worked up an appetite tonight." She blushes.

"Yeah, and it doesn't help that I deprived you of the last five courses at dinner."

"*I* deprived *you,*" she says. "I think that's a more accurate summary of tonight's events." She smiles. "You're not the only one with a God complex, remember?" She shoots me a smart-ass wink.

Oh man, she's delicious. "Let's see what we've got in the kitchen," I say.

"Do you have an apple? Or maybe PB&J?" she asks. "I'm easy to please."

She catches my eye and suddenly we both start laughing. Oh yeah, she's easy to please, all right—sure she is. The girl who's never climaxed once in her entire life is as easy to please as falling off a log.

"Well, with food, anyway." She laughs again, reading my thoughts. For a minute, conversation is impossible because we're both laughing so hard.

When her laughter dies down, she wipes her eyes and throws her arms around my neck. "Thank you for the best night ever." She lays an enthusiastic kiss on my cheek.

I nuzzle into her ear. "I still can't believe I found you."

"Pretty crazy, huh?" She disengages from me. "I never thought in a million years I'd be standing here with you—the woman wizard himself."

I pull out the peanut butter and jelly and bread and place them on the counter, and she immediately gets to work. "You want one?" she asks.

"No," I say. "Gross."

"Then why do you have this stuff in the house?"

"Josh. He could live on PB&J and be happy forever. He's gross like you."

She smiles. "Does he come visit you a lot?"

"About once or twice a month, usually. We hike and climb. He comes to Seattle on business, ostensibly, but then we always wind up playing hooky for a few days to climb. We're planning to climb Kilimanjaro next year."

Her sandwich is made and she takes a big bite. She's adorable.

"You want milk with that? Oreos?"

"Oh, yes, please, Oreos with milk. Mmm."

"I was kidding. You know, making fun of the whole little-kid-food thing?"

Her face falls. "Oh."

"That crap will kill you, you know."

She shrugs. "I love Oreos."

I make a mental note to buy Oreos as soon as humanly possible. I don't want to see that look of disappointment on her face ever again if I can help it.

"Kilimanjaro, huh?" She looks wistful for a minute. "Africa."

"Yeah. Should be pretty epic. Water?"

She nods. "Thank you."

I grab two glasses from the cabinet and fill them with ice water. She's already sitting at my kitchen table and I join her. When I place the water in front of her, she thanks me politely and smiles.

"Have you been to Africa before?" she asks.

"Several times," I say. "You?"

"I've never been out of the country."

"No?"

She shakes her head.

"No passport?"

She shakes her head again.

"Well, jeez, you've got to have a passport. I'll have my assistant send you the paperwork. We'll get it expedited."

"Why on earth do I need a passport—and expedited no less?" Her cheeks are suddenly flushed.

"So you can take off on a moment's notice. You never know."

"Well, shoot. That's what's been keeping me from jetting off to Africa on a moment's notice?" She laughs. "Damn." She's playing it cool, but the sudden rosiness in her cheeks is unmistakable.

I laugh.

"I like it when you laugh," she says.

I tilt my head and look at her. I don't normally laugh this much.

She sighs and leans forward onto her elbow. "I bet being so damned good looking can be hard on you sometimes." She takes a big bite of her sandwich.

I raise my eyebrows at her. I can't tell if she's teasing me or not.

"Nobody around you can ever concentrate. Everyone around you turns into a swooning zombie, lost in a daze of idolatry." She pauses. Her voice shifts to something unmistakably serious. "Nobody tells you anything but what you want to hear."

Yeah, she's definitely serious—at least about that last part.

"I'm totally serious," she says, reading my mind. "*Attractive* people have it easiest—the ones smack in the middle on the good-looks spectrum. People are drawn to them and like them because they're not threatening. On the other hand, people who are supernaturally gorgeous like you, the ones on the very edge of the looks spectrum, they're on the wrong side of the tipping point."

"What tipping point?"

"That point when people start resenting and projecting and feeling threatened. They start thinking you're a jerk when you're not. Or that you're self-absorbed when you're not. Just because you're so ridiculously gorgeous. They judge you differently."

"Yeah, but what if I *am* a jerk and self-absorbed?"

"Oh, well, then, in that case, you're just plain screwed."

We smile at each other.

"But seriously, you probably have to bend over backwards to make people think you're not a total and complete jerk. It's got to be exhausting."

"So you feel sorry for me for being attractive?"

"No, I told you—you're not *attractive*. *I'm* attractive. You're jaw-droppingly gorgeous." She purses her lips.

I lean forward. "You're jaw-droppingly gorgeous, Sarah." Is it possible she really doesn't know that?

"Gah, I'm not fishing for a compliment here." She sighs and squints her eyes at me. "I'm just trying to figure you out." She takes another bite of her sandwich and shrugs. "You're perfect—except for the fact that you're out screwing a different woman every night, that's a little bit imperfect. But, yeah, other than that, I can't find a fault."

I don't know what to say. She's complimented me and punched me in the gut at the same time. I'm sure my face conveys my confusion.

"I'm not trying to beat you up. It's just ... I'm having a hard time reconciling the Jonas who wanted a lifetime supply of coochie with the Jonas sitting here watching me eat a PB&J after renting out an entire restaurant for me."

Goddamn that fucking application. "Well, I think the answer is that the Jonas who wanted a lifetime supply of coochie didn't actually want a lifetime supply of coochie—he was just too stupid to realize it."

She stops chewing her sandwich mid-bite.

I sigh. "Do you think it would be possible for you to forget about my application and take me as I am, right here, right now, sitting here with you? Because right here, with you, is where I want to be. So whatever phantoms of fuckery you see floating all around me, do you think you could, maybe, possibly, just willfully ignore them, and choose to believe the man you see before you is the real Jonas? It would save us a whole lot of time."

She swallows and nods. She places her hand on her heart, as if to steady it.

"Excellent." My heart is leaping, too. "That'd be really great." I clear my throat. "Really great."

She leans back in her chair.

I stare at her, my jaw muscles pulsing.

"I'm sorry," she says.

I shrug.

"You've been nothing but incredible to me. And I keep testing you, waiting for the other shoe to drop. That's not fair."

"It's an understandable reaction, given who I am and what you know about me—and, of course, all you've been through."

She bristles.

Oh shit.

"All I've been through?"

"I mean, no, I don't know what you've been through. I'm just saying, it's understandable, considering . . ." I trail off. I'm about to come up with some bullshit backpedal to get me out of this mess, but then I remember I promised never to lie to her. "I'm just making some assumptions about you. I probably shouldn't do that."

"What assumptions?"

I clear my throat. Oh shit. Here we go. "I assume you had a real motherfucker for a father. You probably saw him hurt your mom, which had to be pretty traumatizing. I don't know if he hurt you too, physically, but, at the very least, he most certainly abandoned you—emotionally or physically or both. And if I'm right, that's scarred you and fucked you up—maybe more than you even realize—and, in particular, made it really hard for you to trust men. Probably a big reason for your ... sexual ... issues." Oh shit. I'm screwed.

She blinks her eyes several times quickly, like I just gave her mental whiplash. She's quiet for a long time.

My stomach drops. I'm an idiot. Why did I say all that? To show off? I'm such an asshole. It's too sensitive a topic. She doesn't trust me enough yet for me to play armchair psychologist with her. If the girl's got trust issues—raging daddy issues—what better way to push her away than to call her on them? Fuck.

"It's spot on," she finally says. "All of it."

My shoulders relax.

She looks down at the half-eaten sandwich on her plate. "He never laid a finger on me—but, otherwise, yeah." Her eyes lock onto mine.

I nod. My heart is racing.

She sighs. "I'm that transparent?"

"No, not at all." I shrug. She's not. For some reason, I just get her.

She bites on the tip of her finger, lost in thought for a minute. "Yeah, I definitely have trust issues," she says.

I exhale. I'm so glad she's not pissed at me. "I know. It's okay."

"I *can* trust, really I can. Just not quickly. It takes me a while. Longer than it should."

"Okay."

"And maybe you're on to something about how this all ties into my ... sexual ... issues." She tilts her head to the side. "I never put two and two together like that. But you're probably right."

I inhale deeply, trying to regulate my breathing.

"So, Jonas."

"Yes."

"Can I ask you a favor?"

"Anything."

"If, occasionally, I wig out, or kind of ... push you away, could you just not hold it against me?"

"Only as long as you keep your promise not to hold the endless parade of coochie against me."

She half-smiles. “Deal.”

“And, anyway, you’ve already wigged out and pushed me away. Repeatedly. And I didn’t hold it against you.”

“That’s true.” Her eyes search mine for a moment. “Thank you for finding me.”

“Thank you for being findable.”

She laughs that gravelly laugh of hers. “That’s not a word.”

“It is now. I’m God, remember? It shall be.”

She laughs again.

“Can I get you anything else?” I ask. She hasn’t touched her sandwich in a while.

“Yeah. Maybe can I see a picture of your family?” she asks.

That’s not what I meant. I was talking about an apple or a cracker. I pause, considering. “Sure,” I finally say. I look around. “Um, yeah.” I go into the living room, and she follows me. “Um. Here. This is Josh and me.” I hand her a business magazine from a couple years ago with Josh and me on the cover. They did a big list of the top thirty business executives in the U.S. under age thirty. Josh and I cohabitated number twenty-five on the list.

“Oh yeah, I saw this picture on your website.”

“Yeah. That’s Josh. We’re twins. Fraternal.”

“He’s awfully good looking too,” she says. “But you’re the one who knocks my socks off, by a mile.” She makes a sound like she’s licking barbeque sauce off her fingers. “You’ve got that ... darkness. A kind of melancholy in your eyes. I can’t resist that.”

I’m floored. “You see that in me?”

“Of course I do. In your eyes.”

My voice goes quiet. “And you *like* that about me?”

“Are you kidding? It’s the best part.”

Where did this woman come from? She’s everything I was looking for when I joined The Club in the first place—what I was looking for and didn’t even realize.

“Any other pictures?” she asks. “Anyone else in your family?”

I’m about to say, “Just my uncle,” but instead, I shake my head. For some reason, there’s a lump in my throat. “Can I show you another time?” I manage to say. I clear my throat.

“Of course,” she says gently. She lays her hand on my forearm.

I nod. That lump hasn’t gone away.

“You know what I want to do right now? I want to hold your face in my hands and pepper your beautiful cheeks and eyes and nose and lips with soft kisses.”

I exhale. I can’t imagine anything better than that right now.

"But seeing as how you hate peanut butter and jelly, I think that would be most unkind of me to do without first brushing my teeth."

Somehow, she's managed to make me smile, just like that. "Good thinking."

She taps her temple with her finger. "I'm always thinking, Jonas," she says. She winks.

I smirk. "That's the understatement of the year."

Chapter 16

Sarah

I'm standing in Jonas Faraday's bathroom, brushing my teeth in Jonas Faraday's sink, staring at myself in Jonas Faraday's mirror. How did I get here? Life is full of surprises; that's for sure.

I close my eyes as I scrub my teeth.

The look on his face when I asked him about his family—that deep sadness that crept into his eyes—just about broke my heart. What happened to this poor man when he was a kid? Clearly, he's not ready to talk about it with me.

From my research, I know Jonas' father, Joseph, died when Jonas was seventeen. But I didn't see anything in particular about how his father died. And, come to think about it, I didn't see any mention whatsoever of his mother. I guess I just assumed she was alive and sitting on the board of some children's hospital or planning tea parties for her local chapter of the Daughters of the American Revolution. But based on what I saw in Jonas' face just now, it's clear she's not alive and well—and whatever happened, he's deeply pained by it.

I place my toothbrush on the counter next to the sink and rinse my mouth out.

There's a soft knock on the door.

"Sarah?" he asks.

"Come in."

He does. "Will you shower with me?" he asks.

"I'd love to."

He steps right up to me like a panther, his muscles taut and overwhelming.

"But first." I reach out and take his face in my hands. "I've been wanting to do this all night long." I kiss his lips gently. It's not a passionate kiss—it's a nurturing one. A kiss that says, *No matter how fucked up you happen to be, Jonas Faraday, I still want you.*

He closes his eyes and sighs deeply as my lips skim past his lips to his eyelids, across his eyebrows, and to the tip of his perfectly sculpted nose. I bring my fingers up to his face and trace his brow line, marveling yet again at the perfect symmetry of his features.

He sighs again, melting into my touch. When he finally opens his eyes, he looks at me with such need—such earnest, raw, vulnerable need—I reach out and hug him to me like he's the lost child I've finally recovered at a busy mall.

He returns my fervent embrace and exhales into my hair.

We stand, embracing for a moment in silence. When he pulls away and looks at my face again, he looks instantly concerned.

"What's wrong?" he asks.

I shake my head. There's nothing wrong, as far as I know. I'm just finding it hard to ignore the fierce emotions swirling inside me. "Nothing's wrong," I whisper. I attempt a smile.

He disengages from me briefly to turn on the hot water in the shower.

When he turns back to me, he brushes my hair out of my eyes.

"How are you feeling?" he asks.

I shrug. "If I answer that question, my strategy for the night will be blown to bits."

He half-smiles. "I mean physically. Down there."

Down there? This from the man who spews words like "pussy" and "cunt" as easily as "hello" and "goodbye?"

"Wow, a kinder, gentler Jonas," I mumble.

He looks sheepish.

"I like it," I assure him. "I'm pretty sore," I say. "You nailed me pretty good tonight, big boy."

"Yeah." His eyes light up. "Twice."

I smirk.

"Let's recharge our batteries a little," he suggests. "Even *I* need to get my second wind. You're killing me."

"Old man," I tease.

He flashes a crooked grin. "We're not in any rush. We've got all the time in the world."

"More than two to seven hours?" I smile so he knows I'm trying to be funny. But, honestly, I'm nervous. If I'm reading this situation wrong, if this is just a one-night, Cinderella-at-the-ball kind of thing for him, I'll be crushed. Am I feeling the way every woman feels after experiencing the divine Jonas Faraday? Is what I'm feeling right now the precise "problem" he described in his application—the female inability to distinguish physical rapture from some kind of romantic fairytale? Are the feelings I'm having exactly what pushed him into The Club in the first place?

"Yeah, longer than two to seven hours," he says softly.

It's vague, yes, but, hey, it's something. I'll take it.

"All I wanna do is touch your skin. Okay? That's all for now."

I nod. Thank God. I really, really don't want to disappoint him—and, of course, faking it is out of the question—but I just don't think I've got enough gas left in the tank to attempt those butterfly flutters for the third time in one night. I'm only human, after all.

Steam is beginning to fill the bathroom and cloud the mirrors.

He reaches behind my back and unzips my dress. Unlike in the bathroom at the restaurant, he gently pulls it up, over my head, prompting me to instinctively hold my arms up over my head. When my dress is off, he surveys my body with fire in his eyes. With one swift motion, he reaches behind my back and unclasps my bra, freeing my breasts. His breath halts as he takes in the sight of them.

He bites his lip.

Without being asked, I take off my G-string and stand before him in nothing but my smile. He looks me up and down, blinking slowly, like he's trying to control himself from tackling me.

"You're incredible," he says, his voice brimming with desire.

I reach out with a trembling hand and unbutton his shirt, slowly pulling it down, off his shoulders. Holy crap, his torso is a work of art. I can't imagine how many hours he's spent in the gym to sculpt his body into such a breathtaking display of the human form. He's glorious.

I run my fingertip over the long, tattooed inscription running down the length of his left forearm. Now that I see it in person, I can tell it's written in the Greek alphabet. But now's not the time to ask him about it—now's not the time for words. And I'm pretty sure I know what it says, anyway. I run my finger down his other tattoo, too, on his right forearm—also in Greek. I don't have a guess as to what this one says, but, again, I don't need to know right now.

He reaches down, pulls off his pants and briefs, and throws them across the bathroom with gusto.

I laugh. But when he turns back to me and stands squarely in front of me, his muscles tensing and his erection at full attention, I stop laughing. Holy hell. I've never seen a more spectacular looking man. And he's looking at *me* like I'm beauty incarnate.

With a loud exhale, he grabs my hand and leads me into the steaming shower. The hot water pelts me in the face and runs down my chest as he stands behind me, gliding his hands over my wet hips, my butt, my back, nudging me with his hardness. I spread my legs slightly and brace myself for him to enter me, but he doesn't, so I turn back around to face him, the hot water cascading around us. His lips are instantly on mine, his hands on my breasts.

I wouldn't have believed it possible after the rigorous sex we've already had tonight, but I'm yearning for him again. But just when I'm about to grab his penis and guide him into me, Jonas pulls away and grabs a washcloth. He pumps some shower gel onto it and glides it across my back and down to my butt.

"Best ass ever," he whispers in my ear.

An all-consuming ache has consumed me. I want him again. I don't care if I'm sore. And I certainly don't care about coming. I just want to feel him inside me again—to be as close to him as humanly possible. I reach for his erection, but he gently guides my hand away.

I glare at him and he smiles.

He pumps some more shower gel onto his hand, and reaches down between my legs. I gasp at his gentle touch, bracing myself for more—wanting more—but he merely cleans me, ever so gently, and then pulls his hand away. He grabs the showerhead off its attachment and carefully washes the suds off every inch of my skin. When he holds the showerhead between my legs, he leaves it there for a moment, letting the warm, strong stream caress me. His kiss is becoming more and more impassioned. I lift my leg, aching for him to enter me again—and he takes the showerhead away. He turns the water off, smirking at me.

What the hell?

He exits the shower, leaving me standing there, dripping and panting. He grabs a thick, white towel off the rack.

Not at all what I expected.

With great care, he wraps the towel around me and grabs one for himself. Without a word, he takes my hand and leads me out of the shower.

What the effing hell? He actually wanted to take a *shower* in the shower?

"Slow burn, baby," he whispers, reading my thoughts. He winks. He dries us both off and leads me out of the bathroom to his bed. "Please." He motions to his bed.

I'm happy to comply. With great fanfare, I crawl onto his bed like a minx—arching my back and sticking out my butt like I'm a wildcat stalking my prey. After a moment, I swing my face back to look at him, smiling broadly.

But he's not smiling. No, he's staring at me, his eyes smoldering, his erection straining. His eyes could cut glass.

Oh man, just that look from him, and I'm on fire. I flip over onto my back and spread myself out, inviting him to join me.

But he doesn't join me in the bed.

I glance up at him.

His eyes are fixed on me.

I raise my arms above my head and spread my legs out wide. "I'm all yours," I say.

His erection twitches, but he stands stock still, not taking his eyes off me.

What's he waiting for?

He takes a deep breath and strides purposefully to his laptop across the room. "I Melt With You" by Modern English—one of my all-time favorite songs—begins playing. My heart soars. This is the last song in the world I'd expect him to play for me. I would have figured him to be a Nine Inch Nails kind of guy.

Jonas is a jungle cat. I'm his prey. He crawls slowly over to me on the bed as the singer from Modern English croons about us melting together. In a flash, Jonas' commanding body hovers over mine, his muscles bulging and tensing as he rests on his forearms on either side of my head.

The song is seducing me, swirling around me, captivating me.

"I love this song," I murmur as his lips press into mine.

"Best song ever," he says, kissing me slowly.

Here I thought he was going to fuck me like a beast again, and he wants to stop this perfect moment and melt with me? My heart is bursting.

He kisses me deeply. His hands are touching me, every inch of me.

He groans with pleasure. "Sarah," he mumbles into my lips. "Oh my God."

I close my eyes. The song lyrics, his strong body pressing into mine, his hands on my skin, his soft lips tenderly kissing me—it's all swirling around me and over me and through me, transporting me to another dimension. This might be the most sublime moment of my entire life.

"You're perfect," he says.

I can't respond. I'm floating, reeling, flying.

His hand finds the wetness between my legs and gently caresses me with the softest, barely-there touch. A soft moan escapes my mouth.

I follow his lead and touch him slowly, gently.

He lets out a long, shaky breath.

I'm suddenly anxious. This is it. He's going to try to make me come, and I know in my heart it's not going to happen right now. I'm sore and exhausted. I've never had this much sex in my life. Even if having an orgasm were possible for me, which is not a sure thing *at all,* what if my body's just not up to it right now? I'll never know if I failed because of my body's current state of exhaustion or if I'm just not capable of it, period.

"Just relax," he coos. "We're not trying to accomplish anything. We're just touching each other, that's all."

He kisses me and I wrap my legs around him, pressing my body into his.

"No pressure," he whispers, pressing against me, nipping at my ear. "We'll just make out."

I don't want this magical night to end in disappointment for him—or for me. I want to be the live wire he thinks I am. But I've never had sex three times in one night in my life, and I'm losing steam. If he finally goes down on me now—the thing he loves to do more than anything—and absolutely nothing happens for me, then what? Other guys have tried, and other guys have failed. What if I just *can't*? I want to give it the ol' college try when I can give it my best.

His hand strokes my cheek. "We'll just pretend we're teenagers tonight. We'll just make out."

It's like he can read my mind. I nod and close my eyes.

The song enraptures me.

I feel his lips on my neck and then on my breasts. He licks my nipples and I can't help but arch my back with pleasure. His tongue is warm, confident. His hands rub my thighs, my belly, and my butt (which he squeezes with enthusiasm). His fingers return to lightly caress the increasing wetness between my legs.

Another soft moan escapes me. I'm suddenly aching for him, longing for him to slip his fingers inside me—I don't care if I'm raw and sore from our previous escapades. I gyrate with pleasure, straining toward him. I reach down and gently fondle him.

He moans.

My head is spinning. I like the feel of his erection in my hand. I like the feel of his warm, taut muscles against my body. I like the feel of his lips on my body, his fingers. Oh God, his fingers have just found the exact spot that drives me wild. I moan. Lord have mercy, he is so effing good at this.

His tongue flickers onto my breasts, my nipples, and then moves south, down to my belly. His tongue visits my belly button and heads to the inside of my thigh. I strain toward the warmth of his tongue, willing him to move to the left and find my epicenter, but his tongue remains on my inner thigh, teasing me. My body is throbbing, yearning for him, apparently oblivious to the self-doubt wracking my brain.

Jonas exhales audibly. His face is perched between my legs. I can feel his warm breath on me. I spread my legs wider, yearning for him. He pauses, his mouth hovering right next to me. Oh my God, I'm throbbing for him. Forget what I said about holding off. I shift, positioning myself, making it easy for him. I tilt my hips up to him.

I'm trembling.

He sighs audibly.

I open my eyes and look up at him.

His face is hovering between my legs. His eyes are on fire. He exhales again and a puff of air teases me.

He licks his lips. He looks like a big cat right now. "There's no rush." Clearly, he's saying that more to himself than to me. He brings his hand to my clit and brushes it ever so gently again.

I shudder. But I don't want his fingers anymore. I want his tongue.

He licks his lips. "I've got to taste you, just once. I have to know what you taste like or else I'm gonna have a fucking stroke."

I nod and close my eyes. Since I first read his words describing his allegedly mind-boggling lingual talents, I've fantasized repeatedly about him using his nimble tongue on me, his somber eyes gazing up at me from between my legs.

"Just one taste."

I nod again. I can't breathe. I'm panting.

Nothing.

Why isn't he doing it? I open my eyes and look down. He's staring at me, clearly waging some kind of internal battle. "I want to lick you so bad," he says.

"So do it already. Jeez."

He exhales like a boxer about to go into the ring. He makes a big show of loosening his jaw. "This isn't it, okay? I'm gonna do this for real later when you're not sore and tired. This is just for me—because I'm an idiot and I can't resist you. Don't get a complex about it, okay? You're not gonna come right now, so don't get all fucked-up in the head about it, okay? This isn't it."

I nod. No pressure. Just a little taste. Got it.

"Don't think."

I nod again and lean back, closing my eyes. "Hit me."

Without warning, his tongue licks me in one clean swoop like I'm a melting, dripping ice cream cone on a hot summer day.

I cry out. Holy fuck, that feels good. My entire body jerks violently at the shock of it.

He makes a low, guttural sound, and then his warm tongue is penetrating me, his lips devouring me. And, just like that, I'm losing my fucking mind. Forget butterfly wings fluttering at a distance—a fighter jet just revved its engines somewhere deep inside me. Holy motherfucking shit.

His mouth abruptly stops its assault and his face is suddenly an inch away from mine.

"Taste yourself," he whispers, pressing his lips to mine. "So good." He plunges his tongue into my mouth, and my entire body bursts into flames. I've never tasted myself before. I'm barely there on his tongue, but I'm there. And I'm undeniably delicious.

The song tells me again how much he wants to stop everything and melt his body into mine.

"I want you inside me," I breathe.

I don't have to ask him twice. I wince at first—I'm pretty raw—but as he burrows deeper and deeper into me, my body relaxes and receives him. His tongue explores my mouth as his shaft begins moving in and out of me, slowly, gently.

"Is this okay?" he asks softly, his voice halting.

"So good," I breathe back. I want to melt with him—to fuse my body into his.

His skin is warm and firm and rippling in all the right places. He's kissing me, touching me, moving in and out of me. I'm lost in the moment. I'm lost in him.

The song restarts from the beginning. He must have set it to play on a loop. I bring my legs up around him, drawing him into me. His hand reaches down and touches the backs of my thighs, my butt.

He groans and thrusts into me even more deeply. "You feel so good," he says. I open my eyes to find his blues eyes an inch away from mine, gazing at me as he moves inside me, the music washing over us. He brings his hand up to my cheek as he gyrates inside of me.

Oh God, the singer keeps telling me Jonas wants to melt with me.

Electricity is coursing through my veins. My heart is leaping out of my chest, overflowing with joy and relief and sheer awe that I'm here, with him, in his house, in his bed. I hug him to me, wanting to absorb him into me. I tilt my hips forward and back in synchronicity with his thrusts, willing our bodies to become one.

"Sarah," he whispers.

I don't know what's happening between us, but I never want it to end.

He yelps and devours my mouth with fervor, his tongue mimicking the gyrating motion happening between our bodies.

That faraway fluttering announces itself again faintly. I hitch my legs up even higher around him, as I high as I can manage, trying yet another means of allowing him entry into the deepest recesses of my body. But it's not deep enough. I need to be on top.

He pulls away from our kiss and looks at me intensely. "I want to taste you again," he says, his voice hoarse.

I shake my head emphatically. "Not this time."

He touches my hair. "I want to taste you."

I shake my head. If it turns out I really am a ten-percenter, I don't want to prove it unequivocally right now—that's not how I want this magical night to end. "Next time," I breathe. "I promise." I push at his chest. "Me on top," I whisper.

His strong arms reach behind my back and cradle me. In one deft maneuver, he's suddenly on his back and I'm on top of him, straddling him, riding him, losing my mind. He's thrusting into me, grabbing at me, groping me, kissing me, groaning, and I'm gyrating my hips to take him into me as deeply as possible. He touches my clit—damn, he's good at that—and that's it. I'm a goner. I can't think, can't form words. I'm losing my mind. The pleasure's incredible.

Something is welling up inside me. I feel like an animal. I throw my head back and groan loudly. I'm losing control. I feel outside myself. I scream his name. I scream it again. Oh my God, I can't control myself. Sounds are emerging from my throat I've never made before. I'm panting. My heart is racing. My head is spinning.

"Sarah," he chokes out.

My body convulses and shudders around him, like a giant internal slap. It happens only once, but it's forceful and undeniable.

"Oh God," he groans. His body shudders and shakes from deep inside me with his release.

There's a long pause. His breathing is ragged. His muscles are glistening underneath me.

The song reaches its chorus again, telling me yet again how Jonas feels about me.

I bite my lip. There's a dull ache in my lower abdomen. I'm still throbbing. Aching. Yearning. I'm not finished.

He reaches up to my shoulders and pulls me down to his face. He kisses my eyelids, my nose, my cheeks. "So much for a slow burn," he murmurs.

I laugh.

"Oh, fuck," he says, and sighs. "You're killing me." Something flickers in his eyes I don't recognize.

"What are you thinking?" I ask.

He sighs. "That I keep fucking this up."

"Oh my God, no, this has been the best night—"

"No, trust me. I'm fucking this up. But, soon, very soon, I'm gonna taste you, and learn you, and lead you to the light."

"This is the light. Right now."

He sighs. "No, you're still stuck in the cave. I told you, I'm gonna give you *both* Valentine's Day bullshit *and* howling-monkey-sex. I haven't delivered on the second half yet."

How can that be? This was the most romantic night of my life and also the best sex I've ever had. Okay, granted, I didn't technically come—I mean, I don't think I did—I'd know it if I did, right? But I was closer than I've ever been, for sure. And, really, it doesn't matter anyway. I've decided I don't care about coming. What we just did was more than enough for me.

"As far as I'm concerned," I say, "we just had howling monkey-sex. It can't get any better than that."

His mouth hitches up on one side. "Oh, Sarah. My poor little bonfire-admiring-green-bean-eater."

I laugh out loud.

He shakes his head and sighs in frustration.

Oh, I don't like that sigh. I smile at him, but I'm uneasy. Obviously, I'm already starting to disappoint him. "I can't imagine anything better than what we just did, Jonas," I say, but even as I say it, I know my words won't convince him. The man wants what he wants. Why, oh why is he so focused on me having an orgasm? Wasn't tonight incredible? Wasn't it enough? It was for me. If I had to choose between having this day over and over, and trading it in for some mythical orgasm that "untethers" me in some vague way I can't begin to understand, I'd pick this night every single time. No orgasm could beat the way I feel right now.

We've stopped everything and melted together.

He kisses me gently. "Just you wait 'til you finally see the light outside the mouth of the cave, baby." He laughs like a villain in a cartoon. "Bwahahahaha!"

I can't help but smile. I like it when he's playful. But I'm anxious. What exactly is he promising? I wonder how long he'll keep trying before he throws up his hands and says, "Forget it."

"But right now, I gotta pee," he says.

He tilts suddenly to the side, throwing me off his lap onto the bed in a crumpled heap. He rolls off the bed and heads into the bathroom, practically whistling a happy tune as he goes, stopping first to turn off the music.

I lie in the bed, looking up at the ceiling. I've never felt so compulsively attracted to another human being like this. I don't want this to end—but what if I can't deliver his "holy grail"?

He returns and scoots next to me in the bed. He's got his laptop with him. He grins at me mischievously.

"I thought we could take a look at my very first note to you—My Beautiful Intake Agent—seeing as how it's what made you throw yourself at me and beg me to find you."

I swat him on the shoulder. "I thought you were a narcissistic jerk."

"Well, I was. *Am.* But you wanted me anyway, right?"

I nod profusely. "Yep."

"Well, then, let's enjoy my narcissistic ramblings together, shall we?" He clicks into his email account to retrieve the document. "Oh, wow," he says, his attention diverted from the task at hand. "I've got an email from The Club. Lovely."

Every hair on my body instantly stands on end.

"'Dear Mr. Faraday,'" he says, reading from the email on his screen. "'Our records indicate you have not been using your membership. Do you have any questions or concerns? Please let us know if we can assist you in any way.'"

I have a pit in my stomach.

"Fuck you," he mutters to his computer screen and looks at me, smirking. His grin instantly vanishes. "Why do you look like that?"

"Why would a sane person spend two hundred fifty thousand dollars on something and not use it?" I feel sick.

"Maybe I'm not sane."

"But they've got to be wondering *why*."

"They got their money; that's all they care about."

I keep having this unshakeable feeling—or is it a premonition?—that violations of The Club's rules don't go unpunished.

"Sarah," Jonas says, "what's wrong?"

I sigh. "I don't know. Never mind. I'm probably just being melodramatic."

"What?"

"I just keep feeling like there's got to be some sort of consequence for what I've done."

"What you've *done*? Sarah, I know you're fucked-up, but are you batshit crazy?"

I don't return his smile.

His face registers acute concern again. "You didn't defy *The Church*. You defied *The Club*. Big difference."

I'm unconvinced. I keep feeling like the shit's going to hit the fan at some point—and sooner rather than later.

"Is there something you're not telling me?"

I shake my head.

He looks wary.

"I'm sure I'm just being paranoid. Forget it." I shake it off. "Why don't you read your cocky-motherfucker-asshole message to me? I could use a good laugh."

He closes his laptop and puts it on his nightstand. "Come here," he says, pulling my naked body to his. I love the feel of his warm skin on mine. I lay my head on his chest.

He strokes my hair. "What you did was a good thing. A very, very good thing." He kisses the top of my head.

I close my eyes, enjoying his embrace, his touch.

He continues stroking my hair. "The best thing."

The anxiety I was feeling vanishes. My entire body relaxes.

"You're safe."

I can't believe his first cocky note to me—well, not to *me,* but to some nameless, faceless "intake agent" who turned out to be me—has led to this exquisite moment.

His hand moves to the curve of my lower back and stays there. "You're safe," he whispers.

"Mmm," I say. I'm drifting.

Jonas' breathing has become rhythmic under my head.

I'm floating between consciousness and dreamland, the words of that first note scrolling through my head like a news ticker: *Nice and slow ... only ever dreamed ... like no man before ... surrender, totally and completely.* I never thought in a million years I'd be lying here now with the author of those words, our naked bodies pressed together, my heart beating against his.

Jonas is asleep underneath me. His chest is rising and falling slowly.

My breathing is beginning to match his.

My mind is blissfully deserting me.

I'm falling, falling, falling. Darkness is overtaking me. But just before I fall completely, just before I slip into serene unconsciousness, one last thought—an admission, really—the exact admission he predicted I'd make in that first arrogant note—flitters across my mind: *"In addition to you being one cocky-bastard-asshole-motherfucker, you're also the man of my dreams."*

Chapter 17

Jonas

"Mmm," she moans.

It's morning. Rain is beating against my bedroom window. We're lying in my bed together, naked, tangled up in my sheets. I don't know when we fell asleep last night, but we must have. The last thing I remember was stroking her hair as she laid her head on my shoulder.

I've been awake for a few minutes, listening to the sound of the rain, enjoying the sensation of her bare skin against mine. I've had a boner from the minute I opened my eyes, but I've let her sleep. Unfortunately, my time is limited this morning—I've got something really important scheduled at the office in about an hour—and since I've decided that Jonas-gets-off-but-Sarah-doesn't is no longer acceptable from this moment forward, sex simply isn't going to happen this morning. No more quickies—no more fucking around. I'm going to do it right from now on. As I've been lying here, feeling her soft skin against mine, listening to her breathing, I've decided not to have sex with her again until I'm sure the situation's perfectly ripe for her to come. No matter what. She doesn't know what she's been missing, but I do. And I hate myself for continually leaving her standing on the proverbial curb while I peel away in a Ferrari. It's not fair to her.

I thought I'd be calling all the shots, but that's not the way things have worked out. Damn, she's bossy. I didn't fully grasp that aspect of her personality until last night. If she'd have let me be in charge like I wanted to be, I'd be lying here right now replaying her first orgasm over and over again in my mind. And giving her an encore this morning. But no. She had to take control, and I had to be a pussy-ass and let her, and now everything's all built up in her mind and she's probably got performance anxiety like a motherfucker. Now, thanks to my inability to resist her, I've got to be especially mindful about next steps. We're at a tipping point here, and I don't want to screw it up.

She's so close. Oh my God. Last night, I felt her body constrict and collapse and shudder around my cock, I'm sure of it. It was brief, just once—but it was *ferocious.* If she'd just listened to me and done things my way, she'd have come by now, I'm sure of it—but no, my crazy little bucking bronco has to go for the jugular every time. And I keep bending to her will because, truth be told, she owns me. Damn. She really does. And the worst part is that, intellectually, I know exactly what buttons she's pushing—exactly what defense mechanism is coming into play—and I *still* can't resist her. It's like I'm playing chess with a girl who tells me, flat-out, "I'm moving *here* so you'll move *there*, so I can take your king"—and yet I'm still dumb enough to move exactly where she tells me to, anyway. Am I stupid or just going crazy? I think it's the latter. I think I'm devolving into a certain kind of madness, thanks to her—an all-consuming madness. And it's fucking amazing.

She moans again and stretches her hands above her head.

Damn. If I'd only known she was that close, I'd probably have done things differently last night. I would have licked her nice and slow, just like I'd planned from the get-go. I just overthought everything, that's all. I was so worried she was too tired, and I didn't want to give her some kind of complex when it didn't work out. But I was wrong. If I'd only done it right, if I'd have let her simmer, anticipate, *yearn* like her life depended on it, it would have worked last night. She's ready to go off like dynamite. But, no, I barreled right in and fucked her exactly like she wanted. Why can't I control myself with her?

She props herself onto her elbow and looks down at me, her dark hair falling around her bare shoulders. "Good morning, Jonas," she says with mock politeness, as if we're just meeting for the first time.

"Why, good morning, Sarah," I reply, mimicking her tone. "So lovely to see you this fine morning." She looks beautiful.

She sighs audibly. "Lovely, indeed." She grins.

I glance over at the clock and grunt. Damn. I've got to get to the office. If all goes according to plan, today's meeting just might change my entire life.

She follows my gaze to the clock. She purses her lips. "I've got a class in an hour," she coos. She touches my face with the back of her hand. "But I suppose I could miss it just this once, if a tragically good lookin' guy with sad eyes and bulging biceps were in the mood to show me the 'culmination of human possibility.'" She flashes me a mischievous smile and leans in for a kiss.

I grimace. Oh my God. This is the worst timing in the history of the world. "I've got an important meeting," I say—and the minute the words leave my mouth, I know they sound like a kiss-off.

She tries to mask her face in nonchalance, but she can't hide the fire in her cheeks. She pulls away, smiling. "Oh, yeah, I should get to class, anyway." Her cheeks are blazing. She quickly begins untangling herself from me, obviously planning to exit the bed as quickly as possible and hightail it out of here.

I grab her arm. "Sarah, no."

She turns to me and feigns a lighthearted smile. "It's fine."

"Listen to me. It's this huge thing with Josh and these guys coming in from Colorado. Life changing, maybe. If it were anything else, anything at all, believe me, I swear, I'd clear my calendar for the whole day—for the whole *week*—and spend every single second with you, right here in my bed, exploring every inch of you, day and night. There's nothing I want more than to be with you."

I've never said anything even remotely close to these words to a woman before, ever—never even felt remotely *tempted* to utter words like these—but as I say them, I know they're one hundred percent true.

Her shoulders relax. "Oh," she says softly.

Jesus, did she really think I was kicking her out? Like, literally, kicking her out of my bed? After the incredible night we just had? I sigh. Of course she did, thanks to that stupid application. I wish she'd never read it.

The smile that spreads across her face this time is genuine. Unguarded.

"Yeah, oh." I push her hair behind her shoulder. "I keep telling you—I can't get enough of you. Please, please, please believe me. I'm telling you the truth—I'll always tell you the truth. Good, bad, ugly. The truth."

She bites her lip. "I can't get enough of you, either." She rolls her eyes. "Obviously."

My cock is tingling with anticipation. Well, maybe there's time, after all?

I look at the clock again. Damn. No. There's no time. I'm going to be late as it is. Sure, Josh can start the meeting without me—but I've definitely got to get over there. Josh is Mr. Personality, Mr. Close-the-Deal—but I'm the one who understands the numbers. He needs me. And this deal is the biggest deal of my life.

I sigh at my predicament. She's as ripe as a summer peach. If I licked her now, nice and slow on her sweet button, she'd go off like dynamite. But I don't have time to do it right, so I shouldn't do it at all.

"I wanna do it when we've got time. No pressure on us."

She nods. "I know."

I grin. "I've got a proposition for you."

"Oh yeah?"

"Well, it's more of a decision."

"Oh? You've made a *decision*, have you?"

"Yes."

"Enlighten me, oh, Lord-God-Master. What have *you* decided?"

"From now on, *I* don't come if *you* don't come."

She pulls back sharply. "What?"

"I don't come 'til you do. I'm all about you from now on. Period."

"Jonas, no. You can't do that. Who knows how long it will take me? No, that's just plain stupid."

"It's not gonna take long, believe me. Next time, if I do it right—when you're relaxed and we've got all the time in the world—you're gonna be dancing in the beautiful sunlight outside the cave. I guarantee it."

"But what if I don't? What if it never happens?"

"Ridiculous. You're this close." I just need to get her out of her head. I just need to take it slow—with lots and lots of prelude. "We're a team. You don't get yours, I don't get mine. I'm all-in, baby."

She twists her mouth up. "Well, damn, that's a lot of pressure."

I sigh, exasperated. "No, the whole idea is there's *no* pressure." I grunt. "How does me being all-in possibly make you feel like there's *more* pressure?"

She shrugs. "Now I've got your satisfaction to worry about, not just mine."

"Jesus, woman. You're impossible. Will you just trust me? If you'd just let me do my thing, you'd realize I'm *excellent* at sex, okay? Like, a fucking master. Aristotle said, 'We are what we repeatedly do. Excellence, then, is not an act, but a habit.' I've acquired a habit of excellence in this particular discipline—just let me do what I'm excellent at."

She laughs. "I wonder how Aristotle would feel about you quoting him for this particular purpose."

I shrug. "Excellence at doing something, whatever it is, is still excellence. I am what I repeatedly do. And so are you." I look at her pointedly, letting that sink in. "What you've repeatedly done has led you to the same frustrating result over and over. And I've let myself perpetuate your habit because I'm a weak-willed, pussy-ass who can't resist you any more than a junkie can resist smack. But I've made a decision. I'm gettin' off the dope. I'm gonna change your sexual *habit* to give you a different result." I wave my hand in flourish. "You're gonna get nothing but sexual excellence from me from now on, baby—*sexcellence.*"

She can't help but laugh.

"So here's what we're going to do and there shall be no arguments—I've had it with your bossy bullshit."

She bites her lip, trying to hold back a smile.

"I hereby grant you, Sarah Cruz, membership in The Jonas Faraday Club—and you're this club's only member, if you're wondering—the mission of which is quite simply the ultimate sexual satisfaction of one Miss Sarah Cruz, the goddess and the muse."

Giddiness instantly washes over her. Wow. It's an instant transformation. She really likes this idea.

I'm only just now formulating my plan on the fly, even as I speak, but it's got me excited, especially seeing the look on her face. Oh man, that look on her face could launch a thousand ships. Yeah, my mind is really clicking now. "You'll fill out an application—revealing all your sexual preferences—and I'll make them come true."

"Wow," she says, her cheeks blazing. "How long does this membership last?" Her eyes flicker with anxiety the second the question pops out of her mouth. She looks like she wishes she could stuff it back in.

Oh shit. My chest is suddenly banging. I didn't think about that. How long am I willing to commit to this little idea?

With each second I pause to consider my answer, her expression devolves further into anxiety. Shit. I've really stepped in it. What am I willing to commit to, right here and now? Shit. Shit. I don't know. Fuck. Why did I barrel right in without thinking this through? There's a lot riding on what I say here. I've got to get this right. I need a minute to think about this.

Her chest is heaving up and down. So is mine.

Wow, her breasts are incredible. I want to lick them. No, back to the task at hand. I glance at the clock again. Shit. I'm late for the most important meeting of my life. My entire body is tingling, not just my hard-on. I'm onto something here, and I don't want to screw it up. I offered her membership in my "club" as a total whim—an off the cuff remark. But holy shit, the look on her face—I had no idea she'd react quite this way. And now I want to deliver on whatever it is she's hoping for.

"Let's talk about it in the shower," I say.

She nods, biting her lip again. Damn, she's adorable.

The hot water is beating down on us. Clearly, she thinks I've moved this party into the shower for some good old-fashioned fuckery, but that's not the plan. No more fast and hard for My Magnificent Sarah—no more letting her go for the jugular to distract me from her insecurities. I brought her in here for three reasons. One, I'm late for my meeting—and I sincerely need to shower and get out of here. Two, I just needed a change of scenery, a minute to think things through. And, three, and most importantly, I just wanted to touch her again. I can't be expected to stare at her breasts during an entire conversation without getting to touch the merchandise.

Her skin is slick under the water. I lather her, sliding my hands down to her ass, nip at her neck, kiss her lips, nudge her with my erection. It's torture not taking things further, but it's a delicious kind of torture. Slowing things down, weaning her from what she's used to doing, might not be what she wants—but it's what she needs. I'm sure of it. So says Aristotle, and so says Jonas Faraday. And, maybe, just maybe, slowing things down is exactly what I need, too. I kiss her, the hot water pelting us, but I can tell she's on pins and needles, waiting to hear what I'm going to say about how long her membership in my club's going to last.

"A month," I whisper into her ear, and instantly regret it. Too short. Offensive. She's gonna freak out and do her self-sabotaging "push me away" thing.

But, no, not at all. In fact, her face is beaming with joy. Holy fuck, she's thrilled. What did she think I was gonna say?

She squeals. She actually *squeals.* She nods profusely and lunges at me. Her kiss is on fire. Her body is grinding into me. Oh my God, she's attacking me. "A month," she mutters.

"A month," I mumble into her lips. "And we do everything my way," I say.

She laughs in my ear. "Right," she says. "But how 'bout you have one last hurrah before my month officially starts—while you're processing my application." She grips my shaft and kneels down in front of me, grinning like a Cheshire cat.

She doesn't ask for permission. Doesn't hesitate. She takes me into her mouth and instantly begins devouring me.

My knees buckle. Holy shit.

I know I said we were gonna do things my way. But ... oh, yeah, wow ... so good. Just like that, good. Oh, she's good. She's ... oh ... she's good at this. I know I said ... She's really, really good at this. I throw my head back. Hot water's pelting me, cascading down my chest, making my skin red and hot. Her lips are slick and wet, her tongue is voracious. The water's so warm and wet, and so is her mouth.

I can't keep letting her . . .

She's talented. She's so fucking talented. And relentless. Oh fuck.

She moans.

My knees buckle.

I look down. She's got one hand on me, and one hand between her legs.

My entire body shudders at the sight.

I reach down and grab her wet hair, pushing myself into her. She moans again.

Fuck. I'm out of my fucking mind. I'm on the verge. Yes. Yes. Yes.

No, wait, no, no, no. I don't want to come yet. No fucking way. There's no way I'm letting her walk out of here today like this. No way in hell.

I pull on the back of her hair, gently, pulling her off me. She looks up at me and licks her lips. She looks drunk. "I'm not finished yet," she says. "I like it." She licks her lips again. Her eyes are blazing. "I like it, Jonas." Her hand is between her legs, working herself.

"I wanna taste you for a minute."

Her chest heaves. I don't need to ask her twice. She stands upright and leans against the marble shower wall, her hands fondling her own breasts. She lifts one of her legs onto shower ledge as an invitation.

I bend down and begin lapping at her, letting the hot water hit the back of my head and stream down my back. Holy fuck, she's delicious.

She yelps and grinds into my tongue. "Oh, yes," she says, her voice muffled by the water. "Oh, God, Jonas, yes." Her fingers are in my wet hair. Her pelvis tilts into me. She shoves my face into her. My tongue finds her sweet button. She moans. "Oh my God," she says. I lick her with a bit more pressure. Her body jerks violently. She's moaning and writhing like crazy.

Fuck. I have a decision to make. If I keep going and she doesn't come, she's going to get all freaked out and become convinced she's hopeless. Better to stop now and leave her wanting more. As a parting shot, I suck on her clit. She screams and her entire body jerks.

I stand up and instantly plunge myself into her. She's all over me, grabbing me, lifting her leg to allow me entry into her. I grab her ass and thrust into her, deeply, the hot water cascading all over and around us.

She's licking my neck, slamming her body into mine. She bites my neck and I shudder.

I reach down and fondle her as I move in and out of her and she screams at the top of her lungs.

I'm shocked. What the fuck is happening right now?

She's frantic. Her movement is urgent, primal. She's totally uninhibited. Oh God, she feels so good. It's like we were born to fit together, the two of us.

"This is the last time," I breathe. "And then it's only about you."

"Don't fucking talk about it anymore," she says. "Just fuck me."

She hops up and straddles me and I hold the full weight of her body in my arms, thrusting into her as deeply as I've ever been inside a woman. Oh God, this is good. She's riding me, up and down, her breasts heaving up and down with her motion, the hot water making her skin slick. I pin her against the shower wall, fucking her like my life depends on it.

She screams my name.

Oh God, this is heaven.

She's unleashed. She throws her head back, and it bangs into the marble wall. She's jerking feverishly against me, sliding around against me, in my arms. She's in a trance.

"Yes," she grunts. "Don't stop."

I begin thrusting harder.

"Yes!" she screams. Her body is frantic.

I'm so turned on right now, I can't ... I can't ... Oh my God, I can't even ... I thrust and thrust, holding her entire body in my arms, and she thrashes around, her wet, slick skin sliding around against mine. I'm drowning—in the hot water, in delirium, in her. She's getting ready to howl, I can feel it. Oh my God, we're close. I've never seen her like this. She throws her head back and moans loudly. She screams my name again, at the top of her lungs.

I'm on the verge. I can't hold on anymore. I'm only human.

Her entire body shudders from the inside out—once—but then stops. I can't hang on. I've never been so turned on in all my life. Oh fuck, I can't stop myself from coming. I'm gone.

She screams my name, jerking violently.

But I'm done.

She moans, disappointed.

Her body isn't shuddering any more.

Fuck, fuck, fuck!

She was so close. She was on the verge. And I couldn't hang on. I just couldn't hang on. I move to touch her clit—she's so close, I want to push her over the edge—and she bats my hand away.

Her voice is raw, almost hoarse. "It won't work now."

I drop my hand. "Fuck!" I shake my head. "Fuck. I'm sorry."

"No, no." She slides her legs back down underneath her. "I saw the light in the distance, Jonas." Her eyes are on fire. "I could see it. I ... I *visualized* it. I was running to it." She's rambling, panting, euphoric. "It's gonna happen, I know it is." She brusquely grabs the showerhead off the wall and urgently cleans herself between her legs as she chatters away. "I know what I'm doing now—I know exactly what I like. I know what to imagine, Jonas." She's beaming at me.

We step out of the shower and I begin to dry her off. She's still giddy, rambling, practically incoherent. "It's gonna happen," she says. She's effusive.

"Yeah, I know, that's what I've been telling you this whole time."

She's giggling. Did she just smoke crack or something? It's like she's high.

"Turn around," I command. She complies, and I dry off her backside with the towel. "Okay, that's it. Your membership just started. Your application has been processed and approved. Back around."

She faces me, her cheeks glowing.

"And the most fundamental rule of the club is that I'm in charge. No more bossy bullshit from you."

"What bossy bullshit? I'm never bossy."

I tilt my head and squint at her.

She laughs. She puts her arms around my neck and I place my hands on her waist.

"God, I've never had this much sex in all my life." She laughs again.

"I should hope not," I say. Even I haven't had this much sex before in such a short window of time. I'm a Sarah-addict on a binge.

She closes her eyes, remembering something. "My body was, like, out of control."

"You were on fire."

"I felt *free*—like I could just let go and ... I don't know. I felt so turned-on, and my body just . . ." She squeals.

I chuckle. "You were right on the edge, as close as you could possibly be. I can't wait to push you over it next time."

"Kiss me," she says.

"Bossy."

She rolls her eyes.

I kiss her, of course. Wow, something's changed. She's like a caged animal set free.

"When can we do it again?" she asks. "I wanna do it again and again and again. As soon as possible. When is your meeting gonna be over?"

"My meeting could end right away or it could go on for days—it just depends how it's going. But you don't get to call the shots, anyway. I'm in charge from now on, remember?"

She nods.

"Say it."

"You're in charge."

"I'm serious. I'm on a mission now. I don't come 'til you do. So don't mess things up for me—I've got as much riding on this as you do."

She nods. She laughs her gravelly laugh.

"Tell me exactly what turned you on so much this last time? Was it the shower?"

She purses her lips, thinking. "No. I mean the shower was crazy-sexy, but that wasn't it. It was the *month*," she says. "Knowing it's gonna be me and you for a whole month, no matter what, made all the difference." She smiles. "The pressure's gone. Poof. No more two to seven hours hanging over my head."

Of course. *Of course*. How could I not understand how much she needed that kind of security right from the start? I put my hand under her chin and make her look at me. "We have all the time in the world."

She beams at me. "A month," she says. She nuzzles into my neck.

I want to speak, but I don't. There's something on the tip of my tongue, something that wants to blurt out of my mouth—but I'm not exactly sure what it is. Or if I'm truly ready to say it.

She doesn't seem to notice I've left something unsaid. She's still bubbling over with enthusiasm. "You're really gonna go a whole month without getting off?"

"It's not gonna take you a month."

"But, hypothetically, if it *did* take me a whole month ... you'd hold off?"

I think for a minute. There's no way I could live without getting off for an entire month. I don't know if I can make it two *days* in this woman's presence. When I made my grand proclamation, *I don't come 'til you do,* I was thinking it'd take two more tries, at most.

"Well, yeah," I say, unsure. It couldn't possibly take a month, could it? "I don't come if you don't." I swallow hard. I can't go a whole month, no way. "During sex," I clarify. "But, hypothetically, if it takes you a while, which it won't, yeah, I might have to jack myself off once or twice in the meantime."

She laughs a full-throated laugh. "There's the Jonas I know."

"But I tell you what. If I do have to jack off, I'll do it to the photo of your boob."

She laughs. "Aw, how sweet."

"So we're making a mutual promise? You're a member in my club and I'm in charge from now on?"

She nods.

"Say it. Say 'I promise you're in charge from now on, Jonas.'"

"For a whole month?"

"Yes."

She screws up her face.

"What?"

"A whole month's a long time to let you be *totally* in charge of me."

I sigh. Yet again, she's a pain in the ass. "Say it."

"Okay, okay. I promise you're in charge for a whole month."

"It's a solemn oath—you have to keep to your word. And I promise this to you: If you let me do what I'm excellent at, you'll leave the bonfire behind and dance in the sunlight outside the cave."

She giggles.

"What?"

"You and your metaphors. You're so cute."

I stare at her, annoyed.

"I'm sorry. Continue. Dancing, sunlight, outside the cave . . ."

"I'm not *cute*."

She looks at me sideways. "You really are. But please, go on. I'll be dancing in the bright sunlight outside the cave, twirling through fields of daffodils and lilies and daisies, with bees buzzing happily around me, in a state of post-orgasmic euphoria. You're so damned cute, Jonas Faraday, you know that?"

I relent and smile. Yeah, I guess my metaphors can get a little overblown at times. It's just the way my mind works—the way it's always worked. I can't help it.

She smirks. "So, how much is this membership gonna cost me, huh?" She squints at me.

"Hmm." I hadn't thought about that. Yet again, I need time to think this through.

"Let's talk about it over breakfast," I say.

"I thought you had to get to the office."

"I do. But I'm already so ridiculously late, what's another half-hour? And anyway, I can't send my baby off to school without a good breakfast, can I? It's the most important meal of the day." I wink at her and she blushes.

Chapter 18

Jonas

"An egg-white omelet good? Spinach, broccoli, sprouts, mushrooms?"

"Ah, so that's why you look the way you do."

"My body is my temple. Well, it used to be—your body is my temple now."

She flashes me a giddy smile.

I pull out the ingredients from the fridge and get to work.

We're both dressed in T-shirts and boxers, but she looks way better in my clothes than I do.

"Okay, so membership fees," I say. "Your membership can't be free, or else you won't value it—it's basic marketing psychology. You have to have some skin in the game."

"I'm definitely in favor of skin in the game." She shoots me a naughty grin.

"As long as it's yours." I glance at her thigh peeking out of my boxers under the table. "So, what I'm thinking is this." I'm doing my damnedest to keep my voice casual, playful, carefree. "How 'bout you quit your job at The Club and come stay here with me for a month."

Her mouth hangs open.

I turn back to the eggs on the stove, my heart racing. "You'll still go to your classes and study, of course, and I'll go to work and work out, of course, but, otherwise, we'll just relax and stop the world and melt with each other—in our little club."

She's silent.

I keep my attention on the food I'm making, but there are butterflies in my stomach. I can feel my cheeks blazing. "Our little club for two," I add lamely, shifting the eggs in the pan.

She's silent, so I steal a glance over at her.

She's not happy. This is not the expression I was hoping to see. I was hoping for another one of those giddy, elated expressions from her.

I try to salvage the situation. "You don't have to worry about a thing. I'll pay all your expenses—your rent, whatever you need—so you can stay here with me and just relax and . . ."

Her eyes are inscrutable.

"And be my sex slave," I add, hoping to make her laugh. Oh, that didn't make her laugh.

"I'm not gonna quit my job," she says evenly. "It's how I pay for stupid things like, you know, tuition, rent, food. I'm not with you because I'm looking for a handout."

Well, of course she's not. I didn't think that for a minute. That was a fucked-up thing to say. "Would you just listen to me? I understand all that, but I'm actually being selfish here."

She opens her mouth to protest.

"I want your undivided attention this whole month. I don't want to share you with anyone or anything. And you said you'd do whatever I tell you to do."

Her expression quite plainly says, *Not this.*

I leave the eggs cooking on the stove and sit at the table with her. "I want you here with me—not doing surveillance on every sexual deviant in Seattle who wants to fuck the Queen of England dressed up like a donkey."

She can't stifle her smile. "Hey, you read that application, too?"

I grin. "I want you here," I say softly. I grab at her thighs under the table. "With me, in my bed, at my beck and call."

Her smile widens.

I push her thighs apart. "Spread eagle."

She chuckles.

"Sarah, I just want you here with me," I say again, softly. "That's your membership fee."

She sighs. "I'm not gonna quit my job."

"You're gonna quit anyway after the school year's up, you said so yourself. So what if you quit a little earlier than you thought you would? I'll pay for everything so you can have sex with me around the clock."

She leans back. "I know you didn't mean to, but you just asked me to be Julia Roberts in *Pretty Woman*—and not the part at the end when Richard Gere comes for her in the white limo, the part at the beginning, when she's a streetwalker in thigh-high boots."

I exhale in frustration. "Sarah, I'm not treating you like a *prostitute*." I throw up my hands. "Don't you understand? I'm treating you like my *girlfriend.*"

Her eyes widen.

We stare at each other for a moment. I can't believe I just said that any more than she can. There's a long pause. Shit. What the fuck am I saying? Have I gone completely insane? A sudden panic washes over me.

She leaves her chair and sits on my lap. In a flash, she's peppering my face with soft kisses, just like she did last night in my bathroom. I close my eyes and let her lips transport me to another place. The panic that was threatening to engulf me vanishes.

"Jonas," she breathes, kissing my cheek, my ear, my eyebrows, my eyelids, my nose. I shiver under the gentle touch of her lips. "You're beautiful, you know that?" she says, still kissing me. "Inside and out."

My heart's thumping so hard, I worry it's going to knock her right off my lap.

"Stay with me," I whisper.

"I can't quit my job." Her tone makes it clear this is non-negotiable.

My heart sinks. For a minute there, I convinced myself I could stop the world and melt with her. For a month. In my house. Just the two of us. Without a care in the world. Fuck everything and everyone else. But that was just wishful thinking. Shit. I probably would have fucked it up, anyway. She probably did us both a big favor by refusing me.

"The eggs," I suddenly blurt. She leaps off my lap and I bound over to the stove.

They're okay—drier than I'd like, but still okay. Luckily, I'd left the heat on low.

I bring our plates to the table and she moans her approval.

"This looks incredible," she says. "Wow." She takes an enthusiastic bite. "Mmm. So good."

I stare at her, enjoying her unbridled enthusiasm. Even when she eats, she turns me on.

"What?" she says.

"You're so voracious."

"I've probably burned, like, eight thousands calories in the past twelve hours. And it's delicious. Wow, you can cook, boy."

"Of course."

"Not of course. I've never known a man who could cook."

"Neanderthals, all of them."

"Your mama taught you well, Jonas Faraday."

My eye twitches. I look away. I can feel color rising in my cheeks.

"Oh," she says. She exhales in frustration, like she's mad at herself.

I know her eyes are on me, but I can't look at her. I need to collect myself. I stand up. I should go in the other room for a minute. I can feel my cheeks blazing. She had me feeling so soft, so weak—I didn't have my guard up. I wouldn't normally have reacted to a throw away comment like that.

She stands up and wraps her arms around me. I start to pull away, but she insists. Her lips are on my cheek and then my lips. I return her kiss. I melt.

"Sweet, sweet Jonas," she murmurs into my lips. "Such a sad little boy."

I nod, kissing her.

"Will you tell me why?" She pulls away and looks into my face. "Will you tell me?"

I shake my head. I'm overwhelmed with emotion.

She puts her forehead on mine and sighs.

Why won't she stay with me? I just want her all to myself. I could make her feel so good, if she'd just let me. I could take the pain away.

She runs her hand through my hair. "Sweet Jonas," she says again. She takes my face in her hands.

I close my eyes.

She kisses every inch of my face again.

Jesus, I feel like crying. Why am I so weak around her? Where's the cocky bastard motherfucker I am night and day with everyone else? That cocky fucker executes high-risk-high-reward strategies on a daily basis and climbs mountains with his bare fucking hands. He's the fucker, not the fuckee. I like that guy. Why can't I be that guy around her? It's like she's discovered an unlatched window into me, and she keeps sneaking through it every time I look the other way.

Enough. I'm acting like a pussy-ass. I'm being soft. I need to pull myself together. I need to regain control.

I peel myself away from her embrace. I kiss her on the cheek and glide over to the fridge. "Orange juice?" I ask, clearing my throat.

She shakes her head slowly.

"Coffee? Cappuccino?"

"Um, yeah, a cappuccino would be great," she says softly. She sits back down in her chair. She looks anguished.

I grab a mug and press the cappuccino button on my machine. I pour a glass of juice for myself. I bring both drinks over to the table.

"Thanks," she says, her mouth tight.

There's a long pause.

Whatever weakness I was feeling a moment ago has receded. I'm back. "Okay, new idea. If you won't agree to my preferred payment plan," I say, "I've got an alternate one." I take my chair.

She purses her lips. She's looking at me like she can see right through me, like she's got x-ray vision—like my bullshit doesn't fool her for a minute. Oh yeah, I'd forgotten about her impeccable bullshit-o-meter.

"Okay," she says, wary. "What's your next brilliant idea, Lord-God-Master?" She crosses her arms in front of her. Clearly, she's ready to reject whatever I'm about to say. Well, then, I'll just have to make her an offer she can't refuse.

"I want you come away with me this weekend."

Instant elation washes over her. She tries to stifle it, but she can't. She uncrosses her arms and leans forward. Her eyes are blazing.

"We'll make it a long weekend—we'll leave Thursday." I'm putting my plan together on the fly.

Oh, wow, she's freaking out—in a good way. This is good.

"That should give us enough time to get you a passport, if we expedite it."

"We're going *out of the country*?" She's losing it. "Oh my God!" Oh yeah, she's definitely losing it. She's squealing. I like this.

I nod. "Hey, membership in this club doesn't come for free."

"Where are we going?"

"Does it matter?"

She laughs. "Not at all."

I think for a minute. I have no idea where we're going. Wait. I know exactly where we're going. *Exactly.* Yes. Oh my God, I'm a goddamned genius. "We're going to one of my favorite places in the whole world," I tell her. "And that's all you need to know." Damn, this is going to be perfect. Talk about a metaphor.

She squeals. "Wow, you drive a hard bargain, mister." She laughs—and there's that gravel in her voice I love so much. "I really hope you're better at negotiating your business deals, because from what I can see, you don't quite grasp the concept of *payment.*"

I laugh. Yeah, I feel good again. It's like my near meltdown a minute ago never even happened. I'm me again. I'm in control. "And one more thing. Before we leave for our trip, I want you to fill out a membership application for me—for the Jonas Faraday Club—describing each and every one of your sexual preferences in intricate detail."

She sighs.

"Tit for tat." I grin.

"It's not necessary," she says. She's stone-faced.

Why am I surprised she's being difficult? Nothing is easy with this woman. Why can't she ever do what I tell her to do?

"Yes, it is," I say. "I want to know everything about you, every single thing you—"

"No, no, I mean, I don't need to write it down." She shrugs. "I can just tell you my sexual preferences right now."

I'm about to protest, to tell her we don't have time for a detailed discussion right now and that, even if we did, I'd rather have it in writing so I can read and re-read her words later, alone in my bed. But she speaks before I can say anything.

"What I have to say on the topic of my 'sexual preferences' is pretty short and sweet."

I bite my lip. I have no idea what she's talking about. But she's definitely got my attention.

"My 'sexual preferences' can be summarized in two little words, as a matter of fact." She twists a lock of hair around her finger. Her eyes are twinkling. Damn, she's a good-looking woman.

She's got my full attention. I can't for the life of me predict what those two little words are going to be. *On top? Doggie style? Hard and fast?* But that's technically three words. *My way? Anything goes?*

She rolls her eyes like she can't believe I don't already know what she's about to say. "*Jonas Faraday*," she says. "My sexual preference is you, Jonas, plain and simple. *You.*" She smiles at me wickedly. "You woman wizard, you."

Chapter 19
Sarah

I pack up my books and shove them into my backpack amid the bustle of students exiting the lecture hall. I've just sat through a particularly interesting constitutional law class about fundamental rights under the U.S. Constitution versus the states' constitutions. The Supreme Court cases we discussed during class were divisive and thought provoking, and I loved every minute of the discussion. And yet, when I looked down at my notebook at the end of class, I'd doodled "Jonas," surrounded by a heart, over and over again in the margin of my notes—and I didn't even remember writing it. What am I, fourteen years old?

"You coming to study group tonight?" a fellow student asks me as he's packing up his laptop.

I pause. I don't know if Jonas is going to be done with his big meeting by tonight—he seemed really unsure of how long it would last. But even if he is, I should study tonight, anyway. I'm going to miss several classes and lots of study time during our four days away—and I already ditched class this morning, too.

"Yeah, I'll be there," I say, even though it pains me to say it. I'd much rather roll around naked in bed (or in a bathroom, or a limo, or a shower) with Jonas than analyze case precedents with my study group. But I've got to stay focused. If I can finish this year in the top ten students, I'll have my entire tuition paid for the next two years. Not too shabby. Yeah, now that I think about it, I absolutely need to study like a lunatic every available minute before our trip, just to make sure I don't fall hopelessly behind while I'm gone.

I sling my heavy backpack over my back and head out of the lecture hall. If I go back to my apartment, I'll surely break down and invite Jonas over, or, if he's still busy, lie on my bed listening to that Modern English song instead of studying. I sigh and take a sharp left toward the library.

He wants an exclusive relationship with me for a whole month? A month! Maybe I should be worried about what's going to happen in a month and a day, but I'm not. I don't care. I want him, and I'll take what I can get. When the limo picked me up for dinner last night, I thought for sure it was going to be a one-night stand—I never thought there'd be a second night with him, let alone a third or fourth—and instead the man brings me to his beautiful home and proposes an *exclusive* relationship with me for a whole frickin' month after only our first night together? And, oh my God, he wanted me to stay with him at his house. He used the word *girlfriend!* True, he was about to pass out or throw up when that word slipped out of his mouth—he's so out of his depths with all this—but he said it, and he didn't take it back. And he didn't run away. And he didn't shut down. Quite the opposite.

And on top of all that month-long-membership stuff, holy crap, I almost came. *I almost came!* Oh, I was *this* close. If he could have held out just a little bit longer inside me, if he could have stayed hard and strong and continued pumping into me and touching me like he was doing. I bite my lip, remembering. He's magnificently talented at touching me—way better at touching me than I am, that's for sure. How does he know exactly where to touch, and when, and how hard or soft? He's got magic fingers, that boy. I was a hair's breath away from total and complete rapture with him. I felt like a wild animal.

And I want to feel that way again. As soon as possible.

My heart's racing just thinking about him. Dang, I've got to calm down and get my mind in study mode.

I've reached the entrance to the library. Before I go in, I pull out my phone.

"Kat," I practically scream when she answers the phone.

"Oh my God, Sarah. You're going to burst my eardrum."

I laugh.

"What happened last night? I'm dying to hear about it."

"It was better than the best case scenario."

She squeals.

"I'm a goner, Kat. I'm so effing gone." I sigh.

"Can you meet for drinks after work?"

"Gah, not tonight. I've got study group tonight. Tomorrow?"

"Can't tomorrow. A work thing." Kat works at a PR firm.

"Wednesday night?"

"It's a date. I'm all yours," she says.

"That's what he said."

"What?"

"Yup."

"Wow. That good?" Kat's bursting.

"Better than good. Incredible. Hot. Amazing. Mind-blowing. *Romantic.*"

Kat lets out a giddy squeal.

"He's taking me away on Thursday for a long weekend—to some mystery locale *out of the frickin' country.*"

"What? Holy shitballs, girl. I'm dying to hear everything."

"Can't wait to tell you. I'll text you about Wednesday, okay? I gotta study for a bit."

I shift my backpack to find the front pocket so I can put my phone away, and it rings. I look at the display screen. It's Jonas. My heart leaps out of my chest.

"Hey," I say, my cheeks instantly hot.

"Hey," he says back. Oh, his voice. I remember his voice whispering in my ear as he made love to me.

"Whatcha doin'?" I ask.

"Thinking of you. Thinking about what I wish I was doing to you right now."

I hope he can hear my smile across the phone line.

"Where are you right now?"

"At school. I just got out of con law and now I'm going to the library to study. You?"

"Still in my meeting. It'll probably keep me busy the rest of the day—but maybe I can see you late tonight?"

What I'm about to say is going to make me sick to my stomach, I know, but it has to be done. "I've got to study all night. I really, really do."

"Maybe I could come over and help you study?" Oh, he's smirking; I can feel it.

I pause. "Here's the thing—and it kills me to say this, believe me—but I really, really have to get my work done before we go on our trip so I can run off and feel zero stress about it. I've got a lot riding on my grades." I want to slap myself for turning him down, but oh my God, I have to do it.

"I totally understand." He sighs. "You know what? It's for the best. I need you totally relaxed on our trip—and, hey, not seeing each other for a couple days will help build the delicious anticipation."

"'Build the delicious anticipation.' You're such a poet."

"Fuck, yeah, I am."

I laugh. Oh God, this man makes my pulse race like nobody else, even over the phone. But no, no, no, I have to keep my eye on the prize. Study now. Sexy time with Jonas later. I have to do everything in my power to get that scholarship at the end of the year or I'll never forgive myself.

"I really do want to see you, but I have so much studying to do."

"No, no, it's fine. No worries. You're right. I'll see you when I pick you up for the airport on Thursday morning. Our slow burn starts now, baby."

"Oh, you're cooking up another strategy?"

"Of course. And this time I'm sticking to it. I've made a solemn oath."

I smile broadly.

"I'll send a courier to your apartment with the paperwork for your passport this afternoon. Our flight leaves early Thursday morning, so we need to get your passport back by Wednesday night. Can you be home in the next couple hours to meet the courier?"

"Yeah, does four o'clock work?"

"Yep. Four o' clock sharp, okay?"

"Got it. Thank you for taking care of that. I'm excited."

"It's my pleasure." His voice lowers. "I'll be counting the minutes 'til Thursday morning."

"Me too."

"Well, I'd better get back in there. I'll send you the details about Thursday."

"Okay. Hey, Jonas?"

"Hmm?"

I'm not sure how to ask this. "Um, since we're not seeing each other for three whole days, can my month officially start Thursday?"

He pauses, not understanding my concern.

"I mean, I wanted to mark the end of my month on my calendar . . ." I don't finish the sentence. Does my month with Jonas end a month from today, or a month from Thursday? I want as much time as I can get.

"Oh," he says, suddenly understanding my concern. "Well." He's considering something. "Your membership is locked in now—no changing your mind—but your membership *period* officially starts on Thursday morning when I pick you up for the airport." His voice is oozing with reassurance.

I exhale in relief. "Sounds good."

"And, hey, how about this—any days we're apart won't count toward the month. Good?"

My cheeks hurt from smiling. "Good. But that'll make it kinda hard to mark the month on my calendar."

"Well, I guess you just won't mark it, then."

We're both silent on the line, but I'm sure he's smiling as broadly as I am. My heart is soaring. Jonas doesn't want to envision the end of this any more than I do.

"We've got all the time in the world, baby," he whispers.

"Okay," I whisper. My eyes are suddenly moist.

"We've got plenty of time."

"Okay," I say again, lamely. "Talk to you later," I manage.

I can hear his humongous smile on his end of the line. "Bye, baby. I'll call you later."

My doorbell rings at four o'clock on the button.

I open the door to find a delivery guy holding a medium-sized box and a middle-aged woman in a post office uniform standing in my doorway. Both of them are smiling broadly at me.

"Sarah Cruz?" the courier guy asks.

"Yes, that's me."

"Here you go." The guy hands me the box in his hands. "I'll go get the rest," he says. He rushes off.

The rest?

The woman in the post office uniform is holding some forms. She's got kind eyes and skin the color of a Hershey's kiss.

"Hi, Miss Cruz. I'm Georgia. I'm here to help you fill out your passport application and get it processed as quickly as possible."

"Wow, thank you. Yes, come in." I show her to the kitchen table, where I put the box down.

I offer her something to drink, which she gratefully accepts.

"I didn't know the post office made house calls. Thank you so much."

"Oh no." She laughs. "We don't make house calls—but anything for Jonas." She smiles like we're sharing some sort of inside joke, even though I have no idea what she's talking about. Why "anything for Jonas"?

"He was so excited to make this happen." She smiles again. "I told him there's no way you're gonna get the passport back in time without a little nudge from me on the inside—and, honestly, I was thrilled to finally get to do a favor for *him* for a change."

"Oh, you and Jonas are friends?" This is already abundantly clear, but it's so unexpected, I can't help asking the question nonetheless.

A look of pure gratitude, or maybe even love, flashes in her eyes. "Jonas is a godsend." She smiles wistfully, but then quickly looks at her watch. "Okay, honey, we're really cutting this close." She spreads out the papers. "Let's do this."

I'm floored. Jonas is a godsend? I'm dying to know more. But she keeps looking at her watch anxiously, so I don't ask her to explain.

The courier returns with several vases of flowers—a ridiculously excessive gift considering the "Valentine's Day" roses already crowding every countertop and dresser and table of my apartment. The courier places one of the vases on the table next to me, and I smile from ear to ear when I see what flowers Jonas has selected this time—daffodils, lilies, and daisies—the exact ones I named when he painted his poetic picture of us basking in the post-orgasmic light outside Plato's cave. I can't help but giggle.

Despite how stressed she must be about getting my paperwork done in time, Georgia flashes a wide smile when she sees the flowers. "Jonas," she says, shaking her head, as if this is exactly the kind of thing she'd expect from him.

Why? Why would she expect such a romantic gesture from Jonas?

She draws my attention back to the forms. "I'm sorry to rush you, but we're really short on time."

"Oh, yes. Sorry." I blush.

The delivery guy returns with bunches of helium balloons emblazoned with messages like "Celebrate!" and "Welcome!" and "Congratulations!" which he releases like doves into my small apartment.

Georgia laughs with me about these latest gifts from Jonas, and then she proceeds to usher me through completing the forms and taking my headshot in front of my white wall pursuant to precise passport specifications.

"I'll head back to the post office and get this submitted for processing right away," she says, gathering everything up. "You should have it back just in the nick of time on Wednesday."

"Do you have far to go?"

"No, not too far. I work at the downtown branch. I'll get everything taken care of in time."

"Thank you so much."

"You're welcome," she says, running out the front door. "Have a great trip."

"Hey, Georgia?"

She turns around, clearly anxious to get going.

"Did Jonas happen to tell you where he's taking me?"

"Yes, he did." She beams at me. "But I'll never tell." She winks and leaves.

I look around. Wow. My bursting apartment looks like a flower shop. Or a Hallmark store. Or maybe the aftermath of a Valentine's Day-baby-shower-birthday-housewarming-graduation barf-o-rama. It's nuts.

I sit down in front of the box with a pair of scissors, my pulse racing, and open it. I pull out the bubble wrap on top and peek inside.

"Oh gosh," I say out loud. There's a package of Oreos. I pull it out, grinning. Oh, Jonas. I peek inside the box again. Two envelopes—a tiny one with something bulging inside it and a flat, letter-sized envelope. I open the flat envelope first. It contains a typed note:

"My Magnificent and Beautiful and Funny and Sweet and Classy and Dirty and Irresistible and A-Little-Bit-Crazy and Smart and Sexy-as-Hell and Ass-Kicking and Insightful and Oh-So-Talented and Fucked-Up (like me) and Tasty (holy fuck!) Sarah,

"Congratulations! Your membership in the Jonas Faraday Club has been approved! Your sexual preferences have been duly noted and meticulously vetted against our sprawling database of potential candidates and, lucky you, you've been assigned one, and only one, uncannily compatible match: Jonas Faraday. Yes, it's true! From here on out, Jonas Faraday will make it his mission (from God, of course) to deliver unto you sexual satisfaction and ecstasy beyond your wildest wet dreams. In other words, you'll be getting nothing but *sexcellence* from now on, baby.

"In order to receive the coveted bounty you so richly deserve, you need only follow the club's singular (but non-negotiable) rule: Member Sarah Cruz must do whatever Club Master Jonas Faraday demands. (That means no bossy bullshit, no hijacking, no hard and fast, and no going for the jugular. Got it?) Again, Miss Cruz, welcome to The Jonas Faraday Club!

"Sincerely,

"Your Hopelessly Devoted Intake Agent,

"Jonas

"P.S. I'll pick you up for the airport this Thursday at 4:30 a.m. Pack casual clothes for tropical weather, including a bathing suit, sturdy hiking boots with ankle support and the thickest tread possible, long pants with moisture-wicking technology, a hat for strong sun, and, of course, something pretty (and easily removable). Please use the enclosed card to purchase anything at all you might need or even remotely desire for the trip—and don't even think about refusing to use it because you absolutely must have the appropriate gear, and, anyway, you promised to do everything I say."

There's a pre-paid Visa card folded into the letter, loaded with $3,000.

This is too much. Too generous. Over the top. But how else can I possibly afford all the stuff he's telling me to pack? I guess I'm going shopping. My stomach is leaping and twisting with excitement. I can't believe this is my life right now.

I pick up the small envelope with the little bump inside of it. Handwriting on its face declares: "*Delicious Anticipation: The Soundtrack.*" When I open the tiny envelope, there's a flash drive inside. I insert it into my laptop and music files pop up onto my screen. My heart leaps. That boy made me a mix tape.

The first song is a classic I know well—"Anticipation" by Carly Simon. I click on the song and listen to Carly sing about the torture of anticipation for a moment. You can say that again, Carly. The next song is called "Slow Burn" by David Bowie. I've never heard of it. I click on it. Sexy. I like it. And, yes, Jonas, I get the message loud and clear. We're going to do this your way, whatever that means—no more hijacking. I smile. The next song is "Lick It Before You Stick It" by Denise LaSalle. I roll my eyes. If the song title is any indication, it's clear what this one's going to be about. I press play on the song—and, yep, the saucy blues singer is singing explicit instructions on how to give a woman premium pleasure through oral sex. Oh, Jonas. Where on earth did he find that one? And, really, would a traditional love song be too much to ask? As if he can read my mind, the next song is utter perfection: "I Just Want to Make Love to You" by Muddy Waters. The title alone feels like a special kind of valentine from Jonas—I've never heard him use the phrase "make love" (except, of course, indirectly, when he selected the Modern English song last night—but in that song the phrase is tucked away in a verse, not front and center, as it is here). I click on the song, and I'm instantly blown away. This is old-school blues—pure and raw and effective. Oh yeah, this song is, most definitely, the musical embodiment of delicious anticipation—sensuous, pained, yearning anticipation. Delicious, indeed.

There's no topping the Muddy Waters song—no way—and yet, there's another song on the playlist. "I Want You" by Bob Dylan. I've heard of Bob Dylan, of course—one of the most influential singer-songwriters of all time—but I don't know this particular song. I click on it. The verse is poetic madness—a jumble of disconnected, almost nonsensical, ideas—and Dylan's delivery is slurring and hard to understand. I know Dylan's one of the greats and all—and he's obviously got a lot to say here—but, honestly, I'm not sure why Jonas picked this particular song. It's definitely not hitting me like the Muddy Waters song did, that's for sure.

But then, oh my gosh, the song arrives at its chorus, and, in the midst of rambling incoherence, there's sudden and succinct clarity. Bob Dylan confesses, quite simply, what he wants: *I want you.* The simplicity of the words combined with the authenticity of Dylan's yearning delivery hit me like a ton of bricks. This song makes me feel like Jonas wants me in a way that transcends our (off-the-charts) physical attraction—it makes me feel like he wants me outside of his bedroom. Or, hell, maybe I'm just hearing what I want to hear.

I grab my phone. "Jonas," I breathe when he picks up. "Can you talk?"

"Of course. Hi."

"I just got my welcome package." My voice is bursting with excitement. So many emotions are swirling around inside me, and hearing his voice is tipping me into near-euphoria. "Thank you."

Jonas chuckles, obviously amused by my exuberance. "Welcome to my club."

I let out a loud sigh. "The music, Jonas. Oh my God."

He pauses. "Sometimes, music says things better than words."

The hairs on the back of my neck stand up.

"I want you," he whispers.

I bite my lip. I wish I could leap through the phone line. "I want you, too."

"Talk about delicious anticipation—I'm already losing my mind." He sighs. "So, did you get your passport worked out?"

I take a deep breath. Okay, normal conversation. Yes, I can do that. "Yeah, Georgia said I'll have it on Wednesday."

"Good."

"I really liked Georgia."

"Yeah, she's great, isn't she?"

I wait a beat, but he doesn't say anything more about her.

Come on, Jonas, tell me why you're Georgia's godsend. "How do you know Georgia?" I finally ask.

"Oh, we met a few years ago." There's a beat. "It's a long story."

I'm quiet. I've got time for a long story.

"Her son interviewed me for this thing at his school." He audibly shrugs over the line.

Hold up. *Georgia's son* was the kid who interviewed him for that middle school career day thing? My brain is having a hard time connecting the dots.

"So are you slipping into an Oreo-induced coma right now?" he asks, clearly changing the subject.

How did Georgia's son wind up interviewing him at his school? "Yeah," I answer, "I've already scarfed down a whole row of Oreos—I can't stop," I answer.

He laughs.

I guess he's not going to tell me anything more about Georgia and her son. I'm dying to know, but I'll let it be. For now. "And, Jonas, the flowers and balloons and the shopping spree—oh my God, the shopping spree. You're too generous. I'm sure I won't need more than a couple hundred dollars."

He scoffs. "No, I want you to get the best hiking shoes you can find—good ones with really deep tread—and those alone will run you a couple hundred bucks. Plus, get some moisture-wicking socks so you don't get blisters—just go to REI, they'll know exactly what you need. Oh, and make sure you get long hiking pants in a breathable fabric."

Why the heck do I need all that stuff? His note said we were going to a tropical place. Doesn't "tropical" mean drinking piña coladas on a beach by day and making hot, sticky, moonlit love by night? Where do hiking boots with deep tread and moisture-wicking socks fit into any of that?

"Where the hell are you taking me?" I ask.

He ignores my question. "And besides all that, get yourself anything else you want, too—maybe a pretty dress, oh, and a teeny-tiny string bikini would look so hot on you, and lingerie, definitely lingerie."

"Wow, you're my very own personal shopper."

He chuckles. "I want you to go crazy, get anything you like. And if it turns out it's not enough money, let me know and I'll—"

"Oh my gosh, no, you're insane. We're only going to be gone for four days, for Pete's sake. I'm sure I'll return the card to you with lots of money left over on it—"

"No, no, spend it all. I won't take the card back."

I'm trembling. I don't know why. "Jonas, you're overwhelming me."

"Good."

"You're sweeping me off my feet."

"That's exactly what Valentine's Day bullshit is meant to do."

I'm reeling.

He sighs. "Sarah, just let me . . ." He pauses. "Hang on." There's an insistent male voice in the background. "Okay," he says to someone. "Just a sec."

Is he talking to Josh? Oh my gosh, he's still in the middle of his meeting. Why on earth did he even take my call?

His voice comes back on the line. "Sarah, just let me do this stuff, okay?" He lowers his voice. "It turns me on to do it—like, seriously, I've got a boner just hearing the excitement in your voice."

His words have an instant effect on me. "I want to kiss every inch of you right now," I whisper, emphasizing the phrase "every inch of you" with particular care.

He moans. "I'd be with you right now if I could, you know that, right?" He exhales. "But this meeting's gonna take for-fucking-ever. Josh and I still have a couple fires to put out to close the deal—and I *really* wanna close this deal."

I sigh. "I totally understand." I better let him get back to whatever he's doing. It sounds important. "Holy moly, when you finally pick me up on Thursday, we're both gonna be rarin' to go."

He sighs. "Seriously. This delicious anticipation thing is gonna be the death of me." He groans. "You better make sure your sweet ass is ready for me on Thursday—because I'll be bringing my A game, baby."

The balloons are making soft poofing noises all around me as they bump against the ceiling and each other. My apartment is bursting with bright colors and thick floral fragrances, thanks to the virtual garden of flowers surrounding me. The bear Jonas sent me before our dinner date is sitting at the table, smiling at me and shouting "Be Mine!" And to top it all off, I've still got the taste of Oreo cookies in my mouth. I'm so frickin' happy right now, I could pass out. *Poof ... poof . . .poof,* the balloons say softly around me. Clearly, they're happy, too.

"Oh yeah, my sweet ass will be ready for you, you can count on it," I say. "You just make damned sure *your* sweet ass is ready for *me,* Mr. Woman Wizard, because, come Thursday, it's gonna be on like Donkey Kong. Oh, and I should warn you: As a paying member of the Jonas Faraday Club, I'm gonna be expecting a helluva lot more than your A game, big boy. You better be ready to bring nothing short of *sexcellence*."

Chapter 20

Sarah

Six hundred forty-three dollars and sixty-four cents. That's what I just spent in a matter of two hours during a whirlwind shopping spree. It's more money than I've spent in a single shopping session in my whole life, but I sure managed to spend it with ease. I got everything Jonas told me to get, and then some, and I still didn't come close to his budget for me. Where did he expect me to shop—Hiking by Prada? True, the high-tech gear I got from REI was on the expensive side, but still, I was never in danger of spending anything close to three thousand dollars—even including the brightly colored tank tops, shorts, string bikini, cover-up, and two sundresses I bought. I didn't bother buying lingerie, despite Jonas' oh so helpful suggestion, because it seemed like a colossal waste of money to me. If there's going to be a situation suitable for skimpy lingerie, I'd rather just wear nothing at all. And, to be perfectly honest, I had an ulterior motive in keeping my clothing expenditures as low as possible—a much better idea for any leftover funds than buying expensive lingerie that Jonas is just going to tear off me, anyway. I just hope Jonas isn't mad when I tell him how I've already dispensed with all the leftover money on his card.

It's only two o'clock and it's already been a long and exciting day—two classes in the morning followed by a giddy shopping spree in the early afternoon. Already, I want nothing more than to go home, pack for my trip (because if I wait for tomorrow to do it, I'm going to stress out), and then curl up for the rest of the night with my contracts textbook. But I've got one more important errand to run before heading back home to study—overnighting my little software engineer his welcome package, complete with a bright yellow bracelet and a pre-loaded iPhone. Normally, I'd go to the post office a half-mile from school to mail a welcome package. But today, I've gone way, way, way out of my way to the post office downtown to send it out.

The minute I walk through the front door of the post office, clutching my outgoing package, I see her. Georgia. She's one of four postal clerks standing behind the long counter, ministering to customers. I step into the line, holding my box, twitching with nervous energy. I steal a glance at her. She doesn't see me. She's laughing with a customer. Her eyes are dancing. She's kind, this woman, genuinely kind.

The line is slowly inching forward. When I get to the front of the line, Georgia is still detained with a customer. I let the person behind me go ahead to the available clerk. And the next person, too. Finally, Georgia looks up, her station available. "Next customer, please," she says, and her eyes lock onto me. She smiles with instant recognition.

"Hi, Georgia," I say when I get to her station.

"Why, hello, Miss Cruz, what a pleasant surprise." She looks around and lowers her voice. "Your passport will be hand-delivered to your place tomorrow evening—we won't have it back 'til then, probably by the skin of our teeth."

"Oh, yes, thank you." I place the box on the counter. "I didn't expect to get it today. I came to overnight this."

"Oh yeah? What brings you downtown?"

"A little shopping for my trip with Jonas."

She eyes me skeptically.

"Well, and visiting you."

She smiles. She knew it.

Georgia asks me all the necessary questions about whether I want tracking and insurance on my package, and we complete my postal transaction.

"Georgia," I begin, tentatively, looking behind me at the growing line, "I was wondering if you had a few minutes to chat."

She purses her lips. Is that amusement? "Actually, yes, right now would be a great time to take my break."

Georgia blows the steam off her hot cup of tea and takes a careful sip.

For some reason, I'm holding my breath. I know she's got something important to tell me, I just don't know what it is.

"A few years ago, my son Trey's little league team had an incredible season, like a once in a lifetime season. They wound up getting a lot of local press because they had this incredible pitcher, you know, a true natural—already blowing everyone away at age twelve with his fast ball."

"And what about your son? Is he really good, too?"

"Oh no, not at all." She laughs. "Every team he's ever been on, he's always the bottom of the order, by far." She laughs again, and I join her. Nothing like a mother's honest assessment of her kid. "But every coach he's ever had has kept him around because that boy's got so much heart. Oh Lord, does that boy shine with pure love of the game. He inspires everyone around him."

Her face glows with pride for a moment. "There's just no quit in him. But he's really small for his age—and not particularly fast, either. Not a great combination." She sighs. "And painfully shy. I've always encouraged him to be on a team because it helps him with his shyness."

I smile. Her face is awash in motherly love.

"So, anyway, when Trey's team had their golden season, the whole city really took notice of them—there was a little parade in the neighborhood when they got back from a big tournament in Vancouver, and the team was interviewed on the local news several times. Jonas' company apparently took notice and was kind enough to invite the boys and their families to watch a Mariners game in their fancy box seats. I'd taken Trey to a few Mariners games before—but always in the nosebleed seats. He was pretty impressed with those box seats, I tell ya. We felt like royalty."

I wonder if that invitation was Jonas' idea? Or was it Josh's? Or maybe a PR firm's?

"And that's when you met Jonas?" I ask.

"Yes. And right away, I knew he was special. All season long, everyone always crowded around that spectacular pitcher on Trey's team—and deservedly so, the kid is just amazing and also bursting with personality—and Trey always hung back, feeling shy and sort of insecure. Well, at that Mariners game, it was more of the same. Everyone was chatting up that pitcher boy—he was cracking everyone up, in fact—and Trey just sat quietly, watching the game, sitting by himself." During much of this story, Georgia has been glancing away, lost in her own thoughts, but now she looks right at me. "Do you like baseball?"

"I've never followed it. My dad wasn't around when I was growing up, and my mom isn't a baseball fan. I've never even been to a game."

Georgia nods knowingly. "Any siblings?" she asks.

"Nope. It's just my mom and me. The two musketeers."

"Yeah, it's just Trey and me, too. It's special that way, huh?"

I nod.

"I can't afford to take Trey to baseball games very often, believe me. But Trey loves it, so I do my best."

We share a smile.

"So, anyway, for the first half of the game, I noticed Jonas in the corner of the box, not talking to anybody, but he kept glancing over at Trey. Trey was totally absorbed in the game, keeping score on his clipboard, just totally fixated. Finally, midway through, Jonas came right over and sat down next to him." She sighs, remembering. "Trey lit up like a Christmas tree, and they wound up watching the whole rest of the game together, jabbering away the whole time." Georgia beams and leans into me. "Trey *never* jabbers away, with anyone."

I bite my lip. I can't imagine Jonas jabbers away with too many people, either.

"By the end of the game, Trey and Jonas were best friends, talking about everything—not just baseball. Jonas asked Trey what he wanted to do when he grew up, and Trey told him he wanted to do something with computers, maybe. Jonas asked, 'No baseball, huh?' and Trey said, 'Naw, I'm too small, too slow.'"

"Well, that really got Jonas going. 'If there's something you want, whatever it is, then you have to go after it relentlessly,' Jonas told him." Georgia looks wistful. "And before we knew it, Jonas was telling Trey how to run wind sprints to increase his speed and eat all the right proteins to increase his muscle mass and giving him a list of books he wanted Trey to read." She chuckles. "He was just really, really sweet. By the end of the game, Trey worshipped the ground Jonas walked on. I don't think Jonas realized what he was getting himself into. As we were leaving, Trey got up the nerve to ask him to come to career day at his school." Georgia rolls her eyes, but she's still smiling. "The kids could either do a written report on what they might want to do when they grew up, or they could bring in an interview subject with a fascinating career—sort of like a human show and tell—and conduct an interview in front of the whole school."

I blush vicariously for Jonas. I can only imagine how little he wanted to do that.

"Honestly, I was shocked Trey wanted to interview Jonas in front of the whole school—he's usually so shy." Georgia's eyes flicker at the memory. "It's like Jonas worked some kind of spell on him."

Based on personal experience, yes, I'm quite sure that's exactly what Jonas did.

"I could tell Jonas was about to refuse, but then Trey explained that a lot of the kids were inviting their dads to be interviewed, and that was that. Jonas said he'd do it. So, anyway," Georgia sighs, but trails off. "I'm sorry—this story is probably so much longer than you bargained for." She takes a sip of her tea.

"No, it's not. It's exactly what I was hoping to find out. So what happened next?"

"Well, Jonas went down to Trey's school and did the interview, and he seemed to enjoy it, too; and after that, he and Trey kept in touch. Jonas sent him a bunch of sports equipment for his birthday, he invited him to a couple more Mariners games, and he even gave him a jersey signed by the entire team. Jonas just spoiled him rotten. Trey was over the moon."

"And you?" I ask. "How did you feel about all this?"

She let's out a huge sigh. "I was thrilled. Grateful. Trey is just the sweetest, most wonderful kid. Just a giant, beating heart. And, you know, growing up without a father has been hard on him, so having a man like Jonas pick him out of the crowd and make him feel special meant a lot."

I nod. I'm swooning. I can relate.

"And then I got sick," Georgia says, her face darkening.

My swoon instantly vanishes. "Oh no, what happened?"

"Cancer."

I reach across the table and touch her hand. "Oh no, Georgia. Oh my God."

"No, I'm fine now. Perfectly fine. This was well over a year ago. And we caught it early, thank God. I had surgery and radiation—no chemo, thank goodness—and I was as good as new, knock on wood." She knocks her knuckles against the wooden table. "But Trey called Jonas and told him, and ... " In a flash, she's totally choked up. She shakes her head. Words won't form in her throat. She looks up at the ceiling, trying to compose herself.

I squeeze her hand.

"I'm sorry," she squeaks out.

She holds my hand silently for a moment. "I'm sorry. I don't know why it still makes me so emotional." She takes a deep breath. "When you're sick, and scared, and all alone, and you've got a child to worry about ... To have someone swoop right in and just *take care of you*, and especially someone who has no reason whatsoever to do it . . ." She tears up again. She grabs a napkin and wipes her eyes. "It was just so unexpected. And so wonderful. He was just a godsend."

My heart is racing. "What did he do?"

"What didn't he do? He sent flowers after my surgery, arranged a car to take me to and from radiation treatments for a whole month. Meals were delivered to our house. My sister's here in town, thank goodness, so I wasn't alone—but she has work and her own kids." She wipes at her eyes. "Everything was so overwhelming. I had to take time off work, get help with Trey. And Jonas just swooped right in and made everything better."

I'm tearing up right along with her. If I didn't already want to tackle Jonas and make violent, savage, primal love to him, I sure as hell do now.

"When treatment was all finished, I got what looked like a bill from the hospital. I thought I was gonna throw up when I got that envelope in the mail; I was so scared to look inside. I knew, whatever the amount, it was going to ruin me."

She unclasps my hand so she can take a sip of her tea with a shaky hand. I follow her lead and take a swig of my cappuccino.

I'm on the edge of my seat, even though I know what she's about to say. There's only one possible ending to her story, after all—but I can hardly wait to see her face when she tells it.

"And when I opened the envelope, it was an invoice, all right—for even more than I'd feared. Trying to pay that bill would have been impossible. I would have had to file bankruptcy. But guess what?"

I shake my head, even though I know what. I'd never deprive her of telling me the fairytale ending to her wonderful story.

"The invoice was stamped 'paid in full,'" she says, her eyes wide. "Can you believe it? The balance owed on the invoice was *zero*. I just couldn't believe it. I cried like a baby." And with that, she's crying like a baby now, too.

I hand her a napkin and pick one up for myself. I'm a puddle right alongside her.

"A godsend," she says in a muffled voice. "He's just been a godsend."

I grab Georgia's hand again, and she grabs mine. Her hand is soft and warm. I have the sudden impulse to bring her hand to my mouth and kiss it—and so that's exactly what I do.

A smile bursts across her face at my sudden show of affection.

She pats my cheek with the palm of the hand. "He's a good one, honey," she says, composing herself. "Hang onto him."

I can't speak, so I just nod and smile.

I want nothing more than to "hang onto" Jonas, believe me. But can a girl, even a very, very determined girl, even a very sincerely smitten girl, hang onto a boy if that boy doesn't want to be hung onto? The answer, of course, is no. It's out of my hands. I'll just have to wait and see if Jonas wants to be hung onto.

I sigh and look up at the ceiling of the coffeehouse. Jonas has my beating heart in his hands. It's his to do with, or not do with, as he pleases. And for the life of me, I don't know where that's going to leave me at the end of all this.

Chapter 21

Sarah

Kat and I shouldn't be here right now. But when it came time to meet Kat for drinks, I couldn't resist killing two birds with one stone and spying on my little software engineer, too. I overnighted him his welcome package yesterday, complete with a bright yellow bracelet, and lo and behold, when I checked his account at lunchtime today, he'd already posted a check-in at a downtown sports bar for seven o'clock tonight. Talk about an eager beaver. And now, here we are at the sports bar, even though we shouldn't be, even though I'm breaking The Club's rules (yet again). But I have to see what kind of yellow-coded woman has been deemed a perfect match for a sweet, hopeful, lonely, normal, yellow-coded man like my sweet software engineer. I hope he finds true love tonight. I really do. I check my watch. 6:45.

Kat and I arrived plenty early. For the past hour, we've been drinking beer and talking nonstop about my night (and morning) with Jonas. Of course, I didn't tell her any graphic sexual details and I certainly didn't mention the whole "yippee, I almost had an orgasm" thing. Kat doesn't know I've never had an orgasm in the first place—I've never told anyone that, other than Jonas—so, obviously, I'm not going to brag to Kat about getting closer than ever with Jonas. Plus, I would never tell Kat, or anyone, about Jonas' particular fixation on getting women off—so that entire topic of conversation was off limits. And yet, even without revealing any sexual details or Jonas' private information, it appears The Story of Jonas and Sarah is still a damned good one, because, throughout the entire conversation, Kat has been "oohing" and "aahing" and gushing and swooning.

"He sounds amazing," Kat says, "which he'd better be to deserve you."

I smile at her.

"So, where do you think he's taking you tomorrow? Jamaica? Tahiti? Borneo?"

"Borneo?" I say, laughing. "Where is Borneo?"

I turn to glance around the bar. Is the software engineer here yet? I look at my watch. We're still a few minutes early yet, but he could come at any time. I look around again. I can't wait to see his Miss Yellow. I hope she's looking for love every bit as much as he is. You never know—maybe their happily ever after will begin tonight, right here, in this sports bar. Why not? I mean, jeez, he's off to a fantastic start—he's not a fucked-up Purple, after all. I smirk to myself. I'm quite fond of my sweet, fucked-up Purple.

I realize Kat's been talking.

"What?" I ask. "I'm sorry, I zoned out for a minute."

"I'm just trying to figure out where he's taking you."

"I have no idea," I say. "Where in the tropical world does a girl need hiking boots with extra-thick tread?"

She grimaces. "Maybe he's going to hurl you into a volcano."

"God, I hope not. Getting chucked into a gurgling pit of lava would not be my preferred ending to this story."

She giggles. "That would definitely be anti-climactic."

I grin. That was a funny choice of words right there.

We both pause to sip our beers.

"So, what did he say about your chat with Georgia?" she asks.

My stomach drops. "I haven't told him about it yet." I blush. "When I talked to him last night, it didn't feel like the right time to tell him about it."

Jonas and I had a heart-racing conversation last night about how much we missed each other and couldn't wait for our trip. He was effusive, and explicit, in telling me just how much he missed me and wanted to see me. Well, and touch me. And kiss me. And taste me. And make love to me. It just didn't feel like the right moment to tell him about my conversation with Georgia.

Kat looks at me skeptically.

"He seemed like he was under a lot of stress to get his deal done before leaving on our trip. I figured it'd be better to tell him about it tomorrow, in person."

Kat pointedly takes a long swig of her beer.

I sigh, exasperated. "*And,* yes, I'm a little bit worried maybe he's going to be upset with me for going to talk to her."

Kat rolls her eyes. "Why on earth would he be upset?"

I sigh, collecting my thoughts. No, that's not it, either. "I don't know. My conversation with Georgia just felt so *game changing*. It made me ... My attraction just went to a whole new level, that's all. And I'd rather talk to him about it in person." I blush.

Kat squeals. "Oh, girl, you're a goner."

I sigh. "Yeah, I'm freaking out just a wee bit."

"Oh, Sarah, don't overthink it. Just *enjoy* it. He's obviously—"

I gasp and grab Kat's forearm. She instantly stops talking.

The software engineer just bellied up to the bar on the other side of Kat.

I crick my neck toward him, but I'm not sure Kat understands what I'm trying to communicate.

The guy takes a seat on the stool next to Kat and acknowledges her with a friendly, "Hi." She replies in kind. Apparently, I'm invisible, but that's okay, seeing as how I'd like to crawl under a rock right about now, anyway.

Wow, he's got quite a spring in his step tonight. He looks nothing like the lonely fellow I saw leaving his building to grab a sandwich all by himself. The man's downright bursting with hopeful anticipation.

I bang my knee into Kat's knee. When she looks at me, I silently mouth the words, "That's him."

Her eyes go wide, and she inhales sharply.

"Are you rooting for Kentucky or Connecticut?" the software engineer asks Kat, motioning to a basketball game on one of the television screens above the bar. As he does, I can plainly see the yellow bracelet on his wrist.

"Uh. Neither. I don't follow basketball," Kat answers. She drinks down the last few drops of her beer.

"Can I buy you another one?" he asks.

Wait just a cotton-pickin' minute. Does he not understand the rules of The Club? Kat's not wearing a yellow bracelet. Why is he hitting on her? Even if she were in The Club, which she's not, it would be up to *her* to decide whether or not to approach *him.*

"Sure," Kat answers. "Thanks."

I practically slap my forehead in disbelief. Why did Kat say yes to him? I bang Kat's knee under the bar again, but what I really want to do is smack her upside the head. She turns to me and shrugs innocently. That's Kat for you. Ted Bundy could offer her a free mojito and she'd gladly accept.

"And for you, too, of course," the software engineer says, grinning at me. "Hi."

I guess I'm not invisible after all. I try to smile back and nod, but I'm freaking out. What the hell is going on here? He shouldn't be talking to us right now. A woman specifically matched to him—a woman who is uncannily compatible with him and his sexual preferences and fantasies and romantic hopes—is going to walk through the door any minute. And she's coming here just to meet *him*. Heck, she might already be here, watching him right this very second, trying to decide if she wants to slip her yellow bracelet onto her wrist and identify herself or turn on her heel and flee.

I make a big point of checking my watch so Mr. Yellow can see that I am *not*—emphatically *not*—wearing a yellow bracelet right now.

"Kat," I say. "I think my watch died. What time is it right now?" I stretch out my wrist, yet again, for the benefit of my software engineer. *See? No bracelet.* I'm hoping Kat will get a clue and display her bare wrist, too.

But before Kat can even process my question, the guy looks at his watch. "Seven-oh-five," he says.

The bartender puts two tall beers in front of us.

"Thank you so much," Kat says, raising her glass to Mr. Yellow. "Cheers."

"Cheers," he replies enthusiastically.

I try to squeak out a polite "thank you," but nothing comes out of my moving lips. I'm really anxious.

Everyone takes a sip but me.

I glance around. Is his Miss Yellow here? I look around the bar for a loner-ish, normal-ish, sweet-looking woman—perhaps a nurse or patent lawyer or dentist or computer programmer?—who's intently watching him from a corner of the bar. Nope. I don't see a single woman in this entire bar paying him any attention whatsoever.

He tilts his head toward Kat like he's about to tell her a secret. "So, I'm crossing my fingers and toes right now that you're in The Club?" His face is awash in hope and excitement.

Oh God, did he really just ask her that? Did he not read a word of the instructions in his welcome package? How could he not understand the way this works? He's a goddamned software engineer! How hard can this be? Does he seriously think every knockout at this bar is here specifically for him? I'm not trying to be cruel here, but come on. The Club matches people up—that's the whole point—and Kat is a frickin' ten. A flaming, raging, unquestionable ten. Every man on planet earth wants a woman like Kat. There is no person alive, no standard of beauty in any culture, that wouldn't view Kat as an ideal manifestation of perfect beauty. And this guy is *sweet*. Unassuming. Normal. But you know, a four, if he's lucky. Well, maybe a five on a good day. And unless he runs a publishing empire or invented the Internet or runs a global organization dedicated to eradicating human trafficking or discovered Justin Timberlake or belongs to Doctors Without Borders, his chances with Kat are slim to none. The Club might boast the ability to make a guy's dreams a reality, but it can't turn water into wine, people. Wow, I'm getting kind of riled up here.

Kat shifts in her chair and turns her head to look at me. Her expression is one of utter befuddlement.

"No," she says softly. "Just here to grab a beer with my friend. Thank you again for supporting the cause." She raises her beer in salute to him. Her tone is gracious. This is not a cruel kiss-off. This is a kind kiss-off.

But he looks totally deflated nonetheless. "Oh."

Poor thing. But what did he expect? That he'd be Charlie and The Club would be his own personal Chocolate Factory come to life? Come on.

There's an awkward pause.

"Well," I say, trying to alleviate the discomfort. And I'm about to say something more—something lame and not helpful, I'm sure—when I'm interrupted.

"Hi there," says a voice from the other side of Mr. Yellow. He turns to look at the source of the greeting, and so do I. And much to my shock and horror and total dismay and confusion, the woman standing on the other side of my little software engineer, the woman who just said hello to him, the woman who's smiling at him and batting her eyelashes—and blatantly displaying a goddamned *yellow* bracelet on her wrist—is none other than Miss Purple from the other night. Stacy. *Stacy the Faker.* The totally hot woman Jonas fucked mere days ago, wishing she were me.

I quickly look down at my hands on the bar. Oh my God, Jonas' penis was inside that woman. I cringe. And his tongue touched her ... I can't finish the thought. I want to barf.

"Hi," my software engineer says, his voice spiking with excitement. "Please, have a seat."

"Well, I don't want to interrupt anything," Stacy says, glaring at Kat. She touches her hair and makes a big show of flashing her yellow bracelet again. "But I was hoping to talk to you for a bit." She shoots daggers at Kat again.

"No, please," Kat says, motioning for Stacy to take a seat. "He's all yours. I'm just here with my friend."

Stacy's eyes lock onto me and then dart back to Kat. And just that fast, her eyes flash with unmistakable recognition.

"Yes, please, have a seat," my little software engineer says. He holds up his yellow bracelet right next to hers. "I've been waiting for you." His head is turned away from me, looking at Stacy, but based on Stacy's wide smile, I'd guess he's smiling broadly at her, too. "I'm Rob," he says, putting out his hand. "Thank you for coming."

"Nice to meet you, Rob," Stacy says, her tone flirty. "I'm Cassandra."

Cassandra? What the hell?

"Do you like basketball?" my little software engineer—Rob—asks, motioning to the TVs.

"I love it." Stacy grins. "Especially college ball. I don't really follow the NBA—until play-offs, of course."

"Same here!" Rob says, elated. "Exactly what I always say."

"You wanna go sit?" Stacy asks, motioning to a corner booth. Her eyes wander ever so briefly to me and flash, just for a nanosecond, with undisguised contempt.

"Absolutely."

The two lovebirds get up and move toward the corner of the bar.

"Well, nice talking to you," Kat says sarcastically to Rob's back when he's out of earshot. She turns to me, her face awash in disgust. "Holy shitballs," Kat says. "What the hell is she doing here?"

I shake my head, thoroughly confused. I open my mouth to speak, but close it again. I have no idea what she's doing here.

"Sarah, she's wearing a *yellow* bracelet," Kat whispers urgently, as if I hadn't noticed. "I thought she was *purple*?"

Now my mouth is hanging open. I don't even know what to say. Even if Stacy were, theoretically, assigned two different compatibility colors (which, based on my understanding, is impossible), how on earth could she possibly be a match for both Jonas *and* the software engineer—two men who are polar opposites in every way? That'd be like saying, "I like incorrigible man-whores *and* virginal boy-next-door types. I like savage fuck machines and guys who love rainbows and baby chicks. I like men with raging God complexes and indefatigable hard-ons *and* mendicants sworn to a vow of poverty, chastity and obedience." You couldn't even say Jonas and Mr. Yellow are two sides to the same coin—they're a frickin' Euro and a nickel. Does not compute.

"I thought the colors don't mix. Purples get matched with purples, yellows with yellows."

"Right. A purple can't even see a yellow's check-ins. It's all separated by color-code."

"Well, then, how did that woman show up to meet *both* Jonas *and* Mr. Software Engineer, too?"

Exactly what I'm wondering.

A guy sits next to Kat at the bar. Wow, he's really cute.

"Hey," he says. "I'm Cameron." Oh boy, he's just her type. Dark, athletic. Gleaming white teeth.

"Hi," Kat replies, instantly distracted from the conundrum of why Stacy is here to meet Mr. Yellow. "Kat." She puts out her hand and he shakes it.

"Cat? Like meow?"

She laughs. Oh, she's already in full flirt mode. "Yeah, but with a 'K.' Katherine. But call me Kat."

"Nice to meet you, Kat. Can I call you Kitty Kat?"

Kat giggles. "Absolutely not—at least not yet. You've got to earn the privilege."

It takes all my restraint not to roll my eyes. Oh, Kat.

"I'm going to the ladies' room," I mumble, getting up from my stool.

Kat peels her eyes off her new admirer just long enough to nod her acknowledgment of my departure.

I steal a glance at my little software engineer—Rob. He's sitting at a table, smiling broadly, deep in conversation with Stacy. Or Cassandra. Or whatever her name is. His face is glowing with excitement. Oh, it's hard to watch—his heart is on his sleeve. I feel sick to my stomach. I can't figure this out. But whatever's going on, it can't be good for him. He came here for love tonight—I know he did—and something tells me he's going to be sorely disappointed. If not crushed.

In the bathroom, my head is spinning. I'm so confused.

Just as I'm drying my hands with a paper towel, the door opens and Stacy bursts in.

She beelines right to me. She's not even pretending she came in here to pee. She bends over to check for feet in the two stalls. Finding none, she whips back up and leans into me.

"I saw you and your friend at the check-in with the hottie, and now, gee, what a coincidence, here you are again, both of you, at this check-in with the nerd. What the fuck?"

I'm speechless. My mind isn't processing fast enough to come up with an explanation for our presence at both locations. But why is she on the offense? What the hell was *she* doing at both check-ins?

"Did the agency send you?" she barks at me. It feels like more of an accusation than a question.

I open my mouth to speak.

"They don't think I can handle this guy on my own, is that it? They think he needs some additional options, just in case I'm not acceptable to him? That's bullshit." She's seething. "I don't need backups. I've never once not closed a guy. Not once. And this one's already slobbering all over me, like they all do."

I shake my head. "No, I . . ."

"This is *my* territory," she fumes, taking a menacing step closer to me. "They think they've gotta send not one but *two* other girls to back me up?"

"Nobody sent us. It's just a coincidence," I finally manage.

"Ha! Fuck you," she seethes, her nostrils flaring. "You tell the agency—was it Oksana who sent you?—you tell Oksana this is *my* account, *my* territory, *my* score—and I don't need anybody checking up on me or making a play for my sloppy seconds." She leans right into my face, her eyes narrowed to slits. "Don't fuck with me, bitch." With that, she turns on her heel and marches out of the bathroom, leaving me standing with my mouth agape.

I steal a glance at my alarm clock. 3:20 a.m. My alarm is set to go off in ten minutes, so I lean over and turn it off with a groan. Jonas is going to be here to pick me up for the airport in just over an hour, and I haven't gotten a wink of sleep all night long. Ever since I laid my head down on my pillow at midnight, I've been tossing and turning, my mind racing, thinking about my horrific encounter with Stacy in the bathroom, and the horrific implications of what she said to me. Worst of all, the thing that's kept me awake above all else, is wondering how I'm going to tell Jonas about all of it. I've been such an idiot working for this disgusting organization. No wonder the women in The Club are so perfectly compatible with the men. They're *paid* to be. Stacy, or whatever her name is, is a frickin' prostitute, plain and simple. For the right fee, she'll be anybody's perfect match. For hours, I've lain here in my bed, staring at the ceiling, the full weight of the situation dawning on me.

I head into the bathroom and brush my teeth. I've got a headache.

I work for an online whorehouse. A global brothel. That's bad enough. But the men buying these women's services don't even know what they're buying. That poor software engineer joined The Club to find love—I'm sure of it. He thought this was a high-priced, exclusive dating service; he really, really did. And even someone like Jonas, who clearly didn't sign up to find his soul mate, at least craved honesty with his partners.

He's going to be furious. Probably humiliated. Most certainly disgusted. I just don't know him well enough to know how he'll react.

It makes me physically sick to think about breaking this news to him. I didn't want to do it over the phone when I got home last night, so I waited—but I certainly don't want to ambush him with the news during our trip, either. Maybe I should have called him with the news the minute I got home? But, no, it just didn't feel right to tell him over the phone.

I hop in the shower, my mind reeling like it's been all night.

When I first got home from the sports bar, I was beside myself, trying to figure out what to do. After a while, I texted Jonas, just to see if he was still awake, perhaps hoping he'd call me and make my decision easy about whether or not to tell him over the phone. He texted back right away to say he couldn't wait to see me, that he was going crazy missing me, that it felt like a month since he'd laid his hands on me.

"Only a few more hours!" he texted. But he didn't call.

"See you soon!" I texted back.

"I've got something big to tell you!" he replied. *"Bwahahahahaaaa!"*

My stomach lurched with anxiety. *So do I,* I thought. But what I texted back was, *"Can't wait."*

Chapter 22

Jonas

I didn't think it was possible, but I've forgotten just how beautiful she is during the three days we've been apart. When she opens the door to her apartment, I feel like I'm being reunited with the girl who waited for me to come home from fighting a brutal war. I can't help taking her face into my hands and kissing her deeply. She tastes good. Minty.

"Welcome to your first day in The Jonas Faraday Club," I say, breaking away from our kiss.

She nods and smiles. But her smile isn't as beaming as I was expecting it to be. Something's off. I can feel it. Is she having second thoughts about going away with me? I thought we were past the whole "I don't trust you because you're incapable of forging intimate human connection" thing. Fuck. How much more upside can I possibly show her? I'm running out of ways to assure her.

"I'm so glad you're here," she breathes, throwing her arms around my neck. She hugs me close and plants a kiss on my lips that makes it abundantly clear she's most definitely not having second thoughts about our trip. But I know I didn't imagine the anxiety that flashed across her face a second ago.

"Jonas," she says, kissing me again and again. "I've missed you so much." I might be crazy, but I feel like she's about to burst into tears right here in my arms. Yeah, something's rattling around in her beautiful head right now—but what else is new.

"Are you okay?" I ask, making her look at me.

She nods. "Just so glad you're here." She kisses me again and my entire body sizzles with electricity.

"If you keep kissing me like this," I mumble into her lips, "we're not going to make our flight."

She pulls away from me, reluctantly. "Are you gonna tell me where we're headed?"

"Ah, ah, ah," I say, holding up my index finger. "All will be revealed soon enough." I motion to a suitcase by the front door. "This it?"

She nods. "Oh, and this." She grabs her laptop off the couch.

I take the computer out of her hands and return it to the couch. "Nope."

"I thought maybe I'd go over my study outlines if we have any free time."

I smirk. We won't have a minute of free time. Do I really need to spell that out to her?

She blushes.

Apparently not.

"No computer, then," she agrees. Her mouth twists into a what-was-I-thinking half-smile.

"Nice to see you're already taking instruction so well."

"A deal's a deal," she says. "I'm paying an arm and a leg to be in this club, might as well get my money's worth." She laughs, clearly still amused by the form of "payment" I've exacted from her.

"You got your passport?" I ask.

She pats her purse. "It came last night, just like Georgia promised."

"Then let's do it." I grab her suitcase and lead her out into the pre-dawn morning to the limo waiting at the curb. The driver comes out and stashes her suitcase in the trunk as I guide her into the backseat, memories of our last limo ride instantly rushing me when she bends over to climb in.

"Surprise," Josh says as she enters the car.

She visibly startles.

"I'm Josh," he says, extending his hand to her as we settle into our seats. "Jonas' brother."

"Oh, yes, of course," she says, turning back to look at me. She's totally confused. "I've seen your picture. So nice to meet you. I didn't know . . ."

"You mean Jonas didn't tell you I'm joining you two on the trip?" He looks at me, appalled. "Why didn't you tell her, bro? That wasn't very nice of you." He turns to Sarah. "That wasn't very nice of him."

I shrug. "It must have slipped my mind." I grab her hand. "I hope you don't mind. Josh is a lot of fun."

"Oh," she says. Damn, she's adorable. "No, I ... That's great."

"Good," Josh says. "Because Jonas and I have so much planned for us." He high-fives me. "Gonna be fucking awesome, bro."

Sarah's speechless.

Josh leans into her. "Jonas and I never travel without each other. Ever. It's a twin thing." He winks.

She's pale. Her hand stiffens in mine.

Josh gazes wistfully out the window as we pull away from her apartment building. "Yeah, it's gonna be amazing. We'll be three peas in a pod all weekend long."

If I blew on her right now, she'd tip over.

I can't do this to her anymore, as cute as she is right now. I laugh. "We're just fucking with you, baby," I say.

Her hand relaxes in mine as she exhales. She swats at my leg and laughs.

"Unless you *want* me to come?" Josh says. "I mean, if you *want* me there, I'll clear my calendar, no problem. Just say the word."

"Okay, enough, Josh. Don't scare her away." I turn to Sarah. Color has returned to her cheeks. She's breathing again. "Josh has been staying with me the last few days while we've been working on our deal—"

"—which we finally closed," Josh says, finishing my sentence and looking at his watch, "about two hours ago." He lets out a hoot of celebration and pulls out a bottle of champagne that's chilling in ice.

"We're just giving Josh a lift to the airport," I explain. "He's catching an early flight back to L.A."

Josh leans into Sarah like he's telling her a secret. "I could have taken a much later flight today, but I wanted to see the woman who's reduced my brother to a mushy pile of goo." Josh succeeds in opening the bottle and I wordlessly hand him three glasses.

Sarah looks at me, clearly wondering how I feel about being called a mushy pile of goo, and I beam at her. I don't mind it one bit. I know the truth when I hear it.

"And you do not disappoint, Sarah Cruz," Josh says politely, handing her a glass of champagne. "Sorry I messed with you. It won't happen again."

"Ha," I say. "Don't believe him."

"Strangely, I wasn't all that freaked out about you joining us on the trip," she says to Josh, "but I admit the whole we-never-travel-without-each-other twin thing got me all kinds of flustered." She takes a sip of her champagne and her eyes light up. "Yum. I've never had champagne this early—but, hey, I make it a policy never to turn down a glass of champagne."

"Duly noted," I say, grabbing my glass from Josh.

"All right, bro, are you gonna tell her the news or should I?" Josh asks.

We've got her undivided attention. She looks anxious. Why does she think big news must be bad news?

I squeeze her hand to reassure her. "Josh and I have been working around the clock these past few days," I begin, my excitement barely containable, "or else I would have been beating down your door like the Big Bad Wolf, believe me."

"Did we ever go to bed last night?" Josh asks.

"No, sir, we did not—though I'm slightly delirious from sleep deprivation so I can't be sure."

"No, we didn't; you're right," Josh says. He looks at Sarah, smiling. "We finished all the paperwork on the deal just a couple hours ago—by the hair on our chinny-chin-chins."

"Are you guys gonna tell me the news? I'm dying here."

"Why, yes, we are, My Magnificent Sarah. Patience." I lean into her ear and whisper, "Stop begging for everything hard and fast, baby."

She blushes. She's so fucking adorable.

I clear my throat. "Raise your glasses, please." They do, and so do I. "And, a drum roll would be awfully nice, if you would."

Simultaneously, Josh and Sarah begin trilling their tongues and slapping their thighs with whichever hand isn't holding a champagne glass. Josh beams at Sarah, laughing at her exuberance. He already likes her, I can tell.

"We are hereby celebrating a new beginning." I shoot Sarah a look that tells her my new beginning includes her. "Sarah, you're looking at the new owners of Climb and Conquer Indoor Rock Climbing Gyms." My smile hurts my cheeks.

"Oh my God," she says, beaming. She clinks my glass and then Josh's. "Congratulations, you guys." She leans over and kisses me.

"Twenty gyms in five states," I say, my skin coursing with electricity. "It's something we've wanted to do for a really long time."

"Something *you've* wanted to do," Josh corrects me. "You were always the one with the dream, bro, from day one. I'm just along for the ride."

"Here's to figuring out what you want in life and going after it," I say, my eyes fixed on Sarah. "Relentlessly."

She clinks my glass again and shoots me the sexiest smile she's ever bestowed upon me.

I wanna tear her limb from limb right now. What better way to celebrate the best day of my life? I turn to Josh. "You're fucking awesome, man, but you're such a cock blocker right now."

Josh laughs. "Sorry."

Sarah giggles. "It's probably good you're here to protect me, Josh. Jonas looks like he could turn into the Incredible Hulk right now."

I smirk. I am, in fact, feeling very Incredible-Hulkish right now, or actually, King-Kong-ish. Yeah, I definitely want to beat my chest, throw her over my shoulder, and climb to the top of the highest building.

"So, is this, like, an investment, or are you two going to personally manage the gyms?" she asks.

Josh and I look at each other. This is an unresolved subject. Josh wants to treat the venture as a passive investment—hire a couple regional managers, oversee things from afar. But I want to make the gyms my passion, the center of my universe. In fact, the minute the deal closed, I didn't give a fuck about doing anything else, ever again. Suddenly, I felt like I'd finally figured out my life's purpose. Fuck Faraday & Sons. I never asked to be a part of it—never *wanted* to be a part of it. Fuck global investments and real estate investment trusts and EBITDA and acquisitions and asset management and weighing tax consequences for every move and counter-move. Fuck it all. I just want to climb rocks and mountains and train to climb rocks and mountains and be with other people who are obsessed with climbing rocks and mountains. And then go home and climb Sarah, my own personal Mount Everest.

"We haven't worked out all the details yet," I say slowly, and Josh smirks in reply. We both know how things are eventually going to shake out. I'm leaving Faraday & Sons. And soon.

"Jonas wants to spend every single minute of the rest of his life climbing mountains," Josh says.

I look at Sarah, my eyes undressing her. "Not every single minute of the rest of my life."

She returns my gaze without flinching. After a moment, she exhales and parts her lips. Oh, yeah, she wants me, too.

"Unless, of course, that mountain is Mount Everest. In which case, yes." I touch her cheek.

Her eyes are on fire.

And, shit, just like that, my cock springs to life. If Josh weren't here, all my careful planning for this weekend would go right out the window. Actually, it's probably good he's here.

There's an awkward silence for a moment as Sarah and I continue to stare at each other, our mutual desire sucking all available oxygen out of the limo. She touches my hand against her cheek.

I close my eyes.

"Oh, wow, you two are gonna burst into a giant ball of flames this weekend, huh?"

Sarah blushes and drops her hand.

I drop my hand, too, but I don't take my eyes off her. "Fuck, yeah, we are," I say. I exhale slowly. "Fuck, yeah."

Finally. We're all alone. Well, as all alone as any two people can be in the first class cabin of a 737, sitting on a runway and waiting for takeoff. But, hey, it's better than sitting in that limo with my fucking brother for another minute. He kept looking at me the way only he does, shaking his head like he's laughing at me with just his eyes. And when the limo pulled away from the curb, he hugged me and whispered in my ear, "Bro, she's totally worth it." And then he winked at me.

I didn't know what he was referring to. She's totally worth the effort it took to track her down? Duh. She's totally worth the expense of hacking into Washington's server? Of course. Or was he referring to something else—something bigger, more philosophical than any of that? Josh doesn't usually get bogged down with philosophy or deep thoughts the way I do, so I can only assume he was talking about the hack job. But I'm not sure. Regardless, after the hug, he just gave me that smart-ass wink of his, hugged Sarah goodbye, and marched off in the direction of his flight with the kind of swagger only a guy as fucking awesome as he is could ever pull off.

As our airplane lifts off the runway, I grab Sarah's hand and she rests her head on my shoulder. She's trembling.

"You afraid of flying?" I whisper into her hair.

She shrugs but doesn't say anything.

We're quiet for several minutes as the plane reaches its flying altitude.

I know it's inhumanely early in the morning, and she said she didn't sleep a wink last night, but still—she seems unusually quiet, like something's troubling her. Is it just being on an airplane? I doubt it, but I don't want to press her. She'll tell me what's going on when she's ready.

"Belize," she finally says when it's clear takeoff has been successful. She sighs and nuzzles into my shoulder. "I still can't believe it."

Unfortunately, I couldn't keep our destination a secret forever. The minute we checked in for our flight, the jig was up, and she squealed like she'd just won the Showcase Showdown on *The Price is Right*. It was exactly the reaction I was hoping for. I wish I could have dazzled her even more by flying her on our company jet instead of going commercial—first, so I could have kept our destination a secret 'til the minute we stepped off the plane, and, second, so we could have flown straight there without laying over in Houston—but my uncle is using the jet for a business trip to London this weekend.

"Wait 'til you see it. I think you'll find it profoundly *inspirational.*"

She looks at me quizzically.

I just smile. I can't wait for everything I've got planned for her. I feel like rubbing my hands together and giving her a really hearty villain laugh, but her hand in mine feels so good, it's not worth pulling away from her to do it.

She leans into me again.

"I have a confession to make," she finally says.

My stomach drops. I knew she had something big on her mind all morning.

"I don't even know where in the world Belize is."

I chuckle. Has her anxiety been about not knowing where we were headed? This is her first trip out of the country, after all. I sigh, relieved. "Central America. Bordered by Mexico, Guatemala, and the Caribbean Sea. Fun fact: It's the only country in Central America where the official language is English—though, of course, they speak Spanish there, too."

Her head remains fixed on my shoulder. It feels nice.

"I'm so excited," she says. With her free hand, she runs her fingertips gently along the tattooed inscription on the inside of my right forearm. Just that simple touch alone makes my breathing halt.

"Do you speak Spanish?" I ask.

"Mmm hmm," she says, sounding drowsy. "My mother's half Colombian—American-born, but her mom was from Colombia. Her father was Irish. She spoke Spanish to me growing up, though of course she speaks perfect English, too."

"And your dad?

She pauses. "American. Spanish-Italian heritage. Cruz is from his Spanish side."

"So he speaks Spanish, too?"

"Nope, just English. But he's also fluent in motherfucking asshole, too."

I can't help but raise my eyebrows at that. But I remain quiet. I wish I could give that bastard a taste of his own medicine.

Her fingertips lightly trace the length of my tattoo again, up and down, up and down, caressing the entire length of my forearm. I keep expecting her to do it, but she never asks me what my tattoos mean. I like that doesn't ask me about them. Most women ask about them first thing, like they're grasping at straws for anything to talk about and can't think of anything else to say. But not Sarah. Somehow, she knows my tattoos aren't fodder for small talk. Somehow, she always just knows.

I exhale. She's driving me crazy with her soft caress.

She's still leaning against my shoulder, not looking at me. "My mom left him when I was ten. Or, more accurately, she *escaped* him. We haven't seen him since. He's never contacted me."

Her fingertips move above my forearm and find my bicep, and begin caressing the muscles of my upper arm, under the sleeve of my T-shirt.

"His loss," I say quietly.

"I don't want to see him, anyway," she mumbles. "Ever."

After a minute, she raises her head up from my shoulder and looks into my eyes. She's holding back tears. "I've got something I need to tell you," she says. "Well, actually, three things. And one of 'em's a doozy."

My stomach drops. "Okay," I manage. "Shoot."

She straightens up and sighs. "I don't even know where to start." She looks like she's going to be sick.

I'm instantly on high alert. "Just say it. I'm a big believer in ripping off the Band-Aid."

She exhales. "I'll go in order from bad to worse."

I nod. "Okay."

"First, hopefully not too bad: I went to see Georgia on Tuesday—at the post office. And I bought her a cup of tea."

I laugh. Oh fuck, I'm so relieved. This is what she was nervous about all morning? "Sarah, I know. She called me. I don't know what you said to her, but she fell, like, head over heels in love with you. She called to tell me to grab you and never let go."

Her eyes light up. "She said that?"

"Yeah." I suddenly wish I hadn't repeated that exact phrase. I mean, I'm smitten here, don't get me wrong, but I don't want to give Sarah the impression I'm anywhere near ready to grab her and 'never let go.' I mean, come on. That's something I don't know if I'll *ever* be able commit to doing with anyone—even someone as incredible as Sarah. "So, anyway," I say, trying to change the subject quickly, "I don't know what Georgia told you, but I don't want you to get the wrong idea about me."

"Wrong idea? No, she said amazing things—beautiful things." Her voice lowers. "Things that made me see you in a whole new light."

"That's what I mean. I'm not that guy." I exhale, trying to figure out how to explain myself without pushing her away. "I'm not myself when it comes to Trey and Georgia. The Jonas Faraday I am for them is the exception, not the rule. Those two just bring something out in me I can't control." I clear my throat. A lump is rising up there.

Her eyes are shining.

I roll my eyes. "Stop looking at me like that. Seriously, I can't run around trying to be everybody's hero all the time—and I don't. I'm vastly under-qualified for the job of hero."

She pauses. "Well, I think you're vastly underestimating yourself." She squints at me. "And I think you're in the process of transforming into Georgia's Jonas Faraday as we speak, even if you don't realize it. And, if you must know, I think the rock climbing gym is happening right now for a reason—it's not a coincidence. In fact, I don't believe in coincidences at all."

She flashes me a know-it-all look that makes it clear she's the smart one here and I'm just along for the ride.

"Well, I think you're a pain in the ass," I say, but I'm smiling broadly.

Damn. I wish I had the courage to say what I'm thinking, but I don't. It's too much. If I did, though, I'd blurt, "You are everything I never knew I always wanted." But it's one thing to say that kind of thing in a Valentine's Day card, and a whole other thing to say it out loud—especially when I'm not even sure what the hell it means. So, instead of saying it and sounding like a total sap, I just kiss her. And I kiss her and kiss her and kiss her again. My heart's racing. If we were alone, I'd rip her clothes off and kiss every inch of her, including her glorious pussy and suck on her clit and make her come right now, to hell with everything I've meticulously planned in Belize. So it's a good thing we're not alone. Because, with God as my witness, I'm going to do everything according to plan from here on out. No fucking around this time.

Oh man, our kissing is turning passionate. Too passionate. If we continue this way, I'm going to be tempted to drag her into the airplane bathroom—and that absolutely cannot happen. I promised myself I'd lead her outside the cave in a way that's worthy of her. I've got it all planned in Belize. And, God knows, fucking this gorgeous creature in an airplane bathroom would most definitely not be part of the plan.

She pulls away, licking her lips. "I have more to tell you, Jonas."

"Okay, okay." I sigh. "What's the second horrible thing?"

She gathers herself. "I spent six hundred and change of the money you gave me for shopping. And, thank you so much, by the way. I had so much fun. I felt like a princess."

I grunt. "Aw man, I really wanted you to go crazy—"

"No, no, that's not the bad part. I'm not gonna apologize for *not* spending three thousand dollars. That was too big a budget—totally ridiculous. I mean, thank you so much, you made me swoon—but I'm not gonna spend money just to spend money."

I smile. I would have been thrilled if she'd spent every last cent of that money spoiling herself—but I've got to admit it turns me on that she didn't. "So what's the big confession, then?"

"I gave all the leftover money on the card to that nonprofit I was telling you about. They provide shelter for battered women, and they also donate suits and work clothes to women going on job interviews."

Before I can speak, she continues. Clearly, she's nervous.

"And there's something I didn't tell you before. It's my mom's charity." She clears her throat. "She started it ten years ago. She runs it. Oh my God, Jonas, it's her life, her passion." Her face is bursting with pride. "So, yeah, technically, I gave the money to my mom, but not to run off and get her nails done or whatever. She'll use it to help a lot of women in need."

There are no words to describe the way I'm feeling right now, so I kiss her again. And again.

She pulls away. "So you're not upset about any of that?"

"Upset? Of course not. In fact, when we get home, I'll make a proper donation to your mom's charity. I'm sorry I didn't think of doing it when you first told me about it. See? I told you, I'm vastly under-qualified to play hero."

"Thank you," she says.

"You thought I'd be *upset* about that?"

"No, not really *upset*, but I wasn't one hundred percent sure how you'd feel about me giving your money away without asking first." She sighs. "And, well, Jonas, I didn't buy a single item of lingerie, either—that's the most appalling part of the whole confession."

I feign indignation. "Don't speak to me ever again."

She laughs. "I just figured lingerie would be pretty useless. Why not just go buck naked and give you unimpeded access to every inch of me, instead?"

"I like the way you think," I say.

So far, her supposed mountain of bad news has turned out to be a whole lot of nothing. Damn, from the way she was looking so nervous a minute ago, you'd think she had something genuinely horrible to tell me.

"So what's the third horrible thing?" I ask. "It's the worst one, right? Should I brace myself?"

She furrows her brow. “Yeah, this one’s really, really bad, Jonas. Really bad.” She’s shaking again.

My stomach instantly twists into a huge knot.

“Remember that software engineer I told you about?” she begins slowly. “The one who joined The Club, looking for love?”

“Yeah, the one who joined for a month,” I say, nodding. Yeah, yeah, yeah, I know—he’s a romantic and I’m a fucking sociopath looking for nothing but endless coochie. She already made that abundantly clear.

“He checked in for the first time last night at a sports bar. So Kat and I went to spy on him.”

I don’t know where this is heading. Something in her eyes is making me dread whatever’s coming next. Jesus, did she go home with him or something? Please, God, no.

She sighs. She’s trembling. She shakes her head, unable to go on.

“Sarah, just tell me.” I’m officially about to fucking freak out.

She shakes her head again.

I pull back from her to look into her eyes. “What’s going on? Whatever it is, it’s okay, I promise.” *Unless you fucked him. That would most definitely not be okay.* I’m about to lose my fucking mind here. “Sarah, tell me.” There’s an edge in my voice I can’t suppress.

“Jonas, the guy couldn’t have been more opposite you in every way—talk about being brainwashed by Lifetime and Disney. Seriously.”

My cheeks blaze. Yes, I know. He’s sweet, I’m an asshole. He signed up for a month, I signed up for a year. He applied to The Club to find love, and I applied to find a year’s worth of no-strings-attached fuck buddies who wouldn’t make me feel like an asshole when I sent them packing night after night. I got it. Is she still judging me based on my application? I thought we were all done with that. Did she have an epiphany that she wants a guy who wears his romantic heart on his sleeve—that she *needs* a guy like that? What is she trying to tell me?

“So, anyway, the guy came to the bar wearing a yellow bracelet—which, like I say, made perfect sense. If *you* were assigned purple, then I knew *that guy* had to be whatever color is the opposite of purple. Kat and I were just dying to see what kind of Miss Yellow was gonna be this normal, boring guy’s one true love.”

Okay, I’m oddly reassured by that last part. If I know anything about Sarah by now, it’s that she doesn’t want normal and boring. She wants fucked up and abnormal and sometimes pretty fucking dirty—

she wants an asshole she can redeem. So, really, she's complimenting me in a twisted kind of way. My heart slows slightly. I wait.

She pauses a ridiculously long time, obviously getting up the nerve to blurt it out, whatever it is.

"Sarah, rip off the Band-Aid," I huff, verging on exasperation. "Come on."

She exhales. "When Miss Yellow showed up in her yellow bracelet ... " She sighs again. "Jonas, she was your Miss Purple. Stacy the Faker."

I'm floored. "What?" My head is reeling. What the fuck?

She proceeds to tell me every last detail about the night, including exactly what Stacy said when she ambushed Sarah in the bathroom.

I run my fingers through my hair, my mind reeling.

Tears have pooled in Sarah's eyes. "I'm sick about it," she chokes out. "I swear I didn't know." She puts her hands over her face. "I work for a frickin' whorehouse," she whispers.

My heart is beating a mile a minute. If I could punch a hole in the wall, I would—but that's a non-starter on an airplane. I run a hand over my face. I can't even process what I'm hearing.

Sarah puts her hands over her face and begins to cry.

I know I should comfort her right now, I know that's the right thing to do, but I want to kill someone. So much adrenaline is coursing through my body it's a good thing I'm strapped down by a seatbelt. I look out the airplane window, trying to corral my racing thoughts, but it's no use. My stomach is flip-flopping and my fists are clenched. Holy shit, I fucked a prostitute. I *licked* a fucking prostitute's cunt. It doesn't matter that it was for twenty seconds; I tongued a fucking pay-to-play pussy. I physically shudder at the disgusting thought. My tongue suddenly feels like it's covered in a thick grime. I can practically hear my father's ghost laughing in my ear.

I unbuckle my seatbelt. My head is spinning.

"I'll be right back," I mumble over my shoulder as I bolt to the bathroom. I know I shouldn't run away, shouldn't leave her crying and all alone. I know I should be reassuring and compassionate, tell her we'll figure this out. *I'm not mad at you,* I should say, *I just need a minute alone.* But I've got to get the hell out of here. I feel like I'm going to be sick.

I slam the bathroom door behind me.

I fucked a goddamned hooker. I've become my fucking father. Fuck me.

In the bathroom, I put cold water on my face. I rinse out my mouth. I stand over the toilet, ready to puke my guts out. But nothing comes up.

After a minute, I rinse my face again.

This is karma, really. Bad things happen to bad people. And, anyway, what did I think I was getting into when I signed up for The Club? Who did I think was out there in the universe, eager to fuck me with no expectation or even desire to feel anything, ever? What kind of woman did I think I'd find matching those criteria? Seriously, what kind of woman yearns for nothing but a good fuck followed by a swift push out the door? I knew there was no such woman—deep down, I knew it. And I just ignored what I knew to be true. Ha! I convinced myself I was looking for brutal honesty, but the whole time, I was looking for lies. And I got what I deserved. I got what I fucking deserved.

I look at myself in the mirror. Water's dripping off my brow.

I licked at Stacy for five seconds before she started howling like I'd blasted her to the moon. I'm good, but I'm not that good. And I knew it. And then I fucked her so hard I practically tore her in half, and she pretended to love every minute of it. So what fairytale did I tell myself to continue believing Stacy had signed up for The Club the way I did? Oh yeah, a woman who looks like that wants nothing more than to get fucked and tossed aside? I knew something was wrong when she left without a word. I knew I was deluding myself. But I didn't care. Josh told me his membership was the "best money he'd ever spent." What the fuck Club did *he* join? Because I knew all along I'd paid The Club to lie to me. Deep down, I knew. Well, now I'm getting exactly what I deserve.

An image floods me—a vision I've tried my whole life to forget. He's binding her arms and legs to the bedposts. Blood is trickling from her nose.

I grip the cold metal sink, trying to steady myself, trying to keep the rest of the images from leaping into my mind, but I can't stop them. They're slamming into me.

He's forcing himself on her, his pants around his ankles, his hairy ass hanging out. He's grunting like an animal. She's screaming. I'm burrowing myself deeper behind her dresses in the closet, but I can't look away. I cover my ears, but I can still hear her blood-curdling screams. He whacks her across the face and bends down to pull up his pants. As he leans over, she peeks over at me in my hiding spot. Her blue eyes are wild. She shakes her head frantically at me. *Don't come out,* she's commanding me. *Stay where you are.* But she doesn't have to command me to stay put—my legs have been frozen since he first dragged her into the room, kicking and screaming.

I run water through my hair and let it drip down my face. I stare at myself in the mirror. I can see my eyes staring back at me now. Those long-ago images are gone, at least for now.

Well, I guess I can't hide from the truth about myself forever. Yeah, I can wear the custom suits Josh always insists I should wear, even though I hate them. I can work out three hours a day and sculpt my body into a façade of perfection. I can read and read and aspire and reach for enlightenment all I like, but I'll never be able to change what I did.

Tears are threatening, but I won't let them come. Even if I were a fucking pussy-ass crier, which I'm not, even if I were "soft," like he always said I am, I'd never let myself cry in a fucking airplane bathroom. But, anyway, I'm not a fucking pussy-ass crier and I'm not soft, so it's a moot point.

If I'd known he had that knife, maybe I would have done something differently. Maybe I wouldn't have stayed in the closet, hiding behind her dresses, frozen with fear. Maybe I would have at least tried to pull him off her. Maybe then everything would have turned out differently.

I unzip my pants and take a whiz.

I'm getting exactly what I deserve. I wanted brutal honesty, huh? Something *real*? I scoff at myself. I was lying to myself. I wanted a quarter-million dollars' worth of pussy, plain and simple. I just wanted to numb the pain, just like my father always did. Where did I think all that pain-killing pussy was gonna come from? Pussy heaven? The Pussy Fairy? I didn't care. I didn't care about anybody or anything but numbing the pain. It serves me right. What kind of sick fuck joins a sex club for a fucking year, anyway? Josh joined The Club for a fun-filled month—just a little vacation—and I'm the sick fuck who joined for a fucking *year*? What the fuck is wrong with me? I'm not normal.

I zip my fly back up.

I wash my hands.

I wipe at my eyes.

I'm getting exactly what I deserve.

As I take my seat again, she looks at me expectantly, tears streaming down her face. She looks half her age—so small and vulnerable. Even before I buckle my seatbelt, even before she can speak, I take her face in my hands and kiss her deeply. She sobs into me, returning my kiss.

After a moment, she pulls away from me. "I should have told you everything before you were stuck on an airplane with me—so you could cancel the trip if you wanted to."

I exhale with exasperation. That's the last thing in the world I'm thinking right now. "Nothing in the world could make me want to cancel this trip with you. Not what you just told me, not the world crumbling down, not the fucking apocalypse. Nothing. I want to be here with you right now, headed to paradise, more than I want anything in the world—and now more than ever." I kiss her again, and her body melts into me.

"Just give me a little time, okay? I don't know how to explain everything I'm thinking right now—everything I'm feeling. It's complicated."

"Okay," she says meekly. She's hiccupping, trying to suppress her sobs.

"Sarah, I'm not upset at you. I promise." I smooth away a lock of her hair that's stuck to her wet cheek. "I'm disgusted, furious, ashamed. But none of it at you."

"I'm sorry," she says. "I didn't know. I never would have taken that stupid job if I'd known."

"I know that. Just give me a little time to think. I can't talk to you about everything right now. I just can't."

She clamps her mouth shut into a thin line and nods.

"It's not you. Sometimes, I have a hard time expressing my feelings out loud. I just need a little time to think everything through, that's all. Maybe listen to some music. Music is what I use to sort out my feelings."

"Okay," she says again. "I totally understand." Without saying another word, she plants a gentle kiss on my cheek, grabs my hand, and leans against my shoulder. Her fingertips begin lightly tracing the tattooed inscription on my forearm and then, slowly, working their way up to my bicep.

I grab my phone and ear buds and scroll into my music library. Arctic Monkeys. I put on my headphones and sit back.

Sarah's fingers are caressing my forearm.

The music is calming me.

Sarah's touch is calming me.

My breathing is returning to normal.

What did Sarah say in that handwritten note of hers, the one she put into the welcome package? "If I were willing to lie to you, like everyone else apparently does—like you actually *want* everyone to do, despite what you delude yourself into thinking you want—things might have been different." She sure saw right through me, right from the beginning, didn't she?

Her hand has stopped moving. It falls into her lap.

Yeah, she had me pegged right from the start.

"My wish for you," she wrote, "is that someday you'll realize what you *want* and what you *need* are two very different things."

Her head flops forward on my shoulder. I glance down at her beautiful face. She's out like a light. I turn off my music and gaze at her for a moment. I love the shape of her lips. Her eyelashes are long and lush. Her fingers are elegant. That silver band on her thumb slays me.

I sigh.

I bring her hand up to my lips and gently kiss her sexy little ring.

Well, if that's her wish for me—that I discover what I *want* and *need* are two very different things—then her wish is never gonna come true. Because sitting here with her, feeling her body rising and falling rhythmically against mine, a wisp of her hair brushing up against my jawline, I'm suddenly quite certain, for the first time in my life, that what I *want* and *need* are one and the same thing. And that thing is sitting next to me, fast asleep.

Chapter 23

Sarah

"Holy moly," I say. "Wow! Oh my gosh!" I can't stop the exclamations of excitement and glee from pouring out of my mouth. "Wooh! Did you see this? Wow!"

After almost twelve hours of travel—two planes, a layover in Houston, and a long, bumpy Jeep ride out to the middle of nowhere—we're finally here at our destination, a secluded resort in the heart of the Belizian jungle. I'm panting like a dog, thanks not only to my excitement, but also thanks to our trek up ten flights of rickety wooden steps in the ink-black night to reach our accommodations. Because Jonas and I are staying in an effing *tree house*—a luxurious, honeymoon-suite *tree house*!— surrounded on all sides by the lush jungle canopy. Holy crappola. Or, holy shitballs, as Kat would say. (*Juepucha,* as my mom would say.) Whatever—it's un-frickin'-believable.

I don't know where I'm getting this sudden burst of energy, but I'm running around the spacious suite, squealing and shouting about every fabulous detail. "Did you see this?" I shout, pointing at the flower petals strewn all over the white bed covers. "And look!" The towels in the bathroom have been twisted and sculpted into two perfect swans. "Woah!" The bathroom shower is even bigger than Jonas' spacious shower at his house. "Ooooh!" A bottle of champagne sits on ice, waiting for us. Holy frickin' moly.

After the steward opens the champagne bottle for us and tucks our luggage away, he explains how to light the mosquito lamps and close the mosquito netting over our bed while we sleep. Jonas hands him a large bill, and he ducks out with a big smile on his face.

"Alone at last," Jonas says, handing me yet another glass of champagne. I think this is my fourth glass over the course of this long day.

"This is the most amazing place, ever," I say, my eyes blazing. I take a sip. "Wow. The best champagne of the day."

Jonas is beaming at me.

"I never thought I'd get to see a place like this in my entire life." I gaze out the screened windows surrounding us. It's pitch black outside.

"Wait 'til you see it in the light," Jonas says. "The jungle's gonna blow your mind." He grabs my hand. "Come here." He pulls me out to the deck. I can't see a thing in the blackness surrounding us.

"What?" I ask, looking around. Light is wafting out of the suite behind us, but looking out toward the jungle, I can't make out a single thing.

He puts his finger to his mouth and tilts his head toward the edge of the balcony. "Listen."

I stand quietly, pricking my ears for any kind of noise in the darkness around me. I smash my body against his and he puts his arm around me. I listen. And I listen. Well, I definitely hear birds. All around me, in fact. Leaves are rustling as animals move around us. Jonas puts his finger to his mouth again, instructing me to keep listening quietly. Yep, birds. And movement everywhere. We stand stock still for what must be a full two minutes. Finally, a screeching howl cuts through the dark night.

I gasp. "What—?"

"A howler monkey," Jonas says quietly, grinning mischievously.

Oh, Jonas.

A moment later, there's another scream, even louder and more piercing than the first one. I burst out laughing.

"They're all around us in the trees." He pulls me close to him. "A little inspiration for you, baby." He kisses me. "Let the monkeys be your guide."

My heart is in danger of hurtling right out of my chest and flinging into the dark night like a Frisbee. "Oh, Jonas. Right here, right now, on this very spot on planet earth, with you"—I point to the ground I'm standing on—"is the most glorious five square inches in the entire world."

His smile lights up the dark night.

"When you said 'tropical,' I pictured us lying on a sandy beach drinking piña coladas," I say.

"Yeah, well, Belize is famous for its beaches. But we're not going to the coast this time. We'll do that next time. This time, we're all about the jungle."

Next time? He's already contemplating a *next* time? I try to suppress a squeal, but I don't succeed.

"But, hey, I can certainly get you that piña colada." He looks at his watch. "But not tonight. We've got a big day tomorrow. Gotta be up bright and early."

"What are we doing?"

"Wouldn't you like to know," he says.

"Yes, I would. But I'll be patient and wait to find out. On this trip, I'm doing whatever you say, Lord-God-Master-Woman-Wizard."

He nods. "Good girl."

In a fit of sudden glee, I twirl like a little girl. "This is like a dream."

He's smiling from ear to ear. It's a welcome change from the storm cloud that's been hanging over him since our horrific conversation on the plane.

I yawn. I don't mean to, but I do. I didn't sleep at all last night, and I caught maybe two hours of sleep today on the plane, if I was lucky. And all the champagne I've had today certainly isn't helping me keep my eyes open.

"What do you say we take a shower," Jonas says, "and then get into bed?"

He's wearing only boxers, glory be, and his taut muscles are on full display. I watch him light the mosquito lamps on either side of the bed, the muscles over his rib cage tightening as he bends over to position the lamp. I'm wearing a tank top and plaid pajama bottoms, my hair tied into a ponytail, and my skin feels squeaky clean and moisturized after our shower together, a welcome sensation after our long and grimy travel day. Showering with him was particularly enjoyable this time, maybe because I was so relaxed. Somehow, I knew he was going to wash me and lather me, and that sex wasn't in the cards. I just knew it. And I was right. He lathered me so tenderly, so delicately, he wasn't so much *washing* me as *worshipping* me. Delicious.

And now, I can't believe I'm lying here in this four-poster mahogany bed in a tree house in the middle of a deep, dark, noisy jungle, basking in the warm night air, as the most beautiful man I've ever laid eyes on climbs into bed and secures mosquito netting around us.

"It's a little cocoon," he says, fastening the net and lying down right next to me. "A cocoon built for two."

"I like that," I say, nuzzling up to him as he scoots his body against mine. His skin is warm. "A cocoon built for two," I repeat.

A monkey screams just outside our window in the darkness and we both laugh.

"That was a good one," he says. "Are you taking notes?"

"Yes, sir." I mimic the sound the monkey just made.

He laughs. "Pretty good."

We lie on our sides, smiling at each other, staring at each other, lost in each other's eyes. After a moment, he rubs the tip of his nose against mine. "Thank you for coming here with me."

"You're welcome," I say. "But you owe me big."

He laughs. "I do, actually."

"You really don't understand the concept of payment, do you?" I ask.

He grins.

I want to kiss him. But tonight I'm going to honor my word and let him take the lead. He's my master tonight. His hands rest comfortably on my waist, not moving, not exploring, not pressing for more. So I rest my hand on his thigh.

"I'm happy," he says.

My heart leaps out of my chest. I can barely breathe. "So am I, Jonas."

He hugs me to him and squeezes me tight. I rest my head against his chest. I wait. Is he going to make love to me now?

After a moment, his fingers lightly skim the curve of my hip.

I follow his lead. My fingertip drifts to the tattoo inscribed on the inside of his left arm.

"Is this Greek?" I ask.

"Mmm hmm," he says. "Ancient Greek."

"Are you Greek?"

"No."

I wait. I've wanted to know the meaning of his tattoos since I first saw his heart-stopping, full-bodied selfie. I smile wistfully to myself. Back then, he was nothing more than an idea—a vision of unattainable perfection, a work of art. Not the flesh and blood man lying next to me now. When I saw that photo, I never would have thought I'd be lying here, touching his muscled arm, drifting off to sleep in his arms. In effing Belize.

I yawn again. Damn. I can't help it. My body is so relaxed and I'm so sleepy. My mind keeps slipping, floating, and then jolting back awake. I don't want to fall asleep. I don't want to miss a thing.

My fingertips track the inscription on his arm again. These words, whatever they are, are the key to unlocking him; I know it. But, somehow, I've known from the start to wait for him to hand me the key in his own time.

He pulls back slightly and displays the inside of his arm to me. "It's a quote from Plato," he says. He waits a beat.

I'm tingling with anticipation at his next words. "Yeah?" I say, breathless.

"'For a man to conquer himself is the first and noblest of all victories.'"

My pulse is suddenly pounding in my ears. "That's the quote you mentioned in your interview with Trey." And it's what I guessed the longer of his tattoos would say.

"Ah, you read that interview, huh?"

"Like twenty times. That interview told me more about you than anything else I could find. And believe me, I was thorough in my research."

He's quiet for a minute as my fingers migrate up to his biceps. Man, I love the feel of his biceps. He's got the kind of arms most girls could only dream about wrapping around them one day. And here I am, my dreams a reality.

"Why did you get that tattooed onto your arm?" I ask.

He's quiet for so long, I begin to wonder if he's ever going to answer me. "Because conquering myself is my life's greatest struggle," he finally says. "It's a constant reminder for me to keep working at it, to keep trying. Not to give up."

When it's clear he's not going to go on, I finally say, "What happened to you, Jonas?"

His body tenses and he shifts uncomfortably. He exhales. "Josh and I were seven." He pauses.

I'm holding my breath.

"My dad was taking the whole family to a Seahawks game—my mom, Josh, and me." He pauses again.

I wait. The light from the mosquito lamp is flickering in the room, casting shadows across his beautiful face. A bird screeches loudly in the jungle, just outside our bedroom window. There's a rustle in the trees.

His voice is low, barely audible. "I worshipped the ground she walked on, followed her around like a puppy. She used to pat me on the head and say, 'Good doggie' and I'd make puppy noises." He closes his eyes, remembering something. "She was so beautiful. And she was *kind*."

I'm afraid if I move or talk or breathe, I'll break the spell and he'll stop talking.

He opens his eyes again and pain flashes across his face. "It was time to go to the football game, but my mother had one of her headaches. She didn't want to go to the noisy stadium."

There's a rustling sound outside our window.

His eyes dart to mine for reassurance.

I nod, ever so slightly.

"Dad was mad. He was like, 'Take a fucking aspirin, you'll be fine.' But I said, 'No, she needs to rest. I'll stay with her and make her all better.' I used to rub her temples when she got her headaches. She always said my touch was the only thing that could take her pain away. She said I had magic in my fingers."

His eyes are moist. I touch his cheek, and he closes his eyes at my touch. He leans his cheek into the palm of my hand.

My heart breaks at this simple gesture.

He continues talking with his eyes closed, his cheek in my hand. "Dad was pissed. He stormed out with Josh. Didn't even say goodbye." I caress his cheek with my thumb and he opens his eyes. His expression is one of unadulterated anguish. "We were cuddling in her bed, snuggling, my favorite thing. I loved having her all to myself. I was rubbing her temples so she could fall asleep." His entire body tenses next to me in the bed. "There was a loud noise downstairs, a crashing noise. She jumped off the bed and I started to follow her, but she said, 'No, baby, stay here.' So I hid in the closet because I was scared. I was shaking." He swallows hard. "And before she got two steps out of her bedroom, there was a man. He dragged her back into the room. She fought against him and he punched her in the face with his fist. She was bleeding out her nose." His voice hitches. "I knew I should run out of the closet right then to help her, but I didn't."

Oh, his voice. I've never heard it sound like this—so small. My heart is aching for him.

"I just stood there, peeking through a crack in the closet door, hiding in her dresses." He inhales, like he's remembering the scent of her. "He tied her up. He ... he ... pulled down his pants. I remember what his ass looked like."

I inhale sharply, anticipating the horror to come. My stomach is twisting into knots.

"She was screaming, but I just let him do it to her. I didn't help her." His eyes are glistening.

I don't speak. I just wait. My heart is banging in my ears.

"I wanted to help her, to pull him off her—I wanted to make him stop. But he was so big and my legs wouldn't work. I imagined myself sneaking out of the closet and finding a golf club in the garage and running back up to the bedroom and bashing him over the head ... But I didn't move." Tears are pooling in his eyes. He looks up to keep them from falling down his cheeks. "Then I realized I could take her pain away after the man left—with my magic fingers. I decided to wait and untie her after he was gone and make it all better with my hands, like I always did." He's choking up. "I didn't know he had a knife." Jonas blinks and, despite his best efforts, big, soggy tears stream down his cheeks. "I didn't know what he was gonna do with that knife—it happened so fast—or else I wouldn't have waited. If I'd known, I would have saved her the minute he punched her. I would have done *something*." Tears are pouring out of his eyes, and out of mine, too.

"Jonas, you were seven," I say.

He lets out a soft groan. "I should have saved her."

"You were *seven*," I say again. "There was nothing you could have done."

"I should have at least *tried* to save her." His voice catches in his throat. "I should have at least *tried* to pull him off her." His body twitches violently, straining to suppress the tidal wave of grief threatening to rise up out of him. "Or I should have died trying."

"Oh, Jonas, no." I take his face in my hands and he melts under my touch. "Oh, baby," I say, pulling him to me. "No."

He nods, unable to speak.

"No," I whisper. "No." My heart is breaking in two.

"If it wasn't for me, she would have gone to the football game like my father wanted her to—she wouldn't have been in the house when the man came. It was *me* who said she needed to rest. It was me who *wanted* her to stay behind so I could have her all to myself. I wanted to be alone with her—no Josh, no Dad. I wanted to touch her and take her pain away. I wanted to lie in bed with her. I wanted her to say I was the only one who knew how to make her feel better." He's on the verge of a total breakdown. "If it hadn't been for me . . ." He can't contain himself anymore. Grief and guilt and heartache and pain burst out of him in a singular, violent release.

There is nothing more heartbreaking than seeing a grown man sob—especially when that man has a hold on your heart like nobody ever has. I hold him to me—rocking him, nuzzling him, stroking his hair—as his anguish rises up and pours out of him like a tsunami.

"It wasn't your fault," I say again and again.

His body twists and shudders.

"Shh," I soothe him. "It wasn't your fault."

After a while, he quiets down. His chest is heaving. He leans his forehead into mine, but he doesn't speak. He's spent.

A howler monkey screams in the dark jungle right outside our window.

He pulls back from me and wipes his eyes with the back of his hand. He moves a wisp of hair out my eyes.

"Did they ever catch him?"

"He was our housekeeper's sister's boyfriend. Our housekeeper had mentioned getting the day off because the family was going out to the Seahawk's game—it wasn't her fault. She had nothing to do with it." He pauses. "He thought we'd be gone. He just came for her jewelry." He sighs deeply. "It was just bad luck we were there—bad luck he turned out to be a psychopath." He sighs again, slowly, trying to control his breathing.

"What about your father?" I ask. I know Jonas' father died about thirteen years ago, when Jonas was seventeen, but I couldn't find anything on-line detailing the cause of his death. "I can't imagine how devastated he must have been."

At my question, Jonas' eyes darken. He inhales deeply and exhales slowly. "My father never got over losing her. The grief—the guilt—it ate him alive. So he turned it into blame. He blamed himself, blamed me. Mostly blamed me."

I shake my head. That can't be true. "No," I say softly.

"Yes. My whole life, I knew it. He blamed me for what happened."

"No. He couldn't have blamed you. You were seven."

"Even Josh knows he blamed me. It wasn't a secret. It's just the way it was. It was my fault. We all knew it. I'm the one that made her stay behind."

A shiver runs down my spine. What kind of man could even think of blaming a child for a horror like that?

"I tried to make up for what I did. But it was never enough. How could it ever be enough?"

I shake my head. Horrible. No wonder Jonas needed years of therapy. "He died when you were seventeen?"

Jonas grunts.

Maybe I should let it be, change the subject. But now that this man has shown me the deepest parts of himself, I'm aching to know every last thing. I wait. But he doesn't say anything. I'm about to say, "It's okay—we don't have to talk about this," when he finally speaks.

"He killed himself."

I moan softly. How much tragedy can one family take?

"He just couldn't ... He never got over losing her. In the beginning, he tried to forget what happened by throwing himself into his company."

I'm surprised at the edge in his tone when he says "his company," especially since that company ultimately became Jonas'.

"And when all the money in the world didn't take the pain away, he turned to booze, and then to women—lots and lots of women—

prostitutes, mainly." He scoffs angrily at this last part. "He had the famous Faraday libido, of course, so becoming a monk wasn't realistic, and yet he didn't want to foul her memory by *feeling* something with another human being ever again, God forbid." He clenches his jaw. "He never told the truth about any of it, acted like all those hot women were falling all over him thanks to his fucking personality, acted like his shit didn't stink 'til the bitter end—but Josh and I knew exactly what he was doing. It was disgusting." He sighs. "He fucked every hooker he could get his hands on for about a year—and then he finally put himself out of his misery."

I'm speechless. Does he not see the parallels between himself and his father? Or does he? I've suddenly got goose bumps.

"My uncle took over the company. Josh went off to college that fall, and I went off the following year, when I was all better." His eyes flicker. "But we both knew, when we graduated, we'd have to come back. We knew we had a duty to become the 'Sons' of Faraday & Sons." His jaw muscles are pulsing.

"Not what you wanted?"

"My dad started Faraday & Sons right after we were born. We were *babies* and he called it Faraday *& Sons*. There was never any question about who we were expected to become." He looks up at the ceiling, lost in thought.

I stroke his cheek with the back of my hand.

His eyes soften. "I like to imagine there's another version of me, the 'divine original' form of me, floating in another realm. A not-fucked-up version of me. In that realm, that one horrible day never happened and I became the man I was originally designed to be." He sighs. "The man I would have been if I didn't get hopelessly fucked up."

"Is that what your other tattoo is about?" I ask, but I already know it is.

He half-smiles at me. "You're so smart, Sarah—you'd give Plato a run for his money, you know that?" He shifts his body and holds his right arm up to display his tattoo. "'Visualize the divine originals.'"

I look down at the lettering. Greek again. "Plato?" I ask.

He nods.

"Why the devotion to Plato?" I ask.

He sighs. "After my dad died, I had a bit of a rough time." He smiles wanly, like this is the understatement of the year. "When all the doctors in the world couldn't fix me, I started reading philosophy—everything I could get my hands on, just reading,

reading, reading, trying to make sense of things, trying not to have a nervous breakdown again, honestly—trying not to go completely insane again. I'd had a total fucking meltdown after everything with my mother, and I'd been in therapy ever since—and doing pretty well, actually—but then I lost it again after my dad ... And I finally figured out talking about my fucking *feelings* just wasn't gonna be enough this time, especially after what my dad said to me in his fucking suicide note."

Oh my God. What did that bastard say to my sweet Jonas as an unanswerable parting shot? I'm afraid to ask, and he doesn't offer any specifics. A chill runs down my spine.

He shrugs. "I knew I needed something more, something wise. Timeless. I needed answers. I read everything I could get my hands on, and when I discovered Plato, I don't know, he just spoke to me, especially his Allegory of the Cave, the one I told you about in the limo." He grins, obviously remembering our eventful limo ride. "I don't know, people always talk about Aristotle—and he was great, of course, obviously—but Plato was Aristotle's *teacher*, you know? Plato was the fucking *forefather* of modern thought, you know? The divine original. His ideas gave me something to latch onto—something to focus on. He had ideas about everything—music, science, death, family, mortality ... love." He blushes.

I feel my cheeks flush. My heart is racing. I touch his cheek again.

He turns his head and kisses the palm of my hand.

"Plato was an idealist." He says the word 'idealist' like he's paying the man his highest compliment.

"But what does it mean—'visualize the divine originals'?"

He looks down at his tattoo. "Visualize the divine originals." He sighs reverently. "It's from Plato's Theory of Forms." Oh wow, his eyes are suddenly animated. Clearly, he's passionate about this, whatever it is. "Plato had the idea that truth, idealism, perfection, it's all an abstraction that exists separate and apart from the physical world we live in."

I shrug. I still don't understand.

He grins. "It's really esoteric stuff. Plato thought there were two realms—the imperfect physical world we live in—the one we experience through our senses, the one filled with pain and imperfection—and also an ideal realm, completely separate, a realm we can't experience, but which we nevertheless innately understand."

"Sorry, I'm still totally lost."

He grins. "So, let's say you see a tree in the physical realm. It's got a couple branches missing. And there's another tree burned in a fire. And another one with initials carved in the bark. How does your mind recognize all of these forms as trees? They're all imperfect, and differently so. And yet your mind recognizes them all as *trees*. Plato said it's because the *ideal* form of a tree—the abstraction of *tree-ness*—exists in the ideal realm. And our minds, our souls, innately understand and recognize the perfect tree-ness in those imperfect trees, even if we've never actually witnessed perfect tree-ness. Tree-ness is what the imperfect trees *aspire* to, and our souls are designed to *aspire.*" His face is flushed, glowing.

I smile at him. This man is stunningly beautiful in every way.

"What? Why are you looking at me like that?"

"You're such a poet," I say.

"No," he replies. "Not usually." He opens his mouth to say something else but thinks the better of it. He clamps his mouth shut.

"So if I understand this correctly, your tattoo means you aspire to the ideal form of Jonas Faraday-ness, like a broken tree aspires to tree-ness?"

He smiles broadly at me. "Exactly. My soul recognizes the divine original of Jonas Faraday-ness, even though that perfect abstraction doesn't exist in the physical world." He sighs. "Basically, I aspire to the un-fucked-up form of me. My soul can envision who he is, even though my physical senses can't. And I just keep visualizing and aspiring."

I cock my head to one side. God, he's beautiful, inside and out. If this man isn't perfection personified, I don't know what is. "You're already him, Jonas."

He shakes his head.

"Yes, you are. You're perfect, exactly as you are."

"No. I'm hopelessly fucked up."

"Yeah, you're fucked up. Of course you are. What you've been through would fuck anybody up. Horribly. But you're perfect—and definitely not hopeless. There's no such thing as hopelessness."

He doesn't understand me.

I sit up on my elbow and look down at his face. "You're scarred, that's for sure." I stroke his brow line. "You've been forced to experience the worst thing a human being could ever endure, and at such a tender age."

He looks away.

"Jonas." His eyes return to me. "You're not a tree. You were innately designed to *feel*—for better and for worse. Which means the perfect form of you was inherently designed to be scarred."

He clenches his jaw.

I sigh. I feel like I'm not expressing my thoughts very well. "If there's a divine original of Jonas Faraday floating around in some other realm, a perfectly unscathed and unscarred version of you, then I'd still choose you. Because if this allegedly ideal Jonas Faraday is perfectly unscathed by life, then he's never *felt* anything." I swallow hard and look him directly in the eyes. "If he's unscarred, then he's never loved," I whisper. "Or been loved."

His eyes flicker.

My heart is going to burst.

"It's *feelings* that leave scars on our hearts. It's *risking.*" A lump is rising in my throat. "It's love," I whisper. "So if the divine original of Jonas Faraday has no scars, he's not perfect, after all." My eyes are pricking with tears. What this beautiful man has been through is unthinkable. "Jonas, we're here on this planet to do one thing: to *love* and be loved." My tears begin to flow. "And nothing else." I wipe my eyes. "Love leaves scars."

He exhales sharply. He's shaking. He opens his mouth to speak, but then apparently thinks better of it.

I lie back down and throw my arms around him, my tears flowing freely. The pain, the grief, the joy at being with him in his arms, the sorrow for all he's been through, the weight he's carried on his shoulders his entire life—it's all just too much for me. I'm suddenly overflowing with emotion. "You're not a tree, Jonas, you're not a tree," I mumble, burrowing into his chest. I can't even think straight anymore. I have to make him understand it wasn't his fault. I have to make him understand he's good—so very good. So very beautiful. He's worthy. He's kind. He's mine.

There's a rustling sound in the darkness surrounding our tree house.

He pulls me close. His body is warm against mine, his muscles taut. His arms feel so strong wrapped around me. He leans into me and kisses me oh so tenderly, even as tears inexplicably continue to pour out of me. His lips are slightly salty, maybe from his tears, maybe from mine. When his tongue gently parts my lips and enters my mouth, it's like he's touching my very soul.

When I first laid eyes on his photos, when I first bore witness to his breathtaking beauty, my body instantly yearned to fuse with his, to take him into me and let him fill me up as fully and deeply as my body would allow. But now, lying here, clothed in my pajamas, nestled next to him in our little mosquito-netted cocoon for two, I feel transported into another world—another realm, as Plato would say.

An ideal realm. And in this realm, it's not my body that yearns to fuse with Jonas, it's my very soul. Yes, he's got broken branches and charred bark—of course—and so do I. But our imperfections don't matter. Because right now, on this particular spot on planet earth, in the middle of a jungle in frickin' Belize, we're perfect.

Chapter 24

Sarah

"Wake up, baby," he coos softly in my ear.

I moan.

"Good morning," he says. "Rise and shine." He kisses my cheek. "Up and at 'em."

I smile, remembering our beautiful, sexless night together. We kissed and cuddled and caressed softly until we couldn't keep our eyes open any longer, and then we fell deeply asleep in each other arms.

I rub my eyes and moan again. "It sounds like jungle sound effects for a movie."

Jonas laughs. "Your voice is so cute in the morning—so gravelly. I love it."

"Coffee," I mumble. I glance at him. He's already fully dressed, bright eyed and bushy tailed, raring to go. His eyes are blazing with excitement.

"Breakfast is out on the balcony waiting for us. Time to get up." He's practically jumping up and down. I've never seen him like this.

I raise my hands over my head and stretch myself from head to toe, purring like a cat. "Best sleep ever," I say dreamily.

He hops onto the bed and crouches next to me. His energy is through the roof. "Do you know what today is, My Magnificent Sarah?"

I smile at him. "What?"

"Today's the day I'm gonna make all your dreams come true."

"You already have."

"Says the girl who's lived in a cave her whole life, staring at shadows. Ha!" He abruptly rolls my entire body onto its side, yanks down my pajama bottoms to reveal my butt cheek, and bites my ass. I mean, really, really, like he literally *bites my ass.*

I yelp.

"Delicious!" he hoots. He snaps my pajama bottoms back into place. "Now go pee or shower or do whatever girly thing you've got to do and meet me on the balcony for some breakfast. Our guide's picking us up in forty-five minutes."

"Guide?"

Without warning, he leaps over me like a panther pouncing on its prey and holds himself in a plank position over my body, his muscles bulging and straining all around me.

I squeal yet again at his sudden movement.

"Yes, guide," he says flatly. He kisses the tip of my nose. "All will be revealed in due time, My Magnificent Sarah, all will be revealed." He leaps off the bed in one sleek motion, turns my body onto its side again, and slaps my ass.

I squeal again.

"Get moving, baby." He bounds across the room toward the balcony. "Time's a wastin'!"

I sit up and look around. Oh my God. Now that it's daylight, I can finally see the source of all the rustling and tweeting and screeching and howling we heard last night. "Holy frickin' moly," I say. Our tree house is surrounded on all sides by a lush, green, almost surreal jungle canopy, stretching as far as the eye can see. "Oh my God."

I leap out of bed, mesmerized by the jungle all around me. Oh man, I really, really, really have to pee, but seeing the jungle up close and personal is more important than any bodily function right now. I join Jonas out on the deck in the already-balmy morning sunshine.

"Incredible, right?" he says, grabbing my hand and leading me to the railing.

My jaw hangs open. "It's like I just leaped into an *Indiana Jones* movie—or, like, a real-life Disney ride."

He laughs. "Exactly. There's no other place quite like this on earth."

"Wow." I can't think of a better word than that.

Somewhere to the left of us, a monkey releases an urgent, plaintive howl.

"Are you taking notes on how to do that?" Jonas asks, laughing.

I dart toward the sound, trying to get a glimpse of the monkey who made it, wherever it is, but the foliage is just too thick to see anything. "I can't see him," I say, frowning.

"Don't worry, we'll see lots and lots of monkeys today. It's easier to see 'em from down below." He claps his hands in excited anticipation. "But, first, you've gotta get your *delectable ass* in gear."

He looks at me like a cat about to devour a mouse and it's suddenly, abundantly clear my butt's about to get chomped again. I squeal and run back inside, laughing, and he follows me, cackling wickedly and stomping loudly right behind me. When he catches me in the spacious bathroom, he wraps his arms around me and picks me up off the ground like I'm a rag doll. He gropes at my butt with exaggerated enthusiasm and nibbles voraciously on my neck.

Yet again, I squeal. I can't help myself.

"Delicious," he says in between bites. "Mmm mmm mmm. Tasty."

And, with that, his erection makes an enthusiastic appearance against my thigh. He gently places my feet back on the floor, but continues holding me tight, his hard-on grinding into me. "If your neck tastes this good, I can't wait to taste the rest of you tonight." He tilts his chin up toward the ceiling and he yells with glee at the top of his lungs. "I'm finally, *finally* gonna lick and kiss and suck my baby's sweet pussy tonight!" His eyes are on fire. "Mmm mmm mmm." He laughs and leans his forehead against mine. "Madness," he says simply, looking into my eyes. He smiles broadly. "Utter madness." Without warning, he slaps my ass again, this time with added gusto (making me yelp), and bounds out of the bathroom, hooting and hollering. "Meet me on the deck for breakfast, baby. You gotta fuel up!"

What have I gotten myself into? I'm slathered in a sticky combination of sunscreen and mosquito repellant—the most high-octane mosquito repellant known to man, so I'm told—slogging through a dense jungle rain forest along a narrow, uneven trail covered in thick mud, vines, tree roots and wet rocks. Miguel, our guide, is hiking through the mud in front of me, charting the least slippery path for us, and Jonas is behind me, variously reminding me to place my feet exactly in Miguel's footprints or watch out for a large root sticking out of the ground or to steer clear of an ant hill the size of a Volkswagen. Thank God Jonas told me to get extra thick-tread hiking boots, or I already would have slipped and broken my neck five different times—or, at the very least, sprained my ankle. It's not the rainy season this time of year, Miguel has told us, but even during this alleged "dry season," as he calls it, torrential downpours nonetheless rain down on this lush inland area at least three times a week. Hence, the sloshy mud I'm currently navigating.

At periodic intervals, Miguel points out a tree or root that he says has healing properties or a particularly nutritious tree nut a person could eat if they were lost in the jungle without provisions, or stops to single out a prehistoric-looking tree with poisonous spines covering its trunk. I feel like I've been dropped into *Jurassic Park.* I keep waiting for a T. rex to ramble into frame and swallow me whole like that guy who gets chomped while sitting on a toilet. Twice, Miguel's stopped to study the path in front of us with narrow eyes and sudden concentration, and when I asked him in a hushed voice what he was looking for, he whispered over his shoulder, "Snake." The phrase that keeps scrolling through my mind on an endless loop is, *This shit is real.*

I still don't know our destination in all this. Miguel has a huge pack on his back, filled to bursting with I don't know what. Jonas also wears a pack, but it seems to be filled with nothing more than sunscreen and jugs of water for the two of us.

"How you doing, baby?" Jonas asks. "You need a water break?"

"No, I'm good," I reply. "Great, actually. Freaking out a teeny bit. But great."

"You're hiking so well. And here I thought your ass was just for show, but it turns out it's functional, too."

I laugh.

"Must be all that dancing," he says.

"How do you know about my dancing?"

"I saw your undergrad transcripts."

I turn back and glare at him.

"Hey, if I'm gonna hack into a major university's server, I'm gonna damn well get my money's worth. You majored in communications, minored in dance. Graduated *magna cum laude*."

I don't know what to say. No man has ever researched me before. But, hey, tit for tat, as he always says—I've certainly researched him more than I care to admit.

"I bet every single guy in every one of your classes wanted to take a big bite out of that delectable ass, too."

I scoff. "I took a lot of *dance* classes, remember? Not every single guy." I smirk.

He laughs. "Touché." There's a beat as he traverses a slippery mud pit. "What kind of dance?"

"When I was young, anything I could find at the rec center. In college, lyrical contemporary, mostly." Under normal circumstances, I could probably talk for hours about dance, but it's hard to chat while concentrating on not falling on my face, getting eaten by a dinosaur, or being strangled by a boa constrictor.

"Do you still dance?"

I smile to myself. I still can't get over how chatty he is with me.

"No. I realized it's not what I want to do with my life. Nowadays, I mostly run or do yoga with Kat. There's hardly time for much else between classes, studying, and work."

Oh crap. *Work.* I didn't mean to bring up The Club. He was in such a good mood, too. Damn. I glance behind me, dreading the look on his face, but he looks unfazed—or, at least, not about to hurl like on the plane yesterday.

He's about to say something, but Miguel holds up his hand—our agreed upon signal for silence—and we stop dead in our tracks. Miguel looks up into the jungle canopy for a moment. He silently points. I look up, trying to zero in on whatever he's focused on, and I gasp. No less than six monkeys are perched in the dense rain forest above—and one of them is leaping from one tree to the next, screeching as he does.

I turn back to Jonas, my face blazing with excitement. He's grinning from ear to ear. He nods and whispers, "Awesome, huh?"

I can't contain my excitement. Real monkeys in a real jungle? I never thought I'd see something like this in my entire life, ever.

Jonas grabs my hand and we watch the monkeys for a full twenty minutes, whispering to each other, laughing, gasping, cooing, our hands comfortably clasped, until, finally, Miguel whispers, "You ready to move on?"

"Let's do it," Jonas says, slapping my ass again.

We hike silently for a good ten minutes. I'm curious where we're headed, of course—and yet, it doesn't really matter. Wherever Jonas is leading, I'm following.

"You know, I was so caught up in my own bullshit yesterday," Jonas says out of nowhere, "I didn't stop to think about how this whole Club thing has affected you. I mean, damn, looks like you're unexpectedly out of a job."

I wasn't expecting him to bring up The Club, and certainly not to offer his condolences about me losing my pathetic job. "Oh, I'll figure something out," I say, stepping carefully over a gigantic vine. "I always do. I'm just pissed about the whole thing. It's gross. People joined to find other, consensual, compatible people—not to be lied to. It just boils my blood to think how they're taking people's money and not delivering on what they promise. It's just a scam, a gigantic fraud." My blood is boiling just thinking about it. "And some of these guys—granted, not lots, but *some* of them—join The Club looking for love—I know you don't believe it, but they really, really do—and they're being totally scammed. They have a dream—maybe it's naïve or stupid or whatever—but they do. And The Club exploits that."

Jonas is quiet behind me.

"So, yeah, big deal, I'm out of a job. I haven't been robbed of a dream." I think of Mr. Software Engineer's face when Stacy told him she only follows college basketball except during NBA play-offs. It was total and complete bullshit. I grunt. I'm pissed. "I mean, I'm not the one who had sex with a prostitute when I thought I'd met the woman of my dreams."

Jonas sighs audibly behind me on the trail.

Oh shit. How I wish I could stuff those last words back into my mouth. I was thinking of that poor software engineer who thought he'd found the woman of his dreams—but it sure sounded like I was talking about Jonas. I glance back over my shoulder. Yep, he's scowling. Damn, I'm an idiot.

We're quiet for a minute, listening to our hiking boots clomp and slosh in the mud.

Jonas doesn't say anything.

I shouldn't have said that. Was I subconsciously taking a jab at him? I don't think so. Dang it. "I'm just looking at the whole thing as a massive life lesson and leaving it at that," I say carefully, hoping positivity will help ease my foot out of my mouth.

"What's the life lesson for you?" he asks. I'm relieved to hear him speak again. His voice sounds calm.

I step over a large rock in the trail. "That I should *always* listen to my gut."

"Your gut was telling you something and you ignored it?"

"Absolutely. I knew deep down something wasn't right. I mean, I never saw a single application from a woman, not once—but I just convinced myself some other intake agent must have been in charge of processing female applicants. And I kept thinking there was no way in hell a woman would ever join a club like that—but I ignored my instinct the minute those fat paychecks started rolling in. It serves me right."

"Hmm," he says, considering what I've said.

We continue hiking in silence again for several minutes.

I glance behind me to get a read on him, but he's looking down, his features scrunched in deep concentration.

"You know what, Sarah?" he finally says.

I don't reply. My heart is racing.

"You're so smart," he says. "But even more than that, you're *wise.* You know that? I just ... wow, Sarah, I just genuinely *like* you."

I instantly stop walking and turn to look at him. My heart has leapt into my throat. I can't suppress the huge smile breaking out across my face. "Thank you."

"You're welcome," he says. He smiles at me. And then he *blushes*. Mr. I'm-Gonna-Lick-Your-Sweet-Pussy *blushes* like we're in fourth grade and he's just asked me to go steady.

"Hey, Miguel, can you give us a minute?" I call out over my shoulder.

"Sure," Miguel says. And because he's obviously a smart man, he traipses ahead into the jungle and out of sight, leaving Jonas and me alone.

I turn back to Jonas. "That's the best thing you could ever say to me. I like you, too. A lot. A lot, a lot, a lot."

"Well, I like you a lot, a lot, infinity," he says. His grin stretches from ear to ear. He looks like a kid right now. Like a glowing, happy, carefree kid.

I throw my arms around his neck. "Thank you for bringing me here."

I go in for the kiss, but he pulls back. "Well, actually, I should clarify one little thing. When I said I *like* you, I was talking about your ass. I really, really like your *ass*." I laugh and smash my lips into his.

His tongue enters my mouth and, holy hell, my entire body ignites like a matchbox lit with a blowtorch. He's instantly inflamed, too, quite obviously, because without hesitation, he grinds his hard-on into me as his hand claws at my T-shirt, untucking it indelicately from my pants and hiking it up. His hand burrows under my shirt and quickly reaches into my sport bra. His fingers are inside my bra, groping me, as his tongue explores my mouth.

That familiar throbbing has returned between my legs, with a vengeance. I'm practically gyrating in his arms like a fish on a line. How we went from feeling like grade school crushes a moment ago to ravenous nymphos, I'll never know. It happened in the blink of an eye.

He moans. "I'm going out of my fucking mind, Sarah." He claws at my pants, and I quickly unbutton them for him. He slips his hand down my waistband and his fingers plunge desperately into my wetness. I let out a loud, low groan and so does he. He's kissing me, touching me, making my knees weak. My body has gone from zero to sixty in a matter of seconds as his fingers slide in and out of me and his tongue explores my mouth. Every inch of my skin is vibrating with my sudden desire for him.

"I'm fluttering," I breathe. "Jonas, ooh, I'm fluttering."

I whip my head behind me to see if Miguel's still out of sight.

"You wanna do it?" I whisper in his ear, pressing my palm against his hard-on. I nip at his lower lip and reach for his waistband, fumbling to unbutton his pants. "Jungle sex," I breathe, struggling with his fly.

He pushes my hand away as his finger continues to slick back and forth from my wetness to my tip. "I don't come 'til you do," he breathes, continuing his fingers' expert exploration.

"I think I'll come," I whisper into his ear. "I'm losing my mind."

With one final kiss, he pulls his hand out of my pants and embraces me. He's instantly in complete control. "I can't risk it." He pulls me to him and whispers in my ear. "This is just prelude, baby, sweet prelude." He smirks when he sees my glare. "I made a solemn vow, remember? I don't come 'til you do. It's my new religion." He kisses my forehead. "You're my religion." He suddenly grabs my butt with both hands. "I love this ass," he whispers. He whips his head over his shoulder. "Miguel!" he yells. "Let's go!" He releases me unceremoniously, leaving me dizzy and confused and raging between my legs.

Miguel appears out of nowhere within seconds.

"You see?" Jonas says in a low voice, scolding me. "If I'd let you have your bossy way, we'd have given Miguel quite a show." He laughs. "I told you—no more fucking around. I've finally got my head on straight."

I'm so aroused, I feel like rubbing my crotch against a goddamned tree—and I wouldn't even care if it's one of those prehistoric ones with the spikes. If he'd only give me the match to light my fuse, I'd go off like a rocket; I know I would.

"You ready?" Miguel says. He looks amused.

"Yup," Jonas says. "What do you think? Fifteen more minutes or so?"

"Yeah, 'bout that," Miguel says.

The minute Miguel turns his back to me to continue down the trail, I reach down and touch myself over the fabric of my pants. I just want to know if the outrageous throbbing I feel on the inside of my panties is palpable on the outside, too. It doesn't seem to be. I glance back at Jonas. He's looking at my hand between my legs, his face illuminated with arousal. I smile at him and wink. *Tonight's the night, big boy.*

We hike for a few more minutes, drenched in sweat, swatting at the occasional mosquito, quietly taking in the sights and sounds of the jungle around us. I still have no idea where we're going, and I'm really starting to wonder.

"I've been thinking," Jonas says out of nowhere, huffing and puffing with the exertion of our hike—or maybe thanks to his current state of sexual frustration. "This whole thing with The Club. It really threw me for a loop yesterday. But now that I've had a chance to think about it, I'm feeling kind of philosophical."

I remain quiet. I've learned not to break the spell when he's opening up—and especially when he's being Philosophical Jonas.

"The way I see it, I dodged a bullet. God only knows what would have happened if I'd gotten what I *thought* I wanted. I'm grateful."

I stop and look back at him. *Grateful?* For getting scammed? For unknowingly having sex with a prostitute?

"If it weren't for The Club," he says, smiling sheepishly at me, "I wouldn't have found you. So, when you look at it that way, it's the best money I ever spent."

Chapter 25
Sarah

"Wow," I say. That's the only thing my brain can come up with.

Miguel, Jonas and I are huddled inside the mouth of a gigantic, breathtaking cave, complete with rock formations and stalactites, as rain pours down mercilessly outside the cave, just a few feet from where we're sitting. The sheer volume of water pounding down from the sky is as if God is standing above, pouring out a humongous bucket of water onto the jungle beneath Him.

I'm shaking from nervousness. Now that we've trekked this long and far into the deep jungle, what the heck are we going to do in this cave? Or maybe I'm shaking because I'm soaking wet from head to toe. The torrential downpour started sheeting down from the sky about ten minutes before we reached the cave, and within seconds of the waterworks, I was as drenched as if I'd walked into a shower, fully clothed.

"There's nothing to be scared of," Jonas assures me, securing the strap on my helmet. "Tilt your chin up." I do. He bites his lip as he adjusts my helmet strap and I'm struck yet again by his sheer beauty. When he's finished with the strap, he places his hands on my shoulders and smiles at me. "There's another opening to the cave about four miles in. It won't take us more than three hours to get there."

"Three *hours?"* I say, shocked. "To hike four miles?"

"Yeah, the trek isn't exactly a straight shot." He smiles. "It's a bit of a hike." He turns to Miguel, and they both laugh, sharing some sort of inside joke.

The hair on the back of my neck stands up. What the hell is so funny?

"Hey, Miguel, why don't you tell Sarah about the cave?"

"Of course. The ancient Mayans, who lived all throughout what is now Belize and Guatemala, believed this cave to be the entrance to the Kingdom of Xibalba—the underworld. This cave, like others in Belize, too, is where the Mayans brought sacrifices to the gods to ensure their continued prosperity."

"Well said, Miguel," Jonas says.

"I've given that speech a time or two." Miguel laughs.

"But, Miguel, what *kind* of sacrifices did the Mayans make in this cave?" Jonas asks the question as if he and Miguel are doing a comedy routine for my benefit. Clearly, Jonas already knows the answer to his question; he just wants Miguel to say it out loud.

"Human sacrifices."

"But exactly what *kind* of humans, specifically, Miguel?"

"Virgins. Female virgins."

Jonas' eyes are dancing. Oh, brother, he's so proud of himself right now. I can't help but smile broadly. Oh, how Jonas Faraday loves his metaphors. Obviously, I'm his virgin—his orgasm-virgin—and I'm about to be sacrificed to the gods. Or, rather, to one almighty god—Jonas Faraday.

Jonas flashes me a wicked grin.

I laugh. "You proud of yourself, Jonas?"

"So proud."

"You really, really like your metaphors, don't you?"

He laughs like a kid on Christmas and pulls me into him. "Yeah, I really, really do."

"You truly are a poet at heart, you know that?" I say.

He leans into me and places his lips right on my ear. "'At the touch of love, everyone becomes a poet.'" He pulls back out and winks. "Plato."

My heart is instantly racing. Did Jonas just tell me he *loves* me? I bite my lip. He did, right?

He grins at me. "Did you get enough to eat?"

I nod. When we took cover in the cave, Miguel laid out a beautiful picnic for us. But I don't want to talk about food. I want to talk about what Jonas just said to me. Did I understand him correctly?

He slaps my ass. "Good." He turns to Miguel. "You got our headlamps?"

"Yes, sir," Miguel replies.

Yeah, I'm pretty sure Jonas just told me he loves me. I didn't imagine that, did I? I didn't just *wish* it, right? I said, *"You're a poet."* And he said, *"At the touch of love everyone becomes a poet."* How else could I interpret that comment, other than to conclude he's been touched by love? By his love for me? Or does he mean he's been touched by *my* presumed love for *him*? Do I love him? My mind is reeling. My heart is racing. Oh, if only Miguel weren't here. If only we were alone right now. There's only one thing I want right now—and it's not a three-mile hike into a blackened cave with Jonas and a guide (sweet as that guide seems to be).

Jonas pulls me to him, but not for a kiss—he's securing a headlamp onto my helmet with great care. "Once we get twenty yards into the cave, there'll be no natural light. It's as dark as ink in there—you can't even see your hand an inch from your face without a lamp."

My jaw is still hanging open. Yes, I'm almost positive Jonas Faraday, the man, the myth, the legend, the Adonis, the Woman Wizard himself, just told me he *loves* me. Unless, of course, he's telling me he feels *loved* by me—touched by *my* love—which wouldn't be a shabby thing for him to say, either. But do I *love* him?

He presses into me and his erection nudges against my leg. "Now come on, baby," he says quietly, grabbing my ass for the hundredth time today. "Let's go sacrifice your virgin ass to the gods."

This is insane. This is utterly, totally, and completely insane. He wants me to climb up *what*? For the past two hours, Jonas and I, with Miguel leading the way, have ventured deeper and deeper and deeper into the jet-black cave, hiking higher and higher along the bank of a winding, underground stream, past stalactites and swarms of bats and dripping cave walls that look like movie sets, wading deeper and deeper into the stream where the bank narrowed and narrowed and ultimately disappeared, climbing higher and higher over wet boulders and through jagged openings, sometimes having to drag ourselves through low rock hangings on our bellies. At one point, Jonas insisted we turn off our headlamps, just to experience absolute darkness, and it was unlike anything I'd ever experienced—truly, the eeriest and most disembodying thirty seconds of my entire life. The cave was so dark as to be disorienting. So dark as to invite panic. The minute I started shaking, though, Jonas sensed it and turned his lamp back on.

"I'm here," he said. "Sarah, I'm right here."

Just before we were forced by the narrowing cave walls to start trudging right up the middle of the deep stream, Jonas retrieved harnesses from Miguel's backpack and secured the thick canvass strappings around my thighs and waist.

"What the hell is this for?" I asked, my voice quavering.

"You'll see," he said, tightening a buckle on my harness.

"I'm scared, Jonas," I whispered.

"I'm in charge, remember?" he said, looking into my face, the light on his headlamp momentarily blinding me.

"In the *bedroom*," I corrected, shaking with cold and nerves.

He flipped up the trajectory of his headlamp so it wouldn't shine directly in my eyes and placed his hands on my cheeks. "My Magnificent Sarah," he said tenderly, looking deeply into my wide eyes. "I would never, ever let harm come to you. You're too precious to me. This is going to be one of the best experiences of your entire life—the perfect metaphor for the indescribable pleasure I'm going to give you tonight. If you'll trust me, completely, you'll thank me when it's over." He leaned in and kissed my wet lips, and my entire body melted into his.

Well, then. A harness it is.

And now, here I am, a harness secured around my body, a rope attached to the harness, standing in jet-black water up to my shoulders, at the base of a subterranean waterfall in a pitch-black cave—and Jonas is casually explaining the best strategy for my climb *up* the waterfall. Miguel already climbed up the rocks of the waterfall like a cat in a tree so he could secure the rope attached to my harness.

"Even if you slip, the rope will catch you," Jonas coaxes from behind me. "And I'll talk you through the whole thing."

I look up. The top of the waterfall is a good fifteen to twenty feet up, and the only way up is by grabbing rocks directly in the path of the cascading water.

Jonas is standing behind me in the deep water with his arms around my waist, speaking right into my ear. He points. "You see that crag right there?"

I nod.

"Just put your right hand *there* and your left hand slightly above, maybe *there,* and then just go slow and steady up, arm-leg-arm-leg, 'til you reach Miguel. He'll pull you up over the edge when you get there."

I nod again.

"You ready?"

I nod again. I'm shaking.

He pushes me forward and up, out of the water, onto a tiny footing at the base of the waterfall, just to the left of the cascading water. The cave is pitch black, other than the small orbs of light cast by our three headlamps. I look up. I can see Miguel's headlamp shining brightly down on us from the top of the waterfall, but I can't see Miguel.

I reach down and feel for the rope attached to my waist. Yep, it's still there. I'm clutching the rock wall, afraid to move. Water is sheeting down a few inches away from me to my right.

"You can do this," Jonas shouts from the deep water behind me. "Just do it, and don't think about it."

I look down at him and almost lose my footing on the slippery rock I'm teetering on.

"You got this," he shouts above the sound of the rushing water.

I look up at my destination at the top of the waterfall.

"I'm here," he shouts. "And I'm not going anywhere. I promise."

Sweeter words were never spoken. I'm still shaking, but I'm suddenly determined. I take a big breath and shimmy to my right, directly into the path of the pounding water. Holy hell, the water is pelting me, pounding the top of my helmet. I reach up and find the crags Jonas designated for my hands, and then I find places for my feet. And I climb. Midway up, I have trouble finding a spot for my right hand, and I'm frozen. The water's pelting me in the face. How did I get here?

"Move your hand up just a little," Jonas coaches. He's out of the water now, standing on the small footing at the base of the waterfall directly beneath me.

I do as he instructs.

"That's it, baby. Damn, you're doing great. Now reach your left hand up. That's it, good."

Before I know it, Miguel's hand is around my wrist, and he's pulling me up, over the lip of the waterfall. And not a minute after that, Jonas is already standing next to me, having ascended the waterfall like he was climbing a step stool.

Jonas clutches me. "You did it!"

I look at him and my headlamp illuminates his face. He's beaming at me. He's elated, triumphant. The waterfall below us is rushing noisily in our ears. But wait. That water-pounding sound isn't coming from *underneath* us, it's coming from *above* us. I tilt my headlamp up, and holy frickin' fuckity fuck fuck, there's yet another waterfall about twenty feet away on the far side of yet another deep pool of dark water yawning before me—only this waterfall is a good thirty feet high.

I swing my face back to Jonas, ready to read him the riot act, but the expression on his face makes me laugh instead. Oh, he's having the time of his life.

Climbing up the second waterfall proves much easier than the first, even though it's twice as high. This time, I just do it. I don't think about it. I don't worry about it. I just trust the rope. And Jonas. And myself. And Miguel. I just let go. It certainly helps knowing this is the last waterfall (which Jonas swore) *and* that our destination (the "back door" mouth of the cave) is only about two hundred yards from this second waterfall (which Jonas swore to be true).

When I arrive at the lip of the second waterfall, my legs wobbly beneath me, I'm aghast. The only thing at the top of the waterfall is yet another small, dark pool of water. This time, thankfully, there's no waterfall, just like Jonas promised—but the blackened pool is enclosed on all sides by low cave walls. There's no trail. There's no light. It's a dead end.

I don't understand. How do we get out of here? Is there some sort of underwater cave we have to dive down to in order to come up the other side and exit the cave?

"Wow," Jonas says, easily climbing over the lip of the second waterfall, "you kicked ass that time, baby. You're a natural. I can't wait to take you indoor climbing when we get home."

"Jonas, how do we get to the mouth of the cave from here?" I shine my headlamp on the nearby cave walls surrounding us. "Where's the opening?"

"Oh, yeah. Um." He looks at Miguel and they share another one of their oh-she's-gonna-shit-a-brick smiles.

"You said the mouth of the cave is only two hundred yards away from this waterfall." I can't keep the edge out of my voice.

"And it is. The mouth of the cave *is* only about two hundred yards away from where we're standing right now—but the *trail* to the mouth of the cave is right ... down there." He points back down to the base of the waterfall.

"What?"

"Yeah. There's a little trail off to right down there—we follow that, and—boom—we're out. Easy peasy."

"Down there? Then why did we climb up here?"

He smiles.

My stomach somersaults. "Oh no."

"There's no other way down."

"No."

"This is how we sacrifice you to the gods." His smile is from ear to ear.

"Jonas, no."

"There's no other way down, baby. No other option. Contrary to what your brain is telling you, contrary to instinct, you're just gonna have to let go and take a gigantic leap of faith into the dark abyss."

I shine my light into the blackness below me. "It's like thirty feet down!"

"Piece of cake."

I grunt with exasperation.

"You want me to go first?" he asks.

I cross my arms over my chest, thinking. There was a high dive at the rec center pool growing up. One summer, when I was eleven, I jumped off it, just to prove I could do it, and I never did it again. I don't like heights. I don't like the feeling of my stomach leaping into my throat. And I *really* don't like the idea of jumping thirty feet into a dark chasm below.

"There's no other way down," he says again.

I glare at him. I'm pissed.

He's anxious. "I wasn't trying to *trick* you, Sarah, I promise. I was trying to *surprise* you." His face contorts with worry. It's exactly the look he flashed at his house when he told me he wasn't treating me like a prostitute but, rather, like his girlfriend. This is the Jonas Faraday that melts my heart, right here, right now.

I grab his hand. "I know." My knees are knocking.

His eyes are pleading with me. His intentions are pure. He's put a lot of thought and effort into this entire trip—into helping me get out of my own way. He's right. I need to get out of my head and take a flying leap. With him.

I look down past the rushing water at my feet into the darkness below. Even with my headlamp pointed down past the ridge I'm standing on, I can't see the water below me—it's just opaque blackness down there. I look back up at Jonas and my headlamp shines in his eyes. He squints and shields his eyes at the sudden bright light. I point my light just to the side of his face and he drops his hand. His eyes are earnest.

"You okay?" he asks.

My heart is clanging in my chest. "Yeah." I exhale loudly. "Let's do it." I nod.

He smiles broadly and squeezes my hand. "I'll jump first. And you come after me." He smirks. "Ha! Of course, tonight we'll do things in the exact opposite order." He winks.

My cheeks flush. Oh yes, tonight. This crazy, beautiful madman has engineered this entire day as a prelude to tonight's main event. I've never wanted anything more in all my life than to make love to this gorgeous man tonight. But I have to survive this ridiculousness first.

"You sure you're okay?"

I nod.

He kisses me on the cheek. "Then I'll see you on the other side," he says. "Bye." He leaps, hooting as he disappears into the blackness.

I hear a large splash, followed by a cheer from below. "Awesome!" he yells up from the darkness.

After a few seconds, a small pool of light shines on the black water below me. "Aim for right here!" Jonas yells up. "Don't think about it; just do it!"

I look at Miguel with my headlamp. His illuminated face smiles at me. He nods his encouragement. I look back down at the small pool of light below me. Jonas' hand flickers into the small orb of light, patting the water. "Right here!" he calls up.

"Fuck it," I mutter. I jump.

My entire body plunges into cold wetness. The water engulfs me completely, past my head. His strong arms embrace me. I'm clutching him, exhilarated, relieved, incredulous, shaking.

"So proud of you," he's muttering as he peppers my face with kisses. "So proud of you," he says again. His kisses are euphoric. "My little virgin sacrifice."

I'm clutching him like he's a lifeboat and I'm drowning. I'm not sure I could command my arms to let go of him, even if I wanted to—which I don't. I don't want to let go of him ever again.

"I'm so proud of you," he says again, in between kisses. "You did it."

He swims to the edge of the water with me on his back, my arms around his neck. When he reaches the shallow part of the pool, he trudges out of the water, cradling me in his strong arms. His legs are under him now, on solid ground. He heads through an opening in the rocks to the side of the waterfall—I can't believe I didn't notice it before I started that second climb. His powerful legs are pumping, his arms sheltering me. I feel weightless. I feel safe. The lights from our headlamps are converging and leading our way out of the blackness. I nuzzle my dripping face into his strong chest.

"Do you see it?" he says after a couple minutes, his breathing labored.

I open my eyes and look ahead of us along the trail—and sure enough, there's a faraway, glimmering light. The mouth of the cave.

"I see it," I say. "Let's run."

He puts me down gently and grabs my hand, and we begin running, hand in hand, toward the light outside the cave. As we run, the light gets closer and closer and brighter and brighter and bigger and bigger; the cave walls become higher and higher and more expansive and open—and our laughter spirals into uncontained delirium. I don't know why we're laughing so hard, but we are.

Finally, we burst out of the cave and into the light together, hand in hand, breathless and howling with our mutual euphoria. The rain from earlier in the day has stopped, leaving behind a glistening, lush wonderland.

"Oh," I say, finally collecting myself. "Oh, Jonas."

He's beaming at me. His face is flushed. "Beautiful," he mutters, and his lips find mine.

Holy moly, this is the best kiss of my life. It's electric. Who knew joining lips with someone could wreak this kind of havoc on an entire body, mind, and soul? His hands find my cheeks as his lips softly devour me. I'm floating, flying, reeling as his mouth continues its assault on mine. I reach for his hair—but my knuckles knock against the hard plastic of his helmet. He pulls away from me, his eyes heavy, and unlatches his helmet with an exasperated grunt. I follow suit. He tosses his helmet to the ground and so do I, and we continue our kiss to end all kisses. Ah, yes, my fingers revel in his wet hair. He pulls me into him, almost desperately, and I swear I can feel his heart beating against mine. After a moment, we pull apart, perhaps sensing Miguel's imminent approach from the cave.

"Tonight," Jonas says, his eyes blazing.

"Tonight," I reply. My heart is racing. Goosebumps cover every inch of my skin. "Hellz yeah."

He laughs. He cradles my back and pulls me close.

I've never felt so connected to another human being as I do in this moment.

I want to kiss him again, but Miguel appears out of the mouth of the cave, shuffling toward us, dripping wet, his large backpack weighing him down.

"Well?" Miguel asks when he reaches us, huffing and puffing. He looks right at me. "How'd you like the cave?"

I look at Jonas. His eyes are on fire.

"Incredible," I say. "But . . ." I motion to the awe-inspiring sights all around me—to the blue sky peeking out from the dense jungle canopy above, to the sun-dappled foliage that looks straight out of the Mesozoic era, to the bursts of color overloading my senses—and, finally, pointedly, to beautiful Jonas himself, standing next to me, his face aglow. "But this is pure beauty, right here." I shoot Jonas a look of unadulterated elation, and he returns it.

Jonas pulls me to him and whispers in my ear. "The culmination of human possibility."

Jonas and I are sitting in the backseat of a topless Jeep, being driven down the Belizian highway in the warm sunshine. My wet ponytail is whipping in the wind, variously bitch-slapping Jonas and me in our faces, making us laugh. Jonas hasn't said a word to me since our exchange outside the cave, but he hasn't let go of my hand, either. I suppose, though, even if he wanted to chat, it would be pretty hard to do, what with the wind blasting us like we're ants in a hand dryer.

Our driver turns on the radio. The song is "Locked Out of Heaven" by Bruno Mars. He turns it up and Bruno Mars sings about sex with a girl who makes him feel like he's discovering paradise for the first time. Jonas nudges me with his shoulder. I nudge him back and laugh. Yep, it's the perfect song. Surely, up 'til now, Jonas and I have both been locked outside the gates of heaven and didn't even know it. But we're inside the pearly gates now, baby—there's no doubt about it.

That kiss outside the cave was ... wow. It was like our souls grabbed onto each other. It was magical. That was heaven, right there. *Ecstasy*—in the way the ancient Greeks described it, as Jonas would say. But it wasn't just the kiss itself; it was everything that happened today that led up to that euphoric moment. I don't think it's an exaggeration to say today changed me. I feel lighter. Stronger. More sure of myself than ever before. Suddenly, I know exactly who I am, as opposed to who I'm *supposed* to be. I'm not a perfect little good girl—not all the time. And that's okay. And I know exactly what I *want*. I want to be my whole self and nothing less, without apology, from this day forward. I want to be true to myself, to the real me, to my deepest desires.

And you know what else I want? I want Jonas Faraday. Holy hell, do I ever. I want to show him every part of me, without holding back. And I want to discover every part of him, too, no matter how damaged he turns out to be. I've never felt like this with anyone. I want to take a flying leap into the black abyss. If my heart winds up getting broken on the rocky crags below, so be it. It was worth it. No matter what happens tonight—whether I have a physical orgasm or not—I've already experienced a spiritual climax of sorts today. And so did Jonas. I know he did.

"Can we stop there for just a minute?" Jonas suddenly shouts above the din of the wind and loud music, pointing to a quaint souvenir shop along the side of the highway. Even from the outside, I can see it's bursting with colorful beach towels and T-shirts, a real tourist-trap kind of place. I can't imagine what he wants to buy there.

Our driver nods and pulls over.

Jonas hops out of the Jeep and turns around to help me down.

"You're in need of a souvenir?" I ask.

He just smiles.

The interior of the tiny store is exactly as I expected—cluttered with mugs emblazoned with "Belize," bars of handmade soap, handcrafted jewelry, T-shirts, wood-carved plates, and colorful tapestries. What does he want to buy here?

"*Hola*," the old woman behind the counter says in greeting.

"*Hola*," Jonas and I reply in unison. I smile at Jonas. His accent is adorably Americano.

Jonas moves toward a rack filled with touristy-looking jewelry and key chains, but then he notices something in the back of the store.

"Sarah, you'd look so pretty in that," he says, pointing to the far corner of the store.

My gaze follows his sightline. He's referring to a white, flowing sundress hanging in the corner, brightly embroidered along the neckline and straps.

"It's beautiful," I say. And it is. It's stunning. But he's already been too generous.

"You like it?"

I nod sheepishly. "But you've already done too much. I've got plenty of clothes."

"The white will be gorgeous against your skin."

I open my mouth to protest. He's done too much already.

"Seeing you in that dress is going to be *your* gift to *me*. We'll call it a bonus payment."

I laugh.

"Go get your size, baby. I want you to wear it for me tonight."

I'm giddy. The dress really is stunning. "Thank you." I have to admit, I'm thrilled. I trot over to the dress rack to look at the sizes while he hones in on a rack filled with jewelry and key chains.

"And pick out a pair of earrings, too," he calls over to me.

"No, Jonas, that's too much. Just the dress."

"Well, then, I'll just have to pick out a pair for you," he says.

I flash him a huge smile and turn my attention back to the dress rack. I hold the dress up. The embroidered trim is breathtaking.

Behind my back, I hear Jonas talking to the old woman behind the cash register. "We'll take the dress—the white one she's holding," he says. "Plus these earrings. And both of these, too. *Gracias*."

"*Están ustedes de luna de miel*?" the woman asks him.

"*Sí*," Jonas replies, smiling.

"*Felicitaciones*."

I whip my head to look at Jonas. He's nodding and smiling at the old woman, but clearly he didn't catch what she said. Based on that Americano accent of his, I gather Spanish isn't his strong suit—but even if he understands a bit, he clearly misunderstood what the old woman asked him. Oh boy, when I translate for him later, he's going to laugh that he replied yes to her question.

Outside the store, Jonas shows me the earrings he picked out for me. They're silver and turquoise—a lovely complement to the dress.

"They're perfect," I gush. "Thank you."

"I thought they'd look pretty with the dress." There it is again—that I'm-treating-you-like-my-girlfriend look. It melts me.

"I love them, Jonas." I kiss him. "Thank you. For everything. You're so generous."

"You're welcome." He takes a big breath. "And there's just one more thing." He reaches into his plastic bag and pulls out two handmade bracelets, identically woven with multi-colored yarn. They're friendship bracelets, basically—the kind of thing crafty teenage girls might make for each other back home. He grabs my wrist and starts fastening my bracelet around it, a shy smile on his face. How cute is this man to give me a Belizian friendship bracelet? One minute he's talking about his hard-on and the next minute he's a fourth grader with a crush.

"You're so adorable," I say, feeling rather fourth-grader-ish myself.

He fastens the other bracelet on his own wrist. "As a member of the Jonas Faraday Club—the sole member—you need a color-coded bracelet."

"Oh yeah." I laugh. "To designate my freaky-ass 'sexual preferences.'" I look at the multi-colored bracelet on my arm. "I'm not a purple?"

"No, you're not a purple." His tone just called me a big dummy. "Neither am I. We're a brand new color—a color designated for just the two of us." He holds his wrist right next to mine. "We're a perfect match."

Chapter 26

Jonas

Fucking finally.

I lick my lips.

As much as I thoroughly enjoyed seeing her in her new white sundress at dinner—and she was even more beautiful in it than I could have imagined—I'm not sad to see that pretty dress crumpled on the floor right now. I reach around her back and unclasp her bra. I love the way her breasts fall when freed from their cruel bondage.

She looks drunk—and not from the rum punch we drank at dinner. No, she's drunk with arousal. Damn, she's ready to go off like a rocket. And so am I.

I press play on the song I've cued up for this moment. "Madness" by Muse. There's no better song to express what I'm feeling. This song is telling her my truth with every word and note.

The minute we walked through the door after dinner, I ripped my clothes off unceremoniously, and she immediately followed suit, pulling her dress off and throwing it onto the floor with a loud whoop. It turned me on. But then again, everything she does turns me on.

"Lie down," I command, motioning to the bed.

She complies without hesitation, crawling on her hands and knees onto the bed like a cat. The sight of her white G-string disappearing up her delectable ass almost brings me to my knees.

"On your back," I order, barely able to breathe.

She complies and stretches herself out to her full length, her dark hair unfurling onto the pillow around her face. Her breathing is shallow. She's already twitching with excited anticipation about what's about to happen to her—oh man, anticipation is eating her alive right now. Well, guess what? Anticipation can move the fuck over—I'm the only one who gets to eat her alive from now on.

The singer from Muse is telling her my truth.

I crawl onto the bed, growling and spreading her legs as I

approach. She arches her back, yearning for me. Without warning, I dive down and bite savagely at her G-string. She shrieks in surprise. I take the fabric in my teeth and shake my jaw like a dog with a chew toy, breaking the elastic waistband and ripping the remnants off her in one fell swoop.

She gasps.

I see my sweet target. It looks utterly delicious. But not yet.

I climb on top of her and kiss her mouth, my hard-on pressing insistently into her thigh. She wraps her arms around me, her pelvis reflexively tilting up and thrusting toward me, inviting me to enter her.

Madness.

I caress between her legs ever so gently, my fingers barely skimming the tip of her, and she moans softly. I dip my finger into her—oh God, she's so ready for me—and bring my finger to my mouth. "You taste so good," I whisper hoarsely. I dip my finger into her again and bring it to her mouth. She sucks it voraciously. "So good," I breathe again, and she nods, writhing under me.

My wet finger glides back down and finds her tip. It's erect—hard and slippery against my fingertip. I can barely breathe.

Madness.

My lips find her breasts as my fingers move in and out of her. Her nipples are hard and at full attention. I lick one of them for a moment and then let my mouth trail down to her belly. She moans softly.

My tongue finds the inside of her thigh.

"Jonas," she whispers, exhaling a shaky breath and arching her back.

I can't hold off anymore. My lips move to her sweet spot, to the glorious pussy I've been yearning to lick for half my life. I kiss her again and again and again, making love to her wetness with my lips and tongue.

"Yes," she breathes, arching her back into me. "Yes."

Madness.

I write the alphabet into her deliciousness, one distinct letter at a time, paying close attention to what her body's telling me to do. When I reach "H," a fierce growl escapes her, so I linger on that letter until her body is writhing and jolting.

When the time is right, when her body tells me to, I move on down the line. I ... J ... K ... L ... M.

Oh, wow, my baby likes "M." Oh yeah, she does.

M ... M ... M ... M ... M ... M.

M is for madness, or so the song keeps telling us.

With each and every letter, with each and every swirl of my

tongue, with each and every kiss of my lips and mouth, I'm telling her the truth about my devotion to her. Emphatically.

N ... O ... P.

She's whimpering. Writhing vigorously.

Q ... R ... S.

"S" usually stands for "sure thing" or, sometimes, "secret weapon"—I can't remember the last time I even made it past "S"—but, no, not with Sarah. Because Sarah's not like anybody else. But I already knew that.

I move on to "T."

Bingo.

Oh yeah, my baby likes her some "T."

"T" is for Taser gun, apparently, because her body is jerking savagely like I've just jolted her with one.

T ... T ... T for My Magnificent Sarah.

T ... T ... T for my sweet baby.

She's gyrating wildly and gasping for air.

Oh yeah, she's losing her fucking mind.

And so am I.

She's unfurling.

Untethering.

Her pleasure is morphing into pain.

By the time I get to "Z," which I follow with a long string of zealous exclamation points, she's hanging on by the barest of threads.

The key is firmly in her lock—and now it's time to turn it.

My tongue teases her tip for a brief moment—but who am I kidding? We're way past the point of teasing. I take her hard cherry in my mouth and suck her like she's never been sucked before.

She howls and thrashes like a wounded animal caught in a trap.

Oh, my baby. Come on.

She grabs the back of my head with both hands and shoves me into her with all her strength, screaming my name, spreading her legs forcefully.

Let go, baby.

Her mind is detaching from her body; I can feel it.

Madness.

I twirl my tongue around and around and around, over and over, grunting and groaning into her. Oh God, I'm either going to come, pass out, or have a fucking heart attack. I can't . . .

She's howling like a fucking monkey right now. She's not human.

I shudder. I'm so turned on, I can't . . .

But, no, no, no, I don't come 'til she does. I don't come 'til she does.

Come on, baby. Surrender.

I plunge my tongue into her, penetrating her as deep as my tongue will go, eating her alive, sucking her, devouring her, willing her to surrender.

I can't hang on much longer.

I skim my teeth across her engorged tip.

She screams.

Let go, baby. Please. Please. Please. Please. Please.

I nibble her, right on her sweet button.

Click.

She unlocks.

Thank God.

She reflexively shudders in my mouth like a window opening and closing in rapid succession. Over and over and over and over she shudders from the inside out, jolting and jerking and convulsing like she's having a seizure—and, oh my God, she's shrieking from the very depths of her soul through it all. She's laying herself bare to me, showing me everything. Oh God, yes, she's surrendering, finally—to the pleasure, to the truth, to me. Yes, to me.

She's pure beauty.

She's perfection.

She's my greatest creation.

My every God-given instinct is to plow into her and let her body constrict and tighten around me—the most delicious feeling known to mankind, the holy grail—but I'd sooner die right now than come without her, and I can't be one hundred percent sure.

Madness.

She twitches powerfully, one last time, and then she's done.

Her shrieking subsides. She's trembling. Moaning. Sweating.

"Jonas," she finally says, her voice catching in her throat. "Yes," she gasps. She puts her hand over her chest, calming her racing heart.

I look up at her from between her legs. Her chest is heaving.

I'm delirious.

"You did it," she whispers. Her eyes are wild. She's seen the light.

Madness.

"Make love to me," she purrs, gyrating. Her breasts are rising and falling.

I climb up to her face and lick her, claiming her. She returns the gesture, lapping at my lips and chin and tongue.

"Make love to me," she purrs again.

I plunge into her, desperate for my release. Her body receives me with a warm and hungry welcome.

"Sarah," I groan, making love to her—glorying in her. We fit together like no two people ever have. Her body was uniquely designed for mine.

She's the ideal form of beauty.

She's the divine original.

With every movement of my body, I'm telling her how I feel.

"Jonas," she whispers in my ear.

I'm gone.

I let go with a loud, deep growl, my entire body seizing and shuddering and releasing.

Sarah.

She's my religion.

I'm her devotee.

She's all-powerful.

I am but her supplicant.

I surrender.

Yes, I surrender.

Totally and completely.

"Madness," I breathe, collapsing on top of her. My body jerks violently again, apparently experiencing some sort of aftershock. "Oh my God, Sarah."

She laughs that gravelly laugh of hers.

"Holy fuck." I'm still shaking. My heart is still racing. "Madness."

Chapter 27

Sarah

"Sarah."

I whip my head up. The last thing I remember, I was tangled up in Jonas. When did I fall asleep? It's the dead of night. The jungle is alive around us.

The mosquito net is opened and Jonas is standing at the foot of the bed. His erection is enormous. Like, holy moly. His eyes are cut from steel. His chest is heaving.

Music blares from Jonas' laptop. This time the song is "Closer to God" by Nine Inch Nails. Every hair on my body stands at full attention. I know this dark song—and I know exactly what it means. The song is telling me exactly what he's going to do to me—how he's going to fuck me. My chest constricts.

Count me in.

This song has always, always turned me on at my very core in the most primal way, making me feel horny and naughty and fucktastic like no other song ever has. Every time I hear it, I secretly imagine myself getting fucked by some beast of a man, without mercy, in exactly the way the song describes. And now, finally, that day has arrived—and that beast of a man is the man of my dreams.

His eyes gleam at me. He reaches out, coaxing me out of the bed.

He's going to fuck me like a beast.

Yes, please. And thank you.

My entire body is pulsing along with the primal beat of the song. I'm already gyrating and Jonas hasn't even touched me yet.

Jonas leads me out into the warm night air on the deck, giving me an eyeful of his backside in the moonlight as he walks. Holy moly, that's quite a backside.

The dark jungle canopy looms beyond us in all directions. He leans my back against a wooden railing and spreads my legs apart like he's about to frisk me. His fingers touch between my legs, and he smiles when he feels how aroused I already am. The tip of his penis penetrates me briefly and I throw my head back in anticipation of being fucked—but he chuckles. He's just teasing me. Bastard.

He grabs a cushion from a deck chair, places it at my feet, and kneels before me like he's saying his prayers. He looks up at me and licks his lips.

I smile down at him. I'm ready.

He leans into me. I feel his warm breath on me.

My chest heaves. Holy crap, the anticipation is killing me.

What's he doing? He's not going in. He's skimming his lips, ever so gently across me, like he's taking in the aroma of a fine wine before swirling it in his mouth. My legs are trembling.

He leans forward and kisses me, lightly, reverently. No tongue. Just soft, adoring kisses, over and over. My knees instantly buckle.

And there it is. Oh God, yes, his warm, wet tongue. He laps at me like he's repeatedly licking an envelope closed. Within minutes, I'm already moaning and writhing like he's been down there pleasuring me for hours. Maybe it's muscle memory from earlier tonight, maybe it's a newfound confidence in knowing where this is headed, maybe it's having him kneeling humbly before me, or maybe he's just "learned me" so frickin' well that any form of resistance is futile, but in record speed I'm already going out of my mind. A guttural sound emerges from my throat as his tongue begins twirling and swirling and shifting my hard clit around. I throw my head back, enjoying the sudden intensity of the pleasure. When he begins sucking and swirling his tongue at the same time—something he's never done to me quite like this before—I grip the railing. I throw my head back again, but it doesn't relieve the pressure building inside me.

I slam myself into his mouth, grinding into his face, forcing him into me. I can't stop my hips from jerking and thrusting into him. I clutch the railing, digging my fingernails into the wood, trying to keep my legs underneath me, but my knees keep buckling.

Oh my God, I'm gonna come. Oh God, yes, holy fuck, I'm gonna come.

I throw my head back and howl. My insides are fluttering, undulating, warping as my knees buckle and melt. I'm practically squatting onto his face, thrusting and smashing myself into him over and over, yearning to take him into me. Oh God, I'm insane right now. Depraved. Ha! I am fucking this beautiful man's face right now. But I don't care. I'm standing on the edge of a deep, dark chasm, and oh God, oh God, oh God, I'm about to leap into the void. He grunts and grabs at my ass, pulling me even closer into his face, gnawing at me with his teeth as he does. I can't stay upright. I can't maintain control. I spread my legs to give him deeper access to me, my hips thrusting into him. This is pure ecstasy. Or agony. Or both. My hands are lost in his hair, pushing him into me. I'm shaking. I'm dizzy. Pain and pleasure have united. I'm ready to come. Right now. *Right fucking now.*

"Now!" I howl. "Jonas! Now!"

He leaps to standing, his erection glorious in the moonlight, and he turns my shuddering, shaking, frenzied body toward the railing. Without the slightest hesitation, he slams into me from behind, feverishly reaching around and touching me as he does so. Oh God, yes, yes, yes, yes, he's thrusting into me, fucking me like an animal, pounding into me, riding me deep and hard and without mercy, fondling me rhythmically all the while. I can't think. I can't breathe. I fondle my breasts, my hard nipples. I reach down and feel him sliding in and out of me, yes, yes, yes, yes, and then I bring my wet finger to my mouth and suck on it, aching to find some way to relieve the pressure inside me.

"Fuck me," I growl, my hips thrusting and tilting to receive him as deeply as possible. "Harder," I groan, and he complies. His fingers massaging me are magic. I'm falling, losing myself, going out of my fucking mind. This is even better than the last time.

"Baby," he grunts in my ear, and my body twitches violently, as surely as if he's just said "open *sesame"* and opened a darkened chamber at the farthest reaches of me. There's a moment of weightlessness, disorientation, like an ocean receding sharply just before a tsunami, and then, finally, finally, a warm wave of intense pleasure slams me from the inside out, seizing every muscle in my body and sending my heart racing.

The first wave is followed immediately by another and another and another and another and another and another, until my entire body is constricting and contracting violently. I begin to say "Jonas" but the only thing that escapes my lips is an animalistic shriek. My entire body tightens and tenses all at once with one final, epic seizure, then releases rhythmically into pulses of pleasure radiating throughout my core.

Jonas cries out savagely as he rams me, his hardness slicing into me one final, merciless time. "Sarah," he cries. "Oh God, Sarah."

He collapses onto my back and sighs, his sweat mingling with mine.

I turn around to look at him, and I'm instantly greeted with his voracious lips.

After a moment, he pulls away from me and laughs. "Wow."

But I can't laugh. I can't speak. My heart hasn't slowed to a normal rate yet. I'm light-headed. Disoriented. My knees are rubbery.

I wobble over to a deck chair and take a seat.

He sits across from me, sweat glistening on his brow.

"Wooh!" he says. "Epic." He's giddy.

I nod. I can't speak. Oh my God.

Several minutes pass as we catch our mutual breath.

"Twice in one night, baby," he finally says, smiling. "Mount Everest has officially been conquered."

Boom. Just like that, I've got a horrible pit in my stomach. I didn't allow myself to think about it, but now I can't help myself. *I'm Mount Everest.* I said so myself. *And Jonas is a climber.* So now what? Does he want to move on to a new challenge—Kilimanjaro or The Matterhorn, maybe? This is a man who wants to get women off more than anything else. No, he *needs* to get women off. I've known that from the start. And he just accomplished what he set out to do with me, and then some. What's left to keep him interested now?

He's still grinning, oblivious to the thoughts racing around inside my head.

"So admit it—you like chocolate a helluva lot better than green beans, don't you?"

I'm too tense to say anything.

"You still wanna lecture me about how sex for a woman is about so much more than coming, blah, blah, blah emotion, blah, blah, blah? Please, enlighten me."

I know he's teasing me, trying to be playful, but I can't deny the anxiety that just crashed down on me like a ton of bricks. He promised not to come 'til I did. And he's delivered on his end of the bargain. So is my climax the end of the road for us? Will he check the box marked "Big O" next to "Sarah Cruz" and move on? Does he even want to continue with the rest of my month-long membership? I look down at the bracelet on my wrist. I feel like crying. I don't want my time with Jonas to end. Ever.

"Well?" Jonas asks, smiling broadly, clearly oblivious to the panic threatening to overtake me.

I clear my throat. "Just because you love making women come more than anything, that doesn't mean it's the only thing." I jut my chin at him. "Not for me, anyway."

His smile vanishes. In fact, his face flashes anger.

"Jesus," he mutters, shaking his head. "Here we go again. Un-fucking-believable."

Wow, he's pissed. I don't understand the sudden rage contorting his features. I open my mouth but nothing comes out.

He leaps out of his chair and glowers at me. "I love 'making women come more than anything'? Fuck! I've had it with your daddy issues, Sarah—your fear of abandonment. I'm not gonna keep paying the emotional debts of your asswipe of a father."

I'm flabbergasted.

He leans down to me, placing his hands on the arms of my deck chair, making me shrink back. "I might be a cocky-son-of-a bitch-asshole, but I'm not a total and complete dick, okay? When are you finally going to trust me? Are you even *capable* of trust? If not, just tell me now, once and for all, so I don't keep banging my head against a fucking wall trying to make you see the *upside* to me."

My eyes are wide. What is happening? He's enraged. What did I say?

He pushes off from my chair in a huff and paces around the deck, his taut muscles tensing like a cat on the prowl. "What more can I do to prove myself to you?" He motions in frustration to the suite, to the jungle—to the entire expanse of Belize. "I'm running out of ideas, Sarah." He looks up to the sky, trying to contain his anguish. "You're so scared of being abandoned—you're turning it into a self-fulfilling prophecy." He grunts.

I shake my head. How did I screw this up so badly, and so suddenly? What did I say that set him off? "No," I begin.

But I can't find the words. Because he's right. He's absolutely right. I've been gripped with fear from day one with him. I've been convinced he was going to own my heart and then shatter it into a million tiny pieces. Yes, I've been waiting for him to do it. And I still am.

He leaps back over to me and cups my face in his hands. He leans his face right into mine. "There's no more 'making *women* come' for me. Haven't I made that clear to you a thousand different ways?" He exhales in extreme exasperation. "There's only making *you* come. There's only getting *you* off. There's only *you,* My Magnificent Sarah. You're the one I want. You're the one I need. You fucking own me—you and your bossy bullshit and olive skin and gravelly voice and big ol' brain and delectable ass and adorable smile. *You, you, you.*" He brusquely grabs my arm like I'm a rag doll and yanks it up. He points to the bracelet around my wrist. "*You.*" He shows me his matching bracelet. "And me." He grunts loudly, like a gorilla. "For a smart girl, you can be such a dumbshit sometimes, I swear to God."

My mouth is hanging open.

He's pacing again. "Didn't you understand the Muse song? *Madness*?"

I shake my head. I guess not. I thought I'd understood it, but I must have missed something. I thought the song meant he planned to lick me into a frenzied state of madness, a temporary state of delirium—mind detached from body. What else could it have meant?

"Madness, Sarah. *Madness.*" He stares at me as if he's just made everything crystal clear.

I shake my head dumbly. Okay, madness.

His eyes are suddenly moist. "I lost my mind a long time ago, Sarah. Like, literally, lost it. And it was so painful." He chokes up. "I swore to myself, never again—no matter what."

He comes back over to me and grabs my shoulders roughly. I recoil instinctively.

His eyes flash and he releases me. "I thought Plato was scoffing at madness, telling me to avoid it at all costs. But I had it all wrong."

I shake my head. I don't understand.

"And then I met you, and I *wanted* to have a serious mental disease. I wanted to go mad." He shakes his head, brimming with emotion. "Plato wasn't telling me to *avoid* it. He was telling me to *embrace* it."

My eyes are wide. My heart is racing. Is he losing his mind, like, for real? "I don't understand."

He grits his teeth. "'*Love* is a serious mental disease,'" he says, making air quotes and drawing out the words. "That's what Plato said. *Love* is a fucking serious mental disease." He's shouting. I can't tell if he's angry or frustrated or passionate or all of the above. He glares at me, his hands gripping the arms of my chair again. "Why would anyone want a serious mental disease? It hurts. It's torture. It's *painful.*" He grunts again. "He said love is *madness,* Sarah. And I thought that meant I needed to avoid it—because I've been avoiding it my whole life." He's losing the battle with his emotions.

I'm speechless.

"But you drive me crazy." His voice is cracking. "And I *want* you to."

I close my eyes, trying to keep my tears at bay. My heart is bursting.

"Do you understand what I'm saying to you?" he whispers.

I nod. I understand completely.

He leans his forehead onto mine. "There's no *women* to get off anymore, you big dummy. There's only *you.*"

I blink and the tears that were pooling in my eyes streak down my cheeks. I nod profusely. I understand.

He clenches his jaw and lurches away from me. He's suddenly angry again. "But if you don't want me, if you don't feel the same way, just tell me now. Rip off the fucking Band-Aid. I can't take it anymore."

Is it even remotely possible he's not one hundred percent certain about my feelings?

"Jonas," I say, my emotions threatening to overwhelm me. "Jonas, look at me. *Look at me.* Yes, I want you. Of course, I want you. You drive me totally, completely, irreversibly crazy."

His chest is heaving.

"Insane in the membrane," I say softly.

He exhales sharply.

"Psychotic. Deranged. Out of my mind."

He twists his mouth.

"Sick in the head. Demented. *Loca.*"

He grins.

"I'm cuckoo for Cocoa Puffs."

He laughs, despite himself.

I stand and wrap my arms around his neck. "I've got a serious mental disease. It's madness."

He kisses me deeply.

"You big dummy," I whisper.

He beams at me. "I knew you wouldn't be able to resist me."

I laugh.

"So this is settled, then?"

I nod.

"No more crazy-ass trust issues?"

"No more."

"No more one step forward, two steps back?"

"Full steam ahead." I pause. "As long as you promise to let me talk about my beloved Maltese Kiki all day, every day."

He bursts out laughing. "Deal."

"But don't worry," I say, my lips hovering an inch from his. "I promise, absolutely no weekend trips to IKEA." I nuzzle my nose against his.

He cocks his head to the side and pulls back. "Well, hang on a second. Let's not be hasty."

I arch my eyebrows in surprise.

"I'm just saying, I mean, it *might* be tolerable, occasionally, to go to IKEA *if* we were to get some of those meatballs while we're there. Have you ever had IKEA meatballs? They're pretty good."

I beam at him. "Yeah, I like those meatballs."

He nods decisively. "Okay, so it's settled. We won't foreclose the *possibility* of going to IKEA, as long there are Swedish meatballs involved." He suddenly grabs my ass with gusto. "Or, maybe we'll just stay home and I'll nibble your *albóndigas,* instead." He laughs. "God, I love this ass."

Wait, how does he know the Spanish word for meatballs? I pull back from him, an epiphany hitting me like a thunderbolt. "You speak Spanish?"

"Yeah. Not fluently, but pretty well."

My heart lurches with my sudden, glorious, heart-melting epiphany.

"What?" He raises his eyebrows, not understanding the sudden flush to my cheeks. "It comes in handy when I travel. What?"

"Oh, Jonas." I kiss him.

Who would have thought the man who's allegedly allergic to "Valentine's Day bullshit" would turn out to be a diehard romantic, through and through? The woman in the souvenir shop asked him in Spanish, "Are you on your honeymoon?" and my metaphor-loving man replied that, yes, we were—while purchasing a flowing, white dress for his "bride" and matching bracelets for our wrists. Oh jeez. How could I have assumed he'd misunderstood her?

"*Estamos de luna de miel,*" I say, kissing him. *We're on our honeymoon.*

He grins from ear to ear under my kiss. "*Claro que sí.*" *Of course, we are.*

Madness.

"You're a poet," I murmur into his lips.

"Nah," he says. "Only with you."

I sigh. "Jonas."

"What?

"You're a cocky-asshole-motherfucker, you know that?"

"Yes."

"But you're also the man of my dreams."

Epilogue

Jonas

After a long travel day, we're finally back in Seattle and trudging up to her apartment door. I'm trailing behind her, holding her suitcase, admiring her backside as we walk.

What a trip.

What a woman.

What a life.

I'd planned so much for our second full day in Belize yesterday—rappelling down a three-hundred-foot sinkhole in the jungle, a late afternoon helicopter ride, swimming in Belize's famed Blue Hole. But that's how you make God laugh—you make plans. As it turned out, we didn't leave our tree house once yesterday, not even to eat. And it was the best day of my life. Well, the second best day.

From the minute we woke up this morning to when the limo pulled up to her apartment building thirty seconds ago, we've been like giddy kids. At breakfast this morning on the deck, when I looked across the table at her, the jungle alive all around us, I felt a kind of happiness surge up inside me that almost took my breath away.

"You're the divine original form of *woman*," I told her. "You're *woman-ness* in the ideal realm."

She gave me that look—the look I'd move mountains to see—the look that makes me want to be a better man.

"You're man-ness," she replied matter-of-factly. "My manly man-ness-y manly man."

I laughed.

And our giddiness didn't end after breakfast.

Through the van ride to the airport and hours of waiting around and two flights, we haven't stopped laughing and sighing and gazing at each other and cooing sweet nothings into each other's ears and stroking each other's skin and laying soft kisses on each other's lips and cheeks—all the while marveling that this is our life. We're on top of the world together—on top of an ideal world inhabited by just the two of us.

We arrive at the front door to her apartment.

The door is slightly ajar.

"What the . . .?" she mutters as she pushes the door wide open. "Oh my God," she gasps.

The place is wrecked—top to bottom, absolutely trashed.

I put my arm in front of her to keep her from venturing inside.

"Stay here," I say, stepping forward.

I can't believe my eyes. When I came to pick her up for the airport four days ago, this place was as neat as a pin. And now it's in shambles. Whatever used to be on the walls and on her shelves and in her drawers now litters the floor. Holy shit, the place is a total disaster area. What the hell is this? Some kind of hate crime?

I feel her body heat right behind me. I reach back and pull her into me. She's shaking.

"Oh no," she gasps.

I whip my head to look at her.

She's pale as a ghost. "My laptop," she says, grimacing. Tears are pricking her eyes. "It's gone."

Oh, Jesus. I suddenly know exactly what this is all about. Damn, how did I not understand instantly?

I grab her suitcase in one hand and her arm in the other and pull her out the door, back to the limo.

"Come on," I command. "You're coming home with me."

She doesn't put up a fight.

She's shaking like a leaf as I guide her into the backseat of the limo. My heart is racing like a bullet train.

I don't even want to think about what might have happened if she'd been home when they came. They couldn't possibly have known she'd be away, could they? Were they planning on her being home when they showed up, or did they come in her absence on purpose, intending to give her a spine-chilling warning?

I should have known when she told me about her encounter with Stacy that she was in danger. Clearly, we're dealing with a sophisticated, global operation with *a lot* of money at stake. They're not going to let some law student in Seattle put their entire organization at risk. I'd bet there are some seriously bad motherfuckers running this whole operation—motherfuckers who'd do just about anything to protect their cash cow.

I put my arms around her in the backseat. "I've got you."

She nods.

They've got her computer. They've got all our communications. All her personal information.

Kat.

"Call Kat," I say, louder than I'd intended. "Make sure she's okay."

She looks at me, confounded.

"Stacy obviously went on a rant to whomever she reports to about some brunette and blonde horning in on her territory, right?"

Her eyes are wide.

"How many other intake agents are there in Seattle?"

"I'm it, I'm pretty sure."

"Okay, then they know the brunette is you; and now that they've got your computer, they know who the blonde is, too."

She looks like she's having trouble processing what I'm telling her.

"There are pictures of you and Kat on your computer?"

She nods. "Tons."

"Emails with her?"

She nods again.

"And she's in your contacts, right?"

Her face bursts into utter panic.

"Call her right now. Tell her we're coming to get her. She's gonna stay with us at my house 'til we get this worked out."

She pulls her phone out with a shaking hand.

"Have any of your emails with Kat ever mentioned The Club?"

She thinks for a minute. She shakes her head. "Never."

"Okay, that's good. But Kat was with you at both bars, so they must figure you told her everything."

"Oh my God."

I take her hand in mine. "I'm not gonna let them hurt you." I squeeze her hand. "This shit stops right here, with me."

Sarah nods at me, but her attention is immediately drawn to her phone. Kat has picked up.

"Kat," Sarah breathes into her phone, relieved to hear Kat's voice. "Are you okay?"

I dial Josh on my phone. He picks up right away.

"Hey, how was Belize?"

"Josh, you gotta come to Seattle. Right now. We've got a situation."

"Something with the deal?"

"No, something else. It's an emergency."

"Are you okay? Is Sarah okay?"

"Yeah, I'm okay. The trip was incredible—Sarah's incredible. She's with me right now. It's The Club. It's total bullshit, Josh. A fucking scam. I'll tell you everything when you get here." I lower my voice and cup my hand to my phone so Sarah won't hear the next thing I say. "I think Sarah's in danger. Like, maybe serious danger."

He pauses briefly. "I'll be able to catch the last flight out if I hightail it to LAX right now. If not, I'll charter something. I'll see you soon."

"Hey, and tell your hacker buddy to clear his calendar. I've got a big job for him starting immediately."

"Will do. See you soon."

We hang up.

Sarah's winding up her phone call with Kat.

"Just get out of there," she says. "We'll pick you up in fifteen minutes. I love you, too."

She hangs up and wipes her eyes. "Her place was ransacked while she was at work. Same as mine—completely trashed. And they took her computer, too." Her voice catches in her throat. "What have I gotten her mixed up in?"

I pull her toward me, but she's too amped up to be comforted.

"The police just left her place. They think it was a burglary—because that's all she thought it was. But now that she knows about my place, she's scared to death."

"You told her we're coming to get her?"

She nods. "She's meeting us at the gas station down the street from her place in fifteen minutes."

"Josh is on his way, too. He'll be at my house later tonight." I kiss the back of her hand. "I don't want you going back there, you understand?"

She nods.

"Ever again. You're staying with me now." I pause. "Indefinitely."

She nods again. No fight at all. I'm surprised. And relieved. And secretly thrilled, even in the midst of my acute agitation. She's really going to be mine now. Every day and every night. Well, damn, I guess there's a silver lining in everything, no matter how horrible.

"Is there anything you need from your apartment? I'll go back later with Josh and get it."

"Some clothes, maybe."

"I'll buy you new clothes."

She doesn't fight me on that, either. Wow, she must really be freaking out.

"My text books," she says.

"Okay. I'll get them." If they're missing or destroyed, I'll buy her new ones.

She sighs. "The only other things I care about are on my laptop." Her voice quavers.

"This is my fault," I say, my stomach somersaulting. "You wanted to take your computer to Belize, and I wouldn't let you." A familiar darkness is welling up inside me. "If it wasn't for me, they wouldn't have your laptop right now." And they wouldn't have been able to identify Kat—or at least not so quickly. Goddammit. Sarah's been mine all of three days and I've already put her and her best friend in danger and probably put a target on my own back, too. Why did I make her leave her laptop behind? And why the hell did I ever fuck Stacy? I knew I was making a massive mistake when I did it—I *knew* it—and I did it anyway. But Stacy's a red herring. The real question is why I applied to The Club in the first place? Was I following my father's path to hell? Was I having another nervous breakdown?

I run my hand through my hair.

Unwanted images are invading my brain—flashes, snapshots, incomplete impressions—all of them unbidden and savage. Blood streaming out of her nose. Her hand grasping and flailing at the rope around her wrist. His hairy ass. The gleam of the knife.

I close my eyes.

I see her glancing frantically over at the closet, pleading with me to stay put. I see the look of fear in her eyes. I see the look of desperation. But for the first time ever, for the first time in twenty-three years, it's not her blue eyes pleading with me—it's Sarah's big, brown eyes.

My stomach lurches violently. I rub at my eyes, trying to erase the pictures in my head. I'm going to protect her this time. Or die trying. I'm not going to fail her this time. I'm not going to let him hurt her again. I'll kill him if I have to—with my bare hands if I have to, before I let him hurt her.

"No," Sarah says sternly. "Jonas, no." She grabs my arm and shakes it. "Jonas, look at me." Her voice is surprisingly forceful. She tugs on my arm.

I comply.

"This is not your fault. Don't say that—don't even think it."

I exhale.

She squeezes my hand. "We're in this together," she says. "Okay? I need you to keep focused. There's no blame here. There's only what we're gonna do about it. No more fucking around. That means both of us."

She's right. What the hell am I doing? This is not the time to give free reign to my demons. I feel like punching myself in the face I'm acting like such a pussy. Right now is about one thing—protecting my baby. At all costs. There's no time to waste thinking about anything else.

Okay, my head is back in the game.

"Was everything backed up on your laptop?" I ask.

She cringes. "No, none of it." She's thinking. "But I shared all my course outlines with my study group just the other day, so I can get those. Oh my God, thank God I did that. Nothing else matters right now except those study outlines. Oh, and my photos—but my mom and Kat have the ones that matter." She sighs. "Crap. I can't believe this is happening."

I look out the window of the limo, watching parked cars whiz by.

Nobody hurts my baby. Nobody even *threatens* to hurt my baby.

I was willing to kiss my money goodbye in karmic exchange for finding my Sarah. I was willing to let bygones be bygones, to chalk it all up to me getting the comeuppance I deserve in the grand scheme of things. Damn, I was willing to walk away and never look back and let those bastards keep shilling their global brothel with no one the wiser. Maybe all the guys joining The Club subconsciously (or even consciously?) know what they're really getting, for all I know. Or if not, maybe they don't want to know. Who am I to make that decision for all of them, I figured? But, oh no, hell no, all bets are off now. Those bastards fucked with my woman—the woman I *love,* goddammit—and now they're going down.

I look over at Sarah, at her elegant profile. She's pursing that beautiful mouth of hers, deep in thought. She senses me looking at her and turns her gaze on me. Her cheeks are stained with dried tears, but she's strong now. She's ready for a fight.

"I'm gonna protect you," I say.

"I know you are," she says.

"I'd never let anything happen to you," I clarify, just in case she doesn't fully understand.

One corner of her mouth tilts up. She nods. She knows.

"I need you, Sarah," I say, my heart pounding.

"I need you, too," she says softly, a lovely grin unfurling across her face.

But that's not what I meant to say just then, not at all. I mean I *do* need her, of course, yes, that's clear to me now. I need her. I want her. I can't get enough of her. But I meant to say something else. Something else entirely. I shift in my seat.

"I'm not going anywhere," I whisper.

Her smile widens. Her eyes crinkle. She's not going anywhere, either.

But that wasn't what I wanted to say, either. I exhale.

I look out the window again. She leans against my shoulder, apparently content. She doesn't need me to say anything more. She knows.

But, no, there's still more to say.

I take a deep breath. "Madness," I whisper in her ear.

She nods. "Madness," she repeats back to me. She squeezes my hand. Yes, she understands. She always understands. *Love is a serious mental disease.* Yeah, she knows. There's nothing more I need to say. I've already told her a thousand different ways.

You're everything I never knew I always wanted. That's the quote I selected for my Valentine's card to her—and I really thought I meant it when I chose it for her. But, damn, I didn't even know her back then—I only knew who I *hoped* she'd be. So that time doesn't count. But, wait, when she called me a poet in the cave, I said, *"At the touch of love everyone becomes a poet."* How much clearer could I have been? That was pretty damned clear. And then, of course, I told her the biggie, *"Love is a serious mental disease." And* I played the Muse song for her, too. I exhale. Yeah, I've definitely told her. There's nothing more I need to say.

I've said enough. More than enough.

I gaze out the window again, my fingers woven into hers.

She shifts her head on my shoulder and sighs.

Fuck.

I haven't said enough.

Fuck.

I don't want to speak in riddles anymore. I don't want to quote Plato or fucking Matthew Perry to tell her how I feel. I want to tell her in my own words, as clearly and as simply as a man can say it.

"Sarah."

She looks up at me.

But the words don't come out of my mouth. I'm tongue-tied.

My heart is racing.

I've never uttered those three little words to a woman before, except to my mother—never even been tempted—but I want to say them now. I want to say them to my Sarah.

I look into her eyes.

My Magnificent Sarah. I'd die before I let anything happen to her. Or kill.

I don't want anyone else.

I love her. I do. I love her.

I love Sarah Cruz.

I need to tell her. I know I do. Right now. She deserves to hear those exact words, especially now.

My heart pounds in my ears.

I look into her big, brown eyes.

She's looking at me with a kind of unadulterated adoration, an unconditional acceptance I didn't even know existed in the world, at least not for someone like me. The look on her face makes me want to throw myself at her feet.

There's a long beat as I struggle to form the words on the tip of my tongue. I want to tell her, I do, but we're racing to pick up Kat. I don't want to share this moment with Kat. I want to say those words for the very first time when it's going to be just Sarah and me, when I can say them to her and *show* her how much I love her at the same time.

My chest heaves.

She squeezes my hand and smiles at me. Her eyes are warm. Kind. "Oh, my sweet Jonas," she sighs. She puts her hand on my cheek. "You're all upside, do you know that?"

I sigh and close my eyes. I'm blowing it. I know I am.

I press my cheek into her hand. God, I love this woman.

"You're nothing but upside, my sweet Jonas," she whispers. She squeezes my hand and puts her other hand over her heart. "It's madness."

Dedication

This book is dedicated to the wonderful ladies who read this book first and responded with a hearty "hot damn and hell yeah": Nicki, Marnie, Lesley, Tiffanie, Colleen, and Holly, plus, my mom, mother-in-law, and aunt. I was thrilled but not surprised when my best girlfriends loved the book—but when my mom, mother-in-law and aunt loved it, too? "We old ladies like the sexy stuff, too," my aunt explained to me. So effing awesome. Thank you, ladies, all of you. I love you all.

The Club Trilogy book two

THE RECLAMATION

Lauren Rowe

Published by SoCoRo Publishing
Layout by www.formatting4U.com

Chapter 1

Jonas

There are two twitching, trembling women standing in my living room right now—and I'm not talking about the good kind of twitching, trembling women. Sarah and Kat are scared shitless right now, freaking out about their places being ransacked and their computers stolen (undoubtedly by the motherfuckers at The Club), and wondering if today's events represent the sum total of the iceberg slamming into them or just the tip of it. And I can't blame them for being scared. Now that Sarah knows the truth about The Club—and The Club *knows* she knows their secret—what might those fuckers be willing to do to protect their global cash-cow-prostitution-ring? Well, I'm not going to wait to find out. I'm taking these motherfuckers down.

I admit I don't have the slightest idea *how* I'm going to take them down at the moment, but whatever I come up with, it's going to be definitive, unequivocal, and effective. End of story. Or, at least, I hope so.

Fuck.

To be honest, I don't think I can do this on my own—I'm definitely not used to wearing a red cape—but when my brother gets here and the two of us put our Wonder Twin powers together, when we combine my brain with Josh's sheer awesomeness, and then throw Josh's hacker friend into the mix, whoever he is, we'll be unstoppable. I know we will.

We'd better be.

How did everything get so fucked up? Only an hour ago, Sarah and I were floating on cloud nine after arriving home from our magical trip to Belize—the two of us gliding up the walkway to her apartment, high on each other and on life, having experienced every form of ecstasy known to man over the past four days. We climbed waterfalls in Belize and leaped into dark chasms and toppled Mount Everest again and again and again and again in our tree-house-cocoon built for two, all the while discovering, with astonishing force and clarity, that the two of us were innately designed for each other in every conceivable way.

Being with Sarah down there in Belize, I felt... I get shivers even thinking about how I felt... I felt *happy,* genuinely *happy,* for the first time in my whole life—or, at least, for the first time since I was seven years old.

Holding Sarah's naked body against mine all night long, touching every inch of her, looking into her big brown eyes as I made love to her again and again, sitting on the deck of the tree house and holding her hand while listening to the jungle all around us, talking with her for hours and hours about everything and nothing and laughing 'til my sides hurt, getting my ass kicked by her every which way, telling her the things I've never told anyone before—even the things I'm ashamed of—just sitting there, mesmerized, watching her eat a fucking mango—it didn't matter what we were doing, that woman made me start believing in rainbows and unicorns and even the crown jewel of Valentine's Day bullshit—happily ever afters. (Really, I should just mail my Man Card to the fuckers at Hallmark and Lifetime with a note that says, "You win, motherfuckers.") What Sarah and I experienced down there in Belize was nothing short of the ideal realm, precisely as Plato described it.

And then, boom, we got back to Seattle and the shit hit the fan. Sarah's place was trashed and her computer stolen. And now she's scared out of her mind, understandably, and I'm standing here like a jackass, my mouth agape, trying desperately to figure out—*What would Superman do?*

I need a foolproof strategy for decimating The Club—and I swear I'm going to come up with one the minute Josh gets here, I really am— but right now I'm just too amped up to think straight on my own. Left to my own devices, all I can think about is wrapping my arms around Sarah and making love to her, tenderly, purposefully, ardently, and whispering "I love you" into her ear as I do it.

I had my chance to say those three little words to her in the limo on the way over here, but, pussy-ass that I am, I didn't seize the opportunity. I wanted to do it, but we were on our way to pick up Kat, and my heart was pounding in my ears, and I wanted to say the words and *show* her at the same time. And then, two minutes later, Kat hopped into the backseat of the limo with us and the two of them started clutching each other and sobbing and the moment went up in smoke.

Okay, fine, yes, fuck me, I blew it. I know I did. I should have told her.

And now we're here in my house—with Kat in tow, of course—and I'm standing here with my usual hard-on for Sarah and my thumb up my ass. I can't stop thinking about making love to her and whispering those three little words into her ear as I do it—and yet I'm mad at myself for even thinking about that right now. Quite obviously, sex is the last thing on Sarah's mind, and I don't blame her. She's scared and worried and frazzled and freaking out, as any sane person would be. What she needs right now, obviously, is a strong man who's going to make her feel safe and protected—not an asshole who's going to keep poking her in the hip with his inexhaustible hard-on. Seriously. But I can't help myself. She just turns me on, no matter the circumstances, even when all hell's breaking loose.

I look over at the ladies. They've moved to the couch, and they're talking softly to each other. Sarah looks on edge. Kat's got her arm around Sarah's shoulders, reassuring her. The two of them look completely exhausted—especially Sarah, who spent all day traveling only to come home to a wrecked apartment.

Looking at the anguish on her beautiful face as she talks to Kat, it's all the more clear I'm a total asshole for thinking what I'm thinking. I need to rein myself in and focus on taking care of her. What I need to do is divorce my mind from my insatiable body. I need to aspire to my best self—the ideal form of Jonas Faraday. I need to visualize the divine original. Yes. *Visualize the divine original.* I take a deep breath. *Visualize the divine original.*

"Can I get you girls anything?" I ask feebly. "Something to eat or drink?"

Sarah shakes her head and opens her mouth to speak.

"You got any tequila?" Kat asks.

I smirk. Sarah's told me all about Best Friend Kat.

"I don't know what I've got in the house," I reply to Kat. "I'll look." I never drink tequila, but Josh loves it. I'm sure he's left a bottle around here somewhere.

I glance at Sarah.

She flashes me a wan smile—but even when she's tired, her eyes are full of warmth. But, wait, is there something else twinkling behind those big brown eyes besides warmth? Is that *heat*?

I try to grin at her, but I'm too jacked up to smile. I can feel my mouth twitching, so I look away. I wish we were alone, just the two of us. I wish this craziness with The Club weren't hanging over us. I wish we were still in Belize.

I head to the kitchen to look for whatever booze Josh might have graced me with on one of his many visits. Bingo. There's a big bottle of Gran Patron in a corner cabinet. I should have known—only the best for Josh.

I rummage around for shot glasses.

I hear Sarah and Kat murmuring softly to each other in the living room. Their voices sound anxious, on edge. Sarah's obviously scared and worried—and nothing else. Yeah, I was definitely imagining that heat in her eyes, probably just wishing it were there. I need to think about what she needs right now and stop thinking about what I want—what I always want. Sarah deserves nothing less.

This whole situation is a giant cluster fuck, I swear to God. Why, oh why did I join The Club? Why, oh why did I fuck Stacy the Faker—or should I say Stacy the Prostitute? Jesus. Why, oh why didn't I let Sarah take her computer to Belize like she wanted to? And why, oh why, oh why didn't I listen to Sarah's intuition?

From day one, even before Stacy accosted Sarah in that sports bar bathroom, Sarah told me, "I keep feeling like there's got to be some sort of consequence for what I've done," as if contacting me against The Club's rules was some sort of mortal sin. "You didn't defy *The Church*," I scoffed, misreading the situation completely. Why didn't I take a step back and really listen to her? She's so damned smart, I should have known to take her seriously, no matter what. If I'd only listened to her, instead of swinging my dick around and acting like I know everything like I always do, maybe none of this would have happened. In so many ways, I've totally blown it here. And now it's up to me to make things right.

I can't find any shot glasses. Juice glasses will have to do. I look in my fridge for a lime. Nope. I pour three double shots of Patron and head back into the living room with a shaker of salt.

I hand the ladies their drinks. "No limes," I say. "Sorry."

"Cheers," Kat says, taking a glass and the shaker of salt from me. "To you, Jonas. Thanks for the hospitality." She raises her glass. "Nice to meet you, by the way."

"Nice to meet you, too. You're everything Sarah said you'd be."

Sarah smirks at me. She knows exactly how she described Kat—"a party girl with a heart of gold."

I clink my drink with Kat's. "Sorry we had to meet like this," I say.

"Yeah, well, at least this time I'm actually meeting you instead of just spying on you in a bar... " She stops. Insert foot in mouth.

I shift my weight and exhale. Wonderful. Yes, Kat, I fucked Stacy-the-Faker-Miss-Purple-Who-Turned-Out-To-Be-A-Fucking-Prostitute the night you and Sarah spied on me at The Pine Box. Nice of you to remind me of that most unpleasant fact—right in front of my girlfriend—as you sit on my couch, drinking my premium tequila.

I scrutinize Sarah's face for signs of humiliation, hurt, or embarrassment, but I don't see any of that. At least I don't think so.

Kat's face flushes bright crimson. "Sorry," she mumbles.

Sarah puts her hand on Kat's arm. "It's okay." She looks at me pointedly. "I don't give a rat's ass about any of that." She shrugs. "I really don't."

Ah, My Magnificent Sarah.

From day one, I asked Sarah if she could just forget the long (looooong) parade of women I've slept with, as well as the year's worth of purple playmates I signed up for in The Club, and she said yes. And she's never once wavered on that agreement. Not once. Because my Sarah's not like anybody else.

Kat whispers something in Sarah's ear. Sarah grins and nods.

Nothing against Kat personally, but why, oh why is she here? I want to rip Sarah's clothes off and make love to her right where she's sitting on my couch. But there's goddamned Kat, sitting there looking at me like she's laughing at me with her eyes the same way my fucking brother does.

"Bottoms up," Kat says. She licks salt off her hand and then knocks back her drink. "Good stuff." She purses her lips and exhales.

I follow suit. Surprisingly smooth. I never drink tequila. It's better than I remember it.

Sarah doesn't knock back her drink. She watches me intensely, like a cat.

Something in her eyes makes me tingle—I don't think I'm imagining that come-hither stare.

"You gonna drink that or what?" Kat says to Sarah, nudging her shoulder.

Not taking her eyes off me, Sarah shakes some salt onto her hand and then slowly, oh so slowly, licks it off with the full expanse of her tongue. She brings the rim of her glass to her beautiful lips and drinks the entire double shot in one fluid motion without so much as wincing. When she brings her head back up, she licks her lips slowly, smirking like the smart-ass she is, her eyes fixed on me.

Holy shit. I'm hard. I've never seen her do a shot before. The way she just swallowed that tequila was so sexy—so *sexual*—I'd give anything to be that tequila right now. Or maybe the rim of her glass. Or, no, wait, the *salt*. Yes, definitely the salt.

She puts her empty glass on the coffee table, leans back on the couch, and puts her hands behind her head. It's a total alpha-male move—the kind of pose a fucking CEO would strike during a hard-nosed negotiation—and it turns me on. She hasn't taken her eyes off me.

I return her smolder.

One side of her mouth hitches up.

Oh yeah, it's on. *It's on like Donkey Kong,* as Sarah would say.

"When will Josh be here?" Kat asks, yet again annoying me with her presence.

"Probably in about three hours," I say, looking at my watch. "His flight just left LAX."

Sarah sighs deeply. Her eyes are like laser beams on me, even though she's speaking to Kat. "Are you tired, Kat?"

My body is electrified. There's no way I'm imagining that look on Sarah's face right now.

Kat shakes her head and begins to speak, but Sarah cuts her off.

"Because I'm *really* tired." She looks like she wants to eat me alive. "I think I'm going to take a nice, hot shower and crawl into bed for just a bit before Josh gets here."

"Oh yeah," Kat says. "I forgot you guys have been traveling all day. You must be exhausted."

Sarah stands. Her gaze on me is relentless. "You've got a room for Kat?"

"Of course. You want me to show you now, Kat? Or do you need to eat something first?"

Sarah sighs audibly and scowls at me. She puts her hands on her hips.

Oh, shit. That last part about offering Kat food was stupid. I'm so bad at this.

"Actually, yeah, I'm—" Kat begins. But Sarah cuts her off.

"Why don't you show Kat to her room *now*. We'll eat in a bit. Is that okay with you, Kat?" Sarah turns her smoldering stare onto Kat and raises her eyebrows pointedly.

Kat raises her eyebrows, too, clearly surprised by the intensity of Sarah's gaze. "Um, sure," Kat says, slowly. When Sarah remains stone-faced, Kat's face suddenly illuminates with understanding. She smiles broadly. "Oh." Kat stands. "Yeah, of course. I'll just help myself to some fruit or crackers or whatever I can find in the kitchen to tide me over. You two go right ahead and get some... *rest*." She says the word "rest" like she's telling the punch line to a joke.

"If you're really starving I could—"

"Oh, for the love of Pete," Sarah huffs. She's pissed. "I've got mosquito repellant and airplane grime all over me." There's an undeniable edge in her voice. "I want to take a long, hot shower, Jonas Faraday. Do you understand me? A very long, *hot* shower—*right now*."

Kat laughs. "Jonas, you aren't normally this dense, are you?"

I feel myself blushing.

"He's usually not, I swear. He's actually pretty smart," Sarah says, rolling her eyes.

"If you say so."

My cheeks are hot. This is why I hate parties. This is why I hate threesomes. This is why I hate crowds. This is why I'm only good at one-on-one interactions. I flash Sarah an apologetic look, but she's not having it. She's glaring at me.

I clear my throat. "Come on, Kat." I pick up her suitcase. "I've got a perfect room for you on the other side of the house—plenty of privacy over there."

"Wonderful," Sarah says, unmistakably chastising me. She flashes a look that makes Kat giggle, and then she beelines out of the living room toward my bedroom without so much as a backward glance.

"Come on, Jonas," Kat says. "I fear for your physical safety if you keep that woman waiting any longer than necessary."

Chapter 2

Jonas

I'm standing in the doorway to Kat's room, trying my damnedest to unclench my jaw and avoid having a fucking stroke. All I want to do is go to Sarah. My body is on fire as I imagine what she might be doing right now in my bedroom—without me—but fuck me, I'm just not wired to be rude to a woman, no matter the situation. And, anyway, it's not Kat's fault she's here—it's mine. I'm the one to blame for this mess, not her.

I've made sure Kat has clean towels in her bathroom. I've told her my house is hers—whatever she wants, feel free to get it, no need to ask. In fact, please don't ask. I've showed her how to use the TV remote because it's kind of tricky. I've told her how to log in as a guest on the computer in my office to check her emails or whatever, seeing as how her laptop was stolen like Sarah's—a thought which makes me ask Kat what kind of laptop she had and quickly tap out a covert text to my assistant, directing her to buy two new laptops and have them hand-delivered to my house first thing tomorrow morning.

"So, you're good?" I ask, my heart thumping in my ears.

"I'm great. Go on. With each additional minute you keep Sarah waiting, you're putting yourself in greater and greater peril." She laughs.

I don't reply. I simply turn on my heel and dart away.

"May God be with you," she shouts to my back.

I tear through my living room toward my bedroom at the other end of the house, my hard-on raging and my heart racing. I'm going to make love to the only woman I've ever loved, nice and slow, and while I do it, I'm going to whisper, "I love you, Sarah" to her, over and over. I'm going to revel in her perfection, glory in her deliciousness—and when she comes (which is something she's gotten quite good at doing lately, I must say), I'm going to say it then, too, maybe even while I'm coming right along with her. That's definitely something I've never experienced before. Talk about a holy grail—a brand new holy grail.

Women have said those three little words to me—several women, in fact—but I've never said them back. In fact, my whole life, I've dreaded those words, avoided them like the plague—mostly because they've wound up torpedoing every goddamned relationship I've ever had, not to mention several extended flings, too. What woman is willing to say those words out loud to a man and never hear them back? It turns out, not a single one. Even if she's determined to be patient at first, to act like Mother Theresa and wait me out, the end is inevitable, if not instant, once she lets the I-love-you cat out of the bag. No relationship can last very long, if at all, when it's suddenly crystal clear only one person's heart is on the line.

But, holy fuck, I want to say those words now. And I want Sarah to say them back to me. What will it feel like to exchange those most sacred and bare words with someone? Well, not just with *someone*—with Sarah?

I can't wait.

But hang on. Wait a minute. I have a thought that stops me dead in my tracks in my hallway. What if Sarah *doesn't* say those words back to me? My stomach somersaults at the thought. What if . . .?

No, I can't think that way. We told each how we feel in Belize. *Love is a serious mental disease,* I said. And then I told her she drives me fucking crazy. You can't get much clearer than that. And then she said it back to me. *You drive me fucking crazy, too,* she said. *Loca. Cuckoo for Cocoa Puffs.*

And on top of all that I played her the Muse song, too. I've never played that Muse song for anyone before, let alone for the woman I love while making her come for the first time in her life. Oh man, that was epic. *Madness.*

I'm rock hard right now.

Yeah, we've definitely said it. *Madness.*

And now we'll take the next step. Together. We'll say the actual words . . .

But wait. What if she's scared of the magic words? Or not ready? What if she's not completely sure . . .?

No, no, no, I can't think that way. That's just my demons talking. That's my "deep-seated fear of abandonment wrought by childhood trauma" talking, as my therapist always explained it to me when my darkness started fucking with me and whispering in my ear. That's the crazy-ass part of me I've got to constantly guard against, push down, snuff out. I know she loves me. And I love her. I know that as surely as I know my own name. I can't let my mind run away from me.

Or my body, for that matter. For the love of God, I've got to control myself—remember she's exhausted and vulnerable and distressed right now. That she's been through a trauma today. I have to be gentle and take things slow. I have to make sure she feels safe and loved—yes, *loved*, above all else. I want to make this memorable and beautiful for her. For both of us. I have to do this just right. I can't turn into the Incredible Hulk on her right now. I have to treat her with kid gloves and make her feel safe and adored. *Worshipped.* To begin with, I'm going to pepper her face with soft kisses, the way she always does for me. And when I do, I'll tell her, *"Love is the joy of the good, the wonder of the wise, the amazement of the gods."*

I open my bedroom door, trembling with excited anticipation.

She's not in the room but I hear the shower running in my bathroom. Her clothes are strewn across the floor, leading quite explicitly into my bathroom. My heart pounds in my chest, crashes in my ears. Damn, this woman turns me on. I rip my clothes off and hurl them across the room. I head toward the bathroom.

I open my bathroom door.

She's in the shower, facing away from me, scrubbing herself with a washcloth as hot water cascades down her naked body. Her backside is pink and slick from the scalding water, her dark hair soaking wet and hanging down her back. Suds float like graceful snowflakes down the small of her back and over her beautiful, round ass. I stand for a moment, just watching her, beholding her breathtaking beauty. She's *woman-ness* personified, the perfect form of woman from the ideal realm, delivered unto the physical world as a gift for the broken and imperfect masses in order to inspire hope and aspiration—well, and to turn me the fuck on.

And she's mine, all mine. Mine, mine, mine.

She turns around and sees me. She smiles. "Talk about not taking a hint. Jeez. I've been wanting you inside me all day long, big boy."

I beam at her, but I don't move. She's so damned beautiful. I'm enjoying watching her.

She tilts her head to the side, letting the water wash over her. She sweeps the washcloth over her breasts.

I just keep smiling at her. She's perfect. I want to remember this moment. I love her. And I'm going to tell her so.

She puts the washcloth on the ledge and runs her bare hands over her hips and belly. She licks her lips. "Well? Are you gonna get in here or what?"

I smile. "I'm just enjoying watching you for a minute, baby. I want to remember this moment."

"Aw, how sweet," she says, but she's clearly being sarcastic. "Don't you know not to make a horny woman wait?"

I bound into the shower. "Words to live by." I take her slick body in my arms. "Say that again.'" I lean in to kiss her.

She laughs that gravelly laugh of hers. "Horny," she says, pressing her lips into mine.

I run my hands over her smooth back, down her ass, over her hips.

"I've been trying to get into your pants for the last hour, Jonas Faraday. Sometimes you really are just a big dummy, you know that?"

I kiss her mouth softly, and then I kiss her entire face, the way she always does for me—but it's not the same when water is pelting our faces. I want to whisper my devotion into her ear, but the shower stream is smacking me in the face.

I want to make her feel safe and protected . . .

She grabs my shaft and begins fondling me with enthusiasm. "Jonas, come on. I've been hot for you all day. Fuck me."

Fuck me? Wow, we're really not on the same page here. I thought she was distraught and needed something gentle and tender and beautiful . . .

"Come on," she says again. Her hands are working their magic on me. I moan.

She lifts her leg onto the shower ledge and guides me into her, then leaps up, into my arms, taking me into her. Immediately, she begins gyrating and sliding against my wet skin.

What the hell? What happened to my damsel in distress?

She throws her head back with abandon. "You feel so good," she groans out, relieved. She's on fire.

"I don't come 'til you do," I mutter.

"Oh, not that again," she moans. "Just don't talk."

She wraps her legs around my back, gyrating, writhing, slithering around in my arms. "Oh, God," she says. "Jonas." She thrusts and jerks in my arms like an animal, kissing me voraciously.

Fuck it. Fine.

I pin her against the shower wall and give her more than she bargained for.

She groans her approval.

She feels so good, oh God, she sure as hell does, so, so, so good, but this isn't what I had in mind. I pivot away from the wall, reach out behind her and turn off the water, still holding her entire body weight in my arms. She's attacking me, devouring me, fucking me, but I walk us into the bedroom as she continues slamming her body up and down on top of me. Holy shit, how I'm managing to even think right now, let alone walk, I have no idea.

I lay her down on the bed and pull out of her.

"No," she screams. "No, no, no! Get back in here!"

Oh God, I love it when she's bossy. When is she going to learn that I'm running this show? I head down between her legs to lick her sweet spot.

"No, no, no," she yells. Her eyes are wild. Her hair is soaking wet. Her olive skin is slick and wet and sexy as hell. "I'm in charge this time, Jonas—" But then my tongue finds her bull's-eye and she moans. "Oh, yeah," she breathes. "Just like that." She arches her back into me. "Oh, Jonas."

I don't know why she always fights me. When will she learn I know what's best for her?

I make love to her with my tongue and mouth, and she writhes against me.

"Jonas . . ." She sighs loudly. But she's still fighting me, battling to exert her will.

I keep working her, sliding my tongue around and around and over and across—employing every little trick that unlocks her. I've learned my baby oh so well by now.

"I want to lick you, Jonas," she says, gyrating. "I want to bring you to your knees." It always comes down to that, doesn't it? She wants to conquer me as much as I want to conquer her.

"No," I mumble, and keep going. I'm too turned on to stop what I'm doing. Oh, how I love breaking my little bucking bronco.

She squirms against me. "Yes," she moans. She lets out a sound I've heard from her before. It means she's getting close. And so am I. Oh yeah, I'm getting really turned on now. But she's still battling me. Why, I don't know. Doesn't she know resisting me is futile?

I keep at her, doing all the things she loves best. Oh God, I love the taste of her, the sounds she makes. There's no way I'm letting her take charge of me right now, no way I'm stopping what I'm doing, no fucking way.

She groans loudly. "I want to lick you, Jonas," she groans out again.

I ignore her. I don't know why her bossy bullshit always turns me on so much, but it does. I'm in a frenzy right now, reveling in her. Nothing can stop me now.

She moans again. "At the same time, baby," she breathes.

My eyes spring open. What?

"At the same time," she says again, shoving herself into me desperately.

Oh, well, that's something else entirely.

I look up at her from between her legs. She's lifts her head and smiles down at me, her eyelids at half-mast, her cheeks rosy. She's got that bad girl look in her eyes I love so much.

"At the same time," she repeats, trembling. She reaches down and grabs a fistful of my hair. "I want to lick you at the same time," she whispers, yanking roughly on my hair. "I've never done that. I wanna try it. Show me." She tugs at my hair again, really hard.

"Ow."

"Come on."

Here I thought I was going to make love to her, slowly, tenderly, whispering my devotion into her ear—and this angel of a woman wants to *sixty-nine* me? For the hundredth time since that first email from My Beautiful Intake Agent landed in my inbox, I'm in awe of her. She's not like anybody else.

I crawl over her, my chest heaving, my hard-on straining. She's spread-eagle underneath me. It's taking all my restraint not to plunge into her right now.

She licks her lips and nods. "At the same time," she says again, this time into my lips. "I wanna try it."

I nod vigorously and kiss her mouth.

She laps at my tongue. "Show me how." She guides me off her onto my back and grabs my shaft. She leans down like she's going to suck me.

"No, no, baby, not like that," I coo softly. My heart is racing. I'm so turned on I can barely contain myself.

She fondles me like she owns me. "How, then?" Her entire body has begun jerking and jolting, she's so aroused.

"You trust me?" My voice is hoarse.

"Mmm hmm." She continues touching me.

I remove her hands from me, gently. "I'm too close," I say. "You can't... "

She smiles. She likes pushing me over the edge as much I like pushing her. We're always at cross-purposes, she and I—too much alike, I suppose.

"You trust me?" I choke out again.

She nods.

"Say it."

"Yes." She shudders. "Yes, Jonas, completely. Come on."

"Lie this way." I point at the bed, indicating I want her to lie face up across the width of the bed.

She complies, writhing, trembling, ready to go off like a bottle rocket.

I pull her shoulders to the very edge of the bed, until her head is hanging off. And then I stand astride her face, one leg on either side of her head, gazing over the full length of her naked body.

I look straight down. Her face beams up at me from underneath my junk. I almost laugh out loud at the sight of her smiling underneath me. I can't believe she just asked to do this with me. And *now* of all times, when the entire world is falling down around us and any other woman would want me to hold her and comfort her and whisper sweet nothings in her ear.

"Baby, listen to me." I take a deep breath. "This turns me on—like, it drives me fucking crazy. So let me get going on you first for a bit, 'til you're just about to come, okay? Don't start in on me 'til you're almost there, like right on the edge, or else I'm never gonna make it. I can barely get through this, even without you sucking me off, it's just so fucking hot for me."

She nods and smiles.

"Promise?" I ask.

She nods. "Yep." But then she lifts her head and licks the entire length of me, from my balls all the way to my tip.

My knees buckle and I shudder.

"Okay, I'm ready now," she says.

I shake violently. "Don't do that again." She obviously doesn't understand how close I am and how much strength this is going to require.

She laughs again.

"Only when you're on the absolute edge," I repeat, my voice much firmer than it probably needs to be—but she needs to understand I absolutely cannot do this if she's going to tease me or start in on me too early. I'm going to need all my strength to do this, physical and otherwise. "Promise me." My voice is stern.

"Jeez," she says. "Okay, I promise, Lord-God-Master."

I exhale and reach down, and then I cradle my arms around her back and pull her entire torso up and up and up, 'til her belly is flush against my chest and her sweet pussy is right up against my mouth. She squeals and instinctively wraps her legs around my neck.

Oh God, I already feel like I'm going to lose it, just holding her in this position. I swallow hard. Her sweet spot is half an inch from my face. Her legs are a vise around my head. This woman is going to be the death of me, I swear to God. I lean in and lick her gently, with hardly any pressure at all. Just a taste.

She shrieks with glee. "This is so wild." She laughs.

But those are her last coherent words. In no time at all, I'm too turned on to be playful or gentle anymore. At this reverse angle—upside down—I can penetrate her, explore her, devour her like she's never experienced before. Within seconds, she's a hot mess, her body jerking against my face, her shrieks and screams and moans and howls a fucking symphony. And I'm losing my mind right along with her.

I convulse with my pleasure, my chest and arm muscles straining. Sweat pours down my back. It's taking every bit of my strength to keep holding her up like this, especially with her jerking around like a fish on a line. And I'm loving it. I don't need any more stimulation than this, don't need anything for myself, couldn't possibly handle anything more... Oh God, oh God, she flutters into my mouth, sending my skin jolting like she's zapped me with a Taser.

She lets out an epic roar and takes my full length into her warm, wet mouth, nice and deep... Oh my God, the way she's sucking on me is... And she tastes incredible... Fuck, oh fuck, she's so fucking talented, even upside down.

If there's a heaven, I think we just found it.

My knees buckle but I readjust.

Holy shit.

Oh God, she's really good at this. So, so good. And she tastes so fucking good.

She's making crazy-ass sounds, and so am I.

This is incredible. I can't . . .

Thank you, God, for letting me experience this kind of ecstasy at least once before I die.

Her tongue does something particularly insightful, and my entire body jerks. I'm not sure if this is pleasure or pain. A swirl of light flashes behind my eyelids. My knees buckle. The sound emerging from me is the sound of a lunatic, but I can't stop. I'm hanging on by the barest of threads. My muscles strain to hold her up. Her mouth is voracious, and so is mine.

Her entire body jerks violently and she lets loose with a pained howl. Her body slams open and shut against my tongue like a window left unlatched in a storm.

I yank myself out of her mouth feverishly, my knees buckling again.

She shrieks.

I want nothing more than to remain inside her warm mouth and see this thing through to its natural, mutual conclusion, but pulling out is an involuntary act, an instinctive act of self-preservation. She's still brand new to climaxing, just a newborn colt, and I'm betting my dick she's gonna clench her jaw like a motherfucker when she comes. I love her, God knows I do, and I'm willing to let her do just about anything to me—*except* reflexively chomp down on my cock like a great white shark on a sea lion.

I throw her down on the bed, quickly pounce between her legs, and slam myself into her, letting her orgasm undulate around me. When my release comes, I'm pretty sure I lose consciousness for a split second. My chest heaves. Sweat pours down my back. I can't breathe. I can't think. I can't... I can't ... I can't do a fucking thing but lie motionless on top of her and catch my breath. I'm not thinking anything coherent right now—other than maybe, "holy fuck."

After a minute, I roll onto my back next to her, shaking and gasping for air. I'm soaking wet. Damn, that was a work out. Fuck. My entire body burns with the exertion of what we just did.

She rolls onto her side and props her head up on her elbow. Her cheeks are flushed. "So that's sixty-nining, huh?" She laughs. "I thought it was... simpler. How the hell does anyone besides a Greek god like you ever accomplish that?"

I swallow hard, still not completely functional. "That was the super-advanced way to do it," I manage to say. "There are several other ways." I breathe deeply. I'm still shaking. That took a lot out of me, in every way. "Much, much easier ways."

She laughs again. "Well, damn, boy, let's try every which way." She grins broadly. "We'll just go right on down the list."

I laugh. She can always make me laugh like no one else can. "I'm in favor of that strategy."

She hoots. "Oh, Jonas. How the hell were you able to hold me up like that? Holy moly." She squeezes my bicep. "You truly are *man-ness,* Jonas Faraday. My manly man-ness-y manly man."

I laugh again. "I could only do it because you're so damned limber and strong. You're the reason that worked."

She beams at me. We've discovered yet another way we're a match made in heaven. I suddenly have an actual, coherent thought: *I love this woman more than I ever thought possible.*

My heart continues racing. "I thought I was going to pass out for a minute there," I say. "I was seeing stars."

"Oh God." She laughs. "That wouldn't have been good with me in that position."

I sit up and touch her face. I'm suddenly earnest. "I'd never let anything happen to you. You know that, right?"

Her entire face contorts like I just gave her a puppy.

I love this woman. I want to tell her so. I want to look into her eyes and say those three little words. I want her to understand they're not just words to me—that they're my new religion. I want her to know I've never said those words to anyone else, that I've been reserving them, waiting my whole life to say them to *her*.

But nothing comes out of my mouth. Again. What's wrong with me?

She beams at me. "I know that," she says softly. "I trust you. That's why this works."

I know the "this" she's referring to isn't the elusive "cascading sixty-nine." No, the "this" she means is "Jonas and Sarah"—the two of us, together. It's our off-the-charts chemistry. It's how she gets me and I get her. It's how she makes me laugh when no one else can. It's how I told her about what happened to my mother—even the parts I'm ashamed of, even the parts that reveal my worthlessness—and she didn't run away. It's how I cried to her, sobbed to her, actually—even though I'd sworn off crying a long time ago. And it's especially how she held me close and cried along with me.

I look over at her. She beams at me.

On second thought, maybe the "this" she's referring to isn't "Jonas and Sarah," after all. Maybe the "this" is just Sarah herself, the new Sarah who's learning to let go and claim her deepest desires. Because now that she's given free rein to what she wants rather than what she's supposed to want, she's becoming a new woman every single day, right before my eyes. I can see it, plain as day. Fuck, anyone could see it. It's in the way she walks, the way she talks. The way she struts. The way she fucks. Maybe I'm just along for the ride, her instrument of self-discovery, a mere conduit to her most powerful self. I don't know. And I don't care. As long as I get to be the one lying next to her, the one making love to her, the one fucking her brains out if that's what she wants, whatever, I don't give a fuck what the "this" is she's referring to. As long as it includes me, I'm in.

I rub my hands over my face. Jesus, this woman is my crack.

There's a beat. I should say it now. But I want to say it when I can show her and tell her at the same time. I don't trust myself with words alone—they've been a struggle for me ever since that whole year as a kid when I didn't speak at all.

She clears her throat. "How is it possible every single time gets better and better and better?" she asks.

"Because we were made for each other," I say softly. *And because I love you.*

Her smile widens. She pushes me back onto the bed and swiftly straddles my lap. She leans down and kisses me tenderly.

I rest my hands on her thighs. "Where the hell did you get the idea to sixty-nine me all of a sudden?" I ask. "That was a pleasant surprise."

She looks at me sideways. "Jonas, I've been reading sex club applications for the past three months, remember? I've been stockpiling ideas the whole time." She winks.

"Oh yeah?" I like where this is headed. "You've picked up an idea or two, have you?" I cross my arms under my head and gaze up at her.

"Yes, sir," she says, her eyes ablaze. She rubs her hands along my biceps. "Maybe just a thing or two... and now that I've got the right partner... the perfect partner…" She leans down again and kisses me. "My sweet Jonas."

My heart leaps. "Sarah," I breathe. I want to tell her. She deserves to hear it from me.

She whispers right into my ear. "Madness."

I exhale and close my eyes.

I know I should be happy to hear this word—she's telling me she loves me in the exact way I've taught her to say it to me—the precise way I've trained her to say it so as not to scare me off. *Love is a serious mental disease,* I explained to her, over and over, quoting Plato—pointedly avoiding the more pedantic but direct route to the same message. I glance away, trying to collect my thoughts. I feel like I'm failing her with all my secret codes.

"Oh, Jonas." She leans down and peppers my entire face with soft kisses—the thing she does that makes me want to crawl into her arms and cry like a baby. "Don't think so much. Thinking is the enemy."

"That's *my* line," I say.

She nods. "Then you have no excuse." She runs her fingers over the tattoo on my left forearm, sending a shiver up my spine. *For a man to conquer himself is the first and noblest of all victories.*

I close my eyes. She's right. I inhale deeply.

She caresses my right forearm with her other hand. *Visualize the divine originals.* And then she runs her fingers from my tattoos to my biceps, to my shoulders, and across my bare chest, tracing every crease and indentation and ripple along the way.

She's right. I need to stop thinking so much. *Love is a serious mental disease.* Yes. *Madness.* Why am I freaking out about the exact words we use? The feelings are there, I know they are—for both of us. The words don't matter.

Her fingers migrate downward to the ruts and ridges of my abs.

I exhale. She knows how I feel. With every touch, with every kiss, she's telling me she does, and that she feels the same way. Why am I over-thinking this?

"Hey, remember my 'sexual preferences' section on my application?" she asks.

She means her so-called verbal application to the Jonas Faraday Club—the application she refused to write out for me in detail because she's a royal pain in the ass.

"As I recall, you summarized the entirety of your 'sexual preferences' with two little words."

Her fingers move to my belly button. "Jonas Faraday," she says, poking me with her finger. She slides her fingers from my belly all the way up to my mouth and begins lightly tracing my lips. I kiss the tip of her finger and she smiles. I grab her hand and pretend to eat the sexy ring on her thumb like I'm the Cookie Monster. Her smile gives way to a giggle. She sticks her thumb in my mouth and I suck on it. She laughs with glee.

"And that's still one hundred percent accurate," she says, pulling her thumb out of my mouth. "*Jonas Faraday.* Mmm hmm." She leans down and skims her lips against mine. "But I think I've got a few... um... *additions* to my 'sexual preferences' section—ideas I've been stockpiling over the past three months. We'll call it an *addendum* to my application." She laughs again and kisses me full on the mouth.

I feel like I'm holding a lottery ticket and she's about to announce I've got the winning numbers. "What kinds of ideas?"

She smiles wickedly. She knows I'm on pins and needles and she's enjoying torturing me. "Well, I'm still formulating the exact specifications of my addendum," she says coyly. "And you're only on a need-to-know basis, anyway."

I frown.

"But I promise you one thing, my sweet Jonas—whatever I come up with, it's gonna bring you to your frickin' knees."

Chapter 3

Sarah

At Josh's arrival, Jonas is a new man. Other than when Jonas and I were going at it like upside-down-intertwined-X-rated-*Cirque-du-Soleil* performers a couple hours ago—and let me just say an enthusiastic *woot woot* and a hearty *hellz yeah* in fond memory of that acrobatic deliciousness—this is by far the most comfortable and confident I've seen Jonas since we discovered my ransacked apartment earlier today.

"Hey," Josh says, putting down his duffel bag and bro-hugging Jonas. "Well, hello, Sarah Cruz." He embraces me next. "Fancy meeting you here."

"Get used to it," Jonas says. He winks at me and I smile back. Jonas has made it abundantly clear he's elated I'm here, regardless of the circumstances.

"So what the hell's going on?" Josh asks, concern unfurling across his face.

In all the chaos of our return from Belize, Jonas hasn't yet told Josh what's happened. And, damn, there's a lot to tell him—not the least of which is how Jonas applied to this depraved thing called The Club, and, oh yeah, how Sarah worked for said depraved club, and oh yeah, how we've recently discovered it's just a global brothel, and, hey, guess what, the bastards just ransacked Sarah's and Kat's apartments and stole their computers. All Jonas said over the phone to Josh was "I need you" and Josh hopped a plane, no questions asked. But now it's time for details.

Jonas moans. "It's so fucked up, man."

Josh sits down on the couch, his face etched with anxiety. "Tell me."

Jonas sits down next to him, sighing like he doesn't know where to begin. He runs his hand through his hair and exhales loudly.

I don't blame Jonas for feeling overwhelmed—he's got a helluva lot of ground to cover. But before Jonas begins speaking, Kat comes out of the bathroom and strides into the room like she owns the place. Josh glances toward her movement, and then away, and then does a double take worthy of Bugs Bunny. The man might as well be shouting "bawoooooooga!" at the sight of her while his eyeballs telescope in and out of his head.

I would have thought Mr. Parties-with-Justin-Timberlake would have a bit more game than a cartoon rabbit—but, no, apparently not. Silly me, I should have known no mortal man, whether he has celebrity friends or not, can play it cool upon first beholding the golden loveliness of Katherine "Kat" Morgan. The woman is every teenage-boy's fantasy sprung to life—the tomboy-girl-next-door who goes off to college and comes back home a gorgeous and curvy and vivacious movie star (except, of course, that Kat works in PR). Why would Josh, unlike so many before him, be immune to Kat's special blend of charm, beauty and charisma?

Kat sashays right up to Josh like he flew to Seattle just to see her.

"I'm Kat—Sarah's best friend." She puts out her hand.

Josh smiles broadly. "Josh." He shakes her hand with mock politeness. "Jonas' brother." I can feel the electricity between them from ten feet away.

"I know," she says. "I read the article." She motions to the business magazine on the coffee table, the one with Jonas and Josh on the cover wearing their tailored suits. "I sure hope you're more complicated than that article makes you out to be."

Josh looks at Jonas for an explanation, but Jonas shrugs.

"If the article is to be believed," Kat explains, "Jonas is the 'enigmatic loner-investment-wunderkind' twin—and you're just the simple *playboy*."

Josh laughs. "That's what the article said?"

"In so many words."

"Hmm." He smirks. "Interesting. And if someone were writing a magazine article about you, what gross over-simplification would they use?"

Kat thinks for a minute. "I'd be 'a party girl with a heart of gold.'" She shoots me a snarky look—that's the phrase I always use to describe her.

Josh smiles broadly. "How come I only get a one-word description—playboy—and you get a whole phrase?"

Kat shrugs. "Okay, party girl, then."

"That's two words."

She raises an eyebrow. "In this hypothetical magazine article about me, they'd spell it with a hyphen."

Oh, man. *Ka-pow.* Talk about instant chemistry. I look at Jonas and I can tell he's thinking exactly what I am—*get a room*—albeit in some warped Jonas Faraday kind of way, I'm sure.

"So what's going on here, Party Girl with a Hyphen?" Josh asks. "I take it we didn't all congregate here to party?"

"No, unfortunately," Kat says. "Though, hey, we did have some of your tequila earlier, so thanks for that." She twists her mouth. "No, I'm just here to support Sarah—and, well, I think I might be some kind of refugee in all this, too." She looks at me sympathetically. "Although I think maybe Jonas is being slightly overprotective having me stay here. I'm not sure yet."

Jonas bristles and clenches his jaw, obviously not thrilled at being called overprotective.

"You're a refugee in all this?" Josh asks. He looks at Jonas, confounded. "What the fuck's going on, Jonas?"

Jonas grunts, yet again. "Sit down."

Josh and Jonas sit.

Jonas takes a deep breath and starts to explain, beginning with Stacy's yellow-bracelet-clad appearance and diatribe at the sports bar, then moving on to our "amazing" trip to Belize and the scary surprise we discovered in my apartment upon our return, and finishing up with his extreme concern that The Club might try to ensure my silence through means more violent than stealing my computer and wrecking my apartment. Throughout it all, Josh listens intently—nodding, pursing his lips, and occasionally glancing at Kat and me. For our part, Kat and I don't make a peep while Jonas speaks, though we exchange a crap-ton of meaningful glances, smirks, and raised eyebrows the entire time.

In addition to engaging in a near-constant nonverbal dialogue with Kat, I also make several observations while Jonas speaks. One—and I realize this is totally irrelevant to the situation at large—holy frickin' moly, Jonas Faraday turns me on, oh yeah, boy howdy, booyah, hellz yeah, whoa doggie, there's no doubt about it. Just watching his luscious lips move when he speaks—and how he licks them when he's pausing to think—and how one side of his mouth rides up a little bit when he's making a wry observation—just seeing the intelligence and intensity in his eyes and noticing the tattoos on his forearms and the bulge of his biceps when he runs his hands through his hair—and a thousand other things about him, too, all of them heart-palpitation-inducing—it's enough to make me want to get all over that boy like tie dye on a hippie.

Gah.

The second observation that leaps out at me while Jonas is speaking is that, man oh man, my supernaturally good-lookin' boyfriend's got the hots for me, too—like, *oh my God,* so, so bad—and, looping back to observation number one, that effing turns me on like boom on a bomb. Perhaps I shouldn't be so turned on by *him* being so turned on by *me*, considering the circumstances—I'm certain I should be consumed with fear and apprehension instead of my hormones right now—but I can't help myself. When Jonas says Belize was "life-changing" for him and calls me "magnificent" and "smart as hell" and "wise," and when he stutters a bit and blushes like a vine-ripened tomato when he says all of it, I feel like he's standing on a mountaintop declaring his raging, thumping, ardent desire for me. *And it turns me on.*

I've never felt so adored and safe and free to be me in my whole life as I am with Jonas. It's like I'm a big ol' vat of mustard—just yellow mustard and nothing else—and up 'til now I've lived my whole life worrying the guys I'm attracted to, the guys who *say* they really, really like mustard, might actually crave a little ketchup or relish or mayo to go along with their mustard, at least occasionally—and who could blame them? And then, all of a sudden, through dumb luck in the most unexpected way, I've stumbled upon the hottest guy in the universe *who happens to have a bizarre mustard fetish,* an insatiable appetite for frickin' mustard to the exclusion of all other condiments! It's like I can't lose, no matter what I say or do or think *because I'm goddamned mustard, bitches.* It's blowing my mind and wreaking havoc on my body to be adored like this, to be *seen* and *understood* and *accepted* so completely. Not to mention fucked so brilliantly. Jonas fucked me so well in Belize, a howler monkey outside our tree house lit a cigarette.

It's like I've been bottled up my whole life and this beautiful man has *uncorked* me. Yes, that's it—I'm frickin' *uncorked,* baby. *Pop!* And now that I am, all I keep thinking about is giving my sweet Jonas, my Hottie McHottie of a boyfriend—my baby, my love, my manly man with sad eyes and luscious lips—pleasure and excitement and thrills and chills and orgasms and assurances and safety and adoration and understanding and acceptance and good old fashioned fuckery like nothing *he's* experienced before—"untethering" *him* the way he's so profoundly untethered *me.*

Gah.

But enough about that. For now. Obviously, we've got bigger fish to fry than satisfying my insatiable lady-boner for the supremely gorgeous Jonas Faraday.

Focus, focus, focus.

Whew.

The third (and more germane) observation I make while my muscled, rippling, smokin' hot, hunky-monkey of a boyfriend speaks to his brother—wooh! I just made myself hot for him again—is that Jonas noticeably doesn't start his explanation to Josh by mentioning any details about The Club—neither its existence nor its purported premise. At first, I'm confused by that omission, but quickly it becomes clear that particular piece of exposition isn't at all necessary... because... wait for it... *Josh already knows all about The Club.* And even more surprising than that, it's also quite clear, based on a couple things Jonas says—for example, "Hey, Josh, did you keep any of your emails from them?"—that Josh himself was a member of The Club at some point before Jonas.

The minute that shocking but fascinating cat lurches out of its bag, Kat shoots me a look that says "holy shitballs"—and I acknowledge her expression with a "holy crappola" look of my own. Very, very interesting. Apparently, neither Faraday apple fell too far from the Faraday horndog tree.

But although I'm surprised to find out about Josh's membership, I'm not fazed by it. Maybe it's because I've processed so many applications, including relatively tame ones from globetrotters like Josh, most of them perfectly normal and sweet. Or maybe it's because, since meeting Jonas, my own rampant sex drive has enslaved me and turned me into a horndog, too—so how could I presume to judge anyone else?

Or maybe, just maybe, I'm so damned grateful Jonas applied to The Club (or else how would we have met?), thrilled by the masterful way he touches me and makes love to me like no one ever has, spellbound by his unquenchable quest to satisfy me, enraptured by his determination to do all things "excellently" that I'm now inclined to view heightened or avid sexual desire as a magnificent superpower rather than something to disparage or snub. Whatever the reason, whatever the journey, whatever the delusion, the bottom line is I'm feeling pretty nonjudgmental about Josh being a past member of The Club right about now.

But that doesn't mean I'm not hella *curious* about it. Because I am.

I don't mean I'm *curious* in some kind of winky-winky code, like “Hello, I’m a freak show who’s *curious* (wink, wink) about her boyfriend’s brother.” Ew. No. Not at all. What I mean is I’m *intellectually* curious to know the details about Josh’s (or *anyone’s*) successful club experience. After three months of reviewing applications on the front-end of the intake process, I still have no idea what happens on the back-end of it—that is, *after* a member receives his welcome package. And I admit, I really, really want to know.

What did The Club deliver to Josh during his membership period? Who were the women and what were they like? Did he see any of them repeatedly? Did he form emotional attachments to any of them? What the heck did they do to him/with him/for him that he felt he couldn’t get outside the clandestine walls of The Club*?* Did he ever suspect what was really going on—that these women were hired to say and do and be whatever he’d requested in his application—or did he buy the entire fantasy, hook-line-and-sinker? And if he *did* suspect the truth about these women, did he care?

And, of course, the granddaddy question of them all, the thing I’m dying to know more than anything else (though I’m not proud to admit it): What did Josh request in his frickin’ application in the first place? Color me curious, I gotta know.

My educated guess is that, given Josh’s good looks and penchant for exploring the world, he’s one of those world traveler/tycoon/professional-athlete types who joined The Club as a simple and expeditious means of finding good sex and compatible companionship wherever he happened to roam—as opposed to being a wack job looking for *bukkake* or for someone to poop on his face. But, hey, maybe Josh isn’t what he appears to be. Perhaps there’s something more wack jobby about him than initially meets the eye. I can’t help but wonder. And judging by the look on Kat’s face, she can’t help but wonder, either—oh my goodness, yes, it’s quite clear to me little miss Kitty Kat’s wondering herself into a frenzy right now.

I’m not surprised by that zealous twinkle in Kat’s eye, to be honest. From the moment Kat found out about my intake agent job, she’s tried relentlessly (though unsuccessfully) to pry every juicy detail out of me about every application I’ve processed. And it wasn’t my intake agent job that ignited Kat’s sexual curiosity—she’s always been this way.

As long as I’ve known her, Kat’s been the boy-crazy one of the two of us, sexually supercharged from an early age, for some reason not shackled by the usual hang-ups and inhibitions that seem to plague other girls, including me. Before Jonas came into my life, I used to watch Kat glide through her interactions with members of the opposite sex and marvel about her supernatural confidence and almost masculine libido. But now that Jonas has "unlocked" me, I have a totally different perspective. In fact, my post-Jonas self might even give Kitty Kat a run for her sexually supercharged money.

I glance at Kat—and when I see her flushed and tantalized face, I suddenly worry my facial expression matches hers. If that's the case, if I look half as revved up as she does right now, then I'm going to hell in a handbasket. Intellectual curiosity or not, no matter how innocent or anthropological in nature my wonderings might be, I absolutely can't be thinking about my boyfriend's brother's sex life. Period. I can't indulge my sexual curiosity, intellectual or otherwise, with or about anyone besides my sweet Jonas—and least of all not regarding his twin brother. I just have to let it go. Some things are not meant to be known by me. Boom. Truth. But that doesn't mean Kat has to let it go, not at all. And by the look on her face, she doesn't plan to.

The next thing I observe during Jonas' telling of his saga occurs to me precisely when he gets to the "and then it turned out Stacy was a fucking prostitute" part of his story. Whereas Jonas quite obviously feels acute humiliation and even suppressed rage all over again simply by *talking* about the fiasco, Josh on the other hand seems oddly calm about the whole thing. Amused, even. He's certainly in no danger of escaping into the bathroom to process his emotions or punch a hole in the wall, that's for sure.

"Huh," Josh finally says when Jonas finishes talking. "Interesting."

Jonas exhales with impatience. His jaw muscles pulse. Clearly, he was expecting something else from Josh.

"Wow," Josh adds, shaking his head. He considers something for a moment. "I'm not sure, bro. I met some really great girls."

Kat visibly scowls.

I can't resist asking at least one, teeny-tiny question. "How long was your membership, Josh?"

"A month."

I'm relieved. That means he's probably not a total wack job. I steal a glance at Jonas. Oh man, he's fuming. At me for asking the question? At himself for joining for a year? Or at Josh's milk-toast reaction to the whole situation? I'm not sure about the source of Jonas' ire—but I figure it couldn't hurt for me to ask one more teensy-weensy question.

"And you... completed your entire membership period... successfully?"

"Oh, yeah. Definitely." Josh smiles broadly. He thinks for a minute. "There's no way all those girls were prostitutes. They were super cool, all of them."

All those girls? *All of them?* How many women are we talking about here?

"They were *all* super cool, huh?" I say, even though I know I should shut the hell up. "Well, Julia Roberts was 'super cool' in *Pretty Woman*, too."

Josh laughs. "True."

Jonas' eyes flash. What's going on in that beautiful head of his? He looks like he's on the verge of exploding.

"How many women could you possibly have gone through in a month?" Kat asks, swooping in to ask the precise thing I'm wondering myself.

Josh's eyes latch onto Kat with laser sharpness.

"I mean . . ." Kat's face turns red. But she can't figure out how to make her question sound pertinent to anything other than her own salacious and highly personal desire to know.

Josh stares at Kat without apology for a very long beat. "A couple," he finally answers slowly. But he's not even trying to sound like he's telling her the truth. He flashes her a broad smile.

Oh boy, he's definitely a Faraday. No doubt about it.

Bam. Just like that, I have a sudden, disgusting thought.

"Josh, did you ever use your membership to meet a 'super cool' girl in the Seattle area?"

Josh's smile droops with instant understanding. He nods slowly. "Once."

Oh no. Please tell me Josh and Jonas didn't both have sex with Stacy the Faker. My stomach churns at the thought.

Jonas' mortified face tells me he gets my meaning, too. "Brunette. Piercing blue eyes—like the bluest eyes you've ever seen—fair skin." It's like he's rattling off a grocery list. "C-cup. Perfect teeth. Smokin' hot body—" He looks at me apologetically. "Sorry, baby."

But there's no need to apologize. Stacy *does* have a smokin' hot body. And, frankly, I like that she does—the hotter the better. My hunkalicious man wanted *me*, sight unseen, based solely on my brains and personality, and he fantasized about me while screwing another woman—a woman with a smokin' hot body. I've got no problem with that. In fact, the thought gets me going like a hungry dog on a ragged bone.

"It's okay." I wink at Jonas. *Woof.*

One side of his mouth curls up, and for one fleeting, delicious moment, I know we're both thinking about our first phone conversation, the one that unexpectedly devolved into dirty phone sex.

Josh is visibly relieved. "No," he says, exhaling "That doesn't describe my Seattle girl. When I filled out my application, I requested only—" He stops mid-sentence. He looks at Kat and smashes his mouth into a hard line.

What? Oh my God. *What?* I've got to know! He requested only... what? Black women? Plus sized beauties? Asian women? A-cups? Men? *Transgenders?* I'm horrible, I admit it, depraved, perverted, going to hell, but I'm dying to know what was on the tip of Josh's tongue. Damn!

But Josh obviously isn't going to elaborate. "Thank God, bro," Josh says. "That would have been just like having sex with *you.*" He mock-shudders, obviously highly amused.

Jonas isn't amused at all. "We're totally off track here," he says, exasperated. "The only thing that matters is that these bastards have fucked with Sarah and Kat, and we have no way of knowing whether they're done fucking with them or if they're just getting started."

Josh leans back on the couch. He sighs audibly. "I don't know."

Jonas lets out a loud puff of air. "What the fuck does that mean?" He stands. His jaw muscles are pulsing. "What the fuck don't you *know*?"

There's a beat as Josh tries to process Jonas' sudden flash of anger.

"You don't fucking know *what?*" Jonas booms. Oh man, he's gone from zero to sixty in a heartbeat.

"Hey, man, calm down. Just... Jesus, Jonas. Sit down."

Jonas' entire body tenses. Every muscle bulges. "Fuck that! Fuck everything except 'What do you need from me, Jonas?' Fuck everything except 'I'm with you, man, one hundred and ten percent!' I'm not gonna sit around and wait to find out if these fuckers have something more planned for us. I'm taking them down."

"*Sit down, Jonas,*" Josh says emphatically. "Let's just talk about this for a minute, rationally."

"Oh, *you're* gonna tell *me* how to be rational? Mr. Buys-a-Lamborghini-on-a-Fucking-Whim-When-His-Girlfriend-Breaks-Up-With-Him is gonna tell *me* to be rational?"

Josh rolls his eyes. "I'm just saying I don't know, that's all. I'm not saying 'I disagree.' Big difference. Just sit the fuck down for a minute. Jesus, Jonas."

"What the fuck don't you *know*? There's nothing to decide. I'm telling you they've fucked with my girl. That's all you need to know! End of story." He's started prancing around the room like a boxer about to get into the ring.

"Jonas!" Josh yells.

Jonas' eyes are blazing.

"Sit the fuck down. Come on."

Jonas grabs his hair in frustration.

"Please."

Jonas grumbles loudly, but he complies. His eyes are on fire. And so is the rest of him. Holy Baby Jesus in a wicker basket, he's so frickin' hot right now, I want to tie him up and make him beg me for mercy.

"Thank you," Josh says politely. He exhales pointedly. "You get so riled up sometimes, man." He shakes his head.

Jonas is trembling. And so am I, just watching him. Oh man, he's a beast—a sexy frickin' beast.

"Okay. Now take a deep breath for a second."

Jonas glares at him.

"Do it."

After a minute, Jonas begrudgingly makes a big show of breathing deeply, as requested, but it's hard to tell if the exercise is calming him down or pissing him off.

"Good. *Good.* Thank you. I'm on your team, bro—I'm *always* on your team. No questions asked, no matter what. Always. One hundred ten percent."

Jonas nods. He knows that. Of course, he does. Without a doubt.

I glance at Kat. She's sitting on the edge of her seat in the corner, her eyes wide.

"Just take a second, man," Josh continues. "Don't fly off the handle. We'll just talk about it, man to man, okay? Talking it through doesn't mean we're having a disagreement—we're just talking it through to consider all angles." Josh keeps his voice calm. Something tells me he's talked Jonas off the ledge a time or two—and maybe even literally for all I know. There's still so much I don't know about Jonas and his demons.

"Don't talk to me like I'm eight years old," Jonas huffs. "I've read that stupid book, too, you know. 'Talking about it doesn't mean we're disagreeing.' Find a new bullshit line, man. That one's stale."

Josh laughs. "It's all I've got—the only thing I remember from that stupid book. Don't take away my one smart thing to say. Not everybody's got a photographic memory like you, motherfucker."

Jonas nods and exhales, regaining control of himself.

Interesting.

"Let's just talk it through," Josh continues. He smirks. "*Talking* about it doesn't mean we're *disagreeing*."

Jonas rolls his eyes. "So I've heard. Repeatedly."

Josh flashes a wide smile.

It seems they've reached some kind of common ground.

Kat and I exchange a "what the hell just happened?" glance. Neither of us speaks.

Josh breathes deeply, in through his nose and out through his mouth, obviously trying to lure Jonas into following suit—and Jonas does. It's like Josh is some kind of gorilla-whisperer or something. And it's working—I can see Jonas calming down with each breath. It's fascinating to watch. And a total turn-on, too.

"Okay. Let's think," Josh says. "What's the point in taking down the entire organization? I mean, really? Just *think* about it, logically. That sounds like an awfully big job—and maybe overkill. Think about it, Jonas. Yes, we've got to protect Sarah and Kat, of course . . ." He smiles at me and then at Kat. "*Of course.* And we will. I promise. But beyond that, why do we care what The Club does?"

I note Josh's adoption of "we" rather than "you" in that last sentence. Very well done.

Jonas shifts in his seat. He's considering.

"Why kill a fly with a sledgehammer when a flyswatter will do?"

A muscle in Jonas' jaw pulses.

Josh barrels ahead. "The Club provides a service—and very well, I might add, speaking from experience. So, yeah, maybe things aren't exactly as they appear, maybe they oversell the fantasy a bit—but so does Disneyland. I mean, you can go ride a rollercoaster anywhere, right?—but you pay ten times more to ride that same roller coaster at Disneyland. Why? Because it's got Mickey Mouse's face on it." Josh nods, thoroughly convinced by his own logic.

Jonas huffs but doesn't speak. His eyes are like granite.

"Maybe all these guys who join The Club want to ride a roller coaster with Mickey Mouse's face on it—and they're happy as clams to pay a shitload to do it. They don't even *want* to know they could ride the same roller coaster without Mickey's face on it for two bucks down the street."

Jonas bursts out of his skin. "Jesus, Josh," he says, jumping back up. "Really?" He's barely suppressing his fury. "'Live and let live?' Is that it? Let these guys go on their merry way while I sit around and wonder night and day if they're gonna come after my baby or not?" He's roaring now, absolutely enraged. "No fucking way."

I stand and put my hand on Jonas' forearm, signaling him to let me speak. He jerks his arm away, fuming. "I expected *you* of all people to understand," he seethes at Josh. "Fuck!"

I take a step back. He obviously doesn't want me to meddle. And he's right. I shouldn't have butted into this brother-to-brother conversation. Not yet. Not now.

"I *do* understand. I'm just saying let's narrow down exactly what we're trying to accomplish here."

There's a long beat.

Jonas is incapable of coherent speech. He's absolutely furious. After a long beat, he motions to me as if he's giving me the floor.

"Josh," I say. I feel the need to choose my words carefully. "Your premise is faulty. When you buy a ticket for Disneyland, you *know* you're signing up to ride a Mickey Mouse roller coaster. Not everyone signs up to ride a Mickey Mouse rollercoaster when they join The Club—but that's what they give them, anyway."

Josh looks genuinely confused.

I feel too stupid to say anything else. I sit back down on the couch, wishing I were invisible.

"What do you mean?" Josh asks me. He sounds remarkably sincere. The tone of his voice makes me look up at him. The expression on his face matches his voice.

Jonas exhales. "She means not everyone is totally fucked-up like you and me." He clears his throat. "Or, at least, like me—you seem to have been cured of your fuckeduppedness by that stupid book."

Josh can't help but laugh at that.

"She means some people are, you know, *normal*," Jonas continues. He sits down on the couch next to me and puts his arm around me. I guess that's his way of apologizing for jerking away a moment ago. If so, I accept his apology.

"What the fuck does that even mean?" Josh finally says. "*Normal?*"

Jonas doesn't answer.

"Okay, fine, let's say there are *normal* people out there. Why the fuck would any *normal* person join The Club?" He seems genuinely confounded.

"To find love," Jonas says quietly. "That's what normal people want. That's what The Club promises to the normal ones. And it's a scam."

Hearing Jonas adopt exactly what I've said to him, whether he believes it or not (I'm not completely sure he does) makes me tingle all over. He's telling me he's got my back along with the rest of my body parts.

Josh laughs derisively.

"It's true," I say, defending Jonas. Defending myself. Defending love, faith, hope, optimism—I don't know what the hell I'm defending. Maybe I'm still hung up on seeing my little software engineer's elated face when Stacy lied and said she only watched college basketball, just like him. Maybe I need to believe that love, and not just sex, is what truly what makes the world go around. Maybe I need to believe there's someone for everyone, no matter how fucked up or depraved. Maybe I just need to believe there are men out there who are absolutely nothing like my father.

Jonas grabs my hand and squeezes it. And with that simple gesture, he's telling me it's Jonas and me against the whole world. Screw anyone else who doesn't believe in true love. We know it's real.

Josh looks incredulous. "Seriously?" There's a beat as he studies Jonas. "Did *you* join The Club looking for love?'"

Jonas blanches. He looks at me, not sure how to respond. But Jonas doesn't need my permission to tell the truth. I know exactly why he joined The Club. And I don't care.

I nod, encouraging him.

Jonas brings the back of my hand to his lips and lays a soft kiss on my skin, his eyes burning with intensity. "No, I didn't."

"Well, neither did I. I can't imagine anyone ever would. That's pretty far-fetched—even if someone's *normal*." He winces at me. "Sorry, Sarah."

I nod. It's okay.

"I'm pretty sure I joined The Club because I was having some kind of mental breakdown," Jonas says softly, almost inaudibly. "Again."

Josh looks absolutely shocked.

"Though I didn't realize it at the time, of course." He looks at me pointedly. "I joined The Club because I didn't understand what was really going on with me, what I really wanted—or what I needed." He squeezes my hand. "I was spiraling, man."

My heart is thumping out of my chest.

Jonas' eyes are boring holes into mine. He's giving me that "I'm going to swallow you whole" look—and, holy hell, I want him to swallow me whole.

Josh clearly doesn't know what the hell to say.

The silence is deafening.

"Well, all righty, then," Kat finally says.

Josh exhales. "Holy shit, Jonas." He rubs his hands over his face, clearly at a loss as to how to handle his ever-complicated brother. "I'm all in when it comes to protecting Sarah and Kat, okay? Whatever it takes—you know that, right?"

"I know." Jonas exhales. "Thanks."

"I just think maybe you're overreacting about—"

"Fuck, Josh!" Jonas leaps to a stand and glowers over Josh on the couch. "These motherfuckers threatened my girl and her best friend. Do you understand? They crossed the fucking line!"

Josh stands and opens his mouth to speak, but Jonas cuts him off.

"I'm not letting them near her."

He pulls me up off the couch and into him like he's defending me from Josh—which is, I must say, a certifiably crazy thing to imply.

"I'm gonna protect her—which means decimating the fuck out of them. Do you understand me? *Decimating them*." He's shaking. His muscles are bulging around me.

"Whoa," Josh says. "Calm down."

"I'm not gonna let it happen again, Josh. I couldn't survive it this time—I know I couldn't. I barely survived it before. You didn't see what I saw—the blood. It was everywhere. You weren't there." He shuts his eyes tight. "You didn't see her." He's flipping out. Oh my God, he's totally flipping out. "I'm not gonna let it happen again. I can't do it again."

His grip on me is stifling, but I wouldn't dream of pushing away, not right now.

Kat's mouth hangs open. I haven't had a chance to tell her anything about Belize—or about Jonas' tragic childhood.

Josh looks anguished. "Jonas... Oh my God."

"I thought *you'd* understand, of all people." Jonas's voice is thick with emotion. "I don't want to do this alone, but I will. I'll do whatever I have to do, don't you understand?" He squeezes me even tighter. "I can't let anything happen to her. Not again. Never again."

Oh my God, I'm turned on. Totally, thoroughly, completely turned on.

Poor Josh's face is stricken. "Ladies, could you give us a minute?" he says. He's at a total loss here. "Please."

Jonas juts his chin and squeezes me even tighter.

"Jonas," I whisper, my lips brushing softly against his jawline. "Talk to your brother, baby. He's on your team." My lips find his neck. His skin is hot. He's shaking. His grip on me is like a vise.

I'm not completely sure what's going on inside Jonas' head, but I'm damn near positive Josh is the one who can help him get his mind right again.

I reach up and touch his chiseled face. "Your brother's on your side," I say quietly. I brush my lips against his neck. He presses himself into me and I feel his erection against me. "Just listen to him," I continue. "He dropped everything to come here for you. Listen to him."

Jonas lets go of my hand, grabs my face with both hands, and kisses me like he owns me. Clearly, his kiss is meant to explain something to Josh, and not necessarily to me, but I'm not complaining. Yowza. He can use my lips to make a point to Josh any frickin' time he likes.

Jonas pulls away from our kiss and looks fiercely at Josh, his nostrils flaring, daring him to contradict whatever statement he's just made with that kiss. When Josh doesn't speak, Jonas does.

"One can easily forgive a child who's afraid of the dark. The real tragedy of life is when men are afraid of the light," he says, his chest heaving.

Chapter 4

Sarah

"Wow, Sarah, what the hell just happened?" Kat asks.

We're sitting on Jonas' balcony overlooking the twinkling lights of the Seattle skyline, drinking wine and finishing the sushi rolls Jonas ordered for us earlier. Josh and Jonas are inside, either talking or beating the crap out of each other. It's not clear which. And I can't stop thinking about that "let me show you what she means to me" kiss Jonas planted on my lips a few moments ago in front of Kat and Josh. Day-am. That was quite a kiss. Wooh! If that's how crazy kisses, then keep bringing the crazy, baby. Please and thank you.

"Oh, Kat, there's so much I've got to tell you."

"Let's start with what the hell Jonas was doing to you in his bedroom earlier. Holy Fornication, Batman! I didn't try to hear, I promise—but it was unavoidable. He was either giving you the best damned orgasm of your life or murdering you—it sounded like you were dying a gruesome death in there." She laughs.

Of all the word choices... Good Lord. "Oh my God, Kat, never, ever say anything like that around Jonas. *Please*." I feel sick at the thought.

Kat's eyes go wide. "Why?"

I tell Kat about the horrific trauma of Jonas' childhood—about my poor, sweet Jonas witnessing his mother's savage rape and murder as he watched from her closet, and how he's blamed himself for her death ever since—with the cruel encouragement of his father.

"Oh my God," Kat says softly. "That's horrible." Kat looks like she feels physically ill. "Wow."

"And on top of that, his father killed himself when Josh and Jonas were seventeen."

"Oh no."

"And his dad left a suicide note that in some way blamed Jonas for everything."

Kat is silent for a long moment. "Well, that sheds a whole new light on Jonas' freak-out in there."

"Yup."

Kat's thinking. "So Josh wasn't there when his mom was killed? Just Jonas?"

"Just Jonas." I exhale. Even talking about this stuff makes me ache all over.

"So judging by the conversation in there, that must be a 'thing' between them—'You weren't there, I was.' Maybe some unresolved stuff?"

I nod. "I can't imagine how their mother's murder has messed them both up—plus their dad, too. Ugh. So horrible."

"Ugh," Kat agrees. She takes a long sip of her wine. "Obviously, Jonas got the worst of it, but God only knows what kind of head-trip Josh has gone through his whole life, too—maybe some kind of weird survivor's guilt or something?" She sips her wine again.

She's so right. I hadn't thought about Josh's journey in all this.

"Talk about a mind fuck for both of them," Kat says. "Just growing up without a mom is tough enough, but add the rest on top of that, too . . ."

I sigh. I feel ill.

"Well," Kat exhales loudly. "Let's talk about something happy now, shall we?"

"Yes, let's."

We clink glasses.

"Here's a happy thought," she says. "Jonas sure has an interesting book collection."

I look at her quizzically.

"I went into his office to use his computer and wound up taking a little tour of his book shelf. *How to Blow Her Mind.* That one looked interesting. *Female Orgasm: Unlocking the Mystery*. Oh, and my favorite: *Becoming a Sexual Samurai: Mastering the Art of Making Love.*" She laughs. "Some interesting reading."

I blush.

"You think Jonas might let me borrow some of his books? I think my next boyfriend should study them thoroughly and take a final exam."

I can't help but smile broadly. "Jonas firmly believes in striving for excellence in all he does."

"Oh, yeah? He *firmly* believes in excellence, does he?"

I giggle and roll my eyes. "Jeez, I walked right into that one."

"As usual." She chuckles at me.

We both take long sips of our wine, grinning from ear to ear.

"So what do you think of Josh?" I ask, looking at her sideways. "From what I could see, you two were like boom goes the dynamite."

Kat twists her mouth but doesn't speak.

"He's exactly your type, Kat."

"I know." She smirks. "*Exactly*. I must say, the guy is hot. But that whole thing about him joining The Club and how much he obviously *enjoyed* it . . ." She makes a face like she's sniffing a dirty diaper. "It was a tad bit Douchey McDoucheypants for my taste."

"Well, Jonas joined The Club, and he's not a douche."

"Well, yeah, as it turns out. But he *was* a bit of a douche at first, you have to admit."

I purse my lips. "No. Jonas was never a douche. He was a cocky-bastard-motherfucker, but never a douche."

"Oh, thanks for the clarification." She shrugs. "Who knows, maybe Josh will turn out to be like Jonas—a knight in shining armor disguised as a cocky-bastard-motherfucker. Or maybe he'll just turn out to be a cocky-bastard-motherfucker disguised as a douche." She sighs loudly.

"I like Josh. He's got a big heart. He dropped everything when Jonas called and said he needed him—no questions asked."

"That true." She smiles. "And I must admit, now that I know about his horrible childhood, I do so desperately want to *fix* him."

"Oh boy. Good luck with that." I sip my wine.

"Hey, you never know—I could be The One Girl in the Whole World Who Can Fix Him. It sure looks like you've fixed Jonas."

"Ha! Oh yeah, as you just now so plainly witnessed, Jonas is totally, completely fixed." I pat my palms together. "My work here is done."

She laughs.

I sigh. "Jonas still has a long way to go to be cured of all that ails him, I do believe. But so do I. We're undertaking a mutual effort."

Kat smashes her lips together, genuinely touched. "I like that."

I bite my lip. I've never said anything like that out loud about any man. But it's true. We're fixing each other.

Kat takes a bite of a spicy tuna roll. "Josh is definitely hot, though, I will say that."

"You're dying of curiosity about him, admit it."

Kat takes another bite of sushi. She shrugs. "Maybe."

"Maybe?" I laugh. "It's written all over your face. You're *dying*."

She laughs. "I'd sure like to know what the hell he was going to say about his application—"

"Oh my God, I know!"

"He was just about to say what he requested," Kat squeals.

"And then he just shut his mouth and stopped talking all of a sudden."

"Mid-sentence!'"

"And looked *right* at you, Kat."

Kat shrieks with laughter. "I was like... yes?... and?... what?... *Yes*? You requested *what* in your application, Josh?" Kat throws her head back, howling with laughter.

"I wanted to scream at the top of my lungs when he didn't finish that sentence."

"Me, too." Kat's laughing so hard she's crying. "I was peeing." She wipes her eyes and exhales. "Oh, Sarah, we're so bad."

"*We're* not bad—*I'm* bad. He's not *your* boyfriend's brother. I can't be wondering this stuff about Josh—surely, I'm going to hell."

"Ah, so Jonas is your boyfriend now? It's official?"

I nod, blushing.

Kat nudges my shoulder. "Awesome, girl."

I'm suddenly too flooded with happiness to reply. I still can't believe he's all mine.

Kat pauses, apparently deciding what to say. "He seems pretty intense, though, Sarah," she finally says. Her tone has shifted. She's warning me. She's wary. "He's not exactly the happy-go-lucky type."

I shrug. Perhaps not. But she hasn't seen what I've seen. She hasn't seen Jonas scale a thirty-foot waterfall like he was climbing a step stool. She hasn't seen him bite my ass (literally) and hoot with glee about getting to lick his baby's sweet pussy. She hasn't seen him laugh until he cried over something silly I've said. He sure seemed pretty happy-go-lucky during all those moments. And, anyway, happy-go-lucky isn't everything. She wouldn't question him if she'd seen the way he cried in my arms when he told me about his mother, or the way he looked when he held his matching friendship bracelet up to mine and told me we're a perfect match.

"He told me he loves me," I say quietly.

"Really?" She's shocked. She wasn't expecting that at all. "In Belize?"

"Mmm hmm."

"Wow. He said 'Sarah, I love you?'"

I hesitate. "Well, no—not in those exact words."

Her face falls.

"It's complicated. *He's* complicated. But trust me, he told me."

She looks skeptical. And I don't blame her. Last Kat heard,

Jonas was Seattle's King of the Man-Whores—with Stacy the Faker one night and me the next. She knows he took me to Belize on a whirlwind trip, of course, but she probably thinks we enjoyed some light-hearted fun in the sun. How could she ever understand what transpired between us down there—how our very souls grabbed ahold of each other? I can barely understand it myself. I'm sure she's worried I'm just another one of Jonas' many conquests—a passing distraction.

"Well, what exactly did he say to you?"

I sigh. There's no way to explain what Jonas said and did in Belize, how he bared himself to me so completely—and how he finally got me to let go and surrender myself to him in ways I've never done before. It's all too personal, anyway.

"Just trust me," I say.

She frowns. She's not at all convinced.

"He told me," I mutter. "Even if he didn't say the magic words."

She nods, but I feel like she's humoring me.

I sigh. She just doesn't understand. Jonas told me his feelings the best way he knows how, and that's enough for me. I love him, even if he can't or won't say, "I love you," even if he *never* says those exact words. When it comes to Jonas, I don't need conventional. I don't need usual. I don't need happy-go-lucky. I just need him.

The hard part, though, I must admit, is not letting those damned words slip out of my own mouth. Every time I look into his mournful eyes, every time I touch his taut skin, every time he makes love to me, every time he looks lost or swallowed alive by his demons, or holds me tight out of some frantic impulse to protect me, every time he makes me climax and scream his name, I desperately want to say those words to him.

But I can't. I know I can't—no matter how powerful the urge. Because, without a doubt, if I say those particular words to Jonas Faraday, they'll scare the bajeezus out of him and blast our nascent relationship to Kingdom Come. I know it without a doubt. And I'm fine with that. I really am. We're mutually stricken with a serious mental disease—madness—something better and deeper and hotter and more beautiful than anything I've ever experienced before. And that's enough. We don't need three clichéd little words to make our love official. We just need each other.

All of a sudden, I can't stand to be apart from him.

I stand, looking at my watch. It's already close to one o'clock. This has been the longest day of my life—I woke up in frickin' Belize this morning, for Pete's sake. I stretch my arms above my head. Back to reality. I've got class tomorrow, homework to do. Study outlines to get from my study group. Oh shit, I've got to find a new job. Damn. And I can't manage any of that without a good night's sleep—not to mention without a laptop or textbooks or any of the clothes from my apartment. But I'll figure all that out in the morning. Right now I want one thing. Jonas Faraday. Inside me.

"Come on," I say to Kat. "Let's go back inside."

Jonas and Josh are sitting on the couch, talking calmly. Good sign.

Without a word, I waltz across the living room, right up to Jonas. I pull him up off the couch, press my body against his, take his face in my hands, and kiss him deeply.

"You take such good care of me," I breathe into him. "Thank you."

There's no better way to tell Kat what Jonas means to me than to show her. If she doesn't believe Seattle's King of the Man-Whores has fallen desperately in love with me, if she doesn't understand the depth of our emotional connection, if she can't see the goodness radiating off him, the kindness, the beauty, that's her problem, not mine. I know who he is and how he feels about me.

"You're welcome," Jonas says quietly. His face is on fire. He leans in and kisses me again—Kat and Josh be damned. When his tongue enters my mouth, my entire body sizzles with electricity. I can feel his erection nudging against me. Good thing, because I've got my own girlie version of an erection throbbing inside my panties, too.

"Have you two made nice?" I ask.

Jonas nods.

"You've come up with a plan to conquer the world?"

Jonas shakes his head in a "yes and no" kind of way. "Sort of," he breathes into my lips. "But Rome wasn't built in a day." He leans down and lifts me up by my hips, making me gasp, and slings me over his shoulder like a caveman. "We'll just have to finish plotting world domination at breakfast." He bounds out of the living room toward his bedroom, my head dangling and bobbing down his broad back as he goes.

"Don't worry about me; I'm fine," Josh calls after us. "I'll just party the night away with Party Girl with a Hyphen."

"Oh no, you won't. I'm going to sleep, Playboy," Kat replies, her voice just barely within earshot as Jonas closes in on his bedroom door. "You'll have to find another Mickey Mouse roller coaster to ride tonight."

Chapter 5

Jonas

I fling her down onto my bed, cue up "Dangerous" by Big Data, and rip her clothes off without mercy. After tearing my own clothes off, too, I sit on the edge of my bed, hard as a rock, and wordlessly beg her to fuck some serenity into me. With a low moan, she straddles me, encircling her legs tightly behind my back, and takes my full length into her. I pull her close, right up against me, and kiss her and kiss her and kiss her, staring into those big brown eyes of hers, reveling in her as my body melds into hers. We don't speak—there's no need—except, of course, for the times I moan her name, which can't be helped.

As Big Data swirls around us, I fuck her slowly, intensely, quietly, filling every inch of her, positioning my cock right up against her G-spot deep inside her. I caress the smooth skin of her back, run my hands through her hair, lick her neck, inhale her—losing myself in her, the music, her skin, her eyes, her scent. I think about absolutely nothing except how amazing she feels and how turned on I am and how awesome Big Data is for making a song so perfectly suited to blissful fucking. I'm not even thinking about making her come, to be perfectly honest—I'm too lost in the moment.

All of a sudden, out of nowhere, she comes like a motherfucker. Holy fuck, the woman explodes like a fucking rocket.

I'm absolutely floored. It's the first time Sarah's had an orgasm through intercourse alone—no tongue, no fingertips, just my cock inside her, filling her up, hitting her G-spot, just my shaft moving in and out of her, rubbing against her clit as we move together. Just my eyes locked onto hers. Just Big Data serenading us with the perfect fucking song—the perfect song for fucking.

It's incredible. The best yet, I might even say.

Our bodies fuse together in a whole new way until I can't tell where she ends and I begin, can't distinguish her pleasure from mine, her orgasm from mine, her flesh from mine. It's like discovering a treasure chest filled with priceless jewels buried six feet under the ocean's deepest floor, when all I'd been searching for was a couple of gold coins in the sand. Fucking epic. Without even trying to, I've discovered a brand new holy grail—this. Right here. Right now.

And yet . . .

I still don't say the words to her. I *feel* them, yes, of course—and thank God for that, because there was a time in my life I truly wondered if I was sociopathic—but I don't *say* them to her. Again.

Immediately after we're done, she falls asleep next to me, exhausted and totally satisfied. The woman is practically purring against me.

But I can't fall asleep. My soul has already started whispering to itself, an unpleasant truth barreling down upon it. I lie next to her for close to an hour, awake, listening to her breathing in and out, my mind reeling. Am I hopeless? Am I incapable of surrendering myself fully to Sarah the way I keep pushing her to surrender to me? Am I a hypocrite? I've been pushing her to get out of her own way—and yet I won't budge out of mine.

And damned if I know exactly what's happening, but the next thing I know I'm making love to her again. I must have drifted off to sleep at some point, at least briefly, because I wake up and I'm inside her, spooning her from behind, fucking her, and she's so wet and warm and fluttering all around me, and... Oh my God. There's nothing like watching my baby transforming into a beautiful butterfly right before my very eyes.

Chapter 6
Sarah

Jonas and I are dining in a fancy restaurant amid a flurry of activity. An army of waiters serves us, a woman sits at my feet giving me a pedicure, an artist paints our portrait from a few feet away, some woman in a toga primps my hair, and diners clatter and chatter all around our table. All of a sudden, Jonas leaps out of his chair, swats everyone away from me like he's King Kong, rips my shimmering gown off, and pushes my naked body onto our table, right on top of our food and lit candles and goblets of red wine and cutlery (including a most unfortunately positioned fork), and begins making love to me. But as he does, he's not his actual, physical self. It's hard to explain, but, in a flash, Jonas splinters and multiplies and becomes amorphic, until he's ten disembodied poltergeists, all of them with ghost lips and magical fingers and bulging biceps and chiseled abs and erect penises—all of them simultaneously embracing me, fucking me, licking me, sucking me, fondling me, groping me, kissing me, and whispering in my ears—all of them enveloping me like a slithering cloud.

And all the while, waiters refill our fallen wine glasses until they overflow, sending warm red wine gushing across my belly and spilling into my crotch and over my clit and down my thighs and between my toes until it accumulates around us into a warm and sensuous pool. The pedicure girl begins massaging my feet with the warm red wine. The hairdresser pours the wine over my scalp until it trickles down my face. And the most titillating thing of all, the thing that turns me on the most, other than Jonas himself, is how the other diners watch us and comment on our lovemaking like they're beholding a masterpiece of performance art.

"He's the most beautiful man in the world," one woman sighs.

"Clearly, but who's *she*?" a male diner asks.

"It doesn't matter. I can't take my eyes off him," another spectator observes.

"She must be something special if he wants her."

"I'm not even looking at her. I can't take my eyes off him."

"He's playing her like a grand piano."

"He's masterful."

"I've never seen anyone do it quite like this before."

"I wish he'd do that to me."

"I wish he'd make me moan like that."

"I'm having an orgasm just watching them."

Jonas' many tongues continue flickering on me, licking up the gushing red wine, his penises penetrate my every orifice, his muscles tense and bulge and contract under my fingertips, and his lips devour and suck and lick the wine off my skin and lap it out of every sensitive fold. It's almost too much pleasure to bear, intensified by the palpable desire and envy of every person watching us.

"She's losing her mind."

"She's gonna come."

"Oh God, yes, look at her. She's on the verge."

In an instant, every one of Jonas' fractured poltergeists converges on top of me, uniting and solidifying into Jonas' actual physical form.

"I love you, Sarah," he says, looking deeply into my eyes.

"Don't leave me, Jonas."

He cups my face in his hands. They're dripping in red wine. "I'll never leave you," he says. "I love you." He lifts his head and addresses our audience. "I love her. I love Sarah Cruz."

My clit, as well as everything connected to it, begins pulsing with emphatic pleasure. It's a sensation so concentrated, so undeniable, so *subversive*, it yanks me right out of my dream and into consciousness, at which point I realize that all the delicious pulsing occurring in my dream is actually happening in real life, too, inside my physical body. Holy frickin' ecstasy, I'm having an effing orgasm in my sleep! I can't believe it—the girl who only recently thought she couldn't have an orgasm at all, under any circumstance, a self-proclaimed Mount Everest Kind of Girl—is coming all by herself, powered by nothing but her own twisted imagination. Oh. My. Gawd. And what an orgasm it is. Talk about conquering the unconquerable mountain. Holy crappola. I feel like my entire pelvis, led by my clit, is going to explode right off my body and zip around the room like an errant balloon.

When my body stops pulsing, I grope feverishly behind me for Jonas' sleeping body and press my naked backside into him. Quickly, urgently, I stroke him into hardness (which isn't difficult to do), and, even before he's fully awakened, I slip his full length inside me and ride him rhythmically, reaching between my legs to feel him slipping in and out of me, touching myself, touching him, rubbing myself against his hard shaft, moaning his name. In no time at all, his mind becomes aware of what his body is doing. His lips find my neck, his warm hands find my breasts and belly and hips and clit, his fingers slip inside my moaning mouth, and his movement inside me deepens and intensifies.

I close my eyes as the pleasure inside me escalates and fills me to bursting. I remember him lapping at the red wine from the sensitive folds of my skin, how the envious diners watched us—and, most of all, how Jonas proclaimed, "I love Sarah Cruz" loud enough for everyone to hear. Lo and behold, warm waves of concentrated pleasure begin warping inside me again, emanating from my epicenter, making my body tighten and clench and release and contract around Jonas' erection.

His arms embrace me from behind and I clutch them around me, moving my body with his, coaxing him to his climax. But, much to my surprise, he pulls out of me, pushes me onto my back, and begins pleasuring me in every conceivable way. He kisses my breasts and neck and face and runs his hands over my thighs and sucks on my fingers and toes and kisses my inner thighs, and, finally, laps at me with his warm and magical tongue, licking my sweet spot with particular fervor—and in record time, I come *again*, this time like I'm exploding and melting at the same time. Holy banana cream pie, how sweet it is.

When I stop writhing and moaning, I can't move. He turns my lifeless form onto my belly and rides his happy, exhausted, horny little pony until he comes, too. And, I'll be damned, when he does, against all odds, I pulse and seize and vibrate yet again, right along with him. Not with eyes-rolling-back-into-my-head intensity, mind you—I'm too far gone for that—but, rather, like I'm his go-kart and he's just revved the engine one final, shriek-inducing time.

And now we're done, both of us completely spent.

He presses against me, holding me from behind.

And I'm a wet noodle. A sweaty wet noodle. A satisfied, sweaty wet noodle. I can't move a single muscle. And I can't speak, either. My vocal chords are non-functional—a couple of useless mucous membranes inside my throat.

Wow. Wow. Wow.

Mind officially blown.

Un-fricking-believable. Incredible. Delicious.

Can I get a woot woot from myself?

Woot woot!

If I could speak, which I can't, I'd scream from the top of every mountain right now: "I'm officially a sex kitten, peeps! I'm *multi-orgasmic,* bitches! Boom!"

I stretch myself out against his body and feel myself slipping into total relaxation. I've never felt quite like this before, so fulfilled, so satisfied—and so frickin' powerful, too. Tonight, I'm reborn, for the second time in my life—the prior time being that magical night in Belize when Mount Everest first toppled—and it's all thanks to this hunky-monkey-magic-man boyfriend of mine, Mr. Fuck Wizard himself. Mr. Most Beautiful Man I've Ever Seen. Mr. Heart as Big as the Grand Canyon. Mr. Sad Eyes. Mr. Tortured Soul. Mr. Divine Original. Mr. Manly Man-ness-y Manly Man.

Mr. Jonas Faraday.

My sweet Jonas.

Oh God, how I love this man.

I close my eyes. My mind yawns and instantly begins drifting into blackness . . .

"Sarah," Jonas whispers, and my mind lurches back to full attention. Something in his voice makes me think he's about to say something important. "Sarah, I . . ." The hairs on the back of my neck stand up, anticipating what he's about to say. He pauses a really long time—an excruciating amount of time—but he doesn't finish his thought.

He inhales sharply and his tone shifts direction. "My Magnificent Sarah," he finally says, stroking the curve of my hip. "Are you awake?" he whispers.

"Mmm hmm." Barely.

"That was a nice wake-up call."

I touch his hand on my hip. He grabs my hand and squeezes it.

"I had a dream that made me a wee bit horny," I mumble softly.

"Apparently. What did you dream about?"

"You. Making love to you. I had an orgasm in the dream, and then I woke up and I was actually having an orgasm."

His breathing halts in surprise. "Oh, wow." He presses himself into me and runs his hands over my belly.

I turn onto my opposite side and face him. "Before you, I thought there was something wrong with me. I thought I was born without some magic button everyone else has."

He inhales deeply, like he's trying to calm himself. He brushes a hair away from my face. But he doesn't speak.

"And now look at me. I'm kicking ass and taking names—I'm a sexual superhero."

He puts on a low movie-announcer voice. "They call her... *Orgasma.*" He smiles and nuzzles his nose into mine. "Orgasma the All-Powerful."

I mimic his announcer voice. "Able to leap tall cocks in a single bound."

"No." He's stern. "Able to leap one and only one tall *cock* in a single bound. Only mine."

"Well, of course." I roll my eyes. "That's the biggest 'duh' of the century, Jonas."

He laughs. He nuzzles my nose again.

"You big dummy," I add.

He shoots me a crooked half-smile. "I just wanted to be clear about that."

"Got it."

We lie in the dark, staring at each other for a moment. I can't remember ever feeling this happy before.

"Thank you," I say simply. "Thank you for helping me discover my magic button. I don't feel like I'm defective anymore. I feel powerful."

He kisses me gently. "You are powerful."

"I had no idea sex could feel so good. You really are good at this."

"No, I'm fucking awesome at this, I told you. But I can't take all the credit. Your body is *designed* to do exactly what it did tonight—get off again and again and again. It's not magic—women don't need a refractory period after orgasm the way men do."

"Refractory period?"

"A period of recovery. Women don't need to recover after orgasm—they can climax again and again, almost instantly after the first time, as long as they get the right stimulation."

I'm blown away. "Are you sure? I always thought some small percentage of women were multi-orgasmic, like porn stars or whatever, and a small percentage of women on the other end of the spectrum can't come at all, and then everyone else falls somewhere in the middle."

"Nah, that's a myth. All women are *designed* to come over and over. Just because most women haven't accomplished it—because they don't know how to do it, don't know it's possible, their boyfriends suck at sex, they've never masturbated and figured out what gets them off, whatever—it doesn't mean they're not *built* to do it. All the parts are there, even if they don't know how to use them."

His eyes are so animated when he talks about this stuff. I could fall asleep at the drop of a hat right now, and he's just getting more and more excited as we talk.

"Your first orgasm is like priming the pump," he continues, fully awake. "The first one might take a while, as we've discovered, my little Mount Everest, but once you're there, once you've reached the peak, your body is ready to do it again and again if you keep yourself open. And the great thing is, it's much easier to get there the second and third times."

I shake my head. Why does he know more about my own sexuality than I do? Why has no one ever told me any of this stuff?

"At the end of the day, female orgasm is always about your head—getting rid of your psychological hang-ups. After you get off the first time, you've just gotta keep your mind open and get the right stimulation—from someone who knows how—and you'll be off to the races every time."

"From *someone* who knows how?"

"Well, from *me*, of course—fuck, don't misunderstand that part. Let me be perfectly clear, yet again: Only from *me*. Always me."

I smile at him. "Jonas Faraday."

"The one and only."

"The sexual samurai."

He laughs. "Ah, you've seen my book collection."

"No, Kat did. She wants to make all your books required reading for her next boyfriend."

He chuckles. "Well, a guy can *read* about this stuff all he wants, but if he doesn't have some God-given talent to start with, it's pointless. It's like being a musician—you can be classically trained to play all the right notes, but no one can teach you to *feel* the music with your soul. Muddy Waters *felt* the music. Bob Dylan *felt* the music. No one can learn how to do that—it's true artistry."

"Ah, so you're a sexual *arteest,* are you?"

He squeezes me. "I am. And you're my canvas." He kisses my neck and grabs my ass at the same time.

"I'll be your canvas any time, big boy."

He's thinking about something. "My whole life, I've had this innate *understanding*. It's like this weird empathy; I don't know what else to call it." He pauses. "I've never told anyone this . . ."

I wait. There's absolutely nothing better than a sentence that starts with, "I've never told anyone this . . ."

"It started when I was little. My mother used to get these horrible headaches, and I was the only one who could make them go away, just by massaging her head the right way . . ." He stops talking.

"It's okay," I finally say. "Tell me."

He shakes his head.

"Tell me, baby. I'm listening."

He shifts internal gears. Clearly, there will be no more talking about his mother. "When I touch you, or fuck you, or taste you—oh fuck, I'm turning myself on again, baby—" He kisses me deeply, his hands firmly on my ass again. *"Albóndigas,"* he whispers. *Meatballs.*

I laugh. "*Siempre tus albóndigas*." *Always your meatballs.*

He smiles at me.

"Tell me," I coax him.

"When I fuck you or taste you or touch you, whatever, it's like I can *feel* what you're feeling—I mean, like, literally *feel* it, you know? And, holy fuck, it gets me off." He grunts, obviously imagining whatever sensation he's talking about.

"I told you—you're a woman wizard, baby. You've got magical, mystical powers."

He sighs and touches my cheek. "I can't wait to keep exploring the depths of you, Sarah Cruz. You're a vast and uncharted ocean, you know that?" He pauses. "You're *my* ocean."

I'm filled with the sudden urge to tell him I love him. He's better than any dream. He makes me feel safe. He makes me feel loved. He makes me feel *good*—so, so, so *frickin'* good. He makes me feel special. I love him. And, oh my God, I want to tell him, in exactly those words.

But, nope. I can't. No way. It's a non-starter.

And that's okay. *I'm his ocean,* he says. Not too shabby. It's enough. It really is.

"Yet again, you're a poet," I whisper.

"Only with you."

He wraps his arms around me and squeezes me. "Sarah . . .," he whispers, "I . . ." He clears his throat. But he doesn't say anything more.

I can feel myself drifting off to sleep. Whatever else he's going to say, it will have to wait until morning.

"Madness," I whisper. And then I close my eyes and slip into a deep and blissful sleep.

Chapter 7

Jonas

Thinking is just the soul talking with itself, or so Plato says. If that's true, then for the last few hours, while everyone else in the house has been fast asleep, my soul's been chatting up a fucking storm with itself. It's okay, though, because while my soul's been pontificating its ass off, my body's been getting shit done.

I washed and ironed Sarah's clothes from her suitcase (all of which were covered in Belizian mud and mosquito repellant). I worked out like a demon (powered by Rx Bandit's awesome new album). I went to Whole Foods and picked up breakfast for everyone (organic berries and Greek yogurt and zucchini-quinoa muffins). I went through my emails (and ignored every one of them except those pertaining to my new rock climbing gyms). I registered and loaded the laptops I bought for Sarah and Kat (which, thanks to my assistant, were delivered to my house first thing this morning). Bringing order and clarity to my environment has allowed me to bring order and clarity to my mind, too—and now, I'm pretty confident about my strategy going forward.

When I first opened Sarah's suitcase and smelled Belize wafting off her clothes, I wanted to charge into my bedroom, scoop up her sleeping body, and whisk her straight back to paradise. Fuck real life. Fuck The Club. Fuck being back in Seattle with Kat and Josh and work and school. But then I thought about what happened in my bedroom late last night (or, technically, early this morning), right here in the paradise of my bedroom, and I quickly forgot all about abducting Sarah back to Belize.

I look out my kitchen window. The sun is rising, illuminating not only my countertops with its soft golden light, but my consciousness, too, suddenly making it impossible for me to ignore a despicable truth: I'm incapable of uttering those three little words to anyone. Even to Sarah.

I sigh.

Before last night, I thought I'd been holding off saying those magic words for twenty-three long years because my soul knew it could only say them in the presence of pure *woman-ness.* I thought I'd reserved saying those words since the age of seven because my soul innately understood I would one day say them to one woman only, the goddess and the muse, Sarah Cruz—the ideal form of woman. But last night in the dark, lying next to her after making love to her in the most intense and mind blowing and intimate ways possible, I realized I'd been making excuses for my emotional limitations all along and that, in truth, I'm fundamentally incapable of surrendering myself to the extent necessary to say those words out loud. Even to My Magnificent Sarah.

What else can I possibly conclude? If those words didn't escape my lips when my baby's body seized and convulsed from nothing but the pleasure of my body filling hers, or when she came in her sleep simply because she'd had a *dream* about me, or when she climaxed over and over for the first time in her life, finally figuring out how to harness her body's greatest power, if all of that wasn't enough to make those three words spring involuntarily from my mouth, then, clearly, I'll never fucking say them.

It pains me to admit that to myself. I want to say those words to her, I really do. But, obviously, I'm too fucked up to accomplish it. I've come a long way thanks to Sarah, but, apparently, there's only so far I can travel on broken legs. No matter what, it seems there's always going to be a non-traversable wasteland inside of me, a bastion of fuckeduppedness just beyond my conscious borders that can't be reached or breached, no matter how beautiful or earnest or amazing the woman who's trying to guide me there. I just have to accept that there are dark, untouchable places inside of me, and adjust accordingly. If I can't say the words to her, okay, I can't. It means I have to work that much harder to *show* her how I feel about her.

And that starts right now.

I flip open my laptop and create a new document—a spreadsheet entitled, "How I'm Going to Fuck The Club Up the Ass."

It's time to show my baby exactly how I feel about her. It's time to show her I can't live without her. It's time to focus on the task at hand and quit fucking around.

Human behavior flows from three sources: desire, emotion, and knowledge. Obviously, when it comes to protecting Sarah, I've got the first two elements in spades, but I'm distinctly lacking in the third category. I need to acquire some knowledge. And fast. I type out what

I know about The Club onto my spreadsheet, add what I don't know, and then sit and brainstorm every methodology I can think of—good, bad, and even just plain ridiculous—for obtaining the information I currently lack.

Last night with Josh, I acted like a fucking lunatic, not to mention an asshole. I know that. I just let my emotions get the best of me. I was pissed as hell at what I perceived to be Josh's lack of loyalty and understanding of the situation, and I let that unfair perception jumble and merge with all the bullshit (real and imagined) years of therapy was supposed to fix (but apparently didn't). But this morning, after my soul's lengthy conversation with itself, not to mention some serenity-inducing fuckery with Sarah last night, I'm feeling more receptive to what Josh said.

Plato says, "Better a little that is well done, than a great deal imperfectly." And, actually, I think that's all Josh was trying to tell me last night, however inarticulately. I think he was trying to say The Club is a huge beast of a mountain to climb, and that if I approach climbing it haphazardly, I won't gain any traction and might even cause an avalanche. What I have to do is develop an effective plan of attack and execute it with supreme and careful excellence. There's too much at stake to do otherwise. What I need to do is frame my mission as "protecting Sarah (and Kat)"—rather than "decimating The Club."

Those two concepts *might* be one and the same—you never know—but they might not be. Right now, I don't have enough information to reach a sound conclusion on the issue one way or another. If destroying The Club turns out to be a component of protecting Sarah, then fuck yeah, that's what I'll do, and gladly. But if something short of that turns out to be a more effective option, then I'll have to be man enough to put my dick away and do whatever's going to achieve my mission. This is not the time to swing my dick around just for the hell of it. This is the time to protect my baby with maximum *effectiveness*.

And it all starts with gathering some knowledge.

"Good morning." It's Kat.

I look up from my screen. "Hi."

"Is Sarah up yet?"

"No, still sleeping like a baby. Same with Josh." Kat's dressed for work. She's got her purse on her shoulder. She's holding her rolling suitcase. "You're leaving?"

"Yeah, I've got to get to work. It turns out Mondays are considered workdays by my boss. Who knew?"

"You think that's wise?"

"I don't have a choice—I've got to work."

I don't respond.

"And, yeah. I think it's wise. I was totally freaked out yesterday, kind of in shock, but today I realize I can't live in fear. I've just got to live my life."

"Have you told Sarah you're leaving?"

"No. I haven't seen her this morning. I texted her."

"How about I put you up in a hotel," I begin. "Maybe just until we have a better grasp of what's going on—"

"No, I'm good. That's nice of you to offer, though. Thanks."

I'd like to keep close tabs on Kat, at least until I've got a better understanding of what I'm up against here. But, hey, she's an adult. Now, if she were my girlfriend, there's no fucking way I'd let her walk out that door right now—but she's not my girlfriend. And, anyway, I'm guessing The Club's real focus, if they have one at all—who the fuck knows what they're thinking?—is Sarah.

I give Kat the laptop I bought for her. Her eyes bug out of her head in surprise, but she nonetheless politely says she can't accept it, blah, blah, fucking blah. I appreciate her politeness, of course, but I don't have time to play "wow, we've both got such great manners" this morning. I've got too much to do.

"Kat, take the computer. Please. Help me alleviate my guilty conscience for putting this whole situation in motion. *I insist.*" In my vast experience with women, "I insist" is the magic phrase that ends all polite pushback regarding gifts and money and who's paying for dinner. It's the ultimate trump card a man holds over a woman. It never fails.

She acquiesces, right on cue. "Well, okay. Thank you so much."

"And I've arranged a cleaning service to come to your place. If your apartment looks anything like Sarah's did, you're definitely going to need some help."

Again, she half-heartedly goes through the social nicety of refusing me until I insist and make her shut the fuck up.

I have a sudden thought. "You know what? I'm gonna hire a bodyguard for you for at least a couple days—"

"No, that's... excessive, isn't it? You can't do that."

"It's not up for debate. I'll email you the information—and the guy's picture—so when he introduces himself, you'll know he's exactly who he claims to be. Just for a few days, Kat. Humor me."

She purses her lips.

"I *insist*. Just while I figure this out, okay? If you don't let me do that for you, then I'll worry about you—and I can't afford the distraction of worrying about you."

She smirks at me. "You're good at that."

"At what?"

"At getting what you want."

I shrug. It's true. So what?

"Thank you, Jonas. For everything. Tell Sarah I'll call her later."

"Will do. Hey, take a muffin with you. You gotta eat."

She grabs a muffin. "Thanks." She begins rolling her bag toward the door. She stops. "You know . . ."

I look up from my computer.

"You might not realize this, but Sarah doesn't normally let her guard down like she has with you—and definitely not so quickly."

I stare at her.

Kat exhales. "I just want to make sure you understand she's not just 'having fun' with you. She thinks this is something serious."

I don't speak. Clearly, she thinks I'm a flaming asshole—the asshole she saw with Stacy the Faker, I presume.

"Sarah always says I've got a heart of gold—but I don't. She's the one who wants to save the world, not me. She's the one who sees good in everyone—not me." She squints at me, clearly implying Sarah foolishly sees undeserved goodness in me. "Trust me, I'm not nearly as nice as she is."

I take this last comment to mean Kat's going to break my legs if I hurt her best friend. I suddenly like Kat a lot.

"She's fallen hard for you, Jonas," Kat says quietly.

This isn't news to me. I already know Sarah's fallen hard for me—she's told me so herself. And, even more importantly, she's shown me so herself. Regardless, though, it feels supremely awesome to hear her best friend confirm that fact, too.

Kat shifts her weight. "I probably shouldn't tell you this, but you need to understand the situation." She takes a deep breath. "She's in love with you." She waits a beat, letting that supposedly shocking revelation wash over me. "And she thinks you're in love with her, too." She grits her teeth—or is she baring them? It's hard to say.

Again, I don't speak.

"Don't crush her, Jonas."

Wow, that last line was delivered with some serious menace. Looks like Sarah's got a best friend who's as fierce as she is. Kat is now officially golden in my book.

"Got it," I say.

She stares at me, obviously annoyed. I guess she was expecting me to say something different.

"Thanks for the heads up," I add lamely.

I like Kat—she's clearly a fantastic friend to Sarah—but my feelings for Sarah are none of her fucking business. There's only room for two—for Sarah and me—in our little cocoon built for two. I don't give a fuck about anyone's opinion of me but Sarah's.

When it's clear I've said all I'm going to say, Kat clears her throat. "Well, thanks again for the computer," she finally says.

"But it doesn't buy your trust, huh?"

She smirks. "Hell no."

"Good."

Her smirk turns into a genuine smile. "Well, okay, then."

"Okay."

She grabs the handle of her suitcase again. "Tell Playboy goodbye for me. Maybe he and I can hang out one of these days—whenever he's done chasing Mickey Mouse roller coasters, if ever."

I return her smile. "I'll tell him you said exactly that."

"Wonderful."

She starts rolling her suitcase toward the door.

"Kat, I think you're forgetting one important thing."

She stops and looks at me, her eyes blazing with pre-emptive defiance. Apparently, she's expecting some sort of knight-in-shining-armor rebuttal from me—and she's already decided that, whatever it is, it's total bullshit.

"Sarah and I picked you up in a limo yesterday, remember? How were you planning to get to work?"

Her face falls. "Oh."

The defeated look on her face makes me smirk. "Let me call a car for you."

Chapter 8

Jonas

"Okay, let's talk action items," Josh says, taking a bite of a zucchini-quinoa muffin. "What the fuck is this?"

"Zucchini-quinoa."

Josh rolls his eyes and puts the muffin down. "Why can't you ever eat anything normal?"

I ignore him and study my spreadsheet. Josh has been helping me brainstorm leads and strategies for the last twenty minutes. Sarah's still asleep, not surprisingly—we were up 'til the wee hours together, discovering Sarah's newfound orgasmic superpowers. Good God, that woman is my crack. *Orgasma.* I can't help but smile.

"All right," I say, looking at my computer screen. "Item one. You and I will forward your hacker guy whatever emails we both still have from The Club."

"Yup. Though I doubt that will yield anything."

"Worth a try."

"One would think they'd be smart enough to use dummies or encrypt their emails or insert fakers, but they might be epically stupid, you never know. And my hacker buddy is really good, so, hey, it's worth a shot."

"Who is this hacker, anyway?"

"A buddy of mine from college. He's solid, trust me—he's helped out a bunch of my friends on the down low with some pretty big stuff."

I instantly wonder why Josh's flashy friends have required the services of a top-notch hacker, but it doesn't matter—if Josh trusts this guy completely, then so do I.

"Action item two," I say. "I engage them in some sort of email exchange. Hopefully, I can get something that helps the hacker and leads us to a power player."

"Good. What are you gonna say to them?"

I consider briefly. "I could thank them for allowing me to partake in their lovely intake agent. I'll tell them she was a thoroughly enjoyable surprise—but that I'm all done with her now, thank you very much, and looking forward to the rest of my membership experience. I'll ask for assurances from the top that my intake-agent detour won't disrupt my membership in any way."

Josh twists his mouth. "That makes you sound like such an asshole. You've had your fun with their intake agent and now you're just tossing her aside?"

I shrug. "Yeah."

Josh raises his eyebrows. "After all the effort it took to find her?"

"They don't know the lengths I went to find her. For all they know, Sarah just picked up the phone and called me after our first emails. Actually, come to think of it, maybe they're not sure if Sarah and I even connected in person. Maybe they think Sarah and I emailed back and forth, she went to spy on me at my first check-in, saw me with the purple prostitute, and that was that. That would be a reasonable conclusion, wouldn't it?"

"Maybe under normal circumstances, but... Come on." He motions to me, as if my mere Jonas-ness somehow makes my hypothetical impossible.

I roll my eyes at him. "Whatever. Either way, they've read my application, so me being a gigantic asshole is exactly what they'd expect."

"You could make it sound like you thought Sarah was part of your membership. Maybe that'd make it more believable that you'd turn and burn her so damned fast."

Josh truly has no idea what I've been doing for the past year?

"Josh, they won't have trouble believing I'd turn and burn her, trust me."

He grimaces.

"Oh really, Mr. Mickey Mouse Roller Coaster? The mere thought is distasteful to your gentle sensibilities?"

He laughs. "The roller coaster thing was an *analogy,* bro—it's not necessarily my life philosophy. As a matter of fact, when I find a roller coaster I particularly like, I prefer to ride it over and over again, exclusively."

"Okay, this is getting gross. Don't talk to me about 'riding' anything ever again, motherfucker. You're making me want to puke."

"It's an *analogy.*"

"It's gross. I don't need that visual of you." I shudder.

He shrugs. "I have no idea what you're talking about. I'm just talking about riding roller coasters."

"Anyway, there's no way they'd believe I thought Sarah was some sort of Club offering. They've got her computer. They've seen our emails. It's clear we both knew she was breaking the rules—I kept assuring her I wouldn't tell them she'd contacted me."

"Aha! Now it all makes sense. I've been wondering why you went ballistic about her sight unseen like that. She was the proverbial *forbidden fruit.*"

"Gee, Dr. Freud, you're so fucking smart."

Except that he's wrong. Josh doesn't have a clue why I lost my shit over Sarah's first email to me—and I'll never tell him because it's none of his business. But, holy fuck, what an email it was. *A Mount Everest kind of girl like me,* she called herself. I still get tingles just thinking about it—and about how many delicious times I've climbed and conquered my beautiful Mount Everest since then.

"I like the part about you saying you're eager to move on with your membership," Josh says. "It makes it seem like Sarah never told you their dirty little secret—or, if she did, like you don't care. Either way, a good thing."

A thought is niggling at me. I pause, trying to pin it down. "Are we sure about that? Does Sarah supposedly not telling me what she discovered help or hurt the situation?"

"How could it do anything but help? If she didn't tell you, then they'll assume she's discreet. Maybe they'll decide to trust her and leave her alone."

"But what if it goes the other way? What if they think she just hasn't had the opportunity to tell me yet? Or she hasn't worked up the nerve? Or what if they think she already told me, and I didn't give a shit, and now she's pissed as hell and about to go on a rampage? Even if they think she hasn't blabbed, they might decide their best strategy is to strike quickly to ensure her continued silence—not to risk it, either way." I know I'm talking really fast, but I can't slow myself down. My heart is racing all of a sudden. What if those fuckers are planning to come after her right now? I have the sudden urge to bolt to my room and scoop her up and whisk her away to a faraway place.

"Hmm. I guess that depends on what kind of criminals we're dealing with here. I mean, it's just a prostitution ring, right? What makes you think they might be capable of physical violence?"

"What makes me think . . .? You mean besides the fact that they simultaneously broke into Kat and Sarah's apartments and smashed both places to bits? That's not enough for you right there?"

Josh's expression is noncommittal—apparently, no, that's not enough for him.

I'm sure my face clearly expresses my exasperation. "Don't get bogged down by the fact that it's 'just a prostitution ring.' It doesn't matter if their particular racket is prostitution, drugs, gambling, identity theft—whatever the fuck—it doesn't matter. What matters is that they're a highly organized crime syndicate with a shitload of money at stake. Do the math, Josh. This is big money. At the end of the day, the specific form of their criminal activity is irrelevant—what matters is that they're not going to let anyone, least of all a dispensable intake agent, fuck with their cash cow."

Josh lets that roll around in his head for a second. "I never thought about it that way. Hmm."

"And, on top of that, I'd bet anything their client roster is a who's who of some ultra-powerful people, too. They've got plenty of incentive to keep their members from learning the truth, through any means necessary."

Josh suddenly looks anxious. "An excellent point."

I'm getting myself all worked up. "They're sitting on a fucking powder keg, Josh. And, as far as they know, Sarah's the one holding the match."

"Shit."

My heart clangs sharply inside my chest. I'm breaking out into a sweat. "I'm just not sure which way to play it. The stakes are too high to fuck this up." I run my hand through my hair. *My Magnificent Sarah.* I can't let anything happen to her. My heart pounds like a motherfucker in my ears. "I just need more information to know what to do."

Josh nods. "Yeah, I see your point. It's tricky." He sighs. "I didn't really understand all that until now." He purses his lips, unsure about something. "Maybe you should just go to the police?"

"I thought about that. This isn't something for the local police—we need the feds. Is the FBI really gonna sick their anti-fraud unit all over this just because Sarah saw a hooker wearing two different colored bracelets? I'm sure they've got more pressing shit to deal with, and I need immediate action."

Josh looks anxious.

"My gut tells me to keep this under wraps until I can serve the whole thing up to them on a silver platter."

Josh nods.

"You know, if I ever do wind up blowing this thing wide open, it might not be pleasant for either of us. At the very least, it might be really embarrassing."

He shrugs. "I'm a single guy. It was one month of my life. I don't give a fuck. No one held it against Charlie Sheen when it came out he had sex with prostitutes all the time. I'll just make like Charlie Sheen and say 'Fuck you—I'm winning.'"

We both laugh.

"Yeah, I don't give a fuck, either. Fuck it."

"Uncle William would shit a brick, though."

"I know."

We both laugh again, imagining our straightlaced uncle—the polar opposite of our father in every way—finding out about our unseemly extracurricular activities.

Josh twists his mouth in apology. "I'm sorry about last night. I just didn't get it."

For some reason, hearing Josh say he finally gets what I've been trying to explain to him makes me feel like the weight of the world has lifted off me, like I'm finally not alone in all this.

"I'm sorry I blew up at you," I say. "Thanks for coming here on a moment's notice."

"Of course. I'll always come when you call, man."

I take a deep breath, panic about the situation and relief that Josh is on board crashing through my body all at once. "Okay, we'll sit on item number two for a bit—think it through some more. I won't email them directly just yet."

Josh nods. "Okay. So what's next on the list, then?"

"Item number three. Find these assholes the good old-fashioned way. We find a real person in The Club, no matter how low on the totem pole, and just keep connecting the dots all the way up until we identify someone we can fuck up the ass. And in the meantime, I keep Sarah safe and out of their crosshairs at all times."

He purses his lips. "You know, we really should ask Sarah what she thinks. She's probably got all kinds of ideas on where to start. I bet she could tell us—"

"No, I don't want Sarah involved in any of this. This is just gonna be you and me."

"Bro." Josh looks at me like I'm an idiot. "She worked for them and she's super smart. She's bound to have an idea or two—"

"I don't want Sarah involved."

Josh throws up his hands. "I'm not talking about asking her to *do* anything. I'm just saying let's ask her for *input*."

"No." It comes out louder than intended. I take another deep breath and collect myself. "You don't know Sarah like I do. If we ask her for *input*, she'll immediately start *doing* something—surveillance or research or snooping around or God knows what. She's not a sit-on-the-sidelines kind of girl. She's the one who emailed me in the first place, remember?"

Josh smiles broadly.

"Yes, granted, that part worked out well," I concede, stifling a smile of my own. That's the understatement of the year. "But the point is, she doesn't sit around thinking, 'golly gosh, wouldn't it be nice to know x y z,' she gets out there and *does* whatever the fuck she has to do to figure out x y z."

Josh sighs in exasperation. "Yeah, but—"

"When she had a question about this friend of mine—remember the time you invited that little league team to our box seats at the Mariners' game?"

Josh nods. "Of course."

"Well, after that, I became friendly with one of the kids and—"

Josh's face contorts in complete surprise.

"It's a long story—totally irrelevant. But when Sarah was curious about my friendship with the kid, what did she do? She paid a visit to his mom at her work and got all the information she wanted." I smile. "She's such a lawyer-in-training, I swear to God. The girl is so fucking snoopy."

Josh gives me his patented laughing-at-me-with-his-eyes look.

"And before she ever agreed to meet me in person, she *spied* on me at my Club check-in—I told you about that, right? That's when I hooked up with that Purple who showed up a week later at some other guy's check-in as a fucking Yellow?"

Josh grimaces in disgust. "Yeah, you told me about that."

"And that's how the shit hit the fan in the first place—Sarah spied on me and the yellow guy, too—just because her *curiosity* got the best of her both times—and that's how Stacy the Prostitute put two and two together and ratted her out."

Josh nods.

"You see? That's Sarah. She gets *curious*—and when she does, she doesn't hesitate to do whatever the fuck she has to do to *satisfy* that curiosity. You don't know her like I do, man. She's a force of nature, that woman. When she sets her mind to something... I don't want her taking charge and hijacking things and unwittingly doing something that puts her on The Club's radar screen any more than she already is. The next time they come after her might not be a simple break-in."

"I get it. I really do, man. Okay? Don't freak out on me—I'm on board. But if we're looking for a place to start connecting the dots, I'm just saying Sarah would know better than anyone what our first dots should be. We should at least ask her."

"No. It's non-negotiable, Josh. I don't want Sarah involved. I'm gonna keep her safe through any means necessary, even if that means benching her from the game."

Josh sighs. "Jonas."

"No. I'm keeping her out of harm's way, both physical and emotional." I lower my voice. "She had a rough childhood, Josh. Her father was a bastard—an abuser." I take a measured breath, trying to calm the raging beast welling up inside of me. "Sarah said she and her mom 'escaped' him. Fucking bastard. If he were here right now, I'd tear him limb from limb."

Josh looks anguished.

"She's been scared enough times in her life. She doesn't need to deal with this kind of bullshit. She doesn't need to be scared. I just want to keep her out of it."

Josh rubs his face and exhales. He doesn't speak for a long beat. "Okay, bro," he finally concedes. "We'll do things your way."

That's exactly right—we'll do things my fucking way. I'm going to keep Sarah out of harm's way and make her feel safe and protected at all times, through any means necessary, no matter what. All my baby needs to do is go to her classes and study her law books and chase that scholarship she wants so badly and help her mom save the world one battered woman at a time and then come home to me and spread her smooth olive thighs on top of my crisp white sheets and let me glory in her and make love to her and lick her and fuck her and kiss her and suck her and show her how I feel. I want her relaxed and happy and satisfied and carefree—not sitting around thinking some boogeyman is coming to get her. And, quite selfishly, I don't want Sarah even thinking about The Club anymore, in any capacity. From now on, she can channel all her sexual curiosity into me. She's all mine now—and I want her undivided attention.

My heart pounds in my ears.

I pull my Club-issued iPhone out of my jeans pocket and toss it onto the kitchen table. "We don't need Sarah's input, anyway. I've still got the keys to their kingdom. The fuckers haven't deactivated me."

Chapter 9
Jonas

"Wow." Josh pauses briefly, staring at my Club-issued iPhone on the table. "I'm surprised they haven't cut you off. They must not be sure if you're friend or foe. Maybe you're right—maybe they don't know for sure what's gone down between you and Sarah."

"Yeah, and they'd better be goddamned positive I'm the enemy before cutting me off. Hell hath no fury like an asshole unjustly separated from his quarter of a million bucks."

Josh lets out a loud puff of air. "Oh my God, Jonas. You joined The Club for a *year?*"

Shit. I've never mentioned that little detail to Josh before. I completely forgot he assumes I joined for a fun-filled month, just like he did.

"That's hardcore, man. Damn."

He's right. I shrug.

"Ha!" He shakes his head, smiling. "I feel totally vindicated. Which Faraday brother is the playboy now?"

I can't help but laugh. Of the two of us, Josh has always been tagged as the bad boy playboy, maybe because he's always so public about his relationships and partying, when all the while it's me who's been burning through women like a lawnmower through tall grass.

"Oh, hey, that reminds me. Kat left a message for you—which she addressed specifically to 'Playboy.'"

Josh looks disappointed. "She left?"

"Yeah, she had to go to work. Said she has to 'live her life.' But she gave me a message for you: 'Tell *Playboy* I'd love to hang out with him some time—whenever he's done chasing Mickey Mouse roller coasters, if ever.'"

Josh groans.

I laugh. "Hey, man, you did it to yourself. You're the one who said all that Mickey Mouse bullshit right in front of her. Dumbass."

Josh looks totally bummed.

"You liked her, huh?"

"Did you *see* her? Oh my God."

"She's just your type."

"She's *everybody's* type."

"Well, she obviously thinks you're a total asswipe."

Josh smashes his mouth into a hard line. "She was sassy, too. I like sassy."

"It's your own damned fault."

"Fuck you. You're the one who signed up for a whole *year's* worth of Mickey Mouse roller coasters, not me. Pervert."

He's got me there. I've got no comeback.

"What the hell did you ask for in your application that you needed a whole *year* of it?" he asks.

"It doesn't matter. I told you—I was having some kind of nervous breakdown. What did you ask for in *your* application?"

"None of your business." Josh's face turns earnest. He fidgets. "Hey, man, I had no idea you were... you know, having such a hard time. I thought you were living large, being a beast. I had no idea you were... you know... "

"Turning into Dad?"

Josh's face flushes.

"It's okay. Neither did I. I'd become quite the expert at distracting myself from the truth."

Josh nods. "Turn and burn," he says quietly.

"Turn and burn," I agree. A series of images from the past year flashes through my mind. Turn and burn, indeed. "But then Sarah came along and kicked my ass, man. Holy shit, did she ever kick my ass. That woman can spot bullshit a mile a way—and she totally called me on mine."

"Sounds like she was exactly what you needed."

"She was—she *is*."

"But next time, if you're having a rough time, talk to me, okay? I never want you to... you know... feel like . . ."

"There won't be a next time."

"Just don't do something stupid."

"I won't. Never again. I promise."

"I've always got your back. You know that, right? I never want you to—"

"I won't."

Josh exhales. "I can't believe you spent a quarter million bucks on The Club—on anything, actually. It's so un-Jonas-like of you."

He's right. I don't spend money frivolously. Clearly, I was out of my mind.

"And Sarah knows you joined for a whole year?"

"Yeah, she's the one who processed my application." I sigh, suddenly wistful. *My Beautiful Intake Agent.* She had me the minute her email landed in my inbox.

"Wow. She knows all the ways you're a total pervert and she still wants you?"

I nod.

"You're a lucky bastard."

"I know."

"Does she know everything else, too? You know, about . . ." He pauses, suddenly unsure how to proceed.

I tilt my head and wait. But Josh doesn't have the heart to finish that sentence.

He swallows hard.

I finish his sentence for him. "Does she know about The Lunacy?"

Josh nods.

It suddenly occurs to me Josh is the only living person (besides doctors and therapists, of course) who knows everything about The Lunacy—the euphemism we use to refer to "the time when Jonas lost his fucking mind." There was nothing remotely funny about that period of my life, of course, nothing at all, but I've since learned that scoffing about it, calling it something as irreverent and light-hearted and dismissive as "The Lunacy," effectively minimizes the pain and relegates it to a distant and containable memory.

I've gotten quite adept at compartmentalizing that stuff into a lidded box inside me, in fact, and now that I'm sane and in control of my mind and body and soul, now that I've come to realize that my father was fallible—that he wasn't God, for fuck's sake, or the supreme arbiter of my worth as a human being, that his suicide note was just fucking *malicious* and not reflective of the objective truth—now that I've figured out how to choose serenity and enlightenment and sanity through visualizing the divine originals and striving for excellence, I'm reborn—a totally different person. I'm a man now, a fucking beast, just like Josh always says—not a mute and frozen boy in a closet or some kind of pathetic pussy-ass seeking his father's forgiveness that will never come. I'm strong now. Especially now that I've found my Sarah.

I put down the muffin I was holding. "Well, I told her about... what happened... you know, on that day when we were kids," I say quietly. The levity of our conversation has instantly vanished. He knows what day I'm talking about, of course—the day that changed both our lives forever, the day that fucked us up irreversibly, especially me. The day we've both tried, in vain, to overcome our whole lives.

Josh looks surprised. And it's no wonder—I never, ever talk about what I witnessed from the cowardly safety of my mother's closet. I've certainly never told any of my other girlfriends about it.

"I also told her about Dad—what he did. You know, just the basics, no details."

Josh nods, clenching his jaw. His eyes flash with sudden hardness.

"But I didn't tell her about... everything that happened right after that. To me."

Josh nods his agreement. "The Lunacy."

I nod. *The Lunacy.* It's my penultimate shame, second only to my life's greatest and most inexcusable disgrace—my unforgivable failure to move from that damned closet and come to my mother's rescue.

"That's good, Jonas. Nobody ever needs to know about that."

"Yeah." I exhale loudly. "I mean, it's irrelevant, right? I'm different now. I've conquered myself."

"Oh, yeah. You totally have. You're a badass now, bro. Just look at you. You're a beast."

Emotion is welling up inside me. I suppress it. I pause, considering my words carefully. I need him to understand what Sarah means to me. "Josh, I've told Sarah things I've never told anyone—not even you." *Because I love her,* I think—but, of course, I don't say it.

"Wow," Josh says. "That's good, Jonas." He gets it. I know he does.

"She understands me." I absentmindedly touch the tattoo on my right forearm. *Visualize the divine originals.* "Sometimes better than I understand myself." I think about Sarah touching this very same spot on my arm and my skin electrifies. "I've never felt like this before," I say softly. *I love her,* I think. *I love her, Josh.* My heart is pounding in my ears.

"Yeah, I can tell." He nods, smiling. "I've never seen you like this about a girl before."

My heart pounds. *Because I love her.*

"So don't fuck it up."

"I won't." God help me, I won't.

Josh exhales loudly and slaps his own face. "Okay, crazy-ass-motherfucker. You know what you gotta do, then?"

I mimic his loud exhale and slap my own face in reply. "Fuck yeah, pussy-ass motherfucker." Slapping ourselves is what Josh and I have always done when we've unexpectedly found ourselves engaged in a conversation about our fucking feelings. It's our mutual way of signaling that it's time to stop acting like crybabies and sack up. I motion to the Club-issued iPhone on the table. "I know exactly what to do."

Josh frowns.

"Hey, I've got to start connecting the dots somehow. I'll start with the only dot I've got. Stacy the Prostitute."

"Jonas . . ."

I scoff. "I'm not gonna *fuck* her, Josh." Even saying those words about Stacy makes my stomach lurch. "Give me some credit."

Josh looks uneasy.

"I'm just gonna check in on the app so I can *talk* to her. I'll butter her up and get her to lead me to her boss. Connect the dots—that's what we said, right?"

Josh grimaces.

"Why do you look like I just gave you a fucking enema? It'll entail nothing but a drink and a quick chat in a crowded bar. Simple."

Josh shakes his head. "Don't kid yourself. It won't be that simple."

"Sure it will. Stacy the Prostitute is just a mercenary—she's chasing the mighty dollar and nothing else. When people are motivated by money, it makes things incredibly simple."

Josh sighs. "But what about Sarah?"

"What about her?"

"She might not think things are as 'simple' as you do."

I stare at him.

"Jonas, think. Sarah might not feel quite so it's-no-big-deal about you meeting up with a woman you've slept with, even if it's just for a 'simple' drink and a chat. Girlfriends are kinda funny that way."

I pause, considering. "Why does she even need to know about it?"

Josh rolls his entire head, not just his eyes. "Oh, for Chrissakes, Jonas, yeah, not telling Sarah would make your fantastic idea even better. Never mind. Forget I ever said a thing about it." Clearly, he's being sarcastic.

"No, really. What's the point in telling her? I'll go meet Stacy at The Pine Box tonight. I'll tell her what she wants to hear—get her to lead me to the next person up the totem pole. Then I come right back home. Done. Simple."

Josh is clearly uneasy. He shakes his head.

"Trust me. Simple."

He exhales. "Just be careful."

"With Stacy?" I laugh. "I'm not afraid of Stacy."

"No, you dumbfuck. I don't mean be careful with *Stacy*." He shakes his head for the hundredth time at me. "I mean be careful with *Sarah*. Don't fuck things up with her. I think you're misjudging this."

I roll my eyes at him. "I'm not."

Why is he worried? This is a great plan. Yes, granted, in a perfect world, Josh's hacker buddy would find these bastards the way he found Sarah for me, and I'd never have to see Stacy again as long as I live. But I can't count on that—Josh himself said so. So I've got to work on Plan B—connecting the dots on my own, one dot at a time, through whatever means necessary.

"Whatcha doin', boys?"

Oh shit. How long has Sarah been standing there?

She's showered and dressed—and, as usual, looking gorgeous.

"Hey, baby," I say, quickly closing my laptop. I stand to greet her. "Just plotting world domination." I smile.

She squints at my closed laptop and then at me, her mind instantly whirring and clacking like the well-oiled machine it is.

I embrace her, leaning in to whisper right into her ear. "Last night was incredible, baby. Epic." I kiss her and my entire body starts tingling. She smells delicious.

"The woman wizard strikes again," she whispers, kissing me back. She leans into my ear. "I'm horny as hell this morning, baby—just thinking about last night." Her eyes drift over to Josh and she instantly pulls away from me.

Fucking Josh. I'm glad he's here, of course—I'm the one who called him and asked him to come, I know—but why the fuck is he here?

"Good morning, Sarah Cruz," Josh says politely.

"Good morning, Josh Faraday," Sarah says. She looks at me again. "Thanks for doing my laundry. Wow. You never cease to surprise and delight me, Jonas Faraday." She winks, and I know she's referring to more than her laundry with that compliment.

"You're very, very welcome. It was my supreme pleasure to do your laundry."

"You're exceptionally good at folding clothes, you know that? Impeccable creases."

I smirk. I love it when my baby talks dirty to me.

"If being a business mogul doesn't pan out for you, you could totally work at The Gap."

Josh laughs.

I glare at him. Fuck Josh. Why is he here?

"Did you *iron* my clothes? They're absolutely perfect, like new."

"Of course, I did."

"Babe, that's insane. Are you secretly a housewife from the fifties under there?" She lifts up my T-shirt and peeks at my abs, her knuckles lightly grazing my bare skin as she does. Just this brief touch of her skin on mine gives me goose bumps.

Josh laughs again, making me wonder, yet again, why he's here.

"Excellence in all things," I say softly.

"Absolutely." She smiles at me. She lowers my shirt but doesn't let go of it.

There's a beat. I want her so much it's taking all of my restraint not to clear off my kitchen table. I can't be in this woman's presence for five minutes without wanting to rip her clothes off.

"So," she says, shifting her weight, "besides creating the perfect form of *laundry-ness* in the ideal realm, what else have you been doing with yourself this morning, my sweet Jonas? You've been a busy bee, I presume?" Her eyes drift over to my laptop on the table and unmistakably land with a crashing thud onto my Club-issued iPhone. It's sitting smack in the middle of the table, a fucking beacon of my degeneracy. Fuck. She lets go of my shirt. Her eyes dart back to me. Oh, wow, shit, her eyes are burning like hot coals right now.

"What have you been up to, Jonas?" There's a sudden edge in her voice.

"Just brainstorming a few things with Josh."

"Why'd you close your laptop when I came in?"

I hesitate.

Her eyes dart back to the iPhone again.

"What's that doing there?"

Leave it to Sarah to go straight for the jugular. No fucking around.

I'd really like to lie to her right now, but I can't. Right from day one, I promised her total honesty. I sigh. "I don't want to get you involved with Club stuff. Josh and I are formulating our strategy. We've got it covered."

Josh shoots me a look that unequivocally says, "Leave me the fuck out of it."

Sarah glances back at the kitchen table and glares at the iPhone again.

I shift my weight.

She bites her lip. She looks at Josh. He does his best to remain stone-faced, but he's doing a terrible job of it. She glares at me.

I smile at her reassuringly. Damn, she's adorable when her face is on fire like this.

"Sure thing." Her voice is cool, though her face is hot. "I've got a bunch of stuff to do, anyway."

Her words don't match her body language at all.

"Can I get a ride to my place?" Her eyes drift to my laptop and then again to the iPhone on the table. Her wheels are turning. Her cheeks are red. She's *thinking.* Her eyes are back on me now. "I'm meeting the police at my place in less than an hour. I've got to file a claim about the break-in."

"Whoa, what? Hang on. I'm not sure we should get the police involved. They can't do a damned thing, anyway, and I haven't decided if—"

She cuts me off. "I need to file a police report in order to make a claim on my renter's insurance. I already called my insurance company—I can get a replacement laptop through my policy, I just need to file a police report first."

Oh, she's going to like this. "I already bought you a replacement laptop, baby." I grin broadly and grab it off the nearby counter. My chest is pounding. I've been excited all morning about giving this computer to her. It's loaded with every bell and whistle known to modern technology.

She's quite obviously shocked. "Oh, wow. Thank you." She smiles at me like she pities me. "But no."

I'm not surprised—that's what Kat said at first, too. "Please take the computer," I say. "Help me alleviate my guilty conscience for creating this whole mess in the first place."

She bristles. "You didn't create this mess, Jonas."

"Sarah, don't overthink this. Your computer was stolen. I've got one for you. End of story."

She raises her eyebrows at me.

I probably shouldn't have pushed my luck with that "end of story" caveman shit. "I'm just saying you need a computer and I've got one for you. Simple. Why not?"

"Why not? Because you're far too generous with your money when it comes to me. There's got to be some boundaries, especially if I'm gonna be staying here with you. If you want to take me to a fancy jungle tree house, to a place I could never afford to go on my own, okay, I'm all for it—I want to see the world with you and experience all the things you love to do. Fine. I'll totally take you up on that. Thank you. But you absolutely cannot pay for my basic needs. It's too much. I can't just put my hand out every time I need something. I'm here for *you*, Jonas, not for a hand-out."

God, I hate it when she says shit like that. It reminds me how fucked up she is. Of course, she's not interested in me for my money, that's undeniable. Jesus Christ. I swear to God, she's got the biggest fucking chip on her shoulder when it comes to that. I exhale sharply in frustration. She's not giving me the reaction I expected. Honestly, I was hoping for one of her little squeals. Or, at the very least, a gushing "thank you."

I don't have time or patience for this right now. I just want her to do what I tell her to do for once in her goddamned life. It's time to pull out the trump card.

"Sarah, please. I *insist*." That ought to do the trick.

"Oh, you *insist*, do you?" She laughs. "Well, so do I. I *insist*. So there."

Wait, what? She's not supposed to say that.

Josh makes a noise, suppressing a laugh.

Fuck you, Josh. Why are you here right now?

She kisses me. "Thank you so much, sweet Jonas. You always take such good care of me. But I've got it covered." She looks at her watch. "Oh man, I've got to get to my place to meet the trusty campus police."

"The *campus* police?" Josh laughs. "Oh, I'm sure they'll crack the case in a jiffy."

She laughs. "I know, right? The campus police will protect me from the baddies at The Club, for sure."

Josh and Sarah share a laugh.

Fucking Josh.

"I'll just report a simple break-in and computer theft—obviously, I won't mention The Club. I mean, jeez, I worked for a frickin' brothel." She shakes her head. "I'm not eager to tell anyone that. I'm not even sure I'd pass the ethics review for my legal license if that ever got out." She furrows her brow, genuine concern flashing across her face.

Shit. I hadn't even thought about that. Could this whole thing with The Club torpedo her law career if it ever got out? I'm sure Sarah's freaking out about that. I didn't even consider that angle. I've definitely got to handle this whole situation with kid gloves.

"I'll just let them make a quick report and then I'll have what I need for my insurance claim." The anxiety that flashed across her face a second ago is gone. She's all business now—my little badass. "I've got contracts class right after that, and then I've got to study in the library." She gasps. "Oh, dang it, and I've got to clean up the mess at my place, too—"

"I've arranged a cleaning service to help you with that." She's got to let me do *something* here.

"Oh, Jonas," she sighs. Her entire body melts. She presses her body into mine and moans softly. "You're amazing, you know that? So sweet." She puts her lips right up to my ear. "You just made me wet."

My cock springs to life.

She continues at full voice again. "But my renter's insurance includes a one-time cleaning service, too, for incidents such as this. I already checked." She smiles at me. "So I'm all good."

What the fuck?

"Well . . ." I begin. I'm flustered. I'm turned on. I can't think straight. I'm pissed she's not doing what I want her to do. "I don't think I can return the computer," I babble.

She laughs. "Of course you can. That's just plain silly."

"Maybe not."

"Oh, Jonas." She kisses my neck softly.

My erection is growing. My skin is tingling under her soft lips.

"I guess you'll just have to donate it to a school, then. Or my mom's charity. Or, hey, give it to Trey—I bet he'd be thrilled." Her mouth moves to my lips. "Thank you for being so thoughtful." She kisses me and runs her hand through my hair. She leans into my ear. "Yep, definitely wet."

I'm rock hard.

Why does this woman turn me on like this?

And why does she have to make everything so damned difficult?

She kisses my neck again.

I tilt her face up and kiss her mouth.

Josh gets up from the table and wordlessly leaves the room.

I want her. Now. On the kitchen table. Right now.

She pulls back from me. "So, how about that ride to my place, big boy? I've suddenly figured out the next item on my *addendum*." She smiles wickedly and winks. "Let's see if we can beat the campus fuzz to my place and let them catch us *in flagrante delicto*, shall we?"

Chapter 10

Sarah

I settle into my seat in the big lecture hall. It's about five minutes before the start of my contracts class. And since it's Take Your Boyfriend to Class Day (or so Jonas Faraday has unilaterally decreed), Jonas takes the seat right next to mine. Weird.

I love spending time with Jonas, of course, more than anything, but sitting here in my law school class with him when he should be tending to his brand new chain of indoor rock climbing gyms or acquiring yet another new company or doing whatever mogul-y thing he should be doing right now seems like a waste of his valuable time and resources, not to mention a bizarre case of "two worlds colliding" for me. How long is he planning to put his life on hold to babysit me? It's not realistic. Not to mention slightly awkward. And, frankly, I'm not even convinced it's necessary. I'd never say it to him (because, holy hell, I saw how he reacted when he thought Josh wasn't on board with his Mission to Save Sarah), but I think Jonas might be overreacting just a teensy-weensy bit here.

I was shocked and scared and freaking out yesterday when we first discovered the break-in at my apartment, and, yes, I lost my mind with worry when we found out Kat's apartment had suffered the same fate as mine, but after the initial shock wore off, I got to thinking about the situation, and I'm not sure The Club poses a genuine threat to me, at least not a physical one. If these guys were violent criminals, then why'd they even bother breaking into my apartment? It would have made a lot more sense to lie in wait for me and take care of things more definitively. My hunch is they were merely gathering information by taking my computer and then decided to trash the place as an afterthought. They're just cyber-pimps, after all. Who's ever heard of a violent cyber-pimp?

I've definitely got to tell Jonas what I think about all this. But this morning just didn't seem like the time to do it—especially after the way he reacted to Josh last night. I figure I'll tackle that issue with him tomorrow—ever so gently—and, in the meantime, I'll just tackle *him.* Whenever I get the chance, that is, because this morning certainly didn't work out as planned.

My big idea this morning was to lure Jonas into "oh no, maybe someone will see us!" sex at my apartment—a safe and seemingly easy way to invoke the spectator-hotness from last night's sizzling dream. I planned to attack Jonas at my place before the campus police arrived, leaving the front door open a crack for Campus Johnny Law to enter. I imagined Jonas and me going at it, hot and heavy in my ransacked bedroom, maybe even with my bedroom door slightly ajar, both of us on the verge of pure ecstasy, until we—gasp!—heard the men in blue stomping around my living room. I imagined the police calling out to me from the other side of my bedroom wall, perhaps concerned for my safety, given the disarray of my apartment.

"Miss Cruz?" they'd say. "It's the police!"

At which point Jonas and I would jolt apart, just in time to avoid being caught by the fuzz with our pants down (literally). The whole idea gets me going like crazy, just thinking about it.

Unfortunately, though, my "Oh no, maybe someone will see us!" fantasy just wasn't in the cards. When Jonas and I arrived at my apartment, the trusty campus police were already waiting inside—the superintendent had let them in, worried something had happened to me—and by the time the police left (after having written out a quick and meaningless report, as predicted), it was time to hightail it over to my contracts class.

I look at my watch. We've still got a few minutes before class starts.

Jonas places the laptop he bought for me on my desktop. He's had it with him in a small carrying case since we left his house, but I thought he'd brought it with him so he could return it.

"This is yours," Jonas says, his voice soft but commanding. "I got it for you because I want to take care of you in every conceivable way."

Before I can respond, he continues.

"If and when you get a replacement laptop through your insurance, you can give that one to your mom or donate it to a school or do whatever the fuck you want with it. But this one is yours, and only yours, Sarah, because *I* got it for you."

He looks exactly like he did when he tied those matching friendship bracelets around our wrists in Belize. I can't help but look down at the multi-colored bracelet around my wrist and then at its match on Jonas' wrist. And just like that, my heart melts like an ice cube on a hot skillet.

"Thank you," I say softly, leaning over to kiss him.

His relief is palpable as he greets my lips with his own.

When his tongue enters my mouth, my body bursts into flames. And when he brings his hands to my face and caresses my cheeks with his thumbs, my heart races and my breathing halts. I'm blazing hot right now, not surprisingly—I've been sexed up like a banshee all morning long, sense memories of last night's intimate festivities (especially my unexpected transformation into Orgasma the All-Powerful) floating through my head (and several other parts of my anatomy, too). Holy hot dam, I'm on fire, ready to go off at the slightest touch.

"Miss Cruz?" My professor's voice rings out into the large lecture hall.

I jerk away from Jonas and wipe my mouth with the back of my hand. Every eyeball in the entire class, including my professor's, is trained on me. I can feel my cheeks blazing crimson.

"Who's our guest?" my professor asks, not a trace of amusement on her face.

"I'm sorry, Professor Martin. This is Jonas," I say. "He's going to sit in on class today, if that's okay with you."

"Well, hello there, *Jonas*," my professor says, her voice softening as she takes in the glorious sight of him—she is a woman, after all. "You have a deep and abiding interest in contracts, I take it?"

I'm expecting Jonas to be mortified by Professor Martin's attention, but he surprises me by being smooth as silk.

"As a matter of fact, I do," he replies. "I'd be grateful if you'd allow me to sit in today."

"All right," my professor says, her entire demeanor warming and melting before my eyes. "We go by last names here," she says. "What shall we call you, sir?'

"Mr. Faraday," he responds, charisma oozing out his pores.

Instant recognition flashes in her eyes. "Jonas Faraday—of Faraday & Sons?"

Jonas nods. "That's right."

"What a nice surprise for us, Mr. Faraday. Welcome."

"Thank you."

"You could *teach* this class, I'm sure. You've negotiated a contract or two in your lifetime, yes?"

Jonas smiles and his eyes twinkle at her. "Maybe once or twice."

She addresses the entire lecture hall, her face suddenly beaming. "If Mr. Faraday is willing, this would be an excellent opportunity for you to learn about how contracts work in the real world." She directs her stare at Jonas again, smiling. "Would you be so kind as to answer a few questions for us today, Mr. Faraday?"

"I'll do my best, Professor."

Professor Martin laughs—something I've rarely seen the woman do.

"Wonderful," she says, bubbling over with enthusiasm. "Why don't you come on up here with me?" She pats a stool up front.

Oh boy, it's on like Donkey Kong. I can feel it. Jonas saunters to the front of the room, his butt a glorious sight in his jeans, his T-shirt clinging to his broad shoulders and muscled back, and I can feel half the class, men and women alike, swooning. When he takes his offered seat at the front of the class and smiles, his biceps bulging out of his short sleeves, the other half of the class falls under his spell, too.

For the next hour, Jonas elegantly and artfully, and with mesmerizing confidence, answers every question the professor and students ask. With the most adorable twinkle in his eye, and the most thoughtful tilt of his head, and an occasional, sensual lick of those luscious lips, he tells us about how contracts work in the world of complex business transactions—how they're formed, negotiated, and what really happens as a practical matter when they're breached (as opposed to what our textbooks say happens). He tells us what role his own lawyers play when advising him regarding multimillion-dollar deals, and, most humorously, why he so often chooses to ignore his lawyers' "impractical and deal-killing" advice and forge ahead, anyway.

"As an entrepreneur, I'm all about stepping on the proverbial gas pedal with a lead foot—getting the deal done. The lawyers, on the other hand, or, as I most often call them, the *effing* lawyers—except I don't say 'effing'" —everyone in the classroom laughs, even Professor Martin, and so do I—though I'm laughing because it's the first time I've heard Jonas use "effing" in place of his favorite word and it sounds comical coming out of his mouth—"tend to perceive their job as convincing me that a sane and prudent person would slam on the brakes. The thing is, in business, sanity and prudence are vastly overrated. The business world rewards risk-takers—the bigger the risk, the bigger the reward."

It's objectively the most interesting and thought-provoking contracts class we've ever had. And the sexiest. The man is gorgeous. Irresistible. Magnetic. Masculine. Brilliant. He's got the entire classroom in the palm of his magical hand. Every woman around me is swooning over this beautiful man—I'm pretty sure I can hear eggs spontaneously popping out of ovaries all around me. Even my professor can't keep her inner fangirl from coming out.

"Such an interesting perspective, Mr. Faraday," Professor Martin gushes when time runs out. "And so well articulated. Thank you so much for joining us. What a lucky surprise." She glances at me when she says the word "lucky" and I blush.

It occurs to me that if Jonas were to ask Professor Martin to come home with him tonight and spread her creamy thighs on his crisp white sheets, she'd say yes. Or, more accurately, "oh, hell yes—let's go right now."

"Come back and join us any time," my professor coos to Jonas in the last moments of class.

"Thank you for your hospitality, Professor," Jonas says, flashing his most outrageously charming smile.

As Jonas walks back up the aisle toward me, everyone applauds in appreciation—and quite a few of them also steal envious glances at me, too.

Why her?

What makes her so special?

I can't believe she gets to have sex with a man who looks like that.

It's as though I can hear their thoughts bouncing off the walls.

He's mine, I send back to them. *Mine, mine, mine, mine, mine.* It's all I can do not to re-enact last night's dream right here, right now, in front of all of them, right on top of Professor Martin's desktop.

"You were magnificent," I tell Jonas when he reaches me at my desk. "So knowledgeable. Confident yet self-deprecating." I smile broadly at him. "Ridiculously charming."

"Thanks. I hated every minute of it." He takes the seat next to me.

"No, you didn't. You *think* you did, but you didn't."

He rolls his eyes. "Is this the part where you tell me what I *think* I want isn't actually what I want?"

"You were in your element. You can't fake something like that. You were brilliant."

"I would rather have been sitting here next to you." His eyes are earnest.

Damn, those eyes of his. They get me every time.

"Let's go to the library," I whisper. "I've got something I need to do."

"Sure," Jonas replies. But then he catches something in my expression that makes him smile broadly at me. "Whatever you say, baby—I'm all yours."

Chapter 11
Sarah

"Tell me about your dream," Jonas says softly. "The one that made you come in your sleep."

We're standing in the massive law library, deep in the bowels of the book stacks. He's got me pinned against a metal bookshelf stacked floor-to-ceiling with thick legal tomes.

He kisses my neck. "Tell me all about it, pretty baby." His erection bulges inside his jeans. He glides his hand up my thigh, underneath my skirt, and onto my bare ass cheek. He lets out a soft moan as his hand gropes me and pulls me into him. "I love this ass."

I'm trembling with my desire for him.

He nips at my ear. "Tell me what turned you on so much that you came in your sleep."

"I'm such a big girl now, aren't I? Coming all by myself like that."

"You *are* a big girl. A beautiful, sexy, irresistible girl."

His hand moves to the cotton crotch of my G-string and caresses me lightly. I lift my leg up and around him, inviting him inside me. His fingers push the pesky fabric of my panties aside and brush lightly across my sensitive flesh.

I shudder.

He brushes his fingers lightly across me again, and when my pelvis thrusts involuntarily toward him in response, his fingers dip ever so gently into my wetness.

I moan softly.

"You like that?"

"Mmm hmm."

I like that a whole lot, thank you, and a few other things, too. For instance, I also like the way every woman in that classroom looked at Jonas like they wanted to fuck him. And I like that they can't have him because he's all mine. And I like how, right before we left the classroom, he cupped my face in his hands and kissed me softly in front of all those staring eyes and then grabbed my hand and brought my thumb ring to his warm lips.

Just behind me in the next aisle over, two students walk by. They're chatting softly as they go. I turn my head and peek at them through the cracks between books. They keep walking past, oblivious to the well-hung cowboy and his horny little pony groping each other just a few feet away on the other side of the bookshelf.

Jonas' fingers continue working their magic on me. A loud moan threatens to escape my throat, so I bite his neck.

"Ow," Jonas says in surprise. "Jesus. Why so violent?"

I stifle my giggle.

Movement flickers in the spaces between the books and someone coughs behind us. We both freeze, grinning at each other like kids removing the lid off a cookie jar.

Whoever it is, they keep moving down the aisle.

"Come on, My Magnificent Sarah." His fingers resume their exploration. "Tell me what turned you on so much."

I unbutton his jeans.

"It was the most erotic dream I've ever had," I whisper.

"I like that word."

"Erotic?"

He nods.

"Erotic... erotic... erotic." Each word is accompanied by a wet kiss on his neck. "*Un sueño erótico*."

He moans softly. Jonas loves it when I speak Spanish.

I lick his neck where I bit him a moment ago.

"Tell me."

I tell him about my dream and why it was so deliriously arousing to me—at least, I try to tell him. Talking is surprisingly hard to do when there are magic fingers massaging your wahoo and soft lips kissing your skin and warm breath in your ear.

When I'm done talking, it's quite obvious he's turned on by my dream, too.

"The red wine was dripping all over your skin?"

"Mmm hmm."

"Over your clit?" His voice has turned husky.

"Mmm."

"And I was licking it up?" He exhales a soft groan.

"You were everywhere all at once."

"Licking you?" Oh yeah, he's really turned on.

"Fucking me, kissing me, touching me, licking me, eating me. All at once."

He grips my ass and pulls me into him. "Sounds like heaven." His lips skim mine as his fingers move in and out of me.

I'm panting. "But it was still *you.* Every mouth and penis and finger was *yours*. That's why it turned me on." I don't want him to misunderstand and think I'm craving some sort of orgy, because I'm not. Even in my dreams, I only want him—one at a time, ten at a time, like a poltergeist, whatever, it doesn't matter, as long as it's him. I only want him. *Jonas Faraday.*

My hand moves into his jeans. He exhales when my fingers find his erection. It's enormous, ready for business. I yank down on the waistband of his briefs and peel back the front of his jeans, freeing his hard-on. He groans as his erection springs out of his pants.

"You're a human Jack in the Box."

He grins. "Only if you're the box."

I bite his shoulder, stifling my laughter.

He nips at my ear. "Back to your dream, baby." His fingers continue manipulating me with astonishing precision. "The people watching—that turned you on?"

"Mmm." I can't say anything more than that. His fingers have found the exact spot that makes me crazy. It's all I can do not to scream right here in the library. My body has begun jerking and grinding like crazy. I'm on fire. "Oh, God, Jonas," I murmur, my pleasure rising. "Yes."

A young woman enters our row, down at the end, headed toward us. We both briefly freeze. She stops dead in her tracks, a stricken look on her face, and quickly strides away in the opposite direction.

We both burst out laughing. I bury my mouth into his broad shoulder again, trying to silence myself.

"We've scarred her for life," Jonas whispers.

"Sucks to be her."

Jonas' fingers resume what they were doing. His fingers slide from my wetness to my tip and back again, over and over. I shudder.

"You like that?"

I nod enthusiastically. "Mmm."

"You like the idea of people watching us fuck?" he clarifies.

Oh, I thought he was asking me about his magic fingers. "Mmm hmm." My hand moves up and down his shaft. His tip is already wet—he's ready to blow. I'm so turned on, I can barely stand.

He lets out a soft moan. "Why?" He exhales. He kisses my lips and the pleasure zings me right between my legs—it's as if a live wire runs directly from my lips to my clit. His free hand grazes my back and unfastens my bra from underneath my T-shirt. He pulls my shirt up and licks my breast. His tongue swirls around my nipple. My clit flutters violently.

I moan. I can't take it anymore. "Now," I whisper.

He ignores me, as usual. He lowers my shirt and grabs my ass under my skirt again.

I grind myself into him. "Now," I say again.

"Why did you like people watching us?"

I raise my leg even higher around him and tilt myself toward him. "Come on, Jonas, right now."

"Patience, baby." He sucks on my lower lip and my entire body convulses. "You never learn, do you?"

I shake my head. It's true. I never learn.

"First tell me why you liked being watched. Tell me why and I'll fuck you."

I'm almost desperate now. I'm tempted to kneel and take him into my mouth—I want him inside me, any way I can get him—but I resist the urge. We are in a library, after all. "Because they all wanted you. Every single one of them wanted you." I stroke him vigorously.

He makes a primal sound and shudders. He yanks on my G-string under my skirt and pulls it down roughly, making me moan in anticipation.

His fingers are spellbinding. Oh my God, he's so talented. I can't stand it anymore. "No more prelude, Jonas," I whisper. "Do it now."

He spreads my legs slightly with his thigh, making me shudder, and shifts his body into position to enter into me. "Who cares if they want me?" He grabs my ass with both hands and lifts me up, pinning me against the bookshelf. "Tell me why it turned you on and I'll fuck you."

He wedges himself between my legs, his tip rubbing deliciously against my clit.

I throw my head back against the bookshelf, bracing myself for him. I want him inside me. I'm shaking. I'm panting.

"Why do you care if anyone else wants me? All that matters is you want me."

He's teasing me wickedly. I'm throbbing, licking my lips, aching. My pelvis is thrusting involuntarily in anticipation of him. "Fuck me right now. Oh my God, Jonas."

"Tell me first."

I groan. "They all wanted you, but they couldn't have you. I liked showing them you're mine. *You're all mine, Jonas*." I whimper. "*Mine.*"

He suddenly withdraws from me and straightens up.

"What the fuck?" he whispers. He stuffs himself quickly back into his jeans.

My cheeks instantly flush with shame.

Oh my God. I thought he'd *like* hearing me say he's all mine. I open my mouth, a confused apology on the tip of my tongue, but then I quickly see that, no, that's not it, he's not reacting to what I said—he's peering through the spaces between the books opposite him, his eyes narrowed to menacing slits. I peek behind me and stare in the direction of his sightline, but I don't see anything.

He whips his head and glares at me, suddenly full of intensity. He grabs my shoulders forcefully. "Stay right here. Don't move from this spot." Without another word, he races down the aisle, fastening his jeans as he goes. At the end of the bookshelf, he makes a sharp right turn and vanishes into the stacks of books.

My mouth hangs open—along with my legs, my bra, my panties, my shirt, and my ego. Not to mention my vajayjay. What just happened? I quickly put myself back together. I'm trembling. What the hell? I wait for him to come back for a good two minutes—okay, maybe for a minute and a half. Okay, fine, for a solid minute. Or so. Maybe less. I've got to figure out what's going on.

I walk slowly toward the end of the aisle, to the spot where Jonas turned the corner and disappeared, my heart pounding in my ears. When I get to the end of the bookshelf, I peek around it, afraid of what I might find. But there's only a couple of students chatting quietly in another aisle. No Jonas. I creep slowly in the same direction Jonas went, my chest tight and breathing shaky.

His eyes were wild when he told me to stay put. He didn't even look like himself for a minute there. He looked like a man possessed. Like a lunatic.

Still no Jonas.

I creep to the perimeter of the maze, goose bumps covering my entire body. Where is he? I keep walking until I reach a small window overlooking the parking lot. I peek out. I can make out his BMW in a distant corner of the lot. That's a good sign—at least I know he's still here somewhere.

A hand grabs my shoulder.

I gasp.

"I told you not to move, Sarah." He's angry. His eyes have that wild look in them again.

"I... What happened?"

"I need to get you out of here. I'm taking you home."

"What happened? What did you see?"

"If I tell you not to move, then don't fucking move, you understand? From now on, you listen to me. This isn't a game."

"What's going on?"

His eyes blaze with sudden intensity. "When we were in the lecture hall, when I was sitting up front, this palooka-looking guy came in the back door and stood there for a couple minutes. He looked like fucking John Travolta in *Pulp Fiction* or something, like he was wearing a two-bit-hoodlum costume for Halloween. Total cliché."

I shrug. I don't understand what that has to do with anything.

He exhales. "He didn't look like a law student."

I still don't understand. I'm sure there are plenty of two-bit-thuggy-looking people milling around any college campus anywhere in the United States at any given time—students, boyfriends of students, fathers of students, janitors, vending machine repairmen, stalkers, rapists, murderers, creepers. I mean, aren't there weirdos and freaks and criminals and people who *look* like weirdos and freaks and criminals at any given place at any given time—especially on college campuses—none of them affiliated in any way with The Club?

"Jonas . . ." I begin.

"I thought he was staring at you in the classroom, but I couldn't be sure—I thought maybe I was imagining things." His eyes are fierce.

I wait.

"But I just saw that same fucker again—right over there—" He motions into the stacks. "And this time I'm absolutely positive he was watching us—one hundred percent sure."

The hairs on the back of my neck stand up.

"When I spotted him, he took off running." He clenches his fists. "Fuck."

"Maybe he was just a student? Or a voyeur?"

He runs his hand through his hair. "Is there a student in your contracts class—or in the entire law school—who looks like a hitman from a Quentin Tarantino movie?"

I shake my head. "Not that I've seen. Bill Gates and Ashton Kutcher doppelgangers, yes. Dancing heroin addicts with ponytails, not so much." I'm trying to make him smile, but it's not working at all.

His jaw muscle pulses. His eyes are steel. "This isn't a joke, Sarah." He's pissed at me.

"I know."

His eyes flicker with something animalistic—he's kinda scary right now, actually.

I sigh.

I can't decide if my sweet Jonas is being overly protective of me (or, worse, maybe even a touch paranoid), or if the bad guys truly are gunning for me as vigorously as he thinks they are. That'd be pretty ballsy, wouldn't it, for the bad guys to waltz right into my classroom in broad daylight?

"You're sure it was the same guy in both places?"

He exhales with exasperation. "I'm absolutely fucking positive. Why the fuck are you doubting me on this?" His jaw is clenched.

"I . . ." I can't finish the sentence. He's right—I'm doubting him. Why? Are my lifelong trust issues rearing their ugly head again? I don't think so. Am I in deep denial about the situation, ignoring real danger as a means of emotional self-preservation? Highly doubtful. Or could it be that I secretly think my gorgeous hunk of a boyfriend is just a wee bit crazy (not that there's anything wrong with that)—that his judgment might be a teensy bit impaired in situations such this (understandably), due to the horrific trauma of his past? I bite my lip. Yup. I'm pretty sure it's Door Number Three. Damn.

I look into his eyes. Oh God, he's got beautiful eyes. And he's looking at me like I'm a rare treasure—the Mona Lisa—and he's just recovered me from the clutches of a master art thief. He pulls me into him and squeezes me tight.

"If I tell you to stay put, then stay put."

I return his embrace. "Okay."

Suddenly, a non sequitur of a thought slams me upside the head and punches me in the gut: *What was your Club-issued iPhone doing out on the kitchen table this morning, Jonas?* Why that seemingly random thought crashes into my brain at this particular moment, I have no idea, but, clearly, my subconscious brain sees some connection between that goddamned iPhone and my reticence to unconditionally adopt his belief in my imminent demise.

He buries his face in my hair and breathes in my scent.

"Don't ever scare me like that again, Sarah." He leans down and kisses me gently. "Come on. I'm getting you the fuck out of here."

Chapter 12

Jonas

I look at my watch. Quarter to seven. Stacy the Faker should be here in fifteen minutes.

"A Heineken," I tell the bartender. He nods his acknowledgment.

I look around the bar.

I hope Stacy doesn't call me out for not wearing that stupid purple bracelet. I know I'm technically required to wear it at all times during Club check-ins, but I threw it into the trash the minute Stacy left my house after our horrible fuck. And, anyway, even if I still had it, there's no way I'd put that thing on my wrist. Now that every part of me, including my wrist, belongs to Sarah, that piece-of-shit purple bracelet would probably sear my flesh like a hot iron brand.

I touch the multi-colored yarn bracelet on my wrist, one-half of the pair I got in Belize for Sarah and me. My mind drifts to the moment I tied Sarah's matching bracelet onto her wrist. The look on her face was so beautiful at that moment, so honest and vulnerable—so pure. I think that's when I knew I loved her for sure—when I tied that bracelet on her and told her she's my perfect match and she looked like she was going to cry.

No, wait, it was before then that I knew I loved her—what am I thinking? *Of course.* It was when she leaped off that waterfall into the dark abyss below. She was scared shitless, but she did it anyway, because she knew I was down there waiting for her in the dark water, waiting to catch her, and that I'd never let any harm come to her. She did it because she was finally ready to take a leap of faith with me—well, that and I'd left her no other way down. I smile at that last part. She wasn't even mad at me for luring her up there with no other option—she understood my intentions. She always understands. And so she rose to the occasion, like she always does—and just let go and trusted me and trusted herself and jumped into the void.

Yeah, definitely, that's the moment I knew—when she plunged into the cold, dark water and threw her arms around my neck, shivering and shaking with fear and adrenaline and elation, and wouldn't let go of me. She clutched me like her very life depended on me, like I was her life raft. And that's when I knew I couldn't live without her because I clutched her right back, just has tightly, just as desperately, if not more so. And every moment since then, I've been clutching her more and more fiercely, becoming more and more sure of my feelings for her—more and more certain she's my life raft, too. I've never been so sure of anything in my entire life, in fact.

The bartender puts my beer in front of me.

I throw down a ten and take a big gulp.

Thank God I didn't throw my Club iPhone away along with that stupid purple bracelet. I was this close to tossing it, actually, but then it hit me I might be able to wipe the damned thing completely clean and give it to Trey—it's a perfectly good iPhone, after all. So I threw it into a drawer in my kitchen, intending to deal with it later, and promptly forgot all about it—until this morning, that is, when I was brainstorming for my "How I'm Going to Fuck The Club Up the Ass" spreadsheet.

As it turned out, it was a huge stroke of luck I'd kept that phone, or else right now I'd have no fucking idea how to begin connecting the dots within The Club to a power player. Josh's hacker already called right before I left for the bar, saying the emails Josh and I forwarded to him are all dead ends, every single one of them, completely untraceable. Josh wasn't surprised at all and took it in stride, but I was deflated. It meant I had to go through with meeting Stacy here tonight. What other option do I have? She's my only lead. I've got to do whatever I can to track these fuckers down and keep Sarah safe.

I take another swig of my beer and look around.

There are some really good-looking people here tonight. But, then again, there are always good-looking people at The Pine Box. That's why this used to be one of my favorite hunting grounds—well, that, and it's within walking distance of my place. That sure used to make things easy. No worrying about whose car we'd take back to my place—we only ever had hers, which also conveniently meant she could easily leave my place in the morning without a messy hassle. Shit, those days of fucking a different woman virtually every night seem like a lifetime ago. I don't even feel like the same guy. Sarah's changed everything in such a short amount of time, just like I knew she would. Just like I hoped she would.

Another long swig of my beer. Fuck it. I chug the rest. I flag down the bartender and hold up my empty bottle. He nods. My knee jiggles wildly. I force it to stop.

A brunette with a pixie cut and large hoop earrings smiles at me from the corner. I look away. The old me would have gone over to her. She's hot. Pretty face. And her whole look screams confidence, a trait that always attracts me. But I don't give a shit. All I can think about is Sarah. She's all I want. I can't wait to get out of here and go back home to her.

Sarah didn't bat an eyelash when I told her I had to slip away for a bit, that I had something I had to do.

"No problem, baby," she said. "I've got a ton of studying to do."

She's so diligent about her studies, so determined to get that scholarship at the end of the year. I love that about her. She sees what she wants and goes after it, relentlessly.

"I won't be gone long," I assured her. "I'll come back as soon as I can."

"Take your time. God knows you can't sit here babysitting me for the rest of your life. I'll be here," she said. "I've got so much to do."

I've never met a woman with such a slender jealous streak. She just trusts me. My stomach suddenly churns at the thought—yeah, Sarah trusts me, and I'm *here*, waiting for Stacy.

"I won't be gone long," I said again. "And Josh will be here the whole time to look after you."

"Okeedoke." She already had her nose buried in a book.

"Promise me you'll stay here and not go anywhere."

She rolled her eyes and looked up from her book. "Jonas, don't act like a weirdo. I've got to study, I told you. I'm so effing behind it's ridiculous. Trust me, I'm not going anywhere."

"But promise me, Sarah. Say, 'I promise, Jonas.'"

"Jeez," she said, scrunching up her nose. "That's not creepy or anything." At my insistent expression, she rolled her eyes again. "Okay, Lord-God-Master, I promise." She flashed me a smart-ass smirk. "You always say I'm bossy, but I think that's the pot calling the kettle bossy."

When my expression remained anxious, she laughed.

"I'll be right here, Jonas. Just go do whatever you've got to do, Mr. Mogul. Thanks to you and your red hot lovin' day and night, I'm woefully behind in my reading for criminal law and torts. I'm gonna study all night long without a single break."

"Well, hang on a second," I replied, forcing her book closed and pulling her into me. "I don't want you studying *all* night long. You're gonna have to take a break at some point for more of my red hot lovin'."

"Well, hmm," she said. "If you *insist.*" She laughed and kissed me. "Duh, Jonas. Making love to you every single night is a given. It's a physical necessity—right up there with breathing and eating and peeing."

I smile to myself. *My Magnificent Sarah.*

I check my watch. Seven o'clock on the button. Any minute now. The hairs on my arms stand at attention at the thought of seeing Stacy again. My knee jiggles again. I can't make it stop. My stomach flip-flops. I banged Stacy so sloppily—and she acted like she was in the throes of pure ecstasy the whole time. The whole thing was just revolting. And then to think she cornered Sarah in the bathroom at that sports bar and threatened her? Okay, I have to stop thinking about all the ways Stacy disgusts me—I've got to put myself in the right frame of mind to charm her.

And there she is. Right on cue, strutting into the bar in a little black dress and sky-high heels. I raise my arm and flag her down. She nods and smiles broadly at me, and even from this distance, I can plainly see the purple bracelet on her wrist. The sight of it makes me recoil, but I force myself to smile.

"Well, hello again," she says, approaching the bar. "*Jonas*."

"Hi, Stacy." I put my hand out to shake just as she leans in for a hug. It's momentarily awkward. I play it off like I'm just a shy dork and quickly lean in to give her a brief hug. Yeah, I guess it's kind of weird to shake hands with someone you've already fucked, huh? I need to get my head in the game and act like I'm happy to see her.

"Chardonnay?"

"You remember. Yes, I'd love it. Thanks."

I order her drink.

Sarah.

This is totally fucked up what I'm doing right now. It feels wrong. I just have to remember why I'm doing it. I'll have a quick drink with Stacy, that's all—with this woman who happens to be a prostitute—a prostitute I've fucked—and get the information I need. And then I'll race home and lick my baby's sweet pussy with extra zeal and make her come, maybe even over and over, if I'm lucky.

"Let's sit at a table," I suggest.

"How about that one over there?"

Stacy points to a booth in the corner—the one where Sarah and Kat spied on me when I first met Stacy. I can see the ghost of Menu Girl sitting there right now, her forearms and hands taunting me with their olive-toned smoothness, her long dark hair cascading around her shoulders from behind her menu. I hadn't even laid eyes on Sarah yet, hadn't even seen a photo of her, but my soul already knew she owned me, even then.

Stacy's eyes are bullets.

Is she trying to communicate something to me by suggesting that particular booth? Is this some kind of a test?

"No, not that one," I say. My eyes are steely. I know they are. I've got to grab ahold of myself and try to channel Charming Jonas right now. Supreme Dick Extraordinaire Jonas isn't going to get the job done. "Over here." I lead her to another booth at the opposite end of the bar and we sit.

Stacy takes a sip of her wine and eyeballs me. "So nice to hear from you again, Jonas. I'm glad you requested me. I was hoping you would."

I nod. "The pleasure's all mine. Thank you for agreeing to see me again."

"Of course. I had a great time with you that first time. I was hoping you'd want an encore."

There's a beat.

I sigh. "Let's talk turkey, shall we?"

She raises her eyebrows.

"I had a little fling with my intake agent—the woman who reviewed my application."

"Oh," Stacy says, seemingly having a genuine epiphany. "*That's* who she was?"

Stacy must be extremely low on the totem pole if she didn't know Sarah's identity until now.

I lean in like I'm telling her a secret. "I'm a bit of an adrenaline junkie. I couldn't help myself—forbidden fruit and all that."

She smiles. Charming Jonas has definitely come out tonight.

"Which one was it? The blonde or the brunette?"

"The brunette. It's always brunettes for me."

Stacy's eyes sparkle. Brunettes always love to hear a man say he prefers brunettes to blondes.

"And brunettes with blue eyes are my absolute favorite."

I'm laying it on a bit thick, I know, but shit, I don't have all day. I want to get the fuck out of here so I can go home to my beautiful brown-eyed girl.

"Who was the blonde, then? Another intake agent?"

"No, just the intake agent's friend. The blonde doesn't know anything about The Club—to this day, she thinks she was spying on some guy her friend met on Match.com." Hopefully, that little tidbit of information will find its way up the totem pole and clear Kat from their crosshairs.

Stacy laughs. "Oh, that's hilarious. I thought . . ." She stops, unsure of how much I know. Obviously, she doesn't want to unwittingly step into a steaming pile of shit.

"You thought they were new girls, poaching on your territory?"

Stacy raises her eyebrows and twists her mouth in acknowledgment.

"Yeah, so I heard. That's why I wanted to see you, actually."

Stacy's eyes narrow. "Oh yeah? Why's that?"

"Well, I'm not gonna lie—I had a really nice time with my intake agent. She was a lot of fun. But it's over now. She got all clingy—you know how that is. I can't stand clingy."

"Oh God, neither can I."

"Well, see, that's what I figured—because you're a pro, Stacy. And I like that."

Her eyes ripple with surprise.

I take a long sip of my beer, eying her. "My intake agent told me all about her encounter with you at that sports bar, when you were wearing the yellow bracelet with that other guy." Stacy reflexively looks down at the purple bracelet on her wrist, like she's trying to remember which color she's wearing tonight. "And I gotta tell you—it really turned me on."

Stacy's face reflects earnest surprise. "It did? What about that turned you on?"

"Are you kidding me? You're not emotionally invested. You staked out your territory—told her not to fuck with you. You're here to do a job and do it well. I respect that. Like I said, you're a total pro. A badass."

She blushes at the compliment. She's buying what I'm selling. "Thank you." She tilts her head and smiles. "So you like a badass kind of girl, huh?" She reaches across the table and strokes the top of my hand.

I instinctively jerk my hand away. The woman makes my flesh crawl. I play it off like I'm reaching for my beer.

"Frankly," I continue, swigging my beer again, "I was relieved to find out the real deal about The Club. Elated, even. The whole reason I joined in the first place was to avoid emotional attachments, you know? Women always get so... *emotional.* It really ruins the fun for me. That's what happened with the intake agent, too. She was a sweetheart, a great girl, but then she got emotionally attached, just couldn't distinguish sex from some sort of fairytale fantasy."

"Sounds like you need a pro." She winks.

"Exactly. Someone I can just be totally *honest* with, you know?"

Stacy raises one eyebrow suggestively. "What would you like to be honest about, Jonas?"

I finish off my beer and flash her my most dazzling smile. "About what each of us wants—what we *really* want."

She leans forward, ready to hear it.

"You're in it for the money." I smile. "And that's good. And I'm in it for the sex. Period. I just want to fuck a beautiful woman, whenever I feel like it, no strings attached. None of the bullshit."

One side of her mouth hitches up. "Well, that sounds good to me." She stands. "Let's get the hell out of here, shall we?"

Oh shit. "Hang on a minute. My idea is a bit bigger than that—bigger than just tonight. Sit down and let me tell you what I have in mind."

She sits back down. "I'm all ears." She licks her lips.

My stomach somersaults. I'm having a flashback of my tongue on her cunt.

"First off, let me just tell you how incredible you are in bed." I'm using the word incredible in its literal sense—*not credible.*

She bats her eyelashes. "It was my pleasure. You were amazing."

"Aw, that's sweet," I say, making myself smile. That's the phrase Sarah uses when she's actually calling me a dumbass. *Aw, that's sweet, Jonas,* she always says, her eyes laughing at me. "But you were the incredible one, Stacy." I feel like I'm going to hurl. "The way you came so fast and so hard? That was just... *incredible.*"

"It was all you."

"I really like it when women come—have you read my application?"

She shrugs. "It's been a little while—remind me." She flashes her most seductive smile.

Yeah, I'm sure she's read more than a few applications since mine. "I really get off on making women come—especially since it's so hard to do. I like the challenge of it. Sometimes it takes me a whole month to figure out how to do it with a particular woman." I chuckle. "Women are complicated."

She laughs and nods. "We sure are."

"But I usually manage it somehow, after lots of practice. Not always, of course, but, usually. But with you, it was right away—boom—and so intense, too. That was just totally *incredible,* Stacy. I haven't stopped thinking about it since."

Stacy smiles. "Yeah. It was awesome."

"So I've been seeing my intake agent lately, like I said, and she's just not like you, Stacy, not at all. One hundred eighty degrees different. She doesn't get off the way you did—not at all—and, lately, I just can't stop thinking about how much I want to be with a woman who embraces her own desires, who knows what she wants—a woman who can let go and surrender to her pleasure without holding back." In other words, I want my Sarah.

Stacy beams at me. "Sounds good to me," she says. "Why don't we start right now?" Clearly, she's politely trying to move this party along. Maybe she's hoping to squeeze in another check-in later tonight if I'd just hurry the fuck up.

"Hang on. I have a proposition for you."

She tilts her head to the side, ready for whatever I'm going to say.

"I'd like to purchase a block of your time."

"Oh." She smiles. "What do you have in mind?"

"Two weeks."

Her smile widens. "You want a GFE."

"What's that?"

"A Girlfriend Experience."

I can't keep my lip from curling. The only GFE I want is with Sarah.

"Right," I force myself to say. "GFE. I'll pay extra, of course—over and above what I've already paid to The Club for my membership. I think that's fair because I want you exclusively. I don't want to wear my purple bracelet, worry about check-ins, etcetera. I just want to take you out of the Club rotation for a couple weeks and have you all to myself. I'd be willing to pay The Club a premium for the privilege—let's say the equivalent of a month's membership?"

"How much is a month's membership?"

"You don't know?"

"No. I get paid per job."

"How much do you get paid per job?"

She pauses. "Five hundred."

She's full of shit. She just doubled her real take. Clever girl. But whatever. Even using Stacy's bullshit number, I quickly do the math in my head. Even if a member checks in every day for thirty days, even after The Club pays their intake agents and whatever other overhead, whoever's running this shit show must clear close to fifteen thousand per month, per member—and they must have thousands, if not tens of thousands, of members. Oh my God, they're making money hand over fist.

"Monthly membership costs thirty thousand."

Stacy's eyes sparkle, though she tries to act like that number doesn't impress her.

"Maybe I could negotiate a deal with your boss to get you a bigger piece of the pie than usual? I could sit down with him and—"

"With *her*."

My heart leaps out of my chest. Finally, a little bit of information.

"Oh, yeah? You're boss is a woman?"

"Yeah."

"Is she a badass like you?"

"That's an understatement."

I smile. "What's her name?"

"Oksana."

"Oksana," I repeat. My skin is buzzing. "Russian?"

"Ukrainian. We call her the Crazy Ukrainian."

I laugh. "Okay, so I'll talk to the Crazy Ukrainian as soon as possible and offer to pay her thirty thousand in fees to reserve your time exclusively for the next couple weeks—and since that will be separate from my club membership, I'll tell them my payment is conditioned on them splitting the pot with you fifty-fifty. How does that sound?"

Stacy looks closer to climaxing now than she did when we fucked. "Oh," she says, her cheeks flushing. "Why do you even need to deal with Oksana? Why not just pay the whole amount to me directly under the table? She doesn't need to know. Just give me the money, and I give you my word—all my time for two weeks, every minute of every day and night if you want. I'll fuck you so good, you won't want our two weeks to end."

Déjà vu. Didn't Julia Roberts say something eerily similar to that at the beginning of *Pretty Woman*? "No, that won't work. If you're suddenly not showing up for other check-ins, won't they figure something's up?"

She nods, reluctantly. "Yeah, probably. But you could just check-in and request me every day, and then pay me the cash directly. It's a win-win-win all around."

Shit. "Hmm. The whole point is I don't want to do the check-in thing. And, anyway, you're sure to get a bunch of other requests during that two weeks—I have to believe you're their top requested girl."

She smirks. "I am."

"I don't want to risk even the chance of sharing you while I'm with you. If we're sneaky about it and they find out somehow, things could really backfire. You might lose your job and The Club might ban me for the rest of my membership period. I absolutely can't risk that. I need this club, Stacy." I flash her my crazy eyes.

She twists her mouth, obviously trying to figure out a way to maximize her take. "I'll take a 'vacation' for a couple weeks—to visit a sick relative or something."

"How about I make sure you wind up with thirty thousand for the two weeks, no matter what?

She nods profusely.

"But I'd still like to do it above-board. I'll pay The Club whatever I have to pay, over and above your fee, to make it work. Does that sound good?"

Her eyes light up. "Perfect."

Jesus. I should hire Stacy to negotiate one of my business deals. She's a fucking shark. "So do you think Oksana will go for it? Is she the decision-maker, or is she gonna have to clear this with someone else?"

"Why wouldn't she go for it? It's all about the Benjamins with her—and, yeah, what Oksana says goes. I told you—she's a badass."

"Great. So how do I contact her?"

"Give me your phone number. I'll tell her to call you." She pulls out her phone.

"No, I'd prefer to contact Oksana. I like being in control in matters such as this—well, in all matters, actually." Just for my own amusement, I flash her my crazy eyes again.

"I'm not allowed to give out her number."

"Is she here in Seattle?"

"No, Las Vegas."

My skin sizzles. *Oksana the Ukrainian in Las Vegas.*

"What's her last name?"

Stacy looks at me sideways. "Why?"

I hold up my phone. "Just wanted to put her in my phone. Is that not allowed?" I play dumb.

There's a beat.

"You don't need her last name."

I pushed it too far. "I'm sorry, I didn't know. This is all new to me. I've never had a GFE before. You know what? I have some business in Vegas, anyway. I'll kill two birds with one stone and pay her in person in cash so she can pay you right away. Do you have her physical address?"

I've said the magic word. *Cash.* Her eyes light up. "All I've got is a P.O. box in Vegas. I'll give you her email address. You can contact her and figure out how to connect."

"Great."

She grabs a pen out of her purse. "I need a piece of paper." She rummages in her bag.

"You've met Oksana in person, I presume?"

"Oh yeah, I started this job in Vegas. I was on the first team of girls, before they branched out to other cities."

Another kernel of information. Las Vegas is their mother ship.

"I was their top girl in Vegas—most requested." She smiles with pride. "When they expanded operations, they gave me my pick of cities," she says.

"And you picked Seattle?"

"I was tired of the dry heat."

"Well, you certainly solved that problem by coming here, huh?"

She smiles. "And I've got family here in Seattle, so . . ."

We sit and stare at each other for a moment in awkward silence. She suddenly looks years younger to me than she did just a moment ago.

"Oksana?" I say, gently prodding her to stay on task and give me that email address.

"Oh, yeah," she says. "Sure thing."

"I'll just input her email address onto my phone." My stomach hurts. I feel like I'm betraying Sarah. And, frankly, I'm taking no pleasure in scamming Stacy the Faker. I just want to be done with this and go home to Sarah.

"Okay." She opens her list of contacts on her phone and scrolls down.

I type the name "Oksana" into my contacts and look up, ready for her to tell me the email address. "Okay, what's the address?"

"Jonas?"

Oh God, no.

Panic floods me like a tidal wave.

This is my worst nightmare.

And my own damned fault.

It's Sarah.

Chapter 13
Sarah

I look at my watch. Five minutes to seven.

I shouldn't be doing this right now—I know I shouldn't. But I can't help myself.

The tip of my nose is cold and turning red in the chilly night air. I hug my sweatshirt to me and keep walking briskly toward The Pine Box. My heart bangs in my chest. I shouldn't be doing this. But I pick up my pace, anyway.

After Jonas left the house, I called Kat to make sure no dancing hitmen had paid her a visit today.

"I'm great," she said. "I'm about to grab dinner with my *bodyguard*." And then she belted out Whitney Houston's famous chorus from *The Bodyguard.*

"What are you talking about?" I asked, laughing.

"Jonas didn't tell you? He hired a professional bodyguard to watch over me. Please tell him thank you, by the way—my hunky bodyguard is way cuter than Kevin Costner."

I was stunned at Jonas' thoughtfulness, yet again, but also anxious to think he deemed a bodyguard a necessary precaution.

"Do you and Jonas want to meet us for dinner?" Kat asked.

"Not tonight. I've got to study and Jonas is out."

"What's he up to?" she asked. "Working?"

"I don't know. He just said he had something he had to do."

Kat responded with a kind of wincing noise that spoke volumes about her mistrust of Jonas.

"What?" I asked.

"Nothing."

"Jonas and I have been joined at the hip since he picked me up for Belize"—quite often *literally* joined at the hip, I thought, smirking—"and now he's all stressed out about protecting me from the bad guys. Poor guy, I'm sure he just needed a little space."

Kat didn't reply.

I grunted with exasperation. "Just say whatever it is you're thinking."

She sighed. "The guy joined a sex club not too long ago, remember. If he were my boyfriend, I'd want to know what he was doing, that's all."

"You don't know him like I do," I assured her. "He's not the dog you think he is."

"I don't think he's a dog. But he's not a perfect angel, either. I'm just saying, if Jonas Faraday were my boyfriend, I'd want to know where he was."

Two minutes later, I was clutching that goddamned Club iPhone in my hand like a frickin' grenade, having found it in only the third drawer I'd opened in the kitchen. Just holding it in my hand made me sick. Until it appeared on the kitchen table this morning, I'd assumed Jonas had gotten rid of the hideous thing after his disastrous night with Stacy the Faker, or, at the very latest, after he'd offered me exclusive membership in the Jonas Faraday Club. Why the hell did he keep it? And if he'd kept the iPhone, I couldn't help reasoning, did that mean he'd kept the purple bracelet, too? I searched for the bracelet in the same drawer where I'd found the iPhone, but it wasn't there, which meant he'd thrown the dastardly thing away, thank goodness—or, I suddenly thought, my heart leaping into my throat, that he was wearing it at that very moment. The latter possibility made my flesh crawl. And my heart ache. And the marrow in my *Fatal-Attraction* bone start simmering. The mere thought of Jonas wearing that frickin' purple bracelet on his wrist, right alongside the Belizian friendship bracelet that matches mine, made me want to boil a little white bunny in a pot.

Opening the iPhone to confirm or debunk my fears wasn't possible—the damned thing was fingerprint- and passcode-protected—and so, in a fit of anger, I threw it with a loud clank into the big trashcan in the garage. And that's when I saw Jonas' car parked in the garage, the engine cold—which made me flip out even further. Either someone had picked Jonas up to take him wherever he'd gone—not a comforting thought—or, in the alternative, he'd *walked* there—also not a comforting thought, in light of a conversation Jonas and I had had in Belize.

We'd been lying in bed in our tree house after making love for the umpteenth time that day, laughing, sharing secrets, divulging our most awkward and cringe-worthy moments. No topic was off limits. We'd told each other about our respective de-virginizations. We'd talked about our past relationships. I'd told him about my two one-night stands, and how ill prepared I'd been for the inevitable brush-offs afterwards, and he'd said he wanted to beat those assholes up for me. And then Jonas had told me a few selected anecdotes from his illustrious career as a shameless man-whore.

"But how did you *find* all those willing women?" I asked, incredulous. "Did you just snap your fingers or what?"

"Well, yeah, most often, they approached me. Other times, I just walked to The Pine Box," he said, "and it was like shooting ducks in a barrel. The bar being walking distance from my house made saying goodbye afterwards super easy—no second car to juggle."

"Wow, you were such a pig," I said.

"I prefer asshole-motherfucker," he said.

"You'll hear no argument from me."

I laughed and kissed him and we made love yet again, the howler monkeys in the trees serenading us all the while.

I keep walking toward The Pine Box, picking up my pace yet again. I'm shivering in the cool night air. I wish I'd grabbed my North Face jacket from my apartment when Jonas and I were there this morning. Damn.

He's not going to be in the bar, I tell myself. *You're wasting your time acting like a clingy, insecure lunatic when you should be studying.*

I know.

He probably just went to the rock climbing gym to blow off some steam.

Then why wasn't he wearing workout clothes when he left the house?

Maybe he had a gym bag in his car.

His car is sitting in his garage.

He probably just needed a drink.

There's a six-pack of beer in his fridge.

Stop being paranoid. You love him, Sarah. And he loves you. Madness, remember?

Of course, I remember. It's all I think about, day and night. Yes, I love him—so much it hurts. And he loves me—I'm sure of it.

Then why the hell are you walking to The Pine Box right now?

Why the hell did he keep that *fucking* iPhone?

I don't know.

And if he kept the iPhone, then isn't it logical to think he kept the purple bracelet, too?

Logical, yes. Probable, no.

Regardless, why did he keep the iPhone in the first place?

Pick up the pace.

It's official. I'm schizophrenic.

Fifty feet away from the bar, I stop dead in my tracks. Stacy the Faker stands in front of the bar in a short black dress, feeding quarters into a parking meter. It's definitely her. I'd know her anywhere.

I can't breathe.

When Stacy finishes with the meter, she turns around and marches into The Pine Box, her impossibly long legs leading the way on her impossibly high stiletto heels.

I sprint to the back window of the bar and peek inside, clutching my chest. I scan the crowded bar through the window.

Maybe he's not in there. Maybe this is just a crazy coincidence. Maybe Stacy's here to meet some other guy from The Club. Maybe—

In an instant, all the "maybes" bouncing around in my head vanish. There he is, standing at the bar, drinking a beer. *Jonas.* My sweet Jonas. Or so I thought.

Stacy approaches him. Jonas hugs her, albeit awkwardly.

My stomach lurches.

I can't breathe.

My head spins.

This makes no sense. Jonas loves me. I can't wrap my brain around what I'm seeing. Tears well up in my eyes. A lump rises in my throat.

Jonas motions to the bartender. The bartender nods.

I can't understand what I'm seeing. This makes no sense. Jonas said he fucked Stacy and the whole time imagined she was me—and this was even before he knew what I looked like. That's what he told me, anyway. He said she faked it with him—that she repulsed him—that he literally gagged—that the whole experience disgusted him. And now he wants to fuck her again? Even though she *faked* it with him?

My eyes widen with my horrifying epiphany.

Stacy faked it with him.

Oh my God.

What did Jonas write in his application about that woman who faked it with him before—the one who unwittingly inspired his lingual quest for alleged truth and honesty in the first place? "I wanted to teach her a lesson about truth and honesty," he wrote, "but even more than that, I wanted *redemption.*"

Oh my God. I think I'm going to barf.

I can barely see Jonas and Stacy through my tears. I wipe my eyes.

They turn away from the bar, looking for an open table. Stacy motions in the direction of "my" table—the one where Kat and I spied on Jonas and Stacy the first time—oh Lord have mercy, I can't believe there's now a *first* time—but after brief discussion they move in the opposite direction to another table.

I scoot around the corner of the bar to gain a better vantage point of them through another window.

Stacy faked it with him, and now he can't resist her. He's an addict and she's his smack, loaded into a syringe and positioned right into his vein. He can't resist shooting her up, regardless of whether he loves me or not. Would loving me change a goddamned thing if he were a heroin addict? No, it wouldn't. An addict needs his fix—loved ones be damned. And this is Jonas Faraday's fix. I knew it from day one, but I wanted to believe I could change him. I thought I was his rehab, his savior, but I was deluding myself. He held off as long as he could. He tried.

Tears squirt out of my eyes.

I grab at my hair and pull on it. I'm out of my head right now. My heart physically aches inside my chest cavity. I've never felt so lost, so alone, so betrayed in all my life. So heartbroken.

When Jonas fucked Stacy the Faker and wished she were me, sight unseen, before he'd ever laid a magical finger on me, well, that was hot, hot, hot—but Jonas fucking Stacy after all that's happened between us, after all we've said and done and *felt,* after everything we've told each other, after that kiss outside the cave in Belize, after all the times we've made love, after all the times I've "surrendered" to him, and jumped off a frickin' waterfall for him, and the bracelets he put on our wrists—oh my God, holy fuckballs, the bracelets!—well, after all that, Jonas fucking Stacy the Faker is a different kind of *hot*—the kind of hot you get when you burn down your boyfriend's fucking house.

My chest heaves.

My mind feels like it's detaching from my body, and not in the way Jonas always refers to—I feel my sanity slipping away. I imagine myself walking in there and slapping Jonas across his gorgeous fucking face and telling him to go to fucking hell. But the thought makes my heart seize and twist and burn. I thought he loved me the way I love him. I thought we'd discovered a mutual madness.

I've got a serious mental disease, he told me.

No shit, you do, Jonas Fucking Faraday. Even after everything we've been through together, you kept that damned iPhone so you could fuck a prostitute who—

I stand completely upright, suddenly having a lightning bolt of a thought. I cock my head like a cockatiel. Hang on a second. This doesn't make any sense.

Hang on a cotton pickin' second.

This doesn't add up.

Jonas would never fuck a prostitute.

I squint through the window and peer at him. He's talking, smiling, looking as gorgeous as ever. He swigs his beer.

He's not wearing his purple bracelet.

I'm frozen on the sidewalk in the cold night air.

Jonas would never fuck a prostitute.

I saw the way Jonas reacted on the airplane when I told him about my encounter with Stacy in the sports bar—how it tortured him to realize he'd unknowingly brought a hooker into his bed. He became physically ill. Mortified. Humiliated. Angry. He wasn't faking that reaction—it was real. And in Belize, on that first magical, sexless night, he sobbed into my arms as he told me about his father's self-destructive obsession with prostitutes during the year before his suicide. Jonas called his father's behavior "disgusting."

I'm shaking, adrenaline coursing through me.

Jonas would never knowingly sleep with a prostitute. Sex is the ultimate expression of honesty to him. Ergo, paying a woman to *pretend* to "surrender" to him would be antithetical to everything he stands for. It would *repel* him, not turn him on.

Inside the bar, two big guys stand up from their table, blocking my view of Jonas and Stacy. I move to the next window, just in time to see Stacy bat her eyelashes at something Jonas has said to her. Obviously, he just paid her a compliment.

What the fuck is going on here? He's up to something, yes. But cheating on me with Stacy the Prostitute? No. What the hell is he doing?

Think, Sarah, think. Think like Jonas.

Stacy reaches across the table and puts her hand on Jonas'. He jerks his hand away like her hand burned his skin. He tries to make it seem like he's grabbing his beer, but oh my God, it's plain as day he can't stand to be touched by her.

I smile. Oh, Jonas. Sweet Jonas. Stupid-Lying-Idiotic Jonas. You're-In-Such-Big-Trouble Jonas. But, yes, undoubtedly, Faithful Jonas.

What could he possibly be saying to her?

Think, Sarah, think.

He had the iPhone out this morning during his conversation with Josh. When I asked about it, he said he wanted to handle The Club on his own, with Josh, and leave me out of it.

I roll my eyes. Oh good God. He's here to get information out of Stacy—and he's charming her to do it. He's complimenting her, telling her what she wants to hear—all so he can gather information for his highfalutin *strategy*, whatever the hell it is. I wipe my eyes. He's just trying to protect me, the big dummy.

Relief ripples through every muscle of my body.

I'm still pissed, though. He may not be a cheater, but he's still an idiot. A big, fat idiot. And a liar through omission. He should have included me in his plans from minute one. What does he think—I'm too fragile and innocent, or maybe not smart enough, to handle his stupid strategy? That I'm going to come undone? I've been doing research and investigations professionally for the last three months, buddy! I figure shit out, man! Who tracked you down tonight like a hungry crack whore looking for her baby daddy on payday? Me! And, anyway, I'm the one who was employed by The Club, for the love of all things holy—doesn't he think I might have an idea or two to contribute to his stupid *strategy,* whatever it is*?* God, I hate Strategic Jonas! Strategic Jonas makes me want to punch him in his beautiful face.

I take a deep breath and watch them, my nostrils flaring.

Whatever he's saying, she's buying it hook-line-and-sinker. She's nodding vigorously. She stands, smiling at him like she expects him to get up with her.

But he doesn't move.

She sits back down, perplexed.

Oh, Jonas.

I smile.

I'm one hundred percent sure he's not here to fuck Stacy. If he were, they'd already be fucking up a storm somewhere. My sweet Jonas is a lot of things, including a dumbass, apparently, and a liar, and an idiot, but a man who sits around drinking a beer and chatting with a prostitute when all he wants to do is fuck, he is not. I can't help but laugh out loud. For a smart man, my sweet Jonas is such a big dummy sometimes, I swear to God.

Chapter 14
Jonas

"Jonas?"

Oh God, no.

Panic floods me like a tidal wave.

This is my worst nightmare.

And my own damned fault.

It's Sarah.

Her eyes are red and wet. Tear tracks stain her cheeks.

"Sarah." That's all I can eek out. This can't be happening right now. This is my worst nightmare. My heart explodes in my chest.

Stacy lifts her wineglass to her lips, a smug smile spreading across her face.

"Sarah," I say again. "Please—"

"There's nothing to say. I know exactly why you're here."

"No, you don't. Please listen." I glance at Stacy. She's grinning like a Cheshire cat.

"You had 'something you needed to do,' huh?"

My stomach leaps into my mouth. My tongue isn't working.

"*Sarah*, is it?" Stacy interjects. "Jonas was just telling me about your problem with emotional attachment—"

"Shut the fuck up, Stacy," Sarah hisses. Her eyes are laser beams.

Stacy smirks, apparently unfazed.

"Stacy, will you excuse us for just a minute, please?" I say, my voice sounding much calmer than I feel.

"No, Stacy, stay here, please," Sarah says. "I want you to hear this."

I stand and grab Sarah's arm. "Sarah, listen to me."

She jerks away from me. "Sit down. I have something to say to you both."

My mouth hangs open. I'm going to have a fucking heart attack.

I can't lose her. Not like this. Please, God, no. I'm officially in hell. "No, listen, I'm—" I reach for her again.

Sarah jerks away again. "If you don't take your hands off me right now and sit the fuck down, I'm walking out that door, Jonas."

Shit. Oh God. This is a catastrophe. I'm light-headed. I sit.

"All I've ever heard from you since day one was Stacy this and Stacy that," Sarah begins, seething.

What? What the fuck is she saying? Yeah, during our very first phone call, I told her about my horrible fuck with Stacy, but—

"And what a 'smokin' hot body' she has . . ."

Oh my God, no. This is crazy. Last night I said Stacy has a smokin' hot body, yes, but only so Josh and I could compare notes about his Seattle girl—

"All I ever hear is Stacy, Stacy, Stacy—how great Stacy is in bed."

Wait, what? Have I had a psychotic break and I don't know it?

Sarah glares at Stacy. "Do you know how many times he's said to me, 'Why can't you fuck me the way Stacy did'?"

The universe warps and buckles and slows to a screeching halt.

Sarah flashes me her patented I'm-smarter-than-you smirk.

Holy shit. She knows. She understands. Oh my God. How the fuck did she figure this out? How did she know I'd be here tonight? And why does she know exactly what line of bullshit I've been slinging to Stacy? A smile threatens my lips, but I suppress it. She's the most amazing woman in the world. Holy shit, she's the woman of my dreams.

Sarah whips her head and glares at Stacy again. "Well, guess what, Stacy—or Cassandra, or whatever your name is—you've fucked with the wrong woman. Jonas Faraday is *mine*—my territory, my score—and I don't need anybody making a play for my sloppy seconds." She leans right into Stacy's face, her eyes narrowed to slits. "Don't fuck with me, bitch."

I can't speak. She's magnificent.

Stacy rises to her feet, ready to rumble.

I get up, too, ready to intercede.

But Sarah doesn't back down. She grits her teeth. "I've written a detailed report about The Club and I've addressed it to the Federal Bureau of Investigation, the U.S. Attorney's Office, and, given The Club's roster of members, the U.S. Secret Service, too."

Stacy's eyes widen. Sarah just called her bluff.

There's a long beat.

"Take a seat, asshole," Sarah says firmly. "Please."

Stacy sits.

And so do I. I'm not sure which one of us she just called an asshole.

Sarah takes the seat next to me and leans forward across the table.

"I've got a message for whoever's running The Club, and I want you to deliver it for me."

Stacy clenches her jaw.

"Tell them I'm not currently planning to send my report to anyone. Frankly, I don't care what The Club does and I'd take no pleasure in publicly humiliating members or their families. But if anything happens to me, or to my friend Kat, or to this man here, or to anyone I care about, if The Club fucks with me or my people in any way, then each of those law enforcement agencies will *immediately* receive that report. I've already made detailed arrangements through multiple resources. It's all set."

Stacy leans back, her face flushed.

"My report is some damned good reading, too, lemme tell you. We're talking hundreds of counts of prostitution and sex trafficking and money laundering under both state and federal laws, plus Internet fraud, wire fraud, racketeering—jeez, I'm guessing a good federal prosecutor could come up with at least a hundred counts under RICO alone—and then there's good old fashioned theft and fraud under state laws, too."

Stacy's nostrils flare.

"I realize it's gonna be hard for you to convey the specifics of my message to the powers that be, Stacy, so just give them the gist and tell them to give me a call. I'd be happy to explain everything in explicit detail."

I'm transfixed. I've never witnessed such an erotic blend of power and beauty and brains in all my life. She's stunning—a goddess—a fucking superhero. Orgasma the All-Powerful, indeed.

"And I've also got a personal message for you, too, Stacy—woman to woman. Fuck you." Sarah smiles. "Whatever you and Jonas talked about isn't gonna happen. He's *mine*." She looks at me. "Tell her you're mine."

"I'm hers."

"I'm not gunning to take you down, Stacy. A girl's got to make a living. You can have anybody but Jonas, any lonely moneybags-wack-job in the greater Seattle area—in the whole world, for all I care. I don't give a fuck. All I care about is this man right here. You got that?"

Stacy swallows but doesn't speak. Her eyes are chips of blue granite.

Sarah smooths an errant hair away from her face and juts her chin in my direction. "Jonas?"

"Yes, Sarah?"

"I'm going to fuck you now—and you don't even have to pay me to do it."

"Thank you."

"I won't do it the way Stacy did it, of course."

"Of course."

"But I'll give it my best shot."

I almost burst out laughing.

"Jonas?"

"Yes?"

"Say goodbye to Stacy."

"Goodbye, Stacy." I stand and pull my wallet out of my jeans pocket. I throw six hundred-dollar bills onto the table in front of her. "Your usual fee plus a twenty-percent tip," I explain politely. I wink.

Stacy's eye twitches.

I grab Sarah's hand and pull her to a stand beside me. "Come on, baby. Let's go fuck each other's brains out."

Chapter 15

Sarah

"So. Fucking. Hot. So. Fucking. Hot. So. Fucking. Hot." Each word he barks at me is accompanied by a zealous thrust of his body.

He's fucking my brains out against the filthy wall of the men's bathroom.

I'm so mad at him right now, I don't even want to speak to him. But fuck him? Yes. As mad as I am, when he said, "Come on, baby, let's go fuck each other's brains out," *right in front of Stacy the Faker,* holy moly, the moment was too scorching hot not to capitalize on it. Every so often, a girl's gotta treat herself to a little I'm-so-pissed-at-you sex. There's nothing quite like it.

"Oh, baby, you fucking killed it," he groans. "So. Fucking. Hot." His thrusts are wildly enthusiastic. "Did you see her face when you told her about the report? So. Fucking. Hot. So. Fucking. Smart." He punctuates each word with another beastly thrust. "So. Fucking. Smart. Oh, Baby. My baby. Oh, Sarah."

His lips devour my mouth.

I'm dangerously close to completely letting go and losing my mind in a whole new, dirty, dirty way. But, no, I'm so mad at him, so hurt, so betrayed, I'm not going to come this time, just to prove my point. It shouldn't be hard to stop myself, for Pete's sake—this bathroom is utterly disgusting. What the hell am I doing in here? I cannot believe I'm having sex in the men's bathroom of a bar. I'm such a dirty, dirty girl. Oh, wow, I just made myself hot. Dirty, dirty girl. Oh God, yes, yes, yes, yes, yes, this feels so good. Dirty, dirty girl. Ow, my head just slammed loudly against the wall.

He stops abruptly, wincing. "Are you okay?"

"Yeah. Don't stop. Come on. Yes, yes, yes." I growl my words loudly and Jonas responds with vigor. "You're in so much trouble," I snarl at him. "You're in so much fucking trouble."

"I know," he says. "I was so bad."

"So bad. Fuck me harder."

"You want it hard?"

"As hard as you can give it to me. Is that all you got?" I stifle a scream.

His hand gropes my breast. His lips suck on mine. His face is covered in sweat. His body heat is palpable.

"I'm gonna get you off and I'm not gonna come myself," I growl. "Just to punish you. You were bad. So. Bad. So. Bad. I'm. Not. Gonna. Come."

"Oh, you're gonna come, baby. Oh, fuck, you feel so good. You like it when I fuck you, baby?"

"That's all you got?"

"You want more?"

"I want all you got."

"Oh God, Sarah. So fucking smart, baby. So. Fucking. Smart. You're a fucking genius."

"And you're a fucking idiot."

He laughs and groans at the same time.

"Turn around," he orders.

I don't obey.

He forcefully turns me around and spreads my legs like he's frisking me. I place my palms on the nasty bathroom wall. He continues fucking me from behind as his fingers reach around and touch me. I'm so wet, so fucking wet, I should be wearing rain boots. Holy mother of God.

"You're not gonna come, huh?" he asks. He bites my neck.

"No." I shudder and moan.

"To teach me a lesson?"

I can't verbalize a response. His fingers are working me with too much skill. I'm delirious.

He growls loudly. He's close.

"Say it," I moan loudly.

He knows exactly what I want. "I'm yours."

Tell her you're mine, I said to him in front of Stacy. *I'm hers,* he said, as if we'd rehearsed it. *I'm hers,* he told her—and her face turned bright red.

That's right. Fuck you, Stacy. He's mine. *Mine, mine, mine, mine.* Oh, God, yes. Yes, yes, yes. I'm fluttering, rippling, close to the edge. I groan loudly.

"Again," I order him. This wall is disgusting. I'm a dirty, dirty girl.

"I'm yours."

"Again." I can't breathe.

"I'm yours. Yours. Yours. Yours. Oh, Sarah. Yours. Yours. Oh, God, Sarah. I'm yours."

"Jonas." The sound that emerges from me is quite similar to the sound I'd make if I were in this filthy bathroom praying to the porcelain gods after one too many mojitos (a comparison I'm unfortunately able to draw through actual experience). I'm splitting into two with my ecstasy. My body is rending, wretching, heaving in painful pleasure—or maybe my body's just reacting to the foul bathroom wall.

Oh yes, oh God, yes, I'm definitely coming. And hard. Motherfucker, I can't help myself. This is just too hot. I let out a guttural growl.

He climaxes right on my heels, letting out a strangled cry of his own.

Holy shit, this bathroom is utterly nauseating.

He collapses onto my back, a sweaty, savage heap.

Damn, that was hot. So. Fucking. Hot.

And I'm so mad at him I could cry. In fact, now that my adrenaline is rapidly receding, I very well might do just that. I tilt my pelvis away from him to force him out of me. I turn around and glare at him.

He smiles broadly: the cat that swallowed the canary.

"You're so fucking hot," he says simply.

Without saying a word, I pull up my panties, push down my skirt, and scrub my arms and hands and face in the sink with hot water. And then, after quickly drying myself with a paper towel, I bolt out the bathroom door. Jonas follows silently behind me.

Some guy stands outside the door of the one-room bathroom as we depart, waiting to go inside.

"She was sick, man," Jonas says in passing. "Sorry."

"Yeah. Sick of waiting around for this asshole-motherfucker to *fuck* me," I say. I don't know why I say it, but I do.

The guy bursts out laughing and so does Jonas.

"Nice," the guy says to Jonas.

I march into the bar area, with Jonas following mutely behind me. I steal a glance at the booth where Jonas and I sat only minutes ago with Stacy the Fucking Faker. She's long gone. Good. Run along and tell your bosses every word I said. *Bitch.*

I beeline over to the bar. "Two shots of Patron," I say to the bartender, gesturing to Jonas and myself.

Jonas stares at me, smirking, but not speaking.

The bartender pours the shots.

"Jonas?"

"Yes, Sarah."

"Pay the man," I say.

Jonas pulls out his wallet and lays down the cash.

I knock back the shot and bite into my lime. I stare at Jonas, defiant. I'm so mad at him, I don't want to speak to him right now.

"You are so fucking hot," he says. He throws back his shot and bites his lime.

I glance to the other end of the bar and gasp. There's a guy at the far end of the bar, staring at me—and, holy crappola, he looks just like John Travolta. Granted, John Travolta from *Look Who's Talking, Too,* but still. I clutch Jonas and he instantly puts his arm around me, sensing my sudden anxiety.

I nudge Jonas' arm. "Jonas, look," I whisper. I motion with my head to the end of the bar.

He looks in the direction I've indicated. "What?"

"Is that him? The John Travolta guy?"

Jonas looks again, squeezing me tight, trying to understand what I'm talking about. His grip on my body is so forceful that it hurts.

"Blue shirt," I whisper.

Jonas focuses on the target and relaxes his grip. "Oh my God, Sarah, come on. You really think that guy looks anything like Vincent Vega?"

"Who the hell is Vincent Vega?" I shake my head. "Is that the John Travolta guy you saw earlier today?"

"'*Who the hell is Vincent Vega?'* Oh my God, you haven't actually seen *Pulp Fiction,* have you?"

"Of course, I have. Never mind. I'm pissed at you. I can't even talk to you right now." Sudden emotion wells up inside me and catches in my throat. Tonight has been a horrible, wretched, death-defying mind fuck. Without another word, I turn away from him and bolt out of the bar.

Chapter 16

Sarah

Jonas hoots into the chilly night air as we walk away from the bar. He keeps leaping into the air like he's doing some sort of touchdown dance. "You were amazing, baby! Holy shit! A fucking genius! And so fucking hot!"

My legs wobble. I'm still flushed with adrenaline and anger and hurt. "I'm not in the mood to celebrate," I mutter, my hand on my chest, steadying myself.

He sweeps me up and cradles me in his arms, just like he did after I jumped off the waterfall in Belize. "I've got you," he says, kissing my cheek. He's jubilant. "You kicked ass in there. Oh my God. Orgasma the All-Powerful strikes again!" He laughs and hoots again.

I don't want to be cuddled by Jonas right now. I'm angry at him.

"Put me down. I'm mad at you."

He laughs.

"Jonas, I'm not kidding. Put me down. I'm really, really mad. And hurt."

He puts me down, elation draining from his face like water swirling down a toilet bowl.

I march ahead of him, trying to collect my thoughts.

"You know I only met Stacy to gather information—"

"Yeah, I know."

"You can't possibly think I wanted to—"

"I don't." I quicken my pace. I'm furious. And hurt. And just plain confused.

"Sarah, I would never, ever—"

"Jonas, just give me a minute. I'm so pissed at you, I can't even speak. Just don't talk."

I can feel him bursting at the seams behind me, but he grants my request—for a solid forty seconds.

"Sarah," he finally says. "I can't stand it. Talk to me."

I stop walking and whip around to look at him, tears in my eyes.

"Oh, baby," he begins, reaching for me. But I cut him off.

"I should be studying right now!" I shriek. "Only the top ten students get a scholarship!" I burst into tears. "I need that scholarship, Jonas, and I haven't studied for a whole *week,* thanks to you." This isn't at all what's foremost on my mind. I have no idea why this is what my brain chose to barf out at this moment. I choke down the sob that threatens to rise from my throat.

He moves to comfort me again, but I put my hands up.

"Don't. I'm so mad at you right now I can't see straight."

He opens his mouth to say something but stops himself.

"I'm a grown-ass woman, Jonas. I'm strong. I'm smart. You should have told me what you were up to. I can handle it—I can *help.* But you didn't trust me enough to tell me the truth."

"It's not an issue of trust. I didn't tell you because I wanted to keep you out of harm's way."

"Bullshit."

He raises his eyebrows.

"You didn't tell me because you didn't trust me not to fuck up your precious strategy, whatever the hell it is."

He rolls his eyes. "No, Sarah, that's not it."

"If tonight were reversed, you'd be just as pissed as I am right now, probably more so."

"You're reading way too much into this."

"Really? Think about it. If I checked in on the Club app without telling you and secretly met up with a guy—*a guy I'd fucked once before*—what would you do?"

He clenches his jaw.

"You think you might wig out just a little bit? Or at least wonder why the *fuck* I didn't tell you?"

He exhales.

"What if I said, 'Oh, don't worry, Jonas, I wasn't gonna *fuck* him, you silly goose—yes, he happens to be the last guy I fucked before I met you, but I was just planning to make him *think* I wanted to fuck him for this super-duper awesome strategy I have—a super-duper awesome strategy I've told you nothing about.'"

He glares at me.

"And what if we add one more little fact to this hypothetical. What if I'd slept with a different guy every single night for the past year—right up until I met you? And then I ran off to a check-in with the very last guy I'd been with? You're telling me you wouldn't wonder just a teeny-tiny little bit what the *fuck* I was doing when I said I had 'something I had to do' tonight?"

He smashes his lips together.

"Ya feeling me on this?" My chest is heaving. Damn, I'm furious. He doesn't understand how close he came to smashing my heart into a million pieces tonight.

There's a long beat.

"I'm a dumbshit," he finally says quietly.

"Felony stupid," I agree.

He looks defeated.

"The problem isn't you meeting up with Stacy. I get what you were trying to do—whatever the hell it was. The problem is you not *telling* me about it—not trusting me enough to tell me."

He sighs. There's a long beat.

"My imagination started playing tricks on me tonight, Jonas." I sigh. "That's why I went to the bar in the first place." Tears well up in my eyes. "Paranoia got the best of me. When I saw your car parked in the garage, I remembered how you said you used to walk to The Pine Box on your 'hunting expeditions' . . ." I wipe my eyes.

He's instantly indignant. "You thought I went to the bar to pick someone up? To *fuck* someone?"

"I thought it was possible."

"How could you think that, even for a second?"

I give him a "duh" look.

"After everything I've—" He shakes his head. "After Belize? After last night? That's what you think of me?"

I glance away.

"I'd never do that to you. Look at me."

I look at him.

"Don't you know you fucking own me?"

"You kept The Club's iPhone."

"To give to Trey."

"It was on the table this morning."

"Because I'm figuring out how to fuck The Club up the ass—to protect my beautiful, precious baby. Everything I do is to protect you. I'm telling you, Sarah, you own me."

"Stop saying that. I don't *own* you."

"Yes, you do."

"No, I don't. If I *owned* you, as you allege, you would have told me what you were up to."

He exhales in exasperation. There's another long beat.

"If I truly *owned* you, there wouldn't have been room for doubt in my mind. By keeping things from me, you left room for me to doubt."

His face is etched with pain.

"Jonas, tonight was horrible. My heart was a whisper away from shattering. I started thinking maybe you couldn't resist teaching Stacy the Faker a lesson about truth and honesty—getting your *redemption* the second time around."

His eyes burst into flames. "How could you think that?"

"Oh, gee! Maybe because I saw you sitting in a bar having drinks with her—*and you didn't tell me about it!*"

He throws up his hands, totally pissed. "Jesus."

"And then I thought, 'Oh, wait, no, Jonas would never fuck a *prostitute*.'"

He nods emphatically, like I'm finally making some sense.

"But that's the problem right there. I shouldn't have been thinking, 'Jonas would never cheat on me with a prostitute.' I should have been thinking, 'Jonas would never cheat on me, period, with anyone.'"

He runs his hand through his hair. "I thought we were done with this. Remember what we said in Belize? Full steam ahead? No more one step forward, two steps back? No more trust issues. You promised."

"Yeah, and we *were* done with this. I kept my promise. I trusted you—completely—until you gave me a reason to doubt you."

He shakes his head.

"Secrets create spaces within a relationship, Jonas—dark spaces. When one person keeps secrets, the other person fills in the dark spaces with their fears and insecurities."

He stares at me for a long beat. "That's profound, actually."

"Thanks. I made it up. Just now. On the spot."

"I like it. It makes a lot of sense." He shoots me a half-smile. "You're pretty fucking smart, you know that?"

I shrug. Tears threaten my eyes.

"Sarah, I do trust you. More than I've ever trusted any woman, ever. I've told you things . . ." He sighs. "I've opened myself up to you in whole new ways."

I shiver in the cold. "Let's keep walking. It's frickin' freezing."

He puts his arm around me as we walk. He's warm. His arm around me is strong. He smells delicious, even after he's just had sweaty sex in a men's bathroom. His physicality is so alluring to me, such a welcome distraction from the rambling dialogue inside my head, I'm tempted to blurt, "Never mind" and just kiss him. But sweeping my emotions under the carpet won't solve anything. It only means they'll come out later, and probably with a vengeance. We need to have this conversation now.

"You made me jump off a frickin' waterfall, Jonas," I say. "And I'm deathly afraid of heights."

He smiles. "I know."

"This whole relationship has been about *me*. Making *me* let go. Making *me* 'surrender.' What about you?"

He doesn't reply.

"You're fucked up, too, you know."

"Royally."

"Well, what's your waterfall? When are *you* gonna jump off a waterfall for *me*?"

We walk in silence for a minute longer.

He stops short all of a sudden. He pulls me into him and kisses me. His nose is cold against mine, but his lips are warm. He abruptly pulls away from me and cups my face in his hands.

"This. This right here," he whispers. "Every single minute I'm with you, I'm jumping off a waterfall. Don't you understand?" His eyes burn with intensity. "You're afraid of heights? Well, I'm afraid of *this*. I'm standing on a cliff a hundred feet tall, and every day with you, I jump. I don't know how to do this, okay? It's all new to me—and I'm terrible at it. So, okay, I'm gonna fuck things up sometimes. But... " He swallows hard, suppressing his emotions. "But every day, I see your beautiful face, every day I get to touch your smooth skin and kiss your spectacular lips and make love to you—oh my God—and talk to you and laugh with you and tell you things I've never told anyone else, *ever*—all of it makes me want to keep climbing higher and higher to the next waterfall, to the next day, and just keep jumping and jumping and jumping into the abyss." He's shaking. "With you."

Tears spill out of my eyes.

"*Because you fucking own me, Sarah.*"

He kisses my wet cheeks. He peppers my entire face with soft kisses. He kisses my mouth. I kiss him back. He presses his body into mine. His lips find my eyelids, my ears, my neck. His hands are on my butt, cradling my back, stroking through my hair.

"I thought I lost you tonight," he whispers.

"You almost did."

His breathing halts. "Don't leave me, Sarah." His kiss is full of passion. "Be patient with me," he mumbles into my lips. "I'm doing my best."

I reach under his T-shirt and touch his warm skin. It's sticky with his dried sweat. The muscles over his ribcage ripple under my fingers.

"I know, baby, I know." His kiss is heavenly. "You're doing so good, baby. So, so good," I whisper into his lips.

"Don't leave me."

My body melts into his. "No more secrets, Jonas."

"I promise," he says. He leans back and looks me right in the face. "I'll jump off any waterfall you want, baby. Just don't give up on me."

A light rain begins peppering our faces and splattering softly onto the sidewalk all around us. Oh, Seattle. You're so predictable.

I nod. "Let's go home," I say. "I just figured out another item for my *addendum*."

His eyes light up.

"You're gonna take a flying-squirrel leap off a waterfall for me tonight, baby—whether you like it or not."

Chapter 17

Jonas

Josh looks up from the TV when we burst through the front door, slightly damp from the rain and revved up like two dogs in heat. He's sitting on the couch, watching basketball and drinking a beer.

"Well, well, well. Aren't you the sneaky one, Little Miss Sarah Cruz? So much for me keeping an eye on you tonight. Sorry, bro, she just slipped out without me realizing it."

"I went to spy on Jonas having a drink with a hooker," Sarah says.

"Ah, so you figured out Jonas' brilliant plan, huh?"

"It wasn't hard."

"And did it piss you off?" Josh asks.

"Oh, just a tad," she says.

"Gosh, Jonas. Too bad someone smarter than you didn't warn you about that very thing."

"Yes, I'm a dumbshit, I know," I say. "You should have seen her. She marched in there, kicked ass, and took charge of the whole thing. She was brilliant."

"Why doesn't that surprise me? I seem to recall suggesting you ask her for her input in the first place."

Sarah laughs. "You should have seen Jonas' face when I first walked in. If I'd blown on him, he would have tipped over." She looks at me sideways, her eyes mischievous. "I liked it."

Oh my God, I've got to get this gorgeous woman into my bed.

"Josh, I'm sorry, man, but you've got to get the fuck out of here tonight. Go to a hotel, whatever," I say. I'm losing my mind. My baby's got something sexy up her sleeve and I can't wait to find out what it is. Whatever it is, it's guaranteed to involve her shrieking like a howler monkey tonight and I don't want Josh sitting out here on the couch eating fucking Doritos while she does.

"A hotel?" He looks at the two of us and instantly understands why I'm kicking him out. "Oh come on, man. I'll just go to my room. It's way in the back. I'll listen to music. I'll put a pillow over my head. Come on. I just want to chill tonight and watch the game. I had a long day."

"No, you gotta get the fuck out. Sorry."

He rolls his eyes. "Fine," he huffs. "Maybe I'll give Party Girl with a Hyphen a call." He looks at Sarah. "Can you text me Kat's number?"

"Yeah, sure, but she's busy tonight. She's hanging out with her new bodyguard. Oh, yeah, that reminds me, Jonas, she asked me to thank you profusely. She says her bodyguard's a total hunk—even cuter than Kevin Costner. And she did quite the Whitney Houston impression for me when I called, too."

I laugh.

"You sent her a *bodyguard*?" Josh asks, incredulous. "Why didn't you just ask me? I would have hung out with her and kept her safe and sound."

I shrug. "It didn't even occur to me. Plus, you've got plenty to do, right?" I beam at Sarah. "And, anyway, after Sarah's magnificent performance tonight, I don't feel all that worried about Kat's safety anymore." I kiss Sarah's nose. "You're so fucking smart, baby." I kiss her mouth. She receives me with enthusiasm. Oh God, how I'm going to fuck this woman tonight. First off, I'm going to make love to My Magnificent Sarah with supreme devotion and expertly calibrated skill—and then I'm going to fuck Orgasma the All-Powerful's brains out yet again 'til she comes like a motherfucker.

Josh clears his throat. "I'm still right here."

I pull away from Sarah and glare at Josh. "Don't you have an acquisition report to analyze?" I laugh. I'm such a hypocrite. I haven't put in an honest day's work since we closed the deal on our rock climbing gyms.

"Yeah, actually, I wanted to talk to you about that for a minute," Josh says. "Sarah, do you mind if I steal Jonas for five minutes?"

"Not right now, Josh," I say quickly. "Sarah's gonna make me jump off a waterfall tonight to prove my unwavering devotion to her."

Sarah swats me on the shoulder. "Jonas!"

"What?" I laugh. I look at Josh. "Let's talk tomorrow."

I grab Sarah's hand and pull her toward my room.

"No, I really need to talk to you tonight, bro. Five minutes."

Sarah drops my hand. "Talk to your brother. I need a few minutes to set up the *waterfall*, anyway." She grins broadly and leans into my ear. "I'll be waiting for you, big boy." She smiles at Josh. "Will I see you tomorrow?"

"Probably not." Josh looks at me, stone-faced. Oh shit. Something's up. "But I'll be back in Seattle again soon, no doubt. I'm up here all the time."

She crosses the room to give him a hug. She whispers something to him and he nods. He kisses the top of her head like she's a little kid and she blushes, nodding. She walks out of the room, but not before flashing me a look that makes me grin from ear to ear.

I sit down next to Josh on the couch. "What's up?"

"I was just about to ask you the same thing."

I sigh. I know exactly what he's referring to. "I know. I've been MIA lately. I'm sorry."

"Just tell me straight. What's the deal?"

I let out a long exhale and rub my face. "I can't do it, Josh. Something's clicked inside me and I can't pretend anymore—about anything. I just can't put on a suit and a fucking mask and try to be someone I'm not. I've never been that guy. I can't keep trying to be him. I'm done."

He exhales. "Are you sure?"

"I never gave a shit about Faraday & Sons; you know that. And now that we've got the gyms, and I've got Sarah, I don't have the stomach for bullshit of any variety anymore. I know what I want."

"Yeah? And what's that?"

"Well, thank you for asking. I want to build Climb and Conquer into a worldwide brand. Not just the physical gyms themselves, but an entire lifestyle brand—clothes, shoes, gear, equipment. Maybe even a blog or magazine. The Climb and Conquer brand will embody adventure, fitness, the pursuit of excellence—each person's individual but universal quest to find the divine original form of himself."

Josh smiles. "Sounds pretty awesome, bro."

"This is what I'm meant to do. I don't care about acquiring shit just to acquire more shit. I've already got more money than I know what to do with. What's the fucking point?"

Josh nods. "Okay. What else?"

"I want to climb. Obviously."

Josh nods. This he already knows.

"All over the world. The highest peaks. With you."

"The Two Musketeers."

"Fuck yeah. The Faraday twins."

He half-smiles at me.

"I've had enough of bankers and financial analysts and fucking lawyers and accountants to last a lifetime. I want to be with people who understand me—people who love to climb."

Josh nods. This part he knows, too. I've never really belonged in the high finance world of Faraday & Sons. You wouldn't know it from the outside—you'd assume quite the opposite from the outside, probably, just because I happen to be good at it—but most of the time, secretly, I'm a fish out of water in that world. Josh knows this about me. He's always known. But no one else does. And I don't want to pretend anymore.

I sigh. "And last but certainly not least I want to be with Sarah as much as humanly possible." A shiver runs down my spine. "I almost screwed everything up tonight, Josh. For a minute there, I thought I'd lost her." I run my hand through my hair. "You were right—things weren't nearly as 'simple' as I thought they'd be."

"Surprise, surprise. Yet another flash of brilliance brought to you by Mr. Book Smarts, Jonas Faraday. I told you so, moron."

I shake my head. "I'm not even gonna say fuck you. That's how right you were."

"Thank you for the much-deserved validation. How can a guy be so fucking smart and yet so fucking stupid?"

"I thought she was gonna leave me. And it scared the shit out of me." I swallow hard.

Josh grins at me. "I told you not to fuck it up, and what did you go and do?"

"Almost fucked it up. If it had been any other girl, I'd be toast right now. I got lucky this time, only because she's so smart. But I can't fuck it up like that again or I might not be so lucky next time."

Josh laughs. "She's good for you, bro. I like her."

"I like her, too."

Josh takes a deep breath. "So is that everything you want? Or is there more on the list?"

"One more thing." I bite my lip, trying to decide how to word this. "I'd really like to pull my head out of my ass and give a shit about something bigger than myself." I pause. I haven't thought this one through very well yet. "Maybe Climb and Conquer could adopt some causes and donate a portion of all proceeds—not for some gimmicky promotion, not to get publicity, but as our basic business model. We can talk about which causes we care most about—I've already got a couple in mind, maybe you've got some, too—but the basic idea is that I'd like to actively and unabashedly try to make the world a better a place, every single day."

Josh tilts his head and looks at me like aliens have overtaken my body. And I understand why. I've never said anything like this before. Ever. Between the two of us, despite Josh's love of fast cars and other assorted high-priced toys, he's the one who's more accustomed to wearing a red cape. He's the one who invites little leaguers or kids with leukemia into our box seats at sports games. He's the one who calls his celebrity friends to ask them to donate a signed jersey or guitar to a charity auction. He's the guy a hundred different people would call first if they were to find themselves in a Tijuana prison or on a desolate highway with no gas in their tank. And, of course, he's the one who's picked me up every time I've fallen down.

I'm suddenly thinking about Sarah—how passionate she is about wanting to help people and make the world a better place. How she puts her money where her mouth is every single day. Josh and I have all the money in the world, but what do we do with it? And then there's Sarah who comes from nothing and is working her ass off to get a full-ride scholarship, just so she can take a job after graduation that pays next to nothing, all so she can help others. My heart's suddenly in my throat. She makes me want to be a better man.

"I'm gonna start being the guy I should have been all along," I say quietly. "The divine original form of Jonas Faraday." I exhale. "The man she would have wanted me to become."

Josh's eyes are moist. He rubs them. He knows exactly who the "she" is in that sentence. He clears his throat, but he's unable to speak.

There's a long beat. The rain outside has gathered strength. It's beating loudly against the windows and the roof.

Josh slaps his face, hard. "Okay, crazy-ass motherfucker. Sounds like a fucking plan."

I slap mine in reply. "Okay, pussy-ass-bitch-motherfucker."

"I'm proud of you, Jonas," Josh says quietly.

"I'm proud of you, too."

We look at each other for a brief moment. The Faraday boys weren't raised to say "I love you" to each other—or to anyone, for that matter—quite the opposite—but Josh and I have just said it to each other in our own way.

"When do you wanna put out a press release about your departure?" Josh asks.

"Give me a couple days at least. I'll write it personally so it doesn't leak before release. And I want to be the one who tells Uncle William, of course—I owe him that much. Plus, I've got to tell my team. I want to assure them their jobs are secure, that we'll keep the team intact, continue pushing forward with acquisitions, blah, blah, fucking blah. And we'll have to put some thought into who should take over managing my team, whether we want to look internally or put out a nationwide search. Or, I guess, you could just assume management of my team along with yours. That would probably make the most sense—you come up to Seattle so much, anyway."

Josh is stone-faced. He doesn't speak.

"What do you think?"

Josh doesn't reply.

"Josh? Any thoughts?"

He exhales loudly. "Shit, man. I don't give a fuck about Faraday & Sons, either."

Chapter 18

Sarah

I expect Jonas to feel apprehensive at first, or maybe even anxious, given the forcible bondage of his mother he witnessed as a boy—and that's exactly why I chose this activity as his metaphorical waterfall in the first place. My actual waterfall in Belize was thirty feet tall, after all, so his symbolic waterfall can't be a frickin' pony ride. I'm just hoping that, with a little bit of coaxing and tenderness, or, as the case may be, a little tough love, he'll be able to view this situation through new eyes—his *adult* eyes—and perhaps replace some of the tortured memories from his childhood with new, delectable, decidedly adult (and pleasurable) memories. Hey, it's worth a shot.

Jonas' bed frame is a sleek design without bedposts, so I need to get creative. I improvise four long tethers using neckties from Jonas' closet and loop them around the base of each leg of his bed. I finish off this brilliant feat of modern engineering with a dandy slipknot at the end of each tether (courtesy of a handy "how to" video on YouTube). The whole setup isn't nearly as simple or functional as the luxurious bondage sheet with soft Velcro cuffs described in reverent detail in one of the applications I reviewed, but, hey, my Jonas-Shall-Surrender-to-Me-and-Thusly-Expunge-the-Remainder-of-His-Demons idea only came to me an hour ago. I think I've improvised pretty well considering the timeframe and what I've got on hand.

I venture into Jonas' closet in search of variously textured items I might be able to tease and tantalize him with during his captivity, but there's not much to choose from. His closet is filled with meticulously hung suits and shirts, perfectly-folded jeans and T-shirts, immaculately lined-up shoes, and an assortment of the latest in athletic clothes, fleeces and jackets. It's quintessential Jonas—simple, well ordered, and beautiful—and absolutely nothing of any use to a dirty little minx like me. The man doesn't seem to own anything even remotely feathered or furry or beaded or fringed—and, hey, no big surprise, there aren't any whips, chains, nipple clamps, butt plugs, dildos, or horse bits, either (thankfully). I smile. My hunky-monkey boyfriend is a man of simple tastes. I like that about him. Even if the Sex Factory were located right next door with an unlimited supply of toys to choose from, I wouldn't want any of it, at least not tonight. First off, I've never used that kind of stuff before and I have no idea how any of it works. But more importantly, that's not what turns Jonas on. As I say, he's a man of simple tastes. And this whole exercise is about turning Jonas on—and forcing him to succumb to a new kind of trust with me.

I take a quick shower and brush my teeth and then crawl onto the bed to await Jonas. I put my fancy new laptop next to me and turn on "Sweater Weather" by The Neighbourhood. I love this song. I close my eyes and stretch myself out, breathing deeply and letting the song wash over me. I begin touching myself, letting images from my dream revisit me—ten poltergeist-Jonases pleasuring me simultaneously. Warm red wine gushing across my belly and spilling into my crotch and down my thighs and between my toes, and Jonas licking the wine off every inch of me. A room full of people watching us. By the time I get to Jonas proclaiming, "I love Sarah Cruz," loud enough for our entire audience to hear, I'm highly aroused and aching for him.

The bedroom door finally opens.

I look up at him, licking my lips with anticipation.

He takes in the web of neckties tethered to the legs of his bed and his face falls.

"No, Sarah," he says simply.

Exactly the reaction I expected. He was unequivocal in his application that bondage of any kind is a non-starter for him. "Non-negotiable," he called it. But that was before he met me. Before I jumped off a waterfall in a dark cave for him. Before we became mutually stricken with a serious mental disease. Before I became Orgasma the All-Powerful. Before he checked in with Stacy the Faker behind my back and made me doubt him.

"Yes," I purr. "Come here, baby."

"Not this," he says. "I'm sorry."

I get up off the bed and go to him. I grab his hands and pull him toward the bed.

He resists. He's immovable.

"I've never done this, either. But I want to do it with you."

I begin unbuttoning his jeans.

He takes a step back. "I won't tie you up, Sarah. Absolutely not."

I smile. "Oh, baby, no. *You're* not gonna tie *me* up. *I'm* gonna tie *you* up."

He inhales sharply. That's not what he was expecting me to say. His face turns pale.

I step toward him again. I touch his lips, his beautifully sculpted lips. "I allegedly own you? Well, tonight, you're going to prove it."

His chest heaves.

"Do you trust me?"

He closes his eyes. "Ask me to do anything else for you. Just not this."

"Trust me," I say. "Come on."

He sighs. "I have no interest in this, Sarah."

"I had no interest in jumping off a thirty-foot waterfall into ink-black water in a darkened cave. But you gave me no choice—and it changed my life. I'm not giving you a choice, either. This is your waterfall."

He lets out a long, controlled exhale.

"Jonas, contrary to my every instinct, I jumped—literally and figuratively. And my body thanked me for it later. And so did my soul. Well, now it's your turn."

He shifts his weight. He shakes his head.

My ire rises. "It's your penance for what you pulled tonight." This is my trump card. "As far as I'm concerned, you've got no other way down."

His gaze is defiant. "'Knowledge which is acquired under compulsion obtains no hold on the mind.'"

He doesn't need to tell me that's yet another quote from frickin' Plato. Screw Plato. "I've got a Plato quote for you, too," I say. "I looked it up, just for you."

He squints at me.

"'Courage is a kind of salvation.'"

He scowls.

"Come on, baby," I say softly. "Madness. Detach your mind from your body. You'll thank me."

He looks over at the bed. "Sarah . . ."

"Madness," I repeat.

He pauses for a long beat and finally takes off his shirt. His muscled chest rises and falls with each anxious breath.

I take in the glorious sight of him—man, oh man, I'll never tire of looking at him with his shirt off. I touch the tattoo on his left forearm. "For a man to conquer himself is the first and noblest of all victories," I whisper, quoting his own tattoo back to him.

He nods.

I pull at the waist of his jeans and he takes them off.

He stands before me naked, his erection defying whatever misgivings his brain might be having.

I look him up and down. He's spectacular. The sight of him never gets old. Day-am.

"Lemme take a quick shower," he says. He swallows hard.

"Hurry."

He's gone.

I crawl back onto the bed, cue up another song on my laptop ("Fall In Love" by Phantogram), and wait—losing myself in my dream again. Wine, poltergeist-Jonases, licking, fucking, spectators. *I love Sarah Cruz.* The throbbing between my legs is excruciating.

I feel his warm skin against mine. His lips on my breast. His hand on the inside of my thigh, creeping up.

"No," I whisper. "I'm in charge this time."

"Let me make love to you," he whispers, his lips trailing down my belly.

I'm tempted to give in, to let go and let him pleasure me all night long.

But holy hell. I put a lot of effort into this bondage setup, and, by God, I'm going to use it. I sit up and push him back. "You do as I command. You're no longer allowed the luxury of free will from this moment forward."

He smashes his lips together.

"I'm serious."

His eyes move from my face down to my naked body. "You look beautiful," he whispers. His erection twitches. "Can't we just make love?"

"Jonas, I just said you've got no free will. Don't speak unless spoken to."

"I can't help it. You're too beautiful. Mesmerizing. You're the goddess and the muse, Sarah Cruz."

I ignore him and scoot off the bed. "Come here."

He rolls his eyes but reluctantly rolls off the side of the bed to join me. He comes to a hulking stand in front of me, his erection straining for me, his muscles tensing in all their glory.

"From here on out, don't speak unless spoken to. My will shall be done."

He sighs.

"If you wig out or something, I'll stop and untie you. Just say… um…" I stop. I've never done this before. Jeez, I'm a terrible dominatrix.

"You're trying to come up with a 'safe word'?" he asks, incredulous.

"Yeah. A safe word." My finger traces a deep ridge in his abs, just above his erect penis. The throbbing between my legs intensifies.

His breathing hitches when I touch him. "Sarah, come on. Just let me taste you. I'm gonna make you shriek like a howler monkey, and then I'm gonna fuck your brains out and make you come again." His fingers lightly graze my breast. "Come on."

I swat his hand away. "I can't stand here buck naked looking at you anymore, Jonas. You're too beautiful. I'm gonna start dripping down my thigh. Are you gonna get on the bed and let me tie you up or what?"

"Sarah," he sighs. "I don't do bondage. You don't understand. I can't."

"You *think* you can't, but you can—with me, you can. With me, anything is possible."

He grunts with frustration. "You don't understand."

I'm getting testy. "You owe me one goddamned waterfall, Jonas Faraday. *One waterfall,* that's all I ask." I cross my arms. "This shouldn't be that hard. Any other man would be leaping onto the bed right now with glee. *Juepucha, culo.*"

He opens his mouth to say something, but closes it again. He shifts his weight. He exhales. "If I do this, it's gonna be just this once. And then we're done with bondage bullshit forever."

I'm noncommittal. We'll see.

"Sarah, you don't understand why this is a hot button for me." He rubs his eyes. "Fuck."

The hairs on the back of my neck stand up. Maybe this wasn't such a good idea. "What? Tell me," I say. I'm suddenly unsure.

"Never mind." His jaw is clenched. "I'll do it." He marches over to the bed and sits, his erection belying his internal struggle. "Let's do it."

"Jonas?"

"It's fine," he says. "You want proof you own me, here it is. Let's go. Tie me up and do what you want to me."

I pause, assessing him. This isn't how I envisioned this going. I thought he'd be apprehensive, sure, but he seems downright pissed. "Okay," I finally say slowly, not sure how to navigate this situation. "So what's the safe word?"

"I'm not gonna need a fucking safe word. What could you possibly do to me that I'd need a safe word?"

"We're supposed to have one."

"Who says?"

I throw up my hands. "I don't know—blogs. I've never done this before." I shake my head. "So you're gonna fight me every step of the way? For the love of Pete, you are the worst submissive, ever. You're totally ruining this whole fantasy for me right now. Damn, I was so turned on, too."

He glares at me. "Fine," he concedes, but his eyes remain hard. "We'll have a safe word." He looks up at the ceiling, thinking.

"Plato?"

That brings out a half-smile. His eyes soften. "Fuck no. Don't bring fucking Plato into our bed of bondage. Jesus. Have some respect for the forefather of modern philosophical thought."

I smile at him. "Okay. How about we keep it simple, then. Stop?"

"No. I always tell you to stop when you hijack me, but I never mean it. I can't resist you, you know that." He motions to one of the tethers on the bed. "Case in point."

"Fine. You pick it, then. It can be anything. Cat, dog, watermelon, Pixie Stix, Dumbledore, whatever."

His smile broadens, despite himself. "I really don't think it's necessary." He has a sudden thought. "You're not planning to actually *hurt* me, right? Not for real?"

"Of course, not. I don't fantasize about pain any more than you do. I'm just gonna, you know, get my rocks off by getting you off."

"You're gonna get your rocks off? Who says that? You're so adorable, I swear to God."

"Jonas, this is not going the way I envisioned it at all." I sit next to him on the bed. "I'm trying to bring you to your knees here, make you surrender to me, drive you crazy. And you're not cooperating at all." I pout.

"Baby," he says, putting his arms around me. "Just let me lick your sweet pussy and make you come and I promise on all things holy I'll surrender to you. You're my goddess—I don't need a fucking necktie around my wrist to prove it. Come on, baby." He brushes his hand between my legs. "Your pussy is calling to me like a siren. I can almost taste it now." He gently dips his finger into me and brings his wet finger to his mouth. "Mmm."

I shudder with arousal.

"Let me make up for what I did tonight by getting you off like a freight train." His hand brushes between my legs and his tongue licks my neck. "You're so ready for me, baby, holy shit." His mouth moves to my mine.

I summon every bit of willpower in my body and pull away from him. I stand.

"Goddamnit, Jonas, this whole relationship isn't about what *you* want. Sometimes, it's about what *I* want, too." I feel heat rising in my cheeks. "And I want this."

He's incredulous. "All I ever think about is what you want. Your pleasure is mine. Always." He stands, his face earnest.

"Well, this is the pleasure I want. Just this once." I jut my chin at him. "You lured me up a waterfall with only one way down. So that's what I'm doing to you. This is your waterfall. Are you gonna jump or not?" My crotch is on fire. I'm not going to be able to hold out much longer without saying to hell with it and jumping his bones.

He sighs. "Yes, I'm gonna jump. You know I am. I can't resist you."

"Okay, then. Let's figure out our safe word already. Jeez." I grab my phone off the nightstand and sit down on the edge of the bed again. He sits next to me, looking over my shoulder at the screen. A Google search of "What is a good safe word?" yields instantaneous results. "Oh, brother," I say, shaking my head. "The trusty 'green, yellow, red system.' That's not obvious or anything."

"Ah," Jonas nods. "People are so clever, aren't they?"

I toss my phone onto the nightstand. "Okay, so green is 'full steam ahead.' Yellow is 'I'm not thrilled but don't stop yet.' Red is 'Stop right now, you fucking freak, I'm totally wigging out.'"

He laughs. "You sound like a pro already." He looks around the room with mock concern. "You don't have a big bag of dildos lying around here, do you? This is just gonna be me and you, right—no foreign objects?"

I smirk. "You'll just have to wait and see. You never know what I might do to you."

"Seriously?" He looks genuinely wary.

I roll my eyes. "Jonas, no, not seriously. I'm not gonna shove a giant dildo up your ass or burn you with cigarettes or pee on you. Just lie down on the bed and trust me. Any time you want me to stop, just say red and I will, I promise." I look at him expectantly. "But after I get started, I guarantee you won't want me to stop." I smile.

He sighs. "Sex should be about pleasure. Nothing else. Not pain."

"Duh, Jonas. Big, fat duh. Have some faith, for the love of Pete. Your pleasure is mine, baby. This is all about pleasure—*your* pleasure. This is just gonna be you and me."

He exhales, yet again. "Okay." He scoots to the middle of the bed. "For you."

"Thank you, Baby Jesus!" I raise my hands to the heavens in gratitude. "Okay, starting now, I'm in charge."

"Just be kind, baby. That's all I ask."

"I know of no other way."

Chapter 19

Jonas

"Too tight?" she asks.

I pull on the restraints. "No."

I can't believe I'm letting her do this to me. If she only knew about the last time I was restrained like this, albeit under completely different circumstances, she'd never ask this of me. Fuck. She's the only person I'd ever let do this to me. Fuck. I never should have said yes.

"Are you comfortable?"

"No."

"Let me rephrase. Do you need an adjustment to your physical environment in any way?"

"No."

"You're a terrible submissive, you know that?"

I sigh. "I should hope so."

She pulls out yet another necktie and places it over my eyes.

"No, baby. Please. Seeing you is what turns me on. Your skin. Your eyes. Your hair. Please."

"Shh," she says. "No more talking."

The song on her laptop ends and the sound of rain pelting the windowpane bleeds into the room.

She secures the blindfold. I can't see a fucking thing. I bite my lip. My heart pounds in my chest. My stomach twists. I feel sick. And yet my dick is rock hard. Go figure.

"Yellow," I whisper.

"I haven't even done anything to you yet."

"Just... the whole thing. Sarah, listen."

There's silence.

"I'm listening," she says softly.

I pause. The rain has gathered strength outside the window. "Never mind."

I can't tell her about The Lunacy. Not now, not like this. She knows I'm fucked up, yes, but she doesn't know I'm *that* fucked up. She wouldn't want me if she knew.

"Did Josh leave?" she asks.

"Please don't mention my brother at a time like this—you're gonna make me puke."

"I need to get something from the kitchen and I'm naked, you big dummy."

"Oh my, aren't you the sassy little dominatrix now? Yeah. He went to the airport."

"I'll be right back."

She's gone. I'm alone with the sound of the rain. Why did I let her to do this to me? I'm fucking blindfolded and spread-eagle with a raging hard-on, trussed up like a calf at a rodeo. There is no other woman I'd do this for in the entire galaxy.

She returns. She places something on the nightstand. Sounds like a cup. Or cups. Something rattling around? Ice cubes in a glass.

Music begins playing. The song is "Magic" by Coldplay. Good song. Surely, she's chosen it to send a lyrical message to me.

"Yellow," I whisper, sending a lyrical message right back to her. I'll see her one Coldplay song and raise her another—my favorite one, in fact—the one in which Chris Martin of Coldplay offers up his very lifeblood to the woman he loves. I'd give my blood to Sarah, too, all of it, every last drop—or, as it turns out, let her tie me up. For me, they're one and the same thing.

"Don't use one of the safe words unless you're serious. No crying wolf." There's a beat. "Wait, are you serious?"

"No, I was just commenting on your choice of Coldplay songs—remarking on the one I'd play for you if I were in charge." Oh, how I wish I were untied right now and making love to her to "Yellow." That song would tell her I love her in the way my own mouth can't—and my body would emphatically prove it.

"Jonas." She's annoyed with me. "No talking. And no Boy Who Cried Wolf with the safe words. As your dominatrix, I have to honor the safe words unflinchingly—I take my vows very seriously."

"Your vows?"

"My dominatrix vows."

I can't help but laugh, even in this situation. Sarah can always make me laugh.

"Okay, Mistress, proceed," I say. "I shouldn't have interrupted your brilliant strategy."

"Based on your gigantic hard-on, it doesn't appear you mind my brilliant strategy all that much."

"My dick has a mind of its own. Pay no attention to the man behind the curtain."

She kisses me. "Seriously, are you okay?"

"Will you just take off the blindfold, please? It's making me claustrophobic."

She sighs. "The blog I read says what I'm about to do is most effective when you're blindfolded—it enhances the sensation."

Her voice is so earnest. I can't resist her. "Fine. Do what you will, Mistress. You own me."

She kisses my lips and giggles.

I instinctively reach for her and the restraints tighten around my wrists. My chest constricts. Talk about sense memory. Déjà fucking vu. My mind hurtles back to that night when they first had me tied up like fucking King Kong. A virtual army of orderlies, or whoever the fuck they were, bum rushed me when I started flipping out. They pumped me with so many drugs after that, I don't remember every detail clearly—but I sure as hell remember the restraints around my wrists and ankles—the ones that felt exactly like these—and how I begged and pleaded with them to untie me so I could put an end to my lifelong misery once and for all. For weeks, my wrists bore deep bruises from how violently I'd thrashed against my restraints during that first horrible night of The Lunacy.

The lyrics to "Yellow" float through my mind. Just like the song says, I'd give her every last drop of blood in my body.

Her soft lips are on my neck, my nipples, trailing down to my stomach.

I reach for her and the restraints pull on me again. I inhale deeply, trying to calm myself, but the ties around my wrists keep pulling me back to the dark movie playing inside my head—to the night my mind finally, painfully succumbed to a decade's worth of torment.

An ice cube on my nipple jerks me back to the present. She swirls it around and across my chest and then down to my abs, her warm wet tongue trailing immediately behind the icy wetness like some kind of erotic Zamboni. Soft skin brushes against my erection—her nipple?—as her lips meander their way down my torso. I shudder.

I want to touch her. I need to touch her. I reach out to her yet again and the restraints tug forcefully on my wrists. My stomach twists.

Even as I climbed the stairs after hearing the gunshot coming from his room, I knew whatever awaited me would push my mind over the edge and into the dark abyss. And yet I continued climbing those fucking stairs, one brutal step at a time, slowly, involuntarily, inevitably, to my doom—his room a monstrous magnet and my body a passive slab of steel.

I'd give her every last drop of blood in my body.

"Yellow," I whisper.

"What part? The ice?"

"No. The blindfold. Take it off. Please." My words choke in my throat. I'm dangerously close to thrashing around, but I breathe deeply and control myself.

Her hands touch my face. She removes the blindfold. Her face is awash in disappointment. "I'm sorry," she says. "I just wanted to try something."

I'm being a total pussy-ass right now. She looks so sad. I sigh. "It's okay, baby. Put it back on. Do your thing. I'm sorry."

"No, it's okay. No blindfold. Just keep your eyes closed, okay?"

"Okay."

"Promise?"

"Yes."

"Swear?"

"Yep."

She throws the blindfold onto the floor and I close my eyes.

I feel her rolling to the side of the bed. The song stops.

A new song comes on. Holy fucking Christ, no, no, no—it's fucking One Direction, "What Makes You Beautiful." Just shoot me now and send me to hell with my father where I fucking belong.

My eyes spring open. "No," I shout. "A fate worse than death."

She glares at me. "Close your eyes. You swore."

I comply.

Her lips are in my ear. "This song is intended to punish you for your despicable actions earlier this evening." Her tone is low and even. "You were a very, very bad boy. You lied to me through omission. You didn't trust me. And that opened the door for me to mistrust you—not a good foundation for a healthy relationship, Jonas. And now I'm going to suck your cock to the dulcet sounds of One Direction to teach you a lesson. And as further punishment, from this day forward, whenever you hear this song in a passing car or in a grocery store, you'll instantly get rock hard, remembering what I did to you tonight."

Well, that shuts me the fuck up—along with the voices inside my head, too. All of us—me, myself, and I—instantly give this woman our undivided attention.

She chuckles, clearly amused by herself, and moves away from my ear.

The abominable song blares at me, making my head hurt and my ears bleed. It's a travesty is what it is—a fucking crime against humanity. But then her tongue licks my cock like it's a melting ice cream cone and I don't give a fuck what song is playing. When she takes me into her mouth, it's really, really warm in there—and extra wet—holy fuck, she's got warm liquid in her mouth that she's swirling around my cock, like she's treating it to its own personal Jacuzzi.

I let out a low moan. I wish I could look at her right now, but a promise is a promise.

Her mouth leaves me.

I instinctively reach my hand toward her, willing her to return to me, needing to touch her, and the restraint stops me. Motherfucker.

I'd give her every last drop of blood in my body, if she wanted me to.

When I first beheld the horror he so meticulously staged for me, I gripped my sanity with all my white-knuckled might, determined not to let go of it—determined not to let him win. If only I'd turned around right then and marched out the door, if only I'd turned my back on him and his malice and his hatred and his decade's worth of blame, if only I'd refused to let him have the last word just that one time, maybe I would have been able to hang onto my mind against all odds, even amid that final, horrific opera he'd performed just for me.

But, no, I didn't turn my back on him and I didn't leave the room and I therefore didn't save myself. Instead, I did the worst thing I could have done. I saw the envelope on his desk, his blood splattered across the neat lettering of my name, and I opened it. Even as I did it, I knew opening that envelope would be my last sane act, I fucking knew it—I knew my mind wouldn't be able to withstand his final parting shot to me any more than his brain had withstood the final parting shot from his shotgun—but I opened it anyway.

She takes my cock into her mouth again, but this time her mouth is icy cold wetness. The intense sensation jerks me out of the horror show in my head and puts me back in the room with Sarah. Surprisingly, the change in temperature feels exhilarating—acutely pleasurable. *My Magnificent Sarah.*

The sound that comes out of me is primal.

"You like that?" she asks. Her voice is gravelly and thick with arousal.

"Yes," I say.

For a few blissful moments, her oh so talented mouth makes me forget all about my restraints. Just as I'm about to lose control and release into her mouth, her mouth leaves my cock, her hand grips my shaft, and her naked body writhes against mine.

"I don't want you to come," she says, panting, her lips touching my ear. "Your job is to stay hard for me. You understand?"

"Yes," I choke out.

"If you're in danger of coming, you're required to tell me so. You can say 'I'm gonna come' all you like, but if you really are gonna cross the line, you'll say 'limit' so I know."

I nod.

I hear the sound of movement at the nightstand.

I shiver with anticipation.

Her face is next to mine again. I smell the unmistakable scent of Altoids mints. Her tongue laps at my lips for one tantalizing second. "I'm going to make your cock feel minty fresh," she says. Her voice is husky.

She takes me into her mouth again. And damn, yes, minty fresh is right.

I'd give anything to see her brown eyes looking up at me from down there, but, fuck me, I promised to keep my eyes closed. I try to imagine what she must look like right now—try to imagine her big brown eyes blazing up at me—but the thought is such a turn on, I have to stop thinking about it or else I'll come like a motherfucker into her mouth. She sucks on my tip gently with just the right amount of pressure and I jerk violently.

"Limit." Holy fuck. "Limit."

Her mouth leaves my cock and finds my belly button. Her lips are warm.

She's moaning, shuddering. This is turning her on as much as me. She crawls on top of me and places my tip at her wet entrance. I jerk my pelvis up, trying to enter her, but she tilts away. I'm a caged lion swatting at a hunk of raw meat that's being pulled on a string just out of my reach. And all the while, that fucking One Direction song tortures me.

I want to reach out and touch her hair. I want to touch her sweet wet pussy and make her come. I want to hold her, cradle her, lick her, fuck her without mercy. I want to make her scream my name.

One Direction, thankfully, stops.

"You can open your eyes now." Her voice is dripping with her arousal.

I open my eyes. Oh God, I could come at the mere sight of her if I let myself. Her cheeks are flushed. Her eyes are wild. A sheen of perspiration covers her face. She's in ecstasy and I haven't even touched her. She's beautiful.

"Limit," I whisper, looking into her eyes.

She moves to put on another song. "Do I Wanna Know?" by the Arctic Monkeys. Yet another reason to love this woman.

She straddles my lap, teasing me yet again, writhing, and bends over to kiss my mouth.

"You're going to lick me now," she says.

"Untie me."

"No."

"Untie me."

"Just give it a chance. Trust me." She flashes her most seductive smile.

"I'm not going to lick your pussy with these restraints on. You're my religion and licking your pussy is going to church."

She doesn't understand. "Trust me, Jonas."

"Red."

She opens her mouth, shocked.

"Red," I say again.

Her shoulders slump.

"You want me to inhabit heaven and hell at the same time. It's not possible. I choose heaven."

Her face droops.

She silently unties my wrists, defeated.

I rub my wrists and sit up to untie my ankles.

When I'm freed of my restraints, I lie back down on the bed in the same exact position I was in a moment ago—my arms outstretched, my legs spread-eagle.

I'm giving her my blood.

"I'm a free man now, baby—and your slave by choice. Do whatever you were about to do and I won't move a muscle. You own me."

She pouts. "Obviously not."

"Come on, baby, my devotion binds me ten times more fiercely than any physical restraint ever could."

She continues pouting.

"I'm in the same position I was in when forcibly bound—but now I'm willingly bound. I'm your voluntary slave. Come on. You own me."

She doesn't move. The look on her face grabs my heart and squeezes it.

"Green," I whisper softly. "Come on."

She looks crestfallen.

"Green, green, green," I say. "Green?"

Her eyes perk up a little bit.

"Green, green, green, green, green, green, green. Full steam ahead. I'm at your mercy, pretty baby."

Her mouth twists into a half-smile, but she doesn't move.

"Come on, baby. You're my religion. Licking your pussy is going to church. And your name's my sacred prayer. *Sarah*."

Her eyes ignite.

"Green," I whisper. "Come on, pretty baby."

She nods.

She maneuvers her body up to my face and places her knees on either side of my head. Slowly, delicately, she lowers herself onto me and sits on my face. With a loud and grateful groan, I begin licking her. Oh thank you, Lord in heaven above, yes, I lick her. Halle-fucking-lujah. It takes every ounce of self-restraint not to grab her ass, but I stay true to my word and keep my arms out to my sides like I'm on the cross. And, in a sense, I suppose, I am.

She gyrates and jerks her pelvis, moaning and groaning as she does, her excitement quickly escalating into powerful thrusts and high-pitched shrieks. Just as her entire body begins to shake, she swivels completely around, panting and sweaty, bends over my torso, and takes my cock into her mouth as I continue eating her glorious pussy.

My Magnificent Sarah, hallowed be thy name, thy kingdom come, thy will be done, on earth as it is in heaven. She's a church hymn, howling at the top of her lungs. With one final, insistent shriek, her body ripples and seizes into my tongue. I yank my cock out of her mouth to avoid her soon-to-be clenched jaw.

When I feel her climax ebb and her body go limp, I leap up, growling like a silverback, and toss her onto the bed. In one fluid motion, I bend her compliant body over the edge of the bed, plunge myself into her wetness, and fuck her without mercy until she screams my fucking name. *For thine is the kingdom, the power, and the glory, for ever and ever. Amen.*

Chapter 20

Sarah

He "safe worded" me and then fucked my brains out. What the hell? And now he's gone mute. We're both just lying here in bed together, one blink away from mutual catatonia, not speaking. I look over at him. Yeah, he's awake. I feel like he owes me an explanation. But based on his silence, I guess he disagrees.

Why exactly did he feel the need to use the safe word with me at that particular moment? I realize he's fucked up, and understandably so, given what he witnessed as a boy, but how could he put on the brakes *right then*? True, I can't imagine what kind of crazy he must battle on a daily basis after seeing what he saw, but I wasn't raping him, for Pete's sake—far from it. Even when I had him bound and tethered and at my utter mercy, my only impulse was to give him as much pleasure as I could muster—and not just any kind of pleasure, but the exact pleasure he always says he craves the most. So why on earth did he need the safe word *right then*?

I wanted so badly to give him a special gift tonight—a new kind of bondage memory to replace the one that's tortuously engrained in his gray matter. And, really, childhood trauma or not, would it have killed him to just let me take the driver's seat in our sex life, just this once? Why can't he just trust me and let go? I've had some childhood traumas of my own, thank you very much, but with each magical day and night we've shared, I'm somehow managing to conquer them.

"Hey, have you actually written that report, or were you bluffing?" he finally says.

This is what he wants to talk about right now? The Club? That's the last thing on my mind.

"What do you think?"

"I think you were bluffing."

"You've been with me twenty-four seven from the minute I

found out the truth. When the heck would I have had time to write a detailed report? I haven't had time to paint my nails let alone write a report like that." It's not my intention, but that last part came out sounding kinda bitchy.

"Are you mad at me?"

I turn on my side to look at him. "No."

"Because you sound kind of pissed."

I take a deep breath and gather my thoughts. He looks at me expectantly.

"No, I'm not mad. I'm just totally freaking out."

His face turns ashen. "About what?"

"Jonas, I haven't studied in a whole week." Tears well up in my eyes, despite my best efforts to hold them back. "So much is riding on my grades and all I've been doing for a solid week is playing sex kitten with you. I've got to study, Jonas. I've got to focus and get some order back into my life and remember why I went to law school in the first place—" The tears break free and drop out of my eyes. "I've got a lot of people depending on me." Oh God, I'm a hot mess. "And now, thanks to my big mouth, I've got to write a damned *Pelican Brief* as soon as possible, too."

He wraps his arms around me. "Baby, don't you realize there's nothing riding on your grades anymore?" He kisses my cheek and wipes my tears with his thumb.

I pull back to look into his face. I don't understand what he means. The top ten students at the end of the first year get a full-ride scholarship for the next two years, which means students eleven and below are shit out of luck to the tune of some sixty-five thousand dollars. This is my ticket to do whatever I want after graduation, including taking a job that pays peanuts but makes me genuinely happy. We're talking about me trying to win life-changing money here, and all I have to do is study my ass off for one short year of my life. And yet, in the home stretch right before finals, here I am playing sex addict night and day with Jonas. I need to get a grip and refocus my priorities.

He rolls his eyes like I'm a silly little girl. "If you get the scholarship, great. That'll be a fantastic accomplishment and we'll celebrate. But if not, I'll pick up the tab. How much could law school tuition possibly be—fifty grand a year? So we're talking maybe a hundred grand total? No big deal. Just consider yourself the lucky recipient of the Jonas Faraday Scholarship Fund." He beams a huge smile at me.

I can't even believe what I'm hearing. *The lucky recipient?* He expects me to hinge my entire future on his fickle beneficence? On a spur of the moment reassurance made in bed? I'm the *lucky recipient,* he says? Well, I've got news for him—I'm not going to pin my entire future on luck—or on his charity, for that matter.

He smiles at me. "Problem solved. The only thing you have to worry about is passing the bar exam at the end of year three. Between now and then, just go to class and do your best, but don't stress it." He touches my face. "I'm sure we'll figure out something you can do with all your newfound free time."

I stare at him, my mouth agape.

"Okay. What else are you freaking out about? Tee it up and I'll knock it out of the park for you, baby."

I sit up in the bed. I can't even muster a response.

"Come on. Whatever it is, I'll fix it for you."

"You really expect me to let you pay my tuition?"

He shrugs. "Yeah."

"I didn't want to accept a laptop from you and now I'm supposed to accept two years worth of law school tuition?"

He smiles broadly. Apparently, that's a yes.

"And you expect me to just sit back and *chillax* about it, as if you paying my tuition six months from now is some sort of foregone conclusion? Like your pillow talk today is an ironclad promise tomorrow?"

His smile vanishes. The playful sparkle drains from his eyes. "What I'm saying to you isn't pillow talk." Oh man, he's pissed.

"You didn't trust me enough to tell me about Stacy tonight, you won't talk to me about the 'hell' I apparently forced you to endure tonight—your word, not mine—and yet I'm supposed to put my entire future in your hands and just believe on faith that six months from now, come what may between us, you'll still be in the generous mood to write that tuition check for me?" Oh, good Lord, I'm shouting. I can't stop the torrent flowing out of me. "What if you get bored with me between now and then—where would that leave me? What if, God forbid, I push just a little too hard, ask just a little too much of the Emotionally Scarred Adonis and scare you away? Hmm? What then? Would you come back to write my tuition check then?"

He looks like I just stabbed him in the heart. He opens his mouth but closes it again. Oh holy hell. The look in his eyes is unadulterated pain. And yet, for some reason, I blaze right ahead.

"You want me to put every single one of my eggs into the basket of a man who likens his feelings for me to a serious mental disease? To *insanity*? Yeah, that sure makes a girl feel über confident about having a long and secure future with a guy." Holy shit, I can't believe I just said that. Up until this very second, I thought I was perfectly fine with our coded language of love.

His face contorts. He shakes his head, but he doesn't speak. His eyes are moist.

"I'm losing myself, Jonas. I just have to get back to standing on my own two feet."

"Why?"

"Why? *Why*?" I open and close my mouth several times, flummoxed. "Why do I have to breathe? Or eat? It's fundamental."

"No, it's not. You don't *have* to stand on your own two feet. Not all the time. When you can't, or even if you just don't want to sometimes, then I'll carry you. I *want* to carry you."

No one has ever said anything like this to me before. Not even close.

"*Estamos de luna de miel,*" he says softly in his horrible Americano accent. *We're on our honeymoon.* He looks at me hopefully.

For some reason, that phrase doesn't make me swoon the way it did the first time he said it to me.

"Except we're not really, are we?" I spit out. "This could all be over next week and where would that leave me? I can't rely on this and let everything I've worked for slip away."

Oh good Lord, whatever knife I stabbed him with a minute ago, I just turned it.

I soften. "I know I'll never be able to understand what you went through as a child," I say. I inhale and exhale slowly, trying to regain control of my voice. "I'll never be able to fully understand why tonight felt like 'hell' for you—but, Jonas, I *want* to understand." My lip is trembling. "I just wanted to replace your bad childhood memories with good adult ones. I wanted to give you pleasure—to try to heal you. And you wouldn't trust me enough to let me try. I'm tired of everything being the Jonas Faraday Club all the time. I just wanted you to join the Sarah Cruz Club for a change."

"This is all because I wouldn't stay tied up while I ate you out?" He's utterly pained.

"No, Jonas. You're so clueless sometimes. Forget about that. Tonight just made me realize how much you're holding back and I'm not."

"Everyone holds back, sometimes."

"I'm not holding back at all."

"You're not holding back at all?" he asks, incredulous.

"Not at all," I say. And it's true, other than the fact that I have to bite my tongue every five minutes to keep myself from blurting, "I love you!" at the top of my lungs. But that can't be helped.

He stares at me, daring me to confess some deep, dark secret I'm keeping from him—as if he's hoping to prove my fuckeduppedness matches his own.

"Well, okay, one thing," I confess.

His face lights up with anticipatory vindication.

"I secretly like that One Direction song."

He laughs, despite the pained look in his eyes.

"A lot," I add. I put my hands over my face. I can't stop the tears from coming.

"Sarah, what's going on?" He puts his arm around me. "Please, please, don't let this be the part where you say I don't 'let you in.'" His face is awash in anxiety. "Please don't say I'm just too fucked up for you." He's holding back tears.

I touch his beautiful face. "No, Jonas. It's just the opposite. You can never be too fucked up for me, don't you understand? That's what I'm trying to tell you. You can never, ever be too fucked up for me, no matter what's hiding deep down inside of you—so stop being afraid to show me everything. I'm telling you to let your freak flag fly loud and proud. I'm telling you I won't run away. I won't reject you. You can trust me." Tears pour out of my eyes. I'm in danger of losing myself to a *bona fide* ugly cry.

His relief is palpable. He kisses me. "Don't leave me."

I snort. "I'm not going anywhere. You're the one who's the flight risk."

His lips are on mine. His tongue is in my mouth. Even if my brain wanted to leave this man, my body would stage a coup. Tears blur my eyes and run down my cheeks. "I just don't understand why you hold back like you do. I'm giving you everything, Jonas. I want the same from you."

"I can't," he whispers.

"Yes, you can."

He shakes his head. "This is all because I wouldn't stay tied up? I don't understand—what happened after you untied me was incredible."

"It's a *metaphor*, Jonas. Come on. I know how you love your metaphors."

"I know it was a metaphor. I'm not stupid. But maybe we enacted a different and even better metaphor than the one you were going for. Sometimes, the best things are unplanned."

"No, I'm pretty sure a better metaphor is not what just

happened—I want *my* metaphor, Jonas, and what I just discovered is that it's just not possible for you." I huff out an exasperated puff of air. "You ready for another Plato quote, hmm? I've become somewhat of a Plato aficionado lately."

His gaze is steady.

"'You can discover more about a person in an hour of play than in a year of conversation.'"

He squints at me.

"And I just discovered a lot."

He glares at me.

"You don't like having Plato used against you?"

Oh boy, he's not happy with me.

"I wanted you to take a leap of faith the way I did when I jumped thirty feet into blackness. And you couldn't do it. Clearly."

He smashes his lips together. "You don't understand."

"Only because you won't explain it to me!"

He's about to lose it. "Why are you doing this? Who cares *why* I didn't want to be tied up. You untied me and we moved forward and it was fucking amazing. We don't have to talk about every goddamned thing we *feel* all the time, do we?"

"Jonas," I sigh. "I know you're not familiar with the practice, but what we're doing right now is this really weird thing adults do sometimes. It's called talking about our feelings. It's okay. We'll survive it, I promise." What was that psychobabble quote Josh used when they disagreed the other day? Oh yes. "*Talking* about it doesn't mean we're *disagreeing*."

"Oh good God, please don't say that. You know not what you do."

I smile and touch his cheek.

He rubs his eyes. "You just don't understand."

"Then tell me."

He's silent.

"This whole time, you've been acting like you're some Kung Fu master and I'm your little Grasshopper in desperate need of enlightenment. But, ironically, here we are: I've surrendered to you mind, body and soul—in every way a woman can surrender to a man, sometimes against my natural instincts—and it's *you* who's holding back on *me*. I can *feel* it. And the closer and closer I feel to you, the more my heart opens and opens and bleeds—the more I start to *need* you—it scares me. It's just starting to feel like there's this gaping void between us that's eventually going to swallow me up and crush my heart into a million tiny pieces."

I'm panting. That speech took a lot out of me.

He rubs his hands over his face. "I told Josh I'm quitting Faraday & Sons. I told him right before I came into the bedroom."

"Oh, Jonas, that's amazing news." I don't understand the connection between this revelation and what we've been talking about, but I'm sure it's coming. I wait.

He waits a long beat and finally speaks again. "I can finally envision the life I want. I see it. I finally know exactly what it looks like."

"That's so good."

"For the first time in my life, I can finally, clearly visualize the divine original form of Jonas Faraday. I've tried to visualize the divine original of myself for so long, Sarah, and I couldn't see him. Or, on my best days, I could sort of see him—but he was blurry or dark or flickering in and out. But now, he's finally crystal clear."

I wait, my pulse pounding in my ears.

His breathing is shaky. "I can see him right in front of me, Sarah." He swallows hard. "He's standing next to you, holding your hand."

My heart leaps. Oh. My. God.

"I can finally see him because you grabbed his hand and guided him into the light."

There are no words.

He stifles a soft yelping noise. "Every heart sings a song, incomplete, until another heart whispers back." His voice brims with emotion. "My song is now complete."

Oh, holy Baby Jesus in a manger.

The time for thinking is done. My brain can go to hell. My body wants to go to heaven. I grab his face and kiss him deeply and then make love to him tenderly until we both fall soundly asleep in each other's arms.

Chapter 21

Jonas

I sit at the kitchen table drafting the press release announcing my departure from Faraday & Sons. Each word I type brings me closer to the man I'm meant to be—the divine original form of Jonas Faraday. Genuine happiness is within my grasp.

Sarah enters the kitchen. She's showered and dressed and ready to kick some ass, as usual. She's got her laptop tucked under her arm and a book bag over her shoulder.

"Good morning, beautiful. Can I make you an omelet?"

"We need to talk," she says.

Not my favorite phrase. No pleasant conversation with any woman throughout history has ever started with those words.

"You wanna talk about your Maltese Kiki?" I ask hopefully.

"No," she answers, unsmiling. She sits down at the table.

I'm filled with unease. My stomach flip-flops.

"I need to stay at my place for a few days, just so I can study and get back on track—"

"No fucking way."

"Excuse me?" she says, her cheeks instantly turning red.

"No fucking way. First of all, I want you here with me, as you know, so I can ravage you at a moment's notice, any time of day. But second of all, and more importantly, it's not safe. I don't want you to be alone for a single minute until we hear from The Club and get a read on how this is whole thing's gonna shake out."

"Well, that's just crazy. What if we never hear from them? What if they trashed my place and took my computer and that's the last we're ever gonna hear from them?"

"I highly doubt it."

"I have a hunch you're wrong."

I let out a long, controlled exhale. This woman is such a pain in the ass, I swear to God. "Let's just say for the sake of argument your hunch is right and we don't hear from them. You're comfortable relying on their silence as some sort of tacit truce? You'll be able to sleep at night—no looking over your shoulder, no wondering if they're coming for you?"

She purses her lips, giving the matter due consideration.

"And what happened to defending all the poor saps who joined The Club looking for true love?"

"I've been thinking a lot about that, during the approximately seven minutes I haven't been having sex with you since we got back from our trip."

I laugh.

"I think I might have been naïve about that. Maybe that software engineer guy was the exception, not the rule, and the vast majority of guys who join The Club want to ride a Mickey Mouse roller coaster, just like Josh said. Maybe they don't care, or even want to know, how The Club supplies the fantasy."

I blink fast a couple times, trying to process what she's saying. "So you're saying if they were to leave you alone, you'd really just leave them alone? Live and let live?"

She shrugs. "Yeah, I think the message I gave to Stacy was honest—if they leave me alone, I'll leave them alone. The only part I lied about was having that report. Oh, and mentioning the Secret Service, too, that was just a total bluff. I've never seen their membership roster."

"Utter brilliance."

"Thank you." She sighs. "But, yeah, I've thought about it, and I'm not sure I care enough to make this the center of my universe. I've got a life to live—things I care a helluva lot more about than taking down a prostitution ring. And, anyway, if ninety-nine percent of The Club's members wouldn't want to know the truth, who am I to ruin the fantasy for them?"

I stare at her for a long time. "Wow. I never thought I'd see the day."

"What?"

"Your Hallmark-Lifetime brainwashing has finally succumbed to cynicism and realism. So you don't believe in fairytales anymore?"

"Oh, I still believe in fairytales, now more than ever." She levels a smoldering gaze at me that makes my heart explode. "It's just that I realized something really important about fairytales."

I wait.

"You can't take them for granted. They're precious. Rare. If you're one of the lucky few who gets to live a fairytale, you best spend your time and energy cherishing it, reveling in it, holding onto it—as opposed to, say, running around trying to take down an Internet sex club." She gives me a look that makes me want to drop to my knees.

My heart is an old, stiff sponge, long neglected on a sink ledge, and it's just been dunked into a warm bucket of water. I get up from the table and walk toward her, my heart-sponge absorbing and enlarging and dripping its bounty with each step. I take her in my arms and kiss every inch of her face and she trembles with the pleasure of it. I take her face in my hands and kiss her mouth and she audibly swoons.

This is one of the top ten moments of my entire life. My baby just called me her Prince Charming.

She traces my lips with her fingertip and then kisses me softly.

It takes a moment before my vocal chords work again. "But what if my gut is right, Sarah? What if they're coming for you?"

"I guess I'll just have to take my chances."

I hug her to me. "I'm not willing to do that. I've got to do whatever's necessary to keep you safe."

She exhales. "What are you gonna do, huh? Go to class with me every day for the next two years, just in case?"

"If necessary, yes."

"Well that's not creepy-intense or anything."

We stare at each other, at an impasse.

"Jonas," she says. "Sweet Jonas. I'm going crazy. I haven't had a minute to myself. I have to study. I have to concentrate. I need to get my hair trimmed. I need to go to yoga. And maybe a facial would be nice, too."

I smile.

"I just need a little space. This has all happened so fast—and, baby, you're really *intense,* no offense—I just need a little elbow room."

"Wait a minute—I'm *intense*?" I glare at her with my best Charles Manson eyes.

She laughs. "I need time to study. Remember all that delicious anticipation before Belize? It was hot. Time apart can be a very good thing."

I grab her hand and pull her back to the kitchen table. She sits on my lap.

"Listen to me. If it weren't for this whole thing with The Club, I'd be semi-normal about time apart. You need time to study? Okay. You want to go to yoga and hang out with Kat? Whatever. I like my alone time, too, believe it or not. All of that's normal. But put that shit aside. These aren't normal circumstances, okay? *It's not safe.* I don't want you to be alone until we have a definitive end to all this. That guy who followed you to your class and then showed up at the library wasn't there to sell you Girl Scout cookies."

She rolls her eyes.

"What? Why did you do that?"

"Do what?"

"Roll your eyes."

She doesn't reply.

"What?"

She's quiet.

"You don't believe I saw him?"

She's still quiet.

"You think I just *hallucinated* him?"

She flashes me an if-the-shoe-fits look.

"You think I'm crazy?" I ask softly, the hairs on my arms standing on end. My stomach twists even as I say those words.

"No, I don't think you're crazy, you big dummy. I think you're overprotective and hypersensitive in this particular circumstance, given what you've been through in your life. I think your mind is playing tricks on you."

"Are you fucking kidding me right now?" I make a sound somewhere between a grunt and a howl. "I can take that shit from Josh, but not from you. I thought you understood what I'm trying to do here—I thought we were on the same page."

She laughs. "It's kinda hard to be on the same page when you don't share your strategy with me."

I make an exasperated sound. "Would you just let it rest already with that? Jesus. It was a good strategy and I was just trying to protect you. I thought you might try to hijack things—which you *did,* by the way."

"And thank God I did. From where I was standing, your strategy looked pretty effing lame."

"How would you know? You were peeking through a window. And for your information, it was an excellent strategy. Stacy was just about to give me her boss's email address when you barged in."

"Oh, really?"

"Yes, really. And then you waltzed in and... yes, you made my strategy look like child's play compared to yours because you're a fucking genius—damn, baby, you were magnificent, you know that? So sexy. You slayed me." I shake it off. "But the point is I was just about to get the information I wanted when you came in and—surprise, surprise—hijacked everything with your never-ending bossiness."

"You are so fucking hot, do you know that, Jonas Faraday?"

My cock tingles.

She smiles at me. "Tell me everything Stacy said before I came in."

I tell her every last thing I can remember from our conversation.

Sarah's wheels are turning. God help us all, she's *thinking.*

"Well, then," she finally says. "It's obvious what we need to do. Let's go talk to Oksana the Ukrainian in Las Vegas. I'm not gonna just sit around, letting my boyfriend follow me to law school every day, waiting for The Club to contact me. I'm gonna write a kick-ass report that'll scare the bajeezus out of them and then I'm gonna hand-deliver it to Oksana the Ukrainian Pimpstress personally. Big risk, big reward, right, Jonas? Isn't that what Professor Faraday preached to my contracts class?"

"In *business*, Sarah. Not with you. I can't afford to take any risk, big or small, when it comes to you."

"Well, I can and will and you can't stop me." She smiles like she's a kid taunting me on a playground. "It's a free country," she adds, just for good measure. "And anyway, don't you have plenty of stuff to do? Like quitting your big, important mogul-job or running your new gyms or getting that flabby body of yours into shape or climbing a rock?"

I sigh. "I don't even have an address for Oksana. Stacy said she's just got a P.O. box. I was just about to get Oksana's email address, but thanks to my bossy girlfriend's impeccable timing, we've got no way to contact her."

"Oh, Silly Rabbit, Trix are for kids. We've already got everything we need to find Oksana."

"We do?"

"Of course, we do, rookie. Leave it to me." She looks at her watch. "And in the meantime, I've got a constitutional law class to attend—*alone*." She gets up from the table. "Oh, and by the way, to keep you company over the next couple days of our Delicious Anticipation 2.0, I made you a playlist—a little mix tape, from me to you." She tosses a flash drive onto the table. "Tit for tat, baby." She winks and turns toward the front door.

"Sarah."

She stops and faces me.

"Sorry to make you waste such a witty exit—'tit for tat, baby'—mmm, it was sassy, clever, and flirty—everything I adore about you—the American judge rates it a perfect ten—but you can forget about walking out that door by yourself. No fucking way."

She groans and sits back down at the table. She opens her laptop.

"What are you doing?"

"Saving my sanity." She clicks into her emails. "I'm gonna lob a Hail Mary." She squints at her screen and begins typing. "Member Services at the club dot com," she says as she types. "That's the only email address I've got for them."

"What email address did they use to send applications to you?"

"All applications and intake reports were delivered back and forth through a drop box." She twists her mouth thinking for a moment. "Maybe your hacker could try to trace that?"

"Good idea. I don't really know how that works."

"Neither do I, but let's ask him."

"Okay."

She looks back at her screen. "I'll keep my email pretty vague—you never know who's going to be on the receiving end of it or whether it might be confiscated down the line by authorities one day. Although, come to think of it, I'm already probably screwed if that ever happens." She sighs. "I'll just keep my cards close to my vest and say just enough to entice them to contact me." She types, rapidly mouthing the words as she goes. "There. I told them I have something urgent to talk to them about—something they're definitely going to want to hear—and to please contact me right away." She clicks her tongue. "Okay. Plan A is to locate Oksana and scare the bajeezus out of her, face-to-face—never underestimate the power of in-person communication. But in the meantime, I'll send this email and cross my fingers they reply. I'm not gonna just sit around and hope something happens—I'm gonna *make* it happen."

"Shocker."

She shrugs. "I've got to do something, Jonas. If every day for the next two years is gonna be Take Your Hot Boyfriend to Class Day, I'm gonna have a frickin' nervous breakdown."

Chapter 22
Sarah

"Can't you maybe just sit in the back of the class and pretend you don't know me? Or at least try not to be so Jonas-y?"

"What does that even mean?"

"It means you don't exactly *blend*."

"Really? You really want me to sit in the back of the class?"

"Yeah, I really do. This is just so totally weird. I won't be able to concentrate on what the professor says if you're sitting next to me making me all hot and bothered. And I guarantee half the class won't be able to concentrate, either. You're just so... Jonas-y."

"Stop saying that. I have no idea what you're talking about."

"False modesty doesn't become you."

He rolls his eyes. "Okay, I'll sit in the back when class starts, okay? I've got plenty to do on my laptop, anyway—some numbers to crunch about the various gym locations. But am I allowed to sit here with you until class starts?"

I look at my watch. "Yeah. We've still got plenty of time. But when the classroom starts to fill up, you best scoot your delectable ass to the back, big boy."

He pouts. "Okay."

"Aw, poor Jonas with the sad eyes."

"I'll survive."

"You know, you could hire a professional bodyguard for me if you're really this worried. Problem solved. Then you could live your life again, and I could live mine, and we could attack each other like animals at home all night long like a normal couple."

"I like hearing you say that."

"Attack each other like animals?" I shoot him a wicked grin.

"Well, yes. But that's not what I meant." He smiles.

"Like a normal couple?"

"No—and, by the way, I don't think most normal couples attack each other like animals."

I try to remember what I just said. "All night long." I smile broadly.

"Nope."

I'm stumped. What else did I say?

"*Home.*" He smiles shyly. Fourth grader Jonas has made yet another appearance on the playground. "I like hearing you call my house your home."

We share a googly-eyed, infatuated smile.

"You're a diehard romantic, you know that?" I say.

"Shh. Not so loud."

"Mum's the word."

He pauses. "So you'd be okay with me hiring a bodyguard for you?"

"No, I'd be mortified. But I bet I could give a bodyguard the slip way easier than I could ditch your paranoid ass—I sure ditched Josh in record time."

"Okay, so much for that idea. Speaking of which, have you spoken to Kat? How's the bodyguard working out for her?"

"It seems her bodyguard is extremely attentive."

He rolls his eyes. "You're telling me I'm paying some guy to screw Kat?"

"Ew, Jonas, no. They're not having sex. Give Kat some credit."

He smirks at me.

"Well, okay, yes. She'd probably have sex with him, but the guy's a professional. Sex with the client is against the Bodyguard Code, isn't it? At least that's what Kevin Costner said in the movie."

"Yeah, right before he slept with Whitney Houston."

"Oh yeah, I forgot about that part. But, anyway, never mind. All I meant was the guy's not at all bummed about his assignment." I laugh. "He should just get in line—it's the way everyone reacts to Kat."

He laughs. "Yeah, Josh was pretty intrigued."

"Really? Aw."

"What did Kat think of Josh?"

"She thought he was... a little Douche-y McDouchey-pants, to be honest."

Jonas looks disappointed.

"Sorry. I think it was the Mickey Mouse roller coaster thing that rubbed her the wrong way."

"No doubt."

"But I reminded her that you were a cocky-asshole-motherfucker when I first met you, so you never know."

"Aw, how sweet."

"So how long are you planning to keep paying that guy to watch Kat, anyway?"

"I don't know. I hadn't given it much thought. However long it's necessary, I guess."

I consider his beautiful face for a moment, the earnest expression on it. The kindness in his eyes. "You're so thoughtful, you know that? You say you're not a natural to wear a red cape, but I think you sell yourself short."

He twists his mouth. "Thank you." He blushes.

Oh good Lord, this boy slays me.

We stare at each other for a long beat. I don't know what he's thinking, but I'm sure as hell thinking, *I love you.*

"If you were Josh, I'd have to slap my face right now," he finally says.

"What?" I laugh.

"Never mind."

I look at my watch. Twelve minutes before the start of class. I'd better get my head in the game.

"Okay, chitchat time over," I bark. "I've gotta get crunked."

He laughs. "Do your thing, baby."

I go through my pre-class ritual. I put a bottle of water on my desk. I open my laptop and open a new blank document. I pull out my textbook, a spiral notebook, and a ballpoint pen from my book bag. (In case anything goes wrong with my computer, I always like to have a good old-fashioned pen and paper handy during class.) I begin writing today's date at the top of my notebook page, but my ballpoint pen doesn't work. Dang it. I rummage into my purse for another one... and discover an envelope. I pull it out, perplexed. Where did this come from? I open it. Inside, there's a check made payable to me in the amount of two hundred fifty thousand dollars from one Jonas P. Faraday. I can't breathe. I keep looking from "Sarah Cruz" to "two hundred fifty thousand dollars and no cents." My brain can't process what my eyes are seeing.

My head swivels to look at Jonas.

He's engrossed in something on his laptop, totally oblivious to what I'm holding in my hand.

"Jonas." I hold up the check with a shaky hand.

He glances over at me. His cheeks burst with sudden color.

"Jonas," I say again. "I can't. What . . .?"

I've never held this much money in my hand in all my life. I'm trembling. I can't believe he did this.

"I didn't intend for you to find that right now," he says.

"Jonas," I say yet again, my vocabulary apparently having been reduced to the developmental level of a toddler's. "No." I can't accept this from him—but I'm electrified that he wanted to do it for me.

"Let me explain my thinking on this," he begins.

"I couldn't possibly accept—"

"Just hear me out, Sarah."

My mouth hangs open. This is crazy.

"You were right. Anything could happen in the next six months. You could decide I'm too fucked up for you, after all. You could get bored with me. You could decide I don't give you enough space... or that I'm not able to express my feelings the way you need me to... Or that I'm too intense." He swallows hard. "Anything could happen. But no matter what might happen between us, I want to make your dreams come true, regardless—even if it turns out I'm not destined to be a part of them.

"So this money is yours, Sarah, whether or not you wind up winning that scholarship, whether or not you wind up wanting to be with me. Put it in your bank account. It's yours from this moment forward, no strings attached. If you get the scholarship and don't need the money for school, then use it for something else that will make your life easier. Donate it to your mom's charity, whatever. But if you don't get the scholarship, then use it to pay for your schooling. Given who you are and what you plan to do when you graduate, this money will ultimately wind up making the world a better place, either way."

I burst into tears.

"Don't cry. I did it to make you smile—not to make you *cry.*"

I can't speak. I'm too overwhelmed with emotion.

"Oh, baby, don't cry."

It's several minutes before I can carry on a coherent conversation.

"But why so much?" I ask. "It's so much money, Jonas—too much. Even if I were going to accept tuition from you, which I'm not saying I'm going to do, I could never, ever accept this. This is crazy."

"Well, now, think about it for a minute. You've got student loans for this first year, right?"

I nod.

"And then you've got tuition for years two and three, if the scholarship doesn't pan out. Plus, you'll have to pay taxes on the money—and trust me, taxes are a bitch. You'll be shocked about how much of this will go to Uncle Sam."

I wipe my eyes, shaking.

"It's really not an excessive amount, considering all that."

I'm speechless.

He reaches over to me and strokes a lock of my hair. "I didn't pick that amount at random, Sarah." He flashes me mournful eyes. "It's my penance."

I shake my head. He owes me nothing—least of all penance. When I whispered into his ear about his "penance" last night in bed, I was just being naughty. This man owes no penance to anyone, least of all to me.

"I'm ashamed I was willing to pay that ridiculous sum to feed my demons. Maybe this small gesture will help balance out my karmic ledger somehow. Or, at least, help me clear my conscience."

Tears gush out of my eyes.

"Good actions give strength to ourselves and inspire good actions in others," he says.

I grin through my tears. "Plato?"

"Plato."

I take a deep, shaky, tearful breath. "Thank you so much, Jonas. There are no words to describe how grateful I am. You're a beautiful person, inside and out. But—"

"No but. Please. Just say yes. Just once in your goddamned life do what I want you to do, woman." His voice is tender. "Please. I beg you, don't be a pain in the ass this time. I need to do this."

I'm gaping like a fish on a line. This money would change my life, there's no question about it. But it's just too much to accept. I look into his eyes, perhaps searching for a sign—something to guide me in my decision-making—and I see love in his eyes. Pure, unadulterated and unconditional love.

"Jonas," I whisper, my head swirling.

"Sarah, I *insist*," he says, softly. And then he graces me with his most dazzling Jonas Faraday smile.

I laugh despite my tears. What mortal could possibly resist this man?

"Oh, well, if you *insist,*" I say.

He smiles.

I shake my head. "Just give me tonight to sleep on it," I say. I put the check back into my purse. "It's just so much money." I put my hand on his cheek. "My sweet Jonas."

I lean forward to kiss him. His lips are magical. I love him with all my heart and soul. I don't know what secrets and pain he continues to harbor deep inside himself, and I don't care—whatever it is, we'll excavate it together. However long it takes, however slowly he needs to go, we'll take it one step at a time. We've got all the time in the world, after all. I'm not going anywhere. I wipe my eyes and my fingers come away blackened with mascara.

"Oh, jeez," I say. "Tell me the truth—does my face looks like the BP oil spill right now?"

He laughs. "No, not at all. You look beautiful."

"I'll be right back." I stand.

Jonas stands, too. "I'll come with you."

"Oh my God, Jonas. The restroom is literally right outside the door—right on the other side of the hallway. Relax. I'll pop in there, pee really fast, wash my face, blow my nose, and come right back here in record time. I promise. I'll be greased lightning. Sit down." I grab my purse, just in case I want to reapply a little mascara after I clean myself up.

He vacillates.

I throw up my hands. "You can't come into the women's restroom with me, Jonas. This is a college campus. They'll put up posters warning students there's a crazy bathroom stalker on the loose. Come on, babe. I know you're paranoid, but please try not to be *crazy* paranoid."

He sighs. "Hang on."

I watch as he strides to the back of the classroom, pokes his head out the door, looks up and down the hallway five or six times, and comes back.

"Okay. All clear." He grins. "I can never be too careful when it comes to protecting my precious baby."

I roll my eyes. "I'll be right back." I kiss the top of his head. "And when I come back, I want you to move to the back of the classroom, okay? This whole I-can't-go-anywhere-without-my-hot-boyfriend thing is starting to embarrass me."

Chapter 23

Sarah

"Oh jeez," I mutter aloud, looking at myself in the bathroom mirror. Despite what Jonas said, my face does, in fact, look like an oil slick.

That check from Jonas really threw me for a loop. I can't remember the last time geysers spontaneously shot out of my eyes like that. It was like I'd been crowned Miss America, received a marriage proposal, given birth to quintuplets, and won the power ball lottery all at once. I've got so many emotions bouncing around inside my body right now, I can't think straight. The only coherent thought I can muster is, "I love you, Jonas," over and over. Damn, that boy is a dream come true.

I turn on the faucet and splash cold water onto my eyes and scrub the errant mascara off my face. I grab a paper towel and wipe my face dry and then blow my runny nose. I'm a train wreck. A mushy pile of goo. The luckiest girl in the world.

I pull a tube of lip gloss out of my purse and apply a little shimmer to my lips. Meh, I think I'll skip reapplying mascara—at the rate I'm going, I'm sure that wasn't my last good cry of the day.

I head into one of two empty stalls, lock the stall door, and sit down to pee.

I hear the bathroom door open. Footsteps enter the room and stop. No one enters the empty stall next to me. That's weird. Whoever she is, why is she waiting on my stall when there's an empty one?

I bend over to peek underneath the partition, but I can't see all the way to the door from this angle. I'd have to get down on my hands and knees to see that far. But there's definitely another human being in this bathroom with me. I wait. No more footsteps. Why is my bathroom buddy standing just inside the door? Did she stop to look for a tampon in her purse? Or is my stealthy bathroom visitor my gorgeous but highly paranoid boyfriend checking up on me?

"Jonas?"

There's no reply.

"If that's you, wait for me outside, you creeper-weirdo."

I hear the lock on the bathroom door click.

"Jonas?" I'm suddenly uneasy. "Is there someone there?"

It's got to be Jonas. Is he sneaking in here for a quickie—inspired by our bathroom escapades last night? I roll my eyes. That was a one-off. I'm not planning to make bathroom-sex a habit. And, anyway, we can't do it right now—class starts in five minutes. Although who am I kidding?—with the right persuasion, Jonas Faraday could convince me to have sex with him anywhere, anytime, even in a gross bathroom stall five minutes before class.

The footsteps walk slowly toward the stall.

My chest constricts. I swallow hard. Those footsteps don't sound like a woman. And they're definitely not Jonas' footsteps, either. That's a shuffle. Jonas doesn't shuffle. Jonas is grace in motion. I pull up my jeans and flush the toilet, my blood pulsing in my ears. I clutch my purse and open the stall door.

Holy shit. It's John Fucking Travolta from *Pulp Fiction*, ponytail and all. A small knife glints unmistakably in his hand. I'm too terrified to make a sound or move a muscle.

In a flash, he yanks me out of the stall by my T-shirt. The knife glints as his hand moves toward my neck.

"Oksana!" I scream. "Oksana!"

He's intrigued enough to pause. He presses the knife into my throat.

But he doesn't slice.

"You're supposed to talk to Oksana," I blurt. "You have new instructions from Oksana!"

A terrified squeal rises up out of me. I try to suppress it, but I can't. I'm a quivering mess. My knees buckle, but he holds me up, holding the knife roughly against my neck. Good thing I just peed, or else I'd surely wet my pants.

"You know Oksana?" He has a thick accent of some kind.

"Yes, Oksana—the Crazy Ukrainian." I try to smirk conspiratorially, but I'm sure I just look like I'm having a seizure. He's not amused. Oh shit. Maybe he's Ukrainian, too. "Oksana in Las Vegas—at headquarters. She has new instructions for you. You're not supposed to hurt me. Things have changed—Oksana will tell you."

"My instruction is to kill you." His eyes are hard.

At this last statement, my knees go weak. He grabs me and holds me up, still holding the knife firmly against my throat—but, still, he's not slicing.

I keep babbling like my life depends on it—because, surely, it does.

"You were supposed to get new instructions last night or this morning. No kill." In my terror, those last two words come out like I'm talking to Koko, the sign language gorilla.

He stares at me blankly, pressing the knife into my neck.

Oh shit, he's got no effing idea what I'm talking about. Stacy hasn't conveyed last night's message to anyone yet—or, if she has, word hasn't made its way up (or down) the totem pole to this guy. He's pressing the knife so hard against my throat, the blade is breaking the skin. My skin under the knife burns.

He grits his teeth and his eyes flash like he's made a decision—and not a good one.

"Two-hundred-fifty-thousand dollars!" I scream.

He pauses yet again, just long enough for me to keep talking.

"Right here in my purse. From the rich guy. Two hundred fifty thousand dollars! Look in my purse. You can have it. And I can get you more."

He pauses briefly, processing what I'm saying, and then puts me in a suffocating headlock while he gruffly opens my purse. He pulls out the check, grunting with pleasure or surprise or malice, I'm not sure which.

"I've been scamming the rich guy all along. He gave me this money, and there's plenty more where that came from. I just sent The Club an email about this earlier today. I want to be partners with you. That's why I emailed you. Call your boss, you'll see. I sent an email. I'm scamming this guy—and I can do the same thing to other new members, too. We can make money together. Lots of money." I'm panting. I'm light-headed.

He holds up the check and leans into my face. "You can get more?"

Oh God, his breath is foul.

"Yeah, lots more—lots and lots and lots and lots and lots." Oh God, I'm rambling. "And not just from him. I can get it from other guys, too. I'll split everything with you. That's what I emailed about this morning—ask them about my email, you'll see. This guy paid his membership fee and now he only wants to fuck me—he wants a GFE . . ." I mentally say a prayer of gratitude to Stacy the Faker for providing this helpful bit of prostitute lingo. "These kinds of guys love a good GFE. They think I'm breaking the rules to be with them—we're Romeo and Juliet. We can do this with all the new members. I'll tell them a sob story about my law school tuition and throw in a sick mom with cancer and they'll fork over big money to feel like my knight in shining armor. We'll split the money."

He's considering. Or, at least, he's not killing me yet.

"I'm not gonna tell anyone about The Club—why would I do that? That's the last thing I want to do. This is my ticket to big money. I love what you're doing to these rich assholes—I want in. Let me be your partner. I'll give these guys the Intake Agent GFE before they ever start using the other girls. I'm the girl they're not supposed to have, the forbidden fruit. This first stupid guy gave me two hundred fifty thousand bucks—and I can get lots more. Call your boss—ask if I emailed this morning like I'm telling you. You'll see—I'm telling the truth. Call and find out. I sent an email this morning."

I'm going to faint. I can't keep talking like this. I'm seeing spots. My chest is jerking and jolting from the exertion of trying to take air into my lungs and speak at the same time. I've never felt so much adrenaline coursing through my veins in all my life. There is no doubt in my mind this man is a heartbeat away from plunging that knife into my chest. I'm shaking.

"Call your boss. Come on, Hugo."

He scrunches his face, amused. It's the first flicker of humanity I've seen from him during this whole exchange. I take it as a positive sign.

"What? Don't tell me Hugo's not your name? Oh man! And you look like such a Hugo, too."

One side of his mouth hitches up.

"When we start working together, I'm gonna call you Hugo. That'll be my pet name for you. You'll always be my Hugo." I smile at him. Or, at least, I try to. I'm sure my face looks more like a raccoon caught in headlights.

He looks at the check in his hand. "You can get more?"

"Much more. I put on a big show last night when the rich guy was at a check-in with Stacy. He *loved* it. Fucked my brains out in the bathroom afterwards and gave me the money. We can do that kind of thing all the time to new members." I try to laugh. "These guys love a good GFE—they're all just diehard romantics underneath it all. Go on—call your boss. Ask about my email this morning. You'll see."

My breathing is fitful. Sweat has broken out over my brow.

Without warning, he puts me into a headlock again, smashing my face against his body, and pulls out his phone. I can't see what he's doing, but I hear the condensed sound of an automated outgoing voicemail message followed by a beep. He leaves a gruff, staccato message in another language. Russian?

I'm going to die at the hands of a James Bond villain.

He yanks me back up by my hair and presses the knife into my throat even harder than before. I feel blood trickling down my neck. My skin is on fire.

His nostrils flare. He jerks his face right into my mine and I squeal, flinching, certain this is it for me—but he holds up the check.

"If you're lying to me, I'll come back and slit your throat."

My neck burns sharply as he lets go of my quivering body—did he just nick me with the knife? Just as I bring my hand up to my neck, a shocking pain in my ribcage burns hotter and fiercer than anything I've felt in my entire life. The intense pain makes my knees buckle and takes my breath away, literally. My legs give way. As I fall, the bathroom spins and twists before my eyes.

A crashing jolt of pain slams the back of my head.

I love you, Jonas.

Darkness.

Chapter 24
Jonas

I move to the back of the classroom, just as she instructed. I'm Sarah's puppy dog, after all—a fucking Maltese named Jonas. Sit, stay, come. Whatever the hell she wants me to do, I'll do it.

The classroom's almost full. A guy takes the seat I just vacated, the one right next to hers. I glance at her open laptop and notebook on her empty desk and feel a pang of envy. I want to be the one who gets to sit next to her—damn, I shouldn't have moved.

I look at my watch. Still a couple minutes before class starts. She'd better hurry the fuck up. What's she doing in there all this time? Putting makeup on? If so, I wish she wouldn't. She doesn't need it.

The professor enters the room and heads down the aisle toward the front of the class. Before he makes it to his destination, a student stops him to ask a question.

I reach into my jeans pocket and fish out the flash drive she gave me this morning. Let's see what songs my baby's compiled for my mix tape. I've never gotten a playlist from a girl before, ever, and I have to admit, I'm excited about it.

I reach into my computer case for some earbuds and shove them into my ears.

The first song is "Demons" by Imagine Dragons. I smile. Oh, Sarah, aren't you clever? I get it. I've got demons and you're going to save me from them. I don't need to listen to this song—I've heard it a million times.

The next song is "Not Afraid" by Eminem. I'm sensing a theme here. This woman is bound and determined to "heal" me, huh? I guess I'd better get used to it. It's just the way she's wired.

"Come a Little Closer" by Cage the Elephant. I'm not familiar with this one. I listen to the song for about thirty seconds, through the end of the first chorus. Love the song. And, yes, definitely a theme. She wants me to "come a little closer"—or, as my various past girlfriends have fruitlessly demanded, to "let her in." Not very original, but surely heartfelt.

The professor moves to the podium at the front of the class and organizes his notes. I look at my watch. She's got maybe another minute, if she's lucky. If she doesn't come in the next thirty seconds, I'll knock at the restroom door and tell her to get her butt in gear. She's so anal about not missing even a minute of class—she made us get here twenty minutes early, for Christ's sake—I'm surprised she's taking so damned long.

I change the page view on my screen so I can see the rest of her selected song titles all at once. My heart explodes. The remainder of her song list forges a decidedly different theme than her initial "let me save you from your demons" campaign: "She Loves You" by the Beatles. "Crazy In Love" by Beyoncé. "Love Don't Cost a Thing" by Jennifer Lopez. "I Just Can't Stop Loving You" by Michael Jackson. And on and on and on. "Love Can Build a Bridge." "All You Need Is Love." "(I Can't Help) Falling In Love With You."

Oh my God.

I bolt out of my chair to a manic stand, wringing my hands, hopping from foot to foot. I need to touch her, kiss her, make love to her. Maybe I'll sneak into that bathroom right now and take her in the stall—no, what am I thinking? We can't have bathroom sex at a time like this. Oh my God. She loves me. We've already told each other this, of course, in oh so many clever and coded ways, but seeing the actual magic word over and over and over on my screen, so starkly, so honestly, so unequivocally—an explicit love letter from my baby to me—it's the greatest feeling in the whole world.

Love is the joy of the good, the wonder of the wise, the amazement of the gods.

"Good morning," the professor begins. "Let's start with the landmark U.S. Supreme Court case of *Lawrence v. Texas* on page one eighty-three of your casebook. Miss Fanuel, will you tell us the holding of this case, please?"

Where the fuck is she? Why is she taking so long?

"Yes. The Supreme Court in *Lawrence v. Texas* held that intimate consensual sexual conduct is part of the liberty protected by the Fourteenth Amendment . . ."

Where is she?

Panic seizes me. She should have come back by now. Holy shit.

She should have come back by now.

Someone screams just outside the classroom door. I bolt out of the room.

A panicked gathering of students stands outside the women's restroom.

"Call 9-1-1!" someone shouts.

I push my way through them into the bathroom.

Blood. Oh my God, no, there's so much blood. It's all over the white tile floor. No, God, please, not again. No more blood. Not again.

I see her bound and bloodied body. The bed sheet is stained a deep, dark red.

I see his brain splattered against the wall. And the floor. And the ceiling. The carpet is stained a deep, dark red.

And now I see my Sarah, My Magnificent Sarah, in a bloodied, crumpled heap, the bracelet I gave her still tied to her lifeless wrist. The white tiles are turning a deep, dark red.

"Call an ambulance!" I scream.

"We called one," someone shrieks. "They'll be here any minute."

I grab at my hair. My body convulses. A howl erupts from me and turns into a gut-wrenching heave. I throw up all over the bathroom floor. Someone tries to come to my aid. I shove them away. Someone grabs at me. I push them away and kneel down on the tile floor next to her.

A guy is bent over her chest, listening for a heartbeat.

Another howl. I pull at my hair.

The guy sits up from her chest and nods at a second guy. There's a collective sigh from the crowd. I push the guy away forcibly. *She's mine.* I scoop her lifeless body up in my arms. I touch every inch of her, patting her down, trying to determine the source of the blood.

"You shouldn't move her," the motherfucker says. I hear the words, but I don't understand the meaning of the words.

My fingers search frantically and find a hole in her T-shirt, right above her ribcage. I touch the hole. The fabric around it is warm and wet and red.

"Red," I say, my voice cracking. She promised to stop if I said red. "Red," I choke out again. But it doesn't stop. Make it stop. "Red." My body wracks with sobs as my mind floats above, confounded, detached from my body, spiraling like an airplane smoking and losing altitude.

I pull up her shirt and a strangled cry wrenches from me. A wound. A gaping, red wound in her beautiful olive skin, just like last time—only this time, there's only one angry hole in her flesh instead of too many to count. I put my fingers on the hole to stop the bleeding, just like I did after the big man left. She always said I had magic hands, but she was wrong. There were too many wounds, too many holes to plug, and my fingers were too small. The magic in my hands didn't work that time—no matter how hard I tried.

But this time, there's only one savage hole to plug—and my hands are big. My fingers are strong. The blood stops gurgling out when I cover the wound and press down. This time, the magic in my hands is working. And yet there's still blood coming from somewhere else. Where's the blood still coming from? I look around in panic. There's so much fucking blood, all over the white tile floor. Her neck. Blood is coming from her neck. I put my fingers on the small indentation in her neck and the blood stops flowing.

"Call an ambulance!" I scream. "Call an ambulance!"

"We already called one. They're coming. The hospital's right here on campus. Any minute."

The other guy leans in and puts his fingers on the hole in her ribcage and I cradle her head in my arms, keeping my fingers on her neck.

"Call again!" I scream. I pat my pockets. I can't find my fucking phone. Did I leave it in the fucking classroom? "Call again!" I howl.

I tried to untie the ropes but the knots were too tight—tried to free her wrists, but my fingers weren't strong enough. The magic in my hands didn't work that time, no matter how hard I tried. *I love you,* I said to her, tears bursting out of me. *I love you,* I wailed, willing her to wake up and smile at me again. *I love you, Mommy.* But she wouldn't wake up, no matter how many times I said the magic words. *I love you.* But my love wasn't enough to save her. *Look at me, Mommy.* But her blue eyes stared into space. *Please, Mommy.* Her blue eyes remained frozen. *I love you, Mommy.* But it wasn't enough.

Sarah's blood is all over my jeans, my T-shirt, my arms, my hands. If I could give her my blood, I would. If I could give her my life, I would. Oh God, I'd bleed myself dry for her.

I feel wetness on my forearms. I pull back. My arms are soaked in her blood. My fingers touch the back of her head, the base of her skull—her hair is matted and wet and sticky. I burrow my finger into the wetness and feel an enormous gash.

I howl at my discovery. My body heaves.

The crowd stares at me, paralyzed, wide-eyed, in shock.

I glare at them all, holding my precious baby in my arms.

Heavy footsteps echo in the corridor, getting louder and louder, approaching. I hear the sound of metal wheels.

"At the end!" someone yells in the distant hallway.

I hug her to me.

"Love is the joy of the good, the wonder of the wise, the amazement of the gods," I whimper, but then a dam breaks inside of me and a lifetime of pressure and pain and sorrow and remorse and rage breaks and a fierceness floods into me.

"I love you," I wail, my voice cracking, my gut wrenching, my heart breaking, my mind hurtling into the abyss. "I love you, Sarah. I love you, baby." I shudder with my sobs, rocking her back and forth. I've never felt pain like this. "I love you, baby, I love you, I love you." I look up at the staring crowd. Why are they staring at us? What don't they fucking understand? "I love her," I proclaim fiercely. They stare at me blankly. Why don't these fuckers understand? "I love her," I scream at them all, but they don't understand how I feel. No one ever understands how I feel—except Sarah. Sarah always understands.

I can't lose her. I won't survive it if I lose her. I need them all to understand. Her blood is mine. I'm bleeding all over the floor. I won't survive without her. I need them to understand. I love her.

"I love Sarah Cruz!"

Dedication

To B, S and C for teaching me every day about deep and abiding love.

Author Acknowledgment

If you are reading this note, you've probably just finished reading *The Reclamation,* which means there's a good chance you just screamed and threw the book across the room (and possibly cursed me out, too). Sorry about that. Trust me, I cried when I wrote that last chapter and felt kind of sick about it. (But it had to be done.) I just want to take this chance to thank you for reading my books. I am writing this note exactly three months since the *The Club Trilogy* first released into the world, and I'm stunned and elated about the reception my books have received in such a short amount of time. As I wrote these books, I cried big ol' soggy tears, swooned, laughed my ass off, and fanned myself, all the while dreaming that one day, ther might be a reader out there who would enjoy my story and maybe even fall in love with Jonas and Sarah the way I have. I hope that reader has been you. Writing is a whole lot more fun when other people actually read what I write, and even more so when they like it (fingers crossed)—so thank you very much for taking a chance on my books. It's a dream come true. If you'd like to connect, please come say hi to me on my Author Lauren Rowe Facebook page and/or shoot me an email at www.laurenrowe.com. Thank you for reading my books!!

Bonus Scene from:

THE REDEMPTION

Lauren Rowe

Published by SoCoRo Publishing
Layout by www.formatting4U.com
Cover design © Sarah Hansen, Okay Creations LLC

Chapter 1

Jonas

I don't want to stop holding on to her, but they peel my body off hers. I stumble backward, my eyes wide. I look down at my shirt. It's soaked in her blood. There's so much blood. It's everywhere.

"No pulse," one of the men says, holding her wrist. He moves his fingers to her throat. "Nothing." He frowns. "Damn. Her carotid's slashed clean through. Talk about belts and suspenders—Jesus." He shakes his head.

"What kind of animal...?" the other man says, but his voice goes quiet. He glances over at me. "Get him out of here. He shouldn't see this."

The men are dressed like firemen—but I don't think they're firemen because there's no fire.

"Body's already cool. I'd estimate a good fifteen, twenty minutes, at least."

I love you, Mommy, I said to her. But she didn't say it back to me. This is the very first time she didn't she say it back to me, ever. When I say it, she's supposed to say, "I love you, baby—my precious baby." That's what she always says, just like that. "I love you, baby—my precious baby." Why didn't she say it this time? And why won't she look at me? She just keeps staring out the window. I look out the window, too. An ambulance is parked in front of our house. The siren light on top is twirling around but it's not making any sound.

I hear faraway sirens. They're getting closer. I usually like hearing sirens—especially sirens that are getting closer. I like it when a police car chases after the bad guy or a big red fire truck zooms past our car. Mommy says when you hear a siren you have to pull over to the side of the road. "There they go to save the day!" she always sings when they pass. But not today.

Today, I don't like hearing sirens.

I move to the corner of the room. I sit on the floor, rocking back and forth. I told her I love her, but she didn't say it back to me. And now she won't look at me, either. She just stares out the window. She doesn't even blink. She's mad at me for not saving her.

"Is this your mother, buddy?" the first man says. He bends down to me.

My voice doesn't work.

She's my mommy.

"Was there anyone else in the house with you two?"

I wanted to be alone with her. I wanted her all to myself. I wanted to take her pain away. I was a bad boy.

"We're here to help you, son. We're not going to hurt you. We're paramedics. The police are coming right now."

I swallow hard.

I stayed in the closet because I thought I could use the magic in my hands after the big man left, but then the magic didn't work. I don't know why the magic didn't work. I was bad.

"What's your name, son?" the other one asks.

"Get him out of here," the first man says again. "He shouldn't see this."

The man bending down to me waves the other man away. "You've got blood on you, buddy," he says softly. "I need to make sure it's not yours. Did anyone hurt you?"

He grabs for my hand, but I jerk free and run to her. I throw myself on top of her. I don't care if I get more blood on me. I hold on to her with all my might. They can't make me leave her. Maybe my magic hands will start working again if I try hard enough—maybe I didn't try hard enough before. Maybe she'll stop staring out the window if my magic starts working again. Maybe if I say, "I love you, Mommy," enough times, the magic will work again and she'll finally blink again and say, "I love you, too, baby—my precious baby."

I lie in my bed on top of my baseball sheets. Josh lies in his bed next to mine on top of his football sheets. Josh usually throws a fit if he can't have the baseball sheets, but this time, he let me have them without a fuss. "You can have the baseball sheets every night if you want," Josh said. "From now on, I'll give you first pick."

A week ago, I would have been happy he said that about the sheets. But now I don't care. I don't care about anything. I don't even care about talking ever again. It's been a week since Mommy went away forever and ever, and I haven't said a single word since then. The last words that came out of my mouth were, "I love you, Mommy" when I was hugging and kissing and touching her with my magic hands that aren't magic anymore—and I've decided to let those be the last words my mouth ever says.

Even when the policeman asked me what the big man looked like, I didn't say a word. Even when I heard Daddy crying behind the door of his study, I didn't say a word. Even when I dreamed about the big man cutting mommy up with a knife and then coming after me, I didn't say a word. Even when Daddy told us last night how the police figured out it was Mariela's sister's boyfriend who made Mommy go away forever and ever, and I heard Daddy say on the phone to Uncle William, "I'm gonna kill that motherfucker," I didn't say a word.

I sit up in my bed.

I hear Mariela's voice downstairs in the foyer. I know she's in the foyer because her voice is bouncing really loud and the foyer is the only place in our house where voices sound big and bouncy like that, especially a voice as soft as Mariela's.

I look at Josh. He's fast asleep. Maybe I should wake him up to say hi to Mariela? But no, Mariela's mine. I'm the one who sits and talks to her in the kitchen while she's cooking us Venezuelan food. I'm the one who helps her wash the pots and listens to her sing her pretty songs in Spanish. I like it when she dips her hands into the dishwater and her brown skin comes back up wet and shiny and looking like caramel sauce on an ice cream sundae. Mariela's skin is so soft and smooth and pretty, sometimes when she's singing, I touch her arm with my fingertips and close my eyes and rub softly up and down. And her eyes are pretty, too—the color of Tootsie Rolls. I like how Mariela's dark eyes twinkle at me when she hands me a pot to dry or when she sings me one of her songs.

"*Señor, por favor*!" Mariela shouts downstairs.

I jump out of bed and bolt out of my room. This is the first time I've left my bed since Mommy went away forever and ever. My legs feel stiff and sore. My head hurts. I promised myself I'd never leave my bed again, but I want to see my Mariela. Even if I made that promise to myself about never leaving my bed ever again, maybe I can make a new rule that I'm allowed to leave my bed only if it's to see Mariela. I run down the steps as fast as I can. I can't wait to hear Mariela's voice calling me Jonasito or singing me one of her pretty songs.

But Daddy's voice stops me in the middle of the staircase.

"Get out of here," I hear Daddy say. He's using his mean voice. "Or I'm calling the police."

"*No, señor! Por favor*," Mariela cries. "*Dios bendiga a la señora. Por favor, déjeme ver a mis bebes. Los quiero.*" *Let me see my babies. I love them.*

"You're the one who told that motherfucker we were going to the football game—you might as well have killed her yourself."

Mariela cries really loud. "*No, señor! Ay, Dios mio, señor. No sabía! Lo juro por Dios.*" Mariela switches to half-English. "Please, *señor*, I love my babies—*son como mis hijos.*" *They're like my sons.* "*Señor, por favor. Esta es mi familia.*" *This is my family.*

"Get out," Daddy yells. "Get the fuck out."

When Daddy's voice is angry like this, especially when he's yelling at Mommy or Mariela, I know I should stay out of his way. But I don't care. I want to see my Mariela.

I run down the steps and across the foyer and jump straight into her arms.

She screams the minute she sees me and hugs me to her. She's squeezing me so tight, I can't breathe.

For the first time since Mommy went away, I speak. "*Te quiero, Mariela.*" My voice sounds scratchy.

"*Ay, mi hijo,*" she says. "*Pobrecito, Jonasito. Te quiero.*"

I wanted the last words I ever said for the rest of my life to be "I love you, Mommy"—but I figure speaking Spanish to Mariela doesn't really count as talking, even if I tell her I love her, because Spanish isn't real. It's just my secret language with Mariela, like make-believe. Even Daddy doesn't understand our secret language, and he's the smartest man there is, so talking to Mariela, even telling her I love her—as long as I'm speaking Spanish—doesn't count as breaking my rule.

Daddy screams at Mariela and tells her to leave.

I grab ahold of Mariela's skirt. "*No me dejes, Mariela.*" *Don't leave me.*

"*Te quiero, Jonasito.*" Mariela's crying really hard. "*Te quiero siempre, pobrecito bebe.*" *I love you forever.*

"No me dejes, Mariela."

"Mariela?" It's Josh. He must have heard her voice and woken up. He runs to her and hugs her.

Mariela kneels down and hugs him while I continue grabbing onto her shoulders.

"*Te quiero,*" she says to Josh. "*Te quiero, bebe.*"

Josh understands my secret language with Mariela, but he doesn't speak it very well. "I love you, too," Josh cries.

"It's time to leave," Daddy yells at Mariela. He picks up the phone. "I'm calling the police."

Mariela holds Josh's face in her hands (which makes me a little bit angry because I wish she'd do that to me) and she cries really hard. "*Cuida a su hermanito,*" Mariela says to Josh. "*Sabes que él es lo sensitivo.*" *Take care of your brother. You know he's the sensitive one.*

"Okay, Mariela," Josh says. "I will."

"*Te quiero, Mariela,*" I say, holding onto her skirt. "*No me dejes.*" *Don't leave me.*

"Oh, Jonasito," Mariela says. "*Te quiero, bebe.*"

Mariela tries to hug me, but Daddy pulls her away from me and drags her toward the front door. I beg Daddy to please let my Mariela stay with me. I scream her name. I tell her I love her. I cry and cry. But no matter what I say or do, Daddy makes my Mariela leave and never come back again.

Chapter 2

Jonas

She looks so pale.

"Blood pressure ninety over fifty," the EMT says. They're crowding around her, edging me out. Space is limited in the back of the ambulance, so I'm sitting down by her feet, clutching her ankle.

"What's her name?" the paramedic asks me.

I see his mouth moving—hear his words. But I can't speak. I promised to protect her. I promised her I'd never let harm come to her. And then I sat in that classroom and listened to fucking music on my laptop while she stood in that bathroom fighting for her life. My entire body shakes.

One EMT holds something down on her neck and the back of her head. Another holds something down on her ribs. An IV is attached to her arm.

"What's her name?" the guy asks me again.

I want to answer him, but my voice doesn't work.

"What's her age?"

I swallow hard. I won't let The Lunacy take over again. I'm stronger now. I'm different now. Sarah needs me.

"Sarah Cruz. Twenty-four."

She moans. Her eyes flutter open.

The EMT repositions himself, making room for me to lean into her. I shove my face into hers.

Her eyes are wide. Scared. A tear falls out the corner of her eye and down her temple.

"Jonas?" she says. Her voice is nothing but the faintest of whispers—but with that one barely audible word from her, my teetering mind lurches sharply away from the brink of darkness and leans toward the light, toward Sarah, toward my precious baby. With that one faint utterance from her, The Lunacy retracts and skitters away like a cockroach after the kitchen light has come on. With that one word from Sarah, my mind reenters my body.

"I'm here, baby. We're on our way to the hospital. You're going to be fine."

"Class starts in five minutes," she says. "I have to go."

"Do you know your name?" the EMT asks.

She looks at the EMT blankly. "Jonas?"

"I'm right here."

"Sit back a little, sir."

I sit back. "I'm right here, baby. Let them work on you." I choke back a sob.

"Do you know your name?" the EMT asks her.

Her eyes are wide.

"Do you know your name?"

She doesn't answer. Her face is pale.

My heart is pounding violently against my chest wall.

"Do you know what today is?" the EMT asks.

"Con law."

"Do you know where you are?"

"Who are you?" she asks the EMT.

"I'm Michael, an emergency medical technician. I'm taking you to the hospital. Do you remember what happened to you?"

She moans. "Class starts in five minutes. You have to let me go." She's strapped to the stretcher.

"Stay still, Sarah. You're hurt. You have to stay still. We're going to the hospital. Tell them your name."

She stares at me blankly. "Jonas?"

"I'm right here, baby."

She bursts into tears. "Don't leave me."

"I'll never leave you. I'm right here." I choke back another sob. I promised to protect her. I promised no harm would come to her. "I'll never leave you, baby. I promise."

The ambulance stops. The back doors swing open.

Doctors surround her and whisk her away. I jog alongside her stretcher through the hallway until someone stops me outside the swinging doors.

"What's her name?"

"Sarah Cruz. C-R-U-Z."

"Age?"

"Twenty-four."

"Any known allergies to medication?"

"She's never mentioned any."

"Do you know if she's taken any medication today? Anything at all?"

I shake my head. "Nothing."

"Does she have any medical conditions?"

I shake my head. "No."

"Are you her husband?"

My entire body quivers. "Yes."

Five minutes later—or is it five hours?— someone finally approaches me in the waiting room. "We're running tests," the guy says. He's wearing scrubs. His eyes drift down to my shirt.

I look down, too. There's blood all over me.

"Were you injured?"

I shake my head.

"That blood is hers?"

I nod.

"She's conscious and speaking. Are you Jonas?"

I nod.

"She keeps asking for you." He grins sympathetically. "The minute we can, we'll bring you back to hold her hand. Just sit tight. We're running a bunch of tests to figure out the extent of her injuries."

I nod again.

"Just sit tight."

The doctor leaves and I sit back down. I'm shaking. My mind is not my own. The longer I sit here, the more my mind hurtles into space. I promised to keep her safe and I failed her. I'm losing it. I need Josh.

I reach for my phone in my pocket but it's not there. Where is it? I don't know Josh's phone number by heart. When I want to talk to Josh, all I ever do is press the button on my phone that says Josh.

My mind is not my own—it's bobbing and weaving and careening through space, trying its damnedest to outrun The Lunacy. And failing miserably.

Chapter 3
Jonas

"You wanna go climb the tree?" Josh asks.

I don't speak, as usual. I haven't spoken since Mommy left two months ago—not even when they sent me away to that mean place right after Daddy made Mariela leave. I never want to go back to that mean place again—I missed Josh and Mommy and Mariela and Daddy and my soft bed and I wanted to go home—and all those doctors cared about was trying to make me talk even though I can't ever talk again.

I knew the whole time I was at the mean place if I did what they wanted me to do, if I said anything at all, they'd let me go home to be with Josh and Daddy again. But they didn't understand my mouth isn't allowed to say anything ever again, not since my mouth said, "I love you, Mommy" and she didn't say it back.

"Let's go climb the tree like we used to," Josh says.

Back when Mommy lived at our house with us, Josh and I used to climb the big tree every day—but now that Mommy's gone I don't care about climbing the tree. I don't care about doing anything anymore. All I want to do is go to heaven with Mommy.

"Come on," Josh says. Josh grabs my hand and pulls me out of my bed.

When I just stand there and don't crawl back into bed, he smiles and grabs my hand again and drags me all the way downstairs, through the kitchen, out the back door, into the backyard, across the field, and to the big climbing tree.

"Come on, Jonas," Josh says. "Let's climb."

Josh starts climbing, but I stand at the bottom of the tree and watch him for a couple minutes. He's so much slower at climbing than me—he's doing it all wrong. Oh my God, it's killing me to watch Josh climb the big tree like he's a fish. Mommy always used to say, "If you judge a fish by how well he climbs a tree, he'll always fail—so why not let the poor little fishy swim, instead?" Well, I'm sorry but it's true—Josh is a dang fish trying to climb a tree. I start climbing after him, but only because I can't stand watching Josh the Fish be so bad at it anymore.

In no time at all, I pass Josh on my way up the tree. When I get up as high as I'm allowed to climb, I sit and look up at the sky, waiting for my brother. When he finally reaches me, he sits and looks up at the sky, just like I'm doing. I don't know what Josh is thinking about, but I'm making pictures in my head with the puffy white clouds.

"You know what I figured out?" Josh says.

I don't reply.

"Mommy's floating in the clouds in the daytime, and at night, she's in the stars. When you see a star twinkle at night, it's Mommy winking at us, telling us it's time for bed."

I don't want to talk about this so I start climbing down. I thought my magic hands would make Mommy all better, and they didn't.

Almost every night since Mommy left, I've dreamed about the big man with the hairy butt cutting Mommy up into little tiny pieces. Sometimes, I dream he's coming after me, too. Once, after I dreamed about the big man cutting Mommy up, I woke up to find Mariela hugging me and singing one of her songs in Spanish—and that made me cry really hard because I was so happy to see her and I've missed her so much. But then I woke up again for real and Mariela wasn't there. No one was there except for stupid Josh, sleeping next to me in his bed, drooling. No Mommy. No Mariela. Just Josh with spit on his chin.

I keep climbing down the tree. The magic in my hands didn't work. And I don't understand why it didn't.

I can hear Josh climbing down after me, still talking about Mommy. But I don't want to talk about Mommy ever again, even with Josh. It makes me think of the blood—so much blood like an ocean of it—and that man's butt when he pulled his pants down. It makes me think about how Mommy looked afraid, but I didn't come out of the closet to help her. Because I was bad.

Josh hops down to the grass next to me.

"Let's get the football and throw it around," he says. He grabs my hand like he's going to pull me toward the shed where we keep all the sports stuff.

I pull my hand away.

"Come on, Jonas," he says, but I stomp away. He follows me. "We can throw a baseball, instead, if you want—we can do whatever you want. You can pick."

This is new. Josh never lets me pick. He's usually so bossy. I kind of want to pick, but I keep marching away, anyway.

Out of nowhere, Josh tackles me. I fall to the grass with him on top of me and he punches me in the stomach and then in the arm and then in the face. I don't fight back. I want him to punch me. Everyone should punch me. I was bad. It's my fault Mommy had to go away. If he punches me hard enough, maybe I can go to heaven with her. I don't want to be here anymore. I want to be with Mommy.

"Why don't you fight back?" Josh says. "Come on!" he screams.

I just lie there and let him hit me. I start to cry and so does he. He's crying and punching. I'm crying and getting punched. After a minute, Josh stops. He sits on top of me, breathing hard. Tears and snot run down his face.

I don't move. I wish he'd punch me some more.

We stare at each other. We don't know what to do. This is weird. We're both crying really hard.

Josh takes a big breath and then he slaps himself in the face. Really hard.

I smile, even though I'm crying. Why'd he do that? That was a dumb thing to do.

Josh smiles really big when I smile. This is the first time I've smiled since Mommy went away. He slaps himself again, even harder, and that makes me laugh.

"If you aren't going to fight back, I guess I'll have to do it for you," Josh says.

I slap myself, too—really hard—and that makes Josh laugh.

"Now doesn't that make you feel better, Jonas?"

It does.

Josh leans down and lies on top of me and we pretend to wrestle, but what we're really doing is hugging and crying for a really long time.

"What the hell?" It's Daddy. "Get up."

Oh man, I know that voice. That's the voice that tells me we're in big trouble. We get up really fast and wipe at our eyes.

"What the hell's going on? I come out here and this is what I see—you boys rolling around in the grass together, crying your eyes out?"

Oh boy, we're in such big trouble.

Daddy covers his face with his hands for a minute. He looks really sad. "If you boys want to cry, okay, but you can't do it where everyone's going to see you and you most certainly can't do it around me. I understand you might sometimes have to cry—but I don't want to see you do it, boys. I'm doing my best to get out of bed each day and I can't be around anyone, even you two, who can't keep his shit together. It's time for all three of us to pull ourselves together and stop fucking around." He shakes his head and makes a weird sound. "If you two boys need to talk about your feelings and cry your little eyes out, then I'll send you to a shrink and you can do it behind closed doors 'til you're blue in the face. But when you're home and in my presence, you boys are gonna start acting like men from here on out. Do you understand me?"

"Yes, sir," Josh says.

I stare at my father, but I don't answer him. I want Mommy.

Daddy's eyes flash at me. "Jonas Patrick, I've had it with you. I've been patient with you up 'til now, thinking you just needed to get it out of your system, but your time's up. It's time to quit fucking around and start talking again. You think you're the only one who feels like the world's crashing down around him?" His voice sounds funny, like he's going to cry. "Your mother was a fucking saint. She was my savior. And now she's gone and who's gonna save me now?"

Josh and I look at each other. We don't know what that means.

"Why don't you think about how someone else is feeling for a fucking change, huh? You're not the only one wanting to lie down and die. Maybe you should stop and think how other people might be feeling—especially considering you're the reason she was here at the house in the first place. If it wasn't for you..." Daddy makes a mean face at me and marches away.

I bolt to the big tree again, as fast as I can, and this time I climb higher than I've ever climbed, higher than Mommy lets me climb—straight up to the very highest branch, the one Mommy says might break if I stand on it. But I don't care if it breaks. Maybe I want it to break.

Once I'm on the very highest branch, I reach my hands up over my head and try my hardest to touch the clouds. But even the highest branch isn't high enough for me to reach Mommy. I need to bring a ladder up here next time. Or better yet, I should climb a mountain—yeah, forget about this stupid tree, I'm going to climb a mountain, the tallest mountain in the whole world. And then I'll go to the tippy-top of it and reach my hands way up in the air and touch the clouds and Mommy will lean down and pull me up. And then we'll lie together in her cloud like it's that blue hammock at Uncle William's lake house and Mommy will smile at me and kiss me all over my face like she always does and we'll be together again forever and ever.

Chapter 4

Jonas

My mind bounces maniacally from one bizarre thought to another as I await word from the doctor. My knee keeps jiggling wildly. I can't make it stop. I'm having all kinds of crazy thoughts—thoughts about things I haven't thought about in years and years. Maybe I'm having some kind of nervous breakdown again. Why hasn't the doctor come out here to tell me what's going on?

I look down. My shirt is drenched in Sarah's blood. I head into the restroom to clean myself.

As I watch Sarah's blood swirl down the sink, I have the intense feeling I've lived this exact moment before.

The yarn bracelet tied to my wrist, the one that matches Sarah's, is covered in blood. I stand frozen for a minute, trying to figure out what to do. I don't want to take off the bracelet, but my sanity won't withstand having her blood on me, either. I pull off the bracelet and run it under the faucet. It's no use. I shove it into my pocket, my hands shaking.

I try to wring the blood out of my wet shirt, but it's a lost cause, so I throw it in the trash and head shirtless out of the bathroom. The hospital gift shop is just a short ways down the hall. Maybe they sell T-shirts for family members stuck at the hospital for long stretches of time.

A nurse makes a kind of yelping noise as I pass her in the hallway. I cross my arms over my bare chest and she looks away, blushing. I stare at her blankly. My mind can't process human interaction right now.

Yep. The gift shop sells shirts—Seattle Seahawks T-shirts. Kind of a non sequitur, considering the situation. But, hey, I need a clean shirt.

I return to the waiting room in my new shirt and sit in a chair in the corner.

I wait.

I've got the worst fucking headache right now. No, that's not true. Sarah's got the worst fucking headache right now, not me. The thought makes tears spring into my eyes, but I push them down. My mind keeps conjuring images of Sarah with lifeless blue eyes, her wrists tied up and her torso slashed with countless bleeding gashes. Holy fuck. It's official. I'm going crazy.

Some kids from Sarah's constitutional law class bound into the waiting room, and when they see me, they instantly swarm me and ask me how she's doing. *What did the doctor say? How are you holding up?*

They've brought Sarah's computer and mine, her book bag and purse, and my phone. I'm so grateful I could cry. It's not the stuff—I don't give a shit about the stuff—I guess it's just nice to feel like I'm not alone. I thank them profusely and quickly excuse myself to call Josh.

When I hear Josh's voice, I lose it. I can't stop myself.

"Hey, man, everything's gonna be okay," he says. "Take a deep breath."

I do what he tells me to do.

"I'll hop a plane right now, Jonas. Hang in there. Don't do anything stupid."

"I won't. But hurry. I can't think straight, Josh. I'm thinking all kinds of crazy shit."

"I'm coming. Just do your visualizations, bro. Breathe. Stay calm."

"Okay. Hurry."

Josh says he'll call Kat and tell her to call Sarah's mom.

Oh shit. Sarah's mom. This is not the way I envisioned meeting Sarah's mother for the first time. *Oh, hi, Mrs. Cruz, lovely to meet you. Sorry I almost got your daughter killed today.* Fuck me. This is all my fault. *Again.* I'm a fucking cancer. Everything I touch turns to blood.

As I return to the waiting room, my heart leaps into my throat. The doctor's standing there, looking around. When he sees me, he beelines right to me, but I'm paralyzed. I can't breathe. I clutch my chest. I can't think. I can't lose her. I won't survive losing her. No amount of deep breathing or visualizations will save me if she dies.

The doctor's mouth is moving. Words are coming out of his mouth.

He's sorry, he says, so very sorry, but there was nothing they could do. She's gone. But no, wait—that's not what he's saying. That's what I'm *expecting* him to say. If my ears are working and I'm not crazy, if I haven't gone totally, completely, batshit crazy, if I'm not just imagining his words and willing them out of his mouth, he's saying Sarah's going to be just fine—and quickly, too. I can't believe what I'm hearing. Am I hallucinating? Having another psychotic break?

"... and if her vital signs remain strong overnight, we'll release her tomorrow," he says.

I can't believe my ears. Blood on the floor has never worked out this way for me. "Tomorrow?" I ask, incredulous. "But there was so much blood." My legs give way.

The doctor grabs my arm and leads me to a chair. "Do you need some water?" he asks me.

I shake my head. "But there was so much blood." I'm still not sure if I'm imagining this.

"Yeah, she lost a lot of blood. The knife grazed her external jugular vein. That's the vein that stands out on the outside of your neck when you hold your breath." He touches a specific spot on his own neck by way of demonstration. "The external jugular bleeds like crazy when it gets cut—as you saw. There's a real danger of the patient bleeding out if direct pressure isn't applied right away—but in her case, luckily, it was. Our searchable exploration down the throat indicated there was no involvement of the carotid, trachea, or esophagus—just a nick to that one external vein. Despite all the blood, the wound itself was fairly superficial, so we stitched it up and that was that."

I feel like I'm waiting for the other shoe to drop. "What about the rest of her?" My heart pounds in my chest. I brace myself.

"Looks like she fell backwards and hit her head on something pretty hard—"

"The sink—the bathroom sink. There was blood on the edge of it."

"Yeah, that's consistent with the injury. Whacked the base of her skull pretty good. Pretty sizeable scalp laceration, mild concussion. Gonna have a doozy of a headache for a couple days, but she'll be fine. Scalp lacerations bleed profusely, as you saw—but again, not life threatening when direct pressure is applied right away, which it was. I'm sure the combination of the external jugular wound and the scalp laceration looked like something out of *Carrie*, but we've got her put back together now and she's gonna be just fine."

"Does she need surgery?"

He smiles. "Nope. We stapled her scalp laceration right up. And the stab wound to the ribcage didn't hit the major blood vessels, the breathing tube, heart or lungs—she got really lucky there—so we stitched that up and she's good to go. If all goes well overnight—vital signs remain strong, no signs of infection—we'll release her tomorrow. She'll be on strict bed rest for two or three days, and after that, I'd say in about a week, she'll be feeling close to her old self."

I'm elated. Shocked. Disbelieving. "She seemed really confused in the ambulance," I say. "Does she have"—I almost can't finish the sentence—"brain damage?"

"A CAT scan of the brain came back normal. Her confusion could have been the result of shock or the concussion—probably a little bit of both. Post-traumatic confusion is common. She seems pretty clear now. A police officer just went in to talk to her."

I let out the longest exhale of my life. "Can I see her now?"

"Right after she's done talking with the police officer, we'll come get you."

I physically shudder with relief, and he makes a sympathetic face.

"She's gonna be fine," he says. He squeezes my shoulder.

"Thank you, Doctor." I sit back down, my head in my hands, trying to focus my spiraling thoughts—but it's no use. My mind is a horse galloping away from the barn, and there's no way it's coming back until I see my baby alive with my own two eyes.

Chapter 5

Jonas

"Miss Westbrook, can Jonas go to the bathroom?" Josh asks, raising his hand.

All I did was look at Josh a little funny and he knew right away what I wanted. Josh has been doing my talking for me for so long, it's like he's inside my brain.

"*May* Jonas go to the bathroom, *please*," Miss Westbrook corrects him.

"*May* Jonas go to the bathroom, *please*?" Josh repeats.

Miss Westbrook looks at me. "Do you need to use the restroom, Jonas?"

I nod.

I don't know why Miss Westbrook always bothers to check with me when Josh speaks for me—he's always right about what I want. I don't mind, though—I like it when Miss Westbrook talks to me. She's pretty. Really, really pretty. Her dark hair is super shiny. I wish I could touch it. And I like how, when she talks to the class, she smiles, even when she's telling someone to say "may" instead of "can" or warning one of the kids to stop talking to his neighbor. Of course, she never has to warn *me* to stop talking to my neighbor—I haven't said a word since before I turned eight, since that day when I was seven when I said, "I love you, Mommy," and Mommy didn't say it back. (That one time I spoke to Mariela in Spanish doesn't count because Spanish isn't even real.)

When I get back from the bathroom, everyone in class is working on the math worksheet. I already finished that one. In fact, I've already finished the entire workbook. I walk toward my desk, but Miss Westbrook calls me over.

"Jonas," she says softly. Her dark eyes are twinkling at me. Man, oh man, Miss Westbrook has the prettiest eyes. They look kind of like chocolate and they sparkle whenever she smiles. "I could really use a classroom helper every afternoon for about an hour," she says. "Someone to help me get everything ready for the next day. Do you think you could be my helper?"

I nod. I don't even have to think about it.

Miss Westbrook flashes me her sparkly smile. Her smile is so pretty it almost makes me want to smile, too. "Wonderful," she says. "When your nanny comes to pick you up today, I'll talk to her about it. Maybe she can take Josh after school for a bit every day while you stay here with me."

I nod again. I'm excited.

After school, Miss Westbrook talks to Mrs. Jefferson about her idea just like she said she would, and she makes it sound like she really needs my help—like I'd be doing her a big favor. I look at Mrs. Jefferson's face, trying to figure out what she might be thinking about the idea, but I can't tell. My stomach hurts, I want to do this so bad.

"The thing is," Mrs. Jefferson says, "Josh and Jonas have a standing doctor's appointment twice a week after school." She lowers her voice. "The therapist."

At that last part, Josh rolls his eyes at me, but I'm too excited about this whole helper-thing with Miss Westbrook to pay any attention to Josh. But, yes, I know what he means. I hate seeing Dr. Silverman, too. Mostly. All we ever do at Dr. Silverman's is color pictures in that stupid coloring book about different kinds of feelings. Or we read from that stupid book, *Let's Talk About Our Feelings*. "Talking lets the feelings out," one of the pages says. "Talking about how we feel makes us feel better," another page says. "Someone might not feel the same way we do—and that's okay," another page explains. "Talking about it doesn't mean we're disagreeing." The last one makes Josh laugh the most. "Talking about it doesn't mean we're *disagreeing*," Josh always says. "It means I'm going to punch you in your stupid, frickin' face."

Every time Josh and I see Dr. Silverman, Josh does all the talking for me. Well, for me and for himself. Josh talks and talks to Dr. Silverman about everything—what he had for breakfast, how he wants to be a baseball player when he grows up, about a dream he might have had the night before—whatever. Sometimes, he even talks about Mommy and how he misses her and how he wishes she could be here with us instead of in the clouds and stars. Josh always cries when he talks about Mommy, but I don't cry. No matter what Josh talks about, even if it's Mommy, I just sit there, coloring in that stupid coloring book, flipping through the frickin' *Let's Talk About Our Feelings* book.

I'd say I hate going to see Dr. Silverman except for one thing. He always plays the best music—the kind of music that makes me feel like my mind is floating in the clouds or riding on a roller coaster. Sometimes, Dr. Silverman's music even makes me forget about feeling sad for a little while.

Dr. Silverman tells me I should listen to music whenever I feel like I have too many feelings inside me. "Music can be like opening a window for your feelings to fly through," he explained to me one time. And when he said it, I got goose bumps on my arms. *Music can be like opening a window for your feelings to fly through.* It was the first thing he'd said to me that made perfect sense. Ever since he told me that, I've been listening to music a lot, especially when I feel like banging my head against the wall. The music calms me down and helps me think straight. So, even though I *mostly* hate going to Dr. Silverman's office, I guess I don't *completely* hate it.

After a visit with Dr. Silverman, Josh always used to say to me, "You don't have to talk if you don't want to, Jonas. I'll talk for you forever if you want." But yesterday, out of nowhere, Josh tried to make me start talking just like everybody else does. "Maybe if you talk—just a little bit—Dad won't make us go to Dr. Silverman's anymore. Come on, Jonas, just make something up—I make stuff up every frickin' time."

At first, I was mad when Josh tried to get me to talk. But today, I think I understand how Josh feels. He's not the one who needs the music, after all.

The more I think about it, the more I'm sure Josh is right—if I said something, anything at all, we wouldn't have to go to Dr. Silverman's anymore. But the thing Josh doesn't understand, the thing no one understands, is that I can't talk ever again. Because talking is against the rules. And there's nothing I can do about that, whether I like it or not.

Miss Westbrook continues whispering with Mrs. Jefferson about what a big favor I'd be doing for her if I became her helper. I feel like my head's gonna explode, I want to do it so bad. Finally, Mrs. Jefferson nods and says, "Well, I guess there's no harm in giving it a shot."

When we get home, Mrs. Jefferson talks to Daddy about what Miss Westbrook said, and, much to my shock, he says I can do it. "Josh doesn't need Dr. Silverman anymore, anyway," Daddy says. "And I suppose Jonas can take a couple weeks off to give this a try. But if it doesn't work, Jonas will have to go back to Dr. Silverman—or, hell, maybe I'll just send him back to the treatment center."

When I hear Daddy say I can help Miss Westbrook, I feel like shouting, "Woohoo!" really loud (but, of course, I don't). I'm so excited about getting to be with Miss Westbrook every day, I don't even freak out that Daddy said that thing about the treatment center.

Later that night, Josh jumps on his bed like it's a trampoline and laughs about how lucky he is and how stupid I am. "Mrs. Jefferson's gonna take me for ice cream every afternoon while you're sitting there with Miss Westbrook," he says. "Sucker."

I roll on my side away from Josh and smile, thinking about how pretty Miss Westbrook is and how her eyes sparkle when she smiles at me. Stupid Josh can laugh at me all he wants—I'll take an hour with Miss Westbrook over a dumb ice cream cone any day of the week.

Chapter 6

Jonas

The cop exits as I walk into Sarah's hospital room. I'm shaking like a leaf. Will she even be able to look me in the eye? Or will she want nothing to do with me?

I stop just inside the door to her room, barely able to breathe. She looks impossibly small. She's got a bandage around her head like she's a Civil War soldier and another one around her neck. She's wearing a hospital gown, but I'm sure she's bandaged under there, too. Oh God, she's pale—though, thankfully, not nearly as pale as she was on the floor of that bathroom. I never want to think about how she looked on the floor of that bathroom again. I bite my lip to suppress a sudden surge of emotion.

Her bracelet's gone. They must have cut it off her. For a moment, the symbolism of her naked wrist threatens to make me lose it, but I stay strong. I'm a fucking beast now. I'm not weak like I used to be.

"Go Seahawks," she says softly. Her voice is gravelly.

I'm confused.

"Interesting time to show your Seahawks pride."

I look down. Oh yeah, my new T-shirt. This woman is bandaged and bruised and literally just escaped death, and she's still got enough gas in the tank to kick my ass. God, I love her. I laugh and cry at the same time and lurch to her bedside. I hug her gingerly, not wanting to break her.

I've never been on the other side of a bloody floor before. Usually, a red-soaked floor simultaneously marks the end of one person's life and my sanity. I don't even know how I'm supposed to react if the story of a bloody floor doesn't have the usual ending.

"I'm so sorry, Sarah," I say, softly kissing her precious lips. "I'm so sorry, baby."

"*I'm* sorry," she mumbles into my lips.

I kiss her again. "You have nothing to be sorry for, you big dummy."

"Jonas," she says.

"I thought I'd lost you," I say, kissing every inch of her face. "Oh my God, baby. I thought I'd lost you."

"Jonas," she says, almost inaudibly.

"This is all my fault. I'm so, so sorry. I fucked up so bad."

"You saved my life," she whispers.

I have no idea what the fuck she's talking about.

"You saved my life," she says again. Her voice is the faintest of whispers.

What? I'm the one who let her go into that bathroom by herself. What the hell is she saying? I have a thousand questions—but before I can ask a single one, Sarah's mom bursts into the room, sobbing and wailing and hijacking Sarah into a sudden whirlwind of rapid-fire Spanish and hysterical tears.

"In English, Mom," Sarah whispers. "Jonas is here."

I understand Spanish fairly well, actually, but Mrs. Cruz talks so fast, I can't understand a word she says.

"Jonas," Mrs. Cruz says, hugging me fiercely.

I'm so ashamed I allowed harm to come to Mrs. Cruz's daughter, I can't even look her in the eye.

"Sarah has told me so much about you, Jonas." Mrs. Cruz touches my cheek. "Thank you so much for your donation. It was delivered this morning—ten times the biggest donation we've ever had. I tried calling Sarah to get your number to thank you, but she didn't answer her phone—" Mrs. Cruz looks at Sarah and bursts into tears.

Sarah squints at me—this is the first she's hearing about my donation to her mom's charity.

Mrs. Cruz hunches over Sarah, bawling her eyes out. "*Qué pasó, mi hijita*?"

"English, Mom," Sarah says softly. "Some guy attacked me with a knife in the bathroom at school."

Mrs. Cruz lets out a pained sob. "Who? Why?"

"I didn't know him. He just wanted what was in my purse. I gave the police a description of the guy—I'm sure they'll catch him. Don't worry."

So, this is the version of events Sarah told the police? What on earth is going on inside that head of hers? I glare at Sarah and she looks away.

"I'm staying here with you all night," Mrs. Cruz says. She pulls up a chair right next to Sarah's bed and drapes herself over Sarah's prostrate body. "Sarah," she says, emotion overwhelming her. "*Mi hijita.*"

I want to be the one sitting next to Sarah, draping myself over her. But, clearly, a mother's love trumps a boyfriend's—especially when the boyfriend's the one who fucked up and let harm come to his girlfriend in the first place.

"Is there anything you need?" I ask. "Mrs. Cruz? Can I get you something to eat? Anything to drink?"

Mrs. Cruz doesn't respond. She's got her head on Sarah's stomach and she's crying her eyes out.

Yeah, I know the fucking feeling.

I wake up in a chair in the corner of the hospital room. When did I fall asleep? I was having a crazy-ass dream—a dream about Miss Westbrook. What the hell? I haven't thought about Miss Westbrook in probably fifteen years.

The room is silent except for the clicks and beeps of the medical equipment. Sarah's fast asleep with her mom still draped over her. Kat's asleep in a chair on the opposite side of the room. I didn't see her arrive. A nurse is changing Sarah's IV bag. I stare at Sarah's heart monitor for several minutes, making sure her pulse is steady and strong, and then I close my eyes again.

My head jerks up. How long was I asleep? Fuck, these crazy-ass dreams won't leave me alone. Am I losing my mind?

Sarah's mom is awake, holding Sarah's hand as she sleeps. Kat's gone. I get up and tiptoe over to Sarah and softly kiss her lips. My heart is heavy—I'm surprised it can beat at all with fifty-pound rocks weighing it down.

"I'm sorry," Sarah whispers when my lips leave hers.

I didn't mean to wake her—but I'm relieved to hear her voice. "I'm the one who's sorry."

"You saved my life," she whispers. She closes her eyes and a tear trickles down her cheek.

I don't know why Sarah keeps saying that. I can only assume it's the painkillers talking because what's happened to Sarah is all my fucking fault.

Chapter 7

Jonas

On the first day of me being Miss Westbrook's after-school helper, she doesn't talk to me all that much except to tell me what jobs she wants me to do. I clean the whiteboard, making sure to erase every little smudge, even off the corners. After that, I sharpen her pencils, making each one the exact same length, and then I staple thirty sets of worksheets, making sure to line up the staples in each and every corner in exactly the same spot.

Miss Westbrook says I'm doing a great job and that I "pay great attention to detail." No one has ever said that to me before. I smile at her—just a teeny-tiny bit—and when I do, she smiles so big at me, I almost laugh. Almost.

The second day is the same as the first, except I pay even more "attention to detail," hoping she'll say something nice to me again. And she does.

"Jonas, you do excellent work," she says. "Anyone can do a *good* job, but it's the special few who care enough to do an *excellent* job. Thank you for caring so much about *excellence*."

I feel all warm and gushy inside. She's the prettiest lady I've ever seen and I like it when she's nice to me.

On the third day, I know all my jobs so well, I finish them in half the time—so Miss Westbrook gives me even more jobs to do. And on this day, yippee, while I'm doing my extra work, Miss Westbrook starts talking to me. She shows me a teeny-tiny diamond ring on her finger—the diamond's so small it's like a grain of sand—and she tells me the ring is how you know she's getting married. I've seen that ring on Miss Westbrook's hand before, but I just thought she wore it to look pretty.

Miss Westbrook tells me her name's going to be Mrs. Santorini in a few weeks and that the man she's going to marry is in the Navy. She explains how people in the Navy are fighting to protect our country and our freedoms. She says we couldn't do any of the stuff we get to do in America if people like Mr. Santorini didn't fight for us. I listen carefully to everything she says. I like the sound of her soft voice. She smells good, too. I especially like her neck. She wears a little gold cross around it and I can't stop looking at it—her neck, not the cross. But I pretend I'm looking at the cross just in case I'm not supposed to look at her neck so much.

On the fourth day, Miss Westbrook sits me down at one of the desks even before I get started with my work. "I have a little present for you," she says. She puts a gigantic cookie on the desk in front of me. "I baked it for you last night."

It's a huge chocolate chip cookie with M&Ms in it—the biggest cookie I've ever seen—and the M&Ms are in the shape of a heart.

For some reason, I feel my bottom lip shaking when I look at that M&M heart.

Miss Westbrook doesn't talk for a really long time. "Go ahead, Jonas," she finally says. "Try it."

I take a tiny bite. It's the best cookie I've ever had.

"Jonas," she says softly. "If you don't want to talk, that's fine. But sometimes I get kind of lonely in the classroom and I'd love a little conversation. Do you think maybe you could talk to me? You wouldn't have to talk outside this classroom if you didn't want to—and you wouldn't have to talk when the other kids are here. But when it's just the two of us here after school, maybe this could be our little cocoon—a cocoon built for two—a magical place where you're allowed to talk, just to me."

We've been learning about how caterpillars turn into butterflies for the last month—we've even got a whole bunch of chrysalises hanging in a big box and we're waiting for them to hatch any day now. We've been learning that a caterpillar has a special kind of magic inside him right from the beginning, but he has to go inside a cocoon for his magic to work.

Maybe talking to Miss Westbrook in our little cocoon-built-for-two could be another exception to the rule? Like how speaking to Mariela in Spanish didn't break the rule, either? Maybe, even if I talk to Miss Westbrook inside our magical cocoon, my last *official* words in the *real* world would still be "I love you, Mommy."

"Can I still call you Miss Westbrook after you get married?" I ask. They're the first words I've spoken since way before I turned eight—since the day Mommy went away all that time ago. I forgot how my voice sounds. I don't even sound like me anymore.

Miss Westbrook's face looks really surprised. She clears her throat. "Of course, you can, Jonas. I'd love that."

For the next week, I chat up a storm with my pretty Miss Westbrook every single day. I tell her about how much I hate seeing Dr. Silverman, except for the fact that he plays music that sometimes makes me feel better. I tell her about how Josh sometimes slaps his own face when I'm feeling sad, just to make me laugh, and that it always works. I tell her about a book on Greek mythology I just read and about how the Greek gods and goddesses are called the Twelve Olympians and they live on Mount Olympus. And, finally, on the tenth day of me being Miss Westbrook's special helper, I tell her about how I'm going to climb the highest mountain in the whole world one day.

"Really?" she asks. "That's exciting."

"Yeah, Mount Everest," I say, standing on a stool so I can reach the farthest corner of the whiteboard. "Because that's the highest one. I'm going to climb to the tippy-top of it and reach my hands up in the air and touch my mommy in the clouds. And she's going to reach down and pull me up and up and up, and then we'll lie down together on one of the puffy clouds like it's a hammock and I'll rub her temples and take all her pain away like I always used to do."

Miss Westbrook has been sitting at her desk while I've been erasing the whiteboard and talking nonstop, and when I look over at her, she's crying. Without even thinking about it, I climb down from the stool, put the eraser down, walk over to her, and brush her tears off her cheeks with my fingertips. Miss Westbrook wipes her eyes and smiles at me. And then she does something that makes me want to curl up in her lap—she touches my cheek with the palm of her hand. That's what Mommy and Mariela used to do all the time to me and it's my favorite thing.

Since Mommy went away, lots of adults have hugged me, or patted me on the head, or squeezed my shoulder, but not a single one of them has ever touched my cheek. Since Mommy went away, I've dreamed about her touching my cheek lots and lots of times—and about Mariela doing it, too—but then I always wake up and I'm all alone and I have to touch my own cheek, which doesn't feel nearly as good as someone else doing it for you, especially someone pretty like Miss Westbrook.

I close my eyes and put my hand over Miss Westbrook's to make sure she doesn't move her hand. Her skin is soft.

"You're a special little boy," Miss Westbrook says. "I hope one day I'll have a little boy just like you."

When Mrs. Jefferson and Josh come to pick me up, for some reason it seems like maybe I could say hello to Josh just this once without breaking the rules. I mean, Josh is really just me in another body, I figure, and talking to myself can't be against the rules, right?

"Hi, Josh," I say.

Josh seems really happy when I say those two little words to him, even happier than he was about getting ice cream with Mrs. Jefferson; so a few minutes later, when we're sitting in the backseat of the car and Josh is singing along to the radio at the top of his lungs, I talk again.

"Shut up, Josh," I say. "You're singing so goddamned loud, I can't hear the fucking music."

Mrs. Jefferson gasps in the front seat.

"Fuck you, Jonas. *You* shut up," Josh replies, but then he covers his mouth with both hands. "I mean, no, don't shut up, Jonas. Keep talking."

Josh telling me to shut up after I haven't talked for so long makes us both laugh really, really hard—or maybe we're just laughing because we're being really bad and cussing like Daddy.

"You big dummy," I say.

"You're the big dummy. What kind of idiot doesn't talk for a whole year? Jesus."

Not too long after Miss Westbrook becomes Mrs. Santorini, she tells the class she's moving to San Diego on account of Mr. Santorini being in the Navy. All the kids seem sad to see her go, but the way I feel about it is much worse than sad. I feel like I'm dying inside.

Miss Westbrook tells the class to work on page fifty-four from our math workbook and she calls me up to her desk.

"Jonas, honey, it's sunny in San Diego all the time. I hope you'll come visit me."

How can I come visit her? I'm just a kid. I don't have a car or an airplane. I have to look away from her pretty brown eyes or else I might cry.

"And I'll come visit you here in Seattle any chance I get." She starts crying. "I promise."

I don't think Miss Westbrook should promise to come back to me. Everybody leaves me—everybody—and they never, ever come back. I wish she would just tell me the truth: She's leaving me just like everybody does and I'll never see her again. Even as I stand here looking at her pretty face, I feel like a big black scarf is floating down from the sky and covering my entire body.

"I like you, Miss Westbrook," I say, trying to keep the tears from coming. It's the first time I've spoken to her when the other kids are in the classroom, too, when we're outside our magical cocoon.

But I can't help it—I have to tell her how I feel about her before she leaves me. Actually, I wish I could say the three words that match my true feelings about Miss Westbrook—but saying those three words to anyone besides Mommy would break the rules.

Miss Westbrook's eyes crinkle. "I like you, too, honey. I'll come back to visit you one day soon, Jonas. I promise."

Chapter 8

Jonas

I open my eyes. Sunshine streams through the window of Sarah's hospital room. A nurse stands next to Sarah's bed, checking Sarah's blood pressure.

"Looking good," the nurse says. "And no signs of infection. The doctor will be in soon to decide if you can go home today."

My phone vibrates with a text from Josh. He just landed in Seattle. Are we at UW Medical Center, he wants to know? I tell him not to come to the hospital, to meet me at home—and to please stop and pick up sick-person stuff like Saltines and Gatorade and Jello and chicken noodle soup on his way. Oh, and Oreo cookies. Sarah loves Oreo cookies.

He texts back, *I've got it covered.*

Thanks, I reply.

Hang in there, bro.

Thanks, I reply. *Will do.*

My phone buzzes again. I look down.

I love you, man.

Josh has never said that to me before, ever. Not in person, not in a text. Never. I stare at my phone for a long time, disbelieving my eyes.

Thanks, I text back. I don't know how else to respond.

I put the phone back in my pocket. If Josh were here, he'd surely slap his face right now, as he should.

The doctor arrives and confirms Sarah can go home and my heart leaps. Oh my God, I'm going to take such good care of my baby. No matter what it takes, we'll figure this out. Together.

Mrs. Cruz shrieks with joy at the doctor's news and starts asking him about his discharge orders. Apparently, she thinks Sarah's coming home with her. I look at Sarah, expecting her to say she's coming home with me, but she doesn't. To the contrary, she nods at her mother. What the fuck? Sarah's not correcting her mother's misunderstanding. Sarah's not saying, "No, Mom. I live with Jonas now." Shit. I guess Mrs. Cruz isn't the one who misunderstands. I swallow my emotions. All that matters is what Sarah wants. What Sarah needs. And, clearly, it's not me.

"I can drive you there," I say. "And help with whatever's needed."

"My mom's got it," Sarah says. "I'm just going to sleep, anyway—take my pain meds and sleep. You should use this time to get caught up on whatever you need to do. I'm finally out of your hair." She grins, but there's no joy in it. "I'll be fine."

I can't speak.

"I think I just need a little mommy time," Sarah says softly. There's apology in her voice. But there's no need to apologize—I understand fully. Everything I touch turns to blood: bloody sheets, bloody carpets, bloody walls, bloody bathroom tiles. Sarah's right. For her own good, she should stay as far the fuck away from me as humanly possible.

A nurse loads Sarah into a wheelchair to transport her to the front of the hospital.

"I can walk," Sarah protests.

"Standard procedure," the nurse assures her.

When we arrive at the front of the hospital, Mrs. Cruz leaves Sarah in my care while she gets her car from the parking structure.

Sarah's quiet. I'm quiet. There's so much I want to say, but not here, not now. Maybe there's never going to be a time to say it. Maybe this is it. Sarah obviously needs a break from me. I just hope a break doesn't turn into forever.

My heart feels like a slab of cement inside my chest. "I'll hire a team to guard your mom's house," I say. "I can't let you go over there unprotected."

"No, I'm safe now, at least for a while," Sarah says. "They think I'm worth more to them alive than dead."

What does that mean?

She swallows hard. "Jonas, I have something to tell you." She pauses, apparently getting up her nerve—but Mrs. Cruz returns with the car before Sarah can say another word.

Sarah looks at me with anxious eyes. Shit, the last time she looked at me like this was during our flight to Belize when she was summoning her courage to tell me the truth about The Club.

I open the passenger side of the car and gingerly load Sarah into the seat. My heart is breaking, aching, shattering. I might be dying, quite literally. Physical death couldn't feel any worse than this.

I lean down to her before I shut her door. "I can't let you go..." My brain intended to say, "I can't let you go there unprotected," but my mouth didn't finish the sentence. *I can't let you go.* Yeah, that about sums it up.

"It's just for a couple days," Sarah says. "My mom needs to be the one who takes care of me—and I need her right now. I'm just going to sleep the whole time, anyway." She shakes her head, stifling tears. "I'm not myself right now, Jonas. I'm overwhelmed. I'm in pain." She looks into my eyes and winces. "Don't worry, baby, I'll call you. I promise. It's just for a few days—just a little mommy time."

I nod as if I understand. But I don't understand. If she's leaving me for good, I wish she'd just tell me the truth instead of promising me something she doesn't plan to deliver. If she's not coming back to me, I wish she wouldn't tell me she is.

"Are you sure you're going to be safe?"

"I'm positive. There's no reason for them to come after me. They left me alive for a reason. I'll tell you about it later, I promise."

"I'll put guards at your mom's house anyway, just to be sure."

"No, don't, Jonas. My mom will freak out. Just trust me. Leave it alone."

I'm dumbfounded. They just tried to kill her and almost succeeded and I'm supposed to "leave it alone"? What the fuck am I missing here?

"*Lista?*" Mrs. Cruz asks.

"*Sí, Mama.*"

"I'll bring your clothes to you—whatever you need," I say lamely. I don't understand what's happening. Is this the end for us?

"I've got a bunch of old stuff at my mom's house. I'll be fine."

I'm speechless. She doesn't even want me to drop off a bag for her?

"I'll call you," Sarah says. But what my brain hears her say is, *Don't call me, I'll call you.*

I shut her door. She reclines in her seat and closes her eyes as the car drives away. I stare at the car until it's out of sight. And then I grab at my hair and swallow my tears.

Chapter 9

Jonas

Almost everyone in my seventh grade class is hard at work on today's stupid assignment. Mrs. Dinsdale said those few of us who've already finished, including me, can read whatever we want while waiting for the rest of the class to catch up. I'm reading a book about mountain climbing and there's an entire chapter about Mount Everest. I guess climbing Mount Everest is kind of a big deal—plenty of people have even died trying to do it. They don't let kids climb it, so it looks like I'll just have to climb rocks and trees and ropes and do sit-ups and push-ups and pull-ups in my room to get myself ready for when I'm older. Oh, and I just heard about an *indoor* rock climbing gym opening in Bellevue. Wow, rock climbing *indoors* sounds so cool I can barely sleep at night just thinking about it. Maybe Dad will let our driver take Josh and me there this weekend.

The door to the classroom opens and—holy shit—oh my God—holy fuck—I can't believe my eyes—Miss Westbrook walks in. She's right out of a dream—even more beautiful than I remembered her from four years ago. Wow.

Until just now, I couldn't even remember exactly what Miss Westbrook looked like, to be honest. She'd become nothing but a hazy fantasy in my mind that I sometimes like to think about late at night when I'm alone in my bed—but the minute she walks through the door, every memory comes rushing back into my head and heart and body. Especially my body.

Wow, Miss Westbrook is as pretty as ever. Even prettier than pretty, actually—she's *beautiful*. Her hair is shinier and a bit darker than I remembered it (which I like a lot). And her lips are much fuller than I remembered them, too. Man, oh man, I'd love to kiss Miss Westbrook's lips. I feel a jolt between my legs just thinking about doing it. Should I go over to her? Or maybe wave to her? I don't move a muscle. Maybe this is just a coincidence. Maybe she's not here to see me. Yeah, I'm sure she's forgotten all about me.

Miss Westbrook scans the room and when her eyes lock onto mine, she smiles. Holy fuck, she's smiling right at me, I'm sure of it. I wave and she waves back. Oh my God.

Miss Westbrook turns slightly to the side and—holy shit—now I can plainly see that Miss Westbrook's gonna have a baby. When Miss Westbrook first walked in, I guess I was so busy looking at her beautiful face and imagining myself kissing her lips, I didn't notice her baby bump. Wow. The beautiful Miss Westbrook came back—I can't believe it—and she's gonna have a baby.

"Jonas," Mrs. Dinsdale says. "You have a visitor. Why don't you two go outside for a little bit? Take your time."

When we sit down on a bench outside, Miss Westbrook hugs me and kisses the top of my head. "Jonas! You're so big! Look at you! Wow!"

My cheeks hurt from smiling. My entire body is tingling. "You came back."

"Of course, I did. I came back to see *you*." She winks. "I never break a promise."

I can't believe she's here. I feel like there's electricity zapping my skin. I wish she would touch my cheek like she did that one time all those years ago. Or kiss the top of my head again like she just did a minute ago. Or, even better, kiss my lips. I'd give anything to get a kiss from her—a real kiss with tongue and everything. Oh my God. The thought makes me tingle everywhere, but especially between my legs.

We talk for twenty minutes. She asks me about school and my brother and what sports I'm playing. She tells me that San Diego is as sunny and beautiful as she thought it'd be, that she's a third grade teacher there, and that she and Mr. Santorini are happy and excited about meeting their new baby in a couple months.

"Oh," she says suddenly, touching her belly. "The baby just kicked. You want to feel?"

I'm not really sure. The whole idea of touching her belly kind of freaks me out. But she doesn't wait for my response. She grabs my hand and places it on the side of her hard stomach and two seconds later something inside of her karate chops my hand.

"Oh my God," I say, laughing. I've never felt anything like that before.

"It's a boy," she says, smiling at me really big.

"Wow. That's cool, Miss Westbrook."

"Do you know what I'm going to name him?"

I shrug. How on earth would I know that?

"Jonas," she says.

There's a long, awkward silence. Is she saying my name to make sure I listen carefully to whatever name she's about to say? Or is she telling me, "I'm naming my kid Jonas"? If she's telling me she's naming the baby Jonas, that's quite a coincidence, isn't it? It's not that common a name—not like Josh.

She rolls her eyes and sighs. "I'm naming the baby after *you*, Jonas."

I can't believe my ears.

She smiles. "Because I hope he'll grow up to be just like you one day. Sweet and smart and kind."

I can't remember the last time my heart has raced quite like this, if ever.

At dinner that night, I tell Dad and Josh about Miss Westbrook's surprise visit and how she's naming her baby after me. I'm floating on air when I tell my story, but the minute I'm done talking, I regret saying a damned thing. Clearly, Dad's been drinking—a lot—and that's never a good time to say a goddamned thing to him about anything at all, especially something you care about.

I grind my teeth, waiting for whatever mean thing Dad's going to say to me to make me feel like shit. I don't have to wait long.

"She wants her baby to grow up to be just like you?" he asks. He takes a long swig of his drink. "I guess she's hoping for a lifetime of fucking misery and pain, then."

Josh shoots me his usual look of sympathy. It means, *Ignore him—he's an asshole.* But ignoring him is easier said than done.

"If she gets her wish and her kid turns out to be just like you," Dad continues, "then she'd better watch Mr. Santorini's back." He laughs and swigs his drink. "That's all I'm fucking saying."

Chapter 10

Sarah

Jonas was right all along—the Ukrainian John Travolta was indeed stalking me in broad daylight. But rather than believe my gorgeous hunky-monkey boyfriend when he said he was "one hundred ten percent" sure of something, I decided the more likely scenario was that he was being overprotective and hypersensitive and maybe even a tad bit crazy. Shame on me.

And, now, thanks to my utter lack of good judgment and my inability to trust him, not only did I get relieved of a good portion of my blood supply, I've also put the love of my life through hell. I've made him relive the worst horror of his childhood—and not only that, I've put him in danger, too. Good God, what have I done? I've promised The Club I can get more money from Jonas—and also from a bunch of other guys, too. But, wait, there's more! Just in case all that wasn't bad enough, I gave the bastards Jonas' money—and it was a helluva lot of money, too.

Of course, Jonas will say the money doesn't matter to him—he'll say he'd pay any amount to keep me safe—but that money wasn't mine to give. The whole situation is just a colossal mess—a cluster fuck, as Jonas would say.

I crawl out of bed, pull back the curtains on the window, and peek across the street. Yup. Still there. Two guys sitting in a car. They've been there for the past four hours. I grab my phone off the nightstand and type out a text to Jonas. "Please tell me those two guys sitting across from my mom's place are yours. Or else I'm going to crap my pants."

"Yes. Sorry to worry you. I should have mentioned it. They're mine."

I'm about to tell him the bodyguards aren't necessary, that Jonas' check surely bought me a little wiggle room in the they're-coming-to-get-me department—but detailing yesterday's run-in with the Ukrainian

Travolta is a conversation I want to have with Jonas in person. "Thank you," I type. "You always take such good care of me."

"You're welcome, baby. I miss you so much. How are you feeling?"

"High as a kite. Painkillers are an awesome perk of being stabbed."

There's a long pause. "I miss you so much," he finally texts.

"I miss you, too."

We've been apart for maybe four hours and I already feel like I'm going through physical Jonas-withdrawal. "I hope you understand," I type. "My mom needs to be the one who nurses me back to health." I'm about to add, *It's a mom thing,* but then I remember Jonas' mom, so I refrain.

And, truth be told, my mom's desire to take care of me isn't the only thing motivating me to stay here with her for a few days. The truth is that I need a little space—time to pull myself together and figure out what I'm going to do, what I'm going to say. I'm overwhelmed. Ashamed. Racked with guilt. I'm in pain, both physical and emotional. And most of all, I can't believe what I've put Jonas through—all because I didn't believe him. I could barely look him in the eye when my mom drove me away earlier today—I just feel so effing guilty.

"I understand," Jonas types. "I'm so sorry," he adds.

Why does he keep saying that? I'm the one who owes *him* an apology. If I'd had faith in him, if I'd trusted his intuition, if I'd believed him when he told me he was sure they were coming to get me, none of this would have happened. There's no excuse for the way I disregarded him.

"You have nothing to be sorry for, Jonas. I'm the one who blew it. Big time."

"Can I call you right now? We need to talk. I want to hear your voice."

I'm not ready to have this conversation yet. I'm still not sure how to explain how I feel. Plus, I'm drowsy as hell. "I just took a pain pill," I write. "I'm pretty sleepy. Talk later?"

He pauses again. "Whatever you need," he finally replies. "I'm here for you."

"Thank you. Talk soon." After a minute, I add, "Madness." I'm overwhelmed and remorseful and groggy and in pain, sure—but nothing, not even powerful painkillers, not even guilt and remorse and emotional exhaustion, not even a couple stab wounds or a bump on the head, can change the fact that I love Jonas Faraday with all my heart.

"Madness," he replies quickly. "So, so much."

I close my eyes and fall asleep.

Chapter 11

Sarah

The doctor told me I'd feel like myself again by day three of bed rest, and, wow, holy moly, he was right. I definitely feel like me again—a slightly beaten up version of me, true, but undeniably me. I open my laptop. Yesterday, a guy from school texted to say he'd emailed me notes from all my missed classes, and I finally feel alert enough to take a look. I click into my emails and my heart drops into my toes. There's an email from The Club.

"Dear Miss Cruz,

"It appears there has been an unfortunate miscommunication between us. We regret any discomfort this might have caused you. Please rest assured we have now acquired full information and look forward to putting the past behind us.

"We are interested in your recent proposal and believe you would make a valuable addition to our organization in the expanded role you have suggested. However, the split shall be seventy-thirty in our favor, not fifty-fifty as originally proposed by you. This is a non-negotiable term and quite fair since we will be supplying the clients.

"We will confirm further details through a Dropbox account within the next few days. But first things first, promptly confirm that you have not released the report you've described to our female associate. Release of any such report to any third party, including but not limited to the agencies you've named, would, of course, preclude the possibility of an amicable working relationship between us.

"Sincerely,

"The Club."

I can barely read the text of the email through my rage. Motherfuckers! They call almost bleeding me dry an "unfortunate miscommunication"? Really? Gosh, how about we sit down and talk things through? *Talking about it doesn't mean we're disagreeing—it means I'm going to stab you.* If Jonas were here, he'd laugh at that. Well, maybe not. You never know with Jonas.

Jonas. God, I miss him. Three days here at my mom's house has felt like an eternity, even in my drug-induced haze. I feel like I'm missing an arm or a leg. No, that's not right—I feel like I'm missing my heart. I've never ached for another human being the way I do for Jonas right now. I physically *need* him.

Speak of the devil, my phone buzzes with a text.

"Hi, baby," he says.

"Hi, boyfriend," I write back. "I was just thinking about you." We've texted and spoken several times over the past three days, but always briefly. Each time, I've told him I miss him and can't wait to see him. Every time, he's told me he's sorry—for what, I don't know. "Been keeping yourself busy?" I type.

"Yeah, went climbing with Josh yesterday. Been working on a business plan for Climb and Conquer. Hard to concentrate. I miss you too much."

"I miss you, too," I write. Why am I doing this to him? To myself?

"Do you need anything?"

"No, my mom is taking great care of me." I pause. I can feel his heartbreak through the phone line. He just wants to be with me. I know he does.

"Can I call you later?" I write. "Just finishing something up."

"Sure."

I can feel the tightness of that word through cyberspace.

"You promise you'll call?"

"I promise."

I *feel* his torture. I know I'm causing him pain. Heck, I'm causing myself pain. But I don't know how to tell him what I'm feeling. I feel guilty, ashamed. Downright depressed. I've put the man I love through hell. I've gotten him involved in something horrible and huge. And now I have to fix things, all by myself—but I don't know how. A part of me just wants to bury my head in the sand and wish it all away.

My mom comes into the room with a steaming bowl of soup and a tall glass of ice water. I close my laptop as she approaches.

"The soup's hot, so give it a minute," she says in Spanish.

"Okay, thanks."

"It's time for your antibiotic," she says. She looks at her watch. "And you can take another pain pill, too, if you want one."

"No," I say. "I think I'm done with painkillers. Maybe just an ibuprofen or whatever."

"Are you sure?"

"Yeah, I'm feeling a million times better. Those pain meds make me sleep too much."

"Sleep is how your body heals," she says. She touches my hair. "You look much better today."

"I feel much better."

"Are you doing schoolwork?" she asks.

"No, just checking my emails."

"Don't do too much. You're supposed to rest."

"I've been resting nonstop for three days. I'm starting to go crazy."

"Do you want me to stay in here with you? We can watch a movie."

Gah. I love my mom with all my heart. She's the best mom in the whole world, she really is. And this whole situation has to be her worst nightmare, even worse than what my father put her through. But oh my God, I'm going frickin' crazy staying here with her. The woman is smothering me with motherly love. Or maybe I just want Jonas.

"Yeah, that'd be great," I say. "Give me twenty minutes to finish what I'm doing on my computer and then we'll pick a movie."

"Okay. Don't do too much. The doctor said you need to rest." She kisses my cheek and leaves.

I open my laptop again. What the hell am I going to reply to these bastards? I can't show weakness, that's for sure. I've got to buy myself more time—time to figure out a game plan. I place my hands on my keyboard again.

"To Whom It May Concern," I type, biting my lip.

My phone buzzes with an incoming call and I grab it. *Georgia.* Wow, I'm elated Georgia's calling me back so soon after our phone conversation yesterday. "Hi, Georgia," I say. I didn't expect her to get back to me so fast. "How are you?"

"I'm great," she says. "How are *you* feeling today? Better?"

"Much better. Each day the pain gets less and less."

She sighs with relief. "I'm so glad to hear it. So, I've got the information you asked for." She sounds excited. "It was easy to get."

Yesterday, when I called Georgia (allegedly to tell her about Belize), I asked if she'd be willing to gather a teeny-tiny bit of post-office-related information for me. When she asked me why I needed the information, I told her a watered-down version of the truth, but the truth, nonetheless: I used to work for an online dating service that I've recently discovered was engaged in illegal activity (the nature of which I didn't specify), and I fear the attack on me at school might have had something to do with my discovery. "So I'm doing a little investigation to see if I'm right."

Of course, Georgia agreed to help me, if she could, although she was understandably worried.

"Okay, here's what I've been able to find out," Georgia says. "There are twelve Oksanas with post office boxes registered in the greater Las Vegas area—Las Vegas, Henderson, Winchester, etcetera. I've got their full names plus the physical address each Oksana provided when she signed up for her post office box."

"I owe you big, Georgia. Thank you. Can you email me the list?"

"Of course," she says. "But, hey, maybe you should go to the police with all of this?"

"I gave the police a statement in the hospital." True. "They think my attack was a random mugging." Also true (because that's what I led them to believe). "Hopefully, this information will lead to something helpful for the investigation." Also true—but helpful to whom and for what investigation I'm not exactly sure.

"Okay, just be careful," Georgia says.

After thanking Georgia profusely and assuring her I'd be careful, we say our goodbyes—and then I sit and ponder the situation for a moment. *Twelve* Oksanas? How am I going to find the right one? Knock on each Oksana's door and say, "Hi! Are you the Oksana who tried to kill me?"

It looks like my strongest play right now is buying myself time. What else can I do? I need time to figure out what to do next and that money I gave them isn't going to protect me forever. I open my laptop and continue typing my reply:

"I sincerely regret any discomfort caused by our 'unfortunate miscommunication,' too—seeing as how it left me dying in a puddle of my own blood on a bathroom floor. To answer your question, I haven't submitted my report to anyone yet, though it took a Herculean effort to stop it from automatically releasing to several agencies, as I'd previously arranged. Luckily, I was able to put the brakes on things at the last minute this time, but I won't be able to stop its widespread and immediate dissemination next time—nor will I even try. *So there better not be a next time.*"

I stop for a moment and consider deleting that last sentence. It's pretty ballsy. Eh, screw it. I'll just go balls to the walls—big risk, big reward, just like Jonas always says.

I continue typing:

"Thank you for your interest in my business proposal. I look forward to finalizing our arrangement, too. A fifty-fifty split is what I'm willing to do. Yes, you supply the clients, but I'm the one who's going to make them pay up. You can lead a horse to your watering hole all you like, but it's me who's going to make him slurp up gallons and gallons of water. In fact, I've recently learned I'm uniquely talented at making horses drink. Fifty-fifty. Take it or leave it, people. But be advised: If you decide to 'leave it,' my report goes live—no second chances. I'm done fucking around.

"The emergency room doctors I've recently visited, thanks to you—did I mention our 'unfortunate miscommunication' left me bleeding out on a bathroom floor?—have told me to take a solid two weeks strict bed rest to recuperate from my injuries. When my health returns and I'm able to walk, let alone ride the horses you plan on bringing to our mutual watering hole, I will let you know. I want this new venture to be a success as much as you do, I assure you—our interests are completely aligned—but I'm only human after all, and having a stab wound on my torso and staples in my head isn't all that conducive to sexy time.

"Sincerely,

"Your Faithful Intake Agent, Sarah Cruz

"P.S. By the way, I've described our recent 'unfortunate miscommunication' to the police as a random mugging. (I'm not fucking stupid.)"

Before I can change my mind, I press send.

Holy crappola. What am I doing? I'm insane. I'm not James Bond. I'm not a superhero. I can call myself Orgasma the All-Powerful all I like, but I'm still just me. A girl made of flesh and bones—and *blood*, as my body so recently proved in spades. I don't know what the heck I think I'm doing. Damn. I need help. *I need Jonas.*

Or maybe I should throw in the towel and just call the FBI already? If that means I won't pass the ethics review for my law license, then I guess I'll just have to live with that. But I don't want to give up on my legal career. Tears rise up in my eyes. I've worked too hard to get here. My mother is counting on me and so are the countless women my mom helps. I can't let them down. I've got to figure this out. I wipe my eyes.

I need Jonas.

I have a stomachache.

I need Jonas.

Jonas. Jonas, Jonas, Jonas. Oh my God, Jonas. My heart and body and soul ache for him. He looked so sad when my mom drove me away from the hospital. I wanted to hurl my body out of the car and leap into his arms right then. But I didn't. I just closed my eyes and cried as the car peeled away, too overwhelmed and in pain and jumbled and depressed and anxious to do anything else.

I need Jonas.

My heart pangs violently. I miss him. I can't be apart from him for another minute. I thought I needed time away to remind myself who I am when I'm not in his intoxicating presence—to battle my addiction to him and regain my sense of self, to get a handle on my studies and figure things out and let my body heal without distraction. I thought I needed to take a break from the madness for a little while. But I was wrong. Oh God, I was so wrong. I need him. My sweet Jonas. The man I love with all my heart and soul. For better or worse.

I pick up the phone and dial him. He answers immediately.

"Baby," he says softly. He sounds out of breath, like he gasped when he saw my name come up on his screen.

At the sound of his voice, I lose it. "Jonas," I bawl.

"What is it, Sarah? Tell me." He lets out a pained exhale. "Whatever it is, we'll handle it." He sounds like he wants to leap through the phone line.

"Come get me, Jonas. I want you. I need you. Please, Jonas. Bring me home."

Chapter 12

Sarah

"I can walk," I say. But Jonas ignores me, as usual. He scoops me up from his car and carries me into his house, straight to his bedroom, and lays me down on top of his white sheets like I'm a porcelain doll.

"Welcome home," he says softly. He's triumphant—the picture of pure elation.

I smile at him. "It's good to be home."

"Say that again," he says.

"Home."

"You're forbidden to leave ever again," he says. "I'm gonna install bars on the windows and doors."

"I'm so happy to be here, I'm not even creeped out by that statement."

He lies down next to me, on his side. "You're so beautiful," he says, softly tracing my eyebrow with his finger. "I missed you so much." He takes my face in his hands. "Never leave me again."

"I won't."

"Never, ever, ever."

"Got it."

"Ever."

"I've learned my lesson. It was physically painful being away from you—or, wait, maybe that pain came from the knife in my side." I smile, but he doesn't. Clearly, it's too soon for knock-knock-who's-there-I-got-stabbed humor.

"I—," he chokes out. He stuffs down whatever he was about to say. "When I saw you on the bathroom floor, I thought you were dead."

"Oh, Jonas, I'm so sorry." I can't even imagine how that must have affected him.

He kisses me gently. "I thought I'd lost you." He wraps his arm over me and kisses every inch of my face. His muscles are taut against my body.

I close my eyes. My fingers find his bicep. "I'm sorry."

"Stop apologizing," he murmurs. "I'm the one who's sorry." He sighs. "Sarah, I need to—"

"Jonas, wait. Listen to me."

He pulls back and stares at me. He waits.

"I know we have a ton of stuff to talk about. Like, tons and tons. But before we start talking and probably never stop, can I ask a favor?"

"You can have whatever you want, my beautiful, precious baby. Forever and ever and ever and ever, whatever you want." He strokes my cheek.

I pause. That was a big statement. Wow. He just made my heart leap out of my chest. I clear my throat.

"Name it, baby," he says, kissing my cheek. "Whatever it is, it's yours. *I'm* yours. Forever and ever and ever. Whatever you want, it shall be yours." He kisses my nose.

Wow, he's making me giddy. Not to mention turning me on. I can hardly speak.

"Tell me," he says.

"I want you to kiss all my booboos."

He smiles. "Your booboos?"

I grin broadly. It's hilarious hearing that silly word come out of his mouth. "Yeah. I want you to give me *besitos* on my booboos and make 'em all better."

"*Besitos*?" he repeats. Jonas always loves it when I speak Spanish to him.

"Mmm hmm. Little kisses. On my booboos."

"*Besitos* on your booboos, huh?"

"Mmm hmm."

He bites his lip. "Whatever you say, my precious, pretty baby. My Magnificent Sarah." His cheeks are flushed.

How did we survive these past three days apart? Why did I feel the need to pull away from him? I can't even remember why I thought I needed space.

I sit up and raise my arms over my head, and he takes off my tank top.

"Oh," he says, wincing at the sight of me.

I look down at myself and shrug. The wound on my ribcage looks way better than it did three days ago. But I imagine Jonas doesn't appreciate all the healing my body has done—all he sees is my current state of disrepair.

I lie back down on the bed, inviting him to kiss my body. “It looks worse than it feels, I assure you.”

He leans down to my torso and softly kisses me. “This booboo right here?”

Goose bumps erupt all over my skin. “That’s the one.”

He runs his fingertip over my stitches and then over the black-and-blue-and-yellowish skin surrounding the gash. “Does it hurt?”

“Not too bad.”

He kisses my wound again and I shudder as my skin comes alive under his touch. His lips move up from my ribcage to the stitched-up gash on my neck.

“And this booboo here, too?”

“Mmm hmm.” I shiver. I’m aching for him.

“Does it hurt when I kiss it?” he asks.

“No, it feels really good,” I say. “Your *besitos* are making me all better.”

“Can I see the back of your head?” he asks.

I sit up and turn my head. He moves my hair and gasps.

“Am I Frankenstein?” I ask. I’m anxious. I haven’t actually taken a peek back there.

“Holy shit. They *stapled* you back together, Sarah.” He lets out a groan of sympathy. “It looks like they used a staple gun from Home Depot on your head.”

I quickly lean back, intending to lie back on my pillow. “You don’t have to kiss that booboo—I’m not a sadist.”

He puts his hand on my shoulder to stop me from reclining. “Hey, sit back up, Frankenstein. I want to kiss all your booboos—*especially* that one.”

I pause. My heart is racing. I don’t know what it looks like back there, but it’s got to be pretty nasty looking. “It’s okay. I don’t want to gross you out.”

“You’re not grossing me out,” he says, turning my shoulders away from him. “I love every inch of you, Sarah Cruz, even the disgusting parts.”

I swivel back around and stare at him. Did he just say he *loves* every inch of me?

He meets my gaze. “Come on,” he says, his eyes smoldering. “Let me show you how much I love every inch of you.”

I’m speechless.

He swivels my head away from him, moves my hair aside, and softly presses his lips against the stapled wound at the base of my skull. “Does that feel good?”

I shiver. "Mmm hmm." Feeling his lips on my stapled skin is turning me on too much to say anything else.

His soft lips migrate down my neck, all the way to my bare shoulder. His hand wraps around my torso and cups my breast.

I feel him shudder with desire behind me—and I'm right there with him. I lie down on my back, and he instantly begins licking my erect nipples—and then my neck. My ear. My lips. His tongue enters my mouth and his hand touches my face.

Oh my gosh, I'm on fire. When my life flashed before my eyes in that bathroom, when I thought I was a goner for sure, what did I think about? *I love you, Jonas.* Of all the thoughts my brain might have conjured in that most vulnerable, raw, life-defining moment, my love for Jonas was everything.

"Sarah," he breathes, kissing me. "I thought I'd lost you." He chokes back emotion. "Sarah," he says again.

"Make love to me," I breathe.

He pulls back, unsure.

"The doctor said sex is okay after three days," I assure him. Okay, technically, I didn't ask the doctor when I can have sex again—but Dr. Sarah is here and she says it's okay. I feel like me again and I want him inside me. Oh my God, do I ever. I want to be as close to him as humanly possible. For goodness sake, the man just said he loves every inch of me, and I'm suddenly desperate for him to prove it, from the inside out.

He touches my face. "I don't want to hurt you."

"Just take it slow."

"Are you sure?"

"I'm sure." I take off my pajama bottoms. I'm yearning for him.

He takes his clothes off and lies down against me, his erection insistent against my belly, his skin warm and smooth against mine.

I'm trembling.

He holds me for a moment, looking into my eyes. "When I saw you in the bathroom... ," he says. But he stops.

"I'm sorry," I say. "That must have been terrifying."

"I thought you were dead."

"I'm sorry, Jonas."

He pauses a really long time.

Something in the way he's looking at me makes me hold my breath.

He inhales deeply. "I love you, Sarah."

My breathing halts. I'm not sure I heard him correctly.

"I love you so much," he says. His eyes are moist.

I burst into tears.

"I love you," he says softly, wiping at my tears. He kisses me.

I know this is the part where I'm supposed to tell him I love him, too, but I'm mute. I can't believe my ears. I'm dumbfounded. I'm spellbound. I return his kiss passionately and throw my leg over him, eager for him to fill me up. When his body enters mine, we both moan loudly at the pleasure of it.

"I love you," he says, his voice husky.

I open my mouth to speak, but nothing comes out. I'm overwhelmed.

"Am I hurting you?" he asks.

I shake my head.

He kisses my lips as his body moves inside mine. His hands stroke my back and butt. I feel nothing but pleasure and love and elation as his body leads mine into synchronized movement. Any pain my wounded body might have been feeling a moment ago has been replaced by pleasure, sublime pleasure. I feel euphoric.

"I love you," he says, his body zealously emphasizing his words.

"Oh, Jonas," I gasp, finding my voice. "I love you, too."

"Oh God," he exhales, shuddering. His lips find mine again, and then he whispers in my ear. "I love you, baby."

I moan and press myself into him enthusiastically. I never knew it could feel so good to hear those three little words.

"I love you, Jonas," I whimper. I'm bursting with joy. I can't believe this is happening.

He pulls out of me, his chest heaving. "I love every inch of you, Sarah Cruz." He gently pushes me onto my back and proceeds to kiss every single inch of me, from the top of my head to the wound on my neck, down to my breasts and belly and the gash on my ribcage, to my hips, thighs, crotch, arms and fingers and thighs and legs and toes, and then he begins working his way back up my legs and slowly up the insides of my thighs, to the sensitive skin right between my legs. By the time he gets to my clit and licks me ever so gently with his warm, wet tongue, I can barely hold it together. I'm arching my back, gripping the sheet, shuddering violently. I'm not sure if I'm going to scream or burst into tears or flames—or if all my stitches are going to simultaneously pop out of my skin like tiny projectile missiles—but, certainly, something's got to give. I can't withstand this pressure building inside me for much longer.

I make a guttural sound. I can't take it anymore. This is too exquisitely pleasurable to bear. *He loves me.* I feel like he's enveloping me in his love, wrapping me in it from head to toe—

delivering me into a dream. But this is way better than any dream, even the one where Jonas became a slithering, sensuous cloud. *He loves me.* And I love him.

His wet tongue leaves my sweet spot, making me cry out in protest, but he ignores me, kissing his way back up my torso, all the way up to my face. Finally, he arrives at my mouth and devours my lips, urgently pressing the tip of his erection against my throbbing clit. He kisses me voraciously, all the while grinding the tip of his penis desperately into the most sensitive spot on my body. Oh God, he's rubbing me, coaxing me, making me cry out, and whispering into my ear all the while.

"I love you, Sarah Cruz," he says, his voice and tip conspiring to push me over the edge. "I love you so much, baby." His voice is gruff as he rubs against me, making me writhe in ecstasy. "I love you with all my heart."

I scream his name as my body releases and shudders, an all-consuming orgasm rippling through me, and he slides his shaft into me, deep, deep inside me. After a brief moment, he finds his release, too.

"I love you," he whispers again, his body heaving one final time.

"I love you, Jonas," I say, shivering.

We lie together for several minutes, neither of us speaking.

Holy crap, that was delicious, even if my wounds have started pulsing angrily at me from the exertion. I don't care about a few throbbing stab wounds—I can take an ibuprofen for that, for Pete's sake. I just experienced unmitigated ecstasy—life-changing, earth-shattering, heart-swooning euphoria. Oh good Lord, this beautiful man *loves* me. And I love him. *We actually said it out loud to each other.* Oh my God.

Jonas kisses my cheek and rolls onto his back, sighing happily. "The culmination of human possibility," he says, flashing me a beaming smile. He's the picture of sheer exhilaration. I've never seen him smile quite so joyously before—never seen his eyes light up and dance without reservation quite like this. It's as if something dark and heavy has lifted off his soul, unburdening him and leaving him light as a feather. He's the most beautiful creature I've ever beheld. Oh, Jonas. My sweet Jonas. I love him with all my heart. And, Lord have mercy, he loves me right back.

Chapter 13
Sarah

Jonas and I are sitting on his balcony, looking out at the city, sipping wine (me) and beer (him), and finally having that heart to heart I've been avoiding for the past three days. I've just told him every single detail about my run-in with the Ukrainian John Travolta in the bathroom and I've also shown him my recent email exchange with The Club, too. He's listened intently to every word, barely breathing.

"You're so fucking smart," he says. "Thank God you had that check in your purse."

"Not thank *God*," I retort. "Thank *you.* I had that check in my purse only because *you* gave it to me, Jonas. You saved my life."

He shakes his head, unwilling to accept this simple but incontrovertible fact.

"Yes, Jonas. Listen to me. Two things saved my life—knowing Oksana's name and having that check—and I have you to thank for both. See? You saved my life."

Jonas takes a swig of his beer, mulling that over. I can almost see the gears inside his brain turning.

"Hey, maybe you can stop payment on that check," I say. "I don't know why I didn't think of that until just now. "

"Hell no. We *want* them to deposit that check—it's a homing device. Couldn't have worked out better if we'd planned it." He clinks his beer to my wine glass. "'Twas a stroke of brilliance, Sarah Cruz."

"I don't understand."

"Once they deposit the check, we'll know their bank of deposit—and we can use that information to find them."

"Oh, wow," I say. "I didn't think of that." I twist my mouth. "But that's assuming they deposit the check. My name's listed as the payee, don't forget."

He scoffs. "Any two-bit criminal can chemically lift the payee name off any check."

"Really? Jeez, that's scary. For a girl employed by a global crime syndicate, I'm not very knowledgeable about organized crime."

"Sarah."

"What?"

He's staring at me, his eyes moist. "I'm so proud of you."

I swat at the air like it was nothing. "All I did was buy myself a little time. I'm just worried about what's gonna happen when I don't deliver the oodles of cash I've promised them." I shake my head, thinking about all my big promises. "How long before they figure out I'm full of crap? How long before they decide to finish the job they started in the bathroom?" My stomach tightens.

"Oh, don't you worry, my pretty baby, we're gonna figure them out long before they figure us out." He puts his hand on my thigh and his palm is warm in the evening air. "You just keep making them think you've got me right where you want me, just like you did in that bathroom. Just like you did in your email to them. We'll use their greed against them and fuck them up the ass six ways from Sunday."

"I'm sorry I threw you under the bus, Jonas," I say. "I wish I could have figured out a way to save myself that didn't drag you into this."

"Are you serious? You were brilliant. You said exactly the right thing." He swallows hard, choking back emotion. "Whatever you had to do to stay alive, I'm glad you did it."

I put my wine glass down and move to his lap.

He puts his beer bottle down and wraps his arms around my back, nuzzling his nose into mine. "So what were the other horrible things you wanted to tell me, my precious baby?" he asks. At the beginning of this conversation, I'd warned Jonas I had five things to tell him, some of them not so great. "Whatever they are, I guarantee you, I won't be upset."

We'll see about that. I've only told him two out of the five things on my list of horribles: One, I gave the bad guys Jonas' two-hundred-fifty-thousand-dollar check. Two, I told the bad guys I've been scamming Jonas and can get them even more money. So far, so good—he seems to think I've handled things brilliantly. But now it's time for items three, four, and five.

"Item three," I say. "I've got a list of twelve different Oksanas who rent post office boxes in the greater Las Vegas area—plus the physical addresses each Oksana used when she registered for her box."

His mouth hangs open. "Wow, that's amazing. Why would I be

upset about..." His face suddenly darkens. "Sarah, how'd you get that information?"

I take a deep breath. "I asked Georgia to help me."

His face reddens and his body jerks beneath me like he's trying to buck me off.

I stand, my cheeks instantly burning.

"How could you even think about getting Georgia involved in all this?" He runs his hand through his hair, trying to contain his anger. Oh man, he's pissed. "That's just... I can't believe you did that." He looks like he's restraining himself from saying more.

I knew he wouldn't like this particular item, but I thought he might just roll his eyes about it. I didn't think he'd be genuinely *angry* with me.

His jaw muscles are pulsing in and out. "I don't want Georgia and Trey involved in all this—what were you thinking?" His voice is controlled rage.

What was I thinking? Well, in a nutshell that I'm going to do whatever I have to do to track these motherfuckers down. That I'm not going to sit around waiting for them to come back and finish the job they started. That I really didn't think I was putting Georgia and Trey in harm's way or else I never would have asked for Georgia's help, for Pete's sake, give me some effing credit.

I'm sure my indignation is written all over my face.

He stands. "Well, Jesus. What did you tell her when you asked her?"

I tell Jonas exactly what I said to Georgia, my voice tight and contained.

He's quiet for a solid minute, leaning over the balcony railing and looking out at the city.

I cross my arms over my chest and wait for the supreme lord-god-master to grace me with his verdict. Does he want to get the bad guys or not? Because I do—and that's all I was trying to do, for goodness sake. I sit back in my chair in a huff and grab my wine. Blood is pulsing in my ears.

He turns around and leans his back against the railing. "You're so fucking snoopy, you know that?"

I'm trying to keep my lip from trembling. I nod. Yes, I'm snoopy. I know this about myself. If he doesn't like that part of me, he's in for a long and tortured ride.

"You just can't help yourself, can you?"

I nod again. It's true. So what? I've always been this way. I can't help it. If he has a problem with the way I am, the way I've always been, the way I'm inherently wired, maybe this thing between us isn't going to work after all. What does he want me to do? Sit around and wait for them to come back and finish the job they started—

"Come here," he says, his voice full of warmth. He holds out his arms.

But I don't move. My cheeks are blazing. I've worked myself into a bit of a tizzy inside my own head and now I need a minute. What did he expect me to do? Sit around and twiddle my thumbs? That's not my style.

He walks over to me and pulls me out of my chair. I resist him for a grand total of three seconds, and then I melt into his broad chest.

"From now on, we're a team." He kisses the top of my head. "No more Snoopy Sarah running around conquering the world all by herself, okay?"

I don't reply. I'm just enjoying the feeling of his arms wrapped around me in the cool night.

"We make decisions together on this thing. And that goes for me, too—two and a half heads are always better than one."

I look up at him. "Two and a *half* heads? Is Josh the half?"

He laughs. "No, though I'll tell him you said that. I'm spotting you an extra half a head because you're so fucking smart."

I nuzzle into his neck. He smells so good. "I'm sorry, Jonas."

He tilts my face up to look at him. "What am I gonna do with you, baby? Hmm?"

I purse my lips. "Kiss me?" I raise my eyebrows hopefully.

He smiles and kisses me.

"Okay. What else is on the list?" he asks. He sounds a helluva lot more wary now than he did a few minutes ago when he so confidently proclaimed I couldn't possibly upset him.

I sigh. "I didn't believe you about seeing the Ukrainian Travolta. I thought you were overprotective and hypersensitive—and maybe even paranoid. I was an idiot. I should have believed you."

He cocks his head to the side and looks at me for a long time. He opens his mouth to say something and then reconsiders. "I understand," he finally says. "It's okay."

I'm expecting more, but apparently that's it.

He shrugs. "What else you got?"

So we're done with that one? Because if we are, I have no idea how it just got resolved. "Um. Well, last but not least, I think it's important for us to talk about how all of this must have affected *you*."

He clenches his jaw but doesn't speak.

"I feel so horrible." My eyes suddenly brim with tears. "I've put you through yet another bloody trauma—the last thing in the world I ever wanted to do to you. It must have been beyond torture for you to find me like that—the whole scenario must have brought up all kinds of stuff about your mother's murder. I'm so, so sorry—"

"*I'm* the one who's sorry." His voice is pure anguish. He sits back down in his chair and puts his head in his hands. "I'm the one who promised to protect you and then let you go into that bathroom, unprotected, all alone, while I sat in that classroom, listening to fucking music—" He's choking up, becoming more and more emotional as he speaks.

"You were listening to music? Were you listening to the playlist I made for you?"

He stops and stares at me, his train of thought hijacked.

I sit on his lap and wrap my arms around his neck. "Were you able to decipher the super-secret coded message I sent you in those songs?" I smile, but he scowls.

Boom. It suddenly hits me like a ton of bricks—this right here is the exact moment I've been wanting to avoid for the past three days—the exact thing that made me retreat from Jonas and seek out a little space. *This.* I don't want to do this. I knew in my bones Jonas would view this entire situation as his frickin' fault—as yet another example of how he's miserably failed to protect the one he loves the most. I knew he'd blur the attack on me with the horror of his mother's murder and wrap the two incidents together into a giant ball of intractable self-blame—and, frankly, I can't handle it. I just don't have the emotional bandwidth to watch to him spiral into yet another tortured round of self-loathing.

This beautiful man has blamed himself for twenty-three frickin' years for his mother's murder. So is he going to blame himself for my attack for the *next* twenty-three years, too? And if so, at what cost to his soul? And to mine? At what cost to our relationship? I'm a compassionate person, but I'm not a frickin' saint. I don't want to deal with this. It's bullshit and I don't have time or patience for it.

"I don't know how you'll ever forgive me," he says, covering his face with his hands.

I leap off Jonas' lap and pace the balcony, my thoughts racing. "Jonas," I begin, adrenaline surging inside my veins. "No."

He looks up at me. He folds his arms over his chest, bracing himself.

I take a deep breath. "No, no, no. Your entire life, you've blamed yourself for your mom's death—*and it wasn't your fault.* Fuck your father, Jonas. It wasn't your frickin' fault. *No.*"

He looks surprised. This isn't what he expected me to say.

"If you and I are going to have a fighting chance, you can't blame yourself for what happened to me the way you've blamed yourself for your mother's death. I'm just telling you, straight up, if you blame yourself this time, with me, it'll poison you—it'll poison me—and then it'll poison *us*."

Now he looks shocked. And hurt. But it's too bad. I'm on a roll.

"You saved my life, Jonas—get it through your thick, tortured head. You're my hero, baby—my savior. It's the objective truth, but it's also the truth I *choose*. Don't you understand? I *choose* to be with the man who saved my life, not the man who's forever trying to undo yet another 'horrible failure' that isn't his fault. Enough with that tormented guy—enough with that self-blaming, *mea culpa* bullshit. In this fairytale—*our* fairytale—you're the guy who rides in on a white horse and kicks ass and takes names and loves me like nobody ever has—because you *are* that guy, Jonas Faraday. This isn't going to work for me if you're going to seek my forgiveness forevermore for something you didn't frickin' do."

He swallows hard.

"If you insist on talking about blame, fine. Let's talk about it. *Once.*"

He opens his mouth to speak, but I hold up my index finger to stop him.

"If anyone's to blame here, it's me. *I'm* the one who broke the rules and contacted you in the first place. *I'm* the one who went to spy on you and the software engineer, making it so damned easy for Stacy to put two and two together and rat me out. And *I'm* the one who refused to let you follow me into that bathroom because *I'm* the one who thought my brilliant and sensitive boyfriend was just being *paranoid*—and maybe even hallucinating."

He winces at that last word. Yeah, Jonas, I just called you crazy-pants.

"And all that's on me. Shame on me, Jonas. *Shame on me.* I'm the one who gave you a hard time for not trusting me completely—not leaping off a waterfall for me—and then I turned around and didn't trust you."

He looks like he's going to cry.

"But I forgive myself for all that, Jonas, and I hope you will, too, because, otherwise, it's going to eat me alive and doom our relationship." The expression on his face is breaking my heart, but I barrel ahead, anyway. "Jonas, I get the whole self-blame-thing when you're seven years old and your dad does a number on you your whole effing life. But when it comes to you and me, moving forward as adults, as equals, the tortured-guy routine isn't gonna end well, I guarantee it." I pause. "I'm not going to be in a relationship with a man who thinks everything that happens is on him. I mean, I know you've got a God complex, but that's taking things too damned far."

His eyes flicker.

"No more blame, Jonas. No more 'I don't know how you'll ever forgive me' bullshit. We move forward without blame or we don't move forward." I jut my chin at him. "Because I'm ready to do this shit, man—kick some ass, baby."

His chest heaves in cadence with mine. His eyes blaze.

"Just as soon as I get the staples out of my head, that is."

His mouth tilts up into a crooked smile.

I raise my hands. "So what's it gonna be, boyfriend? Decide. Are you in or are you out?"

He rises from his chair, his eyes smoldering, and wraps his bulging arms around me. All it takes is one kiss and, in a flash, we're mauling each other, pulling our pants down, consumed by the sudden electricity coursing through our veins. Without hesitation or wind-up, he pushes my back up against the balcony railing, plunges his fingers inside my wetness to find his target, and then enters me deeply, whispering "I love you" and "so fucking hot" and "baby" in my ear as he does it. Oh. My. God. Divine.

I could be wrong—I could be way off-base here—but I'm pretty sure this man right here is telling me, emphatically, that, yes, he's in. *All in.* Inside me, that is, nice and deep and all the way. In, in, in, in, in, in, in.

Chapter 14
Sarah

A noise next to the bed wakes me with a jolt. I squint into the darkness of the bedroom, my eyes slowly adjusting to the surrounding shapes and colors. My heart lurches into my throat. Oh my God. John Travolta from *Pulp Fiction* stands in a far corner of the room, gripping a large knife. When our eyes meet, he grins. I open my mouth to scream, but nothing comes out. He walks slowly toward me, smiling wickedly, the blade glinting in his hand.

I find my voice. "Oksana!" I yell.

He shakes his head. "Not this time, bitch." He raises the knife high over his head, his eyes cold, and plunges the blade into my heart.

I sit up, screaming at the top of my lungs, clutching my chest.

"Shh," Jonas says, gripping my jerking body. "It's okay."

I thrash against his grasp, my throat burning.

"You're dreaming, Sarah. It was just a dream."

I burst into tears and go slack in his arms, my entire body shaking violently.

He pulls me close.

I hiccup, trying to control my sobs.

"It was just a bad dream," he says. "Shh."

A soft rain batters the roof. My heart is racing.

"I'm here," Jonas says. "I'm here, baby. It was just a bad dream. I've got you."

His body is warm against mine. He pulls me close to him and kisses my wet cheeks. I can't stop shaking.

"We have to go to Vegas," I blurt, my voice trembling. "It's time to kick some bad-guy butt. I have to *do* something."

He brushes a chunk of hair away from my face and kisses my cheek again.

"Tomorrow I get the staples out of my head—and then we go," I say.

He pauses a long time. The sound of rain pelting the window fills the silence. "What about your classes?" he finally asks.

"Finals are in five weeks," I say, sighing with resignation. "I'm so far behind, I'll never ace my classes like I wanted to, no matter what I do." I'm sure he can hear the disappointment in my voice. "But on the bright side, I've studied so hard all year long, I could take my finals tomorrow and at least pass every class." I breathe deeply, still trying to steady myself. "I guess finishing middle-of-the-pack is just going to have to be enough for me, whether I like it or not."

He exhales. "You know you don't need that scholarship, right? Whatever happens, I'm gonna take care of you."

I nuzzle into his neck. "I know. Thank you." I want so badly to tell him I love him again, but I bite my tongue. So far, we've only said those three little words to each other during sex—and I don't want to push him too hard. I know it was a big step for him to say those words to me at all, so I settle for my usual three little words. "My sweet Jonas," I say softly.

He squeezes me. "You sure you're feeling up to tackling this?"

"Yep, I'm ready. It's time to kick some butt."

"Well, okay, then." He exhales loudly. "Let's go kick some bad-guy ass. I'll call Josh in the morning and tell him to grab his hacker buddy and meet us in Sin City."

"Why do we need Josh?"

"Josh and I share one brain. Plus, he'll bring the hacker to the party, and we need the hacker."

He's right about that. Yesterday, we discovered the bad guys had deposited Jonas' two hundred fifty thousand dollars at a small bank in Henderson, a town just outside Las Vegas—and Jonas immediately put the hacker to work poking around the bank's mainframe. If we hit pay dirt—if it turns out one of the Oksanas on our post-office-box list has an account at that particular bank—we'll be in butt-kicking business.

"Okay, that sounds good. I'll call Kat and we'll go frickin' *Ocean's Eleven* on their ass."

"Why do we need Kat?"

"Kat always comes in handy in any situation. You'll see. We might not know why or how we're gonna need that girl, but we will."

"But why involve Kat in this stuff? I'm pretty sure I convinced Stacy that Kat's totally clueless about The Club—and odds are high Stacy passed that information along up the chain. Let's just keep Kat off the bad guys' radar from now on."

"No, you don't understand. Kat's the female version of you,

baby—people fall all over themselves when she bats her eyelashes. That's a powerful weapon to have at your disposal. And, anyway, come on—we've gotta have a bunch of good-lookin' people on our team to pull off a Las Vegas heist. Haven't you seen *Ocean's Eleven*?"

He exhales in frustration. "We shouldn't get Kat involved."

"I need her, Jonas. You need your Joshie-Woshie—I need my Kitty Kat."

He sighs. "Okay. Fine. Josh, Hacker, Kat." He rolls his eyes with mock-annoyance. "Who else do I need to fly out to Vegas on a moment's notice for you, boss? George Clooney? Brad Pitt? Matt Damon?"

"Yes, please. All three. Oh, and Don Cheadle, too. I love that guy. How about Ben Affleck, too, just to keep Matt Damon company? If you and I get to have our besties with us, then it's only fair Matt should, too."

"Aw, how sweet," Jonas says.

"Yeah, that's me. I'm a giver." I shrug. "It's just how I'm wired."

He laughs. "Even when you're plotting world domination, you make me laugh."

I sigh. "Sometimes, laughing's the best way to keep from crying."

He squeezes me again. "There's no reason to cry, baby," he says tenderly. "We've got this. You and me. Well, you, me, and Clooney."

I squeeze him back. "And Brad Pitt."

"And Matt and Ben."

"And Don Cheadle," I say. "And Joshie-Woshie and Kitty Kat and Hacker-Guy."

"We're a motley crew," he says.

"And a frickin' good-lookin' one, too."

"We're unstoppable."

We listen to the rain battering the roof for a minute.

"God, I hate Vegas," Jonas mutters.

"Why?"

"*Why*?" He says it like I've just asked him why he hates the Ebola virus. "Crowds. Neon lights. Cigarette smoke. Club music everywhere you go. *Dancing.*" He grimaces like that last item is the worst offender of all. "Not to mention mindless zombies throwing their hard-earned money away on nothingness in a desperate attempt to *feel* something, if only for a fleeting moment, and then trudging back to the bleak reality of their real lives without their fucking rent money." He grunts. "I hate everything about that fucking place."

All this coming from a guy who recently threw his hard-earned money away on nothingness in a desperate attempt to *feel* something, if only for a fleeting moment? I love this boy, God knows I do, but he sometimes slays me with his lack of self-awareness. But I'm in a saintly mood today so I'll refrain from pointing out that bit of irony. "And here I thought Vegas sounded like fun," I say. "Silly me."

"You haven't been to Las Vegas?"

"Nope."

He's surprised.

"Not everyone has been everywhere like you, Mr. Money Bags."

"But Las Vegas isn't an 'oh, I've been everywhere' kind of place. Belize, yes, I understand that, but Vegas? Everyone's been to Vegas."

"Apparently not."

"Huh." He exhales. "Well, then. Hmm." He kisses my cheek. "I guess I'll just have to hold my nose and show my baby a good time in hell, won't I?"

"That's the spirit. Just 'cause a girl's busy taking down a global crime syndicate doesn't mean she doesn't want to have a good time while she's doing it."

"Okay, then. It's settled. Tomorrow we gather our motley but good-lookin' crew and figure out how to fuck these motherfuckers up the ass."

"Sounds like a motherfucking plan," I say.

He kisses my neck. "First things first, though, let's get those staples out of your head tomorrow morning."

"Yes, please. Thank God."

"Although I happen to think those staples of yours are kinda sexy."

I feel his erection against my thigh. "Ew. You're depraved, Jonas."

He nips at my ear. "Everything about you is sexy, even the gross stuff."

"What gross stuff? I don't have any gross stuff."

"Sure you do. Staples... and staples... The list goes on and on." He kisses me again. "And staples." His hand skims the curve of my hip. "And staples." He reaches around and grabs my ass. "How 'bout I get me one last piece of Frankenstein ass before those staples come out tomorrow?"

"You're a sick puppy," I say, laughing. "I like that about you."

Chapter 15

Jonas

Sarah's running through our Las Vegas hotel suite, shrieking and squealing.

"Did you see this?" she yells. "Look at the view! Woohoo!" She starts singing "Fancy" by Iggy Azalea at the top of her lungs.

I exchange a smile with the bellhop. "Over here, sir?" he asks me, motioning with our bags.

"This place is three times bigger than my entire apartment!" Sarah screams, laughing and twirling around. "It's unreal."

"That's fine," I say to the guy. "Thank you."

"Jonas!" Sarah yells from somewhere deep in the bowels of the suite. "Come here."

I tip the bellhop.

"Thank you, sir," he says, smiling broadly. "Would you like me to open the champagne for you, sir?"

"No, I've got it covered."

"Would you like me to describe the full panel of amenities at your disposal here in the penthouse suite or perhaps in the hotel in general?"

"No, thank you. We'll figure it out."

"Very good, sir. Enjoy your stay."

"Jonas Faraday!" she screams. "Get your booty in here."

Damn, I love this woman.

I follow Sarah's voice into the bathroom. She's sitting fully clothed and grinning like a Cheshire cat in an empty bathtub the size of a small Jacuzzi. "Can you believe this?" she says. "Who needs a bathtub this big?"

I can't suppress the leer that flickers across my face.

"Oh," she says, her face turning as lecherous as mine. "I guess *we* need a bathtub this big." Her eyes gleam. "You know, I should warn you, this city's already bringing out the dirty girl in me. I can feel it."

"Oh yeah? I like your dirty girl."

"She likes you, too." I smirk. "Yep, I most definitely feel another addendum item coming on."

"Just as long as it doesn't involve tying neckties around my limbs."

"I learned my lesson about that, don't worry."

I climb into the empty tub with her and she crawls all over me, kissing me. "I'm already having a ridiculously good time."

"We've driven from the airport to our hotel and sat in an empty tub, fully clothed."

"I know—so much fun, right?"

I laugh. "Yep."

She kisses me again. "Hey, maybe there's enough time for a little fun and games before everyone else arrives?"

"Oh yeah, there's plenty of time," I say, kissing her.

"Why don't we fill this thing up and see who can hold their breath the longest?"

"Not exactly the kind of fun and games I was envisioning," I say.

"Ah, you must not understand what I'm planning to do to you while I'm holding my breath underwater."

My cock springs to life. "A breath-holding contest it is. You want some champagne?"

"You know I never say no to champagne."

"Coming right up." I hop out of the tub, my erection straining inside my jeans. Hey, maybe Vegas isn't so bad, after all.

"I feel s-e-e-e-xy, baby," she calls after me. "I'm tu-u-u-rned o-o-o-n, hunky-monkey bo-o-o-oyfriend. Get me that champagne and I guarantee my dirty, dirty girl's gonna come out to pla-a-a-a-ay."

Holy fuck. I pop the cork on the champagne bottle in record time and grab two glasses.

There's a knock on the door. "Hey!"

No, please, God, no. Not yet. Not now.

"Vegas, Baby!" It's Kat, yelling from behind the front door of our suite.

Fuck my life.

Sarah sprints out the bathroom and throws open the front door.

"Woohoo!" Kat shrieks. The two girls hug and scream like they just won the Showcase Showdown on *The Price is Right*.

Even in my current state of disappointment about not getting to be with Sarah in the tub, I laugh. They're pretty adorable right now.

"Wow, Jonas, you really knocked yourself out," Kat says, coming out of her clinch with Sarah. "I bet, like, rock stars and Prince Harry stay in this place, especially with that private elevator to get up here. It's amazing."

"I wanted to show my precious baby an extra good time, seeing as how this is her first trip to Sin City."

Kat and Sarah exchange a look of surprise when I call Sarah "my precious baby"—and, actually, I'm pretty shocked to hear myself use those words in Kat's presence. How did I let that slip out?

"Oh, Jonas," Sarah coos, blushing. "You're so sweet."

My cheeks burst into flames.

"Oh, and thank you for my room, Jonas," Kat says.

"You got checked in okay?"

"Yes, thank you."

Sarah beams at me and I flash her a look of pure longing. I don't want to be having a conversation with Kat right now—I want to be alone with Sarah, kicking her ass in an underwater-breath-holding contest.

"Did you see this view?" Kat squeals, grabbing Sarah's hand. They rush to the floor-to-ceiling windows at the far end of the room. "Just wait 'til you see The Strip at night," Kat says. "The lights are gonna blow you away." She sighs. "God, I love Vegas."

Why am I not surprised?

"I've seen The Strip in movies, but I bet it's really cool in person," Sarah says.

"Oh, champagne," Kat says, seeing the bottle on the bar.

"I'll get you a glass." I steal a pained look at Sarah and she laughs. Well, gosh, I'm glad she finds my agony so hilarious.

There's a loud knock at the door to the suite. "Open up, you beast!"

I open the door to find Josh standing next to a geek-turned-hipster guy with a goatee. After I bro-hug Josh, the hipster introduces himself as Hennessey. I'm not sure if that's his first or last name, but it's all he provides.

"But everyone just calls me Henn," he says, extending his hand.

"Or Fucking Genius," Josh adds.

"You're the only one who calls me that, Josh."

"Well, you are."

"Are you the genius who tracked down Sarah for me?" I ask.

"The one and only," Henn says.

"Then you're a fucking genius in my book, too."

Sarah and Kat bounce happily over to the group.

"Hey, Party Girl with a Hyphen," Josh says to Kat, his eyes sparkling.

"Well, hey yourself, Playboy. It's a crazy, fucked up world when a Playboy and a Party Girl cross paths in *Vegas*, huh?" They both burst out laughing. "It's good to see you again." Josh gives her an enthusiastic hug and she kisses him softly on the cheek—a noticeably warm greeting from both of them. Hmm. Interesting.

Kat introduces herself to Henn and the guy can't muster two coherent words. He might be a fucking genius with computers, but apparently not so much when it comes to pretty women.

After the girls refill their champagne glasses and the guys grab beer bottles from the fridge, we all make ourselves comfortable on black leather couches in the sitting area.

"I'm shocked you splurged on this place, bro," Josh says, glancing around at the grandeur. "So un-Jonas-like of you."

"Would you stop telling me what's Jonas- or un-Jonas-like of me already? Apparently, you have no idea what I'm like."

Josh laughs. "Apparently not."

The hacker flips open his laptop. "Okay, folks. I've got an update on the Oksana sitch you had me working on."

"Fantastic," I say, rubbing my hands together. Other than playing Underwater Oral Sex Olympics with my baby, there's nothing I want to do more than fuck these motherfuckers up the ass as soon as humanly possible. These fuckers almost took my baby away from me—which means they almost killed me, too—and now I don't only want to take them down, I want their blood.

We all crowd around Henn's laptop.

"I was able to hack into that bank in Henderson where your check was deposited—it was easy, actually—I'm constantly surprised how bad online security is at banks—I'd strongly advise keeping your money under a mattress, folks—and anyway, I got into the bank's mainframe and poked around a bit. I was able to cross-check account holders against the list of Oksanas you sent me, and Bingo-was-his-name-oh, I got a hit."

Sarah whoops.

"Our Oksana is Oksana Belenko—sounds like an Olympic ice skater, doesn't she? She's got an account at that Henderson bank *and* a P.O. box in Henderson. Boom shakalaka."

"See? Fucking genius," Josh says.

"You sure that's our girl?" Sarah asks.

"Yeah, it's her. I checked out the physical address she gave the post office, and, of course, it's total bullshit. But there's an Oksana

Belenko registered with the State of Nevada as a member of an LLC that's been running a handful of legal whorehouses in Nevada for the past twenty years—and the address for the business license on the whorehouses matches the address given in the LLC filing."

"So that means we've got a confirmed physical address?" Sarah asks.

"Yep."

"Wow," Sarah says. She pauses, the gears turning inside her head. "So it sounds like Oksana supplies the girls for The Club—" She looks at Josh. "Or, if you'd prefer, the Mickey Mouse roller coasters."

Both Sarah and Kat burst out laughing, but Josh bristles.

"It was an *analogy*," Josh says.

"We know, Joshie, we know," Sarah says, winking at him. "But it's still funny."

I put my hand on Sarah's thigh. She turns me on no matter what she does, but especially when she's kicking someone's ass.

"Yeah, Oksana's like this frickin' old-school *madam,*" Henn says. "Probably not the brains behind all the tech stuff."

"She's probably got a business partner who handles the tech side of things," I say.

"Definitely," Henn agrees. "And whoever that person is, he or she knows exactly what the hell they're doing. Because there's no finding these guys by accident."

Hmm. How the fuck did Josh get hooked up with The Club in the first place? All he said at the time was that some professional athlete buddy of his told him about it, but I never asked him for details. *Best money I've spent in my life*, he told me during our climb up Mount Rainier.

"And even then," Henn continues, sipping his beer, "their storefront is just a shell. Their real shit's gotta be buried way down in the Deep Web. And that's a scary place."

"What's the Deep Web?" Kat asks.

Henn grins broadly at her.

"Is that a stupid question?" Kat asks, blushing.

"Oh no, not stupid at all. I'm just so used to hanging out with computer geeks all day long, I forget normal people don't know about this stuff." He smiles at her again. "I'm glad you don't know what it is. It means you're probably a well adjusted, happy person."

Kat laughs. "I am, as a matter of fact."

"I can tell," Henn says. "Happiness is a very attractive quality in a person."

"Thank you," Kat says, her cheeks flushing.

Josh clears his throat. "So, guys, before Henn launches into The Grand Story of the Deep Web, how about we all do a shot of Patron? We're in Vegas, after all—when in Rome."

"Sounds like a fabulous idea to me," Kat says, her face lighting up. "Do we have Patron in the bar?"

"Of course," I say. "I made sure of it. My brother is nothing if not predictable."

Josh walks behind the bar to start pouring drinks and Kat bounds over to join him.

"I'll help you out, Playboy," she says.

"Why, thanks, Party Girl."

I lean into Sarah's ear. "What's the over-under on those two fucking?"

Sarah stifles a giggle. "I give it forty-eight hours at the absolute outside."

Chapter 16

Jonas

"The Deep Web," Henn begins, leaning back in his chair and rubbing his goatee like he's hosting an episode of *Masterpiece Theatre*. "It's a scary motherfucking place, fellas." He nods at Kat. "And very pretty ladies."

I've heard anecdotally about the Deep Web and I'm sure Josh has, too, but I don't have any practical experience with it. I look at Sarah to see if she knows about this already and she makes an "I have no idea" face.

"Let's start today's lesson with the *Surface Web*," Henn continues, speaking slowly, the consummate hipster-kindergarten teacher.

"The Surface Web," Sarah repeats slowly like she's a member of a cult.

"Yes, my child. Good," Henn says, instantly transforming into Sarah's cult leader.

Sarah and Henn share a smile.

"The Surface Web is the Internet we all know and love—the stuff that comes up when you ask Siri for movie show times or Google a sushi restaurant. But the Internet is much, much more than the Surface Web." Henn smiles devilishly.

"You're freaking me out, Henn," Kat says.

"You should be freaked out. The true Internet—and I mean the *entire* thing—is like an infinitely deep ocean—and the Surface Web is the mere surface of it. Everything below the surface floats around in the ink-black waters of the Deep Web."

"Holy shitballs," Kat says. "How have I never heard of this before? Have you heard about this, Sarah?"

Sarah shakes her head.

"Kinda freaks you out when you hear about it for the first time, huh?" Henn says.

"Totally," Kat agrees. "It reminds me of when I found out there are trillions of invisible microbes on my skin at all times." She shudders.

Josh groans. "Please don't talk about that whole microbes-on-your-skin thing. That always creeps me out."

The Playboy and the Party Girl share a hearty laugh.

Sarah leans into my ear. "Make that twenty-four hours, tops."

I smirk.

"So if normal search engines can't retrieve information that's in the Deep Web, how does anyone find what's there?" Henn asks himself. "Long story short, you gotta know exactly what you're looking for. *Exactly.* The only people you'll find trolling around the Deep Web besides upstanding guys like me are governments and criminals—and when I say 'criminals,' I'm talking jihadists and drug warlords and fucking human traffickers."

"You don't consider yourself a criminal?" Kat asks. There's no judgment in her tone, just curiosity.

"Hell no, I'm not a criminal—I wear a white hat all day long, sister," Henn says. "The only time I ever break the law is for the greater good or when I consider a law to be outdated." He pauses. "Or useless. Or stupid." He pauses again. "Or when breaking a particular law won't hurt anybody." He laughs. "So, yeah, hmm. Now that I think about it, I guess I break the law all the time." He laughs. "But I'm not a *criminal*—I'm one of the good guys."

I glance at Sarah. She doesn't seem at all bothered by Henn's lawlessness—actually, she seems amused. I suppose neither of us has any business being appalled by Henn's wild-west mentality—we already know the guy hacked into the University of Washington to find her for me and that certainly wasn't legal.

"My clients pay me to help them with a particular problem," Henn continues. "And I do. But I leave no trace, take nothing, do no harm—unless I'm being paid to leave a trace, take something, do harm, of course." Henn smirks. "But I only do that kind of thing when I'm positive I work for the good guys."

Sarah squeezes my arm, plainly telling me I'm one of the good guys Henn's talking about.

"For example," Henn continues, "when I poked around that bank looking for Oksana, I discovered a whole bunch of unsecured accounts. I could have taken a couple million bucks if I wanted, easy peasy, but I'd never do that. Why? Because I'm not a thief."

Josh smiles and nods his agreement. It's clear he trusts Henn completely.

"But you might *work* for thieves," Sarah says. "Ever think about that?"

"Nah. If my clients hire me to *take* something, it's always for a very good reason. Like I said, I only work for the good guys."

"But how do you know you're working for the good guys?" I ask. I'm beyond grateful to the guy for what he's done for me—asking him to find Sarah was the single best decision of my life—but hiring this quirky dude to help me take down The Club is an entirely different thing. Am I crazy to trust a guy in skinny jeans with the most important mission of my life? "Everyone thinks their cause is righteous," I say. "Hence, the concept of war."

"Well, yes, of course." Henn flashes a sideways smile at Kat like he's about to tell her a great joke. "But let me show you how I tell the good guys from the bad guys. It's foolproof." He looks right at Sarah. "Sarah, are you a good guy or a bad guy?"

"A good guy," Sarah says.

"And there you go."

Sarah shrugs like it makes perfect sense. "And there you go."

I scoff. "But who would ever say they're one of the bad guys? Who would even *think* that about themselves? People are brilliant at justifying their actions to themselves—trust me, I should know."

"Well, *yeah*," Henn concedes. "But I don't always *believe* people when they say they're one of the good guys. In fact, I rarely do. If I *believe* them, the way I just believed Miss Cruz here, then that's good enough for me."

"Aw, you believe me, Henn?" Sarah asks.

"I do. Indubitably."

"Why, thank you."

"Of course."

I shrug. It's hard to argue with that logic, actually. If I were to boil my own business philosophy down to its barest essence, I suppose I operate in exactly the same way. And, really, what other option do I have right now than to trust this guy? If Josh does, then I guess I do, too. *Indubitably.*

"Sometimes, it's a no-brainer," Henn continues. "Like when a job comes from Josh, for example, I always know I'm fighting for truth and justice and the American way, no questions asked. Because a guy can set his moral compass to Josh—he's *always* one of the good guys, through and through."

"Thanks, man," Josh says.

"Just speaking the truth."

"Well, well, well," Kat says. She shoots Josh an unmistakable smolder. "It turns out the Playboy's a good guy, after all—Mickey Mouse roller coasters notwithstanding."

I lean into Sarah. "Sixteen hours, absolute tops."

Sarah snickers. "Indubitably," she whispers.

"So, Henn," I say, feeling the need to herd cats here. "If The Club lives in the Deep Web, how the fuck do we find them and take them down?" I'm chomping at the bit to fuck these motherfuckers up the ass.

"We need a map," Henn says. "A precise map that gives us a pinpoint location. Once I have that, I can hack in and do a deep dive."

I put my hand on Sarah's bare thigh. I can't wait to do a deep dive with her later tonight in that Jacuzzi tub.

"How do we find this map?" Sarah asks. She puts her hand on top of mine and squeezes.

"We start with our friend, the pimpstress extraordinaire, Oksana Belenko. Whoever she's working with on the tech side of things, there's got to be communications. Or maybe she personally logs into their mainframe. Either way, she'll lead me right to them, one way or another."

"What do you need from us?" Sarah asks.

"A personal email address for Oksana—something you know links right to her."

Sarah shoots me a *mea culpa* look. That's what I was about to get from Stacy when Sarah interrupted my grand strategy at The Pine Box.

"We don't have an email address," Sarah says. "Thanks to me. Miss Bossy Boots." She smiles sheepishly, making me laugh.

"Well, that's what we need," Henn says. "I'll send Oksana malware that'll give me access to her computer. Plus I'll install a good old-fashioned key log, too. But to do that, we need her to open an email."

"What's a key log?" I ask.

"It lets me remotely monitor every key she hits on her keyboard. Easy way to get all her passwords."

I rub my hands together villainously. "Excellent."

"So you'll need to do three things." He looks directly at Sarah. "First, get her email address. Second, obviously, send her an email. And, third, make sure she opens it, preferably in your presence so we don't leave anything up to chance. Do you think you can do all that?"

"Of course I can," Sarah says. "They think I'm scamming Jonas. I'll just find her and say I've come to negotiate my split on the scam."

"No fucking way," I say, probably much louder than required to make my point.

Sarah opens her mouth, shocked. "Jonas, yes. I'll meet her and negotiate my cut and then while I'm there I'll email her something to memorialize the deal. Done-zo."

"No fucking way," I say again, this time controlling the volume of my voice. "You're not gonna meet Oksana or anyone else from The Club all by yourself."

"Jonas, it'll be fine—"

"I'm going with you."

She rolls her eyes. "They think I'm *playing* you, remember? Why on earth would I bring you with me if I'm scamming you?"

"I don't know. Use that big-ass brain of yours to come up with something they'll believe."

She sighs in frustration.

"It's non-negotiable, Sarah. We're doing this together or we're not doing it at all."

She huffs. "Why would I bring you to meet her? It makes no sense."

I purse my lips, thinking. I can't think of anything off the top of my head.

The room is silent, everyone apparently pondering the same puzzle.

"They think I'm *playing* you," Sarah says slowly, like she's thinking out loud. "Why would I bring you with me?"

"I don't know, but it's non-negotiable."

"I heard you the first time, Lord-God-Master." She crosses her arms over her chest. After a moment, she picks up her champagne flute and ambles to the floor-to-ceiling window on the other side of the room. The sun has set as we've been talking and The Strip's frenetic neon lights are on dazzling display below us.

"Wow," Sarah says, staring out at the expanse of lights. "It's beautiful."

Everyone in the room gets up to take in the view alongside her, drinks in hand.

I put my arm around Sarah and she leans into me.

"Let's take a photo, Sarah," Kat says. The two girls smile for a selfie on Kat's phone with the iconic lights as their backdrop. "And one of you and Jonas, too," Kat commands, motioning for us to get together.

Sarah and I cuddle up and Kat takes our picture. It all feels so *normal*. I like it.

Kat looks at our photo. "You two look good together," she says to me, half-smiling. "*Really* good together."

My heart leaps. Sarah's fierce protector just told me she deems me worthy of her best friend?

"Don't post those pics anywhere, Kat," Henn warns. "We don't want the bad guys knowing we're on their turf."

"I won't post them, don't worry. I just want to remember being here in Vegas with my best friend for her first time." Kat suddenly wraps Sarah in an emotional hug. "Thank God you're okay. I was so worried about you. I love you so much."

"I love you, too." Sarah says, nuzzling into Kat's blonde hair.

"I don't know what I would have done if you hadn't pulled through."

"I'm fine. 'Twas merely a flesh wound, Kitty Kat."

I watch them, fascinated. Their exchange is so affectionate and effortless and natural—it makes me envious somehow. I want to be the one hugging Sarah and declaring my love so easily and openly to her.

Sarah whips her head up and gasps. "I've got it," she says.

"You've got what?" Kat asks.

Sarah disengages from Kat. "We use their greed against them."

"That's my girl," I say. "I knew you'd think of something."

Sarah leaps over to me and hugs me. "This is gonna work."

"Of course, it will," I say. "We're an unstoppable team." I kiss her softly.

Henn looks at his watch. "Okay, get your plan figured out and we'll launch first thing tomorrow. I'm gonna work all night on my malware. I want to make sure whatever we send them is ironclad." He grabs his laptop, clearly excited to get to work.

Sarah and I exchange a look. There's a lot at stake here.

"Well," Kat says, her hands on her hips. "While Henn's hard at work cooking up a fancy virus, I guess the rest of us will have to have find *something* to do in Las Vegas. Hmm." She taps her index finger on her temple, pretending to think really hard. "What on earth could we possibly do in *Las Vegas*?"

I look at Sarah, hoping she's thinking what I am: that she's not the least bit interested in being part of a foursome tonight. But nope—one look at Sarah and it's abundantly clear she's thrilled at the idea of going out.

"You like to gamble, Kat?" Josh asks.

"I love it."

"What's your game?"

"Blackjack."

"Lame," Josh says.

"Excuse me?"

"The real fun is craps."

"I've never played," Kat says. "It seems complicated."

"Nah, it's easy. I'll spot you a grand and teach you how to play."

Kat's eyes pop out of her head. "I'm not gonna take your money. I'll just watch you."

"No, you've got to roll the dice for me, Party Girl. You've got first-timer's luck *and* lady-luck on your side, and they only let you roll when you've got a bet on the table."

"Well, then, I'll bet my own money."

"Kat," I interject. "Let my brother pay for your fun. There's nothing Josh Faraday loves more than throwing his hard-earned money away on mindless entertainment."

"That's your idea of helping me, bro?"

I laugh.

"You'd be doing me a favor, Kat. Betting on a first-time roller is the dream of every craps player—it's as exciting as it gets." He smiles. "And I love excitement." Even from here, I can see Josh's eyes flicker when he says that last word.

Kat grins. "Okay, Playboy. I'm in. You had me at 'excitement.' But we're all going out together, right?" She looks at Sarah for assurance.

"Of course," Sarah says.

Damn. I was hoping she'd say her dance card was already filled for tonight with the Underwater Rumba. I clear my throat, trying to catch Sarah's attention. One look at me and she'll know I'm not up for going out.

But the expression on Sarah's face melts me. Oh man, she's so fucking adorable—just bursting at the seams about painting the town red. What am I thinking? Sarah can have sex with me in a goddamned hotel room any time—I've got to nut up and show my baby a good time in the Seventh Circle of Hell.

"Where should we take these lovely ladies to dinner?" I ask Josh.

"It just so happens I know the perfect place."

"Of course you do," I reply.

"Do you ladies think you can handle a night out with the Faraday brothers?" Josh asks.

Both girls squeal with excitement in reply, and Sarah throws her arms around my neck. "Thank you, Jonas."

"You bet," I say softly, kissing her neck. "I'm gonna show you a good time in hell, baby, just like you deserve."

"And then we'll come back here and have an even better time in heaven—in that Jacuzzi tub, just the two of us."

Oh, how I love this woman.

"Henn, you wanna join us for dinner?" Josh calls to Henn across the room. "Yo, Henn?"

Henn looks up from his computer.

"You wanna join us for dinner, man?"

"Oh, Josh," Henn says, shaking his head. "How many times do I have to tell you? You can wine and dine me all you like, but you're never gonna get me into bed."

Chapter 17

Jonas

Okay, I admit it. I'm having fun. *In Las Vegas.* The Apocalypse is nigh. I guess I can count on having fun anywhere, anytime, even in hell, as long as Sarah's by my side.The restaurant Josh selected is superb—Sarah uses the word "ridiculous" at least ten times to describe her food—and the Cirque Du Soleil show we stumble into after dinner, totally on a whim, is spectacular. Every time I look over at Sarah during the show, her face is beaming with an almost childlike joy that makes my heart burst. *So this is what happiness feels like,* I think.

After the show, when the girls gallop off to the bathroom together, I use the opportunity to grill Josh about Henn.

"How well do you know the guy?" I ask. "You sure we can trust him?"

"One hundred percent sure."

"Sounds like we're messing with some pretty hairy shit," I say. "You sure he's *completely* trustworthy?"

"Jonas, I'm sure. He's been my guy since college. He's like a brother to me."

What the fuck does that mean? Henn's "like a brother" to him? Why does Josh need a *friend* who's *like* a brother when he's got an *actual* brother? And why have I never heard of Henn before now, if they're so damned close?

"When I first got to school, I kind of took Henn under my wing when he needed it most," Josh says. "At first, I thought I was the power player in the friendship, but I wound up relying on *him* far more than he ever did on *me*." He shrugs.

My stomach lurches. I know the exact timeframe he's referring to: right after Dad killed himself. *The Lunacy.* Josh went off to UCLA for his first year of college while I stayed behind, school deferred for a year, fighting to reclaim my mind from impenetrable darkness.

"I just needed someone to lean on back then," Josh adds. "And Henn turned out to be that guy."

"I get it," I say. But that doesn't mean I don't feel guilty as hell about it—and, if I'm being honest, jealous that Henn was there for Josh when I couldn't be. Henn is like a brother to Josh? Well, fuck me. The whole idea of Josh needing to lean on someone besides me surprises me—though it shouldn't, now that I think about it. Of course, Josh needed support after suddenly finding himself fatherless and brotherless all at once. Of course, he did.

But what about *after* The Lunacy? Did Josh continue to rely on Henn, even then? I guess I just assumed Josh has leaned on me through the years, despite all my weaknesses and flaws and fuckeduppedness, the way I've always leaned on him. But I should have known. A guy can't lean on someone who has broken legs, or they'll both come crashing down. I look at the ground, emotion threatening to rise up inside me.

"Hey," Josh says softly. "I've leaned on you, too, bro. More than you know. You're the man."

I look up at him. Now that I think about it, I can't remember a single time he's leaned on me. All I can recall are the countless times he's rushed to my aid when I've needed him so badly.

"And I still lean on you, all the time," he says. "All the time."

"You can, you know," I say. "Lean on me. Anytime."

"I know. And I do. You're half my brain, you know that—the better half, except when you're a dumbshit."

"I'm strong now," I say. "You don't have to take care of me anymore. I can take care of *you* sometimes, too. I'm strong now."

"I know you are," Josh says. "You're a beast, man."

"So are you," I say.

I suddenly remember the text Josh sent me as I sat vigil in Sarah's hospital room. *I love you, man,* he wrote. *Thanks,* I replied, emotionally stunted asshole that I am.

"Thanks for your text," I say. "When Sarah was in the hospital."

He knows the one. He nods.

My mouth twists. "It meant a lot."

There's a beat, neither of us knowing what to do.

Maybe I should say more, but that's all I've got.

Josh tries to grin at me, but he fails. His eyes are moist.

Fuck this. This is too weird. I slap my face and Josh laughs in surprise. I'm never the one who slaps first. Ever.

"Are we good, pussy-ass motherfucker?" I ask.

Josh laughs. "Yeah, we're good, motherfucking cocksucker."

I hear the sound of Sarah's laughter. I glance behind us and, sure enough, Sarah and Kat are traipsing noisily toward us from inside the theatre, big smiles plastered across both girls' faces.

"Hey," I say to Josh before the girls reach us, "if Henn's your brother, then he's mine, too. I'm glad he's been there for you."

Chapter 18

Jonas

The Playboy and The Party Girl have been making a killing together at the craps table for the past hour. Josh was right—he can't lose, not with Kat rolling the dice for him. For a ridiculously long time, Sarah and I have watched and cheered and high-fived and even bet more money than we should—but win or lose, my brain is utterly incapable of remaining interested for long in what numbers show up on a pair of dice.

When Sarah whispers to me, "You wanna get outta here?" every square inch of my skin tingles.

"You read my mind, baby," I reply, pushing all my chips over to Kat's mammoth stack and grabbing Sarah's hand. "See you guys later," I call out to Josh and Kat over my shoulder. "Let's go, baby." My cock is already hardening with delicious anticipation.

But, as it turns out, Sarah hasn't read my mind at all. She doesn't want to beeline back up to the suite for water sports like I do—she wants to race into the tattoo parlor on the other side of the casino to get inked with her first tattoo.

Sarah sits on the tattoo artist's table, explaining exactly what she wants him to do. I'm watching her, enraptured and turned on like a motherfucker. All I can think about is tasting her and making her come and then fucking her brains out in that Jacuzzi tub.

"Sounds simple enough," the guy says. "Show me exactly where you want it."

She lies back and without hesitation pulls up her dress to reveal her leopard-print G-string underneath. Wow, apparently modesty's not an issue for Sarah tonight—when in Rome, I guess. Or maybe she's just a lot bit drunk. Or maybe she's finally come to peace with how fucking hot she is and doesn't give a damn who knows it—because, holy fuck, this woman is most definitely smokin' hot. I glance over at the tattoo artist and it's abundantly clear he appreciates the olive-toned canvas he'll be working on.

What the fuck is she doing now? She's peeling down the elastic of her itty-bitty panties, prompting me to lurch forward and reach for her hand to stop her—is she really *that* drunk?—but she stops on her own, just before she gives up the goods.

She points at a tiny swatch of olive skin normally covered by the front of her panties. "Right here," she says, her fingertip touching the exact spot she wants inked. "Boom."

I can't resist. I reach over and touch the spot, too, and she visibly shudders under my fingers. Oh man, what the fuck are we still doing here? Let's get into that fucking Jacuzzi tub already.

"You sure about this, baby?" I ask. The feel of her skin under my fingertips is making me rock hard.

"Hellz yeah," she replies. "The tattoo will be covered up when I'm wearing panties or a bikini—visible only when I'm buck naked—which means no one's ever gonna see it except me. And *you*."

My blood pulses in my ears.

She licks her lips. "You're the only man who's ever gonna see this tattoo, Jonas."

My chest tightens. I nod.

She blinks slowly and grins. "The only one."

"Forever?" I ask.

Whoa. I can't believe I just said that. But, fuck it, I did, and I can't take it back now. *Forever.* Yeah. That's exactly what I want from her.

Her cheeks flush a beautiful shade of scarlet. She shrugs shyly and bites her lip.

"I want to be the only man who ever sees it," I say, my voice low. I motion to the tattoo artist. "Besides this guy."

She swallows hard and nods.

My skin is on fire. I wish I could consummate this pact of ours right now on top of the tattoo table, but since that's obviously not possible, even in a city as debauched as Vegas, I do the next best thing—I take her face in my hands and kiss her like I own her. Our kiss is so full of heat, so deliciously arousing, I can't muster the willpower needed to pull myself away from her. I know in my head the tattoo guy is sitting there waiting for us, but my body doesn't care. She's my crack. And, right now, I want my crack.

I make a big point of pulling Sarah's dress back down over her thighs—*I'm the only man who's allowed to see my baby's panties, motherfucker*—and then I scoop her up into my arms. *Mine.*

"Sorry man," I say to the tattoo guy. "We'll be back to do this another time." I look at Sarah in my arms. "I'll get you whatever tattoo you want before we leave this Godforsaken city, I promise, baby. But right now, I'm taking you straight to our room—straight to that Jacuzzi tub." I lean into her ear so the tattoo guy doesn't hear this next part. "And then I'm gonna dine on some delicious, par-boiled pussy."

Her face bursts into flames.

I reach to pull my wallet out of my pocket, but it's too hard to do while holding her in my arms. "Do me a favor and pay the nice man for me, baby—for his inconvenience."

She grabs my wallet and practically throws two hundred-dollar bills at the guy. She could have given him a thousand bucks and I wouldn't have cared—whatever I have to pay to get the fuck out of here so I can taste my baby's beautiful, sweet pussy underwater in a warm Jacuzzi tub is fine with me.

I kiss her again. "You are so fucking hot," I say.

She's panting.

I bound out of the tattoo parlor with my baby in my arms and beeline through the noisy casino toward the elevator bank on the far side of the lobby. When tight aisles and slot machines and crowds make it impractical to continue cradling her, she hops out of my arms and leaps onto my back, and I continue making my way past gaming tables and cocktail waitresses and drunk bachelorettes wearing tiaras, my hands grasping Sarah's smooth thighs, my cock aching with anticipation. I'm a man on a mission. My legs are pumping. My heart is racing. I hear her tipsy laughter from atop my back. Yeah, baby, I'm a horse racing back to the sweet-pussy barn. Nothing's gonna stop me from tasting my horny little pony as soon as humanly possible.

But my legs suddenly cease pumping. I stop dead in my tracks. What the fuck? Apparently, my legs have a fucking mind of their own because I'm positive I didn't instruct them to stop moving. I look up.

I'm standing in front of a wedding chapel. It's an Elvis-themed chapel, a true Vegas absurdity—but a *bona fide* wedding chapel all the same.

I feel her heart beating against my back, but she doesn't speak. Neither do I.

Fuck. I shouldn't have stopped. Why did my legs stop? I didn't tell them to do that. Did I? They hijacked me and took over. Fuck. Her silence on top of me is as thick as molasses. I feel her chest heaving against my back. Why did I stop?

Because I want to marry this girl.

What?

I want to marry this girl.

Oh my God. I want to marry Sarah. I want her to be mine and only mine, and no one else's, ever again. *Forever.* I want to call her my wife.

But it's not possible.

I could never ask Sarah to pledge herself to me for eternity without first letting her see the non-traversable wasteland inside of me, the bastion of fuckeduppedness I've somehow managed to obscure from her thus far. I can't ask her to vow to love me forever without first telling her every last thing about The Lunacy—and that's something I'm just not willing to do.

Wordlessly, I start walking again, leaving the wedding chapel behind. As I gain speed, I feel the tension leave her body and melt away. She lays a soft kiss on the back of my neck.

I see the elevator bank, including the private elevator leading to our penthouse, off to the right—and I hang a sharp left.

"May I help you, sir?" the woman behind the jewelry counter asks.

"Yes, please. We're in the market for a couple of bracelets."

Sarah slides off my back and stands beside me, grasping my hand.

"There was blood all over my bracelet from Belize," I whisper to her. "I had to take it off."

She nods, her big brown eyes melting me. "They cut mine off at the hospital," she says softly. "I don't know where it is."

"See if you like any of these," the saleswoman says, placing two trays of bracelets on the counter in front of us. "These ones here are men's and those are women's."

I pick up a plain, platinum c-band off the men's tray. It's as basic as you can get. "Can I get this engraved across the face?" I ask.

"Of course," the saleswoman says.

"Sarah," I say, handing it back to her. "S-A-R-A-H."

"Very good." Now she looks at Sarah, her eyebrows raised. "And what about you, miss?"

Sarah peers at the tray of women's bracelets. Virtually all her options are much more elaborate than the simple one I've chosen for myself—full of diamonds and curlicues and chains and colorful gems.

"Do you see something you like, baby?" I ask.

She picks up the female version of mine—platinum, c-band, totally plain.

"No, baby, pick something pretty, something with diamonds. You can have whatever you like."

She grabs the simplest one and hands it to the saleswoman. "Jonas. J-O-N-A-S."

"No," I say. "Baby, listen. Pick one with diamonds on it." I grab a platinum bangle off the tray. It extends all the way around, unlike my c-band, and sparkling diamonds rim its edges. "This is pretty. Or how about this one?" I grab a dazzling diamond tennis bracelet off the tray. "This one is stunning."

The saleswoman puts my bracelet and the one Sarah handed her onto the counter, awaiting our final decision.

"I want the one that matches yours," Sarah says simply.

"Yeah, but—"

"Jonas, listen to me." The tone of her voice leaves zero room for argument. She picks up the matching bracelets off the counter and holds them up, side by side. "I'm the sole member of the Jonas Faraday Club—and you're the sole member of the Sarah Cruz Club. That's all that matters to me—not frickin' diamonds. Our bracelets have to be a perfect match because *we're* a perfect match." She juts her chin at me. "End of story."

Chapter 19

Sarah

I'm bursting out of my naked skin in the rising water, waiting for Jonas to return to the tub with our champagne. I run my fingertip over the engraved inscription on my new bracelet. *Jonas*. I should probably put it on the ledge of the tub so it doesn't get wet, but I don't want to take my new bracelet off. Ever.

I'm aching. Throbbing. Crazy. All I want to do is give this gorgeous man the blowjob of his life. Of course, I want to make love to him, too. And kiss him. And touch him. And feel him deep inside me. And, of course, I can't wait to tell him I love him using the actual, magic words again, too—sacred words it seems we're only allowed to exchange when we're making love—but, holy hell, that blowjob is my first priority. I'm going cuckoo for Cocoa Puffs wanting to take him into my mouth and pleasure him 'til he can't see straight. He gets crazy-turned-on pleasuring me? Well, I've discovered I get crazy-turned-on pleasuring him, too. So there.

I didn't know this about myself until recently, and I've never felt even remotely eager to perform oral sex on any other man, but with Jonas, I've discovered that if I open my mind and touch myself while I've got him in my mouth, sucking on him gets me so aroused, it almost makes me orgasm. I like having him at my mercy—literally and figuratively.

I wanted to drop to my knees and take his full length into my mouth the minute he said the word "forever" in that tattoo parlor, but since I'm a nice girl (and not a crack whore in a back alley), performing fellatio in public wasn't an option (even in a city as perverted as Las Vegas). And then, when he stopped in front of that wedding chapel, holy crappola, he "delivered me unto pure ecstasy" right then and there. I tried to whisper, "the culmination of human possibility" into his ear, but my voice wouldn't work. I knew in my bones Jonas was closing his eyes and pledging forever to me—and willing me to do the same. And so I did. I closed my eyes and thought, "I promise you forever, Jonas." It was every bit as magical as our kiss outside the cave in Belize—maybe even more so.

I touch my bracelet again and close my eyes.

We don't need to stand in front of our friends and family wearing traditional wedding clothes to make our love real and forever. We don't need a piece of paper. Today was our wedding day. And that's good enough for me.

Warm water is rising steadily in the tub around me, relaxing me and making me hella horny. I press my lower back into a blasting stream of hot water. "Aah," I sigh. "Come on, baby," I call to Jonas in the other room. "I'm w-a-a-a-a-i-t-i-n-g."

"I'm opening the bottle, baby," he calls back to me.

I don't blame Jonas for not being the marrying kind of guy because, frankly, I'm not the marrying kind of girl. I mean, seriously, what do I know about marriage? Nothing good. All I know about marriage is that it's when a man hits a woman, sometimes with his fist, sometimes with his belt, sometimes with a kick from his boot. I know it's when a man screams at a woman, seemingly out of nowhere, and sometimes calls her pleasant things like "whore" and "bitch."

I know it's when a man comes back the next day with flowers and tells his wife he's sorry, that he's going to change, that he's stopped drinking—and she cries with joy and relief and everything's good again for maybe six weeks. And then she inevitably says the wrong thing or looks at him the wrong way and he drinks a beer and another and another and then everything starts all over again—only the next time, everything's good again for maybe only four weeks, if you're lucky. One week if you're not.

What else do I know about marriage? I know it's when a nine-year-old little girl spends her nights cowering in a closet with a world map or, when things are really bad, lying in bed thinking of ways to kill her own father without getting caught. It's when, on a particularly bad night right after the girl's tenth birthday, a night when she's seen her mother beaten to within an inch of her life, the daughter calmly crushes up eight Tylenol PM tablets and slips them into her father's beer and waits for him to fall asleep like the worthless fuck he is. And when he does, it's when that little girl uses all her strength to drag her wobbly mother out of the house to an old, dilapidated shed she found only a few blocks away, a shed the girl's been stocking with provisions for the better part of a month. It's when the girl takes care of her mother in that shed and tells her everything's going to be all right, until, finally, after three days, the mother lifts her head and looks at her daughter with a previously unseen glint in her eye and says, "*No más. De hoy en adelante, renazco.*" *No more. From this day forward, I am reborn.*

The water level in the tub is finally at my shoulders and I turn off the gushing faucet. "The tub is filled, baby," I call out to Jonas. "It's s-e-e-e-e-x-y time, big boy!"

"Coming, baby," he calls from the other end of the suite.

So, yeah, Jonas isn't the marrying kind of guy, and that's just fine with me—because I'm not really the marrying kind of girl. I don't need marriage to give myself to Jonas Faraday. I've already done it. And he's given himself to me. *Forever.*

Ah, there he is. My sweet Jonas. Walking into the bathroom with two flutes of champagne and a gigantic woody. Good Lord, seeing this man naked never gets old. He smiles as he hands me my champagne glass and I down every last drop in one long, ravenous gulp.

"Take it easy, baby. This is the good stuff."

"Get in here, Jonas P. Faraday," I say, writhing like an eel. I'm so turned on I can't breathe.

Jonas lowers his glorious body into the warm water, his face glowing with excitement.

"You really like champagne, don't you?"

"You wanna know why?"

"Tell me."

I drift over to him in the tub and grip his delectable erection in my hand. "Because it brings out the dirty, *dirty* girl in me."

"I like your dirty girl."

"And she likes you." I lick my lips. "A whole lot."

With that, I lower myself slowly, slowly, slowly down toward the surface of the warm water—prolonging Jonas' delicious anticipation as long as humanly possible—until, finally, with great fanfare, I take a deep, long, dirty-girl breath, wink at Jonas' exuberant face, and submerge myself under the water.

Chapter 20

Sarah

"I still say it was a draw," Jonas says.

"Oh, please. I totally won," I say.

"I think it's just this next block up," Jonas says, looking at Google Maps on his phone.

"Damn, it's hot," I say.

"Welcome to Vegas."

"Henderson, actually," I correct him.

"Henderson, Vegas—wherever. Hotter than hell, either way. And you didn't *win,"* Jonas says. "If you add up all the minutes I was down there holding my breath in *aggregate*, I totally won. Hands down."

"Yeah but the only reason you were down there so damned long was you couldn't close the deal as efficiently as I could—that shouldn't be a reason to *win*."

He laughs. "Oh my God. That's just men verses women—pure physiology—not a reflection of my skills. And the time it took me probably had a little something to do with all that champagne you drank—dulls the nerve endings."

"Excuses, excuses."

"No excuses—I still did it, didn't I?"

"You sure did. Amen to that."

"Just because you got me off faster than a pubescent boy doesn't mean you *won* a damned thing—the contest was who could hold their breath the *longest,* not who could get the job done *fastest.* "

"No, I changed the contest. It was who could be the most *efficient*."

He laughs again. "You never said that. You're such a cheater."

"I only had to pop up for air once. You had to come up, like, four times. Ergo, I won."

He groans in fond remembrance of last night. "God, you were on fire last night. You are so fucking talented, you know that, Sarah Cruz? You're the goddess and the muse. Mmm mmm. Damn."

I shrug. "'Twas a labor of love."

"Yeah, well, still. You can't unilaterally change the rules of the contest at the last minute. It was never about who could get the job done the fastest and you know it."

"Most *efficiently*."

"Well, then, that's bullshit. I never stood a chance. Before your lips even touched my cock, I was already halfway gone."

"Excuses."

"Not excuses. Facts."

"Are you being a sore loser, Jonas?"

"Ha! No. I'm a very happy loser."

"Wait, is that the place?" I point to a nondescript building on the other side of the street.

Jonas double-checks the address again. "Yeah, that should be it. Fuck, it's hot. How does anyone live in this heat? I swear to God."

We keep walking until we're standing immediately across the street from the building and peeking at it from around the corner of a liquor store. The building is seventies-style cement with blinds covering all the windows and no signage. It's the kind of place you'd expect to see a chiropractor or real estate agent set up shop—just total blah. It most certainly does not scream "global crime syndicate."

"Not what I expected," I say.

"What'd you expect?"

"Like something out of *Diehard,* I guess? A high-rise steel building with mirrored windows filled with bad guys in couture suits wearing earpieces."

Jonas laughs. "Damn, that's quite specific. You expected all that from the fuckers who employ the Ukrainian Travolta?"

"Yeah, like John Travolta's boss in *Pulp Fiction.* He was kind of spiffy looking, wasn't he?"

"Marsellus Wallace."

"What?"

"That was the name of Travolta's boss in *Pulp Fiction*—Marsellus Wallace. And John Travolta was Vincent Vega."

I look at him blankly.

"And Uma Thurman was Mia Wallace—you sure you've seen *Pulp Fiction?* Because I'm beginning to doubt you about that."

I roll my eyes. "Of course, I've seen it. Best movie ever." I crinkle my nose at him. "I've never lied to you about a single thing, ever."

He smiles at me. "I know. You're cute when you get annoyed at me, you know that?"

I purse my lips and peek at the building again. I inhale, trying to steel myself.

"You ready to meet our friend, Oksana Belenko?" Jonas asks.

"Yup." I take a deep breath. "I think." I absentmindedly touch my wrist, but, of course, my bracelet isn't there—Jonas and I decided to go bracelet-free on this particular errand.

"You know what to do?" he asks.

"Yeah. I'm just nervous all of a sudden." I gasp. "What if the Ukrainian Travolta's in there?" I can't believe I haven't thought of that possibility before now.

"Well, then the plan is fucked because I'm killing the motherfucker with my bare hands."

My jaw drops. I wait for him to say, "Just kidding," but he doesn't. "Jonas, no. If he's in there, you have to figure out a way to keep your cool. Promise me you won't kill anyone."

"Nope. If that motherfucker's in there, he's a dead man, plan or no plan. If I tell you to run, you better run like hell."

My chest tightens. I feel a sudden panic coming on. Why didn't I consider what Jonas might do if he were to come face-to-face with my attacker? What might *I* do? I take a deep breath to steady myself. "Jonas, listen. If you do anything not according to plan, you could get us both killed. Or worse."

"What could be worse than getting us both killed?"

"You could get *yourself* killed and not me. Or you could go to prison. Both would be worse. I'd rather die than live without you."

"Well, then, let's pray that motherfucker's not inside that building right now." His eyes are hard. I've never seen him look like this.

My breathing is shaky. "Maybe we shouldn't go through with this. Maybe we should come up with another plan."

"Baby, listen to me." He grabs my shoulders and gazes at me with those beautiful blue eyes of his. "We can't sit around the rest of our lives looking over our shoulders. You know that. It's time to take control."

I nod. Of course, he's right. Coming here to find Oksana was my idea, after all. I take another deep breath. I don't know why I'm suddenly freaking out.

"I refuse to sit around and wonder if they're coming after you again," Jonas continues. "I'm done letting shit happen to me. I'm taking charge."

I nod. I'm glad to hear it.

"So are you ready to fuck them up the ass with me or not?"

"Yeah, I'm ready." I shake it off. "That was just a momentary blip. I'm ready."

He grabs my hand and squeezes it. "All we have to do is get them to open an email. Easy as pie."

I nod. "Okay. You got your phone?"

He holds up his phone.

"And your checkbook?"

He pats his pocket. "Yup." He starts pulling me toward the street.

"Hang on." I drop his hand and step back.

He turns back around and stares at me, uncertain. "You okay?"

"I just had a sudden feeling—almost like a premonition."

Jonas looks at me expectantly.

"I'd kick myself if I ignored this feeling and then it turned out to be right."

Jonas waits.

"Do you think you could write me a check? Payable to me?"

"For what?"

"I don't know," I say. "I just feel like last time, having a check from you is what saved my life. I feel like I should go in there armed with the same protection as last time, just in case."

"Just in case what?"

"I don't know."

He looks concerned.

"I won't use it if I don't have to. But if our Plan A doesn't work out, I think I should have a check from you as our Plan B—"

"Baby, no. There is no Plan B. We're all about Plan A."

"What's the harm? If I don't need it, I'll rip it up afterwards." Adrenaline is suddenly surging throughout my body. The longer I stand here talking about this, the more certain I am that I need it. "Just humor me."

He studies my face. "I'm not gonna leave you alone with them—not even for a minute. You realize that? There's no Plan B."

"Of course. But what if they search my purse or something? That'd be a good thing for them to find, wouldn't it? It would confirm I've got you wrapped around my little finger, just like I've been telling them."

"You *do* have me wrapped around your little finger." He smiles.

I smile back at him. Damn, he's a good-looking man. "That check saved my life last time, Jonas. Maybe I'm being paranoid, but I don't want to walk in there without my good luck charm."

He slowly pulls out his checkbook. "This is not an invitation for you to go off plan. There's no Plan B."

"I know." I hand him a pen from my purse.

"How much? Two-fifty?"

"No, that's too much. A hundred, maybe."

He writes the check and hands it to me. "But we're sticking to the plan, no matter what. I'm only doing this because I trust your gut so damned much." He kisses the top of my head. "Because you're so fucking smart."

"Thank you. I feel better having it." I pat my purse.

He smiles reassuringly. "Just follow my lead. Our plan is foolproof."

"Let's do it."

"No going off plan."

"I know."

"Say it."

"No going off plan. I know."

"Okay. Let's do it."

Chapter 21

Jonas

"I'll tell Oksana you're here," the young woman in the front room says. She looks wary. "Can I get you something to drink?"

"No, thanks. We're good," I say.

"And tell me your names again?"

"Jonas Faraday and Sarah Cruz, here to see Oksana Belenko." I smile my most charming smile and the young woman's features noticeably soften.

"Okay. Just a minute."

She disappears into the next room and closes the door.

Sarah and I look at each other. My heart is beating like a steel drum.

Several minutes pass. I squeeze Sarah's hand. I didn't expect to feel this nervous.

The young woman comes out, followed by a guy of about my age, dressed in a designer suit, his dark blonde hair slicked back. I can almost feel Sarah smirking next to me—she just got her *Die Hard* villain.

"Can I help you?" he says, keeping his distance. He looks pointedly at Sarah.

"Hey there," I say, trying my best to come off like a bull in a china shop. "So great to meet you." I extend my hand like we're long-lost friends. "I'm Jonas Faraday—one of The Club's members." I look at Sarah and smile. "One of The Club's *very* satisfied members, I might add."

Sarah smiles back at me.

He shakes my hand, but he's not nearly as enthusiastic as I am. He pointedly doesn't give his name in reply to my self-introduction.

"I brought our girl Sarah to Vegas for a little fun, you know, and I figured why not kill two birds with one stone while I'm here and do some business with you?"

The guy looks pointedly at Sarah again.

I glance at Sarah under his hard gaze, worried she's going to freak out, but she's cool as a cucumber. She smiles broadly at the guy and puts out her hand. "I'm Sarah Cruz," she says. "I don't think we've met yet." She looks at me. "I've always worked remotely from Seattle, so I haven't met everyone at headquarters yet."

The guy looks behind us toward the front door where we came in. "Is it just the two of you?"

"Yes," Sarah says evenly. "Absolutely. Just us."

"Yeah, Sarah told me to just email you guys, said that would be best, but she's not savvy in business like I am." I wink at her. "Are you, Sarah?"

"Nope."

"She just doesn't have practical experience yet, you know? Smart as hell but no real world experience. She doesn't understand you can get more done with a handshake and looking someone in the eye than with an email." I pull her to me and grab her ass. "What a girl this is, though, I'm telling you. What a girl."

At my rough touch, Sarah throws her head back and laughs. "Oh, Jonas."

"Stacy in Seattle told me Oksana's the one I've got to talk to about buying a block of a girl's time, so I figured, hey, I'll cut a deal with you aboveboard and come down here and buy Sarah from you."

"Jonas," Sarah says, swatting at me playfully.

"He knows what I mean. I'm buying your *time,* sweetheart—obviously, I'm not buying *you.*" I look back at the guy. "That is, unless she's for sale?" I laugh like I think I'm so funny.

Sarah laughs, too.

"Ah, but seriously. I'd like to buy a big block of this girl's time. She's so busy reviewing applications for you guys day and night, she won't give me all the time I want. And, believe me, I want *a lot.*"

I grope Sarah again and she giggles.

The guy looks wary. He doesn't speak. "I'll be right back."

He disappears through a door.

Sarah and I look at each other. We're playing our parts to a tee, just like we planned. But who the fuck is this guy? Where's Oksana?

Die Hard Fucker comes back out after a couple minutes. "Leave your phones and purse with Nina." He motions to the young woman who initially greeted us.

Sarah hands her purse to the woman without hesitation, but I stand immobilized.

"Mr. Faraday, we're more than happy to speak to you within the confines of this building, but we're not willing to risk our voices being recorded for all posterity."

Holy shit. This is the fucker who writes The Club's emails, there's no doubt about it—he talks just like he writes.

"Oh, sure. Yeah, no problem," I say, handing the woman my phone.

Die Hard Fucker pats us down, taking a lot more care frisking every inch of Sarah's body than mine, I notice. Does he trust her a whole lot less than he trusts me? Or is he just enjoying the pleasure of touching her body? I clench my jaw, trying to contain my murderous impulses.

When *Die Hard* Fucker is convinced we're both clean, he invites us into the office. A woman in maybe her late fifties or early sixties with dyed platinum blonde hair and severe eyeliner sits behind a large desk. Introductions all around reveal she's our friend Oksana and that *Die Hard* Fucker is her son, Maksim—though he instructs us to call him Max. Sarah and I take chairs opposite Oksana while Max sits off to the side and stares like a motherfucker at Sarah.

"Great to finally meet you, Oksana," I say breezily after everyone's taken their seats. "I've really enjoyed my Club experience so far—everything's been top notch."

Max clears his throat.

"I'm surprised to see you here," Oksana says evenly. Despite her thick Ukrainian accent, her English is perfect. "We don't take in-person meetings with clients. And our address is not advertised."

"Oh, sure, yeah. Sorry about that. Stacy in Seattle told me exactly where to find you." I feel an unexpected pang of guilt as I throw Stacy under the bus, but I can't think of another way to rationally explain how we've located Oksana. "I hope that's okay. I don't want to get Stacy into any trouble. She's a sweetheart. In fact, I'd originally planned to buy a bunch of *Stacy's* time—that girl is smokin' hot and really talented—"

Sarah stiffens in her seat, emulating barely contained jealousy.

"But then this one right here blew a gasket when I even *looked* at anyone else and my plans changed on a dime." I smirk at Sarah and she nods. "This girl's got a bit of a jealous streak it turns out—she's not too fond of sharing—so a threesome with Stacy was out of the question." I laugh.

Sarah clenches her jaw, playing her part exactly as planned.

"She's a handful this one. A stick of dynamite." I growl that last part.

Sarah flashes a wide smile at Oksana but gets nothing in return.

"Yes, she is," Oksana says. "That's our Sarah for you—quite a handful." Oksana squints at Sarah, apparently trying to figure out her game.

"Aw, I'm sweet, Jonas, you know that," Sarah purrs.

"That's true. As sweet as can be," I agree.

Max hasn't taken his eyes off Sarah the whole time we've been sitting here. I swear to God, if he touches her again like he did in the other room, I won't be able to control myself from strangling him.

"... and he always says I work too much," Sarah's saying. "Isn't that right, sweetheart?"

"Oh, yeah. This girl always has to work. Work, work, work. Poor thing's got school to pay for, plus this horrible thing with her mom's cancer—I'm sure you've heard all about that—" Oksana and her son exchange a look. "And now she tells me her dad just got laid off, too." I exhale loudly. "How much can one girl carry on her shoulders? Jesus. Even after some wacko hauled off and attacked her at school—Sarah, did you tell them about that?"

Sarah shakes her head. "No, I didn't mention it, sweetheart. It was no big deal."

"Are you kidding me? It was brutal," I say. "It's hard to believe there are sick fucks in the world who would want to hurt a sweet girl like this. I hope whoever did it burns in fucking hell." I glare at Max.

"Jonas," Sarah says, her voice tight.

Shit. I'm veering off plan. My heart is pounding mercilessly. I take a deep breath.

"Sorry to hear you were hurt, Sarah," Max says slowly. "Glad you've recovered." He leers at her. "So nicely."

I clear my throat. Motherfucker. I'm clenching my hands so tightly they physically hurt.

"Apparently, there's been a string of rapes at the university," Sarah says evenly. "The police are thinking the attack on me was a botched rape, or maybe just a mugging, they're not sure. But, either way, I'm fine now." She glares at me, warning me to stay on plan. "It was so sweet how Jonas doted on me when I was recovering, though."

"Yeah, the poor thing was hurt pretty bad. And that's what made me realize I want to take care of her, you know? Make life a little easier for her—take some of the weight off her if I can. How much can one girl take, you know? But even after the attack, nope, she just wanted to hop right back into school and work—said she has too many bills to pay, too many applications to review, couldn't afford to take any time off."

Sarah suddenly chokes up, or at least she appears to. Damn. She's good. I know she's acting—but, still, she's breaking my heart.

"Hey," I say gently. "It's okay." I grab her hand. "Everything's gonna be all right."

"I'm sorry," Sarah says. "I'm fine now." She swallows hard. "I've just had so much to deal with lately. It just means so much to me that you want to help me."

I kiss the top of her hand. "I do." I address Oksana. "Maybe I shouldn't admit this to you, but I keep telling her I'll pay her bills for her so she can just quit this intake agent job altogether and concentrate on me, twenty-four-seven, but she says it wouldn't be fair to you guys—that you depend on her too much."

Oksana and Max look at each other. They haven't sent Sarah an application to process since before she left for Belize.

"You know, it's funny. I signed up with The Club so I wouldn't have to deal with emotional attachments but, then, damn it to hell, I got *attached* to this girl right here." I grab her thigh. "No man could resist her. Look at her. She's gorgeous. But business is business, and I know that—I respect that. So that's why I'm here."

"What exactly can we do for you, Mr. Faraday?" Max asks.

"I was just hoping I could convince you to let me buy all Sarah's time for a maybe a month? She's always running out the door to process another application for you guys when I want to fly her somewhere or spend some alone time with her, she's so worried about paying her bills. So I thought maybe if I could convince her to take a paid leave of absence from the job, that would free up some of her time for me."

"I can't quit my job, Jonas," Sarah says, jutting out her chin. "I've got too many people depending on me."

"I know, sweetheart. But you've got to learn to accept my help. I just want to help you."

"Thank you, Jonas. You're so generous."

"I think we could accommodate you, Mr. Faraday," Oksana says. "Sarah's one of our very best intake agents, though, and we rely on her heavily on a daily basis. But, of course, we always want to make our clients happy, whenever possible."

"Fantastic. I'd like to buy her for a month to start with. I can't commit beyond that, at least not yet."

"Exactly the reason I won't quit my job," Sarah says to Oksana like they're best girlfriends. "He won't commit." Now she looks at me. "If you can't commit to me, Jonas Faraday, then I can't commit to you."

Oksana's eyes sparkle. She obviously appreciates Sarah's gamesmanship.

I roll my eyes. "This girl's tough, I'm not gonna lie. Keeps me on my toes." I smile at Sarah and she smiles back. "Obviously, I could have any other girl in The Club—or any girl in the world, for that matter, if you want to know the truth—but I can't seem to get enough of this particular girl. It's crazy. She's just... man, she's a pistol, I'm telling you."

Sarah smirks. "I'm just honest, that's all. I am who I am—take me or leave me."

"Yep, that's what she keeps saying—and I just keep taking her." I laugh like a total letch. "But she won't quit the job and she keeps insisting I have to pay you directly for her time if I want her undivided attention, and I respect that. She's loyal, this one. A straight shooter. I always say in business you've got to be aboveboard and lead with integrity."

Sarah shrugs. "I'd never leave these guys hanging." Sarah lowers her head and appears to become overwhelmed with emotion again. She takes a minute. "Sorry. I was just thinking about my mom and dad again. They've got so much to deal with."

Damn, if this show isn't convincing these fuckers that Sarah's the jewel in their crown, I don't know what will. Give this girl an Oscar.

"Don't you worry about anything, Sarah," I say. I peek at Oksana. Yeah, she's buying what Sarah's selling. "I'm going to help you with all your expenses, sweetheart, I promise. But first things first. What's it going to cost to release this beautiful girl for a month into my care? I want to *own* her—twenty-four-seven." I lick my lips.

"Oh, Jonas," Sarah says. "You're so sweet."

"Twenty-four-seven?" Oksana looks up at the ceiling, apparently calculating something. "Three thousand a day should suffice."

"Ninety thousand for a month?" I say, incredulous. "That seems high."

Sarah bristles and crosses her arms. "That seems *high* to you, Jonas Faraday? For a *month* with me, twenty-four-seven, whenever and wherever you want me? That seems awfully *low* to me."

I put my hands up defensively, trying to appease my impossible-to-please girlfriend, but she looks away, pissed.

Oksana smiles. Oh yeah, she loves Sarah. "We rely heavily on Sarah, that's why she's been so busy with her job. She's our brightest star. You understand she's not one of the girls in The Club, right? She's a highly specialized member of our team. You were never supposed to have her—she's not normally for sale. Someone like that comes at a high premium."

"Oh, yeah, I know that. By the way, sorry I broke The Club's rules to get with her—I just couldn't resist." I smile broadly. "She was just too tempting."

Sarah nods emphatically. *Damn straight.*

"If I understand what you're asking for," Oksana continues, "you'd like us to hold her job for her—guarantee her job will be waiting for her in a month—*and* you want us to continue paying her throughout the entire month she's gone, right? Like a paid leave?"

"Exactly."

"Which means we'll need to hire another intake agent to take her place, at least temporarily—and train that person, too. The whole situation is a huge inconvenience to us. We're running a for-profit organization here, you realize, not a charity."

I remain silent, acting like I'm thinking it over.

Sarah looks at me with pleading eyes. "What if I take a pay cut to make it work for you, Jonas? Because I'd really like to be available for you, every minute of every day and *night,* for the next month." She bats her eyelashes.

"I wouldn't ask you to take a pay cut, Sarah," I say. "Never. You need the money." I sigh. "I wish you'd just let me pay you directly. Wouldn't that be simpler?"

"We'll do it for eighty," Oksana blurts. "But not a penny less. That's my final offer."

"Oh, thank you, Oksana," Sarah says brightly. "You see, Jonas? Oksana's willing to work with you. So will you do the deal?" She gets up from her chair and places her lips right on my ear. "I'll make it worth your while, sweetheart," she whispers.

I know she's just play-acting, but she just turned me on. I turn my head and kiss her mouth. She runs her hand through my hair. Damn, even when we're faking it, she's my crack.

"You know I can't resist you," I say quietly. I pull out my checkbook. "Eighty it is. Payable to The Club?" I ask.

"We'll fill in the payee name ourselves," Max answers.

I fill out the check and hand it to Oksana. I look at Sarah. "It's official. I own you. Twenty-four seven. You're mine."

Sarah's eyes blaze. "For one month."

"Again, sorry I co-opted Sarah against your rules. I just couldn't resist her—no man could have resisted her after what she wrote to me in her email. And then when I found out about her jealous streak, too. Man, that was just too much." I run my finger up Sarah's arm. "She's a handful, this one. A tasty little handful."

Sarah smiles wickedly at me. "Thank you for your generosity, Jonas. I think generosity is such an attractive trait in a man. It turns me on."

I turn to them. "This has been the best money I've spent in my life, hands down. I'm so glad I joined. In fact, I've been going on and on about how awesome The Club is to all my friends. I was just at an international finance convention with some heavy hitters, actually, and I must have told at least twenty guys all about it one night over Scotch—and they all want in, every last one of them. But these guys are all, you know, big-time VIPs—accustomed to highly specialized attention in all things."

"We'll be sure to give them a fantastic experience," Oksana says.

"Some of these guys make me look like a pauper, seriously." I chuckle. "Just obscene amounts of money. I told them I'd ask you to contact them personally, sort of like a VIP concierge type thing, to answer questions, get them signed up, tell them what they'll be getting, assure them they'll be treated like kings. They don't want to sign up like everybody else—they want assurances they'll get the best of the best. These guys don't give a shit about romance, if you know what I mean, they just want premium *service*."

Oksana looks at Max, clearly asking for permission.

"We'll give them platinum service, I assure you," Max says. "Just give them the link to our application portal and we'll get the membership process going per our usual protocols."

"Why don't I just email you their contact info, and you can give them a quick call? I bet you could upsell each and every one of them to a VIP yearlong package for half a mil. Maybe more—maybe even create some sort of special VIP club within The Club, just for these guys? Seriously. Some of them make me look like a hobo." I laugh. "If you give me my phone from the other room, I'll pull up their contacts and send them to you in an email."

"No," Max says, his tone firm. "We don't make telephone contact and we don't solicit new members, ever. No exceptions. If they want to join, they'll have to do it through the appropriate channels, same as everyone else. I designed the protocols myself. We do it this way to ensure maximum protection and confidentiality for everyone involved in the transaction. I'm sure they'll understand that."

Oh, so this fucker designed the site, did he? His mom supplies the girls and he supplies everything else?

"I'm not sure they'll go for that," I persist.

"Jonas, please," Sarah says firmly. "Please respect what Max is telling you. Your friends can't ask The Club to do anything that might compromise confidentiality in any way, regardless of how much money they have. Don't forget, that confidentiality protects me as an employee as much as anyone."

I stare at Sarah. That's not part of the plan. What the fuck is she saying? The plan is for me to send them a fucking email about my rich friends who want to join. Why is she siding with Max?

"Can I be perfectly honest with you about something, Jonas?" Sarah says, but she's looking at Max like they're sharing an inside joke.

"Of course." My heart is raging. What the fuck is she doing?

"If it gets out I've worked for The Club, I might not pass the ethics review for my law license. So it's really important to me that we follow whatever protocols The Club has in place to protect itself—because those protocols protect me, too. I mean, how well do you know these guys? Can you be sure of their absolute discretion?"

I'm speechless.

Sarah looks at Max, unflinching. He smiles at her, heat rising in his eyes. It's all I can do not to leap across the room and wring the fucker's neck the way he's looking at her right now.

"Sarah makes an excellent point," Max says. "Thank you, Sarah."

"Of course. Protecting The Club is in everyone's interest. Especially mine." She looks at me sweetly. "And so is protecting the privacy of members, too, of course." She smiles broadly, full of charm.

What the fuck is she doing? *This is not the fucking plan.*

"I agree," Max says. "Mr. Faraday, why don't you tell me the names of your friends so that when they contact us through appropriate channels, we'll be ready for them." He grabs a pad off Oksana's desk. "I promise, we'll make sure to show them the time of their lives."

"Sure thing," I say, thoroughly relieved. Looks like there was a method to Sarah's madness, after all—she was just gaining this fucker's trust. Good thinking. "Yeah, okay, the names are on my phone. Give me my phone and I'll email you the names."

"No, just tell me the names now, verbally." He positions his pen on the pad.

"Jonas, you can give the list to me later, and I'll make sure they get the names," Sarah says.

I'm speechless again. What the fuck is she doing? *This isn't the fucking plan.*

"Perfect," Max says. "Thank you, Sarah."

Sarah looks at me. "Hey, Jonas, would you mind giving me five minutes to speak to Max and Oksana in private?"

What the fuck? We both agreed I wouldn't leave her alone with these fuckers for a nanosecond. What the fuck is she doing?

"Just for five minutes," she says breezily. "I have some information about a member I need to give them—about the last application I processed—and the information's confidential, of course. This will be my last work-related task for a whole month, I promise. When we walk out that door, no more work." She winks.

I can't speak. This is insanity. No fucking way.

"Just five minutes, sweetheart," she says.

I don't move. No fucking way. *No fucking way.*

"Mr. Faraday, will you be so kind?" Max says, getting up and motioning to the door. "Just for a moment. Nina will get you some coffee." He opens the door leading out to the reception area.

I stare at Sarah. Fuck me. This is not happening. No fucking way.

"Thanks, Jonas," Sarah says. "It'll just take a minute. I promise."

I force my body to stand. I look at my watch. "Five minutes." My eyes are granite. "I'm timing you."

"Great, thanks. I'll be right out."

Chapter 22
Sarah

The minute the door closes behind Jonas, I whip around to face Oksana and Max, my eyes as hard as steel. "Fifty-fifty or I walk," I say evenly, clenching my jaw. "I've got this guy in the palm of my hand, as you can plainly see. He can't get enough of me. He's *addicted.* And now that I've given him my sob story about my mom having cancer and my dad losing his job—he's ready to throw money at me hand over fist. Fifty-fifty or I'm out of here."

Max snickers.

"Sixty-forty," Oksana says. "That's my final offer."

I sit back in my chair and cross my arms. "He's in the palm of my hand, I'm telling you."

Oksana's face has turned to stone. "Sixty-forty," she says. "Take it or leave it."

I wonder what she'd do to me if I leave it? "Fifty-fifty with this guy, and sixty-forty on future guys," I say. "I don't even need you anymore on Faraday—I could keep all this guy's money and you'd never even know it—but I'm keeping you in the loop because I want to work with you on future guys, too."

Oksana and Max look at each other.

"You could keep all this guy's money and we'd never know it?" Max says, chuckling to himself. "You think it'd be that simple?" His voice is pure menace.

"Shh, Maksim. *Dobre,*" Oksana says. "Fine, Sarah. You've obviously done a lot of work on Faraday already—so we'll do fifty-fifty on him and sixty-forty on everyone else."

"All right," I say. "Good. Now that we've got that settled—you'll be happy to know he gave me another check this morning. This time for a hundred thousand."

"That's all?" Max says.

I roll my eyes. "It was just 'fun money' to *gamble* with while we're here." I laugh. "I'm telling you, he's in the palm of my hand."

Oksana looks duly impressed. "Do you have the check with you?"

"Yeah, it's in my purse." I motion to the outside room.

Oksana motions to Max and he gets up to retrieve it.

"I'll squeeze everything I can out of Faraday for the next month, but after that I want more clients," I say to Oksana when Max is gone. "I'm actually enjoying this."

"Ah, you've discovered the power." Oksana laughs. "I always say, as long as a woman's got a pussy and a mouth, it's her own damned fault if she can't get whatever the hell she wants."

I smile through my sudden nausea. "Ain't that the truth. You'd think the man's never had sex before, the way he reacts to me."

"The power of the pussy," Oksana says with mock reverence.

We share a raucous laugh, though I'm seriously trying not to hurl. What a bitch.

Max comes back into the office with my purse, but as he tries to close the door behind him, I hear Jonas' anxious voice on the other side of the door.

"I've paid for her time," I hear Jonas say. "I'm coming back in."

"Just give us five minutes," Max says curtly. He slams the door and locks it and strides across the room, rummaging through my purse as he goes. He pulls out the check and holds it up for Oksana to see.

"Nice work," Oksana says.

"Next week, my mom's health will take a turn for the worse," I say. "And my dad will be in danger of losing his house—to the tune of five hundred thousand."

Oksana nods enthusiastically. "Good."

Max takes the seat vacated by Jonas and leans into my face, placing his hand firmly on my thigh.

I recoil under his touch.

"So did Faraday fix your little problem?"

I don't respond.

Max leans even closer and whispers. "Did he fix the little problem you wrote about in your email to him—your 'Mount Everest' problem, I think you called it?" He licks his lips. "Because if not, I'm sure I can solve your problem in about five minutes."

I lean sharply away from Max's face. "I told the guy what he wanted to hear, that's all—the one thing I knew he couldn't resist."

Max chuckles. His face tells me he doesn't believe me. "You were very, very convincing."

"Maksim, *nemaye*," Oksana says. "Very clever, Sarah."

I grimace. I've only got one thing on my mind right now—getting Oksana to open an email, come hell or high water.

"So let's cut the crap," I say. "I'm willing to forgive our 'unfortunate miscommunication.' But I want to get paid within twenty-four hours, every time, or else I walk—and, believe me, I'll take you down when I go."

"You won't take us down," Max says.

I smash my mouth into a hard line.

"You just said so yourself—you won't pass the ethics review for your law license if it gets out you worked for us. You won't risk that."

I scowl like I'm pissed at myself for revealing my big secret to him. "Maybe I don't care about my law license," I say, trying my damnedest to sound like a terrible liar.

Max grins. "Oh yes you do. I've done my research on you. I'm quite confident you care more than anything about your law license—and that you therefore won't tell anyone about us."

I grit my teeth.

"But that's exactly why we can trust you, Miss Cruz. Our interests are obviously aligned. And that's good."

"If you piss me off enough, I'll send out that report, regardless of what might happen to my law career."

He smiles at me, not buying it.

"Fine," I huff, conceding his point. I cross my arms. "But if you send the Ukrainian John Travolta to hurt me again, all bets are off."

"The 'Ukrainian John Travolta'?" He bursts out laughing.

"Yeah. Like John Travolta in *Pulp Fiction*—only Ukrainian."

Max is highly amused. "I'll have to tell Yuri you said that." He says something to his mother in Ukrainian and she laughs. Max waves the air. "We're not going to harm you, Sarah. You've proved your value. You say you're not 'fucking stupid'? Well, neither are we."

I squint at him.

"You're an entertaining writer, by the way. A spitfire, just like your asshole boyfriend said."

"How do I know I can trust you? How do I know you won't send your hitman after me again?"

His eyes harden. "Because if I say you're safe, you're safe. And if I want you dead, you're dead."

A shiver runs up my spine—I'm six inches away from the man who personally ordered me dead.

"But the good news is I don't want you dead." He touches my

arm and I shudder. "I do hope you weren't too inconvenienced by our unfortunate miscommunication."

"Oh no, not at all. I didn't need all that blood inside my body, anyway," I scoff.

"How bad are the scars?" Oksana asks. "I can't put you on the circuit if you're too scarred." Her tone is pure business.

There's a loud knock at the door. "Time's up," Jonas says loudly. He shakes the door, but it's locked. "Sarah? Time's up. Right now."

Max motions to the door. "Talk to him."

I walk to the door and open it. Jonas looks panicked. Or is that enraged?

"Everything's great, sweetheart," I say cheerily, poking my head out. "We're almost done talking business. We need just five more minutes and then we'll be all done—and I'll be all yours for a whole month."

He's bursting out of his skin.

"Come here," I say brightly.

He leans an inch from my face to whisper something to me, but I kiss him.

"Sarah," he whispers, pulling away, his eyes frantic. "Get out of there right now."

"Yeah, just a couple more minutes," I say at full voice. "And after that, I'm at your service, sweetheart."

"Sarah, now," he whispers fiercely. "*Right now*."

"No," I whisper. "Trust me."

As I close the door on his face, he flashes white-hot anger. I turn back around, making sure to keep the door unlocked. "My wounds are healing surprisingly well," I say, sitting back down. "Thanks for your concern. This one on my neck is hardly anything." I tilt my head so they can get a good view of it.

"Yeah, not too bad," Oksana agrees.

"And the one on my ribcage isn't too bad, either—and it'll get better over time."

"Let's see it," Oksana says. "I need to see for myself."

"Actually, we have a little tradition here at The Club," Max says, his tone suddenly lecherous. "I audition every single girl before we send them out on the circuit—just to make sure they're worthy of our high standards." He looks at his mother and says something in Ukrainian.

My stomach drops into my toes. I glance at the door, suddenly feeling panicked. Holy crap.

"It won't take very long," Max says. "Five minutes." He stands and holds out his hand.

Holy shit. He expects to fuck me in the bathroom right now?

"Maksim," Oksana chastises. "*Ne zaraz*."

My throat is closing up. "Faraday is right on the other side of the door," I sputter. "And he's already wondering what's going on—you saw him. He's freaking out. There's not enough time."

"Maksim, *nemaye*," Oksana says sharply. "*Ne s'ohodni*."

Max scowls at his mother and exhales loudly. "Well, if not today, then before she leaves Las Vegas."

I try to smile, but I'm ninety-nine percent sure I'm failing at the attempt. I have to get out of here—I'm freaking out—but goddammit, I've got to get Oksana to open a frickin' email.

"When can you get away from him for an hour or so? I'll do it right." Max winks. "Tomorrow?"

"I don't know. He's high-maintenance—kind of intense."

"I'll drop whatever I'm doing at a moment's notice."

"Aw, how sweet—you'll take a break from stabbing me to fuck me?" My mind is racing. I've got to think of some reason to send Oksana an email. I'm running out of time.

Max laughs. "You *are* a little firecracker, aren't you? I see why he likes you. This is going to be fun."

"Maksim, *tysha*," Oksana says sharply. "Sarah, I need to see your scars before you leave here. I can't put you on the circuit unless I know what the clients will see. I keep a private catalogue of pictures so I can assign girls to our client's specific preferences."

Think, Sarah, think.

"Faraday's right on the other side of the door waiting for me," I say. "I'm not going to get naked for you right here and now. You saw him—he's suspicious. He could knock down the door any second."

"Well, I need to see your body right now or there's no deal."

Lightning bolt. Hallelujah.

"Okay," I concede. "I'll go into the bathroom and take a naked selfie right now—for your *personal* catalogue only. Hand me my phone. But I'll tell you right now, I'm only gonna take the photo from the neck down and I'm keeping my undies on, too."

Max smiles. "You're just going to take a photo off the Internet."

I throw up my hands, exasperated. "How would I do that? I'll clearly be in *your* bathroom in the photo—and I'll be wearing *these*." I quickly lift up my skirt and flash my red G-string.

At the brief glimpse of my undies, Max's face lights up like a Christmas tree.

"I'll take the photo right now and email it to you. I'll even stand here while you open the photo to make sure it's acceptable to you." I grab a coffee mug decorated with cartoon-cats off Oksana's desk. "And, hey, I'll hold this cat-mug in the picture, too. I can't very well Photoshop a picture of me in *your* bathroom, wearing a red G-string, holding a cat-mug, now can I?"

"*Pravda*," Oksana says, satisfied. "Maksim?"

Max looks dubious for a moment, but then he nods.

I hold out my hand. "May I have my phone, please?"

Max rummages into my purse, pulls out my phone, and scrutinizes it for a long beat.

"It's not set to record," I say. I grab the phone from him and hold it against my mouth. "This is Sarah Cruz and I work for The Club. I've been bilking Jonas Faraday out of his money since day one and I'm about to embark on a fancy new career as a high-priced call girl." I smirk at Max. "Not recording."

He grins at me. "I'll come into the bathroom with you."

"Maksim, *bud' laska*," Oksana barks.

I hope to God that means "no." Without waiting to find out, I beeline into the bathroom with my cat-mug and quickly close the door behind me. The minute I'm alone, my knees buckle. I grab the sink ledge to steady myself. "Holy crap," I whisper, panting. "Pull yourself together, Cruz."

I pull my sundress over my head and quickly take a photo of myself in the mirror from the neck down, holding the mug; and then I stare at the photo of my almost-naked body, my pulse pounding in my ears. This feels wrong. So, so wrong. Then why am I so sure it's going to work?

I shake my hands and exhale, trying to calm myself. What's the worst that can happen here? They try to blackmail me with the photo? They post it to a porn site? I stare at the picture again, trying to imagine it posted on some skeezy porn site filled with topless women. Not the end of the world, right? My face isn't in the photo. There's nothing to identify this particular pair of boobs and torso as mine—other than the scar on my ribcage, I guess. In theory, someone could connect that scar to me—but not definitively. Not like they could with a tattoo. I could always deny the photo is of me, if I had to. I could say they Photoshopped that scar onto the photo.

Gah.

This feels like such a bad idea. What's my alternative, though? They're not going to open an email from Jonas—that much is clear. They don't fully trust him for some reason. But they trust me.

Yep, Plan A is officially done-zo. Now it's time to push ahead with Plan B or accept defeat. *And I refuse to accept defeat.* I embed my photo into the email template Henn gave me, throw my dress back on, and exit the bathroom.

"You want to make sure this isn't recording again?" I hold out my phone to Max with a shaky hand.

"I just won't say anything particularly interesting." He smirks.

"Fabulous." I look down at my phone. "What's your email address, Oksana?"

She tells it to me and my hands tremble as I type it into Henn's email template.

"Max? I'm assuming you want this photo, too?" His expression leaves no doubt his answer is yes. "What's your email address?"

He tells it to me and I quickly type it into my email header—and then I press send. *Oh. My. God.* I'm about to hyperventilate. I'm sure my cheeks are cherry red.

"Okay, I sent it," I say, trying to sound calm, but I can barely breathe. "Why don't you both make sure you got it."

It feels like time moves at glacial speed as Oksana logs onto her computer and opens her email account.

"Do I meet your high standards?" I ask, my voice quavering and my knees knocking.

"Oh yes, very nice," Oksana says, viewing the photo.

Oh my God. She opened my email. *She opened it!*

"You'll be a top favorite for the ones who like spicy," Oksana continues. "The scar is okay. You can blame it on a surgery. Your appendix, maybe, like Marilyn Monroe in the famous photos."

I smile politely at the Marilyn reference, though I have no idea what the hell she's talking about. "What do you think, Max?" I ask. "Do you like what you see?" I try to sound flirty and inviting, but I'm sure I just sound carsick.

Max taps the screen on his phone—*oh my God, he's opening the email!*—and I have to breathe through my mouth to keep myself from fainting.

He studies the picture. "I see why Mr. Faraday's such a big fan of yours." He looks up at me and licks his lips. "I look forward to sampling this tomorrow."

"How much are you planning to pay me for the pleasure?"

He scoffs.

"A smart prostitute never gives it away. Right, Oksana?"

Oksana chuckles. "To Maksim, she does—if she knows what's good for her."

"I always get my freebie," Max says. "But don't worry—I'll make sure you enjoy it, too. I'm very considerate in that way. Especially for a woman with your *problem*."

My stomach churns. "I... I don't know if I can get away." I motion to the door. "Faraday is pretty possessive—"

"You'll figure out a way—if you know what's good for you."

There's an urgent pounding at the door.

"Sarah," Jonas yells. "It's time to go. Right now." He shakes on the door, but it's locked. When did they lock it?

I'm suddenly racked with panic. I've got to get out of this room.

"Sarah!" he shouts. "Time's up!"

"I'm coming," I call back, trying my damnedest to keep my voice light and bright. I whisper to Oksana and Max, "He's really intense."

The door shakes again as Jonas tries to open it.

I turn to go, but Max grabs my arm with a vise-like grip.

"Just think. If Yuri had killed you like I'd told him to, I would have missed out on so much fun." Without warning, he swoops into my face and kisses me on the lips, thrusting his tongue to the back of my throat. I jerk back, utterly repulsed, and he twists my arm. "I guess things always work out for the best." He smiles like a shark. "I'll text you my phone number—and I'll expect your call *tomorrow*."

Chapter 23
Sarah

Just a tip. If you're ever planning on being in a relationship of any kind, but especially a monogamous, romantic relationship, with one Jonas P. Faraday, do not—I repeat, *do not*—do what I just did. Holy shitballs, as Kat always says, that did not go over well.

The minute Jonas and I were out of earshot from the bad guys, even before we'd reached our car, Jonas let me have it. To say he was angry with me is the understatement of the year. To say he ripped into me and created several new orifices in my body doesn't do it justice. For the first time ever, I got to see what Jonas' fury looks like when directed at me instead of his ever-patient brother—and I've got to say, it ain't pretty.

Of course, I cried my eyes out when Jonas started screaming at me, but his meltdown wasn't the only thing making me cry. The countless conflicting emotions simultaneously slamming into me probably had a lot to do with my tears, too. I felt relief, fury, anxiety, righteous indignation, apology, and shame, all at once—but, mostly, if I'm being honest, pure elation and pride that I'd figured out a way to get Oksana *and* Max to open Henn's malware email. And I was pissed as hell at Jonas for being so consumed with anger or anxiety or both that he couldn't appreciate and applaud my savage badassery.

After Jonas' verbal assault had died down and he was finally capable of speaking rationally again, he demanded I tell him every single thing that happened inside that room with Max and Oksana, from the minute he walked out until I joined him again—and I did. Well, almost everything. I didn't mention Max's disgusting demand for a "freebie" or the repulsive kiss he planted on me. What would have been the point of telling him about either wretched thing? I knew Jonas would only turn around, march right back over there, and try to kill the bastard with his bare hands—and I was deathly afraid he'd die in the process. I mean, jeez, I know better than anyone what kind of a monster Max truly is—and I wasn't about to let anything happen to Jonas.

I did, however, tell Jonas about the naked selfie I emailed to Oksana and Max, and that's when my hunky-monkey boyfriend went DEFCON-one ballistic on me. Understandably so, I guess, but, wow, the degree of horror and outrage he expressed about that one itty-bitty photo made me wonder if he'd heard the other thing I said, namely, "They opened the email."

He didn't react when I said it the first time, so I said it again. "They opened the email, Jonas—both of them. It worked. We did it." But he didn't frickin' care. Not in that moment, he didn't, anyway. Nope. He was just angry as hell and nothing—absolutely nothing—was going to distract him from his rage.

I felt empathetic about Jonas' anger to a point. Who would *want* their girlfriend to email a naked photo of herself to a murderous pimp? But come on. At the end of the day, what's the big effing deal? My face wasn't in the photo. It's a photo of a random, naked body, just like all the other bodies on this planet. A neck, two boobs, a belly button, a red-G-string, a pair of legs, and a cat-mug. Big effing deal.

Frankly, if you want to know the truth, I'm proud I did it. I'm Orgasma the All-Powerful, after all, and today I proved it. When Orgasma's on a mission for truth and justice, when she's hell-bent on decimating the bad guys and protecting the innocent, Orgasma stops at nothing to accomplish her mission. Hellz yeah! Orgasma. Will. Be. Victorious. Fuckers!

And, anyway, what the hell was I supposed to do? Go back to the hotel room and say, "Sorry, guys, we did our best—better luck next time?" No effing way. Before stepping foot into that office, I'd promised myself nothing would stop me. And nothing did. So I took a stupid picture of myself—so what? Considering the situation, it could have been worse. And, by the way, did I mention, it worked? Because, holy crappola, *both* of them opened the frickin' email. Boom.

It's been a solid fifteen minutes since Jonas and I have exchanged a single word. Both our chests are still heaving from our argument and my face still feels flushed. I glance at him. He's staring straight ahead, his jaw muscles pulsing in and out. I look out the passenger window of the car, fuming. I can't stop yelling at him inside my head. I'm certainly not going to be the first one to speak.

Jonas pulls our rental car up to the front of the hotel and we wait silently in line for the valet attendant behind several other cars. After a minute, Jonas pulls out his phone and taps out a text. "I'm telling the team to meet us in our suite in ten minutes," he mutters, breaking the silence.

But I don't reply. Screw him. He can't yell at me like he did and then expect me to act like everything's fine. Even before the valet guy opens my car door, I burst out of the car and march into our hotel, not looking back. Jonas is angry with me? Well, the more I think about it, I'm steaming mad at him, too.

Cold air from the air conditioning blasts me as I stride through the lobby toward the elevator bank, but it does nothing to cool my hot temper. He's overreacting, plain and simple. A little anger would have been okay. But a volcano erupting and spewing molten lava at me? Not okay. What he should have done was congratulate me and tell me I'm so fucking smart—that's what he *should* have said. That man needs to take a chill pill and celebrate our victory, no matter how we got it. Yeah, in fact, as far I'm concerned, Jonas can go to hell.

Chapter 24

Sarah

Everyone (besides Jonas) is hanging on my every word. Now *this* is the kind of reaction I'd hoped to elicit from Mr. Volcano. Jeez. When I get to the part about me taking a naked selfie in the bathroom, Kat shrieks, either with shock or glee, I'm not sure which. And when I regale the group with the part about Oksana and Max opening my email right on the spot, Josh whoops and high-fives me while Henn fist pumps the air and scrambles to his laptop to track the progress of his little malware-baby.

But Jonas? He sits in the corner, scowling, watching all of us but not saying a word. I feel like flipping Jonas the bird, to be honest, but I refrain because I'm a fancy lady.

"Bingo," Henn says after a brief moment of looking at his screen. "You did it. We're in. I've got Oksana's computer and that guy's phone. Holy shit, Sarah. Jackpot."

I look smugly at Jonas, but he looks away. Really, Jonas? You're pissed at me? Well, I'm pissed at you.

"Oh my God," Henn says, staring intently at his computer screen. "The bastard forwarded your email to another computer and opened your photo there, too." He chuckles. "Brilliant." He clicks a button on his keyboard and his entire face suddenly bursts into bright red flames.

Oh jeez. Why do I get the distinct feeling Henn just saw my boobs? I blush. "So, Henn?"

His head jerks up from his computer screen like a kid caught with his hand in the cookie jar. "Yes?"

"So now what?"

He swallows hard. "Well, um." His cheeks are still on fire. "I'll snoop around both computers and this Max guy's phone and see what I can find. And then we wait for them to hopefully access their mainframe and bank accounts. I imagine we won't have to wait too long."

"Can you delete that photo?" Jonas asks, his voice tight. "Can you find it and erase it everywhere?"

"Um, sure, no problem," Henn says quickly. "I can delete it right now, if you want me to. I've got total access."

"Yeah, but if you delete that photo off their computers now, won't that tip them off?" Kat asks.

"Yeah," Henn says. "If that photo magically disappears, this Max dude is gonna know something's up for sure—and if he designed their tech like he says, then he's a badass motherfucker of epic proportions and we don't want to do anything to tip him off."

"Well, then, don't delete it. I don't want to give them any reason whatsoever to be suspicious," I say.

"I agree," Henn says.

Jonas exhales and crosses his arms over his chest.

"God, Sarah," Kat laughs. "First the solo-boob shot and now this. You're quite the exhibitionist, aren't you?"

Oh jeez. Thanks, Kat. I steal a quick look at Jonas, just in time to see him clench his jaw. Yes, Jonas, I told my best friend about the left-boob picture I sent you when I was nothing but your anonymous intake agent. *So sue me.*

Kat sees the look on Jonas' face and she winces. "Sorry," she mouths to me.

I shrug and shoot her a "he can go fuck himself" look.

"A 'boob picture'?" Josh asks, raising his eyebrows. "Oh my goodness, tell us more, Sarah Cruz."

"Just a little sexting with this really hot guy I met online," I say, glancing at Jonas—only to find he's still pissed as hell. I roll my eyes. "A hot guy who *used* to have a sense of humor. It's no big deal—all the kids are doing it these days."

"And all the politicians," Josh says.

"And athletes," Henn says.

"And housewives," Kat adds.

"And grandmas," Josh says.

"And some priests, too," Henn says, and everyone (except Jonas) laughs.

"Sarah, you picked the perfect bait for your email," Kat says. "No matter how smart or powerful or rich a guy might be, he's got the same Kryptonite as every other man throughout history. Naked boobs."

"Are we really that simple?" Josh asks.

"Yes," Kat says. "You really are."

"Never underestimate the power of porn," Henn says.

"That's catchy," Kat says. "The porn industry should adopt that for a billboard campaign."

"I don't think the porn industry needs help with their marketing," Henn says.

Jonas hasn't stopped smoldering during this entire exchange. A vein in his neck—which I can now confidently identify as his external jugular vein—is throbbing.

"That was really quick thinking on your feet, Sarah," Josh says, but he's looking at his brother as he speaks. "You went in there hoping to harpoon a baby-whale, and you wound up landing Moby Dick. Great job." He raises his eyebrows at Jonas. "Right, bro? Aren't you proud of her?"

Jonas scowls at his brother.

"I was scared; I'm not gonna lie," I say. "My hands were shaking like crazy the whole time I was in there. But there was no way I was gonna leave that building without implanting that virus, no matter what. There was too much at stake."

"You're such a badass, Sarah," Kat says.

Jonas exhales and uncrosses his arms. I wrinkle my nose at him. I'm a badass and he's just going to have to deal with it. It's all I can do not to stick my tongue out at him.

"Hey, guys," Henn says, engrossed with something on his screen. "Holy shit. Oksana's going into her bank account right now—that Henderson Bank we were scouting out before." He stares at the screen for another ten seconds. "Sha-zam. She just typed in her password. Ha! I got it." He shakes his head. "Oh, man, I love technology."

"So what do we do?" I ask, my heart racing.

"We wait a few minutes for her to log off, and then we go in and snoop around."

"Sounds like the perfect time for me to fill drink orders," Josh says, heading to the bar.

Five minutes later, just as Josh is passing out the last of our drinks, Henn calls us over to his computer screen. "She's logged off," he announces. "Let's go in."

We all gather around Henn's computer like we're watching a Seahawks' game.

"Well, she's already deposited your checks—one hundred eighty thousand big ones," Henn says. "I bet that boils your blood, huh, Jonas?"

Jonas grunts.

"And she just transferred half of it into her savings account. Hmm," Henn says, sounding perplexed.

"What?" I ask. I'm practically breathless. This is all just too exciting to bear.

"Even after today's deposit, Oksana's got only about half a million total in these two accounts." He furrows his brow.

"Hmm," Josh says.

"Hmm, indeed," Henn agrees. "Chump change. These must be Oksana's personal accounts—definitely not The Club's main accounts."

"Damn," I say. "So how do we find the big money?"

Jonas ambles to the other side of the room, away from the group, apparently returning to his corner to sulk again.

"We just have to wait for them to log into their main bank accounts. It could be five minutes, five hours, five days—who knows?—but I guarantee they'll lead us there sooner or later. And in the meantime, I'll take a nice, long gander around their files and data, make copies of everything, see if there's anything of interest. Oh, and I'll listen to Max's voicemails, too. That's so cool you got Max's phone, Sarah." He sips his beer. "Dang, there's a lot to do."

Josh sighs. "Well, it looks like poor Henn's gonna be working through the night again, going through all this stuff." He looks at Kat. "What do you say, Party Girl with a Hyphen—you wanna paint Sin City red with me again?"

"I'd actually like to help Henn, if that's okay," Kat says. "I'm kind of excited about all this." She looks at me. "I have a strong motivation to want to bury these guys."

I grin at her. There's nothing like a best friend.

"Would that be okay with you, Henn?" Kat asks. "Or would I be in your way?"

"No, that'd be awesome. But only if you want to. I mean, Josh and Jonas are *paying* me to do this, so..." Henn sneaks a quick look at Josh, seemingly to make sure he's not stepping on any toes by accepting Kat's help.

But if Josh is disappointed about the unexpected agenda for the night, he doesn't show it. "Could you use my help, too?" he asks.

"Yeah," Henn says. "That'd be great."

"Okay, then. I'll order us room service and the three of us will get to work."

"Make that the four of us. I'll stick around and help, too," I say. "I'm pretty motivated to bury these guys, too." I glare at Jonas. If he's still pissed at me, that's not my problem.

Jonas raises his beer to his perfect lips and takes a long, sexy swig. Okay, I'm still mad at him, I swear I am—but, damn, his lips are luscious when he sips from a bottle like that. It makes me wish I were the bottle.

"Nah," Josh says. "You two kids should go out and celebrate." He looks at Jonas suggestively. "Or stay in and celebrate, whatever floats your boat. Either way, definitely celebrate—you both kicked ass today."

Jonas' eyes flicker at me, but I look away. If Jonas thinks he can yell at me the way he did today and then ravage me like nothing happened, then he's got another thing coming.

Josh grins at me. "The three of us will move our party down to my suite and let you two crazy kids swing on the chandeliers up here."

Jonas takes another long, slow sip of his beer, his eyes holding mine. I jut my chin at him and then look away. If he can't deal with the way today went down, I'm sorry, but that's just too bad for him. I didn't plan to desert him—I wanted Plan A to work out, but it didn't. I had to follow my gut—had to make a split-second decision in order to accomplish the mission. Big risk, big reward—isn't that what Jonas taught my contracts class?

Jonas drains the last drop of his beer, his eyes like lasers, and puts the bottle down. He crosses his arms over his muscled chest and stares at me. This time, I don't look away. Neither does he. I guess we're having a staring contest. Fine.

"What do you say, baby?" he finally says.

When he says the word *baby*, I feel my resolve instantly soften. Damn.

He licks his lips. Oh man, his eyes are a three-alarm fire. "You up for a little celebration tonight?"

I shrug. *No.*

"I think we should celebrate."

I shrug again. *No.* But I know I can't hold out forever. I'm addicted to him, after all.

"Aw, come on, baby." A side of his mouth tilts up, and just like that, heat flashes through my entire body. "You wanna have a little fun?"

"Maybe," I say. But then I remember I'm pissed at him and I steel myself again. "And maybe not." I purse my lips with indignation.

He purses his lips, too—but he's mocking me. "What if I said please?"

I look at Kat. She knows I'm a goner.

I twist my mouth. "Then I'd say *possibly*. But not *probably*."

"What if I said pretty please?" He flashes his full smile.

I smash my lips together, trying to resist him. Of course, I know my efforts are futile, but I'm giving it the ol' college try. I shrug again.

"What if I said pretty please *and* that we can do whatever you want, anything at all, you name it?"

Now he's got my attention. "Anything at all?"

"Anything at all."

"You'll be at my mercy completely?"

Jonas squints at me and bites his lip.

Out of the corner of my eye, I see Kat and Josh exchange a smile.

"Well? Will you be at my mercy or not?" I ask, tapping my toe. "What do you say?"

"Hmm." Jonas walks slowly toward me, his muscles taut. "What do I say?" When he reaches me, he takes my face in his hands. "I say, 'I'm an asshole.'"

Oh, those eyes. Those ridiculously beautiful eyes. "No, you're not. You're a cocky-bastard-asshole-motherfucker," I say softly.

He kisses me gently. His lips are cold and taste like beer. He's delicious.

"You did good today," he says. He kisses me again, this time slipping his tongue into my mouth.

My sweet Jonas.

Gah. I can't resist him. "I'm sorry I worried you," I say. And I am. I'm not at all sorry I did what I did today—it was effective and I totally kicked ass. But I regret the way my actions tortured him. I'm sure today took years off his life. I kiss his luscious lips, taking great care to suck on his lower lip as I depart his mouth. "We do whatever I want tonight—and you get absolutely no say in the matter," I whisper.

He looks wary for a moment, but I hold my ground. He leans into my ear. "No neckties," he whispers softly.

I smile. "Of course not."

"Then, okay, yes, you're in charge. Whatever you want to do."

"Okay, then," I say. "Count me in."

Chapter 25

Jonas

Of all the things we could be doing right now, of all the places we could have gone tonight, my baby drove us to a seedy strip club on the outskirts of downtown. What the hell? We're sitting in our rental car in the parking lot, staring at a flashing neon sign on the club's roof—"The Amsterdam Club." The place looks as seedy as hell—bargain-basement titty bar—definitely not one of the trendy hot spots on The Strip. This is where my baby wanted to come for her big night out? Jesus. I love my dirty, dirty girl, don't get me wrong—she's fucking hot as fuck and smart as hell and she turns me the fuck on, no matter what she does, even when she pisses me off like she did today—but, yeah, hot as she is, my dirty girl is also fucking crazy sometimes. There, I said it. She's batshit crazy.

"What the fuck is this skanky-ass place?" I say. "Why don't we just go back to the suite? I demand a rematch in our breath-holding contest. How about two out of three?"

"A deal's a deal," she says, putting up her hand. "As long as there are no neckties, you're required to do whatever I want tonight."

"How did you even find this place?"

"Google."

"No, I mean—yeah, Google." I roll my eyes. "I'm saying how did you even *think* to find this particular place out of all the strip clubs in Vegas? Why did you take us *here*?"

"Oh, you'll see."

"Why the fuck would I want to watch a dime-a-dozen stripper when I could glory in the exquisite pulchritude that is Sarah Cruz, the goddess and the muse?"

She laughs. "We're here to fulfill an item on my *addendum*. So hush."

Ah yes. Sarah's addendum. When she first hit me with that

word, it sounded so sexy and exciting and mysterious. But ever since she tied me up like King Kong, I've become slightly less enthusiastic every time she pulls out that word. I have a sudden thought that makes me hopeful. "You're gonna strip for me?" Just the idea is making me tingle.

"Let's just go in and have a drink, shall we? Get a little loose. And then I'll tell you exactly what I have in mind."

Uh oh. She's got that crazy gleam in her eye. Shit. I can't resist her when she looks at me that way.

Four Scotches and I'm feeling fan-fucking-tastic right now. I'm not normally a Scotch drinker, but what the fuck—when in Vegas, you gotta act like a member of the Rat Pack, right? Fuck yeah. This place is so fucking old school tacky, four doses of Scotch was the only way I could stomach it. For the past hour, Sarah and I have been making out in the corner of the club like teenagers while naked women gyrate around poles a few yards away from us, and I'm bursting out of my skin wanting to lick her and get inside her. I've yet to see a single stripper who turns me on a fraction as much as Sarah does, though glimpsing an assortment of titties and asses while kissing and groping Sarah's titties and ass has been a certain kind of lowbrow entertainment. I guess it's the same thing as going to the county fair once a year and chowing down on disgusting crap like chicken-fried bacon. Wretched, yes—but kinda fun once every blue moon.

"I'll be right back, baby," she purrs, her cheeks flushed. "I'm gonna get everything set up for us. Don't go anywhere."

She disappears.

I'm hard as a rock. What the fuck is she up to? Is she gonna give me a little striptease? That'd be so fucking hot. Damn, this woman is something else. Never boring, that's for sure. I close my eyes. I can't feel my toes. Scotch will do that to you. I laugh. Where the fuck is she? I'm so worked up right now I might have to insist on a little bathroom action after her striptease. Or, hey, as long as we've been acting like teenagers all night, maybe we'll do it in the backseat of the car.

She's back. She grabs my hands. "Come on," she says. "My sweet Jonas. Come on." She pulls me to her and licks my face. "I'm losing my mind, baby." She drags me toward a dark hallway on the other side of the club.

"Where are we going?"

"The Red Light District." She points to a sign above our heads at the entrance to the hallway flashing "Red Light District."

We stop just inside the hallway, and a security guard trades our cell phones for claim checks. An imposing sign on the wall reads, "Video Taping Strictly Prohibited." After giving up our phones, we stumble into the darkened hallway, holding hands. We stop at a large, blackened pane of glass. "Pour Some Sugar on Me" blares at us from behind the glass.

"What the fuck is this?" I ask.

"A peep show. Like in Amsterdam," she says.

I laugh. "This is absolutely nothing like Amsterdam."

She frowns at me. "How would I possibly know that? Just play along, you snob." She begins feeding tokens into a slot until the black curtain on the other side of the glass rises. A naked woman in a tiny black room bathed in garish red light dances and touches herself for a grand total of about ten seconds. The curtain closes.

I shrug. "Whoop-de-doo. A naked girl. Now let's go back to the suite and fuck like animals."

She laughs and pulls me along to the next window, where we're treated to another naked, gyrating woman bathed in red light in a black box. This time, the song behind the glass is "Talk Dirty to Me."

"It's a porn juke box," I say. "Yippee."

She kisses me. "I can't stop thinking about my dream, Jonas. I want you to make my dream come true."

I stare at her. She can't possibly mean the dream with the Jonas poltergeists making love to her every which way, and the red wine pouring all over her, and the people in the restaurant watching us? Holy shit. *The people in the restaurant watching us.* Oh my God. She's insane. I knew she had some crazy in her—and in fact, I like my baby's crazy—but this is pure insanity.

"You said we'd do whatever I want tonight." She smiles. "This is a gonna get me off like crazy."

She tugs at me, smiling wickedly, and leads me to the end of the dark hallway to a door marked "Authorized Personnel Only." She opens the door to reveal a stripper who, seemingly, is expecting us.

"Baby, thank you, but I don't want a threesome," I say. "I only want you." I know most men have to beg their girlfriends or wives for this particular treat, but I've already done the threesome thing and I've discovered quite emphatically that the format diverts me from what I like best—and, regardless, I don't want to share Sarah with anyone, even another woman.

"No, you big dummy," she says. "This girl's here to help me get everything set up."

"Sarah, listen."

She licks my face. "I want to be a dirty girl tonight." She's panting. "With you. Let's do it, Jonas. Let's be crazy. I want to act out my dream."

"Baby, I'm all for fun and games, but this is really kinky."

Her eyes light up. "Kinky, yes. Good word. Let's be kinky."

I pull back, ready to tell her no—and yet I'm rock hard. Am I appalled or turned on by this whole thing? I can't tell which.

"I've arranged everything for us, baby. No one will know it's us. We'll be wearing masks. I've got bandages to wrap around your tattoos and my scars. You can wear your briefs if you want, I don't care. I'll wear my panties if you want me to—and you can just pull things down or push them aside, whatever we need to do—whatever you're comfortable with." She's talking so fast, I can barely follow what she's saying—or maybe she's talking normally and I'm just fucking drunk. "No one will even know it's us, Jonas," she continues. "We can do whatever we want in the window—anything at all—and no one will know it's us. Maybe people will see us, maybe they won't—it just depends if anyone happens to put tokens in the slot. But that's the turn-on—thinking someone *might* be watching the whole time."

"Why do you get so turned on by the idea of people watching us fuck?"

"Remember the library?" she purrs. "Wasn't that hot?" Her body is jerking and jolting with her arousal. She grabs at my cock through my jeans. "We'll be wearing masks—no one will know it's us. Come on, Jonas. You can lick me and no one will know it's us."

I shudder with anticipation. This is totally depraved.

"Sarah," I begin. This woman turns me on like nothing I've ever experienced before, but I have zero interest in becoming a porn star.

"Just this once," she says. "It's like a bucket list thing."

"Sarah—"

"Pretty please." She licks my face again.

I shiver. Fuck. I don't want to disappoint her. And she's awfully convincing. "I'll make out with you in the black box, but I'm not gonna lick your pussy—certain things are sacred." Truth be told, I might even fuck her in the window if things get too hot for me to resist, but I'm most certainly *not* going to church on her in a disgusting shithole like this.

She's instantly deflated. "Okay," she says. I've plainly taken the wind out of her sails.

I truly do not understand this crazy-ass woman. Aren't women supposed to want rainbows and unicorns and long walks on the beach? What the fuck is this? I can't believe out of the two of us *I'm* the voice of sexual reason in this relationship.

"Will you do me a big favor and pay this nice woman for me?" Sarah asks. "I promised her two hundred bucks to let us take her place in the window for twenty minutes."

I pull out the cash and hand it to the stripper.

"You've set up a table in there, right?" Sarah asks her.

"Yeah," the woman assures her.

"Oh, and there's a particular song I want playing."

"Sure. What is it?"

Sarah whispers to her.

"Never heard of it," the woman says. "You sure you don't want 'Baby Got Back' or 'Talk Dirty to Me' or something like that?"

"No—it's got to be that song."

My interest is piqued.

"Tell it to me again," the woman says, and Sarah leans in and whispers again.

"Okay, I got it. I'll do my best." She motions to a small cardboard box on the floor. "There's the stuff you asked for. I'll be right back."

Sarah laps at my mouth. "I'm so excited."

"Tell me again why you want people to watch us fuck? I don't get it."

"I guess I just... You're so frickin' gorgeous, Jonas. It turns me on to think of you making love to me in front of the entire world."

I study her face for a moment. "You know I'm not going anywhere, right?"

She crinkles her nose. "Even when I pull crazy stuff like this?"

"Even then."

"Even when I scare the bajeezus out of you and don't stick to the plan and piss you off?"

"Barely then—but, yes, even then." I grin. "I'm not going anywhere."

Her voice drops. "Even though there's clearly something wrong with me?" She motions to the cardboard box. "Even though I'm not normal?"

"Even then, baby." I kiss her. "There's no such thing as normal."

What the fuck have I agreed to do? We're standing in the black window box, naked except for our underpants and Lone Ranger masks, with all our respective identifying characteristics wrapped up in white gauze bandages.

"We look like horny mummies getting ready to rob a bank," I say.

At my comment, Sarah bursts out laughing, so hard she has to sit down on the edge of the table. I sit down next to her and she immediately leans into my shoulder, still laughing and holding her belly. Just as her laughter begins to die down and she leans in to kiss me, red lights suddenly shine in our eyes and "Baby Got Back" begins blaring through the speakers.

"What the hell?" Sarah mutters, clearly annoyed at the song selection.

"I think that's our cue," I say. I hold out my bandage-wrapped arms toward her. "It's Frankenstein versus the Mummy—who will prevail?"

Sarah throws her head back and laughs again, but this time she's laughing so hard tears stream down her cheeks from behind her Lone Ranger mask.

Without warning, the black curtain rises, and we suddenly see our reflections in the peep-show glass—which, we can now discern, is one-way glass—a mirror for us, a window for our high-class peeping Tom, whoever he may be. Sarah waves awkwardly at our masked reflections—sardonically greeting our unseen gawker on the other side of the glass—and then bursts out laughing yet again. As usual, Sarah's laughter gets me going, too, and I lose it along with her.

As we laugh together, as I watch this beautiful, sexy, insane but brilliant woman giggling from behind her ridiculous Lone Ranger mask, crazy-ass bandages tied around her neck and torso, Sir Mix-A-Lot serenading us about big butts, I suddenly realize with absolute clarity that I don't want to share my baby with anyone, anywhere, ever—and least of all with a bunch of losers peeping through a window in a rundown titty bar outside of Vegas. This beautiful woman is *my* treasure—not theirs. She wants the world to watch me make love to her? Too bad. I'm the only man who's ever witnessed her reach the highest heights of human pleasure, the culmination of human experience, the most truthful form of expression two people can share—and it's going to stay that way 'til the end of fucking time.

My heart's racing. I grab her hand. "Baby, you've got it all wrong."

She wipes her eyes. "What?"

"Your dream—you've got it all wrong."

She looks at me blankly.

"You think you need to act it out—but the dream's not literal, baby. It's a metaphor."

She still doesn't understand.

"Think about how the dream makes you *feel*—what it makes you *yearn* for. The dream's not literal, Sarah. It's means something different than all this. We could fuck each other's brains out in this window and a hundred people could watch us do it, and it still wouldn't satisfy your yearning."

She crosses her arms over her bare breasts, suddenly modest. Her laughter is gone.

Sir Mix-A-Lot asks the guys in the crowd if their girlfriends have bountiful butts of the variety he's been rapping about.

"Hell yeah," I answer, right on cue with the song, and Sarah's mouth twists adorably. "You do realize this song's making me want to take a big ol' juicy bite out of your delectable ass, right?"

She half-smiles at me, but I can tell she's deep in thought.

I touch her hair. "You ready to go?" I ask.

She nods.

"We'll go back to the suite and you can play whatever song you had in mind for tonight and I'll chomp your ass and lick your sweet pussy and fuck your brains out 'til you swear I'm your supreme lord-god-master—how does that sound?"

She smiles wistfully. "I'm sorry."

"You've got nothing to be sorry about." I push her hair behind her shoulder.

"About today. That I scared you."

"You did." I frown at her. "But you also kicked ass."

She shrugs.

Sir Mix-A-Lot once again proclaims his enthusiasm for large bottoms, in case we weren't clear on that by now.

"I'm sorry about all this." She motions to the black curtain.

"Don't be. It was fun. I mean, look at us right now. Jesus. What a great memory."

"I think I might be a wee bit crazy."

"Sarah, my precious baby, you never need to apologize to me about your crazy. I love every inch of you, inside and out—even your crazy parts."

Her breath catches sharply. She kisses me. "I love you, Jonas." She's trembling in my arms.

Without warning, the black curtain rises and we both stare at our masked reflections in the mirror again, red lights shining in our eyes. When the curtain drops again, I kiss her softly.

"You ready to go back to the hotel and let me make love to you?"

She nods. "Absolutely."

I sigh with relief.

Yet again, Sir Mix-A-Lot professes his abiding affection for ample behinds.

"Right after you take me dancing."

I throw up my hands. "Oh come on!"

She laughs. "I'm kidding." She shoots me a sideways smirk. "But I *do* want to swing by that tattoo parlor on our way back." She winks.

Chapter 26
Sarah

"I love it," he says, his lips an inch away from my new tattoo, his warm breath teasing my skin. "It's so fucking sexy." He kisses my tattoo gently, his soft lips sending a shiver up my spine, and then he licks it. "Is it too sensitive to lick?"

"No." I can barely talk. "Do it again."

He licks it again and goose bumps erupt over my entire body.

"God, it turns me on," he says, licking it again and again. "It's like a buried treasure—and I'm the only guy with the treasure map." His tongue begins sliding downward from my tattoo, making my clit tingle with anticipation.

"Press play on the music," I breathe. "I've got a song cued up for us." I'm already deliriously turned on.

When he gets up to play the song, I touch myself, aching for his return.

The song begins—the song I've been dying to play for him while making love to him. It's "Take me to Church" by the Irish musician, Hozier. The first time I heard the song, I instantly thought *Jonas.* Something about Hozier's combination of intelligence and vulnerability and passion and angst and masculinity perfectly captures Jonas' essence for me—so much so, I've tricked myself into thinking Jonas himself is singing the song. Surely, if Jonas were a songwriter, this is the song he'd write—not just about me but about everything he's been through in his life.

Jonas comes back and begins trailing kisses from my tattoo downward again, closing in on my sweet spot, making me writhe, but quickly, he's too enraptured by the song to continue his concentrated assault on me.

"What is this?" Jonas says after listening for a moment. "Holy fuck."

I smile at him. I know how much music means to him.

"I love it," he says softly. He closes his eyes for a moment, apparently moved by the unmistakable sound of his own soul singing to him, and then he leans down and begins gently kissing the insides of my thighs. When the song reaches its passionate conclusion—*amen*—and then begins again on a loop, Jonas lifts his head and assesses me with hungry eyes.

"Go to church, my love," I whisper, my breasts rising and falling with my arousal.

"Amen," he says.

He yanks my naked body all the way to the bottom edge of the bed and kneels down in front of me. After propping my thighs on the tops of his broad shoulders, he burrows his face between my legs and begins worshipping at my altar like a condemned man desperate to be saved.

Amen.

My orgasm comes fast and hard, and when it ends, Jonas wordlessly scoops up my sweaty body, carries me into the sitting area of the suite, and lays me down on a table. I don't ask what he's got in mind because it doesn't matter. My body is his to do with as he pleases, to manipulate into whatever position he desires, to cull from it whatever pleasure he craves. He's a classically trained cellist and I am but an inanimate slab of wood until my master enlivens me.

Standing at the edge of the table, he places my calves over his shoulders and stands to his full height, lifting my pelvis off the table as he goes and supporting my bottom with his strong hands. He pulls my pelvis into him and enters me, and I moan at the sensation of our bodies joining so effortlessly at this new and exotic angle.

"This is called the butterfly," Jonas says, his voice husky, his body moving magically inside mine. "Because you're my butterfly, baby."

Holy moly. This feels good. We can add this butterfly thing to the long list of sexual positions Jonas has introduced me to that are my new favorite thing.

I've loved every single freaktastic position Jonas has shown me—the ballerina, the seesaw, the "folded deck chair"—all of them. Even the "folded deck chair" turned out to be a blast, even though we didn't actually perform it successfully (how anyone could make that one work, I have no idea)—because, thanks to that hilarious fiasco, I discovered that laughing hysterically with Jonas, especially naked, is every bit as arousing and intimate and pleasurable as having sex with him.

"Butterfly," Jonas groans. "My baby the hot-as-fuck butterfly."

He growls as he rocks his hips into mine, his eyes devouring me.

I arch my back into him, trying to relieve the pressure building inside me, and he pulls at my butt, drawing me into him even closer. I gaze across my torso to the spot where our bodies are fusing, eager to watch his glistening penis sliding in and out of me (a sight that always turns me on), and the unexpected sight of my brand new tattoo makes me moan.

From my vantage point, the tiny lettering of my tattoo is upside-down—Jonas is the only person in the world who'll ever have a right-side-up view of those three little letters—but that doesn't matter. The mere *existence* of the letters is what makes me feel bold and naughty and sexy in a whole new way. *OAP,* my new badge of honor boldly proclaims. It's the short but sweet shorthand for the butt-kicking superhero-crime-fighter-sexual-badass I've become. I look down at my tattoo again. *OAP.*

I groan loudly and Jonas does, too.

The pressure inside me is rising, rising, rising, on the cusp of boiling over.

"You're a butterfly," Jonas groans. "So fucking beautiful."

My body jolts. I'm on the absolute edge. Jonas' proxy lyrically offers me his life through the speakers of my computer—and, thus, so does Jonas in my mind—and I'm gone—unraveling like a spool of yarn—Orgasma the All-Powerful, yet again. Every muscle even remotely connected to where Jonas is thrusting in and out of me seizes. I scream Jonas' name, or at least I think I do—who knows what jumble of sounds actually escapes me as those delicious warm waves undulate through me—and then I dissolve into a relieved puddle, my emotions from this long and exhausting and scary and exciting day too much for me to physically contain.

I expect Jonas to release along with me, but he doesn't. Instead, he pulls out of me, lays my pelvis back down flush onto the table, removes my calves from his shoulders and straightens them up toward the ceiling at a ninety-degree angle from my torso. He crisscrosses my legs into a tight, closed scissor, pulling my ankles over each other in opposite directions, and then enters me again, groaning loudly as he does. A zealous moan escapes my mouth as a whole new kind of outrageous pleasure bursts through my body. Oh God, there's absolutely nothing to impede Jonas' access into me and my tightly closed legs are creating an exceptionally taut fit between our bodies.

He grunts as he thrusts into me deeply, over and over, pressing my legs tightly together as he enters me. A shockwave of delirium careens through me, almost painfully, as yet another orgasm builds inside me. When my convulsing finally hits and my body releases in fitful waves, Jonas uncrosses my legs and spreads my thighs. He pulls my torso up to a sitting position and guides my legs to wrap around his waist.

"Sarah," he says, kissing me voraciously with each powerful thrust. "Sarah," he says again, the word catching in his throat. "Oh, baby, you feel so fucking good."

I've got nothing left to give. I can't even hold myself up anymore, so he cradles my back in his arms as he thrusts. How is he holding on so long? It's got to be the Scotch. Because, holy hell, I'm turning into Jello and he's still going, going, going. I'm melting, oozing, dripping off the table and landing in a giant, quivering puddle on the floor and he's still on fire. He nibbles my ear, kisses my neck, all the while continuing his body's urgent assault. I'm toast. I'm gone. This is too much of a good thing. Pleasure and pain are blurring. My body can't handle anymore. How has he lasted so long? Oh my God, I can't stand it. I've got to push him over the edge.

"I love you," I say. "I love you, Jonas." I bite his neck. "I love, you, baby, forever and ever." I reach down to the spot on his body just beneath our joined bodies and fondle him fervently.

He shudders and groans so loud, it makes me flutter.

"I love every inch of you, baby, inside and out," I growl, continuing to touch him. I bite his nipple. "I love you."

His groan is tortured.

"I love you, baby, every part." I caress him with increased fervor and his entire body spasms. "Even your darkness—even your crazy parts. I love all of you, Jonas." I bite his neck. "Oh God, baby, all of you, even the parts you're hiding from me—even the parts you think I won't love. *I. Love. It. All.*"

He cries out as his body shudders violently and I collapse back onto the table. I'm a marathon runner who's just crossed the finish line. I'm completely spent.

With a loud groan, he collapses on top of me in a muscled, sweaty heap.

"I love, you, Jonas," I whisper, and then I kiss his sweaty cheek. "Every last inch of you, no matter what lies beneath."

Chapter 27

Sarah

I wonder if it's normal to feel like you're physically addicted to another person, to crave a man's touch so rabidly it's like his flesh is a narcotic. To find yourself daydreaming about him like he's some hunk on a movie poster, only to realize he's sitting right next to you on the couch, working on his laptop and munching on an apple. To feel like you were born to interlock your body with his, and only his, like you're two puzzle pieces with no other matches in the whole world. To be certain that, if given a choice at any given moment on any given day between kissing his luscious lips and eating a piece of the finest chocolate, you'd pick his kiss every single time—even on the rare days when you're so mad at him you want to flip him the bird. I wonder if it's normal to love someone so much, you don't just forgive his flaws and mistakes and imperfections and darkness, you don't just overlook them, you adore them and wouldn't have him any other way. Is any of this normal? I really don't know. But if it's not, then I think normal is grossly overrated.

After our marathon lovemaking session, Jonas carries me back into the bedroom over his shoulder caveman-style and lays my prostrate body down on the bed, a cocky grin illuminating his handsome face.

"Order us something from room service, baby," he instructs, rolling me onto my side and slapping my ass.

There's no "please" attached to the end of his command. No "if you'd like." Just the instruction, the ass slap, and an accompanying hoot of glee to the ceiling, followed by him shaking his adorable ass like a proud peacock shaking his tail feathers and strutting into the bathroom.

Maybe I should try to knock him down a peg, remind him it takes two to tango, tell him he didn't accomplish this latest act of *sexcellence* all by himself? But no. I have no desire to dampen his self-congratulatory mood. The truth is, after the way he so masterfully commandeered my body tonight—and always does, for that matter—he deserves whatever praise he wants to heap upon himself 'til the end of time. *Amen.*

Of course, that doesn't mean I'm going to order food from room service any time soon as my lord-god-master has commanded—I can't move a frickin' muscle after what he just did to me. All I can do is lie here like a wet noodle, listening to the sound of him hooting with glee in the shower. To hear him in there, he might as well be standing on the bow of the Titanic, shouting, "I'm king of the world!" Oh, Jonas.

"Amen!" Jonas sings from the shower, obviously trying to deliver one of the lines from Hozier's song. I've never heard Jonas sing before. I smile broadly.

Oh God, he does it again, but this time drawing out his voice like a tone-deaf opera singer. "A-a-a-a-m-e-e-en."

I laugh out loud. Wow, he's terrible—absolutely devoid of any singing ability whatsoever. I'm oddly thrilled by this new discovery about him. It makes me love him even more, if that's possible.

I reach for the room service menu on the nightstand and grab my phone, too. I promised to call my mom every day while we're in Las Vegas to assure her I'm okay and I just realized I never called today. Obviously, I can't call now in the middle of the night, but I figure I'll send her a text for the morning.

I glance at my phone and gasp. I've received a text from an unknown number that makes every hair on my body stand on end: *"When I get my turn with you, I won't take you to a low-class strip club and ask you to cover your beguiling face with a mask. Call me today. I'm not a patient man. M."*

I drop the phone, shaking. My stomach lurches. Oh my God. No.

Max saw us.

He must have followed us to the strip club. How much did he see? I throw my hands over my face, overwhelmed with anxiety and fear and shame and repulsion. I'm in over my head.

Jonas comes out of the bathroom, a white towel wrapped around his waist. "A-a-a-m-e-e-e-n!" he sings, holding out his arm theatrically. "Hey, did you order us some food?" His tone shifts to worry on a dime. "Sarah?"

I'm incapable of speaking. I feel like I'm going to throw up.

He sits down on the edge of the bed. "What happened?"

I hand him my phone, unable to speak.

He reads the text. "Who... ?"

"Max. Maksim."

"What the fuck is this?" He's instantly enraged.

I burst into tears.

"What the fuck's going on? Tell me right now."

I tell him every detail about Max demanding a "freebie" from me earlier today. I tell him how Max said he was glad Travolta didn't kill me like he'd personally ordered, or else he would have missed out on so much fun. And then I admit that Max shoved his tongue down my throat right before I walked out the door.

Jonas grabs at his hair and then gesticulates frantically. "Why didn't you tell me about all this?"

I shake my head.

"How could you not tell me any of this?"

"I was scared."

"To tell *me*? You were scared of *me*?"

"No, no." I exhale in frustration.

He's pacing the room like a maniac. "That fucker followed us tonight."

"I was scared you'd run back there and try to kill the guy."

He grunts. "You were right. That's exactly what I'm gonna do—I'm gonna fucking kill him."

My heart is in my throat. "Jonas, no."

Jonas is so angry he doesn't even look like himself. His entire body is shaking. Every single muscle on his body is tensed and bulging.

He sits on the bed next to me again, his eyes on fire. "Have you told me everything?"

"Yes."

"Everything?"

"Yes. I promise."

He exhales. "What a fucking asshole," he mutters. His lip curls. "He *kissed* you?"

I nod. "It was repulsive." I swallow hard. "And scary." I lose it. My tears come fast and furious. "I'm sorry, Jonas. Today was really, really scary."

He touches my hair. "Never keep anything from me again, do you understand?" His voice is an odd mixture of compassion and rage.

I nod.

"Never. No matter what it is. Ever."

"I wanted to tell you earlier, but you were so mad at me when we left their building, I didn't want to add fuel to your fire. I didn't want you to go back there and try to kill him—and die trying. You were so mad at me—you weren't thinking clearly."

He exhales and hugs me. "I was never mad at you, Sarah. Don't you understand?" He looks into my eyes. "I shouldn't have screamed at you. I didn't handle that right. I'm sorry." He's shaking with adrenaline. "I wasn't mad at you—I was scared at the thought of anything happening to you again. But I acted like an asshole."

I nod. He did act like an asshole. But I understand.

"You poor thing." He grips me tightly. "Jesus."

"I'm sorry I didn't tell you."

"Never keep anything from me, ever again."

"I won't." I lay my cheek on his shoulder.

He pulls back. "Sarah, I can't express this strongly enough to you. This is non-negotiable. Never keep anything from me, ever again."

I nod.

"Promise me."

"I promise. I'm sorry."

He squeezes me and kisses my bare shoulder. "I'm sorry I yelled at you. I shouldn't have done that. You didn't deserve that."

"I forgive you."

"I just freaked out."

"I know."

"Don't keep anything from me again."

"I won't. I promise."

"Good."

"And you promise, too?"

He doesn't respond.

"You promise not to keep anything from me, too?"

He remains silent.

I push on his chest, disengaging from our hug.

"Why are you not saying, 'I promise?'"

"Because I don't promise."

I open my mouth, in shock.

"I can't make that promise—not when it comes to these fuckers. Regarding anything and everyone else, yes, I promise—cross my heart and hope to die, I'll always tell you the truth and never, ever keep anything from you. But when it comes to these motherfuckers, I'm gonna protect you no matter what I have to do, without any limitation on that statement whatsoever, even if that means not telling you something that'd be better for you not to know."

Chapter 28

Jonas

Henn looks bloodshot and bleary-eyed, like he hasn't slept a wink all night. We're all gathered around the table in the suite—the table where my baby became a butterfly so delectably last night—to hear what Henn and his two elves have uncovered about The Club thus far. Kat and Josh don't look particularly well rested, either, but, clearly, those two have slept, unlike Henn—and, if I'm not mistaken, Josh and Kat are sitting awfully close together at the table, too.

"Well, to summarize," Henn begins, "we're dealing with some big shit here, fellas. Like, oh my fucking God." He cracks a huge smile. "Totally awesome."

Sarah and I look at each other with nervous anticipation.

"I've been dive-bombing down this rabbit hole all night, and every which way leads me down yet another rabbit hole chasing yet another Ukrainian rabbit—I'm running a whole shitload of stuff through translation software, by the way, which isn't nearly as good as a human translator, but at least it'll give us an idea—"

"Take a deep breath, Henn," I say. "Slow down and start from the beginning. You're like the Energizer Bunny on meth right now."

Henn stops short and shakes his head. "Sorry, man. I've had like three quadruple-shot Americanos in the past twelve hours, plus two red bulls—"

"Jesus, Henn. That shit'll kill you," I say.

"Occupational hazard." He smirks.

"Just summarize what you know so far."

"Yes. Okay." Henn takes a deep breath. "We got a pretty good lay of the land last night and it's cuh-razy-corn chowder."

I wait.

Henn takes another deep breath. "Almost everything of any interest is in Ukrainian, but there's also a bunch of stuff in Russian, too—Ukrainian and Russian are distinct languages, did you know that?"

I blink slowly, trying to remain patient. "Just tell me—were you able to get into The Club's system?"

"No, not yet. Wherever it is, it's buried deep, deep, deep in the web, way deep. But I'm getting close. I've got lots of breadcrumbs to follow. I'm hot on their trail, fellas. And very pretty ladies." He smiles adoringly at Kat and then as a seeming afterthought shoots a polite wink at Sarah, too.

"You should have seen how Henn figures things out," Kat says. "He's a techno-Sherlock Holmes."

"The man's a fucking genius," Josh adds.

Why is it always like herding fucking cats around here? "What do we know so far?" I ask.

"Okay," Henn says. "Let's start with their scope of operations. Gigantic. Massive. Huge. Colossal. Mammoth. Way beyond what I expected. This is not some podunk mom and pop prostitution ring—not that I have any basis of comparison with another prostitution ring, of course—but, I'm just saying what I've seen has surpassed anything I expected—and, get this, it turns out prostitution is only part of the business."

"What else do they do?" Sarah asks.

"Well, Oksana runs the prostitution side of things, but Max runs a bunch of other stuff—drugs and weapons, mainly."

Everyone's mouths hang open all at once. Holy shit.

"And he's got *a lot* of guys working for him, all over the country, but mostly Vegas, Miami, and New York."

Sarah can't stop shaking her head. She looks totally floored.

I'm reeling, too. "What kind of volume are we talking about?" I ask. "Like, in terms of dollars."

"I don't have access to the banking yet, but I'm guessing the numbers are gonna be big."

"Define big," I say.

"Well, extrapolating on a few things I saw in their records—and I'm only extrapolating at this point—I'm guessing half a billion dollars a year. Maybe more."

Everyone in the room expresses complete shock.

"What about a member list? Any luck on that?" Sarah asks.

"Not yet. The actual data is buried somewhere in The Club's system, which I'm working on getting, but Oksana's got this prized list of VIPs she personally handles herself. She doesn't use real names—it's all managed with codes and nicknames—but I've traced a few things and figured out a few of these guys' identities. So far there are a bunch of CEOs and corporate bigwigs, some high-profile athletes—you know that guy on the Yankees who just signed that huge deal?—and at least two congressmen have been pretty big clients for quite a while. And there's this one guy I think might be a really big deal, some sort of über VIP—but I haven't figured him out yet. But, just from that sampling alone, we're talking about some high-profile people who'd be pretty bummed to find out they've been funding the Russian mafia—or, I guess, the Ukrainian mafia. Although, more on that later."

Sarah and I exchange a look. I didn't think about them as "the mafia." Is that what they are? Shit. My stomach is churning. I've been sitting at the table, my knee jiggling wildly, but now I stand and pace the room.

"The identity of that über VIP guy seems like something we'd better nail down," Henn says. "His emails are double encrypted but I cracked an email from Oksana to Max forwarding one of the über VIP guy's emails—and the guy said shit like 'my security personnel will post outside the door.' He's got security personnel? And they 'post' outside doors? Like, who the fuck says that?"

Sarah looks at me, her eyes bugging out of her head, and I return the sentiment.

"A rock star?" Sarah suggests. "Guys like that always have bodyguards."

"No," Henn says. "Not based on what I've seen."

"Yeah, I know plenty of rock stars with bodyguards—and they don't talk like that," Josh says. He looks anxious.

"I'll keep working on it," Henn says. "Okay, so are you guys ready for your minds to be officially blown?"

"You mean there's *more*?" Sarah asks.

"Oh yeah. The next part is what makes this so much fun." He turns to Kat. "I figured this next part out right after you left last night."

Kat looks at the rest of us sheepishly. "I finally had to get some sleep."

"That's what happens when you don't subsist on a diet of caffeine and nicotine," Henn says.

I steal a quick glance at Josh. He doesn't know what Henn's about to say, either.

"Did you leave to get some sleep, too?" I ask Josh.

"Yeah, I couldn't keep up with Henn, either," Josh says. "I think I left around the time Kat left." He glances at Kat. "Maybe just a little bit later."

Holy shit. They're fucking. I look quickly at Sarah to see if she sees what I see, but she's pale-faced and anxious, not the least bit interested in whether Kat and Josh are having sex.

"So what is it?" Kat asks, on the edge of her seat.

"I'm still waiting to get a bunch of stuff translated—I'm kind of handicapped by all the Ukrainian and Russian, so I'm not finished yet, but you guys, oh my God—Oksana's like some kind of political activist. She's like the Ukrainian Ché Guevara, man. She's in constant communication with these Ukrainian guys about 'Donbas.' I didn't know what that was, so I looked it up, and it refers to some kind of Ukrainian revolution."

"The separatists," I say. This has been all over the news lately.

"Yeah, right? That's what I thought." Henn says. "There are all these messages back and forth with these dudes in Ukrainian and she's spewing propaganda shit, and talking about 'the cause' and they're talking about needed funding and weapons. Like, serious weaponry, guys. Crazy shit. And Oksana keeps saying shit like, 'Keep the faith.'" Henn says this last part in a cartoon-Russian accent.

"Oh my God," Josh mumbles.

"What?" Kat says.

"They're funding the Ukrainian separatists," Josh explains.

"Which means Oksana's funding Putin through the back door," I add.

Kat looks blank. "You guys, break it down for me. Sorry."

"Okay, back in the day, there was the U.S.S.R., right?" I say. "Then it got broken up into all these pieces—Russia and Ukraine and the Baltic states. Well, now Putin wants to put all the pieces of mother Russia back together again, to resurrect the former empire—and he wants the diamond of his new Soviet Union to be Ukraine."

Kat nods. "And is Ukraine down with that plan?"

"No, not the official government. But there's a faction within Ukraine—the separatists—and they want to separate from their government and go along with Putin's reunification plan. So the separatists have waged armed conflicts with their own government, funded by the Russians."

I look at Josh. We're both thinking the same thing: Holy fuck, we gave our money to these people.

Sarah looks the way I feel right now. Mortified.

"Holy shitballs," Kat says softly.

"Yeah, most definitely," Henn says. "Well said."

"We've got to find out who Mr. Bigwig VIP is," I blurt, my stomach lurching into my mouth. "We need to know who all the heavy-hitters are. You said congressmen are involved in this shit, right?"

"Yup," Henn says.

"That could be really, really bad," Josh says.

"Seriously. 'Oh, hi, constituents. Please re-elect me,'" Henn says, putting on his best congressman-voice. "'I added more police to our streets, got a library built, and voted to increase the minimum wage. Oh, *and,* I paid a whole bunch of money to a Ukrainian prostitution and weapons ring to fund the reunification of the Soviet Union. Can I count on your vote during the next election?'"

I can't even laugh. Shit. I didn't see this one coming at all.

"This is too big for us to handle on our own," Sarah declares emphatically. "We've got to hand this over to the FBI." Her eyes widen. "Or the CIA? I don't even know which one. I mean, jeez, I'm a first-year law student at U Dub." She shakes her head. "This is like, a matter of international significance—and that's not even an exaggeration."

She's right. That's no exaggeration. And she's also right—we've got to hand this over to the right authorities. But I don't have the first clue how to handle something of this magnitude any more than she does. "The question is how and when," I say. "We can't just waltz into the FBI and ask for Johnny the Next Available Special Agent and say, 'Hi. There's a prostitution ring in Las Vegas that's laundering arms and money for Putin. Now go on—go get 'em, guys!' Even if they take us seriously, which is doubtful, who knows how long it'll take them to investigate and take meaningful action, if ever? If they take too long, how long before Max and Oksana get paranoid and decide Sarah's not as valuable to them as they thought? The only thing I care about in all this is protecting Sarah."

Sarah groans. "This ain't no casino heist, guys. We're gonna need a helluva lot more than George Clooney to pull this off."

I exhale. "How much of this can we prove as of right now, Henn?"

"The 'Funding the Evil Empire' thing is all circumstantial right now because I don't have the banking records yet. I can prove quite a bit with lots of creativity, putting the pieces together, but to immediately convince anyone else about all this you'd have to have an audience with a long attention span that's willing to listen closely and make certain leaps in logic."

"We can't count on that."

"I know. Everything will be airtight and clear as a bell when I'm able to hack into The Club's actual mainframe—and I'm super close on that."

"We need to be able to show them the money," I say. "That's the key—the only way we're gonna get anyone's attention."

"I agree," Henn says. "I don't have all their accounts or passwords yet—but I'm working on it."

"How long 'til you've got everything you need to make this airtight?"

"A couple more days and I'll be solid. Maybe not airtight, but solid. I mean, I could do this for months and months and still be gathering new information. But as far as having something to use as an opening salvo, something that'll get the good guys' attention quickly and make them take immediate action, I can get you what you'll need in a couple days."

"Excellent," I say.

"Henn, I'm your new best friend," Sarah says. "I'm gonna start collecting and collating the information you find and synthesizing it into one concise document—like a legal brief. We have to have something to hand over to the good guys and get their attention quickly. I'll make it easy for them—outline the facts, The Club operations, all potential criminal counts—RICO, wire fraud, money laundering, racketeering, etcetera, etcetera—and summarize the evidence collected thus far in relation to each count." Sarah's mind is really clicking now. "Kat."

"Yes, ma'am."

"For each and every criminal count, I'm gonna need a piece of supporting evidence—something to show them we're not making this stuff up. I'll tell you exactly what kind of thing I'm looking for, and then you'll go digging through whatever Henn's been able to find so far to get it for me. You'll be my research assistant."

"I can do that," Kat says.

"That's good," I say. "And Josh and I will pow-wow and figure out our best strategy for the hand-off. I agree—we're going to have to turn this over to *someone*—but to whom, that's the question. If we put it in the wrong hands, we might just buy ourselves an even bigger enemy than The Club."

"What does that mean?" Kat asks, her eyes wide.

"It sounds like there are plenty of powerful people on that client list who wouldn't want this scandal to see the light of day."

There's a long beat while everyone lets that sink in. We're about to open a very large and dangerous can of worms.

"It's all gonna come down to the money," I say. "Money talks."

"I agree," Josh says.

"Henn, that's top priority, okay?" I say. "Track the money. Get access to it."

"Roger," Henn says. "Shouldn't take me more than a couple days."

"We can do this," Sarah says, but she doesn't sound convinced.

"Look at the talent in this room. We don't need no stinkin' George Clooney and Brad Pitt and Matt Damon."

"Yeah, but I sure wish we had that Chinese acrobat guy," Henn says. "He was cool."

"The one they stuffed into the little box?" Kat asks. "I loved him."

"Yeah, he was rad," Henn agrees.

"Yen. Wasn't that his name?"

Henn laughs. "Oh *yeah.* Good memory, Kat." He taps his temple. "Brains *and* beauty."

"Hey, guys, sorry to interrupt your profound musings, but I'm kind of getting tunnel vision here," Sarah says. "There's a lot to do and I wanna get started right away."

"Sure thing," Kat says. "Whatever you need, boss."

"Hey, Sarah," Henn says. "One more thing. What do you wanna do about Dr. Evil's text to you?"

Sarah's face turns bright red.

"I'm monitoring his phone, remember? 'I'm not a patient man.' What was *that* all about?"

Sarah obviously can't speak at the moment, so I grab her hand and explain Max's demand for a "freebie" from Sarah and the gist of his follow-up text. (I don't mention the specifics of Max's text—as far as I'm concerned, no one needs to know about Max's reference to a 'low-class strip club' and 'masks'—and, thankfully, Henn has the good sense not to reveal those details, either.)

"What should I do?" Sarah asks the room, her voice small. "Ignore him? Answer him? Hide?"

"Ignore him and hide," I say. "I don't want you saying a fucking thing to that motherfucker."

"I agree," Josh says. "Ignore him and hide."

"No," Kat says flatly. "Answer him and hide. Ignoring him will piss him off, and we don't want to piss that guy off. We want to keep him calm and confident and predictable."

Everyone looks at her, considering.

"Dr. Evil's real boner isn't for Sarah—it's for Jonas."

I grimace. "Jesus, Kat. Please don't say it that way."

"Not sexually. He's got an alpha-male boner for you, Jonas. This is all about a beta silverback wanting to knock off the obvious alpha. He wants what you've got so he can *win*. Hence, his Jonas-boner."

"For Chrissakes, *please* stop saying that," I say.

"So how should I reply to him, then?"

"We have to keep him off your back and convince him you're motivated solely by greed and absolutely *not* by loyalty to Jonas," Kat says. "The more he thinks your interests are the same as his, the safer you'll be. You've got to keep him trusting you. If you ignore him, he'll start getting paranoid."

Sarah looks at me. I nod. Kat's making a lot of sense.

Kat sees my nonverbal exchange with Sarah and seems encouraged. "Tell him that right after your meeting with him, Jonas went totally ballistic—out of his mind with jealousy. Jonas saw the obvious chemistry between you and Dr. Evil and he accused you of lying about never having met him before. Jonas is convinced you two are an item, and he thinks you wanted to be alone with Max just so you two could have sex in the bathroom. And now, dang it, there's absolutely no way you can get away without arousing Jonas' suspicion even more. Jonas the Jealous Boyfriend is watching you like a hawk now, not letting you leave your room without him. Just make Jonas out to be a wacko. Tell Max not to text—Jonas is monitoring your phone—and he's just on the cusp of giving you another humongous check. That way, you play right into his egomania and also appeal to his greed. No matter how much he wants his little freebie to satisfy his Jonas-boner—"

"Okay, Kat, that's enough," I caution.

"—he won't insist on it at the risk of sabotaging the scam. We'll just make Jonas out to be the bad guy and let Sarah sound like she's doing her best to manage him and keep the money rolling in."

Everyone stares at Kat, speechless and impressed.

Kat shrugs. "What? There are two things I know well in this life—PR and men."

"Nice," Henn says, his admiration palpable.

"Hey, I might be dumb, but I'm not blonde," Kat says, and everyone laughs.

Josh flashes Kat an adoring smile. "Does everyone agree with Kat on this? Because I most certainly do."

Everyone expresses agreement.

"Especially the part about how you're not allowed to leave the suite without me," I say. "That part is true. I don't want you going out there without me."

"Trust me, I won't," Sarah says. "Now that I know that creep's out there watching me, I have no desire to leave the suite ever again. I've got to hunker down and write my report, anyway. This is going to be a huge job." Sarah shakes her head in disbelief. "This is so crazy."

"It's totally insane," Henn agrees, exhaling happily. "Isn't it *awesome?*"

Chapter 29

Sarah

It's been a long-ass day. But a productive one. For the better part of today, Kat and I shadowed Henn as he worked furiously on his three computers, and when Henn finally crashed and burned due to total sleep deprivation, Kat and I kept going, doing our best to categorize and prioritize the information he'd retrieved thus far. And as Kat and I worked, Jonas and Josh did, too, brainstorming, researching governmental agencies, and drafting a spreadsheet outlining potential strategies.

Occasionally, the boys bickered until one of them started laughing and the other joined in—and, once, out of nowhere, they got into a heated argument about who would top the list of the best NFL quarterbacks of all-time—and, admittedly, at one point, Kat and I got so punchy we sat fully clothed in the empty Jacuzzi tub to drink a glass of wine—but otherwise, it was a day filled with nonstop work and stress.

In the middle of writing a particularly frustrating section on my report, I looked at Jonas across the room to find him intensely studying something on his laptop, his brow furrowed, and I felt an overwhelming desire to crawl into his lap and say, "To hell with everything—let's go back to Belize." But instead, I suggested he take a break to work out in the hotel gym.

"There's no time for that," he said. "I'm on a mission from God here, baby."

I was about to say his mind might actually benefit from a break, when, without notice, he added, right in front of everybody, "Because I love my baby more than life itself." And then he looked back down at his computer as if that wasn't the most heart-stopping moment of my entire life.

And now, finally, everyone's gone and there's nothing to keep me from crawling into his lap now—or doing whatever else the heck I might want to do to my hunky-monkey boyfriend.

Jonas comes out of the bathroom after his shower, every single inch of his naked body as hard as a rock, and crawls into bed next to me. He flips me onto my back roughly and crawls over me, his erection grazing my belly and his eyes gleaming. "What shall we do first, my lady?" he says. "Shall I take a big bite out of your ass? Or perhaps nibble on your crumpets?" He leans down and nibbles one of my nipples.

"Hang on, sir," I say in a clipped accent, and he pauses—though it looks like it physically pains him to do it. "I happen to have a few very specific thoughts on this subject this fair evening." I pat the bed next to me and he reluctantly obeys, a questioning look in his eyes. "When I was Googling to find that strip club I took you to the other night, I initially searched the term 'peep show Las Vegas,' and you know what came up?"

He shakes his head.

"All kinds of crap about some now-defunct topless musical revue on The Strip starring Ice-T's wife."

Jonas glances at my crotch with pure longing in his eyes.

I smile wickedly. "So then I searched 'peep show sex club,' just to see what might come up, and gosh darn it, Google must have thought I wanted search results for 'peep show *sex.'* Huh. Talk about fascinating reading." I bite my lower lip.

A shadow of a smile flickers across Jonas' face, but he somehow manages to keep his excitement under wraps.

"It turns out there's a sexual position called The Peep Show. Are you familiar with that one, sir?'

He pauses. "Well, actually, that could refer to one of several different things, my dearest lady." He licks his lips. "You'll have to be more specific about your particular item of interest."

I grab my laptop off the nightstand and quickly find the graphic 3-D animation I stumbled upon by accident the other night—two attractive, animated avatars performing "peep show fellatio" with body-jerking enthusiasm.

Considering how many different and sometimes surprising ways Jonas has performed oral sex on me—who knew there were so many ways to do it?—the sight of that "peep show fellatio" animation really shouldn't have surprised me at all. But it did.

All this time, I'd accepted Jonas' paradigm that *my* pleasure was the elusive beast—the hard-earned prize he'd studied and practiced and trained specifically to vanquish—and all the while it never even occurred to me that there might be a thing or two I could learn to maximize *his* pleasure, too. It was like a light bulb went off in my head—and between my legs.

I turn the computer screen toward Jonas and his face lights up. "This," I say, showing him the avatars performing peep show fellatio. "Ring any bells, sir?"

His smile spreads across the entire width of his face. "Why, yes, my lady," he says, his voice edged with suppressed excitement, "it rings bells and whistles and buzzers and clappers and ding-dongs."

I laugh heartily.

"I have indeed heard tell of this 'peep show' sex act to which you refer," he says, his eyes ablaze, "but I've never been so fortunate as to have someone suggest performing it on me." He bites his lip. "*For* me."

I'm floored. I didn't see that one coming. I thought Jonas had done every conceivable sex act known to man. I can't believe my ears. "How is that possible?" I ask, dropping our playful politeness.

"I've never done it."

"But, I mean, I thought when it came to sex, you've already done everything there is to do—and then some."

He shrugs.

"But, I thought... " I shake my head. I'm utterly confused. How is this possible?

He blushes. "It's not the kind of thing I'd ask some random hook-up to do. And I've never had a..." He sighs. "I've never had a girlfriend like you before."

Heat spreads throughout my body. "What do you mean?"

He shrugs again but doesn't answer.

"Your girlfriends have never wanted to do this for you?"

He shakes his head.

"You're going to have to give me more than a headshake here, big boy. 'Fess up. Come on."

He exhales. "It's just never come up."

"Why not?"

"Why don't I lick you and make you come and then we'll talk about this afterwards?" He starts crawling on top of me again, grinning lasciviously.

I push him off me. "This is too fascinating. Tell me first and then I promise it's crazy-sexy-freaky time 'til the break of dawn."

He sighs. "You're such a pain in the ass, you know that, woman?"

"Yes."

He rolls his eyes. "A little over a year ago, I went on a date with this woman and she faked having an orgasm—"

"Yes, I know, the woman who inspired you to seek *redemption* the second time around. I really should buy that lady a bottle of the finest champagne to thank her, by the way, since I'm the one who's benefited more than anyone from the higher learning she inspired."

Jonas smiles. "How about I tell you this story after I lick you and make you come?" He reaches for my inner thigh.

I swat his hand way. "Nope."

He frowns like a little boy denied a cookie.

"Come on. Spill."

He exhales, resigned to his fate. "Thanks to that faker, I started reading up and studying and I realized for the first time what a gift it is to make a woman reach orgasm—how much effort it takes beyond just fucking her. Before then, I just thought, 'If it feels good to me, it must feel good to her.' I thought it was a crapshoot whether a woman comes or not, like out of my control—sometimes yes, sometimes no." He smiles. "I mean, don't get me wrong, my natural instincts were better than most, I'm not a complete Neanderthal—but the minute I started reading and learning, I realized there was so much more to it—so much technique to learn. I realized that if I wanted to make a woman come, I could, every single time. I just had to do it *right.*"

"Oh, God, you're turning me on, Jonas."

His face explodes with desire and his erection twitches. "Then let me lick you and make you scream."

"You'll have to finish your story first." I tease him by caressing my breast.

His chest heaves. "So-then-I-licked-a-bunch-of-women-between-their-legs-and-made-them-come-whenever-I-wanted. The End." He smiles and reaches for me.

I push him away again. "You're so gross."

He laughs.

"Seriously, though. I'm blown away I've finally discovered the one sex act you've never done before."

"Oh, there are *lots* of sex acts I've never done before—and a whole bunch I've only done with you."

Now I'm genuinely reeling. "What? I've been your *first* for some of this stuff?"

"For lots and lots of it."

I blink quickly like he's just given me mental whiplash. I sit up and look him in the eyes. "Babe. What are you talking about? I'm totally confused."

He puts his hand on my cheek and kisses me. "My Magnificent Sarah," he says, nipping at my jawline. "You turn me on, baby. Do you have any idea how much you turn me on?" His hand softly brushes my breast.

Blood rushes between my legs. "No, Jonas. Tell me."

"How 'bout you give me a little taste first—your pussy's calling to me like a siren, woman."

"No."

He pouts.

"Tell me."

He grunts and sighs. "Before I found religion, so to speak, I'd already had plenty of sex, of course, with hook-ups, girlfriends, flings, one-night stands. All the typical stuff—fucking, oral, threesomes—I did it all. But never, ever like it is with you. Never like, you know... " His eyes sparkle. "Going to *church*." His face lights up. "And then *after* I found religion, after I'd started studying and learning and seeking out women to practice on, sex for me was always about making a woman come harder than she ever had, making her *surrender* to me—becoming *God*." He rolls his eyes at that last part.

"Redemption," I say quietly, a light bulb suddenly going off in my head. How have I not understood before this moment how thoroughly Jonas' need for redemption has pervaded his entire life? "Everything you do, even sex, is about redeeming yourself, Jonas. Proving you're not worthless."

He stares at me for a long beat. "Yeah," he finally says. "I guess so." He flashes me those mournful eyes. "Huh." There's another long beat. "So, anyway, I've always wanted to make my sexual partners surrender to me, but I never... " He twists his mouth. "I never wanted to be the one who surrendered." He swallows hard. "So, you know, to answer your question, I haven't done a whole lot of stuff that puts me on the receiving end of things—stuff like The Peep Show. I've always steered things in the opposite direction."

I can barely contain my bodily impulses right now.

"But what about before this past year—before your 'quest for *sexcellence*?' You've had girlfriends before all that—what about receiving from them?"

"Occasionally, sure. But before you, my girlfriends were pretty uptight. I guess I picked girls who made it easy for me to *suppress* rather than *reveal*. Yeah, I've had girlfriends before you, but this is the first time I've been a true *boyfriend* in return—the first time I've *revealed*."

I'm electrified. "But what about all those one-night stands? I can't believe you didn't try sex every which way... ?"

"Think about it. When you fuck a different woman every night, and your only goal is making your partner come hard, you actually wind up being *less* experimental, not *more*. You've got one, maybe two, shots to make this stranger come like a rocket, so you wind up having certain go-to moves you fall back on again and again, just to be absolutely sure you succeed."

"So all those sexual positions we've been doing?"

"I'm trying most of them out with you."

My entire body flutters with excitement. "The butterfly?"

He looks shy. "Just you. My beautiful butterfly."

My clit zings like he's just licked me there. "The ballerina?"

"Who else but you could even stand like that, let alone get fucked like that?"

My head is spinning. "What about that upside-down sixty-nine thing we did the day we got back from Belize?"

"Just you."

"But right before we did it you said it turns you on and—"

"I was talking about sixty-nining in general. I've done *that* before, sure, but not that crazy-ass acrobatic thing. I've always wanted to try that—but who would I have done that with besides you?" He sighs, enraptured. "That was amazing."

I'm ridiculously turned on. "Oh, Jonas." I shake my head. "I thought you'd done everything there is to do with a thousand other women."

He shakes his head. "I licked 'em and made 'em come and then fucked 'em just to get myself off. Nothing like what we've been doing. You're my first on a ton of stuff I've always wanted to try—my sexy little guinea pig."

I feel like a cat in heat, like I want to rub myself against his thigh.

"You've got to be plenty comfortable with someone to do some of the more adventurous stuff we've been doing—there's got to be mutual *trust*."

I grab his face and kiss him and he leans into me, ready to crawl on top of me and mount me. I push him back again and he groans.

"Come on, baby. I'm dying here. I can't wait anymore," he whimpers.

"Too bad." I'm panting. I grab my laptop and call up the diagram labeled "peep show fellatio." I click the back button on the website—an entire site devoted to every sexual position known to man, complete with animated diagrams, detailed instructions, and message boards—and navigate to the website's home page. On the left-hand side of the page, there's a lengthy menu of generalized categories like "face-to-face" and "sixty-nine" and "rear entry," each category linking in turn to a series of more specific sub-options and demonstrative animations. I click the general link for "fellatio" and twelve animated blowjob diagrams fill the screen.

"What about these? Which of these have you already done?"

He looks through the images, his chest heaving. "Oh man," he says. "Wow. Look at that one." His erection twitches. "No. I've just had, you know, the basic blowjob—which is fucking awesome and I'm not complaining, believe me. Oh, and that one, of course, standing up like that, but I'd consider that pretty basic. Oh, and that one, too, sitting down like that."

"But what about this one?" I click on a link.

He shakes his head and laughs. "Nope."

"This one?"

"Uh, no. I don't even *want* to do that one. I'd crush you."

I look. "Yeah, agreed. Scratch that one. I wouldn't survive it. But how about this one? Have you done that?"

"Nope."

"Well, baby, it's your lucky day. Today begins the Twelve Days of Fellatio-Christmas. We're gonna do each and every one of these variations, right down the line—except ones that might literally crush me." I laugh. "I might not be able to pull them all off with particular skill..." I glance down at one particularly enigmatic diagram and make a face. "Some of these look really challenging—I don't even understand how some of these would work from a logistical standpoint—but I promise, I'll give 'em the ol' college try."

"Sarah, you don't have to—"

"I *want* to."

"Baby, listen, when I go down on you, it isn't a tit for tat kind of thing. I *love* eating you out. I get off on tasting you. You're delicious. I don't do it to get something in return—"

I bend down and lick the tip of his penis and he instantly stops talking.

I look up at him. "You like tasting me?"

He inhales deeply. "It's my favorite thing."

"Well, that's how I feel about sucking on you. It's a total turn-on. I fantasize about doing it. I crave it. I dream about it. I like the way you taste. I like the way you feel in my mouth. I like the way you grab at my hair when I'm down there. I like the sounds you make." I lick him again and he moans. "I feel powerful when I do it—like I own you."

"Oh fuck, baby, I'm gonna blow my load before you even get started."

I grip his shaft. "Well, then, I guess we'd better stop talking about it and start doing it. Look at that list again and tell me which one you wanna start with. I'm horny as hell right now."

He looks at the computer and scrolls urgently through the options, his breathing labored.

"Well?"

"I can't pick—asking me to pick is cruel."

"What about this one?"

"Yes, please."

"Or this one?"

"Yes, please."

I laugh. "Which one do you want to try the most?"

"That's like asking me to pick a favorite child. I love all my babies equally."

I laugh again and take another look through the diagrams.

He tilts the computer toward himself. "Hey, why don't we look at all the cunning options for you, too? That'd be fun."

I tilt the computer back to me. "No, this is about *me* becoming a sexual samurai—you've already earned your sword."

"Hang on." He commandeers the computer from me again and clicks on the word "cunnilingus" on the side of the screen. When the options come up, he groans like I've just taken him into my mouth. "Just these little cartoons get me off like a motherfucker. I want to do them all to you right now."

"Haven't we already done them all by now?" I peer at the screen.

"Not this one," Jonas says. He moans. "You've never lain on top of me like that. Oh, I want that. Oh, God, yes, that looks nice. Yes, please."

He's right. It looks incredible. But I shake it off. "This is supposed to be about me doing something for you."

"Yeah, but you *would* be doing something for me, I promise." He moans again. "I'd probably cream rinse your hair if you let me eat you like that one." He points at another diagram in which the woman's head dangles precariously close to the man's penis. He shivers. "Oh, I want to do that one, Sarah. *Please.*" He moans. "Please, please."

I shudder with desire. "That certainly does look delicious."

He quivers again. "Let's do it right now." He reaches between my legs and touches me. When he feels how wet I am, he moans loudly again. "Come on."

"Hang on," I gasp. "Wait, Jonas. *Wait.*"

He pulls his hand back, pouting.

"It's your turn to *receive* right now."

He sighs and looks back at the computer, ignoring me. He clicks on another link. "We've never done this one before, have we? With your leg in the air like that?"

He's missing my point here—I want to be the giver. But I can't resist sneaking a peek at whatever cunnilingus option he's talking about this time. Oh God, it's so tantalizing, it makes my clit flutter just looking at it. "Licking the Flagpole," I read. "Oh, that one looks lovely."

"I want that," Jonas says like a kid in a candy shop. "Me want," he adds, caveman-style. "Me. Want. Now."

I grab the computer. "We're way off track here. This is about me figuring out how to maximize *your* pleasure."

"You couldn't possibly maximize my pleasure any more than you already do, just by being your beautiful, tasty, delectable self."

I blush. "But I really want to try some new things."

He bites his lip. "Okay, fine. I've got a proposal for you, my little samurai in training."

"What is it?"

"We'll do this tit for tat style."

"You really like that expression, don't you?"

"Shh. Listen up."

I make a smart-ass show of giving him my undivided attention.

"This is gonna be Jonas and Sarah's Tit-for-Tat Adventure. Of course, you'll be the Tit—"

"As usual."

"And I'll be the Tat. You'll kick things off each time with whatever configuration of fellatio you desire and I'll humbly and gratefully receive your precious gift—and then it's my turn to do whatever the fuck I want to you, any way I please." He shudders with excitement.

"Isn't that what we do now—you do whatever you want to me, any way you please? What's gonna be different about this?"

"Shh. Now it's *official*—with rules and everything. Tit for tat. You give to me however you like—and then I'll turn around and give back to you, however I damn well please." He licks his lips.

"For twelve days," I add. "It'll be the Twelve Days of Blowjobs for you."

"And the Twelve Days of Tasty Treats for you."

"Jonas, you give me tasty treats every single day. You're not proposing anything new or different here—"

"Just play along, woman. Why on earth do you feel compelled to boss me around and spoil my fun? You're so goddamned bossy."

I roll my eyes. "I'm sorry. Okay." I click back on the fellatio options on the side of the page. "Let's pick your inaugural blowjob." I click on an animated diagram labeled The Jackhammer. "Well, I don't even understand how this one would work. I'd have to pull your penis all the way down in the wrong direction to my mouth. Wouldn't that hurt you?"

"I don't know—I guess we'll find out." He grins broadly.

"And this one—Snake Charmer—can you even do a handstand?"

He laughs. "I'm willing to try."

"Now that's the kind of can-do attitude I like to hear, baby. I tell you what. Let's start with The Peep Show, since that's what got me so hot and bothered in the first place." I grab his shaft and caress it.

He trembles.

"Welcome to the Twelve Days of Blowjobs, baby," I say softly, fondling him.

He yelps with excitement.

"I love you, Jonas," I say.

"I love you more than life itself," he replies. "My Magnificent Sarah."

"Now quit stalling and lie down on your side. You're mine to do with as I please."

He lies on his side, grinning from ear to ear, his erection straining.

"Okay, good." I glance at the computer screen again, trying to understand how this particular game of Twister is supposed to work. "And now I'm supposed to thread my head and neck through your thighs from behind." I get myself into the correct position, singing as I do, "On the first day of Christmas, my true love gave to me, a blowjob in a pear tree." He laughs with unfettered glee, and so do I. "Deck the halls with boughs of blowjobs," I sing merrily from between his thighs, cracking up. "Fa la la la la la la la la." I give him an enthusiastic lick. "Mmmm," I say. "Even better than figgy pudding."

He throws his head back and laughs. "God, I love you, Sarah."

Chapter 30
Jonas

I wake up to Sarah jerking and shrieking in my arms.

"No!" she screams at the top of her lungs, her voice raspy. "No!" She thrashes wildly.

"Sarah, wake up. You're dreaming." I grip her. "Sarah. You're having another nightmare."

She jolts awake, her breathing ragged, her eyes wild.

"You were having another bad dream."

She clutches me and bursts into tears.

"Shh, baby. You're safe. I'm here. It was just a dream." I caress her hair. "Shh. You're okay. I'm right here." After she calms down a bit, I pull her into me and kiss her cheeks. "The Ukrainian Travolta again?"

She nods. She swallows hard and catches her breath. "Only this time, Max was there, too. He was raping me while Travolta held the knife to my throat. And Max kept saying, 'He's gonna kill you when I'm done fucking you,' and I screamed and tried to break free, but my arms wouldn't work and my legs were paralyzed and I couldn't move—"

"Baby, it's okay. It was just a bad dream."

She whimpers again.

"You're safe." I hold on to her fiercely. I swear to God, I'm going to kill those motherfuckers.

She takes a moment to gather herself before she continues. "And then..." She pauses, apparently visualizing something. "My father appeared, out of nowhere." She shivers. "And for a split second, I felt *relieved*, like I thought he was there to *save* me—but then he leaned into my ear while Max was pounding into me and he said, 'Paybacks are a fucking bitch, huh?'"

My blood runs cold.

She trembles. "God, I haven't had a nightmare about my dad in years. I guess all this stuff with The Club has opened up some old psychological wounds."

I stroke her arm. "You used to have nightmares about your father?"

"All the time. For like a year after my mom and I ran away from him, I used to look over my shoulder, afraid he was gonna come up behind me, throw a bag over my head, and drag me away." She inhales deeply and exhales loudly. "And now I keep having that exact same feeling about Max and Travolta—like they're right behind me." She stifles another whimper. "I keep thinking they're coming to get me."

I squeeze her tight. *I'm gonna fucking kill those motherfuckers.*

"Damn. I thought I was done with nightmares about my dad." She wipes her eyes.

"You saw your dad do some horrible things, huh?"

"Yeah," she says quietly. "He used to beat the crap out of my mom—and then he expected me to act like he was father of the year."

"Did he ever hurt you?" She once told me her father had never laid a hand on her, but I wonder if that was completely true.

"He never touched me. I was his princess."

I exhale. I'm hugely relieved to hear that.

"But Jonas."

I wait but she doesn't continue. "What is it?" For some reason, I'm nervous.

"There's something I haven't told you—something I've never told anybody."

The hairs on the back of my neck stand up.

"What did I tell you about my dad? About how we left?"

I think back to what little she's told me. "You said your dad hurt your mom and that the two of you escaped him when you were ten."

"Yeah, that's all true." She sits up onto her elbow and looks down at my face. Her hair falls around her shoulders. "But there's something I've kept secret my whole life. I didn't mean to keep a secret from you—it's just something I've kept hidden from everyone." She touches my face. "But I don't want there to be any secrets between us anymore, about anything, big or small."

My skin breaks out in goose bumps. Is she talking about my secrets or hers? My heart suddenly pounds in my ears. Did Josh tell her everything about me? Is that what she's hinting at?

"When I told you my mom and I 'escaped' my dad, that was true. He used to beat her up all the time." She pauses. "And then came this one horrific night when he beat her unconscious—to a bloody pulp," she says. "She was in such bad shape, I truly thought she was dead."

I hold my breath. I have no idea what she's about to reveal to me.

"When I told you my mom and I 'escaped' my dad, I tried to make it sound like my mom grabbed me and we fled—as if she'd finally decided enough is enough and we ran away."

I nod. That's exactly the scenario I'd envisioned.

"That's the story I tell myself. That's how I make myself remember it. But that's not how it happened."

My blood pulses in my ears.

"The truth is that I did it."

I look at her quizzically.

"He beat the crap out of her one night, so bad I thought she was dead. And when I realized she was alive, I was so relieved, just so frickin' *relieved*, I thought, 'That's it. No more. I'm not letting him kill her next time—I'm not gonna let there *be* a next time.'" She exhales a shaky breath. "So I drugged him and took her someplace where he couldn't find us. She was too weak to fight me on it."

I'm confused—wasn't she *ten*?

"I'd been stashing supplies in this old abandoned toolshed a couple blocks away for weeks, just sort of dreaming about running away, I guess—but I didn't really have an actual plan or anything. And then that night came and all bets were off. So I crushed a bunch of sleeping pills into his beer, like, you know, Tylenol PMs or whatever, and when he passed out, I dragged my mom to that shed. We stayed there for a few days, not making a peep, while she got her strength back. And then one day she woke up and looked me in the eye and said, 'From this day forward, I am reborn.' And that was that. She was done."

"And you were how old?"

"Ten."

My mind is reeling. I knew Sarah was a badass of epic proportions, but this proves she was *born* that way. Jesus.

"For the longest time after that, I worried I'd killed him by accident, like, maybe I'd given him too many sleeping pills—and I kept having nightmares the police were at the door to arrest me. When my mom finally filed for divorce, I realized he must have lived, but then I started having horrible nightmares that he was coming after me to get his revenge."

"When did the nightmares stop?"

"When he remarried and had a son with his new wife, we never heard from him again." She sighs and wipes her eyes. "That's when I slowly started feeling safe."

"Wow, Sarah. That's a lot of stress for a little girl."

She looks at me, astonished. "Says the boy with the saddest eyes I've ever seen." She touches my cheek.

I blush. I didn't mean to make this about me.

She sighs. "I've never told anyone about how I drugged him—not even my mom. She was so out of it, she never asked me for details about that night. Later, I think she was so ashamed she'd taken so much shit from him for so long, she never wanted to talk about him or what happened. And once she'd started devoting her life to helping other women and counseling them to leave bad situations, I didn't want to reveal the scandalous truth that it was her ten-year-old daughter, not her, who'd actually gathered the courage to leave. Well, just at first. My mom was plenty courageous after that."

"You were so brave, Sarah. Wow."

"No."

"Yeah, you were."

"I was more like *determined*. Isn't brave when you know you're doing something scary but you do it anyway? It was more like nothing could stop me. I never stopped to be scared. I just put blinders on and did what had to be done."

I smirk. "I think I've witnessed your 'determination mode' a time or two."

Her mouth twists into a shy smile. She leans down and kisses me. "I've never told anyone that story."

"You have nothing to be ashamed of. You should be proud of that story."

"I'm not proud. I mean, I'm not sorry I did it—maybe my mom would have died the next time if I didn't—but the story kind of proves I'm terminally fucked up, doesn't it?" She smiles. "Or at the very least a wee bit crazy."

Is she trying to get me to tell her about how I'm a wee bit crazy, too? Did Josh tell her about me? Is that what she's hinting here?

"Do you still love me even though I drugged my father and stole my mother out from under him?" She grins at me.

I try to smile back at her, but I can't. I'm suddenly racked with panic. What does she know? Is she trying to tell me something?

She kisses me. "Wow, it feels so good to tell you that." Her hand strokes my bare chest. "I feel so incredibly close to you, Jonas." Her lips press against my neck. She grinds against me. "I've never told anyone that." She kisses my lips. She's obviously getting aroused.

But I'm distracted. Now that she's told me her secrets, do I have to tell her mine? If I don't tell her everything right now, right this very minute, is that the same thing as lying to her? Isn't that what she just implicitly told me? Shit.

Her hand caresses my bicep. Her naked body presses into mine. My erection springs to life.

If I don't come clean right now, isn't that just like when I checked in with Stacy at The Pine Box and didn't mention it to her? What did she say about that? "Secrets create dark spaces within a relationship," she said. "When one person keeps secrets, the other person fills in the dark spaces with their fears and insecurities." She said my silence about Stacy had created a dark space between us—a reason for her not to trust me. Fuck. Will my silence now about my secrets create another dark space?

Her hand caresses my cock and of course it responds to her touch like a champ, as usual.

She moans. "I love you," she says. She wraps her thigh around me, grinding into me.

A normal man would confess his secrets right now. This is the moment for me to come clean. She just told me her deep, dark secret and said it made her feel closer to me to confess it. There are no do-overs for this moment. My heart is pounding. Is not telling the same as lying? Yes, it is. Maybe not before this very moment, but something's changed. I can feel it. I have to reciprocate. That's what she needs from me—what she deserves. And it's what a normal man would do for the woman he loves.

"I feel so close to you," she mutters. "I want you deep inside me."

She kisses me voraciously, but I don't kiss back. I'm paralyzed with fear. I promised not to lie to her. I promised to tell her anything and everything, except maybe relating to The Club. But this doesn't have anything to do with The Club. Shit.

She grips my cock and pulls on my hips, inviting me to make love to her. "Come on, Jonas."

"Sarah, wait."

There's an awkward silence as she looks at me, her eyes wide. She releases me.

"There's something I've got to tell you—several things, actually. Things you need to know about me."

Chapter 31

Sarah

For the last hour, Jonas and I have sat in our PJs on the bed, talking about the aftermath of Jonas' mother's death. I'm afraid to ask too many questions—the man's opening his heart to me like never before and I don't want to break the spell.

When Jonas tells me about his beloved Mariela, I ask if he ever looked for her later in life. He shakes his head sadly. "I never even knew her last name. I was too young. She was just Mariela to me—my Mariela." The ache in his voice is unmistakable. "I don't even remember her face. The only things I remember are her brown eyes and beautiful brown skin." He sighs. "And the way she sang to me in Spanish."

I suppress a grin. The first woman Jonas ever loved besides his mother was a Spanish-speaking, dark-eyed Latina with 'beautiful brown skin'? Um. Hello.

When he explains how he didn't speak for a whole year after his mother's death because he'd wanted the last words his mouth ever said to be 'I love you, Mommy,' my heart smashes into a thousand pieces. It takes all my restraint not to burst into ugly tears at the realization that this gorgeous, sensitive, poetic man let those precious words escape his mouth again for *me.*

And when he tells me about his teacher Miss Westbrook, how she kindly and brilliantly lured him out of his painful silence, how she made him feel *loved* during the loneliest point in his young life, how she nurtured this poor, aching boy when he was so obviously grasping for a drop of kindness, how she so lovingly showed him the purest kind of love through naming her child after him, I thought my heart would physically burst and splatter the poor man with even more blood than he's already withstood. It seems I'm not the only woman to have fallen deeply in love with Jonas' innate sweetness—his mother, Mariela, and Miss Westbrook did, too.

"Oh, Jonas. You poor, sweet baby," I say, moving to hug him.

He holds up his hand. "No. I haven't told you what I need to tell you yet." His face is etched with pure anxiety. "Everything I just told you is mere background—stuff you need to know to understand the context of what I'm about to tell you."

I sit back and shut my mouth. What could he possibly need to tell me that would make him look this anxious?

He takes a deep breath and looks at me with those mournful eyes of his. "At first, when I wouldn't talk, my dad sent me away. To a hospital. You know, a mental hospital. A 'children's treatment center,' they called it."

At *seven*? Right after the poor little guy lost his mother *and* his beloved nanny? That seems like a pretty heartless thing to do to a kid.

"But I wouldn't talk. I wouldn't do anything the doctors wanted me to do. I didn't want to get better. I just wanted to die so I could be with my mom. When they finally let me out despite me not talking, I figured my dad must have missed me too much to make me stay there. I found out later my dad finally broke down and brought me home because Josh had begged and pleaded and cried so much." He smiles ruefully.

I keep forgetting about poor Josh in all this. Good Lord. He didn't have it easy, either.

"And then, after that, through the years, I just always knew there was this threat that at any moment, my father might send me back to the treatment center again. If I didn't talk like I was supposed to. Or if I cried, God forbid. Or if I just wasn't 'man enough,' whatever that meant. It was always hanging over me—say or do the wrong thing, be the wrong thing, think the wrong thing, and he'd say it was because I was 'crazy' and needed the 'fucking doctors to get my head straightened out again.'

"But sometimes I couldn't help it—I just couldn't follow his rules. Maybe I was just too sad to get out of bed for a week. Or maybe I couldn't make myself care about his opinion of me on a particular day. Sometimes, I'd lose my temper and start screaming at him—which became a pretty big problem for him the bigger I got.

"So, anyway, I was in and out of that fucking place for years—in and out, over and over. For long stretches, I'd get to go to school, even make a friend or two. Start to feel like maybe I was normal, after all—and then, boom, I'd have to go back for whatever reason. As I got older, I started to feel angrier and angrier about the whole thing and think I'd rather die than go back there. And then in my early teens, I distinctly remember thinking, 'I'd rather kill him than go back there.'" He swallows hard.

My heart skips a beat.

"He hated me." He runs his hand through his hair. "He just plain *despised* me." His eyes turn moist. "All those years, it was just my father, Josh and me living in that huge house—just the three of us—and two out of the three of us hated my guts."

Tears flood my eyes. Where did Jonas eek out any kind of love in his young life? With Josh, surely—but where else? How the heck did Jonas retain all the goodness and kindness I see in him?

"And all the while, I swear to God, it was my father who was the crazy one, not me. He was the one getting shit-faced drunk all the time, not me. He was the one fucking prostitutes and bringing them to our house and buying Bentleys and Bugattis and Porsches and helicopters and jewelry for his 'girlfriends' and spending money like it was water." He shakes his head. "He was the one who screamed all the time, not me." His eyes suddenly flash like a light bulb just went off in his head. "I'm sorry I screamed at you after we left The Club, Sarah." He wipes his eyes. "I shouldn't have done that. I was just so freaked out at the idea of losing you that I took it out on you." He shakes his head again. "Which makes absolutely no sense." He rubs his face. "Maybe I am fucking crazy, I don't know."

I crawl across the bed to him and hug him. "It's okay. I knew where it was coming from."

He nuzzles into my neck. "There's no excuse to scream at you, ever—you're the gentlest, kindest person I've ever met. You don't deserve that, especially with the asshole-father you had. Please, please forgive me."

"I do. Of course, I do."

"Please don't think I'm like your father."

I scoff at the thought. Jonas is a raw beast in so many ways—physically imposing, daunting, tortured, tempestuous, primal, sexual beyond anyone I've ever encountered—but I've never for a nanosecond thought he'd harm a hair on my head.

"I understand," I say. I kiss his lips and my entire body explodes with outrageous yearning. Oh good Lord, I want to make love to him. I kiss every inch of his face and he melts under me. An outrageous throbbing slams into me, right between my legs. In a flash, I've got a maddening itch and Jonas is the only one who can scratch it. I press my body into his, hungry for him.

He groans, clearly itching the way I am. He runs his hands down my back and pulls on my tank top—but then he jerks away from me, pulling on his hair.

"I haven't told you everything yet," he says, his voice strained.

"Sarah, listen. If I don't tell you everything right now, I never will." He clenches his jaw. "I have to tell you." His eyes are pure pain.

I want to kiss his agony away. I want to feel him inside me and make him feel good and make his hurt disappear and make myself feel damned good in the process. But instead I nod and take a deep breath. "You can tell me anything." I crawl back to my assigned corner of the bed and stare at him, waiting.

There it is again, right there on his face: *Fear.* Really? Does this boy really think there's something he could say that would make me run away? Does he really think there's anything in this world that would make me stop loving him?

"Josh and I call it The Lunacy," he says, exhaling like he's just said an abominable curse word.

I wait.

"I was seventeen. My dad had his usual tickets to the Seahawks game, but he didn't feel great, he said, so he gave the tickets to Josh—Josh always had a thousand friends he could invite to a game. And my dad shocked the hell out of me by asking me to stay home with him and watch the game on TV. 'Let Josh go with his friends,' he said. 'You and I will stay home and make a memory.'" Jonas shakes his head and scoffs. "I was so fucking dumb, I was actually *excited* to stay home with him. I actually thought, 'Wow he wants to spend time with *me*—just *me*? Not Josh, too?' I was like, 'Wow, Dad, that'd be *great.*' I was *giddy* about it—like he'd just offered me some kind of fresh start."

I know what's coming next. Tears pool in my eyes.

"I was in the kitchen, making us turkey burgers before the game. God, I was such an idiot—I was *garnishing* the fucking plates." He lets out a bitter laugh. "Just like I'd seen on a cooking show."

I bite my lip. I know I need to let him get through this, but I'm not sure I can stand to hear what's coming next.

"When I heard the gunshot upstairs, I knew—right then, I knew. I remember I looked down at the plates I was fixing for us, the plates I was *garnishing,* and I actually laughed out loud. I knew right then he'd suckered me." He rubs his eyes. "I should have just walked out of the kitchen, straight out the front door, and never looked back. But I couldn't stop my legs from climbing the stairs, just like he wanted me to do."

He glances out the window of the bedroom. We've been talking for so long, the sun is rising over The Strip. His features are as beautiful as ever, but he looks tired. Exhausted, I'd even say. He licks his lips. They're as luscious as ever. I try my damnedest to think of something to say, but I can't. All I can think about is how beautiful he is. And how sorry I am for all he's had to endure.

"Can we put on some music?" he asks suddenly. "I'd really like to listen to some music for a minute, please."

"Sure. What would you like to hear?"

"Anything. You pick." But he quickly adds, "As long as you don't try to create some poignant moment with some shit like 'Everybody Hurts.'"

I laugh. "Okay. No R.E.M."

"And for the love of God. No 'Hurt' by Nine Inch Nails, either."

"Well, duh. If I was going to be poignant, I'd play the Johnny Cash version of that song."

"Ah, torture. So fucking amazing."

"I know. Makes me cry every time."

"Me, too. His voice slays me."

"Oh, and 'Tears in Heaven,' too," I say. "Talk about a crier."

"Gah. Please, no. Just a little background music to relax me."

"Yeah, yeah, got it. No worries, baby." I get up and fiddle with my computer. "One order of 'Love Shack' coming right up."

Chapter 32

Jonas

"What is this?" I ask.

"'My Favourite Book,'" she says.

"Who is it?"

"Stars. They're Canadian indie pop."

"Where the hell do you find this stuff?"

She shrugs. "I dunno. Just listen."

I close my eyes and let the music wash over me. It's a simple, effortless love song. Soothing. Sexy. Joyful. It's so Sarah.

"It's nice," I say. The song relaxes me. My scrambled thoughts begin to collate and organize themselves. "Thank you."

She blinks slowly at me, like she's caressing my cheeks from across the bed with supernaturally long lashes. God, she's beautiful. A jolt of anxiety flashes through my veins. What if finding out about The Lunacy changes everything for her?

I take solace in her warm brown eyes. No one's ever looked at me the way she does. Her eyes are coaxing me to throw caution to the wind and tell her my secrets.

"Okay," I say softly, girding myself for what I'm about to do. "The Lunacy."

She nods. She's ready.

Fuck it. Here goes. I exhale. "I went into his study. The room looked like he'd stuck his head into a giant blender without a lid."

She winces, but I feel nothing. I might as well be giving her driving directions to the post office. *You turn left on Fifty-Seventh Street and make a right on Seventeenth Avenue Northwest and it's on the right-hand side of the street.*

"He'd hung her wedding dress on a coat rack right next to his desk," I continue. "Wedding pictures were spread out everywhere. His blood and brains were on everything." I clear my throat. Shit. I can't believe I'm about to tell her all this. "I found out later that day would have been their twentieth wedding anniversary."

She bites her lip in anticipation.

"An envelope with my name on it sat on his desk. I knew opening it would be the end of my sanity—but I couldn't stop myself. I had to know—even though I already knew." I sigh. "I guess there's only so long you can outrun your crazy, and I was just sick and tired of running."

She frowns sympathetically, but she doesn't speak.

"'*Everything you touch turns to blood.'* That's what his note said." I laugh bitterly. "Nothing else. Just one final, simple 'fuck you.' No apology. No last fatherly advice or expression of regret or pride or love." I scoff at myself for even uttering that last word. "Not even a goodbye to poor Josh. That was probably the most unforgivable thing of all, what he did to poor Josh—sending him off to cheer at yet another Seahawks game while yet another parent stayed home and died."

She makes a soft moaning noise.

I pause, trying to gather my composure before continuing—but not because this next part makes me want to cry. Quite the opposite. To this day, what happened next makes me want to laugh maniacally. "He had this incredible car collection," I say. "A McLaren, a Lamborghini, a vintage Bugatti, a bunch of Porsches, a couple of Bentleys, even a Lotus. Man, he loved those cars." I shake my head. "I grabbed a couple gas cans from the shed and I doused every last one of them, except for his favorite one, his most prized possession—a vintage silver Porsche 959."

I sneak a cautious peek at her. Her face is neutral, but her eyes are sparkling. Fuck, maybe I'm imagining it, but it almost seems like she's suppressing a smirk.

"I tore out of there in the Porsche—which, of course, he never allowed me to *touch,* so it was particularly gratifying. I had a fantastic view of the bonfire in my rearview mirror as I peeled out, too. That was special."

She nods. Her body language is open, relaxed, fascinated. Maybe even amused? Definitely not freaked out. So far so good. But, surely, this next part won't be quite so easy for her to digest.

"At first, I was laughing, but then I could barely drive through my tears. I was just a fucking wreck. Totally out of my head. I was sideswiping parked cars, running over curbs, doing one hundred on the freeway—just a bat out of hell. It's a miracle I didn't kill someone, a total miracle. To this day, I'm tortured by the thought of what might have happened that day if I'd wound up hurting or killing someone. What if I'd killed some kid's mother? I would have been no better than the fucker who killed my own mother."

She looks at me sympathetically, but she doesn't say anything.

"A police car started chasing me when I got to the freeway and I was like, *Oh yeah? Try to catch me now, motherfucker!* I just floored it, laughing hysterically the whole time. The cops must have thought I was on LSD or something, I swear to God, I was a fucking after-school special—and then another and another cop car showed up behind me until there was a fucking armada on my ass. And I remember, I just started thinking, over and over, like on a running loop, *Kill me, kill me, kill me, kill me, kill me, kill me, kill me.*" I rub my hand over my face. "I just wanted someone to put an end to my fucking misery once and for all."

She bites her lip. That shadow of a smirk I saw earlier, if indeed it was ever there, is long gone.

"And then I thought about Josh and that made me bawl like a baby—to think I was doing this to him on the very day Dad had just blown his brains out. God, it was so heartless of me, but I didn't care. I thought only about ending my own torture and not about the torment I'd be inflicting on Josh. I still can't believe I was willing to fuck up Josh's life beyond repair just to make myself feel better." I twist my mouth, trying not to choke up. "I guess I'd convinced myself I was doing him a favor by finally setting him free."

"Oh, Jonas."

She looks so fucking sympathetic. But is that sympathy or *pity*? Am I transforming from the boyfriend she loves and respects into a pitiful charity case right before her eyes?

"So what happened next?" she asks. "Since you're sitting here right now, I'm assuming suicide-by-cop didn't pan out?"

"Not for lack of trying, though. You know the Montlake canal bridge?"

"Of course. Right by campus."

"I was racing down Montlake toward that bridge with all those cop cars chasing me—I was fucking O.J. in the white Bronco—and I was laughing and crying and totally freaking out the whole time. A total madman. It was just so bizarre, like an out of body experience. And the bridge started opening to let some barge go through in the canal below and the cops started making a perimeter around me, drawing their weapons, and I just... I didn't even think about it. I just gunned it."

Her eyes widen. "Oh my God."

"Yeah."

"You drove that fancy Porsche right off the frickin' bridge?"

"Yep." I make a movement with my hand, imitating the falling trajectory of the car. "Plink."

She winces. "Oh my God, Jonas. How are you even here right now?"

"Eh. It turns out that bridge is renowned for being the worst bridge in all of Seattle for committing suicide. Not high enough. And the car broke my fall in the water." I pause, trying to remember my free fall, but I can't. "By then, I wasn't in my body anymore. I'd *departed,* so to speak. I guess it's like how the drunk guy's always the one who survives a head-on collision."

"Huh," she says flatly, as if I've just told her some fascinating bit of trivia about the average IQ of a turtle.

She's not reacting the way I thought she would. I thought we'd both be crying. I imagined myself trying desperately to convince her I'm fine now, that I'm a beast, that I'm still the same Jonas she knows and loves. But she doesn't seem to be on the verge of tears right now, not like she was earlier when I talked about Mariela and Miss Westbrook. She doesn't seem even remotely tempted to turn her back on me. She just seems oddly *fascinated,* and sympathetic, of course, but not particularly emotional.

"So, yada, yada, yada," I continue, "I didn't die—couldn't even do that right. I was surprisingly uninjured, in fact. A couple of broken ribs. A concussion. And when they pulled me out of the wreckage, I was so uncooperative, so out of my mind, so violent, they threw me into a juvie-psych facility on suicide watch. I don't know how long I was there. Could have been a week. Could have been a month. I really don't know. I just remember being tied up like fucking King Kong and thrashing around."

"How'd you get out?"

"Uncle William eventually got his lawyers on it. I got off with probation and restitution and involuntary psychiatric containment until I was eighteen. I guess my dad's suicide that same day and my prior medical history were considered 'extenuating circumstances.'"

Sarah looks at me intently, studying my face. She's totally unreadable to me right now. I pause. I keep thinking she's about to say something, but she doesn't.

"So is that everything?" she finally asks, her face somber.

I nod, scared to death of what she's going to say next. Is she going to leave me? Is she going to say she doesn't respect me anymore? That I'm not the man she thought I was? "Yes." I swallow hard.

"*That's* 'The Lunacy'?"

I nod again. I can hardly breathe.

She exhales loudly and smiles. "*That's* the big reveal? The dark and horrible secret that's going to make me run away screaming and never come back?"

I don't understand the smile on her face. Is she laughing at me?

"Well, yeah."

"You torched your daddy's fancy car collection, went on a joy ride in the prized Porsche he never let you touch, and then drove his car off a bridge in a desperate attempt to stop the pain that had tortured you relentlessly for ten years?"

Well, fuck. That's a gross over-simplification if I've ever heard one.

"That about sums it up, right?"

"Well, yeah. But, I mean, Sarah, maybe you don't understand. I had some sort of psychotic break that landed me in fucking restraints in a psych ward. That's kind of a big deal."

She shakes her head like she's chastising herself and crawls over to me on the bed. She takes my face in her hands. "I'm so sorry I tied you up, Jonas. I had no idea—"

"How could you know? Any normal guy would have been counting his lucky stars to get tied up by sexy little you." I shrug apologetically. "I'm sorry I'm not a normal guy."

She kisses me.

We're both quiet for a minute. My stomach is churning. I'm freaking out about whatever she's going to say next, but I wait.

She seems deep in thought.

I want to argue my case, tell her I'm all better now, that she can trust me—that I haven't had a major problem since I was seventeen—unless you count joining The Club for a year as a major problem, I guess—that I love her and would never harm her. But I don't speak. My thoughts are spinning out of control. Is she going to leave me? Does this change everything? Does she still love me?

"I thought you were about to tell me you punched a nun or threw a puppy off a cliff. I'm so effing relieved."

Relieved? I can't believe my ears. Maybe she doesn't understand everything I just told her. "Sarah, did you hear me? I crashed into parked cars, drove on the sidewalk. I easily could have killed a kid, a mother, some sweet old lady... and then I *purposefully* drove my car off a fucking bridge, laughing like a maniac the whole time. Did you hear any of that? I came this close to killing some innocent kid who happened to be standing on the sidewalk eating an ice cream cone."

"But you didn't."

"Only because I got lucky."

"Aha! That's the first time I've ever heard you describe yourself as lucky." She smiles broadly. "You see what just happened there? Life is nothing but the story you tell yourself in your own head. So instead of constantly telling yourself The Story of How Jonas Went to the Insane Asylum and Was at Fault for Every Goddamned Thing That Ever Happened to His Entire Family on an endless, self-defeating loop, change your story to The Story of How Jonas Got Super-Duper Lucky One Really Sucky Day."

My mouth hangs open. Why is she being so difficult? This stuff is horrible. Why can't she see that? "Sarah, I'm not sure you understand. I tried to kill myself mere hours after my father killed himself—Josh be damned. How could I even think of doing that to Josh? I was heartless. Selfish. Despicable."

"I think everything you did was perfectly understandable. Sad. Regrettable. Heartbreaking. Outrageous. Yes, pretty fucking crazy. But totally and completely understandable."

Mind officially blown. I shake my head. "No, Sarah. You're taking the 'understanding girlfriend' thing too far." She's just not getting it. I'm damaged. I'm worthless. "Here's something else you don't know: I'm told I punched the first guy who tried to pull me out of the Porsche in the water. I mean, talk about an asshole."

"Oh well, out of everything you've told me, that's the last straw. Sorry, baby, I'm outta here." She smiles.

"How are you so jovial about all this?"

"I'm not *jovial*." She exhales with obvious frustration. "That's not the right word." She squints at me.

I squint back. Why doesn't she get it? I'm hopelessly defective. Horrible. Worthless. Doesn't she understand what she's getting into if she stays with me? I'm not normal. At some point, I'm going to fuck this up. *Everything I touch turns to blood.*

"Are you happy?" she asks.

I pause. Is this a trick question?

"I mean are you happy with me?"

"Oh." Well, that's an easy one. "Yeah, of course. I'm happier with you than I've ever been in my whole life." Actually, happy isn't the right word for how I feel when I'm with her. "I'm beyond happy," I say. "I'm *crazy* happy. It's like I've got a serious mental disease or something." I grin sheepishly.

She grins back at me. "Same here. It's madness, I tell you." She twists her mouth to avoid a smirk. "So, considering my current state of madness, why the heck would I purposefully buy myself a big ol' steaming pile of wretched unhappiness, especially about something that happened thirteen years ago? Why wouldn't I just continue to be happy?"

I'm dumbfounded. I can't answer that question.

"Hmm?"

The woman makes a good point.

"And more importantly, why would *you* want to be anything other than crazy-happy? Wouldn't you just rather enjoy your happiness?"

I feel my lower lip trembling, so I bite it.

She cups my cheeks in her hands again. God, I love it when she does that. "Do you foresee trying to kill yourself again in the near future, love?"

I shake my head. "No. Never."

"Well, okay, then. Good." She drops her hands.

I wait but she doesn't say anything else.

But I'm confused. What does "good" mean? Is that all she's going to say? "So that's it?" I ask. "*Good?*"

She sighs. "Yeah. Good."

I'm incredulous.

She leans in and kisses me softly. "Jonas, failure isn't falling down—it's not getting back up. And you've gotten back up more than anyone I've ever known. I'm proud of you. I see your triumphs, not your failures. I see your goodness. And sweetness. And generosity of spirit. The beautiful kindness that glows inside of you. And I love you for all of it. Just like Mariela did. Just like Miss Westbrook did. Just like your mother did."

That last one makes my eyes water, so I close them. I'm blown away. Is she really going to make this so easy on me? So poetic? So beautiful? She's making me out to be a fucking hero?

"I do have one question, though."

Ah, here it comes. I nod, bracing myself.

"How did you get from Lunatic-Driving-Off-a-Bridge Jonas to Hunky-Monkey-Ass-Kicking-Sexy-Beast Jonas? How'd you get from there to here? I'm fascinated."

Shit. I bite the inside of my cheek, trying to figure out whether to tell her or avoid the topic altogether.

Sarah's eyes are patient. Warm. Curious.

"You really want to know?"

"Duh."

I don't like this part. I've never told anyone about this, not even Josh. All he knows is that I had some "treatments." I've never told him what finally made a huge difference for me. I pause.

"Was there some kind of turning point?" she asks. "Did you have some kind of epiphany? Something specific that helped you turn things around?"

Damn, my baby's nothing if not persistent. I nod.

"Well, what was it?"

I twist my mouth.

"Come on, Jonas. You can tell me anything."

I exhale.

"Come on, baby. Trust me."

Chapter 33

Jonas

My pulse pounds in my ears. Shit. I really don't want to tell her this. I know how bad it sounds. I know how much stigma is associated with this. But I've told her everything else, haven't I? I can't stop now. Fuck it.

"I got a whole bunch of ECT treatments," I say quietly. "Do you know what that is?"

She shakes her head.

"Electro-shock therapy."

She pauses. "You mean they shocked your *brain?* With electricity?"

I nod.

"Wow. That sounds barbaric."

"No, it wasn't like you think. It's not like *One Flew Over the Cuckoo's Nest.* They drug you first. I don't even remember it. It helped me."

"They did this to you when you were *seventeen*?"

"Yeah. I guess ECT is what they do to you when they've tried everything else."

"And that helped?"

"A lot. I don't know why, but it did. And then there was one additional piece of the puzzle. Something life-changing that happened right after my treatments were completed."

She's utterly captivated.

"On my eighteenth birthday, Josh sent me *The Republic* by Plato. His note said, 'I was forced to read this instrument of torture for Philosophy 101. I'd rather pry my fingernails off with rusty pliers than read it ever again. You're gonna love it, bro. Enjoy.' And he was right. I loved it. It introduced me to philosophy for the first time and got me reading everything—Locke, Descartes, Aristotle, Heraclitis, Nietzsche, Sen, Camus, Santayana, whoever. But, in the end, I kept going back to Plato. He was the forefather of modern thought—the one who inspired me to visualize the divine originals and conquer myself. 'For a man to conquer himself is the first and noblest of all victories.'" I exhale. "Are you sure you want to hear all this?"

"Are you *crazy*?" She laughs. "Of course, I do. I'm hanging on your every word."

I pause.

"Come on, Jonas. Continue. I love hearing about this stuff."

I exhale. "All my treatments were over. All charges against me had been expunged from my record thanks to me being a minor. Josh was at UCLA and Uncle William was busy trying to keep the company afloat after my father's death. So I just said, *Fuck yeah, Plato, let's do this shit.* I threw on a backpack and went to visit Plato in Greece—which is where I got my tattoos, by the way—and from there, I traveled all over Europe, wherever the fuck I wanted, all by myself. I climbed, hiked, explored, whatever. I listened to music and read my books and just figured my shit out."

"Oh, come on, Jonas—that's all you did? Climbed, hiked, and read your books? I'm sure you did a little something else, too." She smirks. "I bet all the horny college girls backpacking through Europe went crazy for eighteen-year-old Jonas Faraday with the shy smile and sad eyes."

Leave it to Sarah. Nothing gets past her. Yes, she's exactly right—I've left one particular activity out of my narrative. That trip was when I first got the inkling women might be especially attracted to me compared to the next guy hiking the trail or sitting at the bar. As long as I didn't blow it by being Creepy Jonas or Intense Jonas or Antisocial Jonas or Philosophical Jonas or Asshole Jonas or, God forbid, Crazy-Eyes Jonas, girls actually seemed pretty interested in me—though not being one of those aforementioned Jonases almost always took a lot out of me.

And on those rare and fucking awesome days when Charming Jonas randomly decided to show up, or at least Shy Jonas or Awkward Jonas, I couldn't miss. On those occasions, as few and far between as they were, getting girls was like shooting ducks in a barrel—I had my pick of any young woman on the youth hostel circuit.

"Yeah," I say, blushing. "I learned how much I thoroughly enjoy sex on that trip. That was when I lost my virginity, actually." I can't help but smile broadly. Sex with that pretty Swedish girl wasn't objectively all that great, really, but a guy never forgets finally getting to use his cock as nature intended for the first time in his life.

"I feel like cheering for eighteen-year-old Jonas and throwing confetti on him. That poor boy deserved to have a little carefree fun, don't you think?"

"Yes, I do. And he did."

She laughs.

Why was I so nervous about telling her all of this? She's so damned easy to talk to, so nonjudgmental. The woman is flat-out *kind.* Why didn't I have faith in her?

"Interesting factoid discovered by eighteen-year-old Jonas, though. Most girls don't like dudes who are creepy and intense."

"Really?" She's aghast. "Wait a minute—are you sure?"

"It's true. They run away, their arms flailing."

She laughs. "Well, those girls were all idiots, then. I happen to know it's the creepy and intense guys who make the best lovers." She winks.

I feel like the weight of the world's been lifted off me. "Well, not necessarily. I hadn't quite figured out the *sexcellence* thing yet. Not by a long shot." I laugh again. "I was like a frantic dog with a bone."

"Well, you *were* just a puppy, after all."

"Yeah, a puppy with a big ol' hard-on."

She laughs.

"A big ol hard-on and huge paws and a big ol' tail that knocked drinks off coffee tables."

"Are you sure it was your *tail* knocking those drinks off coffee tables, big boy?"

I laugh. God, I love her.

"So, okay. You weren't quite the woman wizard at age eighteen."

"Not quite. I'm pretty sure I thought the female orgasm was a myth propagated by the porn industry."

She smiles broadly.

"Now, Josh, on the other hand, he was fantastic with girls—or, at least, compared to me. When school got out for the summer, Josh met me in Thailand so we could climb Crazy Horse—which is so fucking awesome, by the way, I can't wait to take you there—and then we traveled together for like ten weeks, climbing and hiking and partying and, you know." I grin broadly. "Fishing."

She knows what kind of fishing I'm talking about. "So Josh taught you how to get the girls?"

I laugh heartily. "The guy was my Obi Wan Kenobi. Before Josh showed up, the only strategy I'd formulated for catching fish was sitting in my boat, all alone, without any gear—basically trying not to come off like a serial killer—and *praying* a pretty fish might by chance leap out of the water and flop right into my lap."

She laughs. "Oh, Jonas."

"And, occasionally, a fish did—lucky me. But Josh? That boy had skills. He could do this revolutionary thing—he could *lure* the fish into his boat with an actual fishing rod and *bait*."

Her face is glowing. "What was Josh's bait?"

"Check this out. He *talked* to the fish. Pretty good, huh?"

She laughs. "What? That's crazy. He should write a book."

"Oh, and he taught me the simple art of buying a girl a *drink*. You know, being a gentleman. Being attentive. *Smiling*. Insane stuff."

"He was a woman wizard in training, sounds like."

I laugh. "Definitely."

I'm amazed. I never in a million years thought Sarah and I would be laughing during a conversation about The Lunacy. I thought we'd be crying—or that I'd be begging, apologizing, reassuring. But laughing? Never.

"You should have seen Josh in action. He was Mr. Smooth—or at least eighteen-year-old Jonas thought so. Josh would always say, 'Jonas, just shut the fuck up and look pretty, okay? Your job is to be the dew-covered web that attracts the girls—*you're the something shiny*—and my job is to be the *spider* who lies in wait and bites their legs off before they know what hit 'em.'"

She bursts out laughing and I join her, yet again.

"So, to answer your initial question, that's when everything started turning around for me—when Josh dragged me all over Kingdom Come in search of big rocks and pretty girls to climb. That's when I started to glimpse the divine original form of Jonas Faraday-ness for the first time in my life, however dim and blurry the image might have been back then."

"Where'd you guys go besides Thailand?"

"Well, I'd already done pretty much all of Europe by myself. So with Josh, it was Asia, Australia, New Zealand, and then a little bit of Central America on the way home. Actually, that's the first time I went to Belize—on that trip with Josh."

The mere mention of Belize is enough to make Sarah's face light up. "Belize," she says, sighing dreamily.

It suddenly strikes me, full force, how much my little caterpillar has transformed since we first huddled together in our Belizian cocoon-built-for-two. I thought I loved her then, and I did, in my own way, but my love was a shallow pool compared to the limitless ocean I feel for her now.

"Belize was just the beginning, my precious baby. I'm gonna show you the world."

Her face bursts with excitement.

"Wherever you want to go, we'll go. You name it."

She squeals. "Oh, Jonas. Thank you."

God, I love this woman. Why was I so afraid to talk to her about this stuff? This entire conversation has felt so *right.* This woman *loves* me. My skin feels electrified. *She loves me.*

"So, what happened once you got home?"

I'm reeling. I can't concentrate. She loves me, despite everything—and maybe even *because* of everything. She's told me she loves me many times by now, of course, but this is the first time I've believed it. *She loves me.* All of me. The real me. Not the pretend me. Not some ridiculous projection of me. *Me.* For better or worse.

"Jonas, what happened when you got home?"

"Um." I smile at her. Damn, she's beautiful.

She raises an eyebrow. "Are you okay?"

"Yeah, I'm great, baby. Never better. Uh, Josh went back for his second year at UCLA. I went off to Gonzaga and later down to Berkeley for my MBA, and when Josh and I finished all our fancy degrees, I took over Faraday & Sons in Seattle, Josh started the L.A. branch, and Uncle William moved to New York to start a satellite office out there. And that's when the company took off like a fucking rocket, beyond anything we'd imagined." I pause. I can't think of anything else to say on this topic. "And-now-I'm-here-with-you-in-Las-Vegas-and-I'm-totally-normal-in-every-conceivable-way-and-I-want-to-be-inside-you-more-than-I-want-to-breathe. The End."

She smiles but doesn't speak, as if she expects me to continue.

"The End," I say again. I put up my hands like I'm saying *ta-da.* "Jazz hands."

She laughs.

Sunlight streams through the window and illuminates Sarah's face. She looks beautiful—sleepy, but beautiful. I glance out the window at The Strip below us and sigh. I hate this hellish place. I miss Seattle. I miss the rain. I miss my crisp white sheets and my home gym and my espresso machine. I want to go home and start building Climb and Conquer into the vision I've got in my head. And most of all, more than anything else, I want to start my life with Sarah.

"The dawn of a new day," she says, following my gaze out the window. "Darkness, be gone." She crawls across the bed and drapes her body around mine. "I know how you love your metaphors, baby, so let this beautiful dawn inspire you. Let there be light in your life from this day forward, filling the nooks and crannies you've previously kept shrouded in darkness."

She's speaking my language. "You're a poet," I say.

"Only with you."

"How are you not fazed by everything I've told you?"

She shrugs. "I dunno."

"But seriously," I say, blood rushing into my face. "If there's something you want to say to me—something you're thinking, anything at all—just say it now. Please. Rip off the Band-Aid. I can take it."

She shakes her head. "Oh, Jonas, come on. It was thirteen years ago. Give yourself a frickin' break already—and give me some credit."

"You're not worried I might be a total lunatic?"

"I already *know* you're a total lunatic."

I wait for her to smile, but she doesn't.

"Jonas, I've known from minute one, from the second I read your application, that you're a wee bit crazy. Duh. But I like your crazy, baby. It makes you sexy."

I'm utterly speechless.

"What happened back then doesn't define you. Has it shaped you? Yes, of course. But that's all. You're my sweet Jonas, no matter what happened then. You're the Jonas who spoke in front of my contracts class—brilliant and charming and intelligent and charismatic. You're the Jonas who caught me after I leaped off a thirty-foot waterfall. You're the Jonas who looked shy and sweet and awkward as he tied a friendship bracelet around my wrist. The guy who sent me Oreos to welcome me into the Jonas Faraday Club. The divine original form of man-ness who makes me come every single time you touch me, baby, even in my dreams."

That last one makes my cock tingle.

She kisses me. "Baby, you're the Jonas who unleashed Orgasma the All-Powerful." She nips at my lips and straddles my lap. "You're the man who saved my life—who gave me everything I needed to save myself and then literally stopped my bleeding with his bare hands." She skims her lips on mine. "And you're the man who's gonna kick some bad-guy ass with me." She licks at my lips. "You'd have to strangle a kitten or kick a girl scout in the teeth for me to run away from *that* guy."

My smile stretches so big across my face, I can't even kiss her.

"It was thirteen frickin' years ago, love. Time to give it a rest. *No más. De hoy en adelante, renaces.*"

Damn. My Spanish is pretty good, but not perfect. I got most of that, I think, but I'm not positive.

"No more," she translates, reading my mind. "From today forward, you are reborn." She grinds herself into my hard-on. *"Renaces—y*ou are reborn. *Renazco*—I am reborn." She kisses my neck.

I shiver. I love it when Sarah speaks Spanish to me, especially when she says something badass like that. "*Renazco,*" I repeat after her.

She kisses my cheek. "*No más. De hoy en adelante, renazco.*"

"*No más. De hoy en adelante, renazco,*" I repeat—but when I say it, it sounds clunky compared to the beautiful way Sarah says it.

"That's right. Exactly right. You're reborn, baby. From this day forward."

I pull at her tank top and she rips it off, followed quickly by her pajama bottoms. I follow her lead, kicking off my boxers, and then I climb on top of her, my heart racing.

She holds my face in her hands. "There are no more dark spaces between us, Jonas, no more secrets. Can you feel the difference?"

I nod. I can. Oh God, I want to be inside her.

She kisses me. "This is how it feels to trust someone completely. Do you understand?"

I nod because, yes, I understand what she's saying. But if it were up to me, I'd have phrased it slightly differently: This is how it feels to be *loved* by someone completely.

Before now, I didn't know how to let Sarah love me, not completely. Before this very moment, I didn't understand how much I'd been holding back and pushing her away. *I* knew how to love *her*—God knows I've loved this woman with all my heart and soul since she leaped off that waterfall into my arms, and maybe even before then—but, as much as I've loved her, I haven't been willing to leap off a waterfall and let her love me back. Until now.

I reach between her legs, eager to touch the part of her that's only for me, and when I feel how wet she is, oh my God, I practically leap out of my skin. I bring my finger up to my mouth to sneak a taste of her deliciousness. There's no sweeter flavor in the world than my baby's wetness and no sweeter moment than right now.

I kiss her mouth and massage her clit with my fingertip, my cock throbbing at the slippery texture of her, the slickness, the delicious hardness, and she shudders and bucks. My hard-on strains mercilessly for her, but I force myself to take my time. We've got all the time in the world, after all—I'm not going anywhere, and neither is she.

I reach deep inside her and massage her G-spot, and she jolts.

"My precious baby," I whisper, touching that magic spot again, and she moans. She's my Stradivarius—and there's no greater pleasure in the world than making her strings quiver. My fingers find her clit again, and she writhes. I can't wait anymore. I slip inside her, all the way, groaning loudly, and she lets out a long, quavering sigh in return.

This is a new feeling for me, a new holy grail—making love to the woman I love with no secrets, no dark places, and no doubt. Standing on top of Mount Everest itself couldn't possibly feel this good. *She loves me.* All of me. Even the fucked up parts.

She gyrates her hips in rhythm with mine and wraps her legs around my back.

"The culmination of human possibility," I groan, my body thrusting in and out of hers.

"Yes," she breathes. "Jonas."

She *loves* me. She *enlightens* me. She *graces* me. She *redeems* me.

A wave of pleasure rises up inside me, threatening to push me over the edge.

"Get on top," I say suddenly. "I need to look at you."

We maneuver until she's riding me, licking her lips, touching herself. I sit back and enjoy the view of her breasts softly bouncing, the curve of her hips, the fall of her hair around her shoulders. I love watching her control how deep, how fast, what angle. It turns me on like a motherfucker when she leans forward and rubs my hard cock against her clit or positions herself so that my tip touches some precise spot deep inside her. It's glorious to witness how well she's learned herself by now, how beautifully she knows exactly what to do to get herself off. What a transformation since day one. Jesus.

I grab her ass and let my palms go along for the magnificent ride. "I love this ass," I groan, clutching her. My fingers migrate greedily to explore every crevice of her and she shudders.

I run my hands up her smooth back and around to her breasts and then let my thumb glide over her angry scar. It's healing quickly. I peek down at her tiny tattoo, her secret proclamation of badassery, and shiver. Holy fuck, I love her. Sheer joy washes over me, palpably, like I've been doused with it from a bucket over my head. *I'm going to marry this girl,* I think. I know this as surely as I know my own name. *I'm going to marry this gorgeous girl and make her my wife.*

I can't hold on much longer. I'm right on the edge.

"Jonas," she breathes, trying to catch her breath. "Oh, oh, oh."

"Love is the joy of the good, the wonder of the wise, the

amazement of the gods," I whisper, my voice halting and straining, and she throws her head back.

She makes The Sound. It means I'm about to be the lucky, lucky boy who's going to feel her orgasm from the inside out if I can just hang on a tiny bit longer.

I touch her clit with supreme devotion and she gasps.

"You're gorgeous, baby," I say, stroking her, luring her, doing my damnedest to push her over the edge. Oh fuck, I crave her release as badly as she does. "You're Orgasma the fucking All-Powerful, baby," I say, trembling, and her entire body quivers. "You're the goddess and the muse, Sarah Cruz." I buck wildly underneath her, trying to hang on. *And I'm going to marry you.*

Chapter 34

Sarah

Fifteen minutes ago, Henn texted an "all hands on desk" message to everyone. "I hit the motherlode!" Henn wrote. And the whole group, except for Jonas, quickly congregated in our suite to hear Henn's news.

"Will Jonas be joining us?" Henn asks. "Should we wait for him?"

"No, don't wait. He went to the gym first thing this morning," I say. "I don't know when he'll be back."

Jonas practically leaped out of bed this morning after our marathon conversation and delicious lovemaking session, saying he wanted to "hit the gym and then run an errand"—but he wouldn't tell me anything more than that.

"You're not going to do something stupid, are you, Jonas?" I asked, looking at him sideways, my heart suddenly pounding in my ears.

"Of course not," he said, his face the picture of pure innocence.

"Seriously, Jonas. You need to tell me—you're not going to hunt down Max, are you?"

He pulled me to him. "No, although the idea of killing that fucker gives me a hard-on. I've got my eye on the prize, baby. Don't worry." He grabbed my ass and nibbled my neck. "Just running an errand."

But I wasn't convinced.

He cupped my face in his hands. "I won't go off plan."

"You promise?" I asked.

"I promise."

I breathed a huge sigh of relief. Jonas never, ever falsely promises anything.

He kissed me, making my entire body melt into his. "I'll tell you about the errand when I get back. See you in a couple hours, My Magnificent Sarah." He practically skipped out the front door.

And now, Kat, Josh and I are huddled on the leather couches in the living area of the suite, staring with nervous anticipation at Henn, who looks like his eyes might pop out of his head with excitement.

Henn lets out an excited breath. "Okay." He pauses for effect. "Are you sitting down?" It's a rhetorical question—we're all sitting down right in front of him.

We hold our collective breath.

"I found 'em—and I got in."

I gasp.

"Oh my God," Kat says.

"You're a fucking genius," Josh adds.

"I *am* a fucking genius," Henn says. "I've got the keys to their whole fucking kingdom—member lists, passwords, emails, code. I'm in."

We all express noisy excitement.

Just when Henn is about to tell us something further that's going to "melt our faces off," as he puts it, Jonas bursts into the suite in his workout clothes and a sweatshirt, his hair matted with sweat. "Hey, guys. I just got your text, Henn. Please tell me you did it."

"I did it."

Jonas bounds across the room, bro-hugs Henn, high-fives Josh and Kat, and then swoops me up into a celebratory hug.

"Did you get your errand done?"

He smiles broadly and nods. "I'll show you later."

Show me?

"What'd I miss?" Jonas asks.

"Nothing yet. Perfect timing," I say. "Henn was just about to tell us something that's going to 'melt our faces off.'"

"The money?" Jonas asks. "Please tell us you cracked the money."

"I cracked the money."

"Oh my God, Henn," Kat says. "You're a fucking genius." She flashes Henn a huge smile and he beams at her.

"I've tracked down twelve different bank accounts in five different banks," Henn begins. He pauses for dramatic effect. "Jonas, you're gonna want to sit down for this next part."

Jonas sits next to me and puts his hand on my thigh.

"Twelve different bank accounts and they've got *cash*—I'm talkin' *cash* just sitting in the bank—totaling, oh, about five hundred fifty-four *million* dollars."

The collective reaction of the group blows the roof off the suite.

I put my face in my hands. I can't wrap my head around this.

"And I've got all their account numbers and passwords," Henn says, smirking. "For several of the larger accounts, transfers are set up for in-person banking only—and most banks require a signature to make transfers over a million, anyway—so I don't think we should get our sights set on grabbing the actual money. We'll just plan on handing over all the account numbers and passwords."

I look over at Jonas. He's deep in thought. "Can you get me printouts showing all the accounts and the balances in each?"

"Sure thing," Henn says. "I can do anything."

"This is unbelievable," Josh says. He looks at Kat, incredulous, and she returns his amazement.

"What about the member list?" I ask.

"Oh, well, that's the second piece of big news," Henn says. "That's the part that's gonna blow your minds."

"Five hundred fifty-four million bucks isn't mind blowing?" I ask.

"Nope." He pauses yet again, a master storyteller. "I've confirmed, with documentary proof, no doubt about it, you can stake your life on it, the member list includes seven U.S. congressmen, two state governors, a Canadian mayor, and . . ." He pauses like he's waiting on a drumroll. "*The fucking Secretary of Defense.*"

Everyone expresses simultaneous shock.

"The dude in charge of the entire U.S. Department of Defense—like, the guy who runs the entire fucking military."

"And sits on the President's cabinet," Jonas adds, his face pale.

Intense panic overtakes me. I feel my heart skip a beat.

Jonas rubs his face. "Shit," he mutters softly.

"Shit is right. Holy fucking shit," Josh says.

We're all silent for a moment, processing this new bit of information.

My heart is quite literally palpitating. "This is gonna be a huge *scandal*," I say. I know that's obvious and I sound like a simpleton right now, but it's all I can muster.

Henn nods furiously. "Insanity, right? The *Secretary of Defense* pays money to a sex club that supplies money and weapons to aid Russian imperialism." He snorts. "Oopsies."

"Not great for the guy's future prospects in politics," Josh adds.

"Not something he'd want to get out," Jonas says darkly.

Holy Baby Jesus in a manger. We're about to unleash a scandal onto the world of epic proportions—information that will surely rock the highest levels of government, all the way to the White House itself. I have no interest in toppling the Secretary of Defense—not to mention various congressmen and governors—or, hell, athletes and CEOs and everyday software engineers, either. And I certainly have zero interest in splattering incidental mud onto the President of the United States. Holy hell.

"When this gets out about the Secretary of Defense, I wonder if it's gonna cause a problem for the President?" Kat asks, reading my mind.

"Of course. The Secretary of Defense sits on the President's cabinet," Josh says. "He's in the inner circle. A guy like that being involved in a large-scale prostitution ring is scandalous all by itself—the press is gonna have a holier-than-thou field day with that little nugget—but add the fact that the guy's been indirectly funding the Ukrainian separatists, and that's the kind of shit that explodes like a political grenade on anyone within spitting distance of the guy—including the President."

"I'm freaking out," I mumble. I look at Jonas and Josh. "What about you two? How bad is this gonna be for you when all of this comes out?"

Jonas and Josh look at each other. "I don't know," Josh answers. He shrugs. "It won't be a shining moment for either of us, I'm sure."

I look down, suddenly nauseated. Josh might suffer minor embarrassment, but Jonas is the one who'll take the lion's share of the heat. Josh joined The Club for a month, after all, while Jonas paid two hundred fifty thousand bucks for a full year's gluttonous membership. Will this scandal obliterate Jonas' reputation in the business community? Will it affect his ability to build Climb and Conquer into the global brand he envisions?

And what about me? In two years, when I graduate from school and the Washington bar processes my application for a law license, will I be able to pass the ethics review? Will they believe me when I swear I didn't know the true nature of my employer?

Jonas squeezes my hand. "We'll just have to figure this out one day at a time. Maybe we can come up with a solution where none of this gets out."

I'm doubtful about that. "How?"

"Leave that part to me and Josh," Jonas says. He looks at his brother for confirmation.

Josh nods decisively, but the look in Josh's eyes doesn't instill confidence.

After a lengthy discussion during which everyone in the room basically shits a brick and says this is way too big for us to handle on our own and oh my God how did we get here and what the fuck are we going to do, we finally decide on an immediate strategy: I'll finish my report *today* with as much supporting evidence as we can put together in such a short amount of time, including printouts showing the balances in The Club's many bank accounts, Josh and

Jonas will put their heads together about our strategy for submitting my report to the proper authorities, and then first thing tomorrow morning, we'll all traipse down to the Las Vegas branch of the FBI and do our best to convince whoever the heck is in charge over there to arrange a meeting with his or her boss in Washington, D.C. What else can we do? This is too big for us to sit on any longer than absolutely necessary and way too big for us to handle without backup from some pretty big guns. Not to mention, we're all paranoid The Club might transfer some or all of their funds out of our reach at any moment.

Just as everyone begins hunkering down to get to work, Jonas pulls me aside.

"I'm all sweaty from the gym," he says, his hands in the pockets of his hoodie. "I'm gonna take a quick shower. Will you join me? I wanna show you something."

He wants to show me something, huh? I'm sure he does. I'm never one to turn down a shower with Jonas, God knows, but a shower right now seems like a waste of valuable time. I've got to get this report completed—and he's got to figure out what the heck we're going to do with it. "I'll take a rain check," I say. "That's how we'll celebrate getting the report done."

He looks disappointed.

"Something to look forward to," I add. Honestly, I'm surprised he's chosen this moment to think about shower sex. I love it, too, but come on—we've got bigger fish to fry.

"Sarah," Kat calls. "Henn's got the bank printouts ready. What part of the exhibit log do you want to attach it to?"

"Yeah, just a sec." I look at Jonas again. He looks like a dorky kid not picked for dodge ball. "Later, baby," I assure him. And then I walk across the room to answer Kat's question.

Chapter 35

Sarah

It's three in the morning and everyone on the team looks half dead. We've been cooped up all day and night together in the suite, barely talking, barely stopping to eat. Every single one of us understands the magnitude of what we're trying to do here—and the potential stakes if we fail. The hard work and long hours have paid off, though, because my report is done. Hallelujah. And it's pretty damned good.

Sure, I could keep writing for another three weeks if I had the time to write my report as thoroughly as I'd like, but time is of the essence and this will have to do. I've outlined the facts, the law, and the evidence as best I can and attached a corresponding exhibit log with proof of every single fact I've proffered. Nothing is speculation. Nothing is guesswork. Nothing is subject to debate. If this report doesn't get the FBI's attention, then I don't know what will.

Josh and Kat leave the suite together, both saying they're off to "get some sleep," ostensibly in their respective hotel rooms (but I'm not so sure). I'm beginning to suspect those two have become more than friends while we've been here in Vegas. I'll have to ask Kat about that tomorrow. Today, I was too obsessed with our mission to veer off track into thinking about anything but that report.

After Josh and Kat have left, Henn calls me over to his computer. I'd asked him to search through The Club's system for one more piece of evidence—something establishing a nexus between the names used during the application process and the codes assigned to member files post-application.

"Will this work?" he asks, his voice weary.

I stand behind him and look at his screen over his shoulder.

He explains the information he's called to his screen.

"Yeah, that's perfect," I say. "Thanks, Henn. I just think we've got to be ultra-clear about everything. No assumptions—no leaps of logic required."

Henn agrees.

Jonas sits quietly in the corner of the room, watching me with burning eyes and tense muscles.

"Jonas, do you want to take a look at this?" I ask.

He shakes his head.

Oh. I know that look. I bite my lip. My hunky-monkey boyfriend is sitting there with a hard-on right now.

"Thanks, Henn. You're a fucking genius," I say.

"So I've been told," he says. He grins and closes his laptop ceremoniously. "Okay, well, if that's all you need, then I'll head out. I've got a sudden intuition I should pull the lever on the one-hundred-dollar slot machine exactly seven times before I go to beddy-bye."

"Good luck," I say. "See you at ten." That's when the whole group's reconvening to head over to the Las Vegas branch of the FBI.

The moment the door closes on Henn, I turn to Jonas. "Will you accept that shower-sex rain check now?" I ask.

He nods slowly. Damn, he's a good-lookin' man.

I stride over to him in the corner, exhausted but excited at everything we accomplished today, and sit on his lap. Oh, hello there. Yup. Jonas is as hard as a rock. I run my fingertips over the engraving on the face of his platinum bracelet. *Sarah.*

"Hi, boyfriend," I say softly.

He smiles and touches my bracelet in return. "Hi, girlfriend." He pulls my face to his and kisses me deeply.

I run my hands over the fabric of his long-sleeved knit shirt, reveling in the feel of his broad chest and sculpted shoulders. I'll never grow tired of touching him. He's a work of art. I move on to his powerful biceps and then to his forearms—and my fingertips detect a different texture underneath his shirt than skin. I poke at the thin fabric above his right forearm. Yes, there's definitely something underneath there besides skin.

"What's under there?"

"My errand," he says, smiling. "What I've been dying to show you." He pulls off his shirt to reveal his glorious chest and abs and sculpted shoulders and bulging biceps—as well as thick, rectangular swaths of medical gauze taped to the tops of his forearms.

"What happened to you?" I ask. But then it hits me. "You got new *tattoos*?"

He smiles broadly.

I'm intrigued. In Belize I asked him if he'd ever thought about getting more ink—especially since he got his sacred Platonic tattoos so long ago—and he said no. "I don't need to tat myself up just for the sake of it," he said. "I'm only interested in marking my skin with ideas that are life-changing and worthy of eternity. Whose ideas besides Plato's could ever live up to that?"

Well, well, well—famous last words. I wonder what new idea suddenly became "life-changing and worthy of eternity" enough for him now?

He picks at the corner of the tape on his right forearm and rips off the bandage with a loud "Ow."

I hold up his arm to get a good look, and when I gasp, his face lights up. I read aloud, tears springing into my eyes, "*No más. De hoy en adelante, renazco.*" These are the words I said to Jonas last night. Oh my God. *My* words are life-changing and worthy of eternity? Tears pool in my eyes.

"*Renazco,*" he says softly, staring into my eyes. "I am reborn, My Magnificent Sarah, thanks to you." He looks shy for a moment, mustering the courage to say whatever's on the tip of his tongue. "*Mi amor siempre,*" he whispers. *My love forever.*

Oh, Jonas. I can't believe he's given *my* words equal billing with Plato's on his body. For eternity. I rearrange myself on his lap and straddle him. "*Mi amor siempre,*" I whisper, kissing him softly.

He returns my kiss deeply, and, just like that, I'm crazy-pants hot and ready to go. But there's a bandage on his other arm, too, of course, and I've got to know what lies beneath. I force myself to pull away from our kiss, though the feeling of his erection poking against my panties is driving me crazy.

"What about that one?" I point to the bandage on his left arm.

He smiles mischievously and begins picking at the corner of the tape.

When the bandage is off, he holds up his arm across his chest to give me a right-side-up view. I can't believe my eyes. The phrase is in English and easily readable by anyone who happens to glance at it.

But that makes no sense—Jonas once told me he'd purposefully gotten his tattoos in ancient Greek because he emphatically did *not* want casual passersby to know what they said. "My tattoos are there to inspire *me*, not the masses," he said. Well, it looks like Jonas Faraday has had a change of heart—on a lot of things, actually.

I read the bold English lettering aloud, this time with a quavering voice. "Love is the joy of the good, the wonder of the wise, the amazement of the gods."

He nods emphatically.

I recall Jonas saying this phrase to me, twice, I think, but both times when we were making love and I was too busy having an orgasm to ask him about it.

"Is it Plato?" I ask, running my fingers over the letters.

He nods. "Plato attributes it to the poet Agathon. It's from Plato's *Symposium*—Plato's lengthy dialogue on the nature, purpose, and genesis of love. *Romantic* love, specifically."

I bite my lip.

"According to Plato, romantic love is initially *felt* with our physical senses, but with contemplation, it transforms into something greater: the soul's appreciation of the beauty within another person."

My heart skips a beat.

"Ultimately, it's through love that our souls are able to recognize the ideal form of beauty—the divine original form of beauty itself." His eyes are on fire. "Which, in turn, leads us to understand the *truth*."

I place my hand over my heart to steady myself. "But Jonas." I'm reeling. "Plato in *English*? Not ancient Greek?"

He nods.

"I thought you didn't want people to understand your tattoos."

"This one, I do."

I hold my breath.

"Plato might have written these wise and sacred words thousands of years ago—but Jonas Faraday is declaring them today."

"Oh, Jonas," I breathe.

"With this tattoo, I'm shouting about my love for you from the top of the highest mountaintop, Sarah. I want the whole world to read it and know the truth—*I love Sarah Cruz*."

I'm melting.

He cups my face in his large hands. "Love is the joy of the good, the wonder of the wise, the amazement of the gods." His eyes are fierce. "That means you, Sarah Cruz. You and me. You're my beauty. You're my truth."

My heart is racing.

"There's never been a love like ours and there never will be again. We're the greatest love story ever told."

I can't believe the man who once professed his disdain for "Valentine's Day bullshit" has turned out to be the most romantic man in the world. I bite my lip.

"We're epic," he says, his eyes burning. "Our love is so pure and true, we're the amazement of the gods."

Who talks like this? Jonas Faraday, that's who. God, I love this man.

He's got that look in his eye—his patented Jonas-is-a-great-white-shark-and-Sarah-is-a-defenseless-sea-lion look. It's the gleam that means he's about to swallow me whole. He kisses me deeply and that's all she wrote—we're both suddenly crazed. He tugs urgently on my shirt and I lift my arms over my head to help him out. He unlatches and removes my bra and sucks at my nipples voraciously the minute my breasts are freed.

"Shower," I gasp, my body writhing with arousal.

He stands, pulling me up with him by my ass. I throw my arms around his neck and my legs around his waist and kiss him fervently, grinding myself into him, attacking him, inhaling him, as he carries my writhing body into the bedroom. He throws me down on the bed and rips off my pants and G-string—holy shit, he *literally* rips my G-string off my body—and then he buries his face between my legs in a frenzy of ravenous animalistic greed. There's no buildup, no finesse, no slow burn. There's no such thing as *sexcellence* this time around, folks. This right here is nothing but a shark tearing into his prey—and it's turning me the fuck on.

When he stands back up licking his lips, he's Incredible Hulk Jonas. A beast. The poet is gone. The romantic is gone. He pulls down his pants and briefs, giving me the view of him that never gets old, and before I can do a damned thing, he scoops me up like a rag doll and carries me to the bathroom, kissing me hungrily all the while.

I grab fistfuls of his hair in both my hands as I kiss him, and he grunts like a gorilla. Oh God, I love that primal sound he makes. He turns the water on behind my back as I writhe around, kissing him and yanking on his hair. Hot water pelts me in the back and cascades down my breasts. I try in vain to slam myself onto his erection, but he evades me.

"Let me down," I say, but I don't wait for his reply to slide down his slick, wet skin to my feet.

"I'm in charge," he says, his voice firm.

But I'm not listening. I get down on my knees and take him into my mouth, sucking on him enthusiastically, as hot water pounds the back of my head. He grabs fistfuls of my hair and gyrates into my mouth, groaning like I'm causing him extreme pain. Oh God, it turns me on to do this. He makes a sound like he's dying—of happiness, of course—and I reach down and touch myself, thinking about the look on Jonas' face when he showed me his new tattoos.

He shudders and growls and grips my hair harder than he ever has—but I don't care about a little discomfort to my scalp, not when I'm making him feel this good. Oh God, I can barely breathe, I'm so turned on. I continue touching myself, sucking on him, visualizing his new tattoos. Jonas engraved *my* words alongside Plato's. He declared his eternal love for me permanently onto his skin, in English, for the whole world to see.

My eyes spring open. My dream. The ten poltergeist Jonases, the dripping wine, the noisy spectators—*and Jonas looking up and declaring his love for me to the entire world.* Oh my God. My dream wasn't about *sexual* exhibitionism—it was about *emotional* exhibitionism—about me wanting Jonas to claim me in front of the entire world. Oh my God, with his new tattoos, Jonas has done just that.

My entire body seizes with a powerful orgasm and I moan loudly (though the sound is stifled somewhat by the vast amounts of penis down my throat). I yelp, trying my damnedest to continue sucking on him as my body ripples from within, but I can't do it.

He pulls out of my mouth. "I'm gonna fuck you, baby," he says.

My orgasm finishes. What did he just say? Hot water pelts my face as I look up at him, in a daze of satisfaction.

"Me," he says, caveman-style, pulling me up off my knees. "Now." His voice is raw. He's in charge. "I'm gonna fuck you."

He pulls me roughly to him, his eyes blazing, and touches me between my legs. I buckle. Oh wow, I'm not done—not by a long shot—I'm still totally turned on. He turns my body around away from him and I passively follow his nonverbal command.

"Bend over," he grunts in my ear. "Bend over and grab your ankles."

I have no thought in my head but to do his bidding—my desire for control is totally gone. I bend over and grasp my ankles. Holy hell, I'm utterly exposed and at his mercy in this position. I shift my grip on my ankles and shudder with anticipation.

One of his hands rubs my back as his other one reaches between my legs from behind and works my clit. He's aiming for another orgasm from me, obviously, and, oh my God, he's gonna get it. Hot water cascades down my back and gushes over my dangling face. I tremble with anticipation. What's he waiting for? My legs buckle and he steadies me.

His fingers are working me too well. The sensation is too intense. I can't remain in this position anymore if he's going to keep touching me like this—I can't maintain my balance while feeling so much pleasure. I bend my legs. I'm too turned on to stay bent over like this. I need to gyrate my body, to rub myself against him, to kiss him. I can't take it anymore. I need a release.

He enters my wetness without warning—and so deeply, so forcefully, and with such unapologetic ownership of my body, I scream—and, much to my surprise, I come, too, instantly.

Jonas thrusts mercilessly in and out of me as I climax, roaring loudly as he does, and in under a minute, he climaxes too, from deep,

deep, deep, deep inside me, bellowing as he does. I shriek in reply. Oh man, we're loud. I love us.

When he's done, he presses his palm firmly into my upper back, signaling me to stay put. I do as I'm told, yet again. He pulls out of me and places the showerhead between my legs.

My entire body vibrates along with the warm stream of water pelting my sweet spot. It feels so damned good, I wobble forward, losing my balance, but he steadies me with a sure hand on my hip. I place my palms on the shower floor and he continues cleaning me between my legs, slowly lathering me with shower gel and then letting warm, pulsing water batter me deliciously.

I'm on the cusp of yet another orgasm. Oh my God, I've got to stand. I can't do this anymore. Blood has rushed into my dangling head and now pulses relentlessly in my ears and eyes. And, jeez, I'm drowning, too, from water cascading down my back and into my nose.

But before I can stand, Jonas kneels down behind my bent-over body and begins lapping at me ferociously—indiscriminately tasting every square inch of real estate back there, his mouth and tongue devouring every part of me even remotely in the vicinity of his usual licking grounds. Holy mother. The sensation of his tongue in forbidden places sends me into overload. Just a couple deep licks of his tongue and I come again, with different muscles than ever before.

The second my orgasm ends, Jonas abruptly grabs my torso and lifts me to standing. I wobble. My legs are rubber.

"I can't," I mumble. "Jonas." I reach for the shower wall to steady myself, but Jonas turns me around to face him. I throw my arms around his neck and rest my cheek on his strong shoulder. I'm totally spent. His skin is slick and taut and delicious under the warm shower stream. His arms are strong around me. Complete satisfaction floods me.

After a few minutes of relaxed silence, Jonas finally speaks. "While I was sitting there getting my tattoos," he says softly, "all I could think about was coming back up to the suite to make love to you."

"Mmm," I say. I'm not functional yet.

"I imagined myself making love to you slowly and tenderly while whispering words of supreme devotion into your ear."

We both burst out laughing at the same time.

"I guess your precious strategy got blown to bits," I say.

"As usual."

"Are you complaining?"

"Fuck no."

"I hate Strategic Jonas, anyway," I say.

"I just wanted to do something worthy of the moment—worthy of you," he says. "I wanted to do something romantic."

"Oh, Jonas." I raise my cheek off his shoulder and look him in the eye. "What we just did *was* romantic. It was Valentine's Day bullshit *and* hot monkey-sex, all rolled into one." I smile broadly at him. "You always give me both."

His eyes sparkle at me. "You were made for me, Sarah Cruz," he says.

"You were made for me, Jonas Faraday." I lay my cheek back down on his broad shoulder and sigh with contentment as he pulls me close. "Thank you for finding me."

"Thank you for being findable."

"That's not a word."

"It is now." He beams a heart-stopping smile at me. "Let's dry off. There's something I want to talk to you about."

We're bundled up in the fluffy white bathrobes supplied by the hotel, sitting on the fluffy white bed. The clock on the nightstand reads twelve minutes before four o'clock. What the hell are we still doing up? We're scheduled to meet the team in six hours to march down to the Las Vegas branch of the FBI. Oh man, I'm fading fast.

Jonas looks nervous. He's plainly trying to figure out what to say.

"You're gonna have to spit it out, baby," I say, yawning. "I'm falling asleep sitting up."

He exhales. "After we're done here, I want to take you on a trip—to a place that's really special to me."

I'm instantly wide awake. "Where?"

"Does it matter?"

"Not at all." I grin.

"It's out of the country—I'll tell you that much."

Holy moly, I'm elated. I've dreamed of traveling the world my entire life, ever since I was little. Whenever my father used to start screaming at my mother, when I knew he was getting all amped up and violence was surely imminent, I used to crawl into my closet with a world map and tune out the bad stuff by imagining myself in faraway places. I never in a million years thought my childhood fantasies would actually come true one day—or that I'd be lucky enough to have a tour guide with luscious lips and abs of steel and sad eyes—not to mention a seemingly inexhaustible travel budget.

"Wow," I say, at a loss for words.

"So that's a yes?" He looks hopeful.

"When?"

"The minute we're done here." His face bursts with excitement.

"You mean before we even go back home?"

"Yeah. I'll have my assistant overnight our passports and I'll take you on a shopping spree to buy whatever you need for the trip and we'll just hop a flight and go." His face is precious. He's a kid on Santa's lap, asking for that one special gift.

I want nothing more than to zip off to some exotic, faraway land with Jonas. But it's not possible—not right now. I kiss his nose. "You're so sweet, Jonas," I say. "Have I ever told you that, my sweet Jonas?"

His face falls. He knows what's coming.

I look at him sideways. "Have you put out your press release yet? About you leaving Faraday & Sons?"

He shakes his head, a second-grader busted for throwing spitballs.

"Have you told your uncle about Climb and Conquer?"

"No." He looks down.

"Don't you think you'd better do all that?"

He sighs. "There was a complication."

"Mmm hmm."

"With Josh. And then you were hurt and in the hospital—"

"But I'm not in the hospital anymore. Why haven't you talked to your uncle yet?"

He twists his mouth. "Because Josh wants to leave Faraday & Sons, too." His face is a mixture of elation and apology. "He wants to do Climb and Conquer with me full-time."

"Oh my God, Jonas. That's fantastic. You must be ecstatic."

"But Faraday & Sons won't survive both of us leaving. Uncle William's semi-retired these days. Who's gonna run the show?"

"And you feel guilty about that? You feel responsible for that?"

He nods.

I grab his hand. "Is this what you want to do with your life, my love? Climb and Conquer—and with Josh?"

He nods. "When Josh said he wanted to join me, it was a dream come true."

"This is what Josh wants?"

He nods.

"Then it's the right thing to do," I say. "You're not responsible for the fate of Faraday & Sons, and neither is he. You didn't ask to be the guardians of it. That company isn't your life's calling—Climb and Conquer is. You're responsible for being true to yourself and your destiny. You have to live your truth. Always."

His eyes soften and warm.

"You've got one life to live, my sweet love. *One*. Make the most of it. Every single day. That's your most sacred job on this earth."

His face flushes. "Thank you."

"You're welcome."

"You're so wise, Sarah. You're smart, yes, but you're *wise,* too."

I love it when he says that. "Butter me up all you like, big boy," I say. "But we're not going on that trip until you've gotten your butt in gear and started your new life. Our trip won't be an *escape*—it'll be a *celebration*. We'll be celebrating the beginning of Climb and Conquer and the end of my first year of law school."

His face falls now that he understands my proposed timeline for the trip.

"Jonas, I can't go away before finals. I've got to study."

He looks utterly disappointed.

"Finals are in four short weeks," I say. "We'll go right after that. Between now and then, you'll get your life in order and I'll study like a banshee, all day, every day, without stopping."

He opens his mouth to protest.

"*Except* that I'll take breaks to have howling monkey-sex with you, of course. I've already told you, Jonas, sex with you is a physical necessity—no different than sleeping, eating and breathing." I roll my eyes. "Duh."

"You read my mind."

"We can leave on our trip the day after finals. How's that?"

He sticks out his bottom lip and pouts.

"You know I'm right," I say.

His pout intensifies.

"You know I am."

He shrugs. "I hate waiting."

"It's just a rain check, that's all, baby. One short month. You just have to be patient."

"I'm not good at patience."

I laugh. "Really?"

He exhales loudly. "Well, it looks like I've got no choice." He shrugs. "Another goddamned round of delicious anticipation, for fuck's sake." He shakes his head. "One month. You'll study and I'll put on my big-boy pants, and every spare minute in between, we'll crawl into our little cocoon built for two and fuck each other's brains out like the sex-crazed caterpillars we are."

I laugh. "Do caterpillars fuck?"

He shrugs. "They do now."

I laugh again.

"But first things first," he says, his eyes turning to granite. "You and me, baby—we're gonna fuck The Club up the ass."

I put my arms around his neck. "You bet, baby. Sounds like a plan."

Chapter 36

Jonas

"We really need to talk to your boss," I say to the newbie FBI agent sitting across the table from me. Fuck me, this rookie agent isn't going to be able mobilize anyone to do a goddamned thing.

"Yeah, well, that's not gonna happen. I'm who you get."

"I'm Jonas Faraday," I say, sounding like a total douche. "And this is my brother, Josh. We run Faraday & Sons in Seattle, L.A. and New York. We'd like to talk to the head of this office."

The kid shrugs. "I'm the only one available to talk to you, sir. Sorry." But he's not at all sorry.

I look at Sarah. Her eyes are bugging out of her head. And rightfully so. This isn't going to work if her report gets thrown onto the pile on this newbie's desk. We need prompt action, and that means getting the immediate attention of someone with a hell of a lot more pull within the FBI than this guy.

"How long have you been an agent?" Kat asks.

When the kid's gaze falls on Kat, his entire demeanor visibly softens. Oh yeah, I keep forgetting that Kat is exceptionally attractive. To me, she's just Kat—Sarah's best friend—the Party Girl with a Heart of Gold. But witnessing reactions like this guy's reminds me she's objectively a knockout.

"Four months," he says.

"Did you go to Quantico for training like they show in the movies?"

"Yeah."

"Wow. That's cool. So what's your assignment? All I know about the FBI is what I saw in *Silence of the Lambs.*" The way Kat's talking to the guy, it's as if the two of them are cozied up together in the corner of a bar, getting to know each other over drinks.

The guy must know Kat's trying to butter him up—and yet his smile says he doesn't care. "Well, new agents are assigned to run background checks for the first year, mostly. And, of course, I'm the lucky guy who gets to talk to all the nice people such as yourselves who come in off the streets of Las Vegas to report the crime of the century."

"Everyone's gotta start somewhere," Kat says, flashing perfect teeth. She leans forward across the table. "So here's the thing, Agent Sheffield. I've come here today off the streets of Las Vegas to report the crime of the century."

He can't help but laugh.

Oh boy, this Kitty Kat just caught herself a fish.

Kat's face turns serious. "Actually, I'm not kidding. I'm here to report the crime of the century."

He sighs. "What's your name?"

"Katherine Morgan. But you can call me Kat." She says this like she's granting him a special favor, like the whole world doesn't already call her by that name.

Special Agent Sheffield's face turns earnest. "Kat," he repeats. "I tell you what. You guys file your report with me and I promise I'll take a long look at it within the next two weeks—maybe even a week. And, if I see something there, I'll most certainly investigate further."

I'm tempted to speak up, but Sarah puts her hand on my thigh.

"Thank you, Special Agent Sheffield," Kat says, smiling. "I really appreciate that. What's your first name?"

"Eric."

"Special Agent Eric." She pushes her long blonde hair behind her shoulder. "The thing is, this is an urgent matter." She leans completely forward across the table again, and the tops of her breasts ride up into her neckline. "This is a career-making kind of case for an agent such as yourself, I swear to God."

I glance at Sarah again. She's suppressing a smirk. I imagine she's seen Kat's charm in action a time or two before.

The young agent looks dubious. "Even if *I* believe you," Eric says, "I'd have to present this to my boss in due course, whenever I could get her undivided attention. And if she's convinced, which isn't a given, then she'd have to present your report to *her* boss in Washington to get anyone to move on this, if it's truly as big as you say. And all that takes time, Miss Morgan. Do you know how many conspiracy theorists walk into the FBI every day to tell us about the crime of the century?"

Kat laughs and shakes her head and her golden blonde hair falls around her shoulders. "I can only imagine," she says. "But you don't actually think we're a bunch of conspiracy theorists, do you?" Kat's eyes are sparkling. "We're just a computer nerd, a law student, a PR specialist . . ." She motions to herself with flourish on the last one. "And two ridiculously rich business dudes with plenty of other stuff they could be doing than filing a report with the FBI. These two guys have been on the cover of *Businessweek,* for crying out loud." She laughs. "Not a crazy among us—well, yeah, okay—I admit I'm a teeny-tiny bit crazy." She holds up her index finger and thumb, slightly apart, to emphasize her point. "But not the kind of crazy you're referring to."

Oh man, she's good. I have to restrain myself from chuckling.

Agent Eric exhales. "I'd be happy to take a look at your report in due course—"

"Agent Sheffield, I'm begging you. Please don't throw our report onto some pile—take a hard look at it right now. Let us explain everything to you, page by page. I guarantee you won't regret it."

Eric looks at his watch. I imagine he's got a huge stack of background checks waiting for him.

"Henn," Sarah interjects, "will you please play Special Agent Sheffield that voicemail we have cued up?"

"Yes, ma'am." Henn presses a button on his computer and the Ukrainian Travolta's gruff voice fills the room for about eight seconds.

When the voicemail ends, Sarah speaks calmly. "That was one of several voicemails our computer expert, Peter Hennessey, has retrieved from the cell phone of Maksim Belenko. He's the brains behind The Club's various operations. In that particular voicemail, a hitman named Yuri Navolska asks Mr. Belenko if he should go ahead and kill his intended target as previously instructed, or, instead, hold off due to newly discovered information."

Special Agent Eric's eyes widen. He's most definitely intrigued.

"That's what a certified Ukrainian translator will tell you in a sworn statement under penalty of perjury—and, of course, Mr. Hennessey will swear that voicemail came from Belenko's cell phone."

Henn nods curtly.

"And since Yuri Navolska was holding a knife to my throat in a bathroom at the University of Washington when he left that voicemail, I can personally vouch for its authenticity."

She's got his undivided attention now.

Sarah continues her assault. "About a minute after leaving that message, Yuri Navolska sliced the external jugular vein in my neck and stabbed me in the ribcage, causing me to fall back and crack my skull on a sink ledge." She tilts her head to the side to display the scar on her neck. "If you need to see the scars on my head and torso, I'll show you."

Agent Eric inhales sharply. "No, that's okay. I believe you."

"Please," Kat says, her voice brimming with genuine emotion. "These guys tried to kill my best friend." All trace of Flirty Kat is gone—she's Earnest Kat now. "Just give us a couple hours of your time." Even I can see how stunningly beautiful Kat looks right now—vulnerability suits her.

"You've got more voicemails besides this one?" Eric asks.

"Several," Henn says. "About all kinds of nasty stuff. Maksim Belenko's a really bad dude—prostitution, weapons, drugs, money laundering."

"This report outlines everything for you in meticulous detail," Sarah says, grabbing the hefty document off the table and holding it in the air. "Every single allegation in here is true and supported with solid, incontrovertible evidence." She lets the report fall back onto the table with a loud thud.

Agent Eric's demeanor has done a complete one-eighty since we first walked through his door. "Okay," he says, exhaling. "Let's dig in. We'll go through the report together, page by page, and if it's everything you say it is, I'll take this to my boss today." He looks up at the ceiling. "But please, for the love of God, don't bullshit me about a single goddamned thing. Okay?"

We all nod profusely.

"If I'm gonna stick my neck out, you've got to promise to tell me the God's truth."

"Thank you," Kat says. "We promise." She shoots him a look like she's just promised him a blowjob, signaling the official retreat of Vulnerable Kat.

"Let's do it," Agent Eric says, getting comfortable in his chair. He looks directly at Kat. "I'm all yours."

Chapter 37

Jonas

We've been here almost three hours walking Special Agent Eric through Sarah's report and accompanying exhibit log. Throughout our discussion, Eric has looked variously excited, overwhelmed, anxious, and ecstatic—but always *convinced.*

"So what do you want me to do?" Agent Eric asks, thumbing through the exhibit log. He's clearly trying to hide the fact that he's shitting his pants right now.

"We want a meeting in D.C. within the next two days with power players at the FBI, CIA, and Secret Service," I say.

Eric keeps a straight face, but I can tell he's losing his shit. "I'm pretty sure I'll be able to convince my boss about all this," Eric says, motioning to the report. "But I doubt she'll be able to pull in those other agencies."

"We're talking about the U.S. Secretary of Defense," I say. "We don't know who within the FBI might be in that guy's pocket."

Eric opens his mouth to protest, but I barrel ahead.

"It's not that I mistrust anyone at the FBI *per se*—I'd say the same thing about power players at the CIA and Secret Service, too. It's simple checks and balances—I'm just trying to increase my odds that this situation gets handled right."

Agent Eric rubs his eyes. "All three agencies within two days?"

I nod.

He shakes his head. "That's gonna be a tough sell."

"Tell me how we can make that happen."

"Deliver the money."

"Done," Sarah says. "A printout of all The Club's bank accounts is at Tab D of the exhibit log. The account numbers are blacked out on that version, but—"

"No, deliver the *actual* money—not a printout. You want the FBI, CIA *and* Secret Service to jump when you say jump? Then make this a turnkey operation for them."

"But we can't do that," Sarah says. "Those accounts require—"

"Yeah, we can," Henn cuts in.

Sarah shoots Henn a "what the fuck?" look, and I'm right there with her. Henn told us the bank accounts require in-person signatures for large transfers.

"We can do it," Henn insists.

"Okay," Sarah says slowly, looking at Henn quizzically. "Even if that's true, we have a problem. If we move the money before law enforcement is ready to pounce, Belenko will immediately guess who screwed him over and come after Jonas and me—and who knows what else they might do?"

"She's right," I say. "We can't move the money to convince you guys to take action—it's got to be the other way around."

Eric sighs and looks up at the ceiling. "You're not bullshitting me? You can do it?"

Everyone looks at Henn.

"We can do it."

"Then I'll vouch for you with my boss," Eric says. "I'll do everything in my power."

Everyone sighs with relief.

"Hey, Agent Sheffield," Sarah says. "I've got a favor to ask of you."

The entire room looks at Sarah in surprise. This isn't something we talked about in advance. What the fuck is she talking about?

Eric purses his lips, apparently waiting to hear her request.

"You do background checks, right?" Sarah asks.

"Yeah," Eric replies. "Every day."

"I'd like you to find two people for me."

Agent Eric raises his eyebrows and so do I. What is she talking about?

"This isn't a demand. It's just a personal favor. But it's really important."

My heart is racing.

"Who are the two people?" Eric asks.

"The first is a woman named Mariela from Venezuela."

I'm instantly short of breath.

Sarah doesn't look at me. "I don't know her last name, but she worked for Joseph and Grace Faraday in Seattle during the years from I'm guessing 1984 to around 1991."

I glance at Josh. His mouth is hanging open. I put my hands over my face, trying to look like I'm deep in thought, or tired, or fighting off a headache. But the truth is, I'm stuffing down tears.

"In 1991, Grace Faraday was murdered in her home, and the man who was convicted of the killing turned out to be the boyfriend of Mariela's sister. You should be able to figure out Mariela's last name by tracing back from the convicted murderer to his girlfriend—and then to her sister, Mariela. Maybe the sister visited the killer in prison? Maybe she was interviewed or gave a statement in the investigation or at trial? Surely, there's some record of the girlfriend somewhere, and that should lead you to Mariela's full name."

I let out a shaky breath and Sarah grabs my thigh under the table. I peek at Josh. His face is in his hands. I can't breathe.

"Hang on," Eric says, taking notes. "Could you repeat all that?"

Sarah repeats everything again slowly, her hand now gently rubbing my thigh. "We need you to find Mariela—and if she's not alive, then her children."

That last part stabs me in the heart. Could Mariela be dead? I do a quick calculation in my head. How old was she when Josh and I were seven? Late twenties? I had no concept of age at the time—everyone was uniformly just an adult to me—but I bet she was younger than I am right now. So how old would she be now? In her fifties, probably?

Eric looks up from his notepad. "Okay. That sounds doable."

My stomach flips over. This kid's going to find my Mariela? I look at Josh and he shakes his head at me, like he's in total shock. I shoot him a look that says, "I'm just as shocked as you are, man."

"Awesome, Eric," Sarah says. "Thank you. And there's one more woman, too. I don't know her first name—but her maiden name was Westbrook."

Holy shit. Josh and I exchange a look of astonishment. Miss Westbrook, too? What the fuck is Sarah doing?

"Miss Westbrook was a teacher in Seattle in probably 1992 and then she married a guy in the Navy named Santorini who was stationed in San Diego."

"What do these two women have to do with The Club?" Eric asks.

"Absolutely nothing," Sarah says. She glances at me with sparkling eyes. "This would be a personal favor to me. I don't have the resources to find these ladies by myself without having their full names, but I think you can do it."

Eric shrugs like that's an obvious statement. He's the FBI, after all. "Shouldn't be a problem." He smiles at her.

"Thank you. I'm gonna need this information as soon as possible, please."

"I'll do my best."

My entire body tingles with anxiety and excitement and a whole bunch of other emotions I can't pin down. What's Sarah planning? I look at Josh again and he's looking at me like I'm an alien, clearly shocked as hell I've told Sarah about Mariela and Miss Westbrook.

"Oh," Sarah says. "I almost forgot. The second woman, Westbrook Santorini, has a son named Jonas—and he's probably . . . " She looks up at the ceiling, calculating. "About seventeen years old by now. Maybe that'll help you somehow."

My heart skips a beat. Holy shit. *Jonas Santorini.* I never thought about Miss Westbrook's baby actually *existing*, and definitely not as a *teenager.* To me, he's always been a baby bump, frozen in time.

"Got it," Eric says, making a note on his pad.

"What's the name of the school where Miss Westbrook worked in Seattle, Jonas?" Sarah asks. "That might be helpful for Eric to know for his search."

My cheeks feel hot. I open my mouth but nothing comes out.

"St. Francis Academy," Josh says.

I look at Josh and he smiles broadly at me. Just like old times.

Sarah puts her arm around my back and squeezes me.

"Okay. I'll do my best," Eric says.

"Thank you," Sarah says.

"Shouldn't be too hard." Eric pushes his pad aside, brimming with excitement. "Okay. I think I've got everything I need." He's trying to play it cool, but he's geeking out. "Now, just to be clear, you're promising to give us full access to everything, right? No limitations? No exceptions? Their operating systems, membership lists, voicemails, code—and the money, too?"

Everyone looks at Henn. He's the only one in this room who knows if we can deliver on a promise that big.

"Yep," Henn says. "Everything."

"But we'll only hand it over to senior level reps from the FBI, CIA and Secret Service. And I want you there, too, Eric—tell your boss we said your presence is a non-negotiable condition of the deal. Tell her I'll pay your way to D.C. if need be, but you've got to be there."

Eric's face lights up. I imagine he hasn't been involved in too many high-powered meetings in his nascent career.

"Okay," Agent Eric says, steeling himself for battle. "I'll go talk to my boss right now. I'll give you guys a call later." He nods at Kat, reassuring her in particular. "I promise I'll give it my all."

"I know you will, Eric," Kat purrs. "I have full faith in you."

Chapter 38

Sarah

"Henn, pass the ketchup," Josh says.

The five of us are eating like gluttons in the Americana restaurant in our hotel. It's burgers, fries, and beers all around—even Jonas is eating a bacon cheeseburger and French fries, two things I've never seen him eat—and we're enthusiastically rehashing our meeting with Special Agent Eric like we're dissecting every play of a Seahawks' game. The general consensus, of course, is that Kat was our quarterback today—and she crushed it.

Henn passes the ketchup to Josh, but he's looking at Kat. "Who's the fucking genius now?" Henn says. "Damn, girl." He fist bumps her.

Kat beams.

"To Kat," I say, raising my beer. All three guys hold up their beers in Kat's honor, too. "You're the reason Eric started taking us seriously," I say. "No doubt about it."

"Aw, thanks," Kat says. "But it was definitely a team effort."

We all raise our glasses again and drink to "the team."

"So how are we gonna get the money, Henn?" Josh asks. "I thought you said most of those accounts are set up for in-person transfer only."

"They are," Henn says. "Which, obviously, means we're going to transfer the money in-person."

We're all silent, not catching his meaning.

Henn looks pointedly at Kat. "Hello, Oksana Belenko."

Kat looks like Henn just said she's been selected to sing the national anthem at the Super Bowl.

"You'll be fine," Henn says. "I'll set you up with a passport and a driver's license—"

"Oh, I don't know," Kat says, sputtering. "I don't know if I can—"

"You *can*," Henn says soothingly. "Today proved that. Indubitably." He smiles broadly. "Don't worry, Kitty Kat." He touches the top of her hand. "I'll hack into each account and shave thirty years off Oksana's age—they won't even question you're her for a second. And then I'll walk into each and every bank with you, right by your side." Henn smiles at Kat reassuringly. Oh, that boy absolutely adores her.

"But will Kat be safe?" I ask.

"I'll make sure of it," Henn says.

"So will I," Josh adds.

This is crazy. Can we really ask Kat to do this? Why are Henn and Josh acting like this is a reasonable request? I look at Jonas, expecting him to be as anxious as I am about all this, but he's nodding emphatically. Have they all gone mad?

A waitress walks by and Kat flags her. "Double Patron shots all around, please." When the waitress leaves, Kat lets out a long exhale. "Okay, I'll do it."

"Kat, are you sure?" I ask. "You don't have to do this."

"Yes, I do. This ain't no casino heist, fellas—and very pretty lady." She winks at me. "This is about taking these guys down so they can't hurt you ever again, Sarah. It's a no-brainer."

Everyone besides me raises a beer in salute to Kat. I'm too freaked out to celebrate. I know all too well the kind of criminals we're dealing with here.

"We'll create an offshore account," Jonas says, forging right ahead. "And funnel everything into it at the last possible moment."

"*Two* offshore accounts," Josh interjects. "I think we're gonna have to take a little finder's fee on the deal—don't you think, bro? Maybe one percent?"

"Fuck yeah," Jonas says. "Great idea. Yeah, five and a half mill sounds about right for our commission. Kat and Henn, you guys will each get a cool mill off the top. You've both earned it."

Kat and Henn look at each other, in total shock.

"Are you *serious*?" Kat squeals. "You're gonna give me a *million* dollars?"

"You deserve it."

Kat squeals again. She stands and hugs Jonas across the table and kisses his cheek in sheer elation like she's won the Miss America pageant. And then she grabs me and kisses me hard on the lips, laughing. She moves on to Josh, obviously intending to plant a chaste kiss on his cheek, but he swoops in and kisses her on the lips. Holy hell, that's quite a kiss—wowza—and Kat's responding like her panties are melting. Good Lord, those two are sizzling hot. I guess that answers the question of whether Kat and Josh are sleeping together.

Henn looks away from their make-out session, crestfallen.

When Kat and Josh finally disengage, Josh says, "I feel like I've been waiting a lifetime to do that."

"Why the hell did you wait so long, Playboy?" Kat breathes, her face blazing.

Wait. *What?* That was their *first* kiss?

Josh chuckles. "Gee, I wonder why."

"So does this mean you're finally gonna tell me?" Kat whispers.

Josh nods. Oh my gosh, his cheeks are on fire.

What the hell are these two talking about? Color me curious.

Kat sits back down, grinning devilishly, but when she sees Henn's face across the table, her face falls. "Oh, Henny. I'm sorry."

Henn shakes his head. "No, it's great. You're both the best." He swallows hard. "Indubitably." He tries to smile.

Josh looks apologetic. "Hey, Henn—"

"No, really." He waves Josh away. "I'm good."

But he's not good. Not at all. Aw, poor Henn.

Kat maneuvers around the table and grabs Henn's shoulders. "You're the best." She kisses him softly on the cheek. "I'm proud to call you my friend."

That's probably no consolation to the poor boy, but it will have to do.

The waitress arrives with the tequila Kat ordered and we all raise our drinks in the air.

"To the Party Girl with a Heart of Gold and the Hacker," I say. "A couple of *mill-ion-aires.*"

"Here, here," Josh adds, his eyes blazing at Kat, and we all knock back our shots.

"Yeah, well, let's not put the cart before the horse," Kat says. "There's still the little matter of actually getting the money."

"Oh, we'll get it—don't you worry," Henn says, trying to imitate light-heartedness. The expression on his face is killing me right now. I guess a million bucks isn't enough to stave off a broken heart.

"What about you, Jonas?" I ask, trying to deflect attention from poor Henn. "They owe you money, too."

"Fuck yeah, they do. Those fuckers took that two-fifty I gave to you—and I'm gonna get it back for you—plus I want the one-eighty I paid them to convince them I'm a fucking idiot."

"Well, plus the two-fifty in membership fees you paid in the first place," I add.

"Nah, I don't deserve that two-fifty back," Jonas says. "I shouldn't get a refund for being a dumbshit."

"Jonas, they took your money under false pretenses," I say.

"No, they didn't." He shrugs. "Regardless, it was my choice to join that place for a fucking *year*. Who *does* that?" He glances over at Josh and half-smiles. "And, anyway, it turned out to be the best money I've ever spent." He winks at me and I smile from ear to ear. I love it when he says that. "All I want is the money they legitimately stole from me, a payday for Kat and Henn, and then the rest of the pot is all yours, Sarah Cruz," he says.

"What?" I blurt.

"Those fuckers almost killed you, baby—they owe you a shitload more than three million bucks. Plus, you've been our fearless George Clooney through all this—you deserve it."

Everyone at the table agrees enthusiastically.

"No, I can't—"

"Sure you can," Josh says.

"Absolutely," Kat adds.

"But what about you, Josh? Don't you want some of the money?" I ask.

Josh laughs. "Hell no."

"But you've been helping us from minute one—"

"Of course, I have. I wouldn't have it any other way." He smiles at Jonas.

I exhale. Wow. Three million dollars? It's tempting, I admit, but it's too much. Don't get me wrong—I'm no saint—if Kat and Henn are willing to take a million bucks out of the pot, then so am I. But *three* million? No. With a million bucks, I'd be able to do everything I've ever dreamed about—buy my mom a house, pay for all my schooling (because, clearly, that scholarship's a pipe dream at this point), maybe put a little money away for the uncertainties of life. But, other than that, I don't need a thing. I'll always be able to take care of myself with my law degree, one way or another. I've got a beautiful place to live with Jonas for the foreseeable future. And if I want to travel, anywhere in the whole wide world, my hunky-monkey boyfriend's already told me I can just name it. What more do I need than all that?

I suppose, since Jonas isn't the marrying kind, I should in theory put money away for the allegedly inevitable day when things go to hell in a handbasket between us and I've got no one in this world to rely on but myself—but the thing is I know that day will never come. For Pete's sake, the man permanently declared his love for me on his skin. He's promised me forever as clearly as he knows how—and I believe him. Yes, even if it proves I'm hopelessly brainwashed by

Lifetime and Hallmark and Disney, I believe my sweet Jonas with all my heart.

"Just don't make a decision about the money yet," Jonas says, gently rubbing my thigh. "Think about it for a little while."

I nod. "Okay, I'll think about it." And, in fact, even as I sit here, I already have a pretty good idea of how to put that money to good use. "So, Henn, how quickly do you think you can—"

I'm interrupted by the arrival of a figure at the edge of our table.

Holy crappola. Oh my God. Holy shitballs. No effing way. This can't be happening. No, no, no. *It's Max.*

Chapter 39

Jonas

What the fuck is Max doing here?

Sarah's body jolts next to me in the restaurant booth like she's been zapped by a Taser gun.

Shit. Did he see us go to the FBI today? Holy fuck. No, there's no fucking way. I made us jump through ridiculous hoops to ensure we weren't followed and I'm one hundred percent sure it worked. Max must have a goon stationed in the hotel who called him when we finally turned up again.

"What do you want?" I ask, putting my arm around Sarah. Wow, she's noticeably trembling.

"Hello, Mr. Faraday," Max says. "Sarah." He glances at the rest of the table but doesn't acknowledge anyone but Sarah and me. "I hope you're still enjoying your stay here in Las Vegas?"

"What the fuck do you want?" I ask.

Sarah squeezes my thigh, probably signaling me to tread carefully. But this fucker thinks I'm a possessive asshole, right? Which I am, actually, so fuck him.

"I had some business in the hotel—what a coincidence to run into you," Max says.

I clench my jaw and glare at him. It's taking all of my self-control not to leap up, grab a fistful of his fucking slick-backed hair, and pummel his smug face. This fucker spilled my baby's sacred blood onto a bathroom floor and left her for dead. This cock-sucking motherfucking fucker of an asshole haunts my baby's fucking nightmares almost every night. I want to rip his head off. I want to slit his throat and watch the lifeblood spill out of him and onto the floor. *I want him fucking dead.*

Sarah can read my thoughts, obviously, because she puts her arm across my body, as if she's holding me at bay. "Hi, Max," she says, her voice quavering. "Yeah, that's one helluva coincidence.

Hey, everybody, this is Max—a friend of mine. These are some friends of Jonas' who met us in Vegas to party—Jonas' brother Josh, Josh's girlfriend Kayley, and his roommate from college, Scott."

Max nods absently at everyone. "I just need to steal you for a couple minutes, Sarah." He puts his hand out like he actually expects her to take it.

"No," I say, crushing her into me. I'm a heartbeat away from grabbing a knife off the table and slashing this motherfucker's fucking throat.

Max snarls at me.

"Hey, guys," Sarah says to Josh, Kat and Henn. "Could you all excuse us for a few minutes?"

They all look at each other, at a loss.

"Um," Josh says, looking at me for a signal.

I nod.

"Sure," Josh says. "Come on, Kayley. Scott. Let's go roll some dice." They leave, looking back at us warily as they do.

Max takes one of the newly vacated seats at the table and my heart leaps into my throat. I could kill this fucker right now. I could reach across the table, grab his fucking head in both my hands and twist with all my might. But, fuck me, I can't. For Sarah's sake—for the sake of the mission—for the sake of the forest and not the trees—for the sake of never having to look over our shoulders again—I've got to control my urges. I clench my jaw like an epileptic on the verge of a seizure.

"This will only take a few minutes," Max says evenly. "Why don't you do a little gambling, Mr. Faraday?"

I lean forward. "Fuck you," I say. "Motherfucker."

Max narrows his eyes.

"I paid you eighty thousand bucks to *own* this woman every second of every day for the next month. And I do—every inch of her, inside and out—every single hair on her beautiful head. So fuck you."

Max smirks and sits back, blatantly surprised.

Sarah leans into me, shaking like a leaf.

"For the next month, this woman is *mine*, motherfucker. I don't want you calling her. I don't want you texting her. I don't want you 'stopping by our table' by so-called 'coincidence' to talk to her. I don't even want you *looking* at her." I wouldn't be surprised if actual steam were shooting out my ears right now. "She's *mine.*"

Max squints and grinds his teeth together. After a moment, he stands, staring at Sarah despite my explicit instructions. "Enjoy your month, Sarah."

"Are you fucking deaf, motherfucker? Don't talk to her. Don't fucking look at her," I growl. "I paid eighty thousand bucks to be the only man who enjoys those sublime pleasures."

Max ignores me and continues staring at Sarah. "I'll expect to see you in my office the minute your month is up. That very day."

"Of course," she says. "I look forward to it."

I whip my head to look at her, about to blow a fucking gasket.

Sarah squeezes my thigh under the table again. "When our month is up, Jonas, I'm gonna have to work again," she says, her entire body quivering against mine. "I've got tuition to pay, my mom's medical bills, my dad's house payment. You know that."

Oh, Sarah. My Magnificent Sarah. I don't know how she always manages to keep her head in the game, even when she's obviously scared to death. "We'll chat about all that later," I say. I glare at Max. "Why are you still here?" I wave at him condescendingly. "Time to shoo, motherfucker."

Max trembles with rage. "I'll look forward to seeing you in a month, Sarah." He shoots daggers at me. "Mr. Faraday, I'd recommend you take care whom you call a *motherfucker*." He clenches his jaw. It's clear he wants to kill me as much I want to kill him. "That's a strong word."

"Mo-ther-fuck-er," I say, drawing out the word. "Yeah, I see what you mean. That *is* a strong word, motherfucker." I lean forward and glare at him. "And so is asshole. And douchebag. Shithead. Asshat." Oh fuck, I want to kill this motherfucker so bad. "*Cock-suck-er*. The list goes on and on, *mo-ther-fuck-er*."

Max shakes his head slowly. "Watch yourself, Mr. Faraday."

"Thanks. I'll be sure to do that, *motherfucker*."

Max stands. He looks at Sarah for a brief moment, his nostrils flaring, and then he turns on his heel and exits the restaurant in a blaze of white-hot fury.

The minute he's gone, Sarah's entire body begins twitching next to me in the booth. I take her face in my hands and she shakes beneath my palms.

"Are you okay, baby?"

She nods and swallows hard.

"You're safe now, baby—my precious baby." I pull her into me. "He's gone."

"Jonas," she breathes, quivering violently against my chest.

"He's gone. You're safe." I stroke her hair—but she continues trembling. Jesus. Her entire body is jolting against me like a fish on a line.

"Jonas," she says again.

"I'm right here." I pull back from her and look into her big brown eyes.

"Jonas." Her voice is strained.

Oh my God, she's a wreck. "Baby, you're okay." I kiss her gently.

"Jonas, please." She sounds like she's got hypothermia. She's practically stuttering.

"I'm listening, baby. What is it? Tell me."

She closes her eyes and tilts her face up to mine. "Take me back up to the suite, Jonas." Her cheeks flush. "Take me up to the suite and fuck my brains clean out of my head."

Chapter 40
Sarah

In addition to Special Agent Eric and his boss from Las Vegas, there are no less than fifteen people in dark suits crowded into this conference room with Jonas and me at FBI headquarters in Washington D.C., all of them with hard eyes and humorless expressions, variously identified as representing the FBI, CIA, Secret Service, DEA, ATF, Department of Justice, and, holy hell, the Department of Defense, too. And, in addition to that whole crowd, there are three scary looking dudes who curtly declined to identify themselves at the outset of the meeting four hours ago and haven't spoken since.

Special Agent Eric, who looks like a kindergartner on take-your-kid-to-work-day amongst this room full of seasoned agents, called us yesterday and told us to get our butts to Washington on the next plane, and that's exactly what we did. According to Eric, my report ignited a firestorm of attention within the FBI, beginning with his boss in Las Vegas and quickly ascending up the chain of command to the highest power-players in Washington D.C.

It seems when two wealthy and respected business moguls (who don't appear on a single government watch list) claim the U.S. Secretary of Defense is unwittingly involved in a billion-dollar crime syndicate that supplies money and weapons to aid Russian aggression—and when those two business moguls are willing to sacrifice their own reputations and maybe even incriminate themselves by coming forward—and when they outline their allegations in a rock-solid fifty-page report with a detailed exhibit log and promise to turn over an easy half-billion to back up their claims, the FBI takes fucking notice. And—holy crappola—so do lots of other scary looking people with fancy badges, too.

It's just Jonas and me sitting here on the proverbial hot seat—Henn, Josh, and Kat (a.k.a. "Oksana Belenko") stayed behind in Las Vegas to make the money transfers at our signal. To say I've been crapping my pants for the past four hours in this conference room would be the understatement of the year. I've tried to sound calm and collected, of course, but I think I've mostly come across as a total and complete spazzoid.

Jonas, on the other hand, has been as cool as a cucumber throughout the whole meeting (other than the few times his knee has jiggled under the table). Jonas been charming. Disarming. Forthcoming. Honest. I'm learning a lot about quiet confidence watching him. He's personable without bending over backwards to make people like him—and as a result, they obviously *respect* him. Watching Jonas handle the room like a boss for the past four hours has made it plain to me why he's been so successful in the business world.

Before walking into this room today, Jonas and I agreed we'd be completely honest at all times, no matter what—and we've stuck with our plan, even when our answers to questions have embarrassed or possibly even incriminated us. And I think we made the right call. Because although the meeting started out feeling distinctly adversarial, I'm beginning to feel like all these hardass people in dark suits actually believe every word we say.

My palms are sweaty. I wipe them on my skirt.

"Who else knows about this?" the Department of Defense guy asks, holding up my report. "Anyone at all besides you two and your three team members?" He looks at his notes. "Katherine Morgan, Josh Faraday, and Peter Hennessey?"

"No one at all besides us five has seen the report or knows anything about its contents," Jonas says, his voice strong and firm. "We sent a few isolated voicemails to a certified Ukrainian translator—but with no context or identifying information whatsoever."

"You're sure? No one else besides you five knows anything about this?" the Defense guy asks, scrutinizing Jonas' face.

I glance at one of the CIA guys, the one who seems most capable of chopping us up and stuffing us into the trunk of his car—and he's hanging on Jonas' every word.

"No one," Jonas says. "It turns out Sarah's unwittingly been employed by a large-scale prostitution ring—not exactly résumé fodder for an aspiring lawyer—and I unwittingly paid a quarter of a million bucks to a prostitution ring to buy unlimited sex for a year." He looks at me apologetically and I smile at him. "And if that weren't enough for either of us to prefer discretion here, it turns out we're dealing with drug and weapons traffickers whose higher agenda is aiding Russian imperialism. If that's not motivation to keep our report on a need-to-know basis, I don't know what is."

The Department of Justice guy snickers and a couple other seemingly senior guys smirk. Good sign.

"We know we're up to our eyeballs in this shit, excuse my language. Believe me, we're not eager to spread the word about any of this."

That seems to satisfy the Department of Defense guy, as well as everyone else in the room.

"As you can understand, my only concern is protecting this woman right here," Jonas says, touching my arm. "We aren't here to expose anyone, including ourselves—and would prefer not to, given our personal involvement. We don't care how you want to go about this, how you want to spin it, what information you might choose to disseminate or not. It's your strategy—your show—and you won't hear a peep from us on any of it. We're only here to give you the information, help in any way we can, and then get the hell out of your way."

That was well said. And not a single f-bomb in the whole speech, too. I guess Jonas is Polite Jonas today.

"At the end of the day, all I care about is fucking them up the ass so hard they can't even fucking hobble when we're done with them," Jonas adds, grabbing my hand.

So much for no f-bombs.

"Ditto," I say. "I have no interest in humiliating or exposing anyone." I look pointedly at the Department of Defense guy, trying to convey I'm talking about his boss, the Secretary of Defense. It must have crossed his mind we could be planning to blackmail his boss. "And also ditto on that whole f-bomb-laden last part." I smile sheepishly. I'm freaking out. I might be Orgasma the All-Powerful behind closed doors with Jonas, but being a superhero in a room like this is seriously testing my self-confidence.

All the big wigs in the room look around, gauging each other's reactions.

"We're the good guys," I say earnestly, looking at all of them. "We're not here to harm anyone—we're here to do the right thing. I just want to keep the bad guys from hurting me or anyone else again." My voice wobbles at that last part and Jonas puts a protective arm around me.

The most senior CIA guy is looking at me like he believes me. And so are the silver-haired Secret Service guy and the FBI woman who looks like she could eat me for breakfast. Oh my God, they *all* believe us. I know they do.

The bigwig FBI agent exchanges a particularly long look with the Department of Defense guy. “And you’ll turn everything over to us?” he says.

“Yes,” Jonas says. “Everything.”

Everyone nods, satisfied.

“Now, with respect to the money,” Jonas says. “My team is in Vegas, ready to make the transfers into an offshore account. I just have to give them the word.” He holds up his phone. “I got a text from my guy five minutes ago, confirming all the money’s still in place and they’re ready to move. But time is of the essence, obviously—Belenko could transfer every dime out of the country any time.”

Jonas’ knee starts jiggling under the table. I put my hand on his thigh and it stops.

The bigwig FBI boss motions to the Las Vegas FBI woman, and they confer quietly for a solid three minutes, shielding their mouths with their hands to prevent the rest of us from reading their lips. Everyone else in the room sits patiently.

“Okay,” Mr. FBI guy finally says, pulling back from his colleague.

I’m not sure what that means. Okay what? There’s an awkward pause.

Jonas fills the silence. “We do have a few small conditions before we transfer the funds to you,” he says flatly.

There’s a collective sigh of wariness throughout the room.

The FBI ringleader glares at Jonas, blatantly mistrustful. If this were a cartoon, he’d be saying, “Dangnabbit!” right now.

Jonas isn’t daunted at all. “I want immunity for everyone on my team regarding our various affiliations with The Club, and also with respect to our investigation.”

Mr. FBI nods. It’s not clear if he’s agreeing to this condition or simply acknowledging the request has been made.

“We’ll help you guys with anything and everything you need from us, answer any and all questions, give you whatever sworn statements you need to aid your investigation. I’ll pay my hacker to fly out here and help you assimilate everything we hand off to you, and I’ll make sure he assists you guys with your investigation, too, if you think you need him. But our five names will be completely expunged from all records. We were never involved with The Club or this investigation in any way. Accordingly, the files we’ll be handing-off to you will not contain any reference to Sarah, my brother, or myself. We’ve wiped the files clean of all such references.” He puts his hand on my thigh under the table.

The main CIA guy and the Department of Defense guy share a glance.

"But believe me, even without mention of us in the records, you'll have everything you need to nail them six ways from Sunday," Jonas says.

The FBI guy is about to speak, but the Defense guy cuts him off.

"Your computer guy altered the files you'd be handing off to us?" he asks.

"Correct. To delete record of Sarah's employment and my and my brother's Club activities."

Mr. Defense guy purses his lips. "Do you still have access to the unredacted data?"

Jonas hesitates, apparently considering his answer. "Yes," he finally says, honestly. I'm glad he answered truthfully.

"Does anyone but you have access to that original data?"

"No."

Defense guy nods. "And you'll provide us with your hacker's services, without limitation?"

"Of course. For as long as you want him."

Defense guy looks happy to hear that. Maybe Defense guy is thinking about erasing a certain someone else's name from all the records, too—wink, wink.

"I'll make sure Peter Hennessey's available to assist you. Trust me, you'll be thrilled to have him on your team—he loves wearing a white hat." Jonas smirks.

There's a long pause, as several sub-groups from different agencies confer quietly.

"We agree to all your conditions," Mr. Defense guy says flatly, without conferring with anyone.

The bigwig FBI guy looks peeved, but he doesn't contradict the Department of Defense guy.

"All right," Mr. FBI says, a brief scowl flickering across his face. "Any other *conditions,* Mr. Faraday?"

"Yes."

Mr. FBI guy bristles. Obviously, that wasn't what he was expecting to hear.

"I'll instruct my team to transfer all but one percent of The Club's funds into an offshore account for your exclusive access," Jonas says. "You'll be enabled to unilaterally change passwords and take immediate and sole custody of the funds."

"And what about the remaining one percent you don't plan on transferring to us?" Mr. FBI guy asks.

"Our finder's fee," Jonas replies. "Five and a half million and change."

Mr. FBI guy walks over to the corner of the room to confer with one of the Department of Justice guys in the back for a moment. "That's a reasonable finder's fee," he says, returning to his chair. "Capped at one percent of whatever funds you ultimately transfer to us."

"There will be several beneficiaries who'll share in that one percent fund," Jonas says. "And I want all of them to partake in their money without taxation—completely tax-free."

FBI guy glances across the room at Department of Justice guy. "No one in this room has jurisdiction regarding individual tax implications on receipts of funds," Mr. FBI guy says evenly.

"But I'm confident *someone* in this room can make it happen, just this once, since it's a non-negotiable condition here," Jonas says.

Indubitably, I think.

Bigwig FBI guy looks at the Department of Justice guy again and gets a nod. CIA guy walks across the room and leans in for a pow-wow with FBI guy.

"As long as you tell us *today* who's going to share in that money, and in what amounts, we will agree to the tax-free status of any amounts distributed from that fund," FBI guy finally says. He sounds annoyed. "But after we cut this deal with you today, it's final. No new names."

"No problem," Jonas says. "I can identify all beneficiaries right now. Jonas Faraday at five hundred thousand, Peter Hennessey at a million, and Katherine Morgan at a million—for an aggregate total of two and a half million—and the balance of the pot, approximately three million and change, will go to Miss Sarah Cruz."

"No, actually," I pipe in, "that's not accurate."

Jonas gapes at me, blindsided.

I've been thinking about the three-million-dollar thing quite a bit since Jonas first suggested it to me, and I'm certain I've got a better way to distribute that money than handing it all to me. "The team members Jonas just identified, including myself, will share an aggregate pot of three and a half million and change. *One* million and change, not three, will go to me. The remaining two million dollars flat will be distributed in equal shares to certain beneficiaries who aren't on our team."

Jonas is dumbfounded.

"In order to maintain the strictest levels of confidentiality about this whole situation, I think the two million dollars should be distributed by the U.S. Government to these beneficiaries instead of by us. Are you amenable to that?"

Mr. FBI guy is noncommittal. "It depends. Let's hear it."

Jonas looks totally confused.

"Okay. The first recipient is Mariela Rafaela León de Guajardo, Jonas' former nanny, currently living in Venezuela with her husband and three teenage children."

Jonas' face turns bright red. He looks down at the table.

"Special Agent Sheffield has tracked down Mariela's contact information. Will you be so kind as to provide that to everyone, Agent Sheffield?"

Eric's face lights up at the mention of his name. "Yes."

"Mariela was deported to Venezuela in 1994. From what I can see, it looks like Jonas' father, Joseph Faraday, pulled some strings with friends in high places to make that happen."

I look at Jonas. He's biting his lip, staring at the table, apparently trying to contain himself.

"I was thinking you might characterize Mariela's payment as some sort of compensation relating to her deportment."

"She'll get her money," the FBI guy says curtly, taking notes. "How the payment will be characterized, I make no promises."

"Okay, that's great. Thank you. The second beneficiary is Mrs. Renee Westbrook Santorini—mother of two and widow of Navy SEAL Robert Santorini."

Jonas shakes his head at me—but it's a "you never cease to amaze me" gesture, not a chastisement.

"Special Agent Sheffield has Renee Santorini's contact information, as well."

Eric nods. He's trying to look serious and professional, I can tell, but he looks like a kid blowing out his birthday candles.

"Mrs. Santorini was Jonas' grade-school teacher. Her deceased husband was Navy SEAL Robert Santorini, based in San Diego and killed in action in 1999. I was thinking you could characterize Renee Santorini's money as something connected to her deceased husband's naval service?"

Mr. FBI guy nods. "I'm sure we can do something along those lines."

I'm on a roll. "Georgia Marianne Walker of Seattle."

Jonas' face contorts with emotion. He clears his throat and looks down again.

"I'm not sure how you should characterize her payment. She's a single mother, a recent cancer survivor, works for the U.S. Postal Service." I pause, thinking. "I don't know what—"

"I think Ms. Walker is about to receive an inheritance as the only surviving kin of a third cousin removed she's never heard of," Mr. Bigwig FBI says, suppressing a smile.

I grin. "Perfect. Thank you."

"Okay, anyone else?" FBI man says, looking up from his notepad. He's noticeably warmed to me during this exchange. I guess he's decided he's not too annoyed with me for making these requests, after all.

"Nope, that's it," I say, smiling at my new best friend. "Mariela, Renee, and Georgia will each share equally in two million."

"No, wait," Jonas says firmly, and my stomach drops into my toes. Have I misread his reaction to all this? Is he upset with me?

"There's one more recipient," Jonas says. "Four beneficiaries will make it an even five hundred thousand per person—and that's a nice round number."

Oh, thank God. He's on board. But who's his fourth? I hold my breath.

"Gloria Cruz of Seattle," Jonas says.

I put my hand over my mouth.

Jonas flashes me the briefest of smiles, but then he's quickly all business again.

Oh, my sweet Jonas. He's already donated a ridiculous amount of money to my mom's charity—and now he wants to give her a piece of this pie, too? This is a huge kindness to my mother, but it's also a windfall for me, seeing as how I'd planned to use half my finder's fee money to buy my mom a house. I beam at Jonas and he plants a soft kiss on my cheek.

"Thank you," I whisper.

He smiles at me warmly but then flashes hard eyes at Mr. FBI guy.

"Gloria Cruz runs a nonprofit for abused women, but we want the money to go to her personally, tax-free. You'll have to figure out a reason for her windfall, too."

"We'll figure something out," Mr. FBI guy says. "Is that everyone?" He looks down at his notes. "Mariela, Renee, Georgia, and Gloria. Five hundred thousand each, tax-free, assuming you hand over all the data as promised and successfully transfer the full half-billion."

"Yes, that's everyone," Jonas says. "And we will."

"Any other conditions?" Mr. FBI guy asks, but his tone makes it clear the answer had better be no.

"That's it," I say, exhaling with relief, but Jonas speaks over me at the same time.

"Yeah, one more thing," Jonas says.

More? What more? Holy crap. Whatever it is, he's clearly pushing our luck.

Several of the more uptight guys in the room moan with exasperation and two guys share a "what an asshole" glance.

What the hell is Jonas talking about?

Jonas pauses. "But I'll reveal our final condition to the highest-ranking members in the room only," he says flatly.

What the hell is he talking about?

"This last demand is on a strictly need-to-know basis."

Everyone looks around, not knowing what to do. Stay? Go? Tell him to fuck off? After a bit of low murmuring and hushed conferring, several underlings stand and leave the room, including poor Eric, who looks none too happy about it.

As Eric walks past Jonas toward the door, he shoots him a long, pleading look, clearly hoping Jonas will exempt him from dismissal. But Jonas does no such thing.

I glare at Jonas with my arms crossed over my chest, tapping my toe under the table. Man, oh man, I can't wait to hear this.

After the door has closed behind the departed underlings, including poor Special Agent Eric, Jonas leans into me, his face an inch from mine. "Will you excuse us, too, baby?" he asks softly. He looks like he's asked me if I'd like one lump or two at teatime.

My jaw drops.

A low-frequency rumble erupts throughout the remaining crowd. Every man in this room just flinched with anxiety on Jonas' behalf—they know they're looking at a dead man.

"There's something I prefer to say to these guys out of your presence," Jonas adds politely.

I blink quickly. Did Jonas just say he *prefers* to say something to all these nice gentlemen (and one lady) *outside* of my presence? I touch my cheeks to prevent my head from spinning wildly on my neck in three-sixties. Jonas *prefers* to say something outside of my presence, does he? Well, what if I *prefer* to hear whatever the *fuck* my fucking boyfriend plans to say to these fucking men (and one woman) about *my* fucking life? After all, *I'm* the one with fucking scars on my body. *I'm* the one who almost bled to death in that fucking bathroom. *I'm* the one looking over my shoulder everywhere I go and waking up in a cold sweat almost every fucking night. And *I'm* the one they'll come after if this whole fucking strategy blows up in our faces.

I open my mouth to protest, but Jonas beats me to the punch.

"Remember that promise I wouldn't make to you?" His eyes are granite. "When I wouldn't say, 'I promise to always tell you everything?'"

I nod. Yes, of course, I remember that conversation. It pissed me off.

"This is why." He clenches his jaw. "Right now is exactly the reason I wouldn't make that promise to you."

A shiver runs down my spine. Jonas anticipated this exact moment?

Jonas' gaze is firm.

Someone in the room coughs. I'm not sure if the guy has a tickle in his throat or if he's just too damned uncomfortable at the exchange he's witnessing to contain himself—but either way, my face flushes. I look around. Well, this is awkward. Everyone in the room is waiting on me to make a decision—will I stay or will I go? I can feel them placing mental bets on whether I'm going to burst into tears, shriek like a banshee, or flip the goddamned table in the next five seconds.

I look at Jonas. His eyes are fierce. Unmovable. He's a savage beast. But he's also my sweet Jonas—the man who loves me like no one ever has. The man I love without condition or reservation. The man who'd lay down his life for me without a moment's hesitation. He's the man I trust with my life.

I sigh. If my sweet Jonas needs to say something out of my presence to protect me, if that's what it's going to take for him to do whatever he thinks needs to be done, then so be it. I'll just have to take yet another leap of faith.

I lean in and kiss him on the mouth. I'm not instigating a make-out session with this brief kiss—I'm demonstrating to everyone in the room, including Jonas, that, yes, I trust this man unconditionally. I pull back from our kiss and lean my forehead against his. He touches my cheek. After a brief moment, I look around the room, defiant. There'll be no crying, shrieking or table-flipping today, fellas (and one badass-looking lady).

"Gentlemen," I say, standing. "And lady." She grins at the acknowledgment. "I'm extremely grateful for all your time and attention today. Thank you. Please know that, whatever Jonas is about to say to you, whatever it is, I'm one hundred percent on board."

Chapter 41

Sarah

I'd wanted so much to see the Lincoln Memorial, the Capitol building, the Washington Monument, the Smithsonian, and the Vietnam Veterans' Memorial during our stay in D.C., a place I've wanted to visit my whole life, but it wasn't meant to be. After yesterday's marathon meeting with "the feds" (the term I prefer to use because it sounds so damned cool), Jonas and I were escorted to our hotel—yes, *escorted*—by two men wearing suits and guns and earpieces—yes, *earpieces*—and deposited into our suite and told in no uncertain terms to stay put.

And those two armed escorts (and, eventually, their two replacements) have remained outside our hotel suite ever since, for close to twenty hours. It's not clear if those nice officers have been assigned to guard our door to keep the bad guys *out* or to keep the good guys *in*—but either way, it's pretty darned clear we're not free to leave our room.

So, of course, Jonas and I have made the most of the situation.

Jonas belly laughs and one of the strawberries I've positioned on his stomach rolls off his naked body and onto the bed.

"Oh jeez," I say, quickly replacing the fallen berry. "Stay still." I continue building my strawberry pyramid with utmost care, squinting and biting my lip with concentration as I do.

Jonas laughs again and yet another strawberry rolls onto the white sheet beneath us.

"Jonas P. Faraday," I scold him. "Control yourself. This is serious effing business, man." I take a big bite of one of my building blocks.

He laughs again.

"A little respect, please. I'm building an edifice of epic importance here." I carefully replace the latest errant strawberry, lodging it into a deep groove in Jonas' abs. "I've got to get my foundation right or the whole structure will fail."

"You're *engineering* a strawberry pyramid?" Jonas asks, laughing uproariously—and another strawberry goes ker-plop at his sudden movement.

"Oh my God," I bellow. "You are the worst human strawberry shortcake ever."

Jonas squeals with laughter. I've never heard him laugh quite like this. He sounds like a toddler being tickled. "Sorry," he chokes out.

I replace the latest rogue strawberry and continue building my masterpiece. "Now, hold still, for the love of God," I command. "Or you'll ruin *everything*."

He bursts out laughing again but quickly composes himself at my icy glare. "Yes, Mistress," he says, trying his best to sound submissive—but when I grab the whipped cream canister off the nightstand, eager to top off my teetering creation with a towering *coup de grace*, he guffaws before I've even creamed him.

Oh my gosh, his laughter is divine. It's the sound of pure, uninhibited silliness—absolute and complete abandon—the sound of joy. And it sends me into fits of giggles, too. I put the whipped cream canister back on the nightstand, laughing hysterically, and begin picking the strawberries off him, one by one, tossing them into the nearby champagne bucket as I go.

"I can't do it, " I say, giggling. "You're hopeless."

"Oh no, don't say that, Mistress. Give me another chance. Have mercy on me." He puts his hands behind his head on the pillow and gazes up at me. "There's no such thing as hopelessness, remember?"

I don't know what he's referring to—but I sure love the way his biceps bulge when he bends his arms like that. I take a big bite of another strawberry.

"Oh come on, My Beautiful Intake Agent," he says, smiling up at me. "'We must accept infinite disappointment, but never lose infinite hope.' A really smart intake agent with a delectable ass once recited that quote from Martin Luther King Jr."

Ah yes. I remember now. I mentioned that quote during our first email exchange, before he even knew my name. I can't believe he remembers that.

I snuggle up to him and place a strawberry at his lips. He takes a big bite.

"I've got a quote for you, too, My Brutally Honest Mr. Faraday. 'Hope is the dream of a waking man.' A beautiful, generous, funny, smart, heroic man-whore with smokin' hot abs and luscious lips and, hey, wow—look at that!—*happy* eyes—"

"Yes, very, *very* happy eyes—"

"Huh. A beautiful man-whore with very, *very* happy eyes once recited that Aristotle quote to me."

Jonas' blue eyes crinkle as he smiles at me. He opens his mouth like a baby bird and I feed him another strawberry.

"So, we're agreed I'm not hopeless?" he asks between bites. "You once said there's no such thing as hopelessness. Do you still believe that?"

"Of course, I do. There's always hope—infinite hope."

"Infinite hope," he repeats with reverence. "Speaking of which, you ready for another round of Tit for Tat, My Magnificent Sarah?"

"How is 'infinite hope' a segue for oral sex, Jonas?"

He laughs. "Everything's a segue for oral sex. How do you not know that by now?"

I throw my head back and laugh.

"So, is that a yes?"

"Only if it involves whipped cream."

"Well, fuck. Is there another way to do it?"

I grab the whipped cream canister. "If there is, I don't want to know about it."

Jonas' phone rings on the nightstand and he scrambles to grab it. He looks at the screen. "Oh shit," he mutters.

I know exactly what that means: Eric's calling. We've known something was up since Eric called three hours ago to say it was time for Kat and the boys to start transferring all the money immediately. But exactly what the feds were planning to do, and when, we had no idea. I guess we're about to find out.

"Hello?" Jonas says, answering his phone. "Hey, Eric. Yes." I can hear his heartbeat from here. He listens for a moment. "All of it?" He rolls his eyes like he can't believe what he's hearing. "You're sure?" He nods at me with wide eyes. *All of it,* he mouths. He flashes thumbs up.

Oh my God. Kat and the boys did it—they got the whole five hundred fifty-four million. Holy crap, we're so effing *Ocean's Eleven.*

"Hang on a sec." Jonas puts the phone to his chest. "The final number's just over six hundred million," he whispers. "They must have made some more deposits." He puts the phone back to his ear. "Okay, sorry, what?"

My heart's beating like a hummingbird's wings.

"Right now?" Jonas motions frantically to the TV remote on my side of the bed and I toss it to him like it's a hot potato. "What channel?" Jonas asks. "*Any* channel?" Jonas turns on the TV and flips past *Sponge Bob Square Pants* to the next channel. Bingo. There it is—a major, live-breaking news event—the kind of national story that lands on every major station at once. "Yeah, we're watching. I'll call you back." He hangs up his phone. "Holy shit."

On screen, a female reporter talks into a microphone and presses an earpiece into her ear. "Breaking News: Terrorist Threat Foiled in Las Vegas" scrolls beneath her on the screen. "... a sophisticated terrorist plot uncovered here in Las Vegas," the reporter is in the midst of saying. Behind the reporter, law enforcement officers in Kevlar vests march in and out of a nondescript building, carrying boxes. Wait, holy crap, that's not just any nondescript building—that's The Club's crappy-ass building, the place where Jonas and I met Oksana and Max.

Jonas turns up the volume on the TV.

"Authorities have confirmed the terrorist organization has been plotting a large-scale attack on U.S. soil—possibly in Las Vegas. Details of the plot have not yet been released."

Jonas grabs my thigh and squeezes it, but I'm too freaked out to squeeze back.

"What we know for certain is that the plot was, indeed, 'sophisticated, imminent and massive,' according to authorities—*and* that the terrorist organization has ties to the Russian government."

"Oh shit," Jonas says. "I think she just declared the start of the second Cold War."

"No mention of the prostitution ring?" I ask.

"I guess not."

"I repeat," the reporter says, as if we didn't hear her the first time, "federal authorities have thwarted an imminent terrorist attack here in Las Vegas—and we're being told by reliable sources that the terrorist threat is somehow related to Russia's recent bid for control of Ukraine."

Oksana suddenly appears onscreen behind the reporter. She's being escorted in handcuffs toward an unmarked car.

"There's Oksana," I gasp. Oksana looks shell-shocked—a deer in headlights.

"So far, fourteen people have been arrested in Las Vegas, four more in New York, and eight in Miami, all with confirmed ties to what's being called the largest Russian terrorist cell ever discovered on U.S. soil."

"Wow," Jonas says. "That's an interesting spin. Do they not know the difference between Russia and Ukraine?"

I can't speak. This is surreal.

The reporter presses her earpiece into her ear. "I'm being told that two of the terrorists—excuse me, two of the *alleged* terrorists—are confirmed dead."

Jonas jerks toward the television screen, suddenly mesmerized.

"Both men were killed in a shoot-out with law enforcement during the raid on the compound earlier today."

Jonas makes a low sound I've only previously heard him make during sex.

"The two men reportedly brandished weapons at law enforcement officers . . ."

Jonas growls softly.

". . . and multiple officers fired shots. Both men died immediately at the scene. No law enforcement officers were injured." The reporter presses her earpiece into her ear. "We're being advised by federal authorities that both men were known sympathizers of the Ukrainian separatist movement, but authorities are not yet releasing their identities."

Jonas looks at me, his face aglow, his chest heaving with excitement. Holy moly, he looks positively euphoric. All of a sudden, he grabs my face and kisses me hard, like a mob boss ordering a hit, and when he pulls back from me, his eyes are on frickin' fire.

"My precious baby," he says. He makes an exuberant noise, his face flushed, and kisses me again. He pulls away again, his eyes sparkling. "Yes," he says. "*Yes.*"

I'm in shock—a wet noodle. This is a lot to take in. They're saying The Club is a terrorist organization? Max and Oksana are part of a "Russian terrorist cell" in Las Vegas? I'd expected to hear the words "prostitution ring" and maybe "organized crime" or "crime syndicate." But "terrorist cell"? I never expected to hear those words in a million years, and especially not "Russian terrorist cell."

Jonas flips through the channels quickly, confirming that, yes, this story is everywhere, and then he mutes the TV. He picks up his phone.

"Eric," Jonas mutters, his voice low and intense. "Yeah, I saw. Fuck yeah. You've got the names?" His mouth tilts up into a crooked smile at whatever Eric's saying on the other end of the line and his eyes flicker ferociously. "Thank you. Yeah, you, too. Absolutely." Jonas hangs up and his smile widens.

Wow, that's quite a grin on Jonas' face—if I were to see it in a snapshot totally out of context, I'd swear the photo was taken while Jonas was getting a blowjob; he looks just that turned on.

"Boom," Jonas says softly, his voice simmering with ferocity.

I pause, waiting for more. But apparently that's all he's going to say.

"Boom?" I ask.

He nods slowly, his eyes on fire.

I wait for more, but it doesn't come.

Should I pretend to be confused by Jonas' one-word proclamation of victory? Because I'm not. I'm not confused at all. The truth is I know exactly what names Eric just said to Jonas—no one needs to tell me which two alleged *terrorists* happened to die today. I continue staring at Jonas' blazing eyes and an overwhelming kind of warmth spreads throughout my body.

"Boom, motherfuckers," I say, my voice as sharp as the knife those fuckers used to slice my throat.

Jonas licks his lips slowly. "That's right, baby." He touches the inside of my thigh. "We fucked 'em up the ass real good, didn't we?"

I bite my lip. This just might be the sexiest moment of my entire life. "We sure did, love."

"I've got the biggest boner right now," Jonas says, lifting up the white sheet to prove it.

"Me, too," I say, motioning to the invisible lady-boner on my naked lap.

Jonas chuckles. "Let me take you away today. I don't want to wait another day to take you to my special place." He gently caresses the inside of my thigh and my skin ignites under his touch.

"In a month," I say. Oh God, I'm on fire.

"I don't want to wait."

"I know you don't."

"I want to go right now."

"I know you do. But you have to wait." I shudder as his fingers brush gently between my legs and drift over my sweet spot.

"I hate waiting."

His expression morphs into his patented Jonas-is-a-great-white-shark-and-Sarah-is-a-defenseless-sea-lion smolder. His fingers brush between my legs again, right over my tip, making me throb.

"We did it, baby," he says. "You're safe." His fingers begin caressing me in earnest. "We're free."

My breathing catches with excitement. He's right. We're free—free to begin our new life together. Free to do whatever the hell we want to do. And I know exactly where I want to start exercising my newfound freedom. Without warning, I crawl on top of him and take him into me, all the way, as deeply as I can, moaning softly as I do.

He exhales loudly. "You're safe," he says, closing his eyes. "My Magnificent Sarah."

I exhale, too, a long, shaky breath, and begin moving slowly, ever so slowly, up and down and around, enjoying every sensation of his body fusing with mine.

"Let me take you away, baby," he moans. "I've got something I want to show you."

"In a month," I breathe.

"Bossy," he says. He touches my breast and groans.

"We'll stop in New York before we go home," I say. "You can introduce me to your uncle and tell him about Climb and Conquer in person."

He gently touches the scar on my ribcage. "Whatever you say, my love," he says, moving his body with mine. "A quick stop in New York it is." His hands move to my hips.

The intensity of my movement increases. He did it. Jonas protected me, just like he promised he would. Oh, yes, yes, yes, my *man* did whatever the *fuck* he had to do to protect me, his *woman*, from the bad guys. And I love him for it. I *fucking* love him for it. Oh, yes, yes, yes, I do. "Thank you, Jonas," I growl, riding him with enthusiasm. "You're my hero."

"You're my everything," he replies. He grabs my butt with zeal. "God, I love this ass." He slaps it.

"Mmm," I say, because that's all the conversation I've got left in me at this particular moment.

He did it. He protected me. We're free. I could cry with joy and relief. I lean down and kiss him, enjoying the feeling of my erect nipples rubbing against his chest. For the first time since those bastards sliced me and stabbed me and left me bleeding out on a bathroom floor, I feel completely safe—carefree, in fact.

"You did it, Jonas."

"*We* did it, baby," he says, his voice straining. He's on the verge of climax. He groans. "We did it together."

Chapter 42

Jonas

Sarah's been talking up a storm the whole time we've been hiking up Mount Olympus behind our guide. Well, actually, she's been Chatty Cathy ever since we boarded our flight for Greece three days ago, obviously relieved as hell to be done with her final exams.

I don't mind Sarah holding up both ends of our conversation during this hike, not at all, because, for the last three weeks, as I've planned and plotted and waited for this special day to arrive, as I've gotten boners in my sleep dreaming about getting down on my knee, as I've daydreamed about asking her the magic question and yearned for the moment when I'm going to slip that ring on her finger (and it's a fucking *epic* ring, by the way), I've increasingly lost my ability to function let alone speak with each slowly passing day. Jesus, by the time we boarded our flight three days ago, I was a total wreck.

I pat the pocket of my hiking pants. Yes, the little box is still there. I let out a long, shaky exhale. I'm ninety-nine percent sure she'll say yes, but it's that one percent chance I'm about to get crushed that's making me crazy. Yes, Sarah loves me, of course. But with Sarah, you never know what she might say or do in any situation. What if she's got some bizarre idea about marriage being the death of a relationship or some other intractable prejudice against holy matrimony, thanks to the shit she witnessed as a kid? It's entirely possible. I don't think it's likely, but she's never once even *hinted* at wanting to get married—and neither have I, for that matter—so you just never know.

I tune into Sarah's chatter for a moment. She's talking about Josh and Kat—about how Kat was headed to L.A. for a long weekend when we left on our trip.

"Mmm hmm," I say. I'm elated to hear things are going well for the Playboy and the Party Girl, I really am—and, actually, Josh hasn't stopped talking about Kat since we left Vegas, so I'm not surprised at all—but I can't concentrate on that right now.

When I planned our trip to Greece, I stupidly thought it'd be best for us to arrive, relax, get over our jetlag, explore Athens for a few days, and *then* climb Mount Olympus so I could ask her to be my wife. I truly didn't understand how anticipating this moment would utterly consume me—how eating, sleeping, and simply conversing naturally would become a fucking impossibility. If I'd known, I would have planned this excursion for the first day of our trip.

"So I *think* I answered the question pretty well," she's saying. "But the whole question was totally ambiguous, you know? I feel like you could argue either side of the issue and be right."

She must be talking about one of her final exams from last week—which one, I haven't a clue.

"Sounds like you kicked ass with your answer," I say. Hopefully, that's the right thing to say at this particular moment.

"You really think so?"

"Yeah, I do."

"Well, that calms me down, then. You certainly know your contracts backwards and forwards. But, hey, what about this question on the torts exam . . .?"

I pat my pants pocket. The little box is still there.

After today, she'll be wearing my ring on her finger for the whole world to see and I'll finally be able to breathe again. Thank God I booked that villa in Mykonos for tomorrow night instead of at the beginning of the trip. If I'd have booked Mykonos for *before* Mount Olympus, I never would have been able to enjoy it, paradise or not. This way, we'll have four glorious days in Nirvana to celebrate our engagement—assuming we'll be celebrating. Oh my God. Fuck me. If she says anything other than yes, I'm going to curl up and die on the spot.

"It's almost like you can feel the ghosts from thousands of years ago, just floating around you, you know?" she says.

"Mmm hmm," I say. I pat my pocket again.

"Like, I dunno, you can feel their collective *wisdom,*" she says. "Like, it's a physical *thing,* just floating in the air."

"Mmm hmm."

The hiking trail isn't particularly demanding nor is it all that scenic on this side of the mountain. But this hike isn't what we're here for—it's just a means to an end. Oh my God, I can't wait to finally spill the beans and tell her why we're here.

"It also makes me think, 'Hey, these were real people,' you know? Like, it makes it so clear these weren't just *names* in an ancient history textbook. They were *people* just like you and me. They ate, slept, made love, cried, laughed, loved... You know what I mean?"

"Mmm hmm."

She stops short and I almost walk into her back. She wheels around to look at me. "Are you listening to me, Jonas?"

"Totally," I say. "Every word. I totally agree with everything you've said." But I don't know what the fuck she's just said. I can't think straight right now. All I can think about is asking this beautiful woman to be my wife—the mother of my future children.

She studies me briefly. "Are you okay?"

"Of course."

"You're acting weird."

My chest tightens. Does she know? "I am?"

"Yes."

"Well, I think I'm just . . . deep in thought."

"About what?"

"You."

She studies me. "Me?"

"Yes."

"Good thoughts?"

"The best thoughts. You're the goddess and the muse, Sarah Cruz. There's nothing but goodness when my thoughts are about you."

"Oh, Jonas." She smiles. "You're so sweet." She turns back around happily and catches up to the guide on the trail. "So, anyway, what part did you like best?"

What part of what did I like best? What the fuck was she just talking about? I try to recall what the fuck she just said. *Real people.* Yeah, that's right. She said they're not just names in a history book, they're real people. She must have been talking about our walking tour of Athens on our first full day here.

"The Acropolis," I answer. "There's nothing like seeing the ground where Plato and Aristotle actually walked. That's what captured my imagination when I was eighteen and it was even more magical to see it with you." Oh my God. Stringing together so many coherent words just took a lot out of me. There's only one thing I want to talk about right now—and it's not the Acropolis. I'm dying to finally let loose with the speech I've been practicing in my head, day and night, for a solid three weeks.

"Yeah, me, too," she says. "That was amazing—especially getting to see it with you." She swivels her head around and shoots me a lovely smile.

I smile back. Or, at least I think I do. Who knows what the fuck my face looks like right now—my facial muscles are not my own.

Holy shit, I'm losing my mind. I've been dreaming of this moment nonstop since we left Uncle William's house a month ago.

Of course, Uncle William fell head-over-heels in love with Sarah the minute he met her. In fact, I'm positive Uncle William reacted so well to the news of my departure from Faraday & Sons because Sarah was there, casting some kind of spell on him. Sure, when Josh joined us on the second night and dropped the "I'm leaving the company, too" bomb on poor Uncle William, that made things a little harder for him to swallow. But, call me crazy, my uncle actually seemed relieved by Josh's news a little bit, almost like he'd been waiting for the Faraday brothers' simultaneous departure from the company for a long time and now he could exhale. All in all, the whole weekend went surprisingly well—and I'm sure Sarah was mostly to thank for that.

"You gonna marry this girl?" Uncle William asked me after dinner on the second night, the minute Sarah had left the dining room to use the bathroom.

"Absolutely," I answered, shocking myself with how easily the word came out. It felt enthralling to admit my intentions out loud—especially to my family. "As soon as humanly possible, in fact."

"That's awesome, bro," Josh said. "Does she know?"

That's when my knee started jiggling under the table. "No," I said, my chest constricting. "Am I supposed to *ask* her if I can *ask* her?" It was an honest question.

Josh laughed. "No, Jonas, you dumbshit. That's not what I meant. I'm just saying if you're gonna surprise the girl, then make sure you blow her socks off. This is the story she's gonna be telling her grandkids one day. So don't fuck it up."

Well, duh, as Sarah says. I already knew that. And yet, at Josh's words, I suddenly felt like I was gonna throw up, and I haven't stopped feeling that way since. All throughout the past month, even as I've been busy as fuck transitioning out of Faraday & Sons and into Climb and Conquer, I've grown increasingly anxious. I'm not nervous about making Sarah my wife—fuck no, that's the thing I'm least anxious about in my whole life—I'm just worried I won't be able to deliver the fairytale proposal my precious baby so richly deserves.

"So this is Mount Olympus?" Sarah says, looking around. "Huh. Not what I expected."

"What'd you expect?"

She pauses. "Oh, I dunno. I thought maybe there'd be an old guy with a long white beard holding lightning bolts up here."

I chuckle. "Actually, little known fact: Zeus is so old by now, he's sitting in a rocking chair at the top of the mountain, doing Sudoku."

She laughs. "It's super cool to think about the ancient Greeks looking up at this very mountaintop, imagining the gods up here."

The guide takes this as his cue (thankfully, because I've just exhausted my ability to converse for the foreseeable future) and he begins a lengthy explanation about Mount Olympus as the mythological home of the Twelve Olympians.

Sarah listens to him with rapt attention as I tune out.

I love how Sarah hasn't once asked me why we're hiking up Mount Olympus. I guess she thinks the mere existence of a mountain, anywhere in the world, is enough of a draw for me to suggest climbing it—which, normally, I suppose, would be true. But today isn't a normal day.

We turn a corner in the trail and traverse over a small crest, and, just like that, we arrive at our destination—a small plateau spanning just below one of the mountain's craggy peaks. I'm relieved to see that our next set of guides is already here, exactly as planned, awaiting us with all appropriate gear.

Sarah stops short on the trail, apparently seeing the crew awaiting us, too. She whips around to face me. "Are you effing kidding me right now?"

She must have seen the two colorful parachutes spread out on the ground.

I smile at her. "No, I am not effing kidding you right now."

She glares at me.

"We're going to jump off Mount Olympus, baby. And then we're gonna paraglide through the air, all the way to the beautiful, white-sand beaches of the Aegean Sea."

She smashes her lips together.

"And it's gonna be fucking awesome."

"Have I mentioned I *hate* heights?"

"Many times."

She blinks rapidly. "Are you trying to make me hate you?"

"Quite the opposite."

"Then you suck at whatever you're trying to do because I *hate* you right now."

I laugh. "Come on, baby. Let me show you what we're gonna do."

Chapter 43

Sarah

I'm shaking. I really, really hate heights. "Jonas, I don't know about this," I say. I'm stuffed into a thick flight suit and the guy who's going to pilot my paraglider is securing my harness and double-checking all his lines, getting ready to jump off the frickin' mountain with me strapped to his body like an infant in a papoose. I can't imagine what part of this idea made Jonas think: *Sarah.*

"Looks good, baby," Jonas says. He steps up really close to me and double-checks the strap on my helmet. "Now remember, all you have to do is sit back and relax and enjoy the panoramic views as they segue from mountains to fields to sparkling sea."

He's quite a salesman, I must admit. He makes torture sound almost lovely.

"Just sit back and enjoy the ride. That's all you ever have to do when you're with me."

"You've already proved that to me a thousand times over—every single night, in fact—and I've *surrendered* to you countless times and acknowledged you as my lord-god-master. Why do you need me to enact yet another metaphor to emphasize your point?"

He rolls his eyes. "Because for once in my life, I'm not talking about sex, baby. I'm talking about *life.* This is a metaphor for *life*—for our life together. I want you to know that when you're with me, all you ever have to do is sit back, relax, and enjoy the ride—because I'll always take care of you."

Well, that was actually a very sweet little speech. He obviously put a lot of thought into it. And yet, I can't help myself from being irritated. I really, really hate heights. "Yeah. You'll always take care of me, other than when you're pushing me off high places, even though I'm scared to death of heights."

He looks distressed.

I sigh. I'm so mean. "Oh, I'm sorry, Jonas." I grab his hand. "I'm sorry. Tell me what you wanted to say. This is all a grand metaphor for *life,* not sex—if I sit back and relax and enjoy the ride . . . Come on, baby. I'm mean and horrible. You put a lot of thought into this. I'm listening. Continue."

His cheeks flush.

"Please. Seriously. I'm listening."

He clears his throat. "Even when something scares you, if you're willing to take a leap of faith—with me—you might discover you enjoy the ride more than you ever imagined possible," he says softly.

"That's lovely. A fantastic metaphor. Thank you for that."

He's gaining confidence again. "Ah, but this is only one of *many* metaphors I've planned for you today."

"Oh yeah? Is today Metaphor Day, my sweet Jonas?"

"Yes, as a matter of fact, it is. Today is Jonas and Sarah's Metaphorical Adventure."

"Oh, how you love your metaphors, Jonas Faraday."

"I really do." He takes a step forward, right up into my face. "May I tell you about the metaphor you've already unknowingly enacted for me today?"

"Please do."

"Our hike up Mount Olympus. 'Twas a metaphor."

"'Twas?"

"'Twas. You'll recall I followed you the entire way up the trail. Do you know why I did that?"

I shake my head, grinning. He's so cute.

"Because I've always got your back, my love—and because I'd follow you to the ends of the earth. 'Twas a double metaphor. I get double points."

I tilt my head at him. He's thought quite a bit about all this, hasn't he?

"Next metaphor. We're standing on the highest peak in all of Greece—Mount Olympus—the home of the gods." He puts his hand on my cheek. "Do you know why I wanted to bring you here—to this particular mountaintop, specifically?"

"Because you're a sadist?" I say softly, but my tone is much friendlier than my actual words.

He takes a long, deep, steadying breath and moves his hand to my shoulder. "Sarah Cruz, I brought you here, to this specific spot on planet earth, for two reasons." He grins. "Double points *again.*"

I smile broadly.

"First, this is the highest peak in all of Greece—which means I am therefore compelled to climb it and shout to the world about my undying love for you."

Oh my God.

"But we're not here simply because Mount Olympus is the tallest peak," he continues. "We're also here because it's the home of the gods, Sarah, which means it's *your* rightful home." His eyes sparkle. "You're the goddess and the muse, Sarah Cruz. My precious baby, you are every Greek goddess, rolled into one."

"Oh, Jonas."

"You're Aphrodite," he says, "the goddess of love, beauty, pleasure, and sex—the hottest fucking sex the world has ever seen, oh my God."

I blush.

"You're Athena—the goddess of wisdom, courage, inspiration, law, justice, strength, and strategy. You're so fucking smart, baby—you blow me away."

I bite my lip.

"You're Artemis—the protector of women. Baby, your gigantic heart—the way you so genuinely care about helping women and making the world a better place—it's my favorite thing about you, by far."

I can't believe he's saying all this. I'm swooning.

"But, wait, there's more." His mouth twists into a crooked grin. "You're my Demeter, too—the goddess of the harvest, life, and sustenance. Baby, you're *my* sustenance. I physically *need* you like a flower needs sunshine and soil and water—you *feed* me, baby, right at my roots. *You give me life.*"

Holy crap—my knees just wobbled.

"And, of course, My Magnificent Sarah, let us not forget, you're also Hera." He pauses for dramatic effect. "The goddess of *marriage.*"

Come again?

He beams at me.

He's speaking metaphorically, right?

"My Magnificent Sarah, you're all of these powerful and revered and beautiful goddesses, all rolled into one."

He wasn't being literal just now when he used the word *marriage*, was he?

"But on top of all that, let's not forget, you're also the *muse*, Sarah Cruz—the inspiration for female beauty itself. You are *womanness* from the ideal realm."

Oh my God. This is all just so over-the-top—so beautiful—so *epic.* "Oh, Jonas," I sigh. For reasons I'll never fully understand, my beautiful hunky-monkey boyfriend is flat-out addicted to mustard and, thank the Lord, I just happen to be a big ol' vat of it.

"And that, my dearest love, is why we're standing atop Mount Olympus, the home of the gods and the highest peak in all of Greece." He sighs like he's greatly relieved, and then he takes another deep breath, apparently gearing up to say something more.

There's more?

"But none of that answers the question why we're about to jump *off* the highest peak in Greece, does it?" He looks like he's bursting to tell me a grand secret.

I shake my head, grinning. He's so damned cute. How on earth did his beautiful mind come up with all this? "Please, love. Tell me why, oh why, we're jumping off this mythical mountain? I'm hanging on your every word."

"Because, lovely Sarah, you and I are ready to leap to the next level. We first leaped off a thirty-foot waterfall together—because that's what we could handle at the time. But now we're ready to leap from heaven itself."

I feel like he just made love to me with his words. Is he making some sort of eternal commitment to me—right here and now? Is this all some elaborate, metaphorical commitment ceremony?

"Which brings me to our next metaphor. We're about to take a giant leap off a mountain, My Magnificent Sarah. And yet, you'll notice I've provided you with a parachute for your landing—well, a paraglider, technically, but for purposes of our metaphor, we'll call it a parachute—because, no matter what happens, no matter how we wind up leaping in life, we'll always do it together—and your safety and protection and comfort will always be my greatest priority."

This is insane. I'm melting here.

Jonas' face is adorable right now—he's euphoric. He's the most beautiful man in the world. And I'm the luckiest girl in the world. Yes, he's metaphorically marrying me right now; I'm sure of it. I touch the bracelet around my wrist.

"I love you, Jonas," I say. Oh good Lord, I want to say so much more than that—but if I know my Jonas, he's been planning this speech for quite some time and I don't want to knock him off his game.

"So you'll jump off Mount Olympus with me, then?" he asks. He looks unsure of my answer.

"Of course, I will, baby. I'll jump off any mountain with you—not to mention any waterfall, tree, ladder, bridge, footstool, or curb—as long as I'm with you."

He practically jumps up and down with glee.

"Oh, Jonas."

"But wait—there's more," he says. He stops to think. He suppresses a humongous smile. "But not now. Later."

My stomach flips. More? My mind is spiraling out of control, having all kinds of crazy-ass thoughts—thoughts I absolutely shouldn't be having. Thoughts he couldn't possibly live up to.

"I'm only sorry I can't pilot you myself. You being strapped to some random Greek dude when you leap off Mount Olympus really fucks up my metaphor. But I figured leaping and dying wasn't really optimal in light of the metaphor I'm going for here."

I laugh. "I'll just imagine I'm strapped to you the whole time."

"Please do."

A pilot approaches. "Are you ready?" he asks us in a thick Greek accent.

"Yeah. I'll be going first," Jonas tells him. "Okay, baby?"

"Great."

"I want to be down there waiting for you when you arrive."

"Another metaphor I presume?"

"No. I just want to take pictures of your face during the landing. It's gonna be hilarious."

I laugh.

"But there *is* yet another metaphor awaiting us down at the bottom—the biggest metaphor of all, my precious baby—which I'll tell you about in great detail after we land."

My stomach flips. Electricity courses through my veins. "Can you give me a little hint?"

"Nope. I'll tell you after you land." Jonas leans in and kisses me. His tongue parts my lips and jolts my entire body. "Enjoy your ride, my precious baby," he says. "Just sit back, relax, and take in the beautiful views."

I have the urge to applaud raucously—holy hell, I've just been treated to the most magnificent declaration of love ever bestowed upon a woman throughout the history of time—this was the *Iliad* of love declarations, people—but I somehow manage to control myself. "That was beautiful, Jonas," I say. "I'm swooning—literally, swooning."

"Really? I'm doing okay so far?" He grins shyly.

What the heck does that mean? "Of course. You're doing great *so far*," I say. "You're a poet—the most romantic man who ever lived. An absolute master of Valentine's Day bullshit."

He grins.

"I pity the poor fool who even *thinks* about declaring his love to a woman after what you just did—I just experienced the divine original form of declaring-love-ness."

Jonas flashes an exuberant smile that lights up his entire face. "It's easy to deliver the divine original form of declaring-love-ness to the divine original form of woman-ness."

A giggle escapes my throat.

He laughs. "So are you ready to leap?"

Well, that sure makes me stop giggling in a heartbeat. Holy crap. I'd kind of forgotten about the actual jumping part. "Sure," I squeak out.

He laughs and kisses me on the cheek. "Then I'll see you down on the glorious, white-sand beaches of the Aegean, my precious baby." He turns to his pilot and flashes him a thumbs-up. "Let's do it."

Chapter 44

Jonas

Here she comes, floating down from the sky like the beautiful butterfly she is. Oh my God, her face is gorgeous right now—bursting with excitement and accomplishment and awe. I can almost hear her squealing from my vantage point all the way down on the beach. I laugh out loud as I crane my neck up to watch her descend. Wow, she's *elated.* I take a million pictures of her with my phone as she waves and mugs for the camera. Oh God, she's adorable in her little helmet with her cute, flushed cheeks. She's positively glowing.

Her pilot yells something to her—I'm sure he's prepping her for landing, probably telling her to stand up in the harness and get ready to hit the ground running. As he speaks, her happy expression completely vanishes. If I had to caption her face right now, it'd be, *Holy shit.* I can't help but belly laugh.

They're coming in fast. There's no turning back. Oh, my poor baby. She looks scared to death—in a sudden and total panic. I feel an acute pang of guilt for forcing her to do this. Maybe there was a kinder way to impose this last, glorious metaphor upon her? Oh well. It's too late now. Here she comes.

Their landing is perfect, thank God—soft as a feather, a gentle touchdown followed by an adrenaline-fueled run. Sarah and her pilot run, run, run together—oh man, look at her go—she's like a pro—for a solid five steps, that is, and then she crumples to the ground in a relieved heap.

I bound toward her, shouting her name as I approach.

She's thrashing around on the ground like an overturned turtle. Her pilot releases her tethers and she springs up off the ground. She runs toward me, shouting at the top of her lungs, and leaps into my arms, squealing and screaming.

"Did you see me?" she shrieks. "I did it!" She wraps her legs around my waist and clutches me, closing her eyes as I pepper her ebullient face with zealous kisses.

"You were amazing," I say. "Incredible!" I kiss her and kiss her and kiss her.

"I did it," she screams. She throws her arms around my neck and squeezes me tight. "I jumped off a cliff! I ran *toward* a frickin' cliff—not away from it—and then I *jumped.* Oh my God, I was crapping my pants, Jonas, but I kept running anyway and then I *leaped.*" She kisses me again, but then she abruptly pulls away and swats at my shoulder, a sudden scowl overtaking her face. "I almost had a heart attack, Jonas Faraday. What the hell were you trying to do to me?" She's trying to sound pissed, but her face is playful. "It's not normal to run *toward* a cliff and jump, you know that, right?"

I laugh. "But it sure is fun, isn't it?"

"So fun."

"You did it, baby."

"I did it. And so did you. *We* did it." She beams at me. "And the view. Jonas, oh my God."

"Gorgeous, right?"

"The most beautiful thing I've ever seen. Just heaven on earth."

"The color of the water—"

"To die for," she says. "I've never seen water that shade of turquoise before."

"And wasn't it relaxing once you were up there?"

"Yeah, once I stopped having a heart attack from the takeoff, I was like, 'Hey, this is really nice.'" She swats my shoulder again. "Until the *landing,* oh my God, you sadist."

I burst out laughing. "You should have seen your face. Priceless."

"Are you *trying* to torture me?"

I kiss her. "No, my precious baby. Quite the opposite." My heart suddenly leaps into my mouth. This is it. The moment I've been waiting for. Oh my God. I take a deep breath. "Lemme put you down."

She unwraps her legs from me and slides down to the ground.

My face feels hot. I can't breathe. This is it. Holy shit. My pulse pounds in my ears. "There's one more metaphor I want to tell you about—the biggest one of all."

She shifts her weight.

I pat my pocket. Yep, the box is still there. "Sarah," I warble. I clear my throat. "My Magnificent Sarah." Oh God, my throat is closing up.

She unlatches her helmet and takes it off. She looks anxious.

I take another deep breath. "Thank you," I begin. Shit. That's not how I practiced this. Where did that come from? I've got to pull myself together and do this right.

She presses her lips together, gazing at me intently.

I take yet another deep breath, trying to gather myself. What did I plan to say? Whatever it was, it feels all wrong now. The only thing I feel right now is gratitude—love and gratitude. Fuck my planned speech. I'll just say what's in my heart right this minute. "Thank you, Sarah," I say. "Thank you for loving me—for teaching me how to be *loved.* Your love is my savior." My lip trembles and I pause, steadying myself. "Your love has given me life."

"Oh, Jonas," she says, her voice brimming with emotion.

I cup her face in my hands. "I got it wrong when I called our love madness. I'm sorry about that. Our love's not madness, baby—our love is what's finally made me *sane.*"

She smiles.

I rest my hands on her shoulders. "Sarah Cruz, when you crawled inside that cocoon-built-for-two with me, when you gave yourself to me, totally and completely, that's when I discovered true happiness for the first time in my life." I stuff down a sudden wave of emotion.

She blinks slowly, suppressing tears.

"And I thought . . ." My voice quavers, so I pause. "I thought there could be no greater happiness than that, than being inside that cocoon with you for the rest of my life." My palms are sweaty. I pat my pocket and feel the little box bulging there.

The pilots and some other people milling on the beach are chatting in Greek around us. Sarah looks like she's about to burst into tears. I feel light-headed.

"I thought our little cocoon built for two was the culmination of human possibility," I say.

Her big brown eyes are smiling at me.

"But somewhere along the line, I'm not sure precisely when, I discovered an even greater joy than being inside that cocoon with you. It was watching you burst *out* of that cocoon and become the beautiful butterfly you were always meant to be, right before my eyes."

Her face contorts with a thousand emotions all at once.

"When you became my beautiful, powerful, delicate, miraculous, glorious, iron butterfly, *that's* when I discovered the divine original form of happiness. *Pure ecstasy.*"

Tears pool in her eyes.

Oh my God. This is it. My heart is going to crack my sternum from the inside.

I take a deep, steadying breath, pull the box out of my pocket, and bend down on my knee. I look up into Sarah's beautiful face and . . . she explodes into tears.

Oh my God. I haven't even asked her yet—*I haven't even opened the box yet.* I'm down on my knee with a *closed* ring box and she's bawling like I just stole her lunch money. Should I stand and comfort her? No, I can't. I'm gonna have a heart attack if I wait another second to say these words to her. I'm a runaway train.

I open the box and she turns into a certifiable maniac—she's crying uncontrollably and laughing with glee at the same time. Oh, my baby. She's a hot mess—and I'm loving it.

She puts a shaking hand to her mouth. "Jonas," she breathes. "Oh my God."

Our pilots and a few other bystanders milling on the beach have gathered around us. I guess a guy on bended knee with a ring translates in any culture.

"You're the goddess and the muse, Sarah Cruz," I say, hoisting the rock up. "I love you more than any man has ever loved any woman in the history of time. Our love is the joy of the good, the wonder of the wise, the amazement of the gods." I pause, not because I'm scared, not because I'm unsure, but because I want to savor the moment. "Our love is the *envy* of the gods, my precious baby." I inhale deeply and look into her big, brown eyes. "Will you marry me, My Magnificent Sarah Cruz?"

She drops to her knees right in front of me, leveling her face with mine, throws her arms around my neck, and kisses me voraciously, almost snuffing the life out of me as she does.

Our small audience on the beach applauds.

"Yes?" I choke out. I can't breathe. Good God, the woman's suffocating me. "Yes?"

"Yes," she shrieks. "Yes!" I grab her shaking hand and begin slipping the ring onto her finger, but she pulls away. Oh God, I've got the wrong hand. She laughs and gives me her other one and I somehow manage to slide the ring onto the correct finger. Oh my God, I can't believe it. She's wearing my ring. It's official. Sarah Cruz is going to be my wife.

Sarah squeals, gazing at her hand. "Oh my God, Jonas. It's breathtaking!"

I hold up her hand and take a look. Wow, it looks even prettier on her hand than I imagined it would. "It's *magnificent,*" I say. "Because nothing short of that would have been worthy of My Magnificent Sarah." I stand and pull her up with me, and then I kiss her like I'm reviving a drowning woman—or maybe she's reviving me.

Our small audience on the beach applauds again and someone shouts, "*Bravo*!"

"My future wife," I say to the crowd, pointing at her. "She said yes."

She laughs. "Oh, Jonas."

"I don't want to wait." I grip her shoulders with urgency. "Let's get married right away."

Her face bursts into flames of excitement. "Whatever you say—my future *husband*." She giggles.

"Baby, take a month to plan the wedding and—"

"Whoa, what?"

"—make it however you want it. Hire ten wedding planners if you want. I don't care what you do, as long as I get to call you my wife a month from now."

She puts her hands on her cheeks like she's the *Home Alone* kid. "Jonas, I can't plan a wedding in a *month*."

"Sure you can."

"No, you don't understand. I need a year—six months at least."

I groan. There's no fucking way I can wait six months to marry this girl. "*Please*, Sarah. *Please*." I'm manic. I'd marry her right this very second if she'd let me. "Spend whatever you want—hire whoever you need. I don't care what you do. Just don't make me wait. *Please*."

She laughs. "You're so effing demanding, you know that?"

I don't care if I'm demanding. Not about this. I absolutely can't wait. Waiting a whole month for this moment to arrive almost killed me—I can't wait more than a month to call her my wife. "Sarah, please, please, please."

She shakes her head, like she can't believe what she's gotten herself into with me, but then she shrugs with resignation. "Okay, baby, whatever you say."

"Anything's possible when you throw enough money at it. Trust me."

She grins and rolls her eyes. "You know what? I don't even care about the wedding. All I care about is being married to you."

"No, no, baby, make it however you want it. Hire whoever you need to make it perfect—pay five times as much as any sane person would pay. I don't care what you do—just please, please, please don't make me wait."

"Okeedokee," she says. She snaps her fingers. "Easy peasy."

I pull her close. I'm so fucking relieved I could scream. "Really?"

"Of course." She kisses me. "I told you—all I care about is being married to you. The wedding's just a party. I can put together a party in a month. No sweat."

I feel high. Adrenaline is flooding me. My cock is tingling. My skin is electrified. "Let's run down the beach to some secluded spot and go skinny-dipping," I whisper, my chest heaving with excitement.

She looks at the rock on her hand and grimaces. "I don't want my ring to come off in the ocean."

Motherfucker. The engagement ring I bought for my future bride is gonna keep me from making love to my future bride right now? Talk about irony.

She motions to the pilots. "Do either of you have an extra parachute we could bring with us on a little walk? We'll bring it right back." She turns to me and grins. "Where there's a will, there's a way."

I smile broadly. She's so fucking smart. And so fucking hot.

One of the pilots pulls a colorful parachute from his pack. "Is not for flying. Is for to practice on the ground," he says. "Is okay?" He hands it to her.

"Perfect. Thank you." Her eyes blaze wickedly at me. "What do you think, baby?"

"I think, fuck yeah."

I grab the parachute in one hand and her hand in the other and we sprint down the beach, laughing the whole time. We run and run, until there's no one around us as far as the eye can see, and when we're sure we've reached a stretch of beach that's ours alone, we lie down in the sand and throw the parachute over us. Filtered sunlight streams through the brightly colored fabric casting glorious swaths of reflected red, blue, and yellow onto the sand all around us.

We're savage animals, both of us, desperate for each other. She rips off her shirt, gasping—her face awash in a haze of reflected blue—and I rip off mine. She pulls frantically at my pants and my cock springs out.

"Jack in the box," she says, panting.

"Only if you're the box."

She laughs—she always laughs at that one.

"The future Mrs. Faraday," I mutter, slipping my hand inside her pants and cupping her bare ass in my palm. Oh shit, I'm hard as a rock. "The future Mrs. Faraday," I say again, just because it feels so fucking good to say it. "You're gonna be my wife."

She groans loudly and nibbles on my lip. Her hand grips my shaft. "My future *husband*."

Her words release a surge of electricity through my veins. "Again," I moan, pulling her pants off.

"My future *husband.*" She works my shaft with authority,

making me shudder, and then leans back into the sand, pulling my cock with her, inviting me inside her, a haze of red-filtered sunlight washing across her beautiful face.

She tugs on me, coaxing me to enter her, but it's not going to happen. I've just asked this glorious woman to become my *wife*—and nothing, not even the indomitable Sarah Cruz, not even Orgasma the All-Powerful, is going to prevent me from taking my future wife to church.

I kneel between her legs and open her thighs and begin worshipping at her altar like the zealot I am—oh God, the future Mrs. Faraday tastes so good—and she moans and quivers under my tongue.

"My future wife," I whisper, licking her again and again. "I'm gonna marry you, baby," I say hoarsely, tasting her the way I know she likes it best—until, finally, deliciously, she arches her back into me, and comes undone.

When her climax subsides, she opens her eyes and smiles at me. "Get inside me, future husband."

That's all the encouragement I need.

"This is the best day of my life," she whispers into my ear, tilting her hips up to greet mine, her face now awash in a haze of yellow.

"Mine too." I kiss her deeply.

She trembles. "Oh, Jonas." She wraps her legs around my back and moves her pelvis with mine. "That was the best proposal ever."

"I did okay?"

"Oh, baby, better than okay. You're a *beast*." She grunts. "Now fuck me like the beast you are."

Damn, this woman turns me on. I do exactly as I'm told.

"Just like that," she says. "*Yes*." She bites my neck.

"Ow." I shudder.

She laughs and bites me again.

"Why so violent?"

She laughs again.

I shift myself so my cock rubs her at a new angle and her body ignites underneath me.

"Oh, God, just like that. Don't stop doing that." She gasps. "Oh, yes, baby—oh my God—yes, yes, yes."

There are no words for this kind of ecstasy because there's never been a love like ours. She's the divine original form of woman—and our love is the divine original form of love. "Sarah," I say, teetering on the edge of my own Nirvana, "I love you."

"Mmm."

The parachute casts magnificent colors around us in the sand, illuminating our cathedral as surely as any stained glass window ever could.

"I love you, baby," I groan, kissing her again and again.

"Jonas," she breathes, teetering right on the edge. "*Yes.*"

"And I'm gonna marry you," I say.

She begins to make The Sound.

"You're gonna be my *wife*."

She's hanging on by a thread.

"Mrs. Faraday."

That does it. She's gone.

And so am I.

She's my savior.

She's my religion.

She's my redemption.

I'm born again.

There's never been a love like ours.

And there never will be again.

Our love is the joy of the good, the wonder of the wise, the amazement of the gods—the culmination of human possibility.

Epilogue

Jonas

"Mrs. Faraday," I whisper softly.

She doesn't reply. She's lying on her belly, her face smashed into her pillow.

I run my fingertips slowly down her back over her tank top, softly singing the chorus from "I Melt With You" by Modern English. I'm a horrifically bad singer, I know this without a doubt—but, for some reason, she loves it when I sing, especially this song.

Still nothing.

"Oh, Mrs. Faraday?" I call out softly. I sing to her again.

"Mmm."

"Good morning, My Magnificent Mrs. Faraday," I whisper. "You awake?"

"I am now," she says, her voice extra gravelly. "How are you already back on Seattle time?"

"I'm not. My body's still on New Zealand time—it's just that my mind is too happy to sleep."

She buries her face in her pillow and groans. "I'm married to a madman."

I poke her ass cheek through her pajama bottoms. "Hey, wifey."

She swats at my hand. "Weirdo."

"Wife?"

"What time is it in New Zealand right now? Because that's what time my body thinks it is."

"Come on, sleepyhead. I've been awake for three hours. I've worked out, done all the laundry in both our suitcases, and answered a hundred emails. And now I'm lonely for my sexy wifey."

"How the hell do you sleep so little, you nutball?" She still won't look at me—she's stubbornly got her face buried in her pillow. "I swear to God you're not even human. You're a frickin' droid."

I sit on the bed next to her and caress the curve of her beautiful ass. I can't help myself—I pull down her pajama pants and lay a soft kiss on her ass cheek. It's taking all my restraint not to yank her pants all the way down and do a whole lot more than that, but I know she's exhausted. "What if I were to tell you I brought you a cappuccino?"

She lifts her head. "Then I would say, 'Why, good morning, dear husband. So nice to see you.' You should have opened with that, you big dummy." She turns over and sits up.

I hand her the mug off the nightstand. "Here you go, dear wife."

"Thank you, dear husband, you're the best—even if you're a nutball and a droid and a weirdo." She takes a sip. "Mmm."

"Did you sleep well?"

"Like a baby. It was amazing to finally sleep in my own bed again."

"There's no place like home." Especially when it's *our* home.

Of course, I loved every minute of our honeymoon—a week in New Zealand (it's the adventure capital of the world, after all), followed by three days in Venezuela, joined by Josh and Kat (Sarah had arranged an emotional reunion for Josh and me with Mariela), and capped off by four magical nights for my baby and me (and our friends the howler monkeys) in our jungle tree house in Belize. It was amazing, all of it—and yet, when it was time to come home, I wasn't at all sorry. In fact, I was chomping at the bit to come home and start my new life with my baby, my wife, the goddess and the muse, Sarah Faraday.

Sarah looks dazed as she sips her cappuccino. "Oh my God, I can't move," she groans. "After all that bungee jumping and rappelling and hot monkey-sex, my body's in a perpetual state of wet-noodledom."

"I'm pretty wiped, too," I admit.

"Yeah, that's why you've already worked out this morning and done all our laundry, you weirdo."

"I told you—I'm too happy to sleep."

"That's sweet," she says, which means she thinks I'm being intense or creepy or both.

"There's a big stack of cards and gifts in the kitchen," I say. "Josh and Kat must have brought everything back for us after the wedding. Do you want to open all that stuff today?"

"Yeah, but later, when I can focus," she says. "I'm just so frickin' *tired*."

I push her hair away from her face. "Even when you're tired, you're beautiful. Do you know that, Mrs. Faraday?"

She sighs happily. "Wasn't the wedding lovely?"

"It was perfect."

Sarah and I have talked about our wedding countless times over the past two weeks, of course, but apparently, neither of us has tired of the topic.

"Didn't Georgia look great?" Sarah asks. "And Trey was so dapper in his suit."

"Your mom didn't stop smiling the whole time."

"Well, except for when she was bawling like a baby."

"No, even then she was smiling."

"And, oh my gosh, the look on Miss Westbrook's face when she saw you, Jonas—oh my God, I could sob just thinking about it. That was a beautiful thing."

I smile. That *was* a beautiful thing. But I could say that about every minute of our wedding day. Sarah planned the whole thing top to bottom—all I had to do was pay the bills and show up like any other guest—and it was glorious. When she walked down the aisle toward me, I truly thought I'd died and gone to heaven. And when she said, "I do"—when she officially became my wife in front of God and everyone—it was the happiest moment of my life.

And then there was the party. Holy fuck, what a fucking party. I mean, Jesus, I even *danced.* All night long. With Sarah, of course, but also with Georgia and her new boyfriend and Trey and Miss Westbrook and her kids (including my namesake himself, who turned out to be quite a strapping young lad) and Sarah's mom and Kat and Josh and Henn and a whole bunch of Sarah's awesome friends. I even danced with Uncle William after the Scotch started flowing, after the band had kicked things into high gear.

I've never had so much fun in my life—good old fashioned, silly *fun.* Well, yeah, I've had plenty of silly fun with Sarah, of course—and with Josh, too—but I've never let loose like that with anyone besides those two, and especially not with a whole room full of people, some of whom I honestly didn't even know. What a stroke of genius on Sarah's part to rent out Canlis for the occasion. What better place to celebrate than the site of our first date?

"Earth to Jonas."

I smile at her.

"What are you thinking about, baby?"

"Our amazing wedding."

"It was amazing, wasn't it? Did you see Uncle William dancing with Kat?" Sarah asks. "He was adorable."

"Yeah. And did you see Henn trying to do some kind of, like, weird break dancing thing?"

Sarah laughs. "I honestly didn't know what the heck Henn was trying to do. I was a bit concerned for his safety."

"And the safety of everyone around him on the dance floor."

She laughs.

"Let's do it again soon."

Sarah shoots me a look that says I'm a complete idiot. "Let me explain something kind of basic to you, love. The thing about having a wedding is that, if you're really lucky, you only do it *once*. The whole concept is specifically designed as a one-off." She smirks.

"Smart-ass. I mean we should throw another party. I've never thrown a party before. It was fun."

Her jaw drops. "Jonas Faraday wants to throw a party?"

"Wait, no. Correction. I want *you* to throw a party and I want to attend. Just like our wedding. You do all the work, make all the decisions, invite everyone, don't bother me with any of it—and then I come and drink and dance and have fun and act like an idiot."

She laughs. "Oh, Jonas. I'll throw you a party any time, baby. It would be my pleasure."

I scoot up against her on the bed and hug her. "Thank you." I kiss her nose. "Wife." I press myself against her body and snuggle close. We lie in silence for a few minutes as I rub her back.

"What's today's date?" she suddenly asks, sitting up, having some sort of epiphany.

I tell her.

"Holy crap. My grades should have posted by now." She grabs her laptop and logs onto some sort of student portal as I peek over her shoulder, holding my breath. "Ah," she says. "Damn."

"What?"

"The good news is I got A's on all my exams," she says, and yet she sounds disappointed.

"That's fantastic. Why do you sound bummed?"

She sticks out her lower lip. "Because the bad news is that I sank like a stone in the rankings." She sighs. "I fell to number twelve. I went down eight spots."

"Number twelve in your whole class? *That's* sinking like a stone?" I laugh. "It's terrific, baby."

"But I didn't get the scholarship." She looks down at her hands—and when she does, I can't help but smile at the sparkling wedding band gracing her slender finger, nestled against her dazzling rock. "I missed the scholarship by two spots."

"Baby, listen to me. Considering everything you went through right before finals, number twelve is fantastic."

She shrugs.

"Don't worry about the scholarship. I told you, you're the lucky recipient of the Jonas Faraday Scholarship Fund. Just be proud of yourself and don't sweat it."

"I don't need the Jonas Faraday Scholarship Fund. I can use my finder's fee money to pay my tuition."

"Nope. I'm your husband now. That means I take care of you. In all things. In all ways. End of story."

She raises her eyebrows at me.

Oh yeah. I forgot she's not a fan of the whole "end of story" thing. "I *want* to take care of you, Sarah—Mrs. Faraday. *Please.*"

She smiles.

"In every conceivable way. For the rest of your life."

"Oh, Jonas."

I kiss her. "I'm proud of you. Just be proud of yourself. Don't sweat it."

"Thank you."

I grab her ass with gusto. "So what do you want to do today, wife? Bungee jump off a bridge? Rappel down a cliff? Fuck like monkeys and imagine our brethren in Belize howling in the jungle all around us?"

"Oh my God, I can't handle any more excitement. For the next week 'til school starts, I'm just gonna lie here and drool and stare at the ceiling."

Well, fuck that. I hope she's not being literal about that no excitement thing—unless, of course, she's planning on letting me lick every inch of her while she lies in bed and stares at the ceiling—because this woman is my crack and I'm not planning to go to rehab any time soon.

She pauses. "Although..."

I perk up. "Yes?"

"There is one thing I'd really like to do today, my dearest husband, if you're up for it."

"Name it, spouse." My cock tingles.

"Well, I've noticed when I'm curled up in the leather armchair in the family room reading my textbooks, there's no end table for my drink."

I look at her funny. What the hell is she talking about?

"And I've also noticed you don't have any shot glasses in your cabinets—"

"*We* don't have any shot glasses in *our* cabinets. We. Our."

She smiles. "*We* don't have any shot glasses."

"Mmm hmm." I'm not quite sure where she's going with this.

"So I was thinking it might be nice to do a little shopping today." She flashes a smart-ass smile, and I suddenly know what game she's playing.

"Shopping, huh?"

"Correct."

"For an end table and shot glasses?"

"Correct. And maybe a few other household items, as well."

Jesus. I can't believe this is what my life has become—*and that I like it.* "And *where* were you thinking about shopping for an end table and shot glasses and various unspecified sundries, Mrs. Faraday?"

"Well, hunky-monkey husband, I know this place where we could miraculously get all of these things and more—maybe even a gigantic, lime-green bean bag chair, too, just for the hell of it—*and* at the same time stuff our faces with some tasty Swedish meatballs."

I exhale with mock anxiety. "Wow, I don't know, baby. Sounds like a big step in our relationship. You really think we're ready for this?"

She makes a big show of considering her options. "Well, it definitely would signify we're taking our relationship to the next level. But I think I'm ready for that, if you are." She grins.

"As long as there are meatballs involved, and as long as I'm with you, I can handle just about anything, even shopping at IKEA. I'll just leave my dick and balls at home, and I'll be fine."

"No, you big dummy. That's not gonna work."

"Why not?"

"Think, Jonas, think. How are we gonna have hot monkey-sex in one of those private family bathrooms if you've left your dick and balls at home?"

Hello, instant hard-on. "Ah, excellent point. I'm glad one of us is thinking."

"Oh, I'm always thinking, Jonas. I assure you."

"That's the understatement of the century, baby."

She laughs. "So it's a date? Mr. and Mrs. Faraday go shopping at IKEA today?"

"Absolutely. But now that you've got me thinking about my dick and balls and meatballs, I'm craving some tasty *albóndigas* before we go."

A look of sheer terror fills her eyes. "Oh no, Jonas. Please, no."

"There's no way to stop me."

"No!" She screams, laughing, but resistance is futile.

I turn her onto her belly, yank down her pajama bottoms, and take a big bite out of her ass—a big, ol' juicy bite. "Mmm. I love this ass," I growl, and then I slap it.

She squeals again.

Oh man, I'm hard as a rock, ready for some good old fashioned fuckery with my sweet wife, My Magnificent Mrs. Faraday.

And yet, on second thought, there's no rush, is there? We've got all the time in the world, my wife and I. I'm not going anywhere, and neither is she. Forevermore. She promised in front of God and everyone and she can't take it back. So why not hold off and let a little delicious anticipation build? It sure sounds like, if I'm a patient boy, I'm going to get to fuck my dirty, dirty girl in a bathroom at IKEA this afternoon, and that's most certainly worth the wait. I hop off the bed and hoot at the ceiling—and then I slap her ass one more time for good measure.

"Come on, Mrs. Faraday," I bellow. "Get your delectable ass in gear. Your husband's got a gigantic boner and he wants to take his hot little wife shopping at IKEA!"

Acknowledgments

Writing this trilogy has been one of the great joys of my life. Thank you to my beloved early readers for your feedback and encouragement, with a special shout-out to my shining star, Nicki Starr. Thank you to my family for always giving me space and support for my writing, even though we all know the process of writing renders me clinically insane (and never more so than when I'm writing three books back-to-back).

In relation to this third book, *The Redemption,* in particular, thank you to the "village" that helped me with inspiration: Thank you to my neighbor, Steve, a retired Secret Service Agent, for the countless hours you spent with me, teaching me about federal investigations, organized crime, and hacking. We were an unlikely pair in some ways, but we sure had fun talking this thing through, didn't we? Thank you to those awesome hacker guys I met in Las Vegas at Mandalay Bay. You happened to be in Vegas for a hacker convention while I was there partying with my girlfriends, and, lucky me, you dudes absolutely styled me with ideas. I'll likely never see you gentlemen again and you'll probably never read this message—but you were so helpful and hilarious, and the free drinks you generously supplied to me were so appreciated, I nonetheless feel compelled to thank you expressly here.

My entire extended family is amazing. Thank you to my mother, mother-in-law, and aunt for reading the books and loving them. I love you all so much. Thank you to my uncle the motorcycle man for reading the first chapter of *The Club* and saying, "Yep," when I asked if it rang true as a male voice—your vote of confidence really encouraged me to keep going and trust Jonas' voice inside my head. Thank you to my uncle the computer whiz for giving me that super-duper, grand idea over lunch one day. Thank you to my Baby Cuz for reading the first chapters to *The Club* and calling me immediately to say, "Cuz, you're a savage beast." Thank you to Cuz for teaching me about the Deep Web. Eek. You can't un-hear that shit, man.

Thank you to my dad for listening to me go on and on about the plotting of these books over lunch one day (sex scenes abbreviated to "and then they have sex," of course). I don't know why I keep creating bastard fathers in my writing when I have the best one on the planet. I love you, Pops. (And I don't even know why I just thanked you here because if you read these books, I don't want to know about it.)

Thank you to Scott, the ER doctor who took so much time out of his busy schedule to help me formulate Sarah's injuries, treatment, and recovery in as realistic a manner as possible. Thank you also to bestselling author (and former ER nurse) Catherine (Fucking) Bybee who also helped me injure poor Sarah in exactly the right way and made me belly laugh as she did.

Thank you to my agents Jill and Kevin—as always, your belief in me, regardless of the name I happen to be writing under or the genre I'm writing in, means so much to me. Thank you to the Author Whisperer for your invaluable feedback and assistance. Thank you to Lisa, Melissa, and Sharon. You ladies rock. Thank you to Alicia for your proofing and editing and to Judi for formatting. I am a lucky girl to have such a great team of people supporting me. And, finally, thank you to the greatest team member of all: my hunky-monkey husband. You are my rock and I love you.

BONUS SCENE
from
The Redemption (The Club Trilogy Book 3)

Jonas

I check my mobile phone on the nightstand.

"Still nothing from Eric?" Sarah asks.

"Nothing."

"God, I'm on pins and needles," she says.

"So am I."

Special Agent Eric called earlier this morning to tell us it was time to direct Kat, Josh and Henn to start immediately transferring The Club's money out of their accounts, but Eric hasn't followed up with us since his early-morning call. We're both dying of anticipation. It doesn't help that we've been stranded in this hotel room since last night.

"Are our guards still out in the hallway?" Sarah asks.

"I think so."

"Well, go check."

"Bossy."

She smirks.

I get up from the bed, taking the sheet with me to cover myself. I poke my head out from our room. Two guys in suits and earpieces are staring at me in the hallway.

"Hey, guys," I say.

"Hey," one of them says. "You two doing okay in there?" He stifles a smile. "It sounded like maybe someone was hurt in there."

The second guy looks down at his shoes and covers his mouth, trying to hide his grin.

"Yeah, we're fine." Fuck it. I can't help bragging just a little bit. "We're actually doing *fantastic* in here." I smile back at them.

"You need anything?" the first guy asks, keeping a straight face.

Number Two Guy is still look down, obviously not as good at hiding his amusement as his partner.

I poke my head back into the room. "Baby, do we need anything, these nice men sitting at our door would like to know?"

"Yeah, some fruit," Sarah calls to me. "We definitely need some fruit."

I poke my head back into the hallway. "The woman says we need some fruit."

"Order whatever you want from room service," the first guy says. "We'll just have to intercept it and inspect it before it goes into the room."

What the fuck? Do they think the motherfuckers at The Club are planning to *poison* us? I'm sure my sudden anxiety is plastered all over my face right now.

"Standard procedure," the first guy adds, obviously reassuring me.

"Okay. Thanks." I shut the door and leap back to Sarah in the bed. "My baby wants some fruit, huh?" I hover over her, my forearms resting on either side of her head. "You mean, in addition to my banana?"

She rolls her eyes. "Sometimes you are so cheesy."

"It's part of my charm, baby."

"That's for sure."

"So what shall we order from room service, pretty lady?"

"Well, champagne would be very nice, sir."

"Of course. I'm always in favor of champagne."

"It brings out my dirty girl."

"Hence, the reason why I'm always in favor of it." I roll to the side of the bed and pick up the hotel phone. "Okay, fruit, champagne. Anything else?"

"And a turkey club sandwich," Sarah adds as I dial. "And French fries. Lots and lots of French fries." She grins. "I've worked up an appetite."

I wink at her. "Whatever you say, baby. Yes, hi," I say into the phone. "We'd like to order room service. Two turkey clubs—one without bacon but add sprouts, please. A huge side of French fries." She grins at me. "Yes, that's right. And a bottle of your best champagne." The attendant starts rattling off their champagne selections. "Whatever's your most expensive bottle, I don't know." I cover the phone with my hand. "That was such a Josh Faraday move right there."

She laughs.

I look at her pointedly, soliciting her further order.

"A humongous bowl of strawberries, whole— *not* cut up," Sarah says with authority.

"Interesting. A huge bowl of strawberries, whole—not cut up," I repeat.

"A canister of whipped cream," she adds, matter-of-factly. "The kind you press the little wand on top and it spurts out. I need a full can."

I raise my eyebrows at her.

She nods at me, emphatically. "You heard me right," she says. "A full can."

"A full canister of whipped cream. The kind you press the little wand on top and it spurts out."

Her face is glowing. "And a whole grapefruit—uncut. Plus a good knife." She winks. "Make sure you say a *whole* grapefruit ."

I shoot her a look of complete befuddlement and she bites her lip. I repeat her last order into the phone and end the call.

"That was an interesting order. This is gonna be an interesting fruit salad."

"You could say that."

"Am I gonna get to eat some of this fruit salad?"

"Nope."

"Hmm." I squint at her. "Am I gonna *like* this fruit salad?"

"Well, that depends."

"On what."

"On whether you're gonna enjoy getting the best blowjob of your entire life."

I twist my mouth, giving the matter mock consideration. "Hmm," I finally say. "I think I'll go with *yes.*"

She laughs. "Baby, you're gonna *love* this particular fruit salad."

I look at the clock. "We've got about twenty minutes 'til the food arrives," I say, crawling next to her on the bed. I run my fingertip over her pelvic bone and take her nipple into my mouth. "What on earth should we do while we wait for the fruit?"

"Hmm," she says, arching her back into my mouth. "Watch TV? Maybe we could catch an episode of *The Golden Girls* or *Full House*?"

I shake my head. "Not what I had in mind." I swirl her nipple around in my mouth and run my hand lightly from one of her hips to the other and back again, skimming her tattoo in between.

"Play cards?" she whispers. Her voice is already getting husky. "Gin rummy?"

I shake my head.

"Twenty Questions?'

"Okay, Twenty Questions."

I skim my fingers lightly between her legs and she shudders. "Ask a question."

"Um. Do you wanna talk about your feelings?"

I laugh. "Nope." My fingertips graze across her wetness.

"Do you wanna talk about *my* feelings?"

"Fuck no," I say.

"Do you wanna fuck me?" She smiles.

"Nope. I mean, yes. But, nope. Not right now." I kiss my way from her breast to her hipbone.

"I give up."

"That's only three questions." I lick her tattoos.

"I'm terrible at guessing games."

"I'm *hungry*. I wanna *eat*." I position myself between her thighs.

She spreads wide for me and moans. "A club sandwich?"

"Nope." With that, my tongue finds her clit and all playful conversation is done.

Five minutes later, she's screaming my name and moaning at the top of her lungs. Damn, my baby's loud. And I love it.

When she's done, I sit up and growl, flexing my muscles. "I'm so fucking good," I say. "Damn, I'm so fucking good."

Her chest is heaving. She's sweating like she just ran a sprint. "Lord have mercy," she says. "You are. That was a really good one. Oh my God."

There's a singular rap on the door. "Food," a staccato male voice says on the other side of the door.

We look at each other and burst out laughing.

"You gave those guys quite an earful," I say.

She rolls her eyes.

"I doubt they minded."

She stares at me, unmoving, apparently assuming I'm going to get the food for us.

I motion to my gigantic boner. "I'm not in any shape to go out there, baby."

"Well, I'm not sure my legs will hold my weight," she says. "You just reduced me to a pile of goo."

"I'm not going out there with my gigantic woody."

She rolls her eyes, wraps the sheet around herself, and heads to the door.

I watch her glide to the door, her hair cascading down her back, her limbs long, her skin glorious. Jesus, I can't get enough of her. I've never felt anything even remotely close to this feeling before. I feel physically ill with this urgent need to call this woman my wife. Now that I've got a firm idea about how I want to propose to her, I don't want to wait to do it. The minute this bullshit with The Club is over, I'm gonna take this gorgeous woman to Greece and marry her the very next day.

"Yes, I'm perfectly fine," Sarah says to the guys in the hall. "Nope. All's well. Thanks for your concern. No, I got it. Thanks."

Sarah comes back into the room with a tray of food and a broad smile, but then she immediately goes back out again and comes back with champagne in an ice bucket. "Aw, those nice men out there are so sweet," she says sarcastically. "They wanted to know if I'm *okay*." She rolls her eyes. "They think they're so frickin' funny."

"Uncle Sam's money, hard at work."

"I guess I should take pity on them. Can you imagine if your job was sitting outside a doorway with another *guy*, listening to a woman have an orgasm on the other side of a wall?" She laughs.

"I'm sure you've made their day."

"And now I'm gonna make yours." She grins mischievously and grabs the grapefruit and knife off the tray.

"Please tell me that knife has absolutely nothing to do with this epic blowjob you've promised me."

She laughs. "I promise." She smirks. "But I can't say the same about the grapefruit ."

I raise an eyebrow.

"Ever had a grapefruit-blowjob?" she asks.

"I can't say that I have, no."

"Well, I've never given one. So we're even." She grabs her computer and clicks onto something. She reads for a minute, nodding to herself. "Okay. I think I got it." She heads to the bathroom and comes back with a thick towel. "Lie down on top of this. This is gonna get hella messy."

"Messy?"

"Grapefruit juice and pulp everywhere, so I've read."

I shoot her a "what the fuck" look.

"Hey, I get to give you whatever blowjob I want for our Twelve Days of Fellatio-Christmas—absolutely no arguments from you, remember? What number are we on?"

"Six, I think."

"Okay, then. I'm still in charge. Lie down on the towel and tell your dick to fasten its seat belt."

"My dick doesn't wear a seatbelt. Ever. It likes to live on the edge."

She laughs. "Of course, it does. Okay, just give me a minute while I get my fruitalicious instrument of pleasure ready for you."

"Fruitalicious is not a word."

"It is now." She grabs the grapefruit and the knife and heads to the small table in the corner of the room.

"Just tell me again: This is all about the grapefruit and not the knife."

"It's about the grapefruit, babe. Duh."

"I don't think you get to say 'duh' in this context, baby. There's no 'duh' about a woman carving up a grapefruit for a blowjob. What the fuck are gonna do with it?"

"You'll see." She smiles. "Patience, love. Trust me—you're gonna love it."

Without further ado, she cuts off both ends of the grapefruit, hollows out a dick-sized hole through the middle of it, and then wordlessly slips that motherfucker right over my tip and down onto my shaft.

"Whoa," I say, instantly tingling like crazy. The cool temperature of the fruit is electrifying, and the acidity is unnerving. "Whoa," I say again.

She leans down and starts sucking me, all the while sliding that fucking grapefruit up and down as she does. And, just like that, I'm about to lose my fucking mind. Oh my God, Sarah's absolutely right. I fucking *love* grapefruit. Best fruit *ever.* And I love Sarah Cruz. If I didn't already want to make this woman my wife, I most certainly do now.

There are no words for what I'm experiencing. The texture and pressure of the wet pulp feel uncannily like a woman—like a cool and ridiculously wet and acidic woman—and, that combined with Sarah sucking on me (like a champ, as usual) feels like I'm having sex and getting blown at the same time. It's an incredible sensation—I'm sure I sound like a dying elephant right now. I grab her hair and yank at it, bucking as I do—and she moans loudly, working my cock with her mouth and that grapefruit with her hand with equal enthusiasm. This is depraved. I love it.

When I come into her mouth with a load roar, Sarah doesn't just swallow my release—she sucks it out of me like she's trying to get every last drop of a milkshake.

After a moment, she pulls her head up, slides the grapefruit off me, peels it, and takes a big ol' juicy bite. "And that, my hunky-monkey boyfriend," she purrs, grapefruit juice running down her chin, "is what the perverts on the internet call a 'grapefruit-blowjob.'" She takes another big bite of grapefruit and laughs.

My heart is still racing. "Sarah Fucking Cruz. You're the goddess and the muse," I say.

"So I've been told."

And I'm going to marry you.

Jonas and Sarah's epic love story continues in THE CULMINATION (The Club #4)

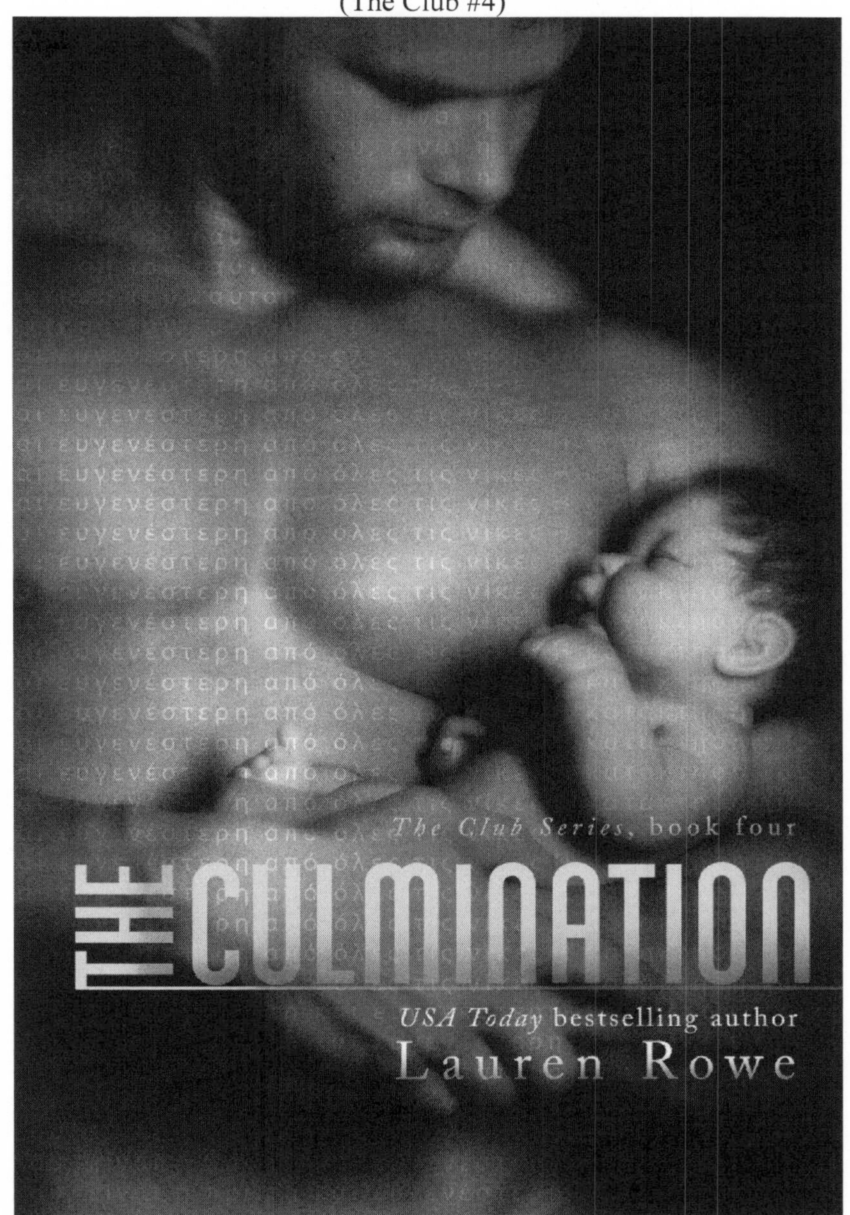

Excerpt from THE CULMINATION (The Club #4)

Chapter 1
Jonas

She giggles. "*Jonas*."

"What? I've got to partake of your crumpets as much as possible before they're off limits to me in a couple months."

"They're extra sensitive these days. Be gentle."

"I can't control myself, baby—they're too delicious to resist." I take her nipple into my mouth and give it a good, strong suck.

Sarah shrieks. "Gah! Go easy, Jonas. They're *sensitive*."

"Oh yeah?"

"Yeah..." But she can't suppress the bloom rising in her cheeks.

"You mean you want me to take it easy doing... *this*?" I give her other nipple an even harder suck.

Sarah shrieks again. "Oh my god. *Take it easy*, for Pete's sake." She laughs. "Holy crap, I can't decide if I love it or hate it."

"You know you love it." I sit up and assess her naked body on the bed. "Damn, woman, just looking at you these days gives me an epic boner."

"These days?"

"Ssh. Play along."

"Sorry."

"My dick grew three inches just looking at you right now." My cock twitches. "Your boobs used to be a handful plus a little extra, and now look at them." I cup her breasts in my hands and marvel at how they overflow from my palms.

She looks down at her breasts in my hands. "I'm the Latina Anna Nicole Smith."

"You're a fucking Botticelli, baby—*The Birth of Venus*. Are you looking at yourself?"

"Yep, I'm looking. That's some serious boobage down there."

"My dick just grew *another* two inches *again*. You're Demeter, baby." I look down at my straining cock. "Jesus, have you ever seen a boner this big before?"

"Every single day since I met you."

"No, baby, look more closely. This time it's different."

Sarah makes a big show of staring at my cock with mocking, wide eyes.

"This is no ordinary boner. It's a behemoth—a revelation. *The divine original form of boner-ness.*"

She laughs. "I thought you weren't a boob-man."

"Whatever gave you that idea?"

"Gosh, I dunno. The bite marks on my ass?"

"Mmm. That reminds me. I'm hungry for some *albóndigas* right now." I reach around and grab a fistful of her right ass cheek, greedily sinking my fingertips into the sexy tattoo she got for me in Thailand, and she squeals. But when I tilt her body toward me, intending to chomp on her ass tattoo like I always do before I get down to business, she gasps and winces sharply.

I release my grip and pull back from her, my heart instantly racing. "Sarah?"

Her eyes are closed. Her brow is furrowed. She brings her hand to her bulging belly and winces again.

"Did I hurt you?" I sit upright, my heart suddenly pounding in my ears. "Sarah?"

"I'm fine." But she winces a third time and curls into a ball on the bed.

I leap up from the bed, my breathing shallow. "Sarah, talk to me. Tell me what's happening."

For the longest five seconds of my life, she doesn't say a word. I'm just about to scoop her naked body into my arms and race her to the hospital when she opens her eyes and exhales with relief. "Whew. I'm okay," she says, her body visibly relaxing. "Oh, man, that was rough." She looks at me sympathetically. "Aw, you look like you're gonna pass out. I'm sorry."

"What happened?"

"Crazy Monkey was just doing Zumba right on a nerve, that's all." She shoots me a crooked smile. "The pain took my breath away for a minute. But everything's fine now—he shifted position." She pats the bed. "Sit back down, love. Tell me more about your transcendent boner to end all boners."

https://www.createspace.com/pub/simplesitesearch.search.do?sitesearch_query=lauren+rowe&sitesearch_type=STORE

About the Author

Lauren Rowe is the pen name of a USA Today best-selling author, performer, audio book narrator, songwriter and media host/ personality who decided to unleash her alter ego to write The Club Trilogy to ensure she didn't hold back or self-censor in writing the story. Lauren Rowe lives in San Diego, California where she lives with her family, sings with her band, hosts a show, and writes at all hours of the night. Find out more about The Club Trilogy and Lauren Rowe at www.LaurenRoweBooks.com and be sure to sign up for her emails to find out about new releases and exclusive giveaways.

Books by Lauren Rowe:

The Club (The Club Trilogy Book 1)—available now
The Reclamation (The Club Trilogy Book 2)—available now
The Redemption (The Club Trilogy Book 3)—available now
The Culmination (The Club Series Book 4)—available August 15, 2015

Additional books by Lauren Rowe:

Josh and Kat's story will be coming in a trilogy of three full-length books, all released in January 2016:

THE INFATUATION: Josh and Kat Part I (The Club #5) (January 5, 2016)
THE REVELATION: Josh and Kat Part II (The Club #6) (January 12, 2016)
THE CONSUMMATION: Josh and Kat Part III (The Club #7) (January 19, 2016)

Countdown to Killing Kurtis (a standalone psychological thriller featuring Lauren's distinctive humor, unique characters, "what the fuck!"-inducing plot twists, and a touch of steam) (available now in ebook, print, and audiobook).

https://www.createspace.com/pub/simplesitesearch.search.do?sitesearch_query=lauren+rowe&sitesearch_type=STORE

Interview with Lauren Rowe:

Q: What has surprised you most since releasing *The Club Trilogy*?

A: How kind readers have been to me. They have bonded with Jonas and Sarah, yes, but they've bonded with me, too. They write me the sweetest notes on Facebook or in emails, and they say the most generous, heartfelt things to me—things that make me tear up, to be honest. I'm amazed that some readers have really felt inspired and touched by the story. That's just the best feeling in the world, especially considering that, on paper, I've written, you know, smut. But I always have believed *The Club* was about so much more than sex. It's about love and hope and becoming who you're meant to be. It's about healing. So the fact that readers have felt that, too, is just the best feeling in the world. My readers call themselves the Love Monkeys, and they send me little monkeys and leave little monkey emojiis on their Facebook posts. It's freaking awesome.

Q: Why do you think readers have taken to Jonas and Sarah so much?

A: They're flawed. They're doing the best they can, just like you and me. They're honest. They're kind. And they crave love above all else. Oh, and they're funny as hell.

Q: Tell me five facts about The Club Trilogy.

A:

1. I wrote all three books back to back without stopping and then released all three books at once (with a slight stagger). That was a long time to be all alone with Jonas Faraday (and Sarah, of course). I think I went slightly insane.
2. When I sat down to write, I knew Jonas Faraday's name and what happened in chapters 1 and 2, and that was it. As I wrote the books, I went on a twisting journey along the way, almost like a reader, basically transcribing the movie I saw in my head.
3. People always want to know how much "research" I did for all the crazy sex scenes in the books. The answer is, yes, I've had A LOT of sex with my husband while writing these books, some of it very interesting, even humorous. During the months I wrote the books, he often said, "Please, for the love of God, never stop writing in this genre."

4. The cover model on all three books is named Damian DeCantillon, a fitness model and actor in New York City. I met him in between writing books 2 and 3, and he was the exact embodiment of Jonas Faraday in my mind. I asked him to be on the covers, and he said he'd have to read the books first. He devoured the books in three days and then called me. "I love these books," he said. "I'm in." It was a dream come true.
5. When I was finished writing the trilogy, I was so proud of it, and so excited I'd written my second, third and fourth works of fiction, ever, I went and got myself inked with the Greek tattoo on Jonas' right forearm ("Visualize the divine originals") in a hidden spot.

Q: How do you make your characters believable?

A: I just become them and then I write the truth. And that's why, sometimes, I lose control of them. I might want them to do or say something, and they stop and stare at me, shaking their heads. And then I go, "Aw, come on, I need you to do this so I can get from point A to B!" That's when they pretty much flip me the bird or laugh in my face and I have to figure out how to get to my next plot point without compromising them (or change the plot point completely). It always works out better than I'd envisioned originally. I always trust the characters.

Q: Is there an author that has inspired you?

A: Anne Rice is my all-time favorite writer. As a teen, I read her erotica called *Sleeping Beauty.* I remember it rocked my world. First of all, though it was written under a pen name, she owned it. She wasn't embarrassed or ashamed, and said it was art with a straight face. I was a teen and a huge goody-two-shoes, so it shocked me to think she didn't care what anyone thought! I was floored that she wasn't embarrassed, or hiding this side of herself. I directly thank Anne Rice for laying the foundation for me to write The Club Trilogy now. Also, her writing is sexy and suspenseful and yet so literate. And she writes about love in a way that is refreshing and different and epic and ageless. I love her so much!! In fact, I even named my daughter after the heroine in my favorite Anne Rice book, *The Witching Hour.* (But I'm super chill and not a fangirl at all or anything.)

Q: Books 1 and 3 of the trilogy are both about the same length (100k words), but book 2 is a bit shorter. Why?

A: Yes. Book 2 (*The Reclamation*) is a full-length book by industry standards, but it is shorter than the other two. The reason is simple. That's the way the story came to me. I didn't want to add scenes just to add length. I wanted to tell the story with the pacing that felt exactly right to me to tell the story as I envisioned it.

Q: Why did you write *The Club Trilogy* under a pen name?

A: I picked a pen name to encourage myself to write without censoring myself whatsoever. Also, I'd written my first novel under my real name in the young adult genre, and I didn't want to confuse readers with such a drastic departure. I did not pick the pen name out of shame or embarrassment. I'm proud of the books and not the least bit embarrassed about the sex stuff. I think I can thank Anne Rice for planting that seed in me as a teen.

Q: You're a singer-songwriter, in addition to writing books?

A: Yes, I am. And I also perform in a dance band that plays cover music at parties and weddings, too. Music is so much of who I am, it's not a surprise that music plays an important part in The Club Trilogy. Quite often, readers tell me they downloaded and listened to all the songs from the book while reading, and that the music heightened their experience with the book. That thrills me to no end because I really thought of those songs a soundtrack to the book. Speaking of which, people ask me for the playlist all the time, so I've included it here.

Music Playlist for *The Club Trilogy*:

Most of the following songs were specifically referenced in *The Club Trilogy*. A few of them merely inspired Lauren Rowe while writing:

The Club (The Club Trilogy Book 1):

White Lies—Rx Bandits
Pony—Far (rock cover of the Genuwine song)
Melt With You—Modern English
Lick It Before You Stick It —Denise La Salle (it's about exactly what the title suggests)
I Just Want To Make Love To You—Muddy Waters
I Want You—Bob Dylan
I Want You—Savage Garden
Do I Wanna Know—Arctic Monkeys
Locked Out of Heaven—Bruno Mars
Madness—Muse
Closer—Nine Inch Nails

The Reclamation (The Club Trilogy Book 2):

Dangerous—Big Data
Sweater Weather—The Neighbourhood
Fall In Love—Phantogram
Magic—Coldplay
Yellow—Coldplay
Come a Little Closer—Cage the Elephant
Demons—Imagine Dragons
Not Afraid—Eminem
She Loves You—The Beatles

The Redemption (The Club Trilogy Book 3):

Baby Got Back—Sir Mix-A-Lot
Talk Dirty to Me—Poison
Take Me To Church—Hozier
My Favourite Book—Stars
Hurt—Johnny Cash
Truly Madly Deeply—Savage Garden
Melt With You—Modern English